Paul Stuart Kemp
in 1972. Bloodgo(
second self-publis
other work which
the Internet. His
www.paulstuartkemp.com.

As an English writer, he has managed to resist the
mainstream American influence, and casts dark tales
throughout major British cities such as London and
Liverpool.

Paul Stuart Kemp lives in Berkshire, England.

also by Paul Stuart Kemp

BLOODGOD

Paul Stuart Kemp

decapita

Published in Great Britain in 2001 by
Decapita Publishing
PO BOX 3802
Bracknell RG12 8FX

Email: mail@paulstuartkemp.com
Website: www.paulstuartkemp.com

All artwork by Paul Stuart Kemp

Photograph of author by Helen Priest

The Author asserts the moral right to be
identified as the author of this work

ISBN 0 9538215 2 8

Set in Meridien

Printed and bound in Great Britain by
Decapita Publishing
PO BOX 3802
Bracknell RG12 8FX

BLOODGOD

CONTENTS

PART THREE
DESTITUTION

PART FOUR
DESOLATION

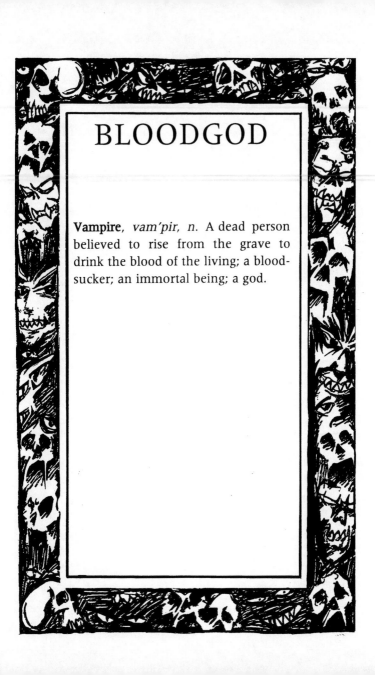

BLOODGOD

Vampire, *vam'pir*, *n*. A dead person believed to rise from the grave to drink the blood of the living; a bloodsucker; an immortal being; a god.

My dearest Kirsty

It is with terrible news that I write this letter to you, for I feel that I may soon be dead. I am lying in a scorching hotel room minutes away from the ship that will be embarking at dusk, but I fear that I will not even make it onboard alive. I have lost all feeling in my feet, and my hands grow too numb to even hold this pen as I write. If I do not make it back to see you again, my beloved Kirsty, I want you to know that I love you so very much, and that I will be thinking of you to the end. But I do not want to list my sufferings here, that will not help me now, but I feel I should give you some explanation of how I came to such a crippling state.

The fear of death gripped me like a vast constricting snake, and I knew not how to shake it off. That grip has since passed, and I look at my final few hours with a sort of helpless melancholy. I will die. That is all I can say. I only hope now that you will be able to forgive me, because I have unleashed something terrible, and it is on its way to you now. But promise me Kirsty that you will never touch it. Burn it, destroy it, run away from it, I do not care. Just promise that you will never touch it.

It was only a few weeks ago that I began my journey to the tiny settlement of Creta el Bullaq, which involved many days of driving through an endless arid desert where I was to meet with Rajesh Minoa from the University of Archaeological Studies. I was glad when I finally reached this place, to have a solid roof over my head, to get away from the incessant blistering heat, to wash with cool water, and to sleep comfortably. But little did I know that my coming to this place would also mark the end of my days.

I waited for Rajesh in the settlement's only bar, as we had agreed, but he did not arrive. When dusk approached I left a note for him at the bar and returned to my room. A young boy appeared before me outside in the dusty street, dressed from head to foot in black sackcloth, telling me that he had important news for me. I assumed him to be a messenger from the excavation site, and asked him of Rajesh's whereabouts, but he could not answer me because he said that he was not from the site. I told him to leave me, suspecting a local village scam, and continued on to bed for the night.

The following morning I went back to the bar, but no one had picked up my note, and no one had left any new messages for me in return. I waited again for him, leaving only for the bathroom and to eat, but the day passed as it had done the day before with no word coming from either him or from the site. The sky darkened as the great hot sun sank beneath the dunes outside, and as I left the bar to return to my room, confused, I once more came upon the young boy, waiting for me outside in the street.

He rose at my approach, and again told me that he had news for me, but I did not know who he was, and nor could he give me reason why I should know. I walked on, ignoring his protests, but he came after me, insisting that he knew who I was, and that he had a great secret to show me.

He described an ancient place, unseen by human eyes for centuries, and that I should go with him to see it. He gave his name as Paneef, as if that matters any more, and there seemed to be something unnatural in the way he moved and spoke when finally I stopped to listen to him. I thought it perhaps to be just a trait of the locals, customs and mannerisms I was unaware of in such a strange land, but my ignorance was to prove to be my downfall.

My concerns were elsewhere, even as I tried to insist that he leave me alone, but he wore a strange glittering pendant about his neck, a gold charm of crescent moons and black feathers that seemed to fascinate me. I can remember that suddenly, now that I have tried to remember why I even went with him. It sparkled, that pendant, and held my attention completely so that I only barely heard his words and pleas. I do not recall even seeing it the first time I met him, but he wore it that second night, and I couldn't help but do as he wished.

There is a knot in my stomach that cramps, and I cannot ignore it as I write this letter to you. It makes me feel sick and doubles me in half by turns. I can feel stabs of pain in my abdomen, and it hurts, oh God, how it hurts. I want it to stop but I fear now that it never will. No doctor can heal me, of that I am sure. I have a sickness for which no medicine exists. It is beyond medicine. I have a disease of evil, a curse, and it is devouring me from the inside.

But I can't continue with any of that. I may not have time enough to even finish this letter if I allow myself to get side-tracked. I want to tell you about Paneef, the boy I met, and I want to tell it all in order.

We travelled deep into the desert after we spoke, an

hour after sundown, because he said we could only travel at night, and I was helpless to do anything other than he instructed. He still wore his heavy black robes that covered every inch of his skin, I remember that, and he carried nothing with him but a flask of water and a small black sack. I distantly assumed, as we headed out, that he would have carried some kind of map with him, but I soon realised as we trekked blindly into the endless wastes of sand, that a map would be of little use with neither sunlight nor landmarks to mark our way.

We drove for nearly two hours into the cooling wastes of the moonlit desert, the coldness growing ever more harsh and unyielding despite the heater inside the jeep. In that time we passed neither tree nor water, but it was only after those two hours that Paneef suddenly told me to stop. We were in a valley of sand, no different from any other valley of sand that we had traversed, and yet he seemed to know exactly where we were.

We left the jeep and went on foot to where a number of stone blocks rose up out of the sand. I was mesmerised by them, perhaps even as much as by the boy's instructions, because I just couldn't believe what I was looking at. There were hieroglyphics etched upon their geometric stone surfaces, carvings that disappeared down beneath the surface of the sand, down into the depths of the desert. Some of them I knew from the great pyramids at Giza, others I recognised from the Rosetta Stone at home in London, but there were others the likes of which I had never seen before. Despite these blocks having been blasted by desert winds for however long they had stood for, the hieroglyphs were still relatively legible, denoting that whoever had carved them had had access not only to excellent tools, but also to the knowledge of how to use them skilfully. I had been taken to an expanse of endless desert known for having never been populated in the country's history. It was impossible for those blocks to have even been there.

It was as I stared at these blocks that Paneef addressed me and terrified me further, again inferring that he knew who I was. He asked me if I especially looked for old temples, and then began to talk about how old temples were even better if they had old stories inside them. The hieroglyphics had already made me nervous, but the words coming out of the boy were just plain scaring me. I remembered then your insistence that I carry a gun in remote digs such as this, and it was only then that I first truly registered the need. I became aware that I was defenceless, even though I was only with a small boy, but a grave feeling of danger seemed to wrap itself around me like a death shroud, knotting at my throat, choking me. If only I had turned back then. If only I had been able to listen to my fears and escape. But I couldn't turn away, not from such a discovery, not from such things in a desert known never to have had a civilisation, and certainly not from Paneef's words that held me rooted to the spot beside him.

But his words got worse, Kirsty. He began to ask me if I preferred old stories to be told by old men, men who had witnessed such things first hand, and would retell them over a campfire. If there was indeed a temple beneath the sand, as Paneef inferred, it would have to be at least a thousand years old for the desert to bury it like it had. Of course the boy could not be telling me that there was someone alive in the temple, someone who had been alive when it had stood its ground against the onslaught of the desert. But his words were just so measured and thought out as though he truly believed in what he was telling me.

I stood and watched as he started towards one of the larger blocks of stone, and it was then that I saw an opening in it. There was a way in, a narrow chasm between two upended blocks, and it seemed that he wanted me to follow him inside to meet this old man who had lived in the depths of the buried tomb for hundreds of years. I stood where I was, despite the mesmerising hold of both his words and the pendant that swung about his neck. Something broke in me then, my fears washing over me like an icy wave, jerking me back to the situation I was in, and I ran stumbling back to the jeep and started the engine.

I wanted to drive, God help me I wanted to drive, but something shrieked at me, something inside, and I knew that I just couldn't leave Paneef to the desert alone. I called back for him to come with me, to leave this madness behind, but he simply stood at the breach in the section of stone blocks, staring coldly back at me. One minute he was there, our eyes locked with some strange connection, the next he had disappeared inside and was gone.

I was sure he'd find his own way back, he was a child of the desert after all, and I waited in the bar for his return. I asked about Rajesh too, but there had still been no sign of him. I called the University, but they too had heard nothing either. I went back to my room and waited and watched for them both, but of either of them I saw no sign.

The day came and passed but Paneef never returned to the settlement, and nor would anyone that I asked trouble themselves enough to go and look for him. If I knew then what I know now, I would have left him to the desert and returned home. But I didn't know - how could I have known? - and so I packed up enough food and water for a day, and the following morning headed back out into the desert to try and follow my tracks back to the hidden temple.

There were no tracks, of course. What little there may have been had long since been blown away by strong winds. But I don't want to get dragged down by pointless detail, though, Kirsty. Such things are of no importance now. The only thing that matters at this moment is to tell you what happened to me that day.

It took nearly two hours to find the temple with a guide, but without one I did not find that same valley until dusk. With the night drawing close I wanted to return to Creta el Bullaq, but I knew that I couldn't leave Paneef out there alone for another twenty four hours, and so I continued my search. I found the opening that I had seen him disappear through, and digging the torch out of my rucksack, I stepped down into the twisted dark labyrinth of the tomb to begin my search.

It seemed as though the temple had been subjected to at least one major earthquake in its lifetime, perhaps even a series of them, because debris littered the staircase like the aftermath of a war. Huge gaping cracks rose from floor to ceiling, and sand drifted in at every breach. The further I descended, the more I realised that the hieroglyphics and stonework were completely unknown to me. I was scared like I don't remember ever being before, climbing alone down crumbling steps with only my torch beam penetrating the total blackness. My footsteps echoed coldly off every hard surface, resounding ahead of me so that it seemed as though a dozen ghostly soldiers accompanied me on my descent throughout those chambers. And yet the most terrifying event was still to come.

As I continued down into the heart of the temple, my torchlight gradually became joined by a luminescence emanating from below the endless stone staircase. A faint red glow came from somewhere near the bottom, a musty smell rising along with the light, and it wasn't until the great stone steps widened and the red glow brightened all around me, that I realised I had been delivered into a vast chamber that burned with lines of torches. It was only then that I came to the conclusion that Paneef must be alive and had lit these torches for warmth and light while he waited out, what I imagined to be, his second night beneath the surface of the desert.

I noticed a shifting of light ahead of me through an archway, shadows playing across the sand-covered floor, and I went quickly towards it thinking I had at last found the boy. The archway led into a long corridor which I hurried down, thinking to call the boy's name as I went. I am glad that I did not call out, because as I came upon another archway, partially covered with heaped rocks and stone, I made out the small dark shape of Paneef, but discovered that he was not by any means alone.

I crouched by that archway for a few moments to watch the two of them talk. Paneef was stood in front of a gaunt old man who was sat hunched over something clasped possessively in his frail withered hands. I watched spellbound as he drew this thing up to his lips to feed upon it, but I did not know then what it was or else I would certainly have fled from the terrible place there and then. It was only as he became full and fell back into his seat, dropping this thing to the floor beside him, that I let out a gasp of shock, and my unobserved viewing came to an end.

I heard no words spoken between them, but no sooner had I seen the old man's eyes flicker in my direction, than Paneef turned also to look at me. I did not know what to do in that moment, as their eyes fell upon me, but it would not be me that would make that decision.

Again something seemed to pass between the two of them, but what was said I couldn't hear. It was Paneef who called out to me to enter the tall stone chamber they occupied, and I did so, only to meet the man whom I was supposed to have met the previous night.

The old man was ashen grey and gnarled with dust and deep wrinkles. He looked gravely ill as he sat twisted in his chair, his hair all but fallen from his peppered scalp, his head lolling as if the sheer effort of staying alive was growing too much for him. His eyes, though, when finally they settled upon me, burned as brightly as the scarlet flames of the torches that lit the room, and they filled me with the deepest dread. His tongue flicked across his lips as I stared at him, and I shivered as I saw the stain of red, stark upon his white teeth. I was confused, Kirsty. I couldn't work out why his teeth would be glistening with red. That was when I looked down at the possession he had clasped so tightly as if nothing else was important to him. I saw that possession lying beside his chair, small and dark, and it still shuddered with the memory of a pulse. It was what he had fed upon. Dear God, Kirsty. It was the body of a small goat.

He spoke to me then, his voice fragile when it came, and he told me that his name was Merricah. He too seemed to know who I was and then rattled off a list of things I must do. I barely heard a word of what he said. My mind was somewhere else. I could barely register control enough to stand upright, I was on the verge of passing out, but all I could do was focus on the red stain of blood on the whiteness of his teeth.

I had to sit down to catch my breath as he spoke, on an elaborate wooden seat across from him, but it was only after a short while that Paneef picked up the flow of Merricah's words. He kept telling me over and over that they knew who I was and that I had to help them find something hidden deep inside the temple. I was confused, I couldn't think straight, and I think then was when I first tried to escape.

They both tried to hold me back, young Paneef with his hands, frail Merricah with his words. I shrugged them both off in equal measure and headed for the archway unrestrained. But I didn't realise that there was reason, and what reason, for their wanting to keep me inside the chamber.

I had not got far. I don't think I had even heard the sounds until I left the corridor and stepped once more into the torchlight near the bottom of the great staircase. Paneef was following behind me, tugging on my shirt and insisting I return with him to Merricah's chamber. I resisted him for only a few seconds more after that, and that was because I now registered the sounds churning ahead of me.

"It is the creature," Paneef hissed. "I can hear it breathing. Can you not hear it?"

I could hear it, of course, or at least I could hear

something. It did not sound like breathing, as the boy had described, but more like the sound of some great enormous engine, with gears and cogs, or like a vast chariot battalion, a hundred strong, grinding and pulsing. I stood and stared into the shadowy darkness, listening to this strange sound of motion, with Paneef tugging me back with all his strength, shouting at me now to retreat before it was too late. My focus flickered across the darkest of the shadows, my consciousness not really grasping anything around me. Not, at least, until I saw it.

It was waiting there, this thing, in those shadows, a creature like a burnished cloud of bruised flesh, with veins of light flickering throughout its body, a transient motion visible inside but unable to be studied because of the subtle shifting of its masses. Pistons came to mind. Yes, pistons. I could see them now, churning and grinding inside.

"It is the creature," Paneef cried again. "It has found us."

To even look upon this thing as real was impossible, and yet I could not help but back away from it. I cannot describe it any more than I already have, my love. There was a monster, in front of me, and I ran from it.

I ran as fast as I could, with this creature's noise of infernal industry churning at my heels. Back into the chamber we dashed, back into sight of that hateful old man. We pushed ourselves through the narrow opening, Paneef and I, just as that thing bore down upon us. But it could not get through, and I stood stricken with terror as I prayed that the stone archway would not crumble beneath its pounding. There were surely more than several tons of stone keeping it back,

23

and the monster seemed to understand this, and backed away from the archway quite readily, accepting this apparently temporary defeat as though it had done it a thousand times, before it retreated into the depths of the corridor where it bellowed frustrated breaths at us.

"There is no other way out," I remember Merricah telling me, as though to answer a question I had not even voiced.

It seemed as though that was the only door, and as I turned back, the creature had already retreated further, back along the corridor, but still berating the solid stonework with whatever it had - tooth, claw or bone. I turned to look at those that I was to share what would be the rest of the night with, and they seemed prepared to tell me more about the reason for my being there, as well as the history of the temple and the terrifying creature that ran throughout its hallways.

"The beast first appeared in this hallowed temple of Kah'Thoth some sixteen hundred years ago," Merricah began to tell me. "Kah'Thoth was my Master, and he ruled this province for many years, making it prosperous compared to other lands. But it was during a single night's terror that so many died that fateful eve. The creature appeared like a sandstorm in the heart of the temple, and then devoured each tribesman in turn as it swept through the chambers and corridors. A hundred different deaths from a hundred different maws, and each one offering no hope but oblivion. I saw my brother Kel'e'cah burned into the ground like tinder, and my sister Jojeh stripped of her flesh. I saw a dozen others, from all tribes, ripped and razored and turned inside out. Their deaths were as sudden as they were unprecedented, and we could do nothing but watch it come."

"We watched our brothers and sisters fall around us like wheat in a heavy rain," he continued, "helpless beneath the destruction that the creature brought. But then, at the height of its frenzy, it suddenly froze and fled. I did not see what had happened, for the fighting between the tribes had already begun. The families had been decimated to a shadow of their former selves within minutes, and yet each side blamed the other for the creature's summoning. Some fled, most fought. And yet that was to be the last day that I ever saw Jackel El'a'cree, the visiting Master of Kar'mi'shah, alive."

I watched him for a while as he laboured to adjust his position in the wooden chair, his eyes closing once again as he relived the terrible memory. I remember asking him how he knew that this Master wasn't dead, although why I even asked that question I still do not know. His reply was straight, however, as though all this madness was somehow real.

"Because the creature has never left the temple," he told me flatly. "It could have hunted the others down. It could have tracked the known worlds for those that had survived. But I believe that it still looks for Jackel. It travels the corridors and chambers of this temple endlessly, searching for him, as it has done so for hundreds of years. It waits, as do I, for the day when the Master of Kar'mi'shah will once again walk these halls."

"But surely then will it not kill him like it did the others?" I found myself saying.

I watched then as the expression on Merricah's face, which had been building with a kind of hope, now descended into one of sadness and loss. It seemed that as much as he thought his own survival or salvation depended on this master of his, he realised that he was as much a prisoner of words as he was of stone walls and vaulted temple ceilings.

"You must find Jackel El'a'cree before the creature does," the old man said to me, clutching desperately at my clothes with his frail grey hands. "You must free him. If anyone can save us all, it will be him."

For some reason I asked him how I could possibly help, but then he began his story afresh, with the understanding that he knew who I was, that he understood how my knowledge of archaeology could decipher the hieroglyphics and texts that kept this Jackel El'a'cree trapped inside his prison.

Oh Kirsty, you have no idea how I felt down there, trapped below the surface of the desert in that nightmarish tomb. I could still hear the distant groans of that monster echoing along the corridors as it continued its search, and I was so afraid. Even now as I write this, I'm sure I can still hear it scraping at the entrance to the temple, assaulting the great solid blocks of stone in its attempt to come after me. I am scared, Kirsty, so very scared. My ship will be leaving soon, to start my journey back home to you, my only desire the thought of your arms to welcome me home. But I feel that I may never feel them again. I fear that I will never see you again. I love you, Kirsty, and I want you to know that. I am lost without you.

I struggle to hold this pen in my shaking hands, it hurts to even keep my eyes open upon this page, but I have to tell you, my beloved Kirsty, the rest of my story, and of the terrible thing that I have done.

I eventually conceded to the old man and allowed Paneef to take me through a series of passageways to a tiny chamber where he believed the Master Jackel El'a'cree was imprisoned. Please do not ask me why I even went, if ever I see you again, because I do not have any answers. There were similar hieroglyphics to those I saw outside the temple, over the archway to the chamber, but they were painted in a deep rich hue of red, perhaps even blood, and they perplexed me with their imagery. Paneef himself would not enter and bade me go alone which I duly did, deep into the prison of paint and symbol.

I wandered slowly inside, the beam from my torch illuminating more hieroglyphics and texts as I went, but it wasn't until I came upon a small box in the middle of the tomb that I found the charred body of another man. Oh Kirsty, I swear I did not do it. I swear I did not know why I went there. But when I shone the beam of my torch across it, I recognised the burnt face of my poor friend Rajesh. I fell to my knees and wept at his side, but my grief was cut horribly short by the sudden echoing booms of the creature somewhere inside the halls of the temple. I was vulnerable, I knew, and I did something which I knew I should not have done. I snatched up the box, Kirsty. I snatched up the box in the middle of the tomb and ran.

The monster's howls boomed louder as I reached the annex to the chamber, and Paneef came swiftly out of the darkness with a whoop of joy in his throat. He wrenched the box from my uncertain hands and darted back the way we had come. I ran after him, screaming for all I was worth, as the booms and the bellows of the creature came louder and louder behind me.

A cry suddenly came from ahead, however, and I turned a corner to find Paneef standing there in a halo of light. But the light came not from a torch or a candle, but from the box itself. The boy stood motionless in a pale orange glow, and I just had time to catch the expression on his face flicker from uncertainty to fear as the fire came. Flames leapt from the box to engulf his meagre frame, licking across his body as it turned him into a living furnace, burning and blackening him and turning his flesh swiftly into ash. The monster's howls came louder at my back then, and I could hear too the pistons of its heart and the grinding of its claws pound against the stone of the floor and walls. There was no longer any time to think. The creature was upon me.

I turned back to see the blackened smouldering husk of Paneef's body tumble awkwardly to the ground, the flames still skipping off his limbs, and saw the box drop from his charred fingers into the sand. I stood for a few moments, just staring at it, my mind blank. The creature rocked the chamber around me, its bellows of rage furious, and it gave me movement. I felt the box in my hand as I stooped to pick it up, and then I was running, back through hallways, and past the broken archway where Merrich lived out his endless days. I heard his frail shouts behind me but I kept going, through the torchlight and up that great staircase of stone.

The pounding of the creature echoed behind me all the way, but still I ran, and it wasn't until I reached the narrow entrance and hauled myself out into the dawn's brightening light that I fell to my knees in a fit of anguish. I lay helpless in the sand, panting and crying out as the creature bellowed and pounded the stone entrance just yards behind me. I waited, and I listened, for it to finally break free and devour me there and then with its terrible jaws, but the great stone blocks kept it back, and I thought that I had perhaps escaped intact.

Oh Kirsty, my fever grows worse, but my conscience troubles me more than my health. I still have the box, and it is packed up along with my belongings already aboard the ship. There is a curse upon me, I can feel it crawling beneath my scalp and in my veins, and its evil is devouring me from the inside. My only hope is that the monster has already given up its assault upon the stone temple entrance. Please forgive me, my love, I did not know what I was doing. If it escapes, then I have unleashed something terrible upon the world. Destroy all my cases if you have the chance. Burn them, commit them to the ocean, I do not care, but just save yourself, and the rest of mankind.

Forgive me.
I love you more than you can know.
Jonathan.

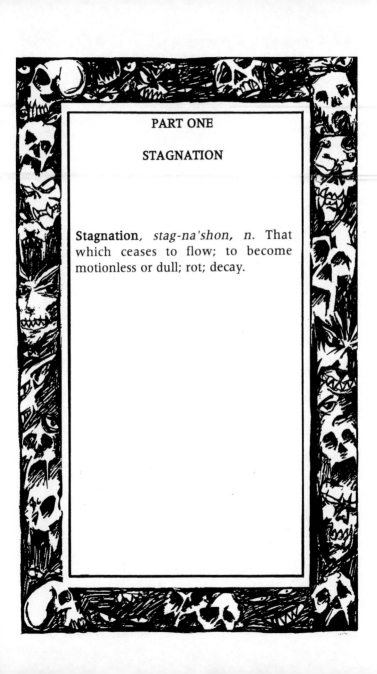

PART ONE

STAGNATION

Stagnation, *stag-na'shon*, *n.* That which ceases to flow; to become motionless or dull; rot; decay.

ONE

FEED

The vampire inclined her head only slightly to confirm the qualities of the man who had come to rest against the bar a little way along from her. Her eyes pierced the space around him, her ears acutely separating the differing tones of breath, heartbeat and pulse. The music in the night-club was pounding, the disco lights dazzling, shrouding, but so many things were clear to her already, more perfect than any words that could ever be exchanged between them, more insistent, even, than her hunger. His qualities were few.

His breath alone wore information like billboards as he exhaled it out before him; alcohol, odours of fermentation, nicotine, all of which indicated that he had consumed many beers and many cigarettes. Yet his breath carried more; stale food, the advancement of tooth decay, lung disease; he was there to be tasted like a book of foulness. Her nose curled slightly in disgust. Her attention drifted back out towards the dance floor again, filtering out the boom of the music, tuning in the pulse and the heartbeats of the dancers. Some had gone since she'd last looked, others had arrived. The man beside her had shifted along the bar a few inches towards her. He would talk to her, no doubt. She inclined her head briefly and captured his scents once again. Her focus shifted towards him almost imperceptibly. Something about his nose, his nasal hairs; there were flecks of white powder adhered to them - speed, she guessed, or possibly cocaine. Her attention flickered towards his eyes. They were partially glazed, barely registering her as he gazed back at her. He couldn't know of her intense scrutiny, not even under the influence of sobriety, and the vampire simply watched his eyes swap views between her cleavage and her legs, his pupils widening frequently. It was sex he wanted, she knew full well. Good, she thought. It would things so much easier, and quicker.

She watched him turn awkwardly and set his drink down at the space on the bar between them. He leaned forward a little, a sour breath slipping from his lips as he wetted them with that coated tongue of his, and then the words came, right on cue.

"What's your name, honey?"

This was a game she had even enjoyed on occasion. With the right guy, or girl, it was sometimes even pleasurable for a while. But tonight, this man was simply disgusting, and it made her feel ill just to register his existence. He was swaying, she could see that without any study, and she wanted to just smack him to the ground right there and then. It was getting late, though, and there were other things that she wanted to pass the night with before dawn, and that one simple desire put momentum into her own words.

"Does it matter?" she replied flatly, her tone even.

The man's smile creased into a grin, his eyes straying once more to her cleavage, widening ever so slightly at the possibility of her breasts. He wanted to touch them so badly, she knew. His ultimate surrender was almost inevitable.

"Yeah, I know what you want," he breathed, the

odours coming like a plague of flies. He leant towards her a little more and placed a hand on one of her knees, his sweat-damp fingers slick as he squeezed it. Her teeth clenched in her mouth, her eyes soured to a sharp acid stare.

"And what's that?" she returned, her fury held momentarily by words.

"Let's get out of here," he urged her, his eyebrow curling as he himself rose from the bar. "It's late."

A flood of cold emotions flashed through the vampire's mind as this human laid himself at her feet. He was there for the taking, but she couldn't help a stray thought rafting inside her head. She had been watching a number of party-goers inside the club - standing, talking, dancing, drinking - and any one of them she could have left with, male or female. Such was the prerogative of the young woman, nobody would have suspected her, or indeed denied her attention. There had been a young black man moving with such rhythm and harmony that she had not been able to take her eyes off him for over an hour. She had seen through his dark silk shirt by the lights blazing above him, his muscles firm and healthy across a rigid torso. His hair had been neatly cropped, his skin unblemished and clean, and yet there had been something about him that declared more than just his weight in blood. To see this young man dance, with the coloured lights playing so beautifully across his black flesh, his hands seeming to caress the air, was intoxicating, something to be admired, and it had been enough to keep her seated at the bar, and enough to keep him alive for another night.

There had been a couple also. They had appeared briefly at the bar a little way along from her, ordering two non-alcoholic drinks. They too were lean, more toned than muscular, and by the healthiness of their heartbeats and only a trace of sweat on their skin, she presumed a fitness agenda played a major part somewhere in their lives. That skin had seemed almost vibrant beneath the artificial lights, strong and firm, and the vampire had thought how pleasurable it would have been to puncture it. But she had not been in the mood to seduce two mortals tonight. She simply wanted to feed and be done with it, and give the rest of the night over to wandering beside the moonlit Thames.

"So will it be my place or yours?"

The man was still there. Indulgence had let practicality slip, and her eyes flickered quickly back to him, the motion resurrecting the gut of disgust. His sweat-greased fingers left slug-trails on the bar as he pushed them between the narrowing breach between them. She felt a bile of rage begin to burn in her throat as he then used those fingers to take hold of her elbow.

"You can finish your drink later if you like," he murmured, inclining his head yet further towards her.

He wants to go now, she thought to herself, and he hasn't even noticed that I don't have a drink. The stench of stale odours escaping his pores was becoming more unpleasant, vying against those that straddled the words suppurating from his mouth, and she realised with no pleasure that she would have to take him quickly before he simply soured her appetite. Her mind drifted back to the young black man on the dance floor, and briefly she even glanced his way, but he was gone now. She turned back to look at this man, this denizen of humanity, and gazed at the grin still attached to his face. He had no grace or charm, nobility or rhythm. All he had was blood. She wanted him dead.

The vampire climbed down off her stool and allowed him to lead her through the night-club towards the door. On the way she noticed at least two different men watching their departure, obscuring their interest by trying to hide their emotions behind lifted drinks. Their expressions turned as she passed them; jealousy for the man holding her arm, sadness for their own indecision or reticence, but mostly anger because they thought she was leaving to have sex with him. How little they knew, she thought, and how different their emotions would be should they have known. She gave one of them a tiny smile, and enjoyed the sight of the flushing of his face, blood rushing close to the surface where his skin grew fragile. She would see him again. Maybe not tonight or tomorrow night, but he would be back to wait and watch for her. It almost seemed cruel.

A chill wind brightened her senses the instant she stepped outside onto the pavement, and he at once seemed different. His eyes were waxy and bloodshot, darkness circling the wrinkles surrounding them. His skin was more pale and neglected, and reeked of odours engrained more deeply within his pores than she had perceived inside. His breath, when he opened his mouth to speak again, seemed even more foul than it had, and she could barely manage to register his words so much did it turn her stomach. She let him walk her along the street a little, his hand finding her buttocks, his fingers seeking out the crease between them, before she tired of him altogether. It must have been at least an hour after midnight, and if she were to play this charade for much longer she knew she would not be back on the street until gone two. Even with the remnants of the day's pollutants still lingering in the air like tainted gossamer, the breeze was sweet compared to this collection of stagnating odours. When they neared an unlit alleyway that led through the streets of Hammersmith in the direction of the river, she took hold of his trousers at the crotch and levered him into it.

"You just can't wait, can you, baby?" the man said, as he pushed his hand firmly up onto one of her breasts.

She could feel the rank sweat from his palm seep into her. Her teeth bared suddenly and a snarl rumbled from the back of her throat. He seemed to take the threat as an urgency of sexual need, and he grabbed hold of her waist with his other hand and pulled her hard against him. She was sick of this game entirely now, and snatching hold of a fistful of hair at the back of his head, yanked his skull back to expose his throat. His cry was stricken immediately, his windpipe forced closed, and his hands left her body altogether as he tried to take hold of her grasp upon him.

Her teeth were extended now, crystalline with saliva, and as her head bowed down towards him, she opened her mouth and sank them deep into his neck. She felt him clutch at her as she broke through the taut surface of his skin, his body flinching and contracting around her as the first gush of hot blood poured over the back of her tongue. The vampire sucked hard upon him as she drank, feeling neither remorse nor guilt, only contentment that such a foul creature would soon be dead.

It was dangerous for her to kill out on the streets, of course, she knew that even as she drank, but the night was precious. Every moment brought wonders to her that other vampires had long ago tired of, the simplest things bestowing worth upon the valueless everafter. There were so many dangers now, negating that immortality. But the decision had been made, and death had joined the unclean air.

She let the body slip from her arms and watched as it collapsed into an awkward tangle of pliant limbs. He seemed almost reverent now that he was bereft of life, but he was just a meal, worth his weight in blood, and that was all. Reality checked rapidly in, however, and her focus narrowed to her own sudden predicament. It would take time to find a place to hide the body, but then what was the point? She knew that it would be found within twenty four hours anyway, whether it be by a skulker, the police or another vampire. Best to be gone now and quickly, she decided, before anyone caught the scent of the corpse on the air and found her with that same scent on both her tongue and lips.

TWO

SHOULD OLD AQUAINTANCES BE FORGOT

It was a feeling of being misplaced and a sense of not being a part of things that was the biggest difference, and it was a difference that seemed somehow to be undoing him from the inside. Jenner Hoard was sitting on the edge of his single bed, gazing out at the dismal rain-threatening sky hanging over the rooftops of Hammersmith, grey and noxious, unappealing, unwelcoming. The dull blue smoke from the cigarette burning in his fingers curled lightly towards the ceiling, a slowly writhing distraction between himself and the city, and he pulled it absently to his lips and inhaled.

There was no consolation to be had from the cigarette, no contentment, no escape, and certainly no pleasure. But it was something familiar - and God just how familiar - but even that seemed awkward in this renewed environment. It had been only hours since his release from Her Majesty's Pleasure, and he had stepped out through those old prison gates with the dream of the moment singing in his heart. The moment itself had been dead, there had been nothing to feel, but he had built that dream in the months leading up to his release, and he had told himself what freedom would mean when finally it came. Yes, he had no bars to obscure the daytime now, and no, there was no schedule anymore for his taking a shit, but it was the rhythm that he'd dreamed of for all those months that he couldn't get into, the rhythm of his life now as a free man, and it was just eating him up like a dull gnawing pack of rats.

His flat had been untended for the two years that he'd been inside, and the smell of damp and mould hung in the air of his bedroom, along with other acrid smells that he didn't want to think about, but he had neither the strength in his limbs nor the will in his blood to reach forward and open the window to let in some of the wonderful fumes that clung to London like swamp water. His stomach ached with hunger, and he put a hand to it gingerly, pressing his fingertips into the grey paunch that had appeared over his time spent inside. He only had what money he'd had returned to him on leaving the prison, plus a few scraps left in the bank which was nothing worth drawing on, and he'd spent it all on food from the market on his way back to the flat.

Money was the source of everything, that much he knew, and even though he had next to nothing at the moment, he had at least allowed himself the luxury, after two year's abstinence, of vodka, the cheapest bottle he could find, some kind of gut-rot with a foreign label, as well as a packet of cigarettes to last him the rest of the week. They both still sat in front of him on the small wooden table, both nasty and both half empty, and he now reached out and took a draft from the bottle before pulling another of the cigarettes from the pack. Lighting it from the short stub still burning in his fingers, he lay back on his bed and watched the two columns of blue smoke entwine slowly together in their soft subtle patterns, and lost himself for a moment in their sheer simplicity.

A car door slammed outside in the street and his eyes flicked back to the window. There was a light drizzle falling now, he could see the subtle pattern of rain dropping against the grey cloud cover like needles. And then a sound came from his front door, and he inclined his head a little towards it as he listened. Easing himself up off the bed, he headed warily out into the hallway. So used to the prison guards placing everything in front of him like a scolded child, it took him a few moments to realise that it was just the sound of mail dropping onto the floor. It was only when he remembered that the postman delivered mail to the mailbox for the whole block of flats, and that it was late in the afternoon anyway, that he realised something was wrong, and moved quickly to the door.

On the floor was a single envelope, and Jenner stared at it for a moment before stooping to pick it up. It was sealed and he quickly wedged a thumb beneath the flap and tore it open. Inside was a note, the handwriting of which was immediately recognisable. He may have forgotten a lot of things while he had been in prison - the smell of a woman, the taste of cheap vodka on his tongue, steak, fresh air, the wind off the Thames - but the neat script of the man responsible for his criminal rise and eventual incarceration was not one of them. It took only another moment for him to pull open the front door and step out into the hallway, but the landing was already quiet. A few soiled rubbish bags littered the doorway of one of the other flats across from him, the stairwell to the right lay empty and silent, but of the messenger who had delivered the note there was simply no sign.

Wandering back into his flat, Jenner closed the door behind him before stepping through into the kitchen to look more closely at the note. It was indeed from Montague, as he had known, and he scanned quickly back over the neat lines to get to the point of the letter as he pulled the new bread and peanut butter out of the fridge with his other hand. Why he had put them in the fridge at all he had no idea, the electricity had not been reconnected, but he spread some of the peanut butter roughly onto a couple of dry slices before folding them in two and taking them back into the bedroom along with the note. Perching on the end of the bed once more, he reread it with utter disbelief.

Montague was insane. Twenty four months he had served in prison for a burglary that had gone wrong from the start. The police had been there seconds after he had entered, and they'd caught him without an excuse. Now here, just hours after his release, Montague had sent him a note asking him to contact him for details of another. It was madness, sheer madness. There was simply no other word for it.

Actually, there was another word for it, a more important word that seemed to fill his head incessantly.

Money.

The water was still connected, which was something, but without the electricity to heat it, he skipped the shower, and simply headed out into the street as he was, keen to know the score on the streets he had been away from for so long. An old acquaintance used to rent a room less than ten minutes away, and he decided to go see what the deal was. Jenner didn't know if Kole still lived there, he hadn't heard from him while he'd been inside, but Kole had also done the occasional job for Montague, and his insights might at least be worth the visit. He was the only person he could think of that might be able to help him get out of the shit that Montague was trying to get him right back into, and might also know if there was a more reasonable way for an ex-con to make some quick money. The last thing he needed was to go straight back inside. No more burglaries, he promised himself, and no more drug trafficking.

Hurrying past the market, he started suddenly as he heard his name yelled from amongst the tangle of busy stalls. With his thoughts still wrapped inside Montague's games, his first reaction was to run. Reality kicked in almost immediately, however, and he turned his head, locating who it was straight away. It was the beautiful girl waving her arm over her head from the depths of a crowd, a leopard print hat perched elegantly on her head, a matching jacket snug around her shoulders. It was Emma, dear sweet Emma. It was a friendly face, too friendly perhaps for his first day out, and he just wasn't in the mood for the questions that he knew she would have about his life spent behind bars.

"When did you get out?" she wanted to know, throwing her arms lovingly around his shoulders as she reached him.

"This morning," Jenner told her, reluctantly accepting her overwhelming embrace, his mind still wrapped tight with the worries of making a living.

"And you didn't call?"

It was a simple enough excuse to tell her that he had no cash for a phone call, which was the truth after all, but he received the answer he thought he was going to get; she opened her purse and offered him what notes she had. His reluctance to re-ignite their relationship was exceeded only by the grisly ache still gnawing at his stomach, and despite the guilt he felt for intentionally misleading her, a trait a convicted criminal should have long since left behind, he accepted her offer of dinner.

Sitting awkwardly at a window table at the Peking Palace, Jenner stared out at the ever-increasing traffic rushing past while Emma began talking opposite him. He had nothing to say to her, and so he let her carry most of the conversation, and watched occasionally as she put on a consoling face whenever she asked him about the awfulness of prison life.

He'd been a thief when she'd met him, and she'd found it a deeply thrilling addition to a lifestyle that was paid for by her father. All this he knew, and if it wasn't for his conscience, he would have taken her for every penny he could get his hands on. It was strange, this conscience of his, he thought to himself as he watched her grin at him over the rim of her wine glass. He could go to bizarre lengths to break into mansions or institutions and steal files or jewels, and then evade both the security and the police for just a fraction of what he could get by sitting back and letting Emma pay for everything he wanted. But then it occurred to him on each occasion that he thought this way, that she simply wouldn't look twice at him if he wasn't a criminal in the first place. He was an object to her, pure and simple. That was the truth, and that was why he felt so indifferent about her. Sure, the sex was good, and she was a beautiful woman to have on his arm and to look at, but she didn't seem interested in him in the slightest, only what he was and what he did. It made her rich friends gasp at the sheer audacity of it.

Jenner felt her touch his hand and he realised that she'd said something that needed a response. He hadn't heard a word she'd said, but then had he ever?

"I want to know if you'll come over," she said again. "Everyone will be there."

Jenner nodded briefly. He didn't know what he was nodding for, but she smiled anyway. She was happy. It was such a stupid situation that even if he didn't turn up for anything she had planned, she just thought him even more of a rogue, and therefore more adorable. He hated her shallowness, but then she was buying him dinner, and thought that she at least deserved to have him hang around long enough to eat it.

After the meal came and went, and they were leaving the restaurant, the subject of Jenner's electricity and telephone came up, with the result that Emma offered to pay to have them both reconnected. Only once they were outside in the street, and with the dilemma of them walking their separate ways, did Emma push things further still, suggesting that she stay the night with him.

"We can be together again," she whispered. "Like we used to be."

"I don't think so, Em. I'm not feeling right."

"That's okay," she said with a mischievous grin. "You can lie back and I'll do all the difficult stuff. Just like I used to do."

Her hands were on his chest now, tracing delicate circles up across his face and then teasing through his dark hair. Jenner stepped away from her, away from her touch, but she simply stepped after him, that smile of hers still on her lips.

"Tell me we can," she said breathlessly, pressing her lips gently against his neck, her other hand tracing a path down across his stomach to his groin, where it cupped him firmly.

"Look, Em, I don't feel like it tonight. I... I'll have to call you."

"Yeah, right," she toyed. "Like I haven't heard that one before. You say you'll phone, and then you won't, and then I'll have to come over, and beg you to let me stay -"

"I don't want you like that anymore," Jenner heard himself saying. God, why was he even saying it? He hadn't had sex for two years. "You don't love me, you never have."

"What do you know about love?" she said bluntly, her kisses still coming passionately across his neck. "I'm just some object for you to use. And you love that, don't you?"

Her hands were toying with him more forcefully now through the fabric of his jeans, and after such abstinence how could he do anything but comply?

"Don't you want to use me?" she breathed, her voice shallow, seductive.

His eyes flickered closed as he felt her fingers and lips against him, caressing him where for two years there had been nothing but harshness and rough prison laundry. Her touch was insistent, perhaps even loving, and despite his former feelings of not being a part of the world, he allowed himself the pleasure of it. His attention had been stolen entirely by her, until the blaring horn of a car somewhere along the darkened street snatched him from her affection, and his eyes flickered open, revealing to him the reality that had skipped his notice. They were stood on the pavement on a busy London street, while passing drivers watched her feel him up. He grasped her hands firmly, instantly stopping their motions. Her eyes found his, afraid, but willing. He let her go, wanting just to be gone and away from the scrutiny of the eyes on the rainy dark street, but Emma was not prepared to be done with him just yet.

Jenner stared at her, almost helplessly, as she slowly lifted the hem of her dress and showed him the white silk knickers that she wore underneath, right in the middle of the street. It was becoming more than he could bear, and he felt the eyes of the drivers turning to watch this spectacle as they made their ways home bear down on him like some vast colossal weight. How often had he dreamed of a woman, naked and willing for sex? Every night and every day for the past two years. Now here was the beautiful Emma, offering him anything he wanted, begging him to take her, and all he wanted was to be alone. Quickly he took hold of her hand, more to be away than anything else, her dress swishing back across her thighs once more, as he hauled her along the street after him in the direction of his flat.

She giggled at his roughness, even as he dragged her across the road to the disdain of passing pedestrians. She bent to lick the fingers that held her, even as he cursed her out loud. She urged him on, even as he began to lose his temper with her and pushed her angrily against the wall of his building before dragging her upstairs to his flat.

She stood her ground once she was inside, and leant back against the door, her fingertips slowly playing across the white silk underwear that she exposed for him once again. Then, as he watched, she asked him one last time to take her to bed. Jenner had the means in his own underwear, he could feel it straining at the front of his jeans - how could it not be with such stimulation? - and his thoughts went briefly to Kole, and to Montague, and to the problems he still had with his money, before he snatched her up in his arms, carried her through into the bedroom, and hurled her down onto the bed.

He took her there and then, on the unmade bed beneath the yellow pallor of the streetlamps flooding in through the grimy top floor windows.

Emma was willing, of course, crying and yelping and turning her body to any device he wanted, clawing and moaning as he pleasured himself of her. It had occurred to him on occasion in the past to perhaps try and pleasure her, but she had never seemed tempted to mention it, and he had never seemed interested enough before to use anything other than what he was currently using. So when finally he exhausted himself and rolled off and away from her, she uttered not one single word of complaint, not even as she wrapped her arms tightly around him, but simply let him drift into a welcome, if shallow, sleep in his own bed.

THREE

SEDUCTION

The night was cool, the air less polluted than it had been, and a crisp white moon pierced the sullen sky, bathing Covent Garden in a perfect radiant glimmer of light. The small paved square heaved beneath a weight of surging bodies, the stone buildings condensing the clamour of human voices into a dull focal din, as Saturday night drew a vast crowd to the bars and clubs, each and every one of them eager to nullify their senses with alcohol, to parade themselves in desperate rituals of sexual frenzy, and to crawl blindly into the blissful arms of whoever might have them.

The vampire stood tall and motionless beside the grand white columns of the ancient monument building, hidden from prying eyes inside a veil of darkness, vigilant, preying, watching everything before him as though it were a third-world market. The human condition, he thought to himself, so frail, so ambitious, and yet so prone to distraction that it seemed almost unkind to take their pitiful fleeting lives from them. A literal paradox was what made them pitiful, so fierce were they and yet so weak, so transient and yet so fully aware of their own existence. Poor dumb creatures, one and all.

Strings of helpless mortals threaded their way through the amassing throng as he watched them, some dressed up for the night, others dressed down for want of attention. A group of seven individuals caught his attention, less than nineteen years all of them, circling in a drunken state near to where he haunted the shadows. They were loud in both their laughter and their costumes, hugging each other and strangers alike, and dressed in little more than white cotton bedsheets. Togas, he guessed they were aiming for.

His eyes pierced the uncertain darkness between them, the moonlight overhead vying for dominance over the gaudy bright lights that flooded the square, as he inhaled the rich aromas and internal rhythms of each of their bodies. Ripe, young and fresh, their blood would be so very sweet. And it would come freely and eagerly too, flooding from their bodies in a torrent that would slip down his throat with a consummate and passionate ease. It would be bliss, too, and it would be right. One of them would die this night.

The loudest of their number was female and overweight, confident and brash, and he studied her coldly as she forced her way through the bustling crowd, leading the group to the next bar. She commanded the most sobriety, he could see, her gaze even with clarity, the most likely to put up a fight, although against his formidable strength a fight was too great a word. Two young males followed in her wake, drawn by her lavish attentions towards them, all three of them trailing so sickly a stench of hormones and sexual want that it nauseated him with its potency. There were better kills than this, and out of the four children that followed, only one of them staggered out of step with the rest, drunk to the point of incompetence.

Her eyes were glazed and uncertain as she clung

helplessly to the fluttering costumes of those that led her, her infirm body buffeted from side to side by the masses that harangued her inept and ragged progress. The vampire tracked her doggedly as the group made their cumbersome way through the clamouring crowd. It seemed almost coincidence that her face drifted up out of her stupor towards him, that uncertain sight finding him even through the shroud of darkness that he had folded around himself. The vampire stepped out from behind this cloak of shadows only marginally, enough so that the bright moonlight overhead caught his pallid features, but not nearly so much that the remainder of the crowd should suddenly see him.

The girl found him beneath the pale moonlight more readily now, and as the vampire beckoned her towards him with a simple motion of his hand, he watched with a cruel seductive satisfaction as her hand slipped the guiding rein of the friend she trailed and came, unquestioningly and with a coy smile, up the wide stone steps and into the shrouded sanctity of the vampire's powerful darkness.

Guiding her away from the sight of her friends behind one of the tall white pillars of the monument building, the vampire moved so very close to her that they were almost touching. Her scent bewitched him immediately with a natural perfume of health and youth, even through the stagnating odour of sweat and alcohol that reeked from her pores and sought to sicken him. Her bloodshot eyes betrayed the confidence she was trying to create for this stranger, uncertain and dilating, but the vampire saw through it all with an eye practised at bringing death. She could not cheat him. He would soon open her veins and taste her blood.

"I think I've had a bit too much to drink," the girl confessed, swaying inside the cradle of his arms.

"Alcohol will do that to you," the vampire said simply.

"My name's Shiri," she went on, her smile blossoming helplessly into an inebriated, if uncertain, grin. "I go to one of the colleges here. Is that where you go?"

"No."

Distilled from the corruptive odours, the aroma of her body was still alluring, blissful even, and the vampire inhaled her intoxicating scent appreciatively as she spoke. He studied her with a practised eye, distantly but still entranced, even as she pushed a mop of unruly sweat-damp hair out of her eyes to try to see him better, staggering back against the pillar from the suddenness of the motion. It seemed to partially embarrass her.

"My friends are just over there," she continued, with a giggle and a vague movement of her hand. "Why don't you join us? You're more than welcome. We're having a bit of a celebration tonight."

The vampire did not answer her, and he watched as her grin faltered for a moment. She was weak, and would be so easy to prey upon. He held her face with one hand, delicately.

"I saw you," he whispered to her, "and I thought we felt a connection. I thought you maybe felt it too. Is this not the case? I think, perhaps, that if I have made that mistake, then I have embarrassed us both."

She looked at him, uncertain of how to respond.

She tried to smile.

"You feel as though you're more of a solitary

person than your friends, don't you? You feel as though they don't understand you. You're different, and you spend much of your time on your own."

"How do you know that?" she suddenly yearned to know, her smile dropping.

"We share that loneliness, Shiri. The heartache, the pain of feeling misplaced, of being isolated. We are different from other people. We share that pain. That is what I thought we felt."

The girl stared at him, her smile waning further beneath the weight of his words.

The human condition.

It was so very frail.

So very predictable.

"It hurts," she agreed, her eyes flickering with sadness now.

"You're too beautiful to feel such pain, Shiri," the vampire continued breathlessly, his face almost brushing against the sweet smoothness of her skin. "Someone like you should never have to feel alone. Neither of us should."

Her hair literally shimmered with youth, so fragrant and so warm. He wanted to touch it, to grasp it, to feel it against his cheek and neck as he imagined biting down into her throat and taking her life.

"When was the last time you were told that?" he whispered, restraining himself from taking her there and then.

She shook the notion away, tears welling swiftly.

Despair seemed close, so readily close.

There would be no fight.

"You should be told that," the vampire continued, "because you are. You are beautiful, Shiri, so very beautiful."

"You're messing with me now," she told him. "I'm going back to my friends."

"No, Shiri," he took up her hand now, clasping that smooth resilient skin. She was perfect. So fresh. So very young. "I want you here. With me. Say you will."

"Let me go. I want to go back to my friends now."

"Do you?" he exclaimed, intensely. "Do you really want your friends? Do you want them even though they won't tell you how beautiful you are? Do you want them even though they can't hold you and tell you how much they care about you? They don't care, and they don't love, and they haven't even stopped to come back to look for you. But I'm here, Shiri. I'm offering myself to you. I'll do anything you ask me, and I'll never complain. Just come with me, and I will make it all alright. I promise I will make it all go away."

The girl stared up at him, helplessly, and he watched with a cold and unfaltering gaze as the despair and the confusion that racked her poor tortured heart blossomed rapidly inside her. He would have that heart too, he promised himself. He would puncture it and tear at it, and suck the last of her blood out through it even as it beat its last dying rhythms. He would kill her without guilt, without remorse, and he would leave her still corpse behind him as if she had never lived at all.

"Yes," she finally uttered quietly to him, breaking the silence between them.

"Do you want me to take you away from all this?" the stranger asked.

"Yes," she murmured again.

"And you want me to love you?"

The girl could only manage a shallow nod this time.

"Then let us go, my love. It is late."

And so they left Covent Garden swiftly and without attention, with the din of human voices harrying the air behind them, and the stench of stale alcohol and human sweat on the breeze like a rancid cloud at their backs. Beside him, the girl was already sniffing back the progress of her tears, swallowing that loneliness down inside her body where it had lingered for so many years already. Through his touch upon her skin, the vampire could feel her chest shudder with despair, and he knew that he would have to be quick in his despatch of her, lest she open up completely and bring attention to those who might do him harm.

He guided her effortlessly away from the square and out into a darkened thoroughfare, his arm now clasping her shoulder firmly. Leading her up the cold grey steps to a small sheltered doorway, he heard a brief but pitiful sob, and then he grasped the back of her head quickly with one hand and exposed her taut young throat to the unfeeling blackness of the night. He paused momentarily at the sight of her pale bare skin, his teeth already lengthened into fangs and slick with saliva, inhaling her heady scent like a potent drug as the smell of her youth overtook him. She was beautiful, this girl, intoxicating, and a wave of conflicting emotions suddenly broke over him even as he sank his teeth deep into her throat and punctured her skin. The girl struggled only briefly, her arms flinching as a fragile gasp skipped somewhere inside her. The vampire held her solid in his strong restricting grasp as he forced himself down even harder upon her, crushing her tiny body as he drank, and drawing the hot sweet fluid out of her body.

Her arms dropped to her sides even before he had drunk his fill, her white cotton toga unravelling and falling open to expose her small young breasts. The vampire gazed down upon her nakedness almost indifferently, and realised the irony in his seduction, promising her love and devotion, but ignoring her body now that it was offered, even in death, for him to play with if he so chose.

He gazed down upon her upturned face now. So beautiful she truly was, this girl no more than nineteen years old. Her dark hair flowed back from her brow like a rich silken veil, her eyes still open to the creature that had killed her, but now they stared up vacant and hollow, no thoughts present behind their cold dull sockets. He watched her for a few moments as he weighed her tiny frame in his arms, so tender and so young, a vessel of blood that would now only rot and decay. She would have parents, he presumed, who would grieve and berate whatever god they prayed to, for allowing their precious daughter to perish so early on in her years. But what was her life anyway? Just a passing moment, a receptacle for transferring one form of energy to another. She had been born from the combined potential of two adults and had cultivated it into a form that he could use himself. He had chosen to take it all, however, to use up all that potential and leave nothing in its place. She was dead now, a corpse that would wither over time, until the earth rotted her bones and used whatever it could to nourish itself. Was he not simply doing the same thing? Playing his part in the cycle of things?

Mortality.

It was a shallow promise indeed.

To offer so much but give so little, and all with ungodly conditions.

The vampire let her body slip down into the small

sheltered doorway, and he stood gazing down at her bare breasts and her dull vacant eyes one last time, before gliding down the cold grey steps and off into the tangled depths of the moonlit night.

The smell of blood was in the air once more, and death filled the night like a clinging shroud of cold wet muslin. The hunters would come, he knew. Perhaps not quickly, and perhaps not until daybreak, but they would come.

And when they came and found the body of the dead young girl, they would ask their questions, and they would gather their weapons, and their fury would increase tenfold as a vengeance for his head would become insurmountable. A battle would become inevitable one night, he knew, and on that night it would be interesting to see who would finally stand the victor, and who would finally turn to dust.

FOUR

BLOOD DEAL

The phone rang for the first time in Jenner's flat just two days later. It was another cold and wet morning, a filthy drizzle clinging to the sprawling greyness of London, and the thief found himself once again in bed with Emma. It was something that he had told himself he would not do, but she had that way with her, of touching him, of coaxing him, and for a convicted criminal, he seemed to be powerless against it.

He glanced across at her as the phone continued to ring in the living room. She was beautiful, he could never deny that, and she was always sweetest towards him when he played at being bad. He'd done some things in his life that he was none too proud of, but nothing serious, nothing like murder or any shit that might actually have hurt someone. Just burglaries mainly, from those that could well afford to have some stuff lifted, as well as the occasional delivery of some new weird drug that Montague had managed to lay his fingers on. She loved him for all his rebellions, though perhaps love was not quite the right word, and he could tolerate that. The notion came into his head suddenly to kiss the part of her forehead where stray wisps of her silken hair had fallen across it in wonderful feather-like curls. But the notion was fleeting - and what if she should catch him? - and so he simply left her and slipped out from beneath the sheets to pick it up the still-ringing phone in the next room.

"You didn't return my message," the voice on the other end of the line said. Jenner recognised the low deep tones of Montague's voice as soon as he lifted the receiver.

"What do you want?" Jenner asked him, rubbing the sleep from his eyes with his thumb and forefinger.

"You," Montague replied bluntly.

"I don't think that's ever going to happen again, do you?"

"I want your services again," Montague continued. "I've had people watching your flat, Jenner, and I know that you've got no money - although I see that the lovely Emma has made your acquaintance again."

"That's none of your business."

"Oh, I think it is," he observed. "You are my business, and I want you back again."

"I'm not interested."

"If you'd read the note, Jenner, you'd realise that I'm offering you a lot of cash, more than I paid you before. Ten grand for one night's work. You can't tell me that you're not interested in that?"

Jenner kept his silence and closed his eyes as he took in a deep breath. That bastard Montague, he knew exactly what to say and how to say it. Sure, he was penniless, they both knew that, and they both knew that Montague's money could set him up for a while.

"You know I've got other jobs as well, don't you?" Montague said on the silent line. "More trafficking. I could get you one tonight, if you wanted. A simple delivery to Watford. Five grand."

Jenner was gritting his teeth now. He so desperately wanted to tell Montague to go fuck himself, recalling the sight of those armed policemen dashing across the grass towards him at that house he'd broken into. He'd promised himself he would be clean of all that from now on. He knew he couldn't face another single night in jail, let alone years, but he knew that he would always be struggling without work like this. Of course he could make quite a life for himself, fleecing Emma for as much as he could get his hands on, but he just couldn't bring himself to treat her like that, no matter how easy it would be.

Jenner had broken a sweat now, the cool air of the living room chilling it, and he could hear Montague's breathing on the other end of the phone, chewing, no doubt, on one of those huge cigars of his. He couldn't do it, he thought to himself, and lowering his hand he replaced the receiver back on its cradle with a click. It just wasn't worth it.

He stood for a few moments staring into middle distance, his head a swirling mess of money and deceit. Then he heard a footstep in the hallway behind him and he turned startled to find Emma standing in the doorway, his shirt from last night wrapped loosely around her naked body. She was smiling at him, a half-smile of uncertainty as she studied the unease in his expression.

"Who was it?" she enquired.

Jenner looked dumbly at her, his thoughts still swirling from the conversation. Did Montague really have someone watching them? He gazed at Emma as she left the doorway and came towards him, tugging the shirt around her more tightly as it began to slip from her shoulders.

"On the phone," she continued. "Who was it? Something bad?"

Slowly Jenner nodded.

"Yeah, something bad," he said, and confessed that it had been Montague on the phone, asking him to go back to work for him again.

"That bastard," she snapped. "Don't you dare work for him again. It was him that put you away, remember?"

"Of course I remember," Jenner yelled, as he stormed past her. "It was me that did the time."

Emma hurried after him, and put her hand on his shoulder as she reached him in the kitchen.

"I'm sorry, honey," she said gently. "I didn't think."

"It's okay," Jenner said to her, turning to frame her face with his hands. She was still beautiful even in this unflattering light. Perhaps they should go away somewhere, just the two of them. Would she even want that? "I know I shouldn't take it out on you. But I think that perhaps you should spend some time away from here, okay?"

"Why?" she wanted to know, putting her hands against his now.

"I think he's got someone watching the flat. It's just better that you're not here if something's going on."

"You're not thinking of seeing him, are you?"

"It's money," Jenner explained, "and that's all it is."

"I've got money," she said. "All that you want."

"I don't want your money," Jenner snapped, regretting his words almost immediately as he watched her pull away from him. Her eyes were wide with something close to disbelief, perhaps even offence, and tears began to well suddenly as she then turned and ran back in the direction of the bedroom.

Jenner turned and smacked the sink with his fist as he gazed out through the window, down into the street below. He wondered just how much shit he could take in one lifetime when his eyes suddenly settled on a car parked there, its driver looking back up at him. Jenner frowned as he recognised the face. It was one of Montague's thugs. He'd met him once many years ago when there had been a huge deal going down in one of the unused wharves. A real piece of shit.

Quickly he turned from the window and dashed through to intercept Emma, but she had already pulled on her dress and was stumbling into her stilettos on her way to the front door.

"Where are you going?" Jenner wanted to know, as he took hold of her arm, but Emma simply wrestled it free, and yelled back at him.

"I'm more than just a wallet, you know. I wanted a future for us. I offered everything you could want, and you just throw it back at me. You know where I am. Come and find me if you ever figure out what it is that you really want."

Jenner went to reason with her, to explain just what was going on inside his head, or at least to tell her to be careful of the fucker that had been watching them out in the street. But she was not going to listen to anything he had to say now, and he wasn't even certain why he wanted to let her know, and so he kept his words and watched as she stormed out of the flat, slamming the door shut after her.

Stepping back through into the kitchen, he went to the window and looked down into the street once more. The car that had been parked there was now gone.

Jenner ran a hand through his hair as he exhaled gravely. Just what was he to do, he wanted to know, as he watched Emma leave the building and storm across the street? The phone began to ring again in the living room, and he stood for a moment just watching her stride along the pavement while he thought. It was volatile, this thing with Emma, and it nearly always had been, at least from the point where he had realised what a weird bitch she could be. Unless that was her just caring too much. What did he know anyway? Sure, she had money, but at least when he took Montague's cash there was no emotional expectation. He stepped back into the hallway and then into the living room. The phone continued to ring, and ring, as he stood in the doorway and watched it. Money was money though, he told himself, and even though it was against his better judgement, he knew Montague would at least be as good as his word. Five grand for tonight, he thought to himself again, and then he slowly crossed the room and picked up the handset.

It would always be a pick up from the same place. Ten o'clock, Euston Station, he made his way to one of the black rubbish bins. Stashed inside a small plastic bag wedged behind it was the vial, a small metal cylinder less than three inches long and only slightly thicker than a pencil. He knew what it contained, or knew its name at least, and could only reckon on the price paid for it by the buyer he would shortly be meeting. Payment would have been made days, maybe weeks, ago, and with Montague continuing to sell the stuff, he had hired Jenner back into the fold to do the running for him. Quick and simple, and no dirt on his own hands.

The Blood Of The Ancients, they called it. He had been given a history lesson on the merits of such a potent liquor by one buyer six years ago, eager, it seemed, to spread the word of this wonder-drug to anyone willing to listen. At the time, Jenner had been curious on these frequent runs he had made, and why anyone would pay so much for so little an amount. Some, like his one-time midnight tutor, would down the scarlet fluid within seconds as though they had not had a fix in days. Others would gracefully nod their appreciation and disappear back into the shadows of the night. After that encounter, he had not been so bothered, but tonight he was doubly so. He only felt contempt for these mysterious buyers now, and as he sped north in the back of the black taxicab towards Watford, he only wanted his cut. Five grand in his pocket for just this one trip and he could put quite some distance between himself and London once and for all. At least that was the idea. The parole board might have something to say about that, and a second stretch for violation of it was certainly something that he didn't want. He cursed Montague afresh, despite the lure of his money, for landing him in such a shit situation all over again.

As Jenner lit a cigarette and replaced the pack inside his jacket pocket, his hand brushed against the plastic bag that contained the vial. The light blue smoke curled around him like a nurturing fog as he was rocked back and forth inside the taxi, and he unwrapped the bag carefully to take a look at the vial. It was made of a dull grey metal, and in the rolling yellow light cast through the window by the passing streetlights, it looked nothing like steel or aluminium, and he wondered briefly what it was. Perhaps some strange special material used in hospitals or pharmaceutical companies, he mused to himself. That would make sense, considering the nature of its contents. He studied the cap and noticed for the first time its unique coating. It would be obvious if the seal had been broken, covered as it was by a sort of hard red wax. He didn't know what kind of a percentage he got as the trafficker, but whatever it was, it sure made the vial a special purchase.

He knew the address of the location by heart, even after such a break, a back alley behind a local nightspot. Everyone asks to go to the club, the driver had told him, but never to the alleyway behind it. At least not at the beginning of the night, he'd added with a grin.

It was quarter past eleven when they arrived, and the street was heaving with clubbers outside. As the taxi driver pulled up at the kerb, Jenner handed over a twenty and asked if he could wait for him. The driver shrugged as he pocketed the note, and said that if he wasn't here when he got back then somebody else had probably offered him more. Jenner stepped out of the back of the taxi with a comment on his breath and wandered across the pavement and past the door of the nightclub. Flocks of beautiful women were staggering on both their way in and on their way out, cajoled every inch of the way by packs of yearning men. Jenner tried to keep his mind on his delivery, but with so much to look at, and so many short skirts and bare legs, it was difficult.

He passed the majority of the crowd and turned into the unlit alleyway that ran round behind the club.

There were a number of bins pushed back against the wall, as well as a few stacks of empty crates and boxes, and he negotiated his way slowly in the dark towards the rendezvous point. He could have done with a torch or even the flame from his lighter, but he knew the strict guidelines set out by Montague's buyers - total darkness always.

He came to a halt for a moment and stared hard into the darkness. It was such a stupid thing for him to be doing, coming here alone, but he knew the risks and was sufficiently content to have the money counteract them. He wasn't sure if anyone was waiting in the dark for him or not, but he only had to wait a few moments before a voice suddenly addressed him, a male voice less than a yard from his face.

"You've come alone?" the voice whispered.

The proximity startled him, but he remained outwardly composed.

"I always come alone."

"You have The Blood?"

Jenner reached into the inside pocket of his jacket and retrieved the small metal vial. Holding it out into the darkness, he could not even see the buyer's hand as it was taken from him. Then he heard the buyer once more, but was not certain whether he even intended himself to be heard.

"How long I have waited for you," the buyer seemed to say to his purchase. "How long I have waited and prayed that this moment would arrive."

Jenner went to say something but resigned himself to simply leaving quietly. It was no business of his what the vial contained, nor what was done with it, and so he continued to make his way slowly back through the unlit alleyway. It was only after he had taken perhaps a dozen steps that a cry of agony suddenly split the air and he glanced over his shoulder, fearful.

A sour smell had already coloured the air around him, and the first instinct in his gut was to run. So the dope freak had fucked himself up on the fix, he thought to himself as he knocked over boxes to his left and right, so what? He had seen addicts fuck themselves up before, on cocaine and heroin, but this somehow seemed different, more violent perhaps. Whatever it was, it wasn't his business anymore, and as he reached the busy pavement with the cries still splitting the night behind him, a sweat now on his skin that the cold night air was already chilling, he found that his hands were shaking. He breathed a partial sigh of relief as he caught sight of the taxi still waiting there for him, but he didn't dare throw a glance over his shoulder to see if anything had emerged out of the alleyway after him as he headed for the cab. Taking hold of the taxi door, he threw himself inside, glancing out through the back window only once the cab had put some distance between them.

The crowds were dotted everywhere on the pavement still, writhing and bustling like vermin, but there seemed nothing untoward amongst them, no attackers and no murderers. Slumping back in his seat, he exhaled gravely as he closed his eyes, his imagination painting vivid and horrible pictures of death and assault, his sinuses pricking once again with the memory of the stench that had soured the alleyway.

When his eyes finally flickered open again, and he had dragged a cigarette nervously out of his pocket, they found those of the taxi driver's returning his gaze in the rear view mirror. Jenner went to open his mouth, his cigarette poised hesitantly in his fingers, in an attempt to explain his behaviour, but the driver simply cut him short.

"I don't want to know," he said flatly. "Seems there's plenty going on without my knowing. I'd just like to keep it that way, if you know what I mean."

There's plenty going on without my knowing too, Jenner thought to himself, sparking a flame out of his lighter before holding it up against the end of the cigarette. Drawing deeply on it, he realised how much his hands were still trembling, and inhaled another rich lungful as he rolled his head to one side and gazed out absently at the dark streets that passed by.

There had to be some answers about this stuff he was trafficking somewhere, he thought to himself. If it was that dangerous, and he had no doubt now that it was, then there just had to be something. Yes, he got paid a lot to keep his mouth shut and his fears to himself, but if it was going to lead to him losing his head, then perhaps it wasn't that much after all.

The drive back from Watford seemed to take forever, and every stranger that stood on every street corner seemed to gaze at him as though he had somehow brought death to an innocent man, and that they should report him immediately to the police, and drag him back to that hellhole prison. His heart rate barely slowed a beat in the back of the taxi from the rate it had drummed in the alleyway, and although his hands had stopped shaking, his head would do nothing but keep turning over images of bank notes coated in blood. Rain was beginning to fall now, its crystalline droplets snaking across the windows in frantic patterns as the taxi sped through the dark

London streets, glittering with the reflections of the streetlamps, enticing him with their clarity from the other side of the glass, clean and clear where he couldn't get at it, while he gazed helplessly from inside the cab, in a choked box of smoke and death and indecision. He knew that it was uncalled for to visit Montague unannounced, but he leant forward and asked the driver to make a detour anyway. Money might buy his silence, he thought, but he reckoned that his life was at least worth a question or two.

PART TWO

DISRUPTION

Disruption, *dis-rup'shon*, n. Act of rending into parts or dividing into states; breach; rupture; a place of broken parts.

ONE

NEWS

The child vampire halted for a few moments to gaze in both directions along the banks of the Thames, grasping the cold black metal railings with her tiny fingers as the cold November wind snatched at her long golden curls, snaking them across her cool white angelic face. She was searching the twisted shadows of the embankment, her sharp eyes piercing the crooked shapes and hollow blackness given substance by the tall yellow lamplights, but it was not for food that she searched this night, but for another of her kind. Death was in the air once again, a strange unnatural death, and it had made her afraid, afraid for her own safety and for that of her closest companion.

Callie left the railings and moved swiftly towards Chelsea Bridge, a place that had once been a haven for them, a sanctuary of deep shadow that had kept them safe from prying eyes. But the solemn archways were now lined with electric bulbs that stole that darkness and flooded what had once been secret with a piercing white light, visible to all. It was almost as if the mortals were trying to drive them from their haunts and out into the open air where there was no place to hide. Even as she approached the bridge she could see that the brightly lit archways were vacant, but she stepped onto the bridge anyway, hoping that from a different

71

viewpoint she might at least be able to find Alexia amongst the tangled shadows somewhere along the river. She needed to speak to her urgently about the death in the water, further west near the parliament buildings, and within easy reach of where they had made their new home.

Her tiny body barely cast a shadow as the strings of light cloaked the bridge with a stark illumination. The wind whipped up off the river, snatching her hair in writhing swathes, as her eyes sank down towards the surface of the surging water. Where was Alexia, she wanted to know? There was news that needed to be told, safety that needed to be found. This was no natural death, no natural death of a vampire anyway. They all knew the limitations of their immortality, even someone as young as she, but this was no work of a skulker. This was something else, something beyond words, beyond explanation. The black waters swirled beneath her feet, their motions mesmerising, confounding. It sought to steal her thoughts, to drag her to distraction, but she fought it, knowing that to let down her guard against those that would do her harm, would invite her own demise all too quickly.

"Callie."

The voice startled her even as she focussed her attention, her eyes snatching glimpses of the bridge around her, searching the glittering lights and starkly lit metalwork for the creature who had addressed her. It was bright, the speaker should have been easy to see, and yet she could discern no one else on the bridge beside her.

Then came a laugh, a hollow and cold laugh, and she knew immediately who had called her. She voiced his name now, out into the night, even though she could still not find him amongst the glittering lights illuminating the bridge.

"Venice," she murmured.

She watched now as the other vampire slipped up and over the edge of the bridge where he had been perched, hidden from casual view by a cloak of darkness that he'd folded so effortlessly around himself. He stood before her now, his hands deep in the pockets of his long black coat, his face a white unfeeling mask, regarding her. She returned his cold stare, not wanting him to know that she had not seen him when she had searched the shadows of the bridge. His ability to remain motionless and unseen even in half-light was extraordinary, and sometimes even Alexia was not aware of his presence when the mood took him to watch events unseen. But she was not about to let him know of his continued superiority. She was not about to let him know of anything.

He'd said in the past that it made his kills all the more enjoyable, this ability of his; the secrecy of lying in wait, the deception, the confusion of his prey. He'd apparently been dead for over four hundred years, travelling mostly through the darkened backstreets of Western Europe, and over the course of those years he had chosen which human traits to shrug off, and which ones to keep alive and hone. Callie had always thought him somewhat secretive, even in the comparatively short time that she'd known him, but she knew that she could never disregard his skills as either a hunter or a killer. He was a demon. A cruel and evil taker of life.

"What brings you here?" Venice enquired.

Callie refused to answer at first, not wanting to discuss anything with him. But something inside her made her confess, and made her explain her purpose in returning to the bridge.

"I'm looking for Alexia," she told him finally. "I need to speak to her."

"I have not seen her," he replied slowly. His teeth gleamed behind his lips as they formed the words. "I think perhaps she'll be out looking for something to warm her, no?"

Callie stared at him. She didn't like Venice one bit. Not since he had appeared a few years ago and joined them. Alexia had said he could stay if he wanted, and he did, and so that was that. But that didn't mean that she had to like him. At least he didn't share the flat with them. That was something. She didn't know where he went in the moments before dawn, and didn't much care. She was just glad that he wasn't able to stand over her while she slept.

Callie suddenly averted her gaze from his curiosity and shifted her position on the edge of the bridge.

"What do you need to see her about that's so important?" Venice wanted to know.

Callie swallowed uneasily as she shifted her weight.

The discomfort she felt whenever she was alone with him disturbed her greatly, especially now with the death of one of their kind so close. She knew she should tell Alexia first, to let her make a decision about what they should do, but Venice had seemed to realise her discomfort, and seemed to be pressing her for more information. She was sure he could read her thoughts, read them like a book, even manipulate them into doing whatever he wanted. She didn't like it, but then how could she prove such a thing? Callie turned away, not wanting to get caught up in one of his mind-games, but Venice continued to speak.

"We should talk a while," the other vampire said to her. "We have never really spoken, have we? There are probably many things that we could discuss."

"I have to find Alexia," Callie persisted.

"And you will," Venice chided. "Just indulge me a little, won't you?"

Callie turned back and studied the creature in front of her, his black eyes burning intensely behind the perfect white mask that was his face. It was a face that had no movement other than that which he commanded, his body too a phenomenon beyond words, with no human movement recognisable in the way that he carried himself. Only his shoulder-length black hair moved about him as he stared at her, the night breeze ruffling it as it swirled across the cold metal struts of Chelsea Bridge, this mannequin-man that had travelled the earth for centuries, watching and wandering, and stealing both life and breath.

His unblinking eyes seemed almost to reach inside her very being, to gaze in upon her thoughts, and to look out through her eyes and watch himself, as if only to discover just how she saw him. It unnerved her intensely, but the stare was hypnotic, irresistible. Then he seemed to whisper to her without moving his lips. It was her news that he wanted, news that she did not want to tell him. It was important, surely, but not sufficiently so that he go to lengths such as these to learn of it. Yet for all the power that she could feel within him, a power that commanded both her attention and her obedience, she was sure that he would do her no harm. Callie felt herself edging towards him, and tried to oppose his will, even as she felt her lips part to deliver the news of the death that she had witnessed.

"The police have found a body," she heard herself saying, "in the water near Lambeth Pier."

"What about this body?"

"It was caught up amongst a load of debris."

"A dead human, that's hardly anything to trouble Alexia with."

Callie paused.

She did not want to continue.

And yet the words just continued to come.

"A vampire," she said. "Not human."

"Another vampire has been dusted?"

"No, not dusted. Killed. The police have his body."

"Body?" Venice murmured quietly, almost to himself, his tone, like his expression, still a mask, devoid of any emotion. "How is that possible?"

Callie shook her head slowly. She could feel him still inside her head, trespassing, probing and searching her thoughts even as she formed them.

Venice seemed to look away now, although she missed the movement, and in that moment his touch went from inside her head. She moved back a little, almost as if she had been held by a series of threads that had now become unravelled, and she had to step through the altercation they had just had to realise what she had told him. Callie had known the severity of the situation at the pier when she had seen the bloodless corpse floating in the river. That was why she had been so frantic to find Alexia. Now Venice knew too, but Callie guessed that he would be unlikely to help their cause. If the police started asking questions about the nature of the body, or even started searching a wider stretch of the river, then who could tell what consequences that might have, not only for them, but also for the rest of the vampires hiding in the city.

Venice suddenly turned back to look at her, the movement throwing Callie off-balance for a moment.

"Alexia said she was going to walk the area," he told her. "Why don't you check some of the streets and then head further east along the river."

"But that will take me nearer the pier."

"That's right," Venice told her, pressing his hand against her long golden hair.

"But what about you?" Callie persisted.

Venice's stare suddenly became ice.

"I will search the wharves."

"The wharves? What are you going to find there?"

The breath Venice took was cold and harsh.

"Rewards can be found in the unlikeliest of places," he whispered close to her face. "Remember that. And never question me again."

Callie stood her ground as she watched the other vampire depart, his lithe frame fleeting as he left the floodlit bridge and disappeared into the darkest depths of the night. Her eyes tracked him almost superstitiously until he drew his veil of darkness around himself once more and stole what little she could discern from her sight altogether.

Gazing back along the river in the direction she had first come, at its dark and murky depths that wound slowly north and then east, she wondered about the vampire that guarded the territory of the parliament buildings. Known only as The Howler, he was notorious city-wide as the most brutal and vicious of all the London vampires, and Callie knew that she should not have been anywhere near that place at all. She had only strayed as far as Lambeth Pier because she had been tracking a young mother with a pushchair. She had not been intent with the kill at all - it was not often that she had the courage to even attempt to take a human life - but she wanted to at least keep vigilant, to track and to learn, and know that she could take a life if she so chose.

Callie knew also that searching the streets for Alexia alone, with the smell of death once more in the air, was inherently dangerous. And if Alexia was out looking to feed, as Venice had disclosed, then she could be absolutely anywhere. Not a comforting thought if The Howler was taking the lives of their own kind so very blatantly in front of them all.

TWO

SUSPICIONS

Montague stood by the tall leaded windows in his top floor study, cloaked by the long heavy velvet curtains, and watched Jenner Hoard as he clambered out of the taxi that had just pulled up in the street below. It was a foul night outside, cold driving rain lashing hard across the courtyard, its spears of water lit brightly by the lamps that burned throughout his estate. Such a wretched night it truly was, but he would gladly have braved its chill and its damp, rather than remain in the company of the lady who graced his home this night.

Her name was Catherine, and she was a vampire, the most hard-hearted vampire that he'd had to deal with so far. He was never truly sure of her real agenda, or with whom her allegiances really lay, but in only the handful of times he'd been unfortunate enough to have been contacted by her - and over the past six months it had been more than a few - she had always brought with her a sense of dread. To those who only caught a fleeting glance, her appearance denied her virtually any air of menace - her skin shone like purest marble, her face seemed exquisitely sculpted, and her long dark hair shimmered with the richest of browns - and yet she stood with a stillness that made Montague uneasy, and spoke with a coldness that froze his bones. She had no mannerisms, no body language, her eyes simply looking, her lips forming only words. Every movement seemed planned, every head-turn or footstep necessary. Her walk made no noise across any surface, so that whenever she entered or exited a room, it gave the appearance that she was gliding.

Montague could feel her eyes of ice pricking him even now as he watched Jenner at the intercom by his iron gates. It caused him to feel afraid, even though there was nothing else, apart from this feeling of dread, to confirm that she was even still in the room. There was no sound of breathing, no impatient finger-tapping, nothing but silence and the beating of his own heart loud in his ears. Even if he was to turn, and she allowed herself to be seen by him in the shadows of this single lamplit room, he would probably still not be certain she was there. Catherine almost always wore a full-length cloak of black that seemed to envelop her into the very darkness around her, and she'd worn it tonight when she had appeared in his study, her white face appearing from beneath it like the moon on a cloudless night.

He willed Jenner to hurry, as the gates rolled slowly open and the runner started across the courtyard. No more did he want the penetrating loneliness of the room, Catherine's incessant gaze the only thing to accompany him. He wanted his runner to be here and their business to be dealt with quickly, whatever the consequences of that might be, just so that Catherine would be gone and out of his house.

She had plenty of accusations for them, he knew. She'd brought grave concerns from those she worked for, nameless ones that would have him dead should such accusations be confirmed. But even with such rumours being as ill-founded as some of them were, there were no assurances to be had from that. He made deals with vampires, pure and simple, immortal beings who possessed powers beyond his imagination. There were secrets, of course, secrets that would surely have brought his death some time ago had they been more widely known. But like all secrets, however, only those that knew them could profit by them. Montague knew more than most, but he was smart enough to realise that he didn't know them all. No doubt after the events of tonight, Jenner would be wanting an insight into some of them too, a wish that Catherine would undoubtedly impede. He just wanted to allay her suspicions, and then be rid of her.

The shadows in the lamplit room shifted slightly behind him, and he knew Catherine was growing impatient with him. He could not hear her footsteps on the plush carpet, but he could feel her moving silently across it towards him, and then, when she laid a hand on his shoulder, he could not help the shiver of cold, as it ran from her touch and down throughout his body.

"I'm still waiting," Catherine said softly at his ear.

Montague kept his vision on the courtyard outside, even as Jenner disappeared from sight into the entrance, and willed him to ascend the stairs swiftly to appear with news of the death in Watford, news that he had already received from Catherine herself only moments ago.

"This runner of yours," Catherine continued, "does he know that he carries The Blood Of The Ancients?"

"Yes," Montague said to her, adding quickly, "but he does not know what it is. He has the sense not to ask questions. But I feel that he may ask them tonight."

"And what will you tell him?"

Montague turned his head a little so that he could see her. Her face seemed almost luminescent in the gloom of the dimly lit study, her features showing no expression except for those penetrating eyes of hers. It was perhaps the coldness in that stare rather than the threat in her words that chilled him. Merciless, heartless, and devoid of all feeling.

"What will you tell him?" she asked again, her fingertips pressing slightly more firmly into the flesh of his shoulder now.

"I will tell him nothing," Montague conceded, breaking the hypnotic gaze between them to return his sight to the cold and rain outside.

Her touch suddenly lifted from his shoulder, but he resisted the urge to cast a glance over it to see if she was retreating back into the shadows of the room, to resume her vigil once more near the doorway.

Jenner will be here in moments, he thought to himself, and with those moments so precious, dare I ask another secret of her?

"Do you know how The Blood comes into this world?" Montague enquired, his sight still fixed on the rain lashing down into the courtyard outside.

"What concern is that of yours?" Catherine asked quietly, her voice as distant as if the dark depths of the shadows were a cloak that enveloped her words as well as her body.

Montague shrugged lightly.

"I'm just curious, that's all."

"Curious?" Catherine murmured. "I don't believe that."

Montague shrugged again, as if to leave it at that, but the vampire would not leave such a thing go unanswered.

"Why would you be curious about such a thing?" Catherine continued. "It is the substance that keeps you alive. It is the commodity that makes you rich. If it were not for The Blood, you would be viable prey, and as such, you would have been dead a long time ago."

"Maybe," Montague conceded, with yet another shrug. "But I was just concerned that if something were to happen to me, whether you yourself would be able to continue to traffic The Blood or not."

There came a silence after that so suffocating that the hammering of the rain in the courtyard outside suddenly became noticeable. He could hear the sound of his own blood, thudding nervously in his head, and even the stillness of the air in the room seemed strangely audible. Then her voice came again, seething but still quiet, to dispel the rise of those reticent sounds and answer him.

"No," she said simply. "I do not know where The Blood comes from."

"You don't know who brings it to me?"

"No."

"And you only know of some of my runners?"

"Yes."

"The ones where some of your kind were killed -"

"Enough," Catherine raised her voice for the first time. "I will not continue this enquiry. It is pointless. I would rather kill you now than suffer any more of your questions."

"But you can't," Montague confirmed immediately, turning at last to look into her cold hard eyes. "Your Master would not let you. Unless he knows of another dealer?"

Catherine said nothing this time, but it startled him to see her jaw muscles clench for just a moment. It was the only time he had seen her facial muscles move other than through speech, and it turned something inside him. Perhaps there was a weakness here after all, he thought to himself, a hand that could be brought out and played later on. But he knew that it was wise not to push too much at the moment. There was nothing to be gained now, he realised, but breathing space. If she was uncertain at this moment, then no one would do anything just yet. Unless she really suspected Jenner of the murder in Watford. But it still seemed unlikely. Inside, Montague was suddenly smiling, and for the first time too in her presence.

"Your runner is on the stairs," Catherine told him from the shadows.

Montague listened but could hear nothing but the quiet of the study. He knew he had only seconds alone with her before Jenner appeared. Time for another.

"Are you originally from Kar'mi'shah?" Montague asked the vampire, the question posed as lightly as a passing comment.

"What concern is that of yours?"

"Again, I'm just curious."

"I am losing my patience with you, mortal," Catherine threatened, her voice chilling. "You have no concept of the danger of your knowledge."

"You are, aren't you?" Montague persisted.

"I was made a vampire in Kar'mi'shah, yes," she confessed. "And I was raised in the Faraoh tribe under Jackel El'a'cree."

"And you miss your home?"

"Of course I miss my home," she said. "How could

84

I not?"

"Then it must hurt all the more to know that others of your kind are passing between our two worlds and you are not."

"What is your point?"

"That there is a pathway to your home, and you cannot find it."

Once again he saw those jaw muscles clench, and once again Montague knew that he was pushing his luck more than was healthy. But he also knew that it was knowledge such as this that would pay dividends for him later on. He himself had no legitimate knowledge of where this portal was, and for all he knew there could be many, or none, but that was irrelevant. It was his contacts that gave him The Blood, and it was only he that knew who they were.

"Those that bring you The Blood," Catherine said to him. "They would not tell you where this pathway is?"

"Why would they?" Montague asked her plainly. "Wherever they bridge our worlds is the source of their livelihood. If it becomes known, their profit is gone."

Montague stopped as he heard the pad of footsteps out on the landing. He had sown enough controversy in her mind, he thought, to at least keep himself breathing for another night or two. He would never be truly safe, he knew, but when playing this close to fire, safety was something that he'd learnt to live without a long time ago. He knew the dangers he faced whenever he dealt with these creatures, but the prices they paid were high, and as a middleman his profit margin was unbelievable. He understood too their immortality, their deftness with shadows, their necessity to consume blood from human prey, but his fear was compromised to a certain degree by their willingness to deal with a mortal in order to have what they desired. He knew they would all have it otherwise, of course, to feed upon him and have him dead, but not one of them was unwise enough to actually try it. But times were changing, it seemed. Deaths were becoming commonplace amongst the vampire community, their immortality compromised by organised groups of humans known as skulkers. Someone seemed to be leaking information, at least in part, about some of his deals, and Ki'ma was the last of the vampires to die. That was the information that Catherine had brought with her tonight, and the subsequent reason for Jenner hurrying to him from that very same scene. There had been four other vampires killed in the past six months alone, and Catherine had come here, amongst other things, for answers, the patience of those she worked for finally at an end.

"At last," he heard the vampire breathe impatiently beside him, and Montague watched as her narrow frame became shrouded by the shadows once more, until she seemed almost to dissolve into them entirely, even her pale face appearing little more than a translucent mask hanging gently in the air.

A rap on the door to his study snatched him from this apparition, and he took his eyes from the still-shifting darkness to call him in. The door opened and he saw the partially silhouetted frame of his runner standing in a halo of brighter light streaming in from the landing.

"It's unprecedented for you to come in person for your money," Montague declared.

"I didn't just come for the money," Jenner told him.

"Oh?"

"I want to know more about that drug I've been delivering."

"More?" Montague said. "I didn't realise you knew anything."

Jenner stared at him, perplexed and angry, but Montague continued before anything else could be said, stepping away from him to resume his place by the tall leaded windows.

"If you're going to tell me about what happened tonight, Jenner, there's no need, because I already know."

"Already know what?"

"That he's dead."

Jenner staggered forward a step.

"And I was hoping that you would be able to give me a reason why."

Jenner crossed the study floor after him now.

"How do you know he's dead? I've just left him."

"Let's just say I've been told," Montague said, as he turned to face him. The urge in him rose to glance into the motionless shadows, but he fought it and kept his eyes on Jenner. "Did anyone follow you to the drop off?"

"Of course not."

"And you didn't see anyone waiting for you near the alleyway?"

"What are you talking about? It was the drug that killed him."

"The drug?" Montague said. "Of course it wasn't the drug."

Jenner stared at him, bewildered by what he was being told.

"His head was taken off by an axe, Jenner.

Someone was waiting for him. And for you too most likely."

"I didn't see any of that."

"You're saying he was fine when you left him?"

"Well, no."

Montague stared at him, waiting for him to continue.

"I heard a scream," Jenner started, beginning to get agitated now, "but then I just took off. I thought it was just some bad shit that had fucked him up. It was dark, Montague, I couldn't see anything. I don't hang around to see if they're alright, or if they fancy a lift home. I give them the shit and then I leave."

"But they don't normally get decapitated, though, do they?"

Jenner gazed helplessly at him now, his hands beginning to shake once again.

"I don't need this, man," he said, running his hands nervously over his face. "Things were never this bad before I went inside. Look, just give me my five grand and I'll get out of here."

"I'm afraid it's not that easy."

"Don't you give me that shit," Jenner cried.

"There are other interests involved here."

"Fuck your interests," Jenner yelled. "Just give me my money."

From his place in front of the window, Montague could see Catherine as her frame suddenly loomed out of the shadows, her great cloak of black billowing out behind her, as if she intended to take Jenner there and then from behind and devour him. Montague didn't want that, at least not yet. He had other plans for him, Catherine's second request that she had brought with her tonight. He put his hand past Jenner's shoulder, to try and urge the vampire back, but he knew that he had no control over her. She would quite happily kill them both if she saw fit, but tonight she seemed undecided, and held her position just behind the runner.

"I have to find out more about what went on," Montague continued.

"I'm telling you what went on."

"I mean, who's killing these people."

Jenner stared agog at him.

"There's been more than one?"

Montague nodded.

"I want out of this right now," Jenner exclaimed, turning towards the study door, his hands clamped to his head in despair. "Things were never this bad two years ago."

"There were rumblings, though."

"But nothing like this," Jenner reiterated, his gaze fixed on the floor now.

"He knows nothing," Catherine's voice came almost silent in Montague's ear, her sudden proximity startling him. "But I would kill him anyway if you did not have such feelings for him." Her voice was soft like a breath, and inaudible to his runner.

Montague went to speak but she cut him short. It seemed she did not want his runner to know of her just yet. Before she turned, however, she added a short but serious threat.

"I will be back. And if I find out you are involved in some conspiracy against us, you will pray that you die quickly before I find you."

Montague watched as she drifted away, back towards the door to the study, before slipping silently through it and away without so much as a footfall.

Exhaling gravely, he looked back to discover Jenner staring at him, a frown fixed upon his brow. Montague shook his head a little as if to say 'don't ask', and then he crossed the study to take a seat behind his huge wooden desk.

"I am not ignorant of the things that go on," Montague said to him, reaching into one of his desk drawers, "nor am I ignorant of the dangers that I put you in. But I pay you good money for what you do, Jenner, and I trust you implicitly."

"I can feel an 'and' coming on."

The single lamp on the desk illuminated half of Montague's face and threw deep shadows over the remainder, creating stark creases in his living mask as he smiled at Jenner's comment.

"I'll give you your five thousand for tonight, Jenner, that's not an issue," he said, pulling a small packet out of the drawer and placing on the top of his desk, "but I have another request regarding your services as a liberator."

"You mean thief," Jenner corrected. "But never mind any of that shit. I still want to know who might've tried to cut my fucking head off with an axe."

"You don't want to know," Montague told him sternly.

"I think I do," he insisted, leaning forward on his desk.

Montague pursed his lips and then pushed the packet towards him.

"What's that?" Jenner wanted to know.

"Your five grand," Montague told him. "Take it and leave. I won't stop you, but I also won't ask for your services again. Take it and we're done here for good."

His words caught him off guard for a moment, and rattled around inside his head like cold hard marbles. Done here for good? Only this morning he had wished for a way out, a chance to start again, and here Montague seemed genuinely to be offering it to him. Five grand could see him okay for a few months while he looked for a regular job, a new break, and at the very least it might belay his guilt for a while about Emma. But there was something else lurking there at the back of his mind that nagged at him, and it brought confusion with it, confusion in abundance. What else could you ever do, it seemed to say to him, after all the things that you've seen and done? How can you ever load a truck, or drive a van, when you've seen things of mystery in darkened alleyways, and made deals in derelict wharves, and run across waste ground with police dogs snapping at your heels? How can you work for a few pounds an hour when you've seen five grand in just one night?

Jenner looked from the packet on the desk to Montague and then back at the packet. He simply couldn't do anything but this. He knew it, and Montague knew it too. Money was everything, and he couldn't do anything without it. He was hopeless without it, and that was the truth. Grinding his teeth in both confusion and desperation, Jenner pulled out a seat opposite Montague, and listened to what he had to offer him this time.

THREE

HOME

The vampire Alexia stood on Millbank, her back to the Tate Gallery illuminated behind her across the road, and looked out over the moonlit river. To all intents and purposes she was simply staring into middle distance, her hands deep in the pockets of her long dark overcoat, her thoughts lost or unrecoverable as though in some nightly dream. Her long blonde hair billowed like silken sheets as the wind whipped up off the river to chase it across her face, yet her sharp eyes remained focused and steadfast on the handful of glittering lights on the water further up the Thames. She could see three small boats bobbing there, their pilots throwing searchlights across the surface of the water, looking for clues that they would no doubt never find.

Her acute sense of smell picked up the tang of sweat on their pallid flesh, of fear, she imagined, as well as from their labour. She inclined her head slightly to try and make out their voices more clearly, but the wind - it whipped up again - was blowing from the east, and it made it difficult to hear just what they were saying. After a number of gusts had rifled across the water, she gave up, and turned her back on the fast-flowing waters to gaze back up at the great grey facade of the famous Tate Gallery.

She sighed appreciatively as she recalled wonderful

moments spent wandering alone through its nightime halls. How she'd adored the art that had hung upon its walls all those years ago. Not the modern efforts of today, produced so quickly with ignorant slabs of gaudy colour or tasteless texture, but the fine art worked and produced so many decades ago, fresh and vibrant and glowing from their hey-day. How she had loved to stroll along the river at the turn of the century, when painters arrived daily from across the Channel, and sought inspiration under the spell of London by twilight. She used to watch them sketch and plan for hours by candlelight, spellbound by the magic that would appear before her eyes in charcoal and pencil. Seldom did any of them paint by night, except some of them locked away in their dank studios, but the sheer feeling that came from seeing life captured by paint when she had witnessed them - wet canvases hanging from walls with such delicate touches of colour - oh, it had been too much to bear at times.

The wonder of sunlight, something she had not seen in over one thousand years of immortality, came to life in front of her eyes in just a few strokes of paint, glittering across the river, and sparkling on dew-laden lawns. Oh, the romantic headiness of those days sometimes used to make her feel so wonderfully vulnerable, and she'd let herself be seduced so many times in bars and in moonlit streets by those very same artists. But ultimately she had seen them all to their graves; natural deaths, of course, for the sensual artists that they were. Now she had only a handful of those miracles she'd seen worked hanging on the walls just across the road to remind her. It was a sad, but inevitable, end.

The patter of panicked footsteps somewhere off to her left snatched her momentarily from her memories, and her head turned instinctively to find their maker. The images of gleaming blue skies and sun-dappled leaves laid down luxuriantly with knife and brush flickered briefly in her mind's eye, until they became extinguished completely.

Out of the darkness came little Callie, her young angelic face gazing frantically in all directions. Her eyes were wide with fright and Alexia could smell a pall of fear in her, different to what she had smelt in the sweat of the policemen on the river, but more of a kind of dank rot that permeated her pale white skin. No heartbeat skittered inside the chest of the young dead girl, of course, not as she had heard it all those years ago gripped by the stranglehold of death, but it was obvious that something was indeed wrong for the child vampire to be so terrified. Alexia moved swiftly towards her, deftly avoiding the traffic of the early hour and intercepting her before she could disappear.

"What's wrong?" Alexia urged her quickly, and watched as Callie's eyes took a moment to register the sight of her.

"The body..." Callie stammered.

"By Lambeth Pier?" Alexia asked, and watched as the girl nodded her head. "Yes, I know. I've been watching them take the body away."

"You saw that it was a vampire that was killed?" Callie asked her.

"Yes," was all that Alexia said.

"How could they have killed him like that? Drained all his blood. It's not possible."

Alexia could not answer her, and went down on one knee in front of her and pushed her hand through

Callie's long golden hair. It was dangerous for them all, she knew, but Callie just seemed so young and precious. She had the body of a child, but Alexia had to frequently remind herself that the girl was already over forty years old.

"Will it never be safe for us?" Callie asked.

"I will do my best to make it safe for you, I promise."

"But what about you?"

"I've lived a lifetime."

"But we're immortal. You told me we would live forever."

"This is no life, Callie," Alexia said at last, "running and hiding. For centuries, man has slowly been coming to terms with sharing his world with us. They've put up resistance for decades, some fighting back, some even taking the upper hand."

"So why can't we just take it back."

"It is not that simple, Callie. We're not completely invulnerable to them. They've learnt our weaknesses, and they've learnt to prey upon them. It is a dangerous time, and it is not just humans that we have to fear. There are threats lurking inside our own ranks. There has been turmoil for years, clan fighting clan, vampire fighting vampire, and there has been no Master to bring order to the chaos. That is why we have to hide in order to simply survive."

Callie gazed up at her, any argument she might have had frozen upon her lips. What could she say? There simply were no words.

"We should be off the streets," Alexia declared at last, beginning to start away. "There is too much death in the air. Way too much."

The streets of London were still relatively busy even at two thirty in the morning, and they travelled swiftly through the dark streets towards Knightsbridge. Skulkers could be hiding almost anywhere, and it seemed that they were growing stronger and more dangerous all the time. Taking her human prey earlier was stupid, she knew, but she needed to feed nightly, and at least taste human blood every once in a while. Of course it was true that killing animals drew less attention, but their blood lacked the richness that they needed. It was an insane situation, but it was all that they had.

The top floor flat in Knightsbridge was perfect. With access to the rooftop she could see out over Hyde Park and much of the surrounding area. She'd bought it many decades ago and had never regretted it, but it was only in recent times that the turnaround in the hunter-prey scenario had occurred. Humans had always had their superstitions, however, and the bravest of the superstitious had always struggled to put their fears to the test. What hadn't worked had brought about their deaths. What had worked had resulted in laws of salvation, weaknesses penned in books and tomes. There were still one or two myths, of course, there always had been in these things, but most of the rules ran true.

The stake through the heart was number one, naturally, but bury a stake through the heart of anything and it'll kill them. Sunlight, sure, but sealing yourself in a coffin or similar was usually not a problem except for those who had not planned sufficiently well enough in advance. Garlic? That was a joke surely. Alexia actually quite liked the smell of it, except once cooked and on someone's breath. But it was the crucifix that was the biggest puzzler of them all. Only those who had accepted Christianity in life but renounced the church in death was affected by it, and it was still to this day a wonderfully profound spectacle to behold; that of the mortal's expression as a vampire stalks unaffected towards him, the cross slipping from between their bewildered fingers. She had seen it herself a thousand times. It never failed to amuse. Her home was in Kar'mi'shah, a world away, and Christianity had never taken much of a firm hold. There were a few small churches, she recalled, but they were so isolated and of so little consequence to the greatest cities that it hardly mattered.

Shapeshifting was another misconception held by the human populace of both worlds. Not all vampires could transform themselves. She had been sired in Tooma, a district of Kar'mi'shah, over a thousand years ago, and had become part of the Faraoh tribe through marriage. Most clans were not shapeshifters, but the Faraoh clan was. It was the Faraoh clan to which the Master Jackel El'a'cree had belonged, and it was he who'd had the power to transform himself into any creature he'd so desired. In his temples he'd preferred the image of the jackal itself, but had taken many different guises in front of his mortal worshippers; the crocodile, the bull, the eagle, but nearly always with his human body beneath. They were gods to their followers, and they were worshipped devoutly. It was the mortals who built them their temples. It was the mortals who carved out their portraits in stone. And it was the mortals who went to them to have the evil spirits drained from their blood. It was all good. Until it all stopped.

Callie clambered up through the skylight and came

to sit beside Alexia on the dark slates of the rooftop. Alexia acknowledged her arrival but did not interrupt her vigil.

"What do you see?" Callie asked her, as she followed the vampire's gaze over Hyde Park.

"The past," Alexia told her. "Always the past."

"I cannot see it," Callie said, gazing into the darkness of the park.

"I am glad of that," Alexia said. "It is something that you do not want to see."

"Do you mean the clans again?"

Alexia nodded slowly.

"I want to see your family," Callie said, turning to look at her. "You make them sound so regal. I bet they wouldn't hide in the shadows or run away."

"I want to see them again too," Alexia told her.

"Will you take me with you?"

"I would if I could, sweet one."

"But you don't think there's a way back home?"

Alexia shook her head.

"I don't know of one."

Callie seemed to leave it at that then, and together they stared in silence over the empty blackness of Hyde Park for a while, its expanse devoid of all human life, but busy with rabbits, owls and foxes. They had fed on worse.

"Will you tell me what happened?" Callie asked.

"To what?"

"To your family."

"Why do you want to know?"

"Because it makes you sad. If I knew what happened, I could perhaps try to help."

Alexia turned her head to look at her now. Callie's large oval eyes returned her gaze, and she did seem genuinely interested, but Alexia still saw the child whenever she looked at her. A child could not possibly understand, no matter how much she insisted.

"One day, perhaps," Alexia replied, turning to look back at the darkness. "One day."

FOUR

THE BACK GAME

The rain was coming down harder when Jenner finally stepped back out into the night. It was probably getting close to three o'clock, and the cold dank sky was a solid heavy black. Pulling his collar up against the downpour, Jenner dashed across the courtyard and let himself out at the gates. He found no taxi waiting, and realised quickly that it would mean a long trek back through the silent London streets before he would find anything that remotely resembled a taxi rank still operating at such a late hour.

He had only covered perhaps a hundred yards, certainly no more than two, when the sound of a vehicle splashing its way down the street behind him became audible over the rain. Absently, Jenner stuck out his thumb, hoping that what luck he might have remaining might grant him a lift closer to home. He heard the vehicle slowing, the splashing of the rain-lashed street growing louder, and glanced expectantly over his shoulder, squinting through the rain at the dazzling headlights. It pulled up abruptly beside him, a dark panelled van, and then the side door slid swiftly back to reveal one of its occupants reaching roughly for him. The whole abduction took no more than five seconds, and Jenner could recall little of what actually happened, as he was hauled off the pavement and thrown headlong into the unlit interior of the stranger's van, the resultant blow knocking out both his sight and his consciousness with a dull and heavy thud.

The van was still in motion when his eyes reopened. The coarse weave of the carpet was harsh against his face and hands, and as the memory of the incident returned, it came to him that he was still lying where he had been thrown. Ahead of him he could see one of them sitting behind the driver, gazing absently out through the windscreen, dressed from head to foot in black. But even in the darkness of the interior he could still make out the rifle the man was cradling, and it looked powerful and deadly. Turning his head only marginally and very slowly he found a third occupant, also decked out in full black combat gear, only this one returned his gaze, staring down at him with a practised contempt. Jenner caught sight of his hand tensing on the grip of his rifle, and saw too the purpose echoed in the man's cold eyes, intense and focussed. It seemed pointless to try and keep up a charade of still being unconscious, now that the two of them had exchanged such a lengthy gaze, and so Jenner eased himself awkwardly round and into a sitting position.

The man seated behind the driver turned to regard him now, once Jenner was upright. A dull pain throbbed at the top of his head where he had hit the inside of the van, but he tried his best to keep his trepidation back, knowing that whatever happened, their intention was inevitable, and his death was undoubtedly much on their mind.

The man who had first seen him wake kicked his

leg with his boot to get his attention, and then lowered his rifle towards him, before proceeding to enquire just what business he might have with the owner of the big house.

"You mean Montague?" Jenner uttered, putting a hand to his head that continued to throb harder with each passing second.

"We know his name, now tell us your business with him."

"We have no business," Jenner replied. "We're just old friends from way back."

The rifle was lowered and then squared at his head, the barrel becoming nothing more than a small black dot that seemed to have no possible end, and then it dawned on him that a bullet waited for him somewhere inside. It was a sheer and sudden notion of oblivion that forced his unexpected U-turn.

"He puts work my way, you know?" Jenner confessed hurriedly. "Nothing heavy, just a bit of this, a bit of that."

"Be more specific," the rifleman commanded.

"I don't know - robberies, burglaries, deliveries - the usual sort of thing."

"Is that it?"

Jenner nodded agreeably, and the wash of pain in his head crippled his sight in a single pulse of black agony.

"He's definitely the one," he heard one of the others say. Probably the one sitting behind the driver. Jenner squinted through the dark shifting haze behind his eyes and saw the two rifle carriers regarding each other.

"You're sure?" the first one said.

The second nodded, and the first one turned back

to stare down at Jenner.

"My friend here thinks you know more than you're telling."

"No, no, that's it, I swear."

"What about Watford?" the man behind the driver snapped, shoving his rifle in Jenner's direction. "That was you, wasn't it? Tell me the fucking truth, or I'll break your skull myself."

"Okay, okay, that was me. But I never killed that guy, honest."

"I know you didn't kill him, you idiot, because it was me that was waiting for him."

Jenner stared at him, and then the weight of the whole situation suddenly pounded him like a vast colossal wave. They were the killers, that much they had confessed. Three killers driving about London in a van with rifles and God knows what else, murdering people, and here he was, defenceless at their feet.

His own death could not be avoided now surely. Two rifles were already pointed at his head, and both holders were severely pissed with him. They were obviously nothing to do with the law, that much was at least certain, so that could only really mean some demented vigilante group intent on clearing the criminals off their patch of the world. They already knew about Montague, they knew about the drug, and now they knew about him. He was fucked.

"So what are you going to do with my body then?" Jenner suddenly burst out. "Dump it in the river? You dumb fucks."

"Hey!" the second rifleman yelled. "Shut your fucking mouth or we *will* kill you."

"You're going to anyway. Just get the fuck on with it."

The first gunman lurched forward out of his seat and smacked the butt of his rifle hard into Jenner's stomach, punching the air out of his body and causing him to crease in agony.

"We ain't going to kill you, fucker, so just shut up and do what we tell you."

The rifleman slumped back in his seat and lowered the barrel of his rifle back down upon his prisoner. Jenner continued to coil in pain, but he forced himself to regain at least some kind of composure as he sucked some wind back in through his teeth. Sure, if they'd have wanted to kill him, they could have just topped him as he left Montague's house. There was no reason to bring him along, except that they wanted information. Jenner regarded them both now, sitting and looking back at him with contempt, their hands gripping their weapons with an unnerving familiarity.

"What do you want to know?" he conceded quietly.

"That's better. Now, we want to hear everything you know about the vampires."

Jenner stared at them.

"The what?"

"Vampires. We know you've been dealing with them. Just tell us what you know about them - where they nest, places they haunt, that kind of shit - and we even might drop you back at your own doorstep."

Jenner stared agog at them both, disbelieving and a little wary now.

"You're shitting me..."

"We ain't shitting you," the gunman behind the driver blurted out. "Now fucking tell us. We know you're involved. I saw you myself in the alleyway just a few fucking hours ago."

"Look, I don't know what you think you're on about, or what you think I've been up to, but I just don't believe in any of that stuff."

"Demons roam the earth," the first gunman said solemnly now, as though he was about to recite a speech that he had recited a hundred times before. "There are dozens of them in London alone. We find them, and then we dust them. It's as simple as that. Now, one more time, we want to hear everything you know about them."

Jenner looked from one to the other, their faces locked with expressions of severity and purpose. They weren't shitting him. Or if they were, they were fucked up on some mind-drug and were actually believing what they were saying. Either way, they had those huge guns to back them up.

"Look," Jenner began again calmly. "I can't tell you anything about vampires, except what I've seen in films, and I don't think that's going to help you any."

"Who do you think that was that you delivered The Blood to in Watford?"

Jenner stared at them blankly.

"I don't know. Just one of Montague's customers."

"You didn't think it strange, someone drinking blood in an unlit alleyway?"

"It's only some drug. What do I care if someone wants to get high behind a nightclub. I don't give a shit what they do to themselves."

"And what about when they kill a human being in order to feed off their blood? Do you not give a shit about that either?"

"There ain't nothing like that going on. Christ, what's up with you guys?"

"There are demons walking the same streets as us,

and it's our duty to stop them. Every time they're allowed to feed, another one of us dies. It's a battlefield out there. They're evil and unnatural and they must all be killed. Help us, Jenner. Help us to destroy them. It's your duty as a human being."

Jenner looked from one to the other again, and it slowly became clear that they were deadly serious. He glanced then, for the first time, around the inside of the van, at the crosses and the stakes and the axes that hung from specially designed fittings. These people were an organised group, and there wasn't a doubt in his mind that they truly believed in what they were doing. He just couldn't believe it himself.

"You know my name," he said suddenly, looking back at them. "How about returning the favour. Just so that I know we're all on the same side.

"Very well," the first rifleman said. "My name is Rocket. That there," he nodded towards the gunman behind the driver, "is Vapour. The one driving is Grunt."

"Excuse me," Jenner said testily, "but they're not the names your mother gave you. How about your real ones?"

"We have no real names any more. We are skulkers, we live outside the everyday world, and we have nothing but clan names."

"Listen, Rocket, I don't know what to say to you, really. All I know is that I was paid to deliver a drug to a customer in Watford. Vapour here topped him as I left. That's really all I know. You say he was a vampire. Who am I to argue? I just want to get back to my flat and get a few hours sleep before morning."

Rocket seemed almost to listen to him with something close to accepting this as the truth, but it wasn't until he glanced across at Vapour, who shrugged, that he actually told him so.

"We can't keep you here all night, Jenner," Rocket told him, "but just remember what we've told you. Vampires live among us, they walk our streets, and they watch us from the shadows, even here in this busy city of London, and you, my friend, are playing a very dangerous game with them."

The van pulled up at the side of the road suddenly, and Rocket hauled back the van door to reveal the foul wet London night once more. Jenner eased himself to his feet and stepped out of the van, back onto the rain-lashed pavement, as Rocket cast him one final stare to offer him a warning that was to echo in his head for the rest of the night.

"Demons walk our streets," he told him. "You must help us to destroy them. It is your duty."

FIVE

MEETING

Venice stood in the unlit alleyway, enveloped by the heavy shadows of the wharves, and watched the horizon to the east grow steadily brighter as dawn threatened. A messenger had brought news of this meeting to him earlier that night, and there had seemed urgency about the rendezvous then. It seemed likely that the immediacy would mirror the news Callie had brought, news that she was insistent Alexia hear first. But he was equipped with information now, as always, and ready to hold an even hand with the battle-scarred vampire.

The Howler had killed one of their own kind, blatantly, it seemed, a deed so far from good sense it was untrue, and then simply abandoned the bloodless body in the Thames. How he had even managed such a deed was beyond possibility, but he had done so, and it would surely only add credence to a name already synonymous with death. This was a dangerous event, and dangerous for them all. Casta Mica'tore had undoubtedly been one of the first to know, and now he knew too. There would need to be a certain amount of clearing up to do, but no doubt Casta would have his own people see to that, and would merely require his usual services of him.

A cold wind suddenly whipped through the alleyway and lifted his long black hair, but he neither moved his head nor his hand to pull it back from his face. The wind settled, and then dropped, and his hair fell once more back across his shoulders. His memories drifted like his hair on the wind, whipping back a few decades to the seventies, and to his first meeting with Alexia, the vampire who, like Casta, had been sired outside of this world. That particular meeting had been a chance encounter, but his being in the vicinity had not.

He had been on Chelsea Bridge when he'd first seen her half-dead body held in the grasp of the freezing Thames, and he had scaled the bridge down to the water's surface before hauling her out. How much longer she would have survived would never be known, of course, but her injuries had been severe. Their relationship had grown over time, although not entirely coincidentally. There had always been motive, but of that she did not know, and still to this day did not know. On the surface of things, everything was well, but then if she had known the truth of why he had stayed with her, Venice was certain that the situation might not have been so pleasant.

He didn't know the connection between Casta and Alexia, still didn't, and to a degree didn't really care, but there was a bond now between Alexia and himself that over the course of time he did not want to see compromised. She had integrity, it seemed, and a sense of pride. Perhaps he valued that in her because he knew that he lacked it in himself. And truth - he laughed inside at the absurdity of that - what was the truth? Truth was something he had abandoned a long time ago before they had even met. He had been told things about her, been led to a city where she could be found, and then left to watch and ask questions. What would Alexia do, Venice wondered to himself, if she was to ever find out that she was the subject of reports brought back to a third party? They were immortals and could not be easily killed, but that didn't mean that she wouldn't at least try.

A cold chill passed over his body like a descending cloud, and he became aware of something crawling behind him in the darker depths of the alleyway. The thoroughfare had been empty when he'd arrived, and he had heard no one enter while he watched the sky. Venice pulled his forward sight into himself and projected it back through the alleyway behind him without turning his head. The boxes and debris that littered the dank rotting matter of the ground were undisturbed, and he could sense neither heat nor smell from anyone else. He inclined his head only slightly and sniffed at the air. Still nothing, and yet the chill of being watched continued to creep over him.

He had never been wrong about sensing the presence of anyone before, not even another vampire, and he doubted that he was mistaken now. Swiftly he turned, a master in the depths of shadow, and saw the alleyway devoid of life. The litter remained untouched, as he had seen, and the boxes stood undisturbed. Inside, he frowned, but his facial expression remained passive and did not move. His acute sight scanned the darkest of the shadows with voracity, adamant that there was something there to be seen, but he could simply not detect it. It began to trouble him, that one sense could not confirm another, but there was not even so much as a rat hiding in the foul damp darkness. But then, in a blinding instant, all of his senses suddenly reeled, as a voice came out of the darkness to shatter all the certainty that he'd had.

"I am here," the voice simply stated.

Venice swallowed hard. He could pinpoint the

source of the voice, it was within yards of him, but there was simply nothing there to see. This was wrong. There was power here, power wielded like he had never seen before. He was worried, something that he had not been for a long time.

"Casta?" he tentatively asked.

A figure emerged from the very darkness Venice had been pressing his sight into, a figure wrapped in the deepest of black cloth, his face stolen from the light and utterly imperceptible.

"A body has been found," Casta began, "a body in the river near Westminster, a body with no blood, and no breath, and a song of death that's been hushed. But you already know this, don't you? You've already heard the song that's been silenced?"

"I've heard," was all Venice could answer. He had always questioned the other vampire's sanity, the words he used coming out confused and almost in verse. It made him anxious, uneasy that such madness should be mixed so unequally with so potent a magic.

"And so soon, too," Casta continued. "The nights grow ever colder and they scream with a stifled torment. Ssh, you can hear them even now. Listen, Venice, listen to their cries. The wolf that lives on the river fights to hurt us, to hurt the lambs that live along that stretch of water, and you know who owns the face beneath the fur, don't you?"

"The Howler."

"Indeed. The Howler. And it seems that he has stepped over the boundaries of what keeps us together, snuffed out a candle that burned so very brightly, and left the ragged corpse - and he did leave it so very ragged - for the shepherd to find. We must be ever more vigilant because of what he has done. We must examine our eyes, Venice, seek out the veils and expose the lies that they would tell us."

"Is that why you choose to hide yourself so?"

"My cloak?" Casta clarified simply.

"If that's what you would call it."

"You would change your garb for one of sackcloth, to appease the gods of blindness? I hardly think that is in your nature, or indeed in your scope."

"Extra deceit is always beneficial. Where might I get one?"

"Take nourishment not from the blood of fools, but from the words of books. Ignore the night and grow weak as you learn. It is necessary. It is cold. But you will fail. I can see your empty skull more clearly than you can."

Venice stared at him, uncertain of what to say.

"Study your art," Casta murmured. "Magic is there but you must be willing to cradle it inside you. But it is a bad animal that will scratch you if you do not devote. Scratches take time to heal, and they can hurt so very cruelly."

Venice tried to discern any detail of the vampire before him as he listened to him ramble, but it seemed as though he was simply made of the darkness, leaving nothing there for him to see. No light penetrated the air around him, and even the word silhouette would imply more sight of him than there was.

"The Howler threatens us all," Casta continued. "He brings a plate of poison to our table and offers each of us a bowl. I cannot feed. I must abstain. But my thoughts now turn to you."

"Me? What can I do?"

"I want you to destroy him. I want him dead and soon. He cannot be allowed to sit at our table. Not now. His manners defy all creatures, of fur and of flesh, of wool and of web."

"Are you sure it was him?"

"A question on your lips?" Casta scolded.

"No, I just -"

"I tell you it was him." Casta said. "I tell you it was him, and I want him dead. Do it."

"But if I go to him, he will kill me."

"And I will not?"

A growl of intent rumbled between them, and Venice gazed into the hollow chilling darkness. His choices had grown thin over the past few years. Death was everywhere, even for an immortal, and in the moment that followed, Casta posed yet another question, but one that seemed light and almost sane.

"What news of Alexia?" he asked. "How fares she?"

The nature of the question caught him off-balance for a moment, and he struggled to provide a lengthier answer than the one he managed to utter.

"I... have not seen her tonight."

"Oh?"

"No, Callie came looking for her with news of the body, but I... I said that I hadn't seen her."

"That's a pity."

Venice stared helplessly. These discussions of her behind her back always seemed to be leading somewhere, as though there was some secret agenda, and tonight it seemed almost as though it was linked with this death in the river. He felt like he wasn't being let in on it, and he didn't like it. It was certainly something important, this agenda of his, and it had been going on since Casta had first brought him to London over twenty years ago. It had annoyed him then, and it continued to annoy him now, but Casta was not the sort of vampire that you could simply just accuse.

"I feel there's a secret," Venice began, composing himself.

"Oh?"

"That Alexia is a part of something."

"We are all a part of something, Venice. The spider knits us together like that. It is her way. I have seen the web where we all live and it glistens so very brightly. I see the thread to which you cling, my friend, and it is so very fragile, so very fragile indeed."

"Something's going on," Venice persisted, battling against the tide of his words. "Something that I'm not a part of."

"If there was something going on, would I not tell you?"

"I don't know. Would you?"

The figure of Casta Mica'tore loomed suddenly from the shadows, and came so close to Venice that he wanted to step back, but he knew that he couldn't. Not even when the shallow light from the streetlamps in the road flickered across the cruel distortions of Casta's face, and Venice saw once again the horrific scars and lacerations across his cheeks, forehead and throat. The vampire's injuries had healed little over the few decades that he'd known him, and it brought to mind that they were probably as good as they were going to get. Scars covered most of the skin that was visible, and his nose was disjointed and ragged from where it had presumably been broken or torn at some time, perhaps by the very spider or wolf of which he so frequently spoke. His eyes still burned, though, intense and with a fury, and they frightened him as they seemed almost to penetrate his very being.

"Have I done something to warrant your distrust?" Casta asked, the edge in his voice as hard as the ground beneath their feet.

Venice hesitated, searching for words that would not enrage him.

"Then clearly I have," Casta said.

Venice could feel the vampire's touch on his skin, even though there was no contact between them, and it was cold, chilling. He guessed that he had not fed tonight, for he could also not detect the smell of blood about him. Perhaps he did not have to feed. Perhaps he had risen above even that base necessity.

"Tell me how I have offended you?" he said, his lips barely moving, his eyes unblinking.

"You ask all these questions about Alexia," Venice found himself saying. "They must all be for some reason."

"And they are."

"So if they're for a reason, there must be an agenda."

"That is my business," Casta said, as he backed away from him a little, retreating ever so slightly into the shadows so that they concealed his face once more. "You would have us keep no secrets from each other?"

"No, but I've come to think more of Alexia than just a meal ticket."

"Have you?" Casta said gravely. "My only hope is that you have not become too fond. That would be a shame."

Venice could feel his icy gaze upon him, but finally he relented and turned to avoid his eyes.

"Alexia already makes her way to Westminster to meet The Howler," Casta continued. "Stop him, Venice. Stop him before he hurts her. The Howler nudges the web on which we all stand, shaking the threads and fluttering them like gossamer. But the spider would have it no other way. You are in her plan. She smiles down upon you with teeth that would pluck out your dead heart."

Venice stood and stared at the vampire shrouded in black cloth in the veil of the unlit alleyway. His form was already protean, his skin shifting, his power to confuse his senses unworldly. Venice wondered about the vampire's sanity once again, and more specifically, about the harm such madness could measure out. The Howler was a legend of death, a legend known by them all, and the vampire that he had dumped in the river was simply his last abomination. If Alexia was indeed on her way to meet him, then she would undoubtedly be devoured by him also.

"Go after her," Casta ordered. "If you do care anything for her, then do not let The Howler get close to her. My eyes will watch you wherever you go."

Venice found himself nodding his agreement.

Casta's eyes burned intensely as he studied him, and then he simply retreated without another word, back into the shadows of the alleyway that seemed to draw up and envelop him like a shroud, knitting itself around him as though it were made of the very threads that kept him together. He stood for a few moments just gazing at the space where the vampire had been. The chill had gone from his body, and the touch that had been on his skin disappeared. Turning, he gazed back up at the ever-brightening sky once more, his previous thoughts returning once again to the past.

He regretted that night now, that first night when he had met the ancient vampire Casta Mica'tore. It had been in a park in Milan in the late nineteen seventies when he had still been dizzy from the blood of a young couple in love. Casta had appeared before him as he lay recovering from the intoxicating meal in a grove of fruit bushes. He had promised him so many things that heady night, promises of kinship in a higher order, and he had delivered them too, in part. But it was the deceit, the constant regurgitation of things said with Alexia and how she spent her time, that had been growing tiresome. But it was even more than that. He resented the intrusion that Casta demanded, the unrelinquishing need for knowledge about her. He had no choice but to continue now, of course, no choice at all. His years of deceit with her could not be turned around, even if she was unaware of them, and he would not be able to face her with the truth anyway. Casta had also put into place his network of the undead, Venice was certain of that, and perhaps that was his web. He had spies everywhere, spies like creeping insects, and who knew how far across London, or indeed how far across this world, those eyes stretched? He knew about the body in the river. He knew that Alexia had gone to see The Howler. Wasn't he himself just another of Casta's spies?

Stepping out from the cool darkness of the alleyway, Venice gazed up at the night's sky once more. He would not have long before the sun broke the horizon, a few hours at most, and he would somehow have to manage to overtake her on her way to Westminster Bridge. What he would say if they met he had no idea, but that was something that he didn't have time to concern himself with. Casta wanted The Howler dead, and that was what he had to do. It was a game with no choices, and played with its current rules, no winners either.

Venice crossed the road swiftly and headed back out along the river, past the brightly illuminated arc of Chelsea Bridge and on towards the parliament buildings. He had known Alexia for twenty years, and after dragging her from the freezing waters of the Thames, she had accepted him without question. She'd never asked anything of him in that time, nor pursued any details from his past. Now for him to betray her once again gnawed at him more than it had ever done, and for a reason that he couldn't quite fathom. Guilt had never played a great part with him, at least not as far as taking the lives of the mortals that continued to feed him. But there was something about Alexia that allured him to her, and that, surely, was troubling enough. He had never felt such things for anyone before, be they mortal or immortal, and after a span of over four hundred years, it seemed a strange time to start.

The illuminated spires of Big Ben dominated the blue-black sky as he turned a corner, and he stood for a moment just gazing up at the pearlescent gothic clock faces that blazed out across the starless night. His eyes tracked down towards the bridge that spanned the great surging river, but found no sign of either Alexia or The Howler across its span.

His first words to her, when at last he would come face to face with her, had still not formed in his head, and even as he hurried on towards Parliament Square, he formed arguments in his head that he or she might have later, as he planned how he might use his bare hands to rip out the cold Howler's heart, and bring it all the way back to Casta Mica'tore.

SIX

THE BREAK-IN

It was four thirty by his watch, the rain had let up, the sky had been left a dark soup of cold dank air, and the words of the skulker Rocket still rattled around inside his head. He'd taken a taxi across town after he'd left them, not wanting to let them know about the next job that Montague had set up for him. He'd never heard of these skulkers, and as little as he liked Montague, he wasn't about to shop him to a bunch of deadbeats with a van full of assault rifles.

Vampires, he thought to himself, as he darted across the deserted street, the yellow pallor of the streetlights overhead glimmering dimly across the wet tarmac of the road. What the hell were they on? There was no such thing as a vampire. Everyone knew that. If they'd tried to pin this story on him in some far away Eastern European country, one of those bizarre ones where all sorts of weird shit went on, then he might have bought it. But this was London. Things like ghosts and demons just didn't go on.

The address he'd been given was only a few streets away from the British Museum, a plush studio in a modernised row of tall red-brick apartment buildings. Security would be reasonable, Jenner guessed, but not impossible, and with his knowledge of the local backstreets and thoroughfares, it would make little difference once he was outside again with the merchandise.

He stood for a few minutes just gazing up at the building, thinking about Emma, the past, and all that he'd done with his life, whilst trying to forget all about Rocket and the other two skulkers. His education had been paltry to say the least, and life growing up with only his beggarly father had taken its strains. When finally the old man had died and left him their squalid flat to call his own, he'd ended up spending more time on the miserable luckless streets than was healthy, and that was when he had stumbled upon Kole. They'd done a bit of thieving here and there, nothing too serious, as well as turning over the odd shop. It had been Kole who'd first been introduced to Montague. It had only been a matter of time before Jenner had found him too. That had been over six years ago, and it had turned out that Kole had been more able to say no to some of his more dangerous offerings than he'd been. Jenner had tried to see Kole once again, just after the interrupted visit his first day out, but there had been no reply at his door. It was tough on the streets, even with a roof over your head, but especially so when you're broke and desperate. Montague had shown him the opulent insides of buildings he would never have otherwise seen. He'd introduced him to wealthy people he would never have otherwise met. And the money? Hell, that was what it was all about, wasn't it? But when you got it quick, you lost it quick, and you always ended up going back for more. Some would say it was unfruitful and pointless. And if Jenner was ever likely to admit it to himself, then he'd be numbered amongst them as well.

Montague had told him that the service door to the rear of the building would be left unlatched by his contact, whoever that was, and when he skirted round to the unlit entrance, Jenner found two tall bare metal double doors. There were no handles or locks, and he assumed that there would just be a push release mechanism from the other side. Gently he pressed his fingers to the gap between the doors, his nails trying to prize open the unlocked door without pressing it closed completely. To his surprise, the door swung open quite readily, and slipping silently into the unlit corridor beyond, he made his way into the building.

The passageway led to a grand main chamber, and from his vantage point of an unlit doorway, he could see a flight of stairs, two lifts and a desk where a security guard was sat back dozing. The lift would instantly draw the attention of the guard, and so he moved swiftly across the chamber floor towards the staircase, and took them to the top floor. It was a long climb, his prison days taking its toll on what little fitness he'd possessed going in, and by the time he reached the landing from which the doors to the studios ran, Jenner was breathing hard. He took a moment to catch his breath - it would be a short escape if he had to run now - before stepping across the lavish carpet to the door of studio two. Even though it was so early in the morning, and he'd been told that the occupant was not home, he still pressed his ear gently to the door and listened. There was no sound, either from the apartment or from the rest of the building, but it was only then that he realised that he'd not brought any equipment with him, and he certainly had nothing resembling a lock-pick. It had not occurred to him that there might be things he would need to relearn, procedures and tools that he had taken for granted years ago. The checklists that he'd prided his successes on had become second nature, and now after such a break, he suddenly realised what was missing from this current break-in. Perhaps his confusion over whether to even continue trafficking or thieving had clouded what skills he'd had, he had no way of knowing. It was just another reason to finally decide one way or another what he would have to do.

His fingers hovered over the handle to the studio door, as his mind fought with what he was doing. He was breaking into someone's home, forcing his way into their lives, just so that he could take something from someone he didn't know, only to give it to someone else he didn't know. It was wrong. He knew it was wrong. But he was broke. He had no money, there was no food in his cupboards, and the prospect of his ever achieving anything ever was slim at best. He had no choice but take the tainted cash that Montague offered in abundance. What else was there?

The immediacy of his situation returned. He was stood in a building where he didn't belong, faced with a locked door to a flat that he didn't own. There were only two choices and one of them had to be made now - go forward or go back. A rumble in his belly seemed almost to make the decision for him, urging him to mischief just for the sake of its hunger. Feed me, it seemed to say to him. Feed me as well as yourself. There was nothing else he could do, nothing but use brute force against the door that held him back from Montague's money, and hope that no one would hear. It was crazy, he knew, but then it was his own fault after all. Some criminal, he thought disparagingly, and then braced himself as he put his shoulder hard to the door.

The bang seemed to reverberate throughout the

entire building, and Jenner stood motionless as he prayed for it to die. The door stood firm, however, and gritting his teeth, he composed himself and then aimed his right foot at the lock with all his strength. The crack of the lock and the resulting thud of the door slamming hard against the wall behind seemed to rock the entire landing, and Jenner knew that his time inside was compromised considerably before people came running. He thought of even taking flight there and then, but knew that he couldn't. If he failed, then Montague had other people, people who would be willing to bend his arms into new and interesting shapes.

Once inside the studio, he played the narrow beam of his torch from wall to wall, looking for signs of the luggage or equipment that Montague had described. A box had been brought back from an expedition, he'd told him, and due to the nature of the return journey, it was still likely to be found amongst the crates it had been stored in, unpacked and presumably undisturbed.

He found what he was looking for almost immediately in the front room overlooking the light-speckled city. In the corner of the room, a stack of flight-cases and baggage stood in an orderly pyramid, but there was one in particular that stood out from the rest. A holdall had been almost completely wrapped up in black tape, and the sheer sturdiness of it grabbed Jenner's attention. He went to it, swiftly, and felt the object that was inside. There was no time to unwrap the bag and check the contents, and as unprofessional as it was, he simply snatched it up and ran, hoping that the box he could feel inside was the same box that Montague's buyer had paid so much to possess.

A police siren echoed out in the street below even before he had reached the top floor landing. There were many flights of stairs to descend and Jenner hurled himself down all of them in seconds, hoping that he could reach the ground floor before the officers or the guard sitting at the security desk caught sight of him. As it was, they all reached the entrance hall at the same moment, and it was only the thief's awareness of what was actually happening that propelled him out of the chamber first, and on towards the rear door that he hoped would still be unlocked.

As Jenner stumbled out into the alleyway at the back of the building, the headlights from another police car lit up the brick walls and debris littering the damp ground as it sped towards him, its blue lights seeming to strobe the very air around him. He heard the tyres skid on the wet matter as he took to his heels, voices yelling at his back as he ran, but he ducked down another passageway as the police car accelerated behind him in pursuit.

Jenner was certain that if he could make it out onto the Tottenham Court Road, it would only be a quick run to Regent's Park where he knew he'd be able to lose them for sure. He hit Gower Street at full sprint, and narrowly missed a pursuing officer on foot who made a grab at him as he passed. Jenner let out a yelp of surprise at the sight of him, and picked up his pace to try and increase the distance between them. It was not going to be such an easy escape after all, Jenner couldn't help thinking, as he was pursued down a connecting street and finally into the Tottenham Court Road. The officer was keeping pace with him, yard for yard, but as Jenner dashed across the road to the opposite pavement, the police car from the alleyway sped from a side street, its siren once again piercing the night air.

Jenner had no choice but to abandon the main road and try to lose the car via the footpaths, despite the officer on foot who was barely twenty yards behind him now, and showing no sign of slowing. Jenner, meanwhile, was still breathing hard, and his head was beginning to feel like a soup. His chest was hurting with a fierce ache, and he so desperately wanted to stop, but he knew that he could not give up this pace until he had lost the policeman trailing him.

Across another junction he raced with the officer still in pursuit. The siren from the car had faded as it had been forced to make a detour some way back, but there was still this one man to lose. It occurred to him briefly that he could try and make a stand, raise his fists and attempt to battle his way to freedom. But he knew that he was in no condition to fight. As soon as he stopped he knew he would just collapse in a fit of exhaustion.

Regent's Park suddenly loomed into view from out of the night, and as much as it pained him, Jenner stretched out his aching legs to try and gain a few more yards between the two of them. He chanced a quick look over his shoulder, and was pleased to see the officer flagging behind. He was still running, but his mouth was open and he was gasping for breath. Jenner felt relief inside, even though his own body was aching, as he crossed the road towards the big iron gates that surrounded the park. Tucking the stolen holdall firmly inside his jacket, he hurled himself at the gates, knowing that he had only one chance to get up and over. If he had any problems scaling them, the policeman behind couldn't fail to grab hold of him, even if he was as exhausted as the thief.

So it was with a ragged breath drawn from somewhere deep inside that Jenner leapt at the railings and hauled himself up. Perhaps it was the fear of prison again, or the distant recollection of the last time he had scaled these railings all those years ago, but he somehow found the strength to sail up and over, and continue onward into the darkest depths of Regent's Park.

As he hit the ground, he fell forward with a gasp for breath, and stole a look behind him at the perplexed face of the officer as he came to a stumbling halt. He could see him plainly now - one hand out to the railings, his body hunched over, his chest heaving - and realised that he was probably about the same age as he was. From the light cast down by the streetlamps, Jenner could see his eyes wide, his expression one of defeat, as he stared in bewilderment at the criminal who had finally bested him. Jenner did not take in this welcome sight for long, but gave himself the pleasure of a few deep breaths, and then forced his legs to move, and carry him on for at least a few hundred more yards into the dark enveloping shroud of the park, where he would be able to rest more fully for a while.

He would wait a few hours, he decided, and then take his time crossing the park to the opposite side where he would hail a taxi to take him back to his flat. He knew he'd need at least a few hours sleep before taking the box to Montague, so that he could decide with a relatively clear head, and perhaps a relatively full stomach, just what he could do with his future plans for breaking and entering, and robbing people of their wealth. But he knew, on a conscious level, that it had to stop, and now, but he had to at least convince himself that he would give the matter some considerable thought.

SEVEN

THE HOWLER OF WESTMINSTER

Alexia grew anxious as she crossed Parliament Square and caught her first glimpse of Westminster Bridge through the brightening haze of the approaching dawn. There was plenty of traffic around the parliament buildings, even at this early hour, the drivers cutting and diving across the insane pattern of lanes like buzzing drones, and yet a sudden calm descended around her that seemed to detach her from it all. There was only one thing that took hold of her senses now, and that was the bridge that was home to the most harrowing of all the London vampires, the creature known only as The Howler.

The streetlamps overhead cast their pallid glow down upon her as she took her first tentative steps towards the bridge. Even now she recounted the endless anxieties in her head - the reasons for not confronting The Howler, the benefits of retreat - but the dangers facing them all were growing by the day, and it had to be known whether or not he was openly taking the lives of their own kind in the face of the immortal populace.

The bitter salt of the river pricked her sinuses as she stepped onto the bridge and gazed down at the Thames surging beneath her, and she shuddered at the promise of the creature that lived in the archways just beneath her feet. She had ventured this far past the Houses Of Parliament only once before, and that had been the night she had met The Howler face to face. He had glanced at her only briefly, enough time for her to catch nothing but a flashing glimpse of bared teeth, before he had smelt the scent of vampire. No more than a heartbeat had passed before she'd lost contact with the ground and felt the tarmac of the road hard at her back. She had been beaten badly that night, the pain in her bones crippling her more than the icy cold of the river, once he had despatched her over the side after he was done, its currents seeking endlessly to drag her under. That had been the night she had met Venice too. He had found her clinging desperately to the supports of Chelsea Bridge, and had it not been for him, Alexia was certain she would not have survived. Ever since that night, and for over two decades now, they had stayed close together in the depths of London's dark underworld.

Those twenty years had passed without further incident at the hands of The Howler because she had stayed well clear of his territory. That was to come to an end tonight, because she now stepped out from beneath the towering monolith of Big Ben and onto the bridge itself, on a matter that could endanger them all throughout the capital. Even if it meant risking her own existence in order to do so.

The wind blustered suddenly over the bridge, and she had to push her hair from her face as it snaked across it. The booming of the river below seemed to heighten too, and she tried hard not to swallow her fear in case it should awaken The Howler's bloodlust too readily, for he was surely watching her as she made her way towards his home. The wind gusted again and seemed to rattle the very structure of the bridge, and Alexia staggered to keep her balance beneath its onslaught. It was only as she looked up again that she noticed a figure standing looking at her, where no one had been standing before.

It was The Howler.

He had grown larger still since last she had seen him, and he stood motionless in the middle of the pavement some fifty yards ahead of her. His hands were thrust deep into the pockets of a long dark coat, his long black hair blown sideways on the wind as it continued to bluster across the bridge. Suddenly, nothing else seemed real - the cars that sped in both directions across the bridge, the din of city life that always filled the air, the surging mass of the Thames beneath their feet - everything was illusory. Somehow, they were the only two beings left alive in the whole world.

The nervous anxiety inside Alexia seemed to echo throughout her entire body, her thundering blood causing her limbs to shudder, her head to drift and shake. Her feet were suddenly incapable of movement, and her mind seemed beyond the effort of creating a single coherent thought. The Howler's sight was locked with hers, and although his face seemed incomplete and shrouded by darkness, she could feel his raven-black eyes burrowing deep inside her, like rats eager to claw their way into her skull, to seek out and devour her mind.

Then The Howler took a step towards her.

It was a slow step, a casual step, and for a brief and irretrievable moment, she dared give hope to the possibility that this was not The Howler, but a simple mortal human out taking the night air. Then the second step came, more urgent than the first, and her doubts resurfaced once again. The third seemed not to touch the pavement at all. And the fourth never came. The Howler was in flight, and covered those few dissolvable yards between them in a single uncertain moment. Alexia drew breath to cry out, but The Howler already had his fingers deep in her throat, stifling the scream before her lungs had even tensed.

The ground went from beneath her as she was taken up into the night sky, the lights from below now swirling in an uncontrollable nonsense as she was dragged round and round. Her arms flailed for purchase, and she tried to cry out again as she caught sight of two great blustering wings that sprouted now from The Howler's back. But his other hand was pushed hard into the soft organs just below her sternum, and the agony of his fist stole her fight. She felt herself being turned tightly, and now sighted the bridge as she was hauled back down towards it.

Alexia managed a swift gasp of air between The Howler's fingers, just moments before she was thrown hard against the side of the bridge. Pain came instantly as she hit it, her consciousness registering a single thud as her head impacted. The world was suddenly somewhere very far away, dark and uncertain, until it came rushing back in a thunderclap, and she became aware of being hoisted upwards by her clothes, her weight restricting her breathing as they pulled against her chest and throat. The next thing she was aware of was the coarse ground scraping hard on her face and hands. Her eyes flickered open briefly and she became conscious of wooden boards, the swirling mass of the river far below her between splintered cracks. A voice came after a series of fractured and shuddering breaths, low and guttural, distant at first but then suddenly very close to her.

"You should not have come back," it growled.

Alexia tried to push herself up onto her elbows, but her body seemed unable to obey her, her muscles simply shuddering and without strength when she tried to use them.

"Who..?" she tried to say, but blood spilled quickly from between her lips, and she halted her question as she painfully swallowed it back.

"You want to know who I am?" The Howler enquired, his voice grating in his throat. "You know who I am. I am the one who owns the bridge, the one who sits on the clock face and watches the city while its people sleep through the night. I am the one who sees it all, and I bow down to no one."

"I... I know who you are. Are you going -"

"To kill you? Probably, this time, yes."

Alexia lay still as she concentrated on her pain. Her chest burned and her throat was tight with a sharpness that crippled her voice. Her muscles ached and her knuckles felt raw, and her head was a single pulse of pain. She tried to focus on the black waters hurtling past below the platform The Howler had made beneath the archway of the bridge. He said he would kill her, and yet she wondered why he had not already done so. She had to ask the questions she'd come with, and ask them quickly, or else she would be dead before he had even drawn his next ragged breath.

"We saw the body at Lambeth Pier," Alexia managed to say. "We saw the dead vampire."

The statement seemed to perplex The Howler for he remained silent for a moment. But then he said:

"I saw it too. What of it?"

"Why would be a more suitable question," Alexia

stated, managing to push herself up onto her side.

The pain doubled in her chest, and she coughed suddenly, and violently, and felt the thick hot fluid of her own blood on the back of her tongue once again. Her eyes found those of The Howlers again, black and hollow, and cavernous like twin voids. He was studying her.

"Do you think that I killed him?" he growled.

"Every one of us thinks you killed him."

The Howler's eyes seemed to draw her into them as he stared at her. Was there emotion there? Did he somehow care?

"You have spoken with every other vampire in the city?" he eventually asked.

"It's a small city," she lied, with an attempt at a shrug.

Alexia heard The Howler exhale, and saw his eyes flicker for a second.

"If you know every other vampire, then I could give you a name, and you could tell me where I might find them," he said to her.

Alexia was perplexed.

"I'm not a directory," she told him. "You want to kill somebody, you go find them yourself."

Her retort belied the terror she still felt. This creature no doubt had both the desire and the means to kill her, and yet for some reason he hadn't. She thought that he would spare her this time too, but she had nothing to base this on. It was only a vague hope, and she did not want to push her luck. She glanced back at him and found him gazing down at the river. Then, as he looked back up, he said:

"You must believe that I did not kill him, could not kill him, in such a way."

His words stunned her utterly, but the pain in her

body was giving strength to her own.

"Why should I believe you?" she demanded. "You sought to kill me before, and now you try to kill me again."

The jaws of The Howler clenched and a growl rumbled once again at the back of his throat. Alexia stiffened but did not back away.

"I know that with each passing night we must be more careful because the humans grow stronger," he told her. "But mine is another destiny. I am bound to the duty of but one single death. It is not yours, and nor is it my own."

"Then who?"

The Howler's black eyes turned once more towards the great booming waters of the Thames.

"I cannot tell you," he said, "but I think that of all the other vampires, you are perhaps the greatest threat to me."

"Me?" Alexia exclaimed. "What can I do?"

"I am not sure whether you are even aware of your own involvement, but what you may be certain of, is that you are involved."

"In what?"

"In what?" The Howler cried, almost with incredulity. "In the only event that has ever mattered more than the birth of the very first Ancient. The massacre of our tribes."

Alexia stared agog at him, his words battering her more than his blows had done. What did he know of the creature that had decimated her family? It was true that it was the only important event she had ever known since her birth into immortality, what other event could there possibly be? But how could he think that she had something to do with it, and how had he

134

come to know of it himself? Had he been a member of one of the other tribes, or even a secret member of her own? She had never seen him before until she had reached London in the early 1900's. So what, then, did he know of Kar'mi'shah?

"Where are you from?" Alexia asked him, attempting to haul herself up into a sitting position, the movement sending knives of pain throughout her chest.

"I will tell you nothing, woman, but know that when I find your other, I will gut him and kill him, and rain the sky with his blood."

Alexia stared at him, thinking him insane. More than insane. With his ability to attack her like he had, perhaps he was just as dangerous as the creature that had killed their tribes. The other of whom he spoke baffled her utterly - the other what? - and it was apparently obvious in her expression for he clarified his target to her the moment after.

"It is the one who created the demon that slew our families that I seek, the one who plotted and dreamed of destruction for us all. I know the name of whom I speak, I saw him that night as he brought forth that terrible demon and unleashed it upon us all. I saw you too, before and during those events. That is why I would kill you now. But I know that he hides from me, and I know that one day the two of you will meet again. Then the death to which I am bound will come, and I will take the head from his shoulders, and the blood from his veins, and sup upon them both as though it were my last and final meal."

Alexia watched dumbfounded as he turned his head away from her and gazed out across the city, as though he could somehow see this villain hiding amongst its shadows. His chest was heaving, not with the effort of their brief battle, but with the rage that had consumed him for hundreds of years. While she had grown to cherish this city, and deal with her losses and even let herself be charmed by the enigmatic artists who had come to this most beautiful of rivers, he had sat and watched and waited with a fury in his heart. There could be no doubt that he had been watching her too over those years, presumably since she had arrived in London, and that now, in itself, brought an unease to her. But for him to be harbouring intent of her death as well as conceiving a part for her in some vast and brutal conspiracy, then that was something else entirely.

"Tell me one thing at least," Alexia said to him at last.

The Howler turned his head to look at her.

"If you did not kill that vampire down there -"

"Then who did?" he finished.

Alexia nodded.

"I saw who it was," The Howler told her. "Or rather what it was."

Alexia looked at him, as he seemed somehow unable to explain, lost for words for just a moment, perhaps even afraid himself.

"It was during my nightly vigil," he started finally. "I was sitting on the parliament building, on the ledge just above the clock face that overlooks the river. There was a cold wind that night too, and I listened to it and breathed it in as it whistled across the stonework. Suddenly the cold went from it, and was replaced by something else. I could feel the heat of a desert wind, and I could taste the sand on its back. I looked down to study the river, but could see nothing but the surging current, as powerful as always. Then I noticed a shadow rolling across the surface of the water. It was almost impossible to see, black against black, yet it was definitely there. The shadow slowed as it approached my bridge, then lingered a moment. I watched, strangely not daring to move in case this thing, this shadow creature, should glance up at the face of the clock and find me sitting there, watching. But then I saw, glad that the wind stole my scent, that vampire who had dared to stray across my bridge. The shadow swept across the water, then washed rapidly up and over the bridge towards him. Teeth came from that shadow. I saw a mouth open from nowhere, a gaping wound in the air that sucked him off the pavement and deep into nothingness. I watched spellbound as he was passed through the body of the creature, his body dissolving as rapidly as his blood, before finally he was excreted, out into the river."

"And he was dead?" Alexia asked quietly, trying to study the almost imperceptible movements within The Howler's expression.

"Oh, he was dead," The Howler replied, "butchered from the inside out, and yet without being dusted or dissolved. I waited until the shadow had drifted out of sight, and then I flew down to where the body rode the currents of the river. I could see the deepest bite marks covering his neck, hands and face, and anywhere else there was flesh exposed. All that was left was a ragged bloodless corpse."

"I... had not seen the body so closely myself," Alexia said quietly.

"But now you know that it was not I that killed him."

Alexia looked at him.

"I guess that I do," she murmured quietly.

The Howler studied her for a moment, and then

told her that she could go.

Alexia did not say anything in reply, but simply eased herself towards the edge of the wooden platform before reaching out to the brickwork. Pain seared throughout her body as her fingers found purchase and she put weight to them. She didn't want to show any sign of defeat to the creature that had crushed her to such a state, if perhaps he even cared, and so she silently swallowed back the agonies that crippled her and climbed. Her limbs were leaden, yet somehow she managed to haul herself upward, up and over the railings at the top, before finally collapsing onto the cold hard concrete of the pavement.

She was a vampire from a world far away, the same as he, and yet there seemed to be something unknown to her that would forever keep them as enemies. He knew things that she did not, secrets that he had harboured for centuries. His anger had kept him focussed, that much was certain, whereas perhaps she had lost her way. She had given up hope of ever finding a way back home, but that now seemed utterly redundant. There was a fight still raging here in London, a battle that was not yet over. Surely everything was lost when the tribes had been decimated and her Master killed, and yet here was The Howler, waiting and watching for the vampire he knew was responsible. Who that vampire was she had no idea, but The Howler seemed to think that she did. And that was deeply troubling, for she truly had no idea.

Her head was pounding to near blindness as she hauled herself to her feet, and she realised through the agonies that wracked her body that nothing would be resolved here tonight. Starting back towards the parliament buildings in a half-stumble, her mind straining for clarity, the danger of her immediate situation came to her. Through the haze of pain she suddenly realised how vulnerable she really was. It was a long walk back to Knightsbridge, and even if there weren't any Skulkers out on the streets looking for an ancient unworldly scalp to treasure, then just about any passing mortal could do her harm, if they so wished. This was London, after all.

EIGHT

JACKEL IN A BOX

The moonlight glinted off something to his right and he stooped to see that it was a bright shiny coin, peeking out at him from amongst the dark tangle of grass and leaves. Quickly he scooped it up, cheerful at his good fortune, but as he did this, his eye was caught by another coin winking at him just a few yards from the first. As he knelt down to pluck this off the grass and drop it into his pocket, so he realised that there were more, the ground seeming to be littered with coins, all glittering and fresh from the mint. He had no idea who might have dropped the coins, and gave the matter only a fleeting consideration, before he began filling his pockets, drawing great handfuls of the bright shiny coins up into his possession, all thoughts of his former poverty now driven from his head, now he had found such bountiful wealth.

The coins were everywhere. Money covered the ground. He could hardly see the grass anymore. He was up to his knees in it now, and he couldn't pocket them quickly enough.

No one else knew it was here, surely, that was his first thought. His next, and it came almost immediately after the first, that he would undoubtedly have to kill in order to keep it his. His trousers bulged with this new wealth, his jacket weighing him down so much that his back was beginning to ache. But it was a good ache, an ache that signified the end of his scraping by, and the start of a new and fruitful age.

It was then that the coins began to slip between his fingers as he continued to force them into spaces that weren't there. At first he just put it down to sweaty palms, the coins slipping against his greasy skin. But the more he thrust his hands into the piles of coins, the more he noticed their sliding away, and also his hands coming away slick and wet. He looked down now at what he was doing, and saw beneath the cool moonlight, the dark liquid that dripped from his hands. It was a deep scarlet, this liquid, and it ran freely and quickly across his skin, leaving rich dark rivulets behind in its wake. It smelt sickly sweet as he put his nose near it, but no sooner had he done so than the ground spurted up like a torn vein, coating his face and throat in a cruel shower of the stuff, saturating his hair and clothes, and drenching him utterly so that he reeked of it.

It was blood, he immediately realised.

Oh my God, it was blood.

Jenner tried to stagger back away from it, but he was up to his knees in it now, his body weighed down considerably from the sheer weight of coins bulging out his pockets, and he achieved nothing more than falling backwards into its filth. He lay there sprawling, in a soup of blood and money that even now was rising over him like a tide, spilling up over his arms and chest, seeking to drag him down, and drown him in its grim viscous sea. He tried calling out, but as soon as he opened his mouth the tide simply swelled to fill it, choking him as it sought out his throat, the blood searching out his lungs, the coins his stomach.

Jenner urged what strength he had left to sit

upright once more, his hands clasping for any purchase they could find, but the sheer weight of the money held him fast. Blood continued to break over him in thick glutinous waves, blurring his sight and stealing what last remaining gasps of breath remained in his body. His thoughts began to slip from him, abandoning his head with unnerving eagerness, his mind conjuring nothing but his deepest primal fears of death and drowning. And then his body began to shudder, his limbs to shake and convulse, as the last of his life became bludgeoned out of him.

His eyes shot open in a panicked heartbeat, and his lungs managed to snatch a rasping rapid intake. The sky was clear and dark above him. Trees waved and whispered beneath the pull of the gentle night breeze. The weight of the money had left his bones. And the blood had receded. Jenner found himself alive.

He sat up, his heart pounding furiously with the echoes of the nightmare, and grabbed snatches of the depths of Regents Park. It was dark and quiet but for the moonlight overhead, the wind through the leaves of the trees and the distant rumble of the city beginning to stir for yet another approaching day. He must have fallen asleep, he quickly realised, hauling himself onto two unsteady feet, his limbs still shaking from the encounter, the images in his head put there by Rocket's insistent talk of vampires and blood-drinking. He glanced back the way he had come, through the trees and tangled bushes, but of any police pursuit there was no sign. At least that was something, he conceded, and looked around him some more.

The horizon was light in the east with the

approaching sun, and the air was relatively clear, the damp gone and promising a fine day. There were still no sounds, except for the city and the wind, but then his eyes suddenly went to a copse of trees off to his right as though he felt he was being watched. He stared hard into the utter darkness of its shadows, searching for a glimpse of someone, and there, could it be, the uncertain silhouette of someone standing there, returning that same intense scrutiny? No, it couldn't be, he thought, even as he sought hard to separate torso from trunk, limb from branch. Why would anybody be standing in the middle of Regents Park, at - he glanced at his watch, pressing the light button so that he could make out the digits - five fifteen in the morning, just to watch somebody who had dozed off amongst the bushes? No, it was just his imagination, his mind and body jittery after such a disturbing dream.

It was six forty five when Jenner finally slammed shut the door to his flat and trudged through into the kitchen. Dropping the holdall on one of the counters, he took up the kettle and shook it to see if there was any water in it, before filling it at the sink, setting it back down and switching it on. Going to one of the cupboards, he snatched up a mug and the coffee jar standing beside it and set them both down next to the kettle while he waited impatiently for it to boil. Gazing out through the window at the brightening street, Jenner pushed his hand over the stubble on his chin as he turned over the terrifying realism of his dream.

It seemed like it had actually happened, his sheer greed drowning him in the blood of those he had hurt.

Symbolism, he guessed they called it. It sounded like shit, but it kind of made sense. Especially now. Just where was his life heading, he wanted to know? Breaking into people's homes, stealing their stuff, dealing drugs to those destined to have their heads lopped off with an axe. And for what? Money, that's what. It was all fucked up. All of it. Once he handed the box over to Montague he would get his hands on ten grand, which was no bad sum of cash for a night's sprint through the city. But at what cost? It sure wasn't healthy, but it was profitable. He clamped his eyes shut and screwed his hands through his hair.

It was all fucked up.

All of it.

And he was fucked up most of all.

"Shit," he suddenly yelled aloud across the kitchen, desperate to release some kind of tension.

His eyes opened and flickered without direction around the kitchen - the oven, the fridge, the sink with its tiny unkempt stack of used plates and mugs - until finally they settled on the holdall that he'd set on the counter. He stared at it for a moment, wondering just how such a small thing could be the source of so much disruption, causing someone to pay Montague to have it stolen, and then Montague paying him a cut to do the dirty work for him. He picked it up and looked at it, turning it over in hands still grimy from the dirt of the park.

Lengths of strong black tape bound it fast, a hurried effort to conceal its contents permanently. It was certain that whoever had done it, definitely didn't want anyone else to ever get inside.

Pulling open a drawer, Jenner rummaged amongst what sparse utensils he had, before taking out a pair of scissors to begin hacking away at the tape. It was tough tape, and several layers thick, even in the thinnest of areas, and it turned out to be easier just to cut through the bag where it became visible. As a hole opened and he managed to slice it wider, the box that was held inside tumbled through, but he was not quick enough to catch it in time and it hit the floor with a clatter and skipped briskly across the tiles.

Jenner bent to retrieve it with a grunt as he tossed the shredded bag to the ground. There looked like a spatter of dried blood across one of its corners, and the blackened film of fire damage caking most of two sides. But the rest seemed fairly intact, and it made him wonder why anybody would want it so much.

It seemed fairly unremarkable to look at. It had a few pictures on it, a handful of symbols, and perhaps it might even be valuable because of its rarity or age, but that was about it. Turning it slowly over in his hands, his fingers traced the subtle patterns of the pictures, the strange symbols and marks, some painted, some roughly engraved. It was as he turned the box, however, his eyes seeking conundrums amongst its many details and previously unseen motifs, that the strange revelation came. There seemed to be no way to open it.

Jenner turned it once more, and studied each of the six flat sides more closely. There seemed to be no lock, no latch and no hinge, and it was then that the symbols marking every surface suddenly became all the more curious because of it. It could almost have been a solid block, but that suddenly seemed so ludicrous a notion.

Jenner started as the kettle began to boil beside him. He had forgotten all about the coffee, as well as the hunger that had nagged at his belly on his way back to the flat, and he now set the box back down on the counter next to the mug and the coffee jar, filling the mug from the kettle, before pulling the pack of cigarettes from his jacket pocket. Lighting one, he drew deeply on it as he stared at the box, its coloured surfaces and magical symbols becoming more mesmerising by the second. Just where had this thing come from, he wondered? Morocco? The Middle East? Egypt? South America? A number of the symbols seemed familiar, but not so much that he could place them. A dog here, a moon there, a triangle with a squiggly line underneath that could have been either a snake or a stick. The smoke from the cigarette was curling round him now, shrouding him in a comforting but distracting cloud of fog, and he took up the box once more, as well as the mug of coffee, and wandered through into the living room to continue his study.

Perching on the edge of the sofa, Jenner set down his coffee and began to rub away the specks of blood that had splashed across the box, carefully carving it out of the grooves with his fingernail where it became stubborn, and wiping the black soot off with the sleeve of his jacket. The more that he looked at them, the more the symbols seemed just that - a few lines to depict fire or water or an animal. There seemed nothing genuinely mystical or powerful in any of them, but they were intriguing nevertheless.

The sun was considerably brighter the next time he glanced up to look out of the window, and he wondered briefly just how long he had been sat there studying the box. The traffic was busy now, he could hear it swelling and screeching on the other side of the glass, and his attention wandered to the coffee table in front of him. The cigarette that he had drawn on earlier, but perhaps had only drawn on it twice since he had lit it, had burnt down to a stub before extinguishing itself completely. His coffee was untouched, cold, and now had a grim discoloured film over its surface. Jenner glanced at his watch, and was surprised that it read ten forty five. Where had the time gone? He looked at the images on the box once more, and traced his fingertips back across it. The markings that were carved had been carved quickly and roughly, certainly not the work of a craftsman. The painted symbols were the same - quick rough scraps to get the job done, nothing more. Why anyone would pay so much money to have this, he thought, was beyond him. But then he wasn't an eccentric idiot with money to spare.

There came a knock on his door, and Jenner lifted his head absently from his study of the box. It was probably another of Montague's runners, come to find out what was taking him so long with the delivery, or perhaps just to trade his money for the merchandise and take it away with them. With all his curiosity in the box, he had completely forgotten about the deal, as well as his rendezvous with Montague.

Jenner set the box down on the coffee table and pushed himself to his feet. Wandering through into the hallway, he pushed his hand through his hair as he opened the door. Almost immediately he regretted his nonchalance, the allure of the box stealing his common sense temporarily, as he found himself helplessly gaping at two uniformed officers that stood astride his open door. Before he could even utter a word or attempt to slam the door on them, one had already stepped across the threshold to take hold of him, the other now reaching for a night-stick that hung within eager reach from a hoop on his belt.

Jenner's mind was swirling suddenly, images flashing through his head of prison bars and flashing lights as he tried to rally them into cohesion. He only vaguely recalled the burglary just hours before, as well as his ragged escape attempt through Regent's Park. He'd thought that he'd lost the police altogether and made it to safety, but he was obviously out of practice in such things because of those two terrible years spent in prison.

Prison.

The word leapt out from the others like a flare. It was then that it suddenly dawned on him that that was exactly where he was now headed. The two police officers had a hold of each of his arms, and as he stared at them now, he saw the slightly bemused expression on their faces as though they had expected more of a struggle than what they were currently getting.

"You have the right to remain silent..." he heard one of them say, distantly, as though he was standing yards away from him.

Jenner looked from one to the other now, as his mind struggled to comprehend just what was happening to him. He realised that he was in his own hallway - they had crossed the threshold and forced him back against the wall - and he was standing between the doorways to the kitchen and living room, but that was about it. What happened next, and he was to at least remember that it was momentous, was simply a blur of scarlet, but much more than that he would never truly grasp.

The grip on his arms went, that was the first thing

of significance, and then he saw what he thought was a black rabid dog fly between him and the arresting officers. A flash of white needle teeth streaked through this hot haze of red, and he found himself looking down upon a heap of two broken bodies, a spray of blood fanning out across the floor from where they had both been opened up.

The black dog was there still, snarling and growling with an insurmountable hunger, only now it had two human arms and two human legs, and a human face that looked up at him through a mask of blood that churned down across a human throat. The teeth of the beast were still embedded in this human-looking mouth, and they gleamed like glittering diamonds, stark against the taint of butchery that surrounded them. And then they disappeared from sight altogether, as they became embedded in the raw and ragged flesh of the two dead officers, as the man bent his head once more to drink upon the hot fresh blood that had once been flowing uninterrupted in the police officers' covered and unbroken veins.

NINE

SEEKING SANCTUARY

Venice had seen what little exchange there'd been on the roadway of Westminster Bridge. He'd also seen the great shroud-like wings unfold from The Howler's back. He had even seen The Howler unfurl them and use them to haul Alexia up into the cold night's sky. He'd wanted to rush to her rescue. He'd wanted to storm across the bridge and beat The Howler back, saving Alexia from this assault before breaking him in two. But to see the size and fury of him kept him back. Fear, that was what kept him back, fear of this other vampire, and he could do nothing but watch, frozen to the spot, and bear witness to her beating.

Shortly after that, Venice had managed to claw his way down to the level of the river where he'd struggled to pick up threads of a conversation he was surprised they were even having, but what few scraps he did manage to catch above the rushing din of the Thames were useless. His keen vision had been able to furnish the sight of her battered body, and he had been certain that he would witness her total defeat, and watch the dumping of her carcass into the plunging waters below. But no. It seemed that The Howler was more in the mood for exchanging words tonight, rather than blows, but it had still been a sad sight to watch a pitiful Alexia haul herself back up the brickwork of the bridge before collapsing onto the pavement above.

How could that be, though? Casta had told him that The Howler would literally destroy her. Casta had foretold that she would be torn limb from limb, and that he must get to The Howler ahead of her in order to strike the first lethal blow. But this was not the scene that Casta had painted for him, despite his palette of colourful language. There had been a conversation, things said, but the content of such things he was ignorant to. Perhaps it was this content that Casta was afraid of, could that be it? Perhaps such a meeting between Alexia and The Howler was something that Casta wanted to avoid, perhaps even permanently. And yet their first and only meeting, as far as Venice knew, had ended with her near death. That seemed more in keeping with Casta's concerns. It was most perplexing.

Not wanting to intervene in their private war, Venice had remained at the edge of the bridge, waiting for Alexia to make her own stumbling way towards him. She did not see him, however, not even as she shuffled slowly past him. But it was only then, as she passed by so very closely, that he saw the true extent of what The Howler had done to her. Her once beautiful face was now battered and raw, and blood tracked freely down her flawless skin from several gashes. Her legs seemed badly crippled for she found it difficult to walk, and she hobbled along the pavement awkwardly. One hand she held to her ribs, the other to her head, and it was a depressing sight to see the woman he'd seen grow so strong, return to a similar state to when he'd first met her, also at the hands of The Howler.

Even as he joined her and kept pace by her side,

she did not look up, and as he studied her for a few steps he could see that her eyes were clenched with agony. Her heightened senses seemed gone, and it wasn't until he spoke that she even acknowledged him at all.

"What are you doing here?" Alexia wanted to know.

"Did you ever know me not to be around when you're in trouble?"

Alexia managed to grimace a smile at his reply.

"You do seem to be making a habit of finding me near-crippled," she said.

"That's twice now," Venice told her. "I hope there won't be a third."

"You and me both."

"Why did you go to see him again?"

"It's a long story."

"I've got a lifetime to listen."

"And complicated."

They continued through Parliament Square in silence for a while after that, Venice preoccupied with steering what conversation they might have later, and Alexia simply concerned with walking upright and staying conscious. She was a killer the same as he, but this wasn't the first time that he'd seen her vulnerable. They both knew the risks on the streets of London, every vampire in the city knew them, and it was dangerous for any one of them to wander even the darkest routes alone. But here was Alexia, not only alone, but wounded to the point where a couple of mortal youths could best her. It was not good.

His thoughts drifted to the exchange he'd had with Casta Mica'tore in the alleyway, and to the truths hidden inside the madness of his words. Was he simply little more than another of his puppets, he wondered, another life ensnared in the web of his beloved spider? He'd walked the earth for hundreds of years, and seen more countries than most, and yet here he was, reduced to the level of a servant, and not an honest one either, although he'd never been much of an angel in his past. His existence now, though, was something different. He'd found roots in London with Alexia, and not just because Casta had brought him here and given him reason to stay. Defying Casta was not something that he wanted to do, but looking at the woman struggling onward beside him made him realise that perhaps there were choices that could be made. Casta's magic was powerful, and he was sure that he'd only seen the surface of its might, and it was not something to be taken lightly. He was in a dangerous situation, more so than any of the other vampires out roaming the streets. He'd managed to find himself caught not just between mortal hunters, but between his own kind too. His friends were few, he knew that, but he also knew that honesty would only thin that number down further. He could never tell Alexia about his relationship with the vampire known as Casta, not even if he decided never to work for him again. His thoughts raged in circles in this way as he walked with Alexia through the streets of London, and it wasn't until they reached the front door to her flat, that he realised how far they had actually walked together.

"Are you coming in?" Alexia asked him.

Venice declined with a shallow bow of his head.

"I have things I need to do," he told her, "and I think the best thing for you is rest. You don't need me here anymore anyway."

"But I do still need you," she added, and then slipped inside, away from the night.

Venice stood on the doorstep of her apartment

building for a while after that, gazing up at her window. No light would come from behind the heavily-draped room, but he was happy to know that at least she was off the streets and safe inside. Then he himself turned, and disappeared swiftly into the lamplit streets of Knightsbridge, and deep into the heart of darkest London.

Alexia lay back on her bed, one hand pressed against her aching ribs, the other held at her brow, and gazed up through half-lidded eyes at the white plastered ceiling. Perhaps the flat was not the safest place to be at the moment, she thought, and told herself that as soon as Callie returned they should talk about leaving her beloved London - perhaps even for good - and finding somewhere new for them to live.

There was much from her brief exchange with The Howler that still troubled her, and most of it was from what he knew about the horrors that took place in Kar'mi'shah. Her own recollections of what had happened were still hazy, but he seemed clear. He spoke as though he knew that someone was responsible. He spoke as though he knew who that was. And worse still, he spoke as though he held her partially responsible herself.

But how could that be? She had lost most of her tribe herself. How could he believe her capable of plotting to destroy her own family? It just made no sense. She'd seen virtually no one from Kar'mi'shah during her years living in London, but she knew of some that lived here. They were not from the Faraoh tribe, however, and after the holocaust that had decimated so many of the vampires, every tribe beheld each other as the enemy. They would kill each other on sight, she knew, even today after so many years,

154

and it was because of that more than anything else, that she kept her distance from them. But after this conversation with The Howler, where she had virtually been named as an accomplice to the horror of that fateful night, she felt perhaps that she should break this feud between the clans, or at least make an attempt to put things straight. She was still not sure how The Howler fitted in to all this, she had not even known that he'd originated from Kar'mi'shah, but there was one person that she knew of who was more likely to know than any other. And he was one of the Masters from another tribe, the tribe of the Wraiths.

She had only seen Koulan on a number of occasions, and only during rituals in the temples of Kar'mi'shah. She had not seen him in this world, and she had never even spoken to him, but she knew where he was reported to haunt, and she knew too that he lived with other surviving members of his tribe. It was dangerous, she knew, to try and see him, and his guards would probably attempt to kill her before she had even managed to gain an audience with him. But the feuds had gone on for too long, and if what The Howler said was true, and the wars between them all were still raging as strong as ever, with spies and assassins across the globe, then the sooner the elders got together, the safer it would be for all of them once again.

But it was not just other vampires that they had to fear. The humans that would indiscriminately destroy them all grew in every way too, and more and more of them were joining their secret ranks year after year. It was becoming more of a war than a struggle with these mortals, as more and more of them began to believe in the demons that passed by their own doorsteps. Of course vampires had to kill to survive in this world, but the hunters were becoming the hunted, to coin a cliché, and they were being forced to avoid their human prey altogether.

She knew a number of these human hunters - they were commonly becoming known as skulkers within the vampire community - by name. Some worked together as closely knit groups, sharing resources and information, while others preferred to work alone. One thing was certain, however, and it was true for them all - times were getting more dangerous for all vampires, and even though she was immortal, she was still as scared of death now as she was when she was mortal.

She was not ignorant of the advent of the Internet either, although she rarely had the opportunity to view what was going on, only when she could coax a victim back to their home to glean what she could. It troubled her greatly that humans were becoming more resourceful, intuitive even, and she had once stayed online until dawn after she had fed, to study a number of their chat-zones. What she had seen had terrified her.

Long gone were the codes and metaphors, it seemed. Skulkers were blatant now, openly discussing names, dates and locations of meetings and kills. She had witnessed a conversation between two such hunters once - calling themselves [ATI]Blessed-Angel and [PSK]Rocket - discussing a vampire one of them had slain called Matra'abor'el. Blessed-Angel had graphically explained how he had tracked Matra to a warehouse, where he had ensnared her with a series of pre-painted hexes, before staking and dusting her. Alexia had wept as they had spoken online. She had

156

known Matra, and had last seen her in the early 1920's, when she had planned to travel north throughout England. Blessed-Angel had apparently caught up with her on the outskirts of Edinburgh, tipped off by an unknown source, before killing the immortal.

Alexia had left the conversation to scroll unwatched down the screen, leaving the flat quickly, the owner's body still slumped lifeless beside the monitor. She'd been careful to cover her tracks after that night. She'd taken only a few human lives, forcing herself to feed mostly on stray pets or native animals, so that only the fewest questions could be asked of the deaths she left behind her. But the relative safety this afforded her, as well as that of Callie's, had its drawbacks, however. The quality of animal blood was poor, and seldom nourished them sufficiently. But these were desperate times, they all knew that, and as such their choices were minimal.

It occurred to her, as it had occurred to her many times in the past few decades, that she could return to Europe. Things would have changed since last she was there too, of course, and she knew that she'd be lying to herself if she thought that it would be any safer. Skulkers spanned the globe via the Internet. Vampires across the continents would be in equal disposition. There would be no refuge in this world. Their only hope was to somehow find a way to return to Kar'mi'shah where they could resume their lives as Gods, worshipped and praised in their own palatial temples. That was the only clear thought in her head now, and it was a thought that The Howler had resown there. Her dream of home had come back, and it was certain that it would only bring with it the same frustrating disappointments that it had brought before.

There was no way home.

That was the simple truth.

Her heartache before had lasted decades until she had come to terms with it. Now The Howler had brought all that heartache back, and with it a renewed longing to see those radiant skies over her beloved Kar'mi'shah once more.

Her eyes flickered closed with the agonising dream that she knew could never be realised, the pains in her chest and limbs ebbing in dull rhythms in the swirling void behind her eyelids. She wasn't sure if she drifted into partial sleep, or simply slipped consciousness briefly, but when next she opened her eyes again, she was aware of someone watching her in the darkness.

"I wasn't sure if you were awake or not," came a voice.

It was Callie.

She was perched on the edge of the bed peering over at her, a faint halo of light around her straying in from behind the heavy curtains across the windows, partially silhouetting her, but giving her the appearance of something holy. Alexia felt weak as she looked up at her. Daylight was coming, if it wasn't already here, and she had not fed during the night. She would heal little before the next sunset, especially with no fresh blood in her body.

"You seemed so still," Callie continued, interrupting her thoughts. "I wasn't sure if you were still with us."

"It's okay," Alexia returned, pushing herself up a little, the pain in her chest thankfully reduced to a severe dull ache. "I'm not gone yet."

"What happened?"

"The price of knowledge was high," Alexia told her,

almost able to add a smile.

"Who did this to you?"

"The Howler."

"He found you?"

"No, I went looking for him."

"You went looking for him? Why? He nearly killed you last time, why did you think he wouldn't try again this time?"

"I didn't know. But it was just something that I had to do."

"You saw the body he left behind," Callie continued. "That vampire was shredded. Torn to pieces. He could've done the same to you."

"You must know that no vampire could ever be capable of such a killing."

"Then what is?"

"I don't know," Alexia said, looking at her. "But the thing is, neither does The Howler."

"You had a conversation with him?" Callie still seemed shocked by what she was being told.

"This isn't the time for this, Callie. I wanted to wait until I saw you first, but I really think we should go."

"Go where?"

"Away. And as far away as possible from here."

Callie seemed to ponder the weight of this for a moment, and Alexia wondered briefly about how connected the child vampire might actually be to this city. London was her home after all, all she had known, and perhaps she was asking too much in requesting that she leave it.

"I want to stop in Camden first, though," Alexia added, touching the girl's hand.

Callie glanced up at her, distracted.

"What's in Camden?"

"There's someone there that I think I should talk to."

She watched as Callie pursed her lips, a human trait she rarely saw her use.

"Are we leaving the city altogether?" she asked tentatively.

"I'm not sure," Alexia told her honestly. "But I have to see this someone first before I can make any decisions. It's been a long time, and I only hope that things will have changed."

"And if they haven't?"

"Then it won't really matter what we decide to do. We'll be dead."

TEN

LUNCH WITH GOD

Jenner's eyes struggled open to view a darkened room. He could tell that it was his flat, and that the curtains in his living room had been drawn, and also that it was still day because of the feeble shaft of grey sunlight that managed to find its way between the gap in the curtains and into the room. His head was dizzy, and pounding a little, and for a moment he could only barely recall standing in front of an open doorway staring at two policemen that morning. It was only then that he remembered those two policemen, and yes, they had been holding him, grasping his arms tightly while he stood in the hallway. He'd not been arrested though, his lying here in his own flat was proof of that.

Jenner sat up on his sofa. Blood rushed to his head with the movement, bludgeoning the inside of his skull with such a brutal force that he had to clamp it with one hand and take hold of the arm of the sofa with the other in order to keep himself conscious. Sickness crawled into his stomach now too, clutching at his innards, twisting them, knotting them. But there was something else though, too, something that nagged at him, a dreaded image that he couldn't quite remember. Something white. Something red.

And then it came in a rush.

The black dog.

Jenner stood up hurriedly and gazed around the room. His head pulsed with blackness almost immediately and he grabbed hold of the sofa again as he stumbled forward a half step. His eyes flickered open quickly, straining through a glutinous sea of pulsing black shapes, but even through them the room seemed empty. He fought to focus on his watch, confirming the time as four thirty five.

"Shit," he exclaimed aloud.

It was four thirty five.

Montague would be wanting to know where the box was.

Oh my God, he thought. The box.

Jenner started towards the door, his hand still clutching his head as he went, but jerked sideways as he caught sight of the man torn from the shape of the black rabid dog staring back at him from the corner of the room.

As though he had wrapped the very shadows of the room around himself in order to wear them like a cloak, he stood tall and motionless, his unblinking eyes shining brightly out at him from the gloom, his pale face like some kind of theatrical mask. He seemed to regard him in silence as they both stared at one another, but then he took a step forward, partially shrugging off the shadows that seemed to clothe him, and allowed himself to be seen more clearly by the dim light of the room.

"You have finally woken," the man observed, quietly and simply.

"Yes," Jenner managed to reply, squinting his eyes through both the ache in his head as well as the murk of the room. "I must... have fallen asleep."

"Stronger you will soon be," the man continued. "It

is to be expected. I will not hold such lengthy replenishment against you."

"What... happened?"

"You have done what I thought could not be done. I am grateful. I am in your debt."

Jenner stared at him, his head only slowly beginning to order itself, his thoughts shuffling and uncertain, dark and clouded. He dimly asked him just what that meant.

"You have set me free," the man said plainly, his words measured and equal, monotonous.

"Set you free?" Jenner repeated. "Who are you?"

"Who am I?" the man asked slowly, as though he did not understand the question. "I am Jackel El'a'cree, Master of Kar'mi'shah, Master of the Faraohs."

"Who?"

The man narrowed his eyes at this response, his sight still burning and intense, and Jenner thought he could hear a deep breath of agitation escape him.

"If you do not know who I am," he stated, "then I should deem it necessary to demand your name."

"My name is Jenner Hoard. This is my flat."

"Your flat?"

"Where I live."

"Where you live?" the man's calm had gone, replaced with a temper that was fraying. "By the blessed moon, if you live beneath my sky, then you bow down before me. If you wish for continued existence, then you devote your praise upon my name." He shook his head. "Enough of this. Where are the others? Send for them immediately."

"Look, I don't know who you are -"

"I am Jackel El'a'cree..." the man faltered, and

gazed, open jawed and suddenly bewildered, at the thief who stood feebly before him. His lips then closed and he sniffed at the air. "What year is this?" he asked quietly.

"1999."

His eyes flickered closed as he continued.

"And what country?"

"England."

"Who do you worship now?"

"Worship?

"Yes, worship."

"You mean personally?"

"Just give me a name, damn you."

"I don't know. Jesus Christ, I guess."

The man then took a shallow, if not altogether happy, breath.

"I see," he said.

The severity of his situation came to him as he stared at the remains of the two dead police officers still lying in his hallway. He stood for a few seconds just simply trying to allocate names to body parts. Here was a skull, and there a rib cage, but amongst the tangled matted mess of their blood-soaked uniforms and black tarnished boots it was difficult to tell much more. Their flesh had seemingly been ripped from the bone, devoured, chewed and wrestled. The cloth of those uniforms and the leather of those boots had been scuffed and ripped as though they had been in some drawn-out battle, the glint of a belt buckle or wristwatch the only thing to brighten the mass through the darkened pulp. Looking at this sight for only a few seconds was enough, however, before

Jenner felt the knot of sickness twist in his stomach once again and he stumbled past and through into the kitchen, retching across the tiled floor in an attempt to reach the sink.

The stench of vomit hug sourly in the air, refusing to leave via the window even after it had been cleared up. Jenner leant against the sink as the early evening air drifted in, chill but grimy from the traffic-busy street below. There were fumes in the air, a sharp tang of diesel mixed with monoxides and other pollutants. It made the air almost too thick to breathe, and it felt as though it was coating his throat and lungs even as he took it in. His eyes played idly across the soot-blackened flats opposite, their windows dark with the city's filth, taller high-rises and office buildings looming grimly above them, encroaching over the city like a living black mass, preparing to swamp them all with a wave of brick and choking dust.

A car horn resounded aggressively along the street below, blaring out its impatience to the knotted snake of metal grinding its way towards the flyover. It shook him from his distant thoughts only briefly, and he became strangely aware of the permanent rumble that always hung over London, no matter where you were in its depths; of lorries, and of cars, of horns and of sirens, all blurred together into a single horrible cacophony, a dull booming din that his ears had long since switched off to - except at obscure times when the din somehow manages to get through. It seemed to blurt out a single sharp point of focus every now and then, as though the city screams to be heard, and no one that lives inside its limits can hear it or do anything about it.

Jenner turned his head slightly and listened to the

silence of his flat, dead and hollow compared to the city's incessant monotone. The man who had called himself Master of Kar'mi'shah had barricaded himself inside Jenner's bedroom since their brief exchange, and Jenner had been left to decipher what few insights this murderer had offered him.

For one, just what did Master of Kar'mi'shah mean? Jenner had sat in the living room gazing out at the Hammersmith streets for a while asking himself that, but of course every other question was just as mystifying and unanswerable as the last. The man called Jackel El'a'cree had told him how he had been imprisoned inside the box he had stolen from the apartment building. He had said that he'd been trapped inside it for centuries. He had also said that whoever had cast him into the box, had been both clever and powerful enough to keep him there as well. And it was shortly after that, with Jenner being unable to understand any of it, that Jackel El'a'cree had withdrawn to his bedroom.

Jenner had heard the din of breaking furniture. He had pounded on the door already wedged fast, and no amount of shouting had brought this intruder out into the open. It had only been as he had wandered back through the flat towards the kitchen that he had stumbled upon the bodies of the police officers again, and set his worries whirling afresh.

He had leant against the kitchen counter for some time after cleaning up his own vomit, gazing out through the window at the rooftops of London, trying to breathe steadily, not daring to return to the hallway, and even thinking once again about the skulker's final words to him, about the evil that walked the same streets as he. But as the sky slowly relinquished the sun to the horizon, and the day began to darken

166

towards dusk, it became apparent that the bodies, like his guest, were here to stay.

Reluctantly stepping back into the hallway, Jenner glanced down only briefly at the grizzled corpses still entangled on the floor, as he made his way back through to his bedroom once again. Knocking gently against it, he called to Jackel and waited for a reply. When none came, he knocked again.

"I need your help," Jenner said to the closed door, unsure of what he was saying even as he listened to the dead silence on the other side. "Something has to be done about these two policemen."

Again there was silence, and Jenner stood waiting for a few minutes hoping that the man would unblock the door and step outside to meet with him. He didn't want to think about what would happen in the meantime if more officers were to arrive on his doorstep only to find their colleagues lying gutted beyond all recognition on the floor. His life would undoubtedly be over, of that he was certain.

Pressing his ear to the door, Jenner listened to the hollowness of the room once again. There was simply nothing to hear. He tried the handle and put his weight to it, but it still would not budge. Exhaling gravely, he trudged back into the living room, perched on the window sill, and settled down to watch the streets carry their freight of commuters home from their offices, from normal life to normal life in the space of one simple and unremarkable day.

PART THREE

DESTITUTION

Destitution, *des-ti-tu'shon*, n. Want; poverty; comfortless.

ONE

A SIGHTING OF HORROR

Milestone stood on the railway bridge gazing down at the canal that ran alongside it, the moonlight glimmering brightly across its black mirrored surface. He didn't want to be feeding on rats or dogs, like Koulan had instructed them all to do so many years ago. He wanted the thrill of killing live prey, human prey, to taste their hot rich blood on the back of his tongue, and feel the ecstatic moment as his teeth pierced their firm cologne-scented skin. All that Koulan had told him he knew was true, but where was the life in hiding and getting by? Either he was going to live or he wasn't, and living like a slave was not living at all. He was a vampire, and the vampire had a desire that stemmed far beyond rules. It was a desire for blood and blood only, and there was such love and devotion in that. Koulan could do what he liked with him, what did he care? His only concern was his next feed, and on the victim who would most readily supply it.

A shuffling from somewhere along Camden High Street lifted him from his thoughts, and he glanced down in its direction. His eyes narrowed as his acute vision pierced the gloom of the shadows cast by the pallid streetlights, and there, in between the tangled shapes of empty shop tables, he caught sight of a vagrant. Milestone's teeth broke into a cruel grin at the

171

sight of him, a wanderer, homeless and with no one to know him, to miss him, or to ever come looking for him. Slowly the vampire eased himself forward until he was leaning over the edge of the bridge, his midnight eyes trained on the throat of his prey, and then he was gone, dropping down from the cold grey metal bridge and down into the secret shadows of the street.

Hugging the darkest parts of the shop doorways, Milestone moved swiftly towards the old man. He could already smell the alcohol on his breath - beer and whisky, if he wasn't mistaken - and he grinned once more as he enjoyed the notion of how easy this kill would be. The blood would not be as pure as the gentry to the west of the city, but it would still warm him thoroughly on this cold night. He was within twenty yards of him when he stopped in the arch of a doorway to watch him. The man was leaning against a stall laid out in front of one of the shops as he struggled to find his cigarette with the flickering match he was holding.

After a few moments, Milestone could see the tobacco finally take, its flakes glimmering brightly with the flame of orange, before the vagrant drew deeply on it, closing his eyes and nodding his head back a little with relative pleasure. Milestone took another few silent steps towards him, the shroud of night his unassailable cohort, the vagrant still blissfully unaware of either his presence or the fate that awaited him.

The vampire's senses were choked with both the sight and the smell of the vagrant - the skin of his neck sagging and dappled, a sweat breaking on his wide brow - but he did not notice the signs of danger that emerged suddenly just a few hundred yards beyond him. Not until it became too late to escape, and his own fate was sealed.

He looked past the vagrant now, his concern escalating rapidly by the new warnings his heightened senses were giving him. He stepped out from the shadows suddenly, past the old man and out into the street. The vagrant started as he caught sight of this strange young man appear from nowhere, and stumbled back away from him, confused and disorientated. But Milestone ignored him now, his blood, his sweat and his neck, an intolerance that only sickened him. His only concern lay now with the disturbance further along the street, where a strange shifting presence, that neither his sight nor his smell could penetrate, was approaching rapidly.

He could smell the stench of death, that much he was certain of - how could he have missed that before? - and maybe even the aridity of a hot desert wind somewhere within its cloak. He could also make out the dim hollowness of an ethereal shadow as it passed over the tarmac of the high street. It was like nothing he had ever seen before, not even in all his decades as a vampire, and he just stood and gazed at it, his forehead knotted like old weathered rope.

He had never felt fear before, not real fear. Perhaps intimidation from the likes of Koulan on one or two occasions, but never real fear. He was immortal, he'd always thought, what could ever destroy him? But then, even as he sought to see through the shimmering cloak that surrounded this thing, he caught sight of the creature that lay beneath, as one of its folds lifted suddenly.

Then his feeling of fear came rapidly, and dropped him helplessly to his knees.

The first thing he saw was teeth, row upon row of razor-sharp teeth, and behind them the deepest scarlet of its red and bloody maw. He suddenly became aware of the vagrant staggering somewhere behind him, he could hear his slurred voice wailing about something, but why he was even listening to such a pointless mortal, he had no idea. It was just so much worthless noise in the face of this dispassionate and violent creature.

The vagrant was at his back now, he could hear his feet shuffling across the tarmac, his voice uncertain from the alcohol in his body. Even when Milestone felt him lay a hand on his shoulder, the thought rose in his mind to kill him quickly just to be done with this annoyance, but it then seemed obvious that the old man couldn't even see this creature himself.

Milestone turned quickly in the few moments that he knew he had left, and ignoring the vagrant, glanced back towards the underground station. There was not a single vampire to be seen; no guard, no sentry, nothing. They were all gone.

They knew, that was all he could think.

That, and Koulan had been right.

Milestone glanced back. The creature was suddenly upon him now. His vision clouded with tears of terror in an instant, and the sight of its teeth came only in snatches. The thud of its heart carried on the dead air towards him and pounded at his head. His tongue and throat suddenly felt thick, the stench of death decaying the very air around him, and his stomach clenched as though he were about to vomit, a human reflex that he had not felt in a such a very long time, yet he still put a hand to his mouth involuntarily. It came away bloody, however, and he realised that his mouth and nose were bleeding. He looked down, and saw that a long razored shaft had somehow penetrated his chest. The demon had already started its assault, piercing his body and ripping it open from the inside. There was no pain, no confusion. He saw it all so very plainly.

Milestone coughed violently, and heaved a mouthful of blood up over himself. His eyes rose as he choked back a terrified scream. The pain was coming.

The invisible cloak that seemed to surround the creature lifted, and beneath it came a wall of barbed teeth that descended swiftly upon him, scooping him deep inside its jaws and shredding back his flesh as it devoured him.

Milestone felt his scalp open, and the top of his skull juddered away from him with an explosion of intense agony. He felt his blood run freely from the wound, down over his neck and shoulders like soup, and he began to cry openly as scraps of ragged flesh slipped from his back. Layer upon layer of razored teeth enclosed around him, drawing him in deeper and deeper into that terrible throat, and he felt every torment and every torture as it ground away his bones into dust and shards.

His consciousness would not let him go, however, not even as he saw the mechanism of the beast at work inside, a hard thumping mass of sickening engine, turning and churning, with no hope of exhaustion.

A wash of scarlet marked the place where he had stood, he could see that through the closing jaws behind him now, and beyond that the street just ahead of the fluttering ethereal veil of its body.

Still the teeth of the creature continued to grind and berate his limbs and body, his blood drawing up and out of every fissure that opened. His toes popped and his fingers broke, the agony excruciating as he was slowly unmade, back into his basest parts. Blackness began to come, slowly at first, but then in pulsing fits, until his consciousness finally disappeared altogether.

The creature finished its meal, drained back the blood it had stolen, and then shat out the ragged corpse of the vampire back onto the street, with nothing more than a deep rumbling belch of satisfaction to mark its departure. The vampire known as Milestone was no more.

TWO

WHAT ELSE CAN BE TAKEN?

Jenner woke shaking and shivering the next morning to the sound of birdsong, a single bird, presumably just outside the window or up on the roof. It was a simple herald to mark the warm morning sunshine that streamed in through the window, but he had spent the night on the sofa, bent double and uncomfortably, and his body was wracked with aches and stiffness, even as he pushed himself up into a sitting position. It had not been a dreamless sleep, however. Images had visited him, dark and foreboding, almost as if they had been put there by the man still living on the other side of his bedroom door. They had been nowhere near as terrifying or as bloody as the images that had taken him over in the coldness and the dark of Regents Park, but they had been harrowing nevertheless.

The sleep he had drifted into the previous night had at first been an empty void, a sleep so heavy and oppressive that it seemed to carry him down into its depths and hold him there, as though he was at the bottom of some pit, but with no sides and no top or bottom, and certainly no hope of escape. There seemed to be no purpose in his being there either, or any reason, or any time, only his being there in the depths of a never-ending blackness, forever and ever. But then a story seemed to unfold around him, a strange far away story of temples and gold, of kings and regency. White-robed worshippers bowed low before him, and a vast pale moon rose high above his head. Priests with heads of different shaped animals offered gifts and blessings, while seas and rivers altered courses to deliver bountiful treasures at his feet. Fields grew rich and fertile at his touch, while women became heavy with child at his word. Life blossomed before him, and his name became the world. The dream was a wonderful sight, and yet it rattled quickly into despair. People were dragged away, temples cracked and toppled. Gifts fell to dust, and food rotted in poisoned gutters. Life went away, death moved quickly in, and the darkness that had been everything before, became everything once again.

He ran his hand trembling through his hair, easing his neck to either side, his muscles complaining with the effort, before hauling himself to his feet and shuffling through into the bathroom, the images reluctant to leave his head. The stench in the hallway hit him like a thundering wall as opened the living room door, however, harrowing his thoughts and crippling his innards. His empty stomach heaved instantly, doubling him in half, and he reached the bathroom door stumbling, retching the bitter contents of an empty stomach up into his mouth, an evil palette of cruel bile and yellow acid. He spat the vile fluid out into the toilet, heaving a few shuddering breaths into his lungs before swallowing back a few mouthfuls of water from the sink to try and steady himself. Checking his pallid complexion in the small mirror, he recomposed himself as best he could as he relieved his bladder, and then stepped warily back into the hallway.

As soon as he set eyes upon the bloody mass still littering the patch of filthy carpet opposite the front door, he knew something was wrong, and his thoughts went back once again to the words of the skulker Rocket, of demons and vampires and blood-drinkers, even though this was the work of the sick murderer still camped out in his own bedroom. The bodies were not as he had left them the previous night though. They were now scattered across the floor as though they had been picked at, shards and scraps discarded or dropped, footprints and marks staining the area around it. But it was as he stepped closer still, putting his hand over his nose and mouth against the foul odour, that he realised just what was different.

The bones had gone.

Where there had been bones before, there was now nothing but the remains of blood-soaked clothes and scraps of gnawed meat. Where there had been an arm, there was nothing but a bloodied sleeve. Where there had been a rib, nothing but a punctured knotted organ. And where there had been a skull, there was nothing to see but a severed collar and a scrap of torn scalp. Jenner was loathe to touch any of it, the sight of it sickening beyond measure, but he forced himself forward to nudge some of the hardened matter over with his foot to see exactly how much remained. Of any white bone, whether intact, splintered or shard, there was simply no sign. It was just meat now.

Slowly Jenner turned his head to gaze back down the narrow hallway in the direction of his bedroom. The whole flat was still silent, the deadened quiet of his bedroom seeming more like a desolate church graveyard than the bustle of a busy London district, and an evil chill crept throughout his body as the realisation of what must have happened dawned on him. The Master of Kar'mi'shah must have left his room in the middle of the night without waking him, desecrated the two dead policemen by stripping the bones out of their bodies, and then returned back to his bedroom with them.

His heart was pounding rapidly now, thudding in his head and chest like a hammer, and his nausea grew like a knot in his stomach once again. Slowly, he headed back along the passageway towards his bedroom door, uncertain as he went whether he was either angry or afraid. But this time he pounded hard upon it, hammering his fist with all his strength against the wood and yelling for the man inside to come out. The silence that came only infuriated him more, and he kicked out at the door now - once, twice, three times - as hard as he could, in an attempt to get inside. But the occupant had barricaded it well, the door held fast, and the Master of Kar'mi'shah would not come out.

Panicking, and with his chest heaving with both exhaustion and despair, Jenner stood and stared at it, but knew deep inside that he had no alternative but to leave it alone yet again. The killer would have to come out again sooner or later, Jenner thought to himself. He would just have to make sure that he'd be around when he did.

He returned to the kitchen to find something to put in his aching stomach. The stench of death still filled the flat, souring the air, but he knew that he would have to at least try and eat something. Regardless of what might happen, whether it be from the hands of the police or from Jackel El'a'cree himself, he knew he would have to have some energy in his muscles to either fight or flee. He found some bread going hard from exposure to the air, but could stand only butter to flavour it, and forced three slices, swallowing them down with water from the sink. It took the edge off his hunger sufficiently to take his mind off it, and he gazed out through the window to take a look at the grey early morning. There were already a number of cars speeding past down in the street below, and again Jenner envied both them and their lives. How simple it must be to leave their families to journey to a daily place of work - an office or a shop - and then return home in the evening to love and laughter. He ran a hand over the coarse stubble on his chin, thinking how his appearance might look to anyone gazing back at him, before he turned away from the window and walked nervously back past the bodies to the living room, where he took up his unnerving vigil once more on the sofa.

The traffic outside faded and the flat fell into silence once again, and he listened to it for a while, its depths strangely captivating, almost as though there were many levels to quiet, different planes separating one from the other. The more he listened, the more sounds became audible, subtle and barely perceptible, but he heard them now that he gave them attention, perhaps even giving strength or credence to them.

Pipes were creaking somewhere in the building, from one of the other flats, no doubt, and the bird that had woken him earlier, now joined by others, sang in bright but muffled patterns of chorus. Outside, further still, he could hear the distant traffic grow louder, a conversation started up down on the pavement below, and now the clatter of something metallic echoed nearby. Inside, he became aware of his own heart beating, his blood thudding rhythmically around his body, in his ears and in his head, and now that he was keeping still, he could feel it flowing through his hands and feet. And then came a creak, a floorboard, and this in a space somewhere between the street outside and the blood within his body. It was a creak from a floorboard in his bedroom. And it came from the other side of the living room wall.

Jenner listened hard, straining his ears against the silence that now seemed so impenetrably thick, but the pipes and the birds and the talkers outside were insistent now that they'd been heard, that they should always be heard. He tried to filter out these sounds, but through them, the floorboards would creak no more. He settled back uneasily, closed his eyes, and listened to the world, hoping that the man in his flat would soon emerge once again into the quiet hallway, so that he could take hold of him, and beat, if necessary, whatever answers he wanted out of his skull.

A knock came at the door, and Jenner started, his eyes open in an instant, his dream-dazed mind unravelling the conundrum of mysteries swirling in the darkened room. He checked the curtains and found them open, and found too that night flowed in through them, the only light illuminating the room coming from the yellow streetlamps out in the road. Jenner listened to the world for a few moments in the midst of the darkness, the grumble of the city, the creak of the building, but more importantly for any sound of the occupant in his bedroom as well as for the caller on the other side of his front door.

The knock came again, only slightly more insistent. What if it were the police, his brain thought quickly, tracking down the last call of their colleagues. He felt his skin grow cold, and noticed that a clammy sweat had broken out all over his body. He was trembling too, and fearful that the law was waiting just outside his door, ready to drag him back to prison.

Slowly he got to his feet, thinking now that it could perhaps be Montague, or more likely one of his runners, checking up on both him and the box that he knew he should have delivered by now. The knocking came a third time as he crept out into the hallway, but his attention was snatched immediately by the space left behind where the two corpses had lain. Where this morning he had seen just a bloody mess after the bones had been taken, now even that mess had gone, leaving little more than a dark stain to harden the carpet.

Jackel must have left his bedroom yet again, Jenner realised, to take up the last of the bodies and steal them back to his room. Slowly he turned his head to gaze in both horror and utter disbelief at the bedroom door. It was still closed and, presumably, still barred as before. His head was thick was unanswerable questions, but he still continued to the front door for some reason, barely able to comprehend the consequences should there be more police on the doorstep, or hell, even Montague with questions of his own.

Surely, he reasoned, as his fingertips felt the cold metal of the handle, the police would have broken down the door should they have suspected his guilt in the disappearance of the two officers. The further thought that sprang into his head from this was, would the creature in his bedroom tear forth and save him a second time? But he had no time to think through such thoughts. His hand had already gripped the handle and was turning it, pulling open the door to reveal a face that not even he had considered to be part of any of his questions or fears.

"Emma," he stammered, barely comprehending her features as she rushed at him and threw her arms around his shoulders.

"Where have you been?" she cried, hugging him tightly to her. "I've been calling for five days, but there's been no answer."

Jenner stared at her as she relinquished her hold on him a little, his mind confused by what she was saying.

"I didn't know if you were still angry at me after our fight and was just refusing to pick up the phone in case you thought it was me."

"No, of course not," Jenner replied. "I've been here."

Emma hugged him again, and began pressing kisses into his neck, thanking God under her breath that he was alright. Jenner wondered, as he let her express this affection upon him, just what she had meant by five days. It had only been the day before yesterday that they'd had that stupid argument.

Hadn't it?

His mind began to turn over, a grave feeling of sickness creeping once more into his stomach, and he put a hand to it as he began to wonder whether she was actually telling the truth or not. What would she have to gain by lying, and especially over something so ludicrous as losing a week of his life? What if she had been calling for five days, and he hadn't heard her? But then he supposed that she had been phoning fairly frequently and he'd never left the flat. Another fear crept up on him, and he hurried back through into the ill-lit living room to check the phone.

He checked the phone line going into the wall, half expecting to find that Jackel had ripped it out, but it sat there, undisturbed and untouched, the white cord sitting neatly in the box behind the television. Confused now, he looked at the phone itself beneath the yellow pallor of the streetlamps. The receiver was sat in its cradle, just as it had been, and there seemed no reason why the phone should not be ringing. But as he heard Emma behind him, and she flicked on the light switch, so he saw, by the stronger light from the bulb overhead, just what Jackel had done.

The receiver still sat in its cradle, yes, but the section of the phone that produced the ringing tone had been smashed, the black plastic casing ragged in a circle as though he had punched something hard and sharp through it. He must have done it when the ringing had first disturbed him, before it had woken the owner, and had managed to leave the phone line itself intact. Emma was beside him now, gazing down at the broken phone base, a murmur of confusion already on her lips.

Yet more thoughts ran through his head, adding to those already swirling there, about the box he had stolen from the apartment building, about the visitor who had appeared from nowhere, and about the consummation of the two dead police officers. Now he was starting to become less concerned with who this Jackel El'a'cree was and why he had felt the need to smash his phone, and more with just how to get him the fuck out of his flat, and out of his life forever.

"What happened?" Emma murmured beside him.

"I don't know," Jenner replied absently, uncertain

if she was talking about the phone or the whole situation, of which she was undoubtedly ignorant.

Emma laid her hand on his shoulder.

"Tell me," she said softly.

Jenner turned his head a little and looked into her warm brown eyes. Always she had been there for him, in one way or another, no matter how indifferently he'd treated her. It was only now, however, that he wondered why. He'd always thought that it was for her own selfish whims, using him as some kind of trophy for her friends. But she had been eager to be with him that first day she'd seen him after his release. She'd returned after that night too. And now she seemed genuine that she'd been phoning for days, even though it had only been the day before yesterday. Her touch upon his shoulder was light but reassuring, and it felt good to have it there. One good thing in a supposed week of death and decay.

"I'm not sure if I could tell you even if I wanted to," Jenner said to her finally.

"Try," she persisted, giving his shoulder a gentle compassionate squeeze.

Jenner took a breath and returned his gaze to the rooftops over Hammersmith, and to the grey sky that hung down as if to smother them.

"I spoke to Montague a couple of days ago," he started, "and he told me about a job he'd got lined up."

"You were talking to that bastard?" Emma cried, incredulous. "What were you thinking?"

"I know, I know. But what could I do? I'm no good for anything else."

"Don't say that."

"It's true, Em. And his money could've bought me a fresh start."

186

"Parole offered you a fresh start," Emma told him. "Why did you need to go back to him of all people?"

"I don't know, Emma," Jenner said ruefully. "I just didn't seem to have any other choice."

He stood for a few moments, his attention distracted by a car attempting to parallel park down in the street below, and making several bad attempts, before he continued with the events of what he believed had been the previous night.

"Montague wanted a box stolen. There was a place over near the British Museum, a residential place, that had just received a load of stuff back from some dig in Egypt. It seemed a pretty easy trip. He'd said he'd got someone on the inside, some security guy, but that's another story. Anyway, I got in, got out, alerted the police, and then ran off with them on my tail."

"But you managed to escape?"

"Yeah," Jenner told her, with a humourless grin. "But I hadn't been back long when two of them turned up on my doorstep and tried to take me away."

"So what happened?"

"That's just it, Emma. I don't know."

He turned again to look at her. Her brow was knotted, bewildered yet concerned, but it was her eyes that gave him hope. Then, and for perhaps the first time, he moved towards her and took hold of her, hugging her to him with a warmth he wasn't sure he even possessed. It felt good to have her in his arms, to draw her close and feel the heat of her body, and he hugged her now as he had never hugged her before, lovingly and with need, and as he breathed her in, he caught the sweet delicate aroma of her hair, and it smelt wonderful. As he gently let her go, he looked into her deep brown eyes once again and confessed the events to her of which even he himself was not sure.

"Something happened," he told her, under his breath for fear the man in his bedroom might hear. "Something bad."

"What?"

"A creature appeared in the flat, a creature that came from somewhere that makes no sense. It tore at the two policemen, ripped them apart, and then drank from their bodies."

Jenner watched as her brow sank lower, her hand rising over her mouth in either horror or disbelief. How could he blame her for what she was thinking? It was unbelievable to him and he'd lived through it. All of it. Every last grisly occurrence. It surprised even him when she answered him with something close to acceptance.

"Is that what the stain is in the hallway?" she asked quietly.

Jenner nodded grimly.

"That's where the bodies were," he explained. "But he's taken all that was left."

"What have you done?" she asked with a whimper, taking a step back.

Jenner picked up her accusation quickly, and went after her, eager to dispel the horrors that she was building rapidly inside her head.

"It wasn't me," Jenner insisted, taking hold of her arms in desperation. "You must believe me. No one in this world has ever trusted me before, but please, I beg you, you must believe me now."

Emma gazed hard into his eyes, searching, God bless her, for some shred of sanity in the words that he spoke. Her eyes, those warm brown eyes, welled with tears as she stared at him, her tongue running across her lips that had become dry.

"I believe you," she finally said quietly. But then asked: "Where are the bodies now?"

"He's taken them," Jenner explained to her again. "He's taken them into my bedroom and bolted the door."

"He?"

"The creature became a man, a tall man who told me how I'd saved him. He said he was a great leader, a king or a god or some fucking thing. He's a lunatic, Emma. And now he's hidden himself away in my bedroom."

"I don't understand any of this," she began, turning away from him and stepping back across the living room floor.

"I know," Jenner said, going after her. "I don't understand any of it either. But please," he took hold of her arm again, "I need your help."

Emma turned and tried to smile. He could see that she tried, but it just wouldn't come.

"I'm sorry," she said. "But I just don't know what you're trying to tell me."

"Go to Montague," Jenner told her. "Tell him I'm in trouble and that I need him to come here."

"Can't you tell him yourself?"

"I can't leave the flat, Emma. Don't you understand. If I leave, he might leave."

"But isn't that what you want?"

Jenner stared at her for a moment. Yes, that was what he wanted. At least that's what he thought he wanted. This man, if indeed he was a man, seemed a strange and powerful being. Perhaps he wanted to talk more with him, listen to his tales of strange lands and strange creatures, or perhaps he just wanted to smack him with something in a fit of revenge.

His mind was shifting again, uncertain, and the feeling of sickness began to rise in him again, but he managed to keep his focus on Emma. His lips parted to tell her to go, to put her own safety first, but he fell silent as his attention became distracted by a movement from the hallway, a shadow passing briefly across the wall.

His eyes went to the light there, to the shadows marking their territory, and then he shuddered as the threshold suddenly became filled with the dark and ominous figure of the Master of Kar'mi'shah.

"You are not alone," he said simply, his body silhouetted in the doorway.

Emma turned in an instant, startled by the sudden presence of this stranger.

"Who are you?" she demanded to know.

The man in the shadows stepped into the room a little way until the light from the bulb overhead gently caught his expressionless features.

"Lady, my name is Jackel El'a'cree. I have been a prisoner for many years, but now I am free."

"A prisoner?" she said, glancing back over her shoulder at Jenner. "Were the two of you inside together?"

"You have been denied freedom too?" the stranger directed his comment to Jenner. "We share more than I had at first realised. But in answer to your question, Lady, no, we were not prisoners together. However, it was your acquaintance here who released me, and for that I will be eternally in his debt."

His eyes flicked between them as he spoke, but it was the only thing about him that did move. His hands lay at his sides, motionless. His body stood upright, and neither swayed nor turned. Nor too did his head, but simply faced the direction of his body, his eyes only moving as he addressed them, his lips parting only to form words.

"Lady," he continued, his hand rising slowly, palm up, requesting Emma to take it, "can I beg a moment of your time."

Jenner stepped forward quickly to intercept his request.

"What do you want with her?" he demanded angrily. "And just what the fuck have you done with those two officers?"

"Those two men that would do you harm," Jackel El'a'cree said, "have been put to a far greater use. Even now I am fed, and growing stronger all the time. I shall soon be able to leave, but it would be dangerous to leave alone. You can understand the strength of companionship, surely?"

His words sickened him, as much for his apparent insight into his relationship with Emma as for the thought of the two dead officers, their flesh gnawed and torn and sucked dry of blood. His words inferred that he had consumed them, bones and all, but surely that was not possible. And what was this talk of his leaving? Without Jackel in his flat to account for the death of the two policemen, he would have no alibi, no matter how impossible.

"You're going?" Jenner managed to say.

"And soon," Jackel confirmed. "When I have company for my journey and I have fed enough to restore sufficient strength."

This second reference to feeding confirmed the implication of the two dead officers and it was simply too much to take. The urge to see what had become of them suddenly overcame him, and he pushed past the man and out into the hallway, reaching the open bedroom door within a few strides.

The choking stench was the first thing that grabbed his attention, grasping it like an insurmountable stranglehold, even before he had crossed the threshold. The second was the sheer state of his room, ransacked and violated, debris littering the floor like a battlefield. His bed lay smashed, the mattress lying ripped and shredded and on its side against the wall. His chair too had been smashed, its legs used with the wooden parts of the bed frame to construct some kind of altar in the corner of the room. A small fire had been lit there in a rough makeshift hearth, and as he stepped closer, he discovered the source of the foul stench that hung so thick in the stale air.

The man now standing in his living room had used his own excrement as well as scraps of wood to fuel his fire. A number of bones from the hallway lay heaped in the hearth also, as well as bits of their blood-soaked uniforms. The churning of his stomach had subsided as he'd spoken with Emma, but now as he gazed down at this disgusting sight, it started up again, knotting his insides with the promise of convulsion.

Turning away, he snatched a breath, but the air was still foul and it only caused his stomach to heave. He put a hand to it, trying desperately to keep hold of the vomit even as it pushed slickly between his fingers. As he had taken his eyes off the altar, he'd seen little else of his room as he'd tried not to retch across his carpet. But now, as he scanned the remainder of his room, it became obvious that the man had ransacked every part of it, pulling out drawers and breaking them before scattering their contents, pulling what few pictures he'd had out of their frames, and voiding both his bladder as well as his bowels just about anywhere he saw fit. All that was left was a sickening mess of defiled and filthy possessions, and faced with the terrible sight of it, he simply removed his hand and let his mouthful of puke out onto the floor along with the rest of it.

Stumbling back out into the hallway, weakened from both exhaustion and sickness, Jenner clawed his way back along the wall towards the living room. As he reached the threshold, however, his head light and distant, he stopped in his tracks as he caught sight of Jackel El'a'cree, standing at its centre with his back to the streetlit window, his head pressed hard against the gentle curve of Emma's soft white neck. Emma herself seemed an almost willing partner to this deadly embrace, her arms limp at her side, her eyes closed with an almost serene expression on her face. Blood trickled from the place where his mouth clamped hard against her, and all Jenner could do was watch as Jackel drank deeply from her, while the words of the skulker Rocket came back once more into his head.

Vampires live among us, he'd said.

There are dozens of them in London alone.

This man, surely, was one of those vampires, and he stared back at him now with an almost animal pleasure. Somewhere in the weight of that stare, what few scraps of energy and anger remained in him, dissipated rapidly, and Jenner sank to his knees as he witnessed helplessly the last of Emma's life ebb away. She had almost certainly been on the edge of death as he had entered the room, and nothing he could have done could have saved her. Jackel had taken her as he'd fled to see his room, and her death had been his fault, trading the fear for his possessions over the life of his beloved Emma.

Beloved.

The suddenness of the word startled him.

Yes, she had been his beloved, and he had loved her, after all the years he had known her and the time he had spent with her. But now it was all over. She was dead, killed in the arms of this butcher who had already consumed the two policemen. The vampire's words suddenly took on a far graver meaning. He'd asked him if he understood the strength of companionship. He'd thought he had. But now here, faced with the death of his beautiful Emma, he truly felt the real strength of it, now that it was gone and snatched away from him.

He watched, dumbfounded and numb, as Jackel slowly lifted his head from Emma's neck, and ran a thin red tongue swiftly across his lips. A gasp of pleasure escaped him, and as his lips parted, so Jenner caught sight of the two blood-stained fangs that hung down from his palette like needles. Jackel's eyes were glazed as he looked at him, burnished and cold, and misted with satisfaction after his consummation of her. Jenner saw then, the two puncture wounds on Emma's neck, the marks where Jackel El'a'cree had fed.

For some reason then that he couldn't quite fathom, his fingers went to his own neck, and almost immediately found two similar puncture wounds, clotted and dry, where Jackel had fed from him. It suddenly became clear, in the moment that their eyes locked, how much of a debt Jackel owed him. He would drink from him, but not so much that it would kill him. This was some kind of prize, it seemed. To

194

nourish this vampire, but also to keep his life. It seemed certain that this was where his weakened state and sickness had come from. Not just from nausea brought on by the stench of death in his flat, but also from forced blood loss.

"What have you done?" Jenner gasped, his voice hoarse with both fear and anguish.

"I have needed to feed," Jackel commented simply. "Companionship for my departure had to follow."

"But... you said you were in my debt. How could you do this to me?"

"You, I am grateful to. She, I am grateful for."

Jenner could feel his head growing lighter, his throat becoming tight with anguish, his chest stricken and aching. His own violation was one thing, but the death of Emma at the hands of this creature was something far worse.

He fell forward onto his hands, prostrate and powerless, as he watched the vampire gently guide the lifeless body of Emma down onto the sofa, laying her down in front of him, her eyes still closed as if in the depths of some blissful swoon. Then, as Jackel stood up once more to his full height, the light from the street outside came almost afresh at his back to cast deep shadows across his face. It was a terrifying sight to behold this cold and unnatural murderer standing before him in his own home.

Jenner struggled to keep hold of his consciousness, but it was rapidly becoming elusive, his mind losing its grasp on the distorting vision of Jackel El'a'cree before him. And then it all went in a shuddering heartbeat - the flat, the room, and the vampire - and he blacked out completely, leaving the Master of Kar'mi'shah standing over him, stronger and more omnipotent than ever.

AT CAMDEN

Alexia's injuries were still causing her discomfort but she was glad that they had decided to take the initiative and seek out Koulan without delay. It took them a little over an hour to reach Euston Station, by which time sunrise was imminent, and it was then just a short walk to Camden. There were already a lot of people about, trudging the early morning streets on their way to work, but no one gave them anything more than a passing glance. A mother and her daughter, or so it seemed, out early to catch a bus or train. No mortal would have dared presume the truth, or even to guess what secrets might lie behind such a simple façade. Only her wounds would draw unwanted attention, her face bloodied, her battered body supported by an eight year old child. But her ribs would soon heal, and her cuts would scar quickly and then disappear altogether. Then she would once again be unmemorable to the eyes of scrutiny.

A buzz of commotion caught her attention before they had even reached Camden High Street, and once they turned a corner she had her fears confirmed. Fifty yards from the underground station, a small crowd had gathered to study something lying in the road. Alexia held her breath as they walked ever closer, their destination seeming to have drawn the attentions of more than a few mortals. The nearer they got, however, the more she realised that it was vampire blood, not human blood, that she could smell in the air, a sour echo of the body that had been discarded in the Thames.

There were already a number of people hunched over the body, if indeed that was what it could be called, while others stood from a viewable distance. A siren was wailing a few streets away, she could hear it echoing off the buildings of the city, and so she chanced just a brief glimpse before hurrying on.

Between the tangle of pedestrians she could see a mangled body, its ragged clothing saturated red with blood. She smelt the odour of vampire more strongly now, her worst fears validated as she saw the long bared teeth protruding from the scrubbed and open skull. She gazed down with pity in her eyes at the sight of him, and her thoughts went back once again to the death of her friend Matra'Abor'El. But this had not been the work of a skulker, that much was already clear. No human could have butchered a corpse like this, and it was obvious that this body, as well as the body from the Thames, had been despatched by the same being. This vampire had been crushed, snapped and skinned, and then desanguinated from a thousand different puncture wounds. His head, battered as it was, was twisted back on itself, the neck partially splintered and jutting out through his torn throat. The ribcage was blackened with dried blood and cracked open, the organs inside scattered across the street like soiled knotted rags. His crushed limbs were tucked up beneath his body at awkward angles, and made the whole corpse look as though it had been compacted. Even from such a distance, it was obvious to Alexia that it had been virtually drained of all its blood, every scrap of flesh razored and squeezed dry. It shocked even her to see death dealt so savagely. But then the siren filled the air suddenly as a police car turned the corner and sped towards them. Alexia looked up and quickly, snatched from her whirling thoughts, and tugged at Callie's arm, ushering her away from curious eyes, and on towards the underground station.

The doors to the station were open, the black iron gates pulled back against the wall, and the two vampires hurried down the steps and into the cold wind-braced depths. Moving swiftly past the guards, their sight uncertain in their elusive early morning shift, they reached the platform that would lead them down to Koulan. They swept down between the electrical lines, seen by no one, and disappeared deep into the dark blustery maze of underground tunnels, heading swiftly into a world where light did not belong.

A rush of chilling air signalled the approach of an early train, and pressing themselves hard against the grimy tunnel walls, the two vampires braced themselves as it flashed past. Through the strobing windows of the carriages, they could make out a few of the early morning passengers gazing distantly out into the blackness, none of them catching sight of the two ghostly apparitions that returned their gaze. It was a strange world, that of the mortal, Alexia thought as she watched them carried on their way. Wonderfully simplistic in their comprehension of things, their worries of things unimportant, their burdens of fleeting fancy. She could barely recall how she had fretted as a human, so long ago was it now, but she suddenly envied them all, and their ignorance of what they were, and more importantly of what was now stalking the streets, night after night.

The last carriage of the train rattled past and Alexia and Callie stepped back out into the darkness of the rough-walled tunnel. Ahead of them, where no mortal eyes could possibly see, lay the narrow entrance that led to Koulan and the remainder of his tribe. It seemed strange to her, as they crossed the electrical lines together, that there had been no guards posted anywhere inside the station or in the tunnel so far. But with the chaos that they'd witnessed in the street outside, she could hardly blame them for not wandering too far from the sanctuary of their lair. It was dangerous for her to come here, and she knew she risked Callie's life too just by bringing her, but these were all dangerous times, and she just hoped that Koulan would see that they were all held together in the same helplessness nightmare, and that perhaps they now needed each other more than ever.

Nearing the narrow ragged entrance of the tunnel, Alexia instructed Callie to wait behind her while she crept forward alone to see if all was safe. She had never directly spoken to Koulan, Master of the Wraiths, but she had known of him and his high standing in Kar'mi'shah, and she knew of it here too in London. He kept a considerable clan down here, despite all that had happened, and she knew that her life was in jeopardy just by her being this close to them. Still, things might have changed in that time, she thought. Perhaps he'd realised, the same as she, that this was no longer a time to be at each other's throats. This was a time to work together, for the collective good, when all the world seemed to be against them.

Cautiously she moved her head nearer the

entrance, her smell detecting little but the stale musty odour that filled the tunnel, of pigeons, of fumes, and of animals that had died down here long ago. It was difficult to tell much at all through the mixed stench of London's rot, but she eased her torso through the breach nevertheless, hoping that a welcome would be just that when it came.

Her luck held for only a few moments, however. No sooner had she stepped through the tunnel entrance and turned her head to call for Callie to follow, than a hand reached out of the darkness and grasped her throat. Alexia choked instantly beneath the grip, and clawed at the hand with all her strength. But despite her considerable force, and the skin that was even now beginning to come away beneath her nails, the hand remained firm, and dragged her forward and down roughly into the dirt.

"Speak your business," came the growling voice, a second hand taking hold of a fistful of her hair and forcing her head back hard.

"I... I came to see Koulan," Alexia managed to say as the grip relinquished sufficiently enough for her to speak.

Callie had stepped through the entrance now, and taking in the scene in front of her, rushed at the guard, her tiny fingers finding his eyes quickly in the unlit passageway.

"No," Alexia cried out, but the guard had already flung her effortlessly into the solid wall of the passage.

Alexia heard Callie loose a whimper as she tumbled awkwardly to the ground, and finding some inner strength, forced herself to her feet despite the hold still on her. Grasping any part of her assailant that she could, she let out a shriek of rage as she battered him back, her fist finding what she hoped was his jaw and nose. The guard retaliated instantly, and Alexia felt a sharp stab of pain as he connected with her chest, the blow finding the ribs already broken there. It was then, as the waves of agony coursed through her body once again, that she slumped to her knees, and realised that Callie had found her feet once more.

Through the swirling darkness she could detect the vampire's tiny frame as it wrapped itself around the body of the guard, and she could smell instantly too the tang of his blood in the air as the girl sunk her long sharp teeth deep into his neck. The assailant howled in pain, and Alexia took the moment to lash out at him, striking him with all her strength and succeeding in taking his legs out from beneath him. He landed hard, and taking what little chance they both had, she grasped Callie by her arm, and dragged her away from him before fleeing deeper into the cavern of the Wraiths.

She hoped that the guard was not going to be the first of many, and even as Callie voiced the same concern, she realised that things had probably not changed after all, and that Koulan was still just as likely to tear them both limb from limb as soon as he set eyes upon them.

A light glimmered somewhere up ahead, and she slowed her pace as her fears resurfaced. Behind them came the growl of the guard, incessant and raging, on his feet once more and in pursuit. They had been lucky to escape him once, she knew, and she knew too that if he caught up with them before she could reach Koulan to explain her being here, then everything was lost. The guard was strong, stronger than both she and Callie combined, and it had been a fortunate blow that had sent him to the ground. She was not so stupid as to think otherwise, and nor was she stupid enough to think that they might manage it a second time.

The light in front of them grew steadily brighter as they turned a shallow curve in the tunnel. The guard's growls bellowed now as he made rapid ground on them, his footsteps fleeting over the rough surface of the floor, his frame sprinting on all fours like a savage dog. Then, as they dashed through a rough entrance, they found themselves entering a long vaulted chamber, electric lights burning on the floor at its centre and casting stark flickering shadows up and over the walls and deep into its many hollows. The heads of a dozen or more vampires turned as they entered, and Alexia stumbled to a halt in front of them, Callie skidding on a carpet of loose stones in her wake. A number of the vampires rose from their seats, others stepping out from the hidden depths of shadow. Growls rumbled in their throats as teeth became bared for blood, their faces distorting in fury at the sheer audacity of this unwelcome intrusion.

More grotesque faces appeared from the shadowed vaults hewn in the rock walls, disturbed by the sudden appearance of these two strangers, while others swept down from the heights of the ceiling, from roosts that Alexia had not previously seen. Yet another stepped out from a further annex to her right. And from behind them, the guard came swiftly to a halt, his feet dashing across the rough floor, his snarl of fury rasping in his throat. Alexia stood for a few moments, Callie's hand grasped tightly in her's, as she took in this whole terrifying scene. A second count revealed the number of vampires present to be closer to thirty, and it took just a second for her to doubt her faith in coming here.

It was not often that she felt fear as a vampire, not even at the hands of The Howler, but she thought it likely now that at least one of these vampires would do her serious harm. She took a defiant step forward regardless, and even as the growl behind her increased and Callie's grip on her hand tightened, she opened her mouth to speak.

"I'm looking for Koulan," she called out.

Her voice was louder than she had expected, and it rattled around the hard dark caverns of the chamber. The eyes of thirty vampires glared at her in silence, burning like dozens of tiny orange fires, and her fears doubled as she wondered whether they might actually get out of this place alive. But she repeated her request, as outwardly confident as before, and hoped that someone would respond to her. It took a hollow moment, but somebody did. And he stepped slowly out of the crowd to speak to her.

"What is it that you want here, Faraoh?" he asked.

"I want to see Koulan, Master of the Wraiths."

"I heard you before. But tell me what you want of him."

The vampire continued towards her, his eyes narrowing as he studied her. He wore a long black leather coat that stretched almost to the floor, and beneath that a dozen gold chains hung down over his bare chest, each one carrying a talisman or charm. His step was silent over the stony ground, and he seemed to almost glide across its surface, until he came to rest just a few yards from her.

"Who are you?" he said.

"My name is Alexia," she told him, "and I am from Kar'mi'shah. I need to talk to Koulan about what happened there, and what is happening now in this city."

"And what is happening now?"

Alexia stared at him in disbelief.

"Have you not left this place? Have you not seen the death on your very own doorstep?"

"We have seen."

Alexia gazed at him. How could he be so indifferent about these bizarre deaths, deaths that had claimed their own kind? There had been two vampires killed in as many nights, and with no clue as to what had butchered them in such hideous ways, any one of them could be next.

"Is Koulan here?" she continued, her anger beginning to dispel the fears that had wracked her. "I need to speak to him immediately."

The vampire stared at her, apparently dumbfounded now at this stranger's demand to see his Master in his own den. Alexia was adamant, however, and stood defiantly before him, awaiting an answer. It was then, from the back of the ill-lit chamber, that a voice came, low and deep.

"I am Koulan."

Alexia turned in the direction of the voice, and there, emerging from the darkest of the shadows, stepped a huge dark figure, his long black cloak shrouding his body. As he stepped closer and the electric lights began to illuminate him, so Alexia managed to make out a face. His features were broad, his hair cropped tight against a pale weathered skull, and his lips were pressed firmly together as though they contemplated with the deepest concern the problem of her even being in his shelter.

"Why are you here?" Koulan asked her flatly. "You must know that this is no place for you."

"I need help," Alexia began.

"Help?" Koulan bellowed. "From me? I don't think

you know your place, girl."

"I know who you are -"

"Do you?" Koulan exclaimed. "Do you really? This is a clan of Wraiths. You are a Faraoh. You are my enemy. I should kill you now for what your tribe did to mine. Do you know how much of my family I lost?"

"I... have a fair idea."

Koulan took a threatening step towards her.

"I should take out your throat right now," he growled, "just for your very being here."

"Then why don't you?" Alexia retaliated. "Go on, tear out my throat. What would that achieve? Would it bring back those you lost? Would it get you back your home? I've lost many people too. My husband, my Master, my family. Both our tribes suffered. We are more alike than you think."

"It was a Faraoh that conjured that creature. It was a Faraoh that brought death to our families."

"Enough!" Alexia cried, taking a threatening step towards him this time. "This argument has gone on too long. How can you say that a Faraoh conjured that thing? No one knows where it came from, and no one can do anything about what happened that night. All we know is that it decimated most of our tribes, and took the lives of those we knew. We are trapped here now, Koulan. You and I and everyone in this room. We are forced to live like vermin because of that creature, and we have to stop blaming each other for the terrible massacre that decimated our families."

Koulan stared at her, his words momentarily held in his throat. It seemed that he knew what she was saying was true, or at least part of it. They had both lost so many people, and the struggle between the tribes afterwards had killed so many more. It had to stop, now, and before any more were killed.

"You know of the death out in the street above, don't you?" Alexia asked him finally.

Koulan nodded gravely.

"A vampire," she continued. "And one of your own, too, I suspect."

Koulan nodded again.

"His name was Milestone," the Wraith admitted. "He was brash and foolhardy. There was nothing I could have done that would have stopped it."

"You say it as though it was your doing."

"In a way," he said, "I guess that it was. But in the end, all things come back to haunt us."

Alexia looked at the furrows across his face, furrows of torment and age-long tiredness.

"What do you mean?" she asked him.

Koulan took a breath and gazed round at the stone-faced vampires that studied their conversation from the silent depths of the darkened cavern. He looked back at her with a sudden sadness in his eyes, his voice reduced in both tone and volume.

"Yes, you are right that we have no life down here. We hide ourselves away, and we eat what vermin we can find, but it was a decision that I made a very long time ago. Yes, we have survived with very few casualties, but at what expense? Tensions are high. We are miserable. We all want to return home to Kar'mi'shah, but it was I, as Master of the Wraiths, that made this decision. It is I, trying to control us all, that has led to Milestone's death."

"Do not blame yourself, Master," came a voice. It was the vampire who had first spoken to Alexia. "He rebelled at every chance. He hated this life, and he didn't care for your rules. But he respected you, deep down, and he knew that you were right. That was why he never left."

"You cannot comfort me, Jay. I know that this is no life for the Gods that we were. We are less than criminals here, and I have made us so."

Koulan turned to Alexia at this point.

"How much do you remember of Kar'mi'shah?"

Alexia looked hard at him. His question confused her.

"I remember my life there," she said. "The temples, the servants. But why ask me about that now?"

"And your Godhood?"

"We were worshipped, yes, but that was only as it should have been."

"I want us to leave this place, I really do, but I fear that it is more dangerous now that it has ever been to go above the surface. I suspect that the events that happened over those last few days in Kar'mi'shah are about to be re-enacted now. I have tried my best to piece together what I remember of those last few days - names and places, motivations and alibis - but nothing makes much sense to me. And yet I cannot help feeling that there is so much more going on than I can possibly know."

"What exactly are you trying to remember?"

"I'm trying to remember the vampire who instigated it all."

Alexia stared at him in shock.

His words echoed those of The Howler.

They could simply not be true, could they?

"Surely it was a creature that we didn't know of," Alexia stated. "A dormant beast. A demon of the wastelands. There was nothing anyone could've done."

"No," Koulan corrected her. "There was something

we could have done. If only I could figure out just who had done what, then perhaps I can find a way of securing all our futures. I believe that someone from your tribe invoked that creature to destroy the Master Jackel El'a'cree, but his plan somehow went wrong and he ended up destroying more than he'd envisaged. If I could find out who that was, then maybe it would all make sense. And then if I could find him, I would take his head from his shoulders for what he has done."

"But how can you be so sure that this creature was conjured?"

"It was a terrible beast that decimated most of my tribe," Koulan told her. "Down here in this chamber, hides what is left. We hide from everything now. Nowhere is safe."

"There is little to fear outside," Alexia told him, "if you are careful. This is no life for any of you, you have seen that. How long can you continue to hide in the dark like the rats on which you feed? How much longer can you continue until these tensions become too much?"

"It is the only way until I can find out who betrayed us."

"And how long have you been looking?"

"Since we first arrived here."

"And you are no closer?"

"Each day brings renewed clarity," Koulan explained, almost desperately, "and one day he will show himself to me - perhaps in a vision, perhaps in the flesh - but one day he will, and then I will take out his eyes."

Alexia looked at this man standing before her, this Master of the Wraiths, with something close to pity in her eyes. While she had tried to come to terms with all that she had lost, with learning to live in a new alien city, and finding new loves and companions, Koulan had imprisoned his own tribe down here in the dank rotting depths of the London underground system. He had wracked himself into such a desperate state, blaming himself and blaming others for the holocaust that had befallen them all. Was it any wonder than he seemed such a wreck, this former elder of a Kar'mi'shah clan, to have undergone an endless spiral of torment and revenge? His eyes were cast once again at the floor, as though he was searching amongst the muck and the dirt for answers that still eluded him centuries afterward. Alexia asked him just what it was that he could remember.

"Jackel was set to reveal news in front of all the assembled tribesmen," Koulan began slowly, "news of his final sole possession of The Curbane, the source of The Blood Of The Ancients. The Curbane, as you know, was the most sacred site of all the vampire clans, the place where the Ancient Ones had gone to die to spill their Blood. It had also been the source of many wars between the tribes, wars that had raged long before you were even born, and probably still rage to this day. Jackel El'a'cree was the most devoted and respected of any of the clan Masters, his word feared throughout the temples of Kar'mi'shah. But on that night, word must have spread from one of his own tribesmen, conspiring against him, and it was this that brought about our downfall."

His eyes flickered up to find hers now.

"It was midnight," he continued, "and the tribes were present at the Raza pyramid. The elders met at the altar, waiting for Jackel to appear with this great news of his. As you may remember, there were angry voices on all sides, each vampire critical of each other, suspicious, wary. Finally Jackel appeared from one of the annexes to the vaults, his sacred chambers where only he and his protector, Cal'Beha, were permitted to enter."

"Cal'Beha?" Alexia uttered.

"That was his name."

"I've never heard of him."

"I myself had seen Cal'Beha only once before, when one of the other tribesmen had made an attempt on Jackel's life. It had been a small gathering in a sealed temple chamber, and Cal'Beha had moved swiftly from the shadows, so swiftly in fact that even I had not been aware of his presence, let alone see him descend from the lofts to take off the would-be assassin's head. The skull hit the marble floor just yards in front of Jackel El'a'cree's feet, the lifeless body falling after it. The protector stood growling for a few moments as though he were expecting a second assault. But if there had been one planned, it did not come. That was the only time I saw Cal'Beha. And from that day on, there were no more subsequent attempts on Jackel's authority."

"Until the night the beast arrived," she murmured quietly.

Koulan looked at her.

"Now you see," he said.

"I hadn't thought about it that way until now," she confessed, "but your words do make sense."

"So you see why I try to remember who did what on that night."

"Are you suggesting that this demon was sent to take Jackel El'a'cree's life? A creature so powerful that not even Cal'Beha could stop it?"

"Why not? It is the only thing that makes sense to me."

"But why did it try to kill us all?"

"Perhaps the creature slipped the control of its conjurer. Perhaps it was simply too powerful to be controlled. Ever since that night, I have been trying to ratify that suspicion of mine, find some shred from my memory, but there is simply no proof that that is what happened."

"There must be somebody that you suspect."

Koulan shook his head slowly.

"That is where I fail," he said quietly. "It could have been anyone, and no one."

Alexia asked him what that meant.

"Any of the tribal elders would have wanted to command the clans and have the power that Jackel possessed. Any of their tribesmen, not content with their standing, could have had the desire to rise up through the ranks, been devious in their plotting, and sought to show every vampire in Kar'mi'shah that they were a force to be reckoned with. It could even have been one of the mortal slaves or priests wanting to put an end to the blood-drinkers altogether. There's just no way of knowing. At least not with all of us stranded here so far away from home."

"But you said something about no one?" Alexia prompted.

"I did," Koulan confessed. "There is not a single being I know, apart from Jackel himself, who could have possessed the knowledge or wisdom capable of conjuring such a creature. It takes more than a few rites and a magic talisman to bring forth a demon with enough force and venom that it could have devoured

211

our brothers and sisters in such a way that it did. That is where I fall short in my findings. I can not think of one single name to put on the guilty list."

Alexia watched as his eyes fell wretchedly to the uneven surface of the floor once again. She herself had lost her family. Some through death at the behest of the creature, others simply left behind. She wasn't even sure how she herself had escaped intact. She could recall only ragged images, blood mostly, but there were screaming mouths, sheets of fire, and teeth, so many teeth that they ripped through her mind. She thought that her husband had somehow saved her, but how could that have been possible? The creature would have, and probably had, consumed him on sight as it had done to so many others that night. She had mourned his passing, nevertheless, as if he had died that terrible night. But there was simply no way home, no way to return to Kar'mi'shah, where the living may be waiting, and the dead be laid to rest.

FOUR

WHAT HIDES IS FOUND

A cross the street from the runner's flat, Catherine stood on the roof of a three storey terraced house, waiting for him to emerge. She had watched the moon rise for the past seven nights, calculated its slow ascent and arc, in the hope that Jenner Hoard would dare to venture out into the night. She was used to waiting, but it surprised even her how long he could remain in his pit.

The light from the streetlamps below was meagre and a dim yellow, and would certainly not illuminate the rooftops above them should anyone even be looking for her. The runner Jenner Hoard would be oblivious to her presence, of course, even if he had been alerted to the danger by his benefactor Montague. If only her Master would allow her the pleasure of killing them, she thought, as she watched the curtained windows of the flat. If only he would see reason in their dispatch. Vampires were being killed by humans. So grave a crime was that in itself, but surely here was proof. One had plotted to the other in a bid to steal the resting place of the legendary Master of Kar'mi'shah. Such a relic was sacrosanct, there were no two ways about it. Even for it to be looted from wherever it had been hidden should be sufficient to have their heads, but for one mortal to steal it for another, that was sheer suicide.

Or so she had thought.

Her Master had seemed to think otherwise, and it was that that so infuriated her.

Tiny black bats circled below her in flitting paths, and Catherine allowed herself to be distracted by them for a while. The curtains in Jenner Hoard's flat had not moved, yet movements in the shadows inside spoke of his continued presence. What he could be doing for seven nights solid she couldn't imagine, but her sources had informed her that he had not left by sunlight either. She could see that a thick layer of dirt and fumes covered the windows of his top floor flat, and even from across the street she could hear little but a single slow heartbeat from inside. It could only be that of the runner's, and yet it seemed to be coming from the living room of the flat, and not from the bedroom.

The television had been on but he'd hardly paid any attention to it. The death of his beloved Emma had not been off his mind since he had witnessed Jackel El'a'cree taking her life. He'd passed out shortly after that, his head light from blood loss at the behest also of the vampire, who had fed from him so very frequently, it had seemed.

Emma had died, but he had lived.

It made no sense.

When he had woken to find himself sprawled on the floor of his own living room, he had found Emma gone. Jackel had laid her on the sofa where he now sat after he had drunk from her, but now there was nothing there but an empty space. The bedroom door was once again barricaded, denoting that the vampire at least still resided in the flat. But he had promised that he would soon be leaving, but only once he had his companion. Jenner had waited for his request to go with him, but that request had never come. More and more as he thought about it, he felt like he was nothing to him but nourishment, pure and simple. But it was the disappearance of Emma that now distressed him more.

He imagined her poor body abused as the two officers' bodies had been, torn and eaten, their blood drained, their bones removed and burned. She had always been there for him, compassionate and devoted, and this was her reward. It occurred to him that he had never once even told her how he felt about her - hell, did he even know himself? - and now he would never get that chance. His eyes went to the living room door behind him, as though he somehow hoped that she would be standing there, alive and well, with her arms wide to embrace him.

The threshold stood empty, of course.

There would be no welcome for him tonight.

From the gaps between the window panes, her keen senses could just make out the smell of staleness, perhaps even faeces, and wondered why such a smell should be coming from this room. It was then, as she tried to discern these things, that she heard a sound, almost like sand shifting across a desert floor, but it did not seem to come from the flat, but from somewhere a few streets away.

Barely audible, even to her acute senses, but eerily distinctive, it seemed so out of place in a city the size of London. She tried to return her attention to the runner's flat, shaking off such unnecessary distractions, but it lingered. The heartbeat in the living room was all that mattered, she told herself. But the key to the deaths of the London vampires lay somewhere between the two sounds.

The crawl of the shifting sands grew steadily closer, and it demanded her attention, simply by its sheer unprecedented rhythms, and Catherine pursed her lips in agitation as she glanced down the length of the street, away from the flat, in the direction of the approaching sound.

At such a late hour there was nothing there to see, nothing strange that any mortal would recognise anyway. The shifting and fall of the sand grew closer still, and she was sure that whatever made that sound should be where she was looking. A howl of wind accompanied the shifting sands, and Catherine began to feel anxious that there was something there to be seen, but her eyes were simply not able to sift through the layers of darkness to find it.

She opened her eyes to the blackness of the street and searched the deepest of the shadows, seeking to make out this interruption to her surveillance of Montague's runner. The sight that she found, when at last she found it, was little more than another shadow, and yet it was a shadow that burned with movements of its own, and pounded with a pulse of a singularly horrid rhythm.

Catherine had seen this thing before. This was the creature that had decimated most of her tribe. It was below her now, a pulsing cloud of shifting forms that was sweeping through the streets of the city. Where was it going, she wanted to know? Was it coming for her? Like it had come so many years before when she had somehow mercifully managed to escape its talons? Suddenly her hands were shaking, her whole body trembling with abject fear. The demon was back.

She felt that fear ragged in her throat as she stood on the roof of the three storey building and watched this thing come towards her. A chill had crept across her body, and the sight of it devouring her family so many years ago jerked back into her head like a whipcrack. She had to snatch herself free of these images as it closed in upon her, coming down the street towards her with disturbing speed. But it wasn't until the creature suddenly veered away from her and began to scale the building opposite, that she realised that it had not come for her.

Catherine watched bewildered as it clawed its way up the brickwork towards the living room window of the top floor flat, the glass shattering beneath the sudden colossal onslaught that came. Its shadowy mass obliterated most of the surrounding wall as it hauled its weight of shifting forms over the threshold of broken glass and splintered wood, like a snake heaving rib after rib over the edge of a step. A howl of fear pierced the night air from inside the flat, a human voice, Jenner Hoard's no doubt, and Catherine forced herself to attention, stepping even closer to the edge of the rooftop in order to witness the assault upon the runner's flat.

Her thoughts were spiralling out of control even as she looked inside and saw Jenner, not dead, but very much alive, and lying sprawled across the carpet trying to claw his way back from the beast. Terror spread across her face as she watched, as she tried to unravel this mystery unfolding before her eyes. Here was a creature that had decimated most of the Gods of Kar'mi'shah, but had passed by this simple human as though he did not even exist. Why would it destroy this mortal's flat if it were not even interested in him? Why should it even be here?

So many questions. No forthcoming answers. But then her thoughts suddenly seemed to connect in one single heart-shattering jolt. Jackel El'a'cree was alive.

A low rumble caught his attention briefly, and Jenner turned his head towards the window as though perhaps there was a lorry passing outside in the street. A shadow cast by something passing between the pane and the streetlamps washed briefly across the glass, and then suddenly that glass, and the frame that held it fast against the night, shattered inward, as something dark and massive forced its way into his flat.

Jenner loosed a scream as he tumbled off the sofa and threw himself sprawling across the floor as the wall came apart with a thunderous boom, shards of brickwork crumbling down onto the floor in a great billowing cloud of dust. His hands shook with terror as he scrabbled out of this thing's way, forcing his back hard against the wall, away from this sight, his body shuddering with absolute fear and shock.

Was this what Jackel had meant by a companion? Some vast terrifying creature that should simply not exist.

It had no discernible eyes, this thing, nor any head in which to keep them, but whatever it used to see, Jenner now felt the weight of it, as it turned its terrible gaze upon him. He felt the intent of its stare, heavy and oppressive, and he feared for his own life in that moment, certain that it had come to destroy him. But then that terrible and bludgeoning weight suddenly left him, and the creature turned away, disinterested in both him and his worthless life.

It berated the floor as it hauled its length away from both him and the opening it had torn in the building, and Jenner could see its shape more clearly now as he watched it begin a fresh assault upon the wall that joined the living room and his bedroom. It was still nothing more than an unidentifiable shape, a shape with roving bruised colours that burned beneath a shadowy cloak, harsh forms churning and grinding in sickening motions, and teeth, so many teeth that he could never hope to count them even if he'd sat through the whole of the night to study its weird contortions.

It broke through the wall and disappeared through the jagged chasm it had made, dust and debris choking the air as it swirled in great clouds behind it. Through it he could still see the colours of its flesh, of deep reds and purples, but now there were lights, glittering sparks of fury that lit up the inside of its colossal frame, illuminating cages of ribs and spines, claws and talons. Hearts seemed to thump and pulse in deep confounding rhythms, forcing clots of blood through dark straining arteries. Veils of matter seemed to streak out ahead of it, violating the air and causing myriad distractions, while tendrils of ether played out from within this mass to grasp and claw at the ceiling and walls that surrounded it.

Its great thumping hearts continued to beat their rhythms as he watched, the colours of its mass glittering as they swapped hues like broiling clouds. Just beyond this thing he could see movement somewhere - Jackel, no doubt - and watched spellbound as his flat continued to shake beneath the creature's fury. A motion somewhere to his right caught his attention, and he flashed a glance quickly towards the shattered frame where the window had stood. He jerked suddenly as out of the darkness of the night a woman appeared, holding effortlessly to the wall from the outside as though she were simply floating there, her long dark hair drifting on the wind, her pale skin unblemished and almost radiating its own faint light like a cold white theatrical mask. Her eyes, he could see, were focussed entirely on the gaping hole broken through the bedroom wall beyond him, and at the creature just beyond that. And he watched spellbound, unable now to take his sight off this woman, as her eyes suddenly flickered towards him, and forced him to shiver beneath the iciness of her stare.

Their eyes seemed locked together for what seemed like a day, as though they were somehow connected in ways that he could never possibly know, but it was in that stare that he realised that this too, surely, was also a vampire. There was no way to confirm this, of course, but he somehow knew by the sight of her and by the stillness of her body as she regarded him with almost no respect and almost total contempt. Still she hovered, outside at the threshold to his world, unable to move, unable, it seemed, to enter. Jenner continued to stare at her, helpless in his own flat, even as the war continued to rage in his bedroom just a few yards away from him.

"What happens here?" the woman suddenly demanded of him, her voice like granite as it came out of the night.

Jenner stared at her, his throat stricken with

absolute anguish. This woman was beautiful, perhaps even perfect, but she could barely contain a mask of fear that flickered frequently across another that was cold and threatening. There were no lines or marks on her radiant white skin, and only her lips moved as she spoke, her unblinking dark eyes regarding him with utter hatred.

"I asked you a question," she seethed, her voice cutting through the din that raged in the very next room.

Furniture was breaking, and now cries of agony came with it. Lightning sparked somewhere in the building, and an angry ball of flame lit up the room like a flare. The floors shuddered wildly as yet another assault rocked the flat, and filaments of furious light strobed across the ceiling, scorching the plaster and igniting anything that could sustain a flame.

"He killed Emma," Jenner managed to say, his trembling hand lifting to point to the place where her dead body had been laid. His eyes went there now too, but all they found was that same empty space where the vampire had taken her corpse.

"Where is Jackel El'a'cree?" the woman demanded.

"He told me that I had freed him," Jenner said.

"Is he here?" the female vampire cried, almost desperately now.

"The Master of Kar'mi'shah. He said that I had set him free."

The woman stared hard at him now, her eyes betraying her dumbfounded state.

"You?" she hissed, unable to believe the apparent absurdity of his statement. "How could you have done such a thing?"

"I took a box," Jenner explained, his back still

pressed hard against the wall, his limbs shaking as he wrapped them now around his body. "I opened it."

"But you are not a God," she seethed. "You have no power." And then more quietly, "Perhaps I have underestimated you."

All this she said from outside the window. She had not entered, or made any attempt to enter. Jenner took his sight away from her as the din of shattering glass erupted suddenly from inside the bedroom, snatching his attention from her as a flash of livid colour burned throughout the flat. Instantly the creature bolted forward further into the room, its tendrils recoiling after it like electrified snakes, back into the depths of its pulsing forms. On it raged, even further into the bedroom, as though in pursuit of the first intruder. A cry filled the night ahead of the beast, and Jenner watched as the far wall crumbled beneath the escape, the heavy stench of sweat and blood roiling in the vacated space left now in the air as the beast dragged the broken debris of the flat after it. Suddenly, all that was left in its wake was a mess of rubble, shards and scraps of burning leftover matter.

Jenner lay slumped for several minutes afterwards, just watching the gaping holes that now opened out onto the night sky over London, as his chest beat heavy rhythms. His breathing was ragged but gradually it slowed, and so too did his pulse, as he became accustomed once more to the returning silence of his flat. His attention once again strayed to the obliterated window of his living room, and to the woman still waiting at the wall outside. The sounds of the city returned as he stared at her - the distant rumble of traffic, a dog barking somewhere nearby - but none of this brought any normality with it. It was just surreal, a reminder of just how normal other people's lives were, compared to his own. How could he ever drive a van, his mind suddenly returned to? How could he ever load a truck, when he had witnessed events such as these? Death would be welcome, he thought. Why had Jackel not brought it?

Jenner pushed himself slowly forward onto his knees, and edged across the carpet through the broken glass to where the mysterious woman still gazed in disbelief at the carnage left behind. Her gaze came back to him as he approached, still icy as she regarded him strangely, almost as though he was as much a threat to her as the creature had been. Jenner stopped and simply looked up at her. Who was she, he wanted to know, this woman hanging from the window of a third storey building? And how did she come to be a part of such unnatural things?

"Why do you look at me like that?" the woman asked him suddenly, her voice dry and raked.

"Like what?" Jenner asked.

"Like I am a ghost. You know who Jackel El'a'cree is. You know who I am."

Jenner stared at her but kept his silence.

"I'm not sure what has gone on here," she murmured, "nor how you managed to free the Master of the Faraohs, if indeed that was what really happened, but it will be known, you can be sure. Your employer Montague is in even greater danger that I had at first suspected. If, between the two of you, you have managed to free him for your own profit, then you will both die painful and horrific deaths. This I can promise you, for I will do the deeds myself."

These words she spat with venom. There was so much hate in her, a hate for which he had no explanation, never having seen her before, and he still

223

had no clue as to even her name. That she knew Montague was now no secret, and just confirmed to him how dangerous Montague's world was. He cursed himself, even as he looked up at her, that he should have just taken the packet with the five grand and not asked those questions that he'd had. What was knowledge anyway? Nothing but a vessel for death, it seemed. He saw that now, saw it now that it was too late. It had taken Emma's life, that knowledge, and now surely, it would take his own.

His thoughts began to churn once more with guilt for Emma, for all the things that he had never said to her, and for all the things that he never would. But even these were stolen as the vampire in front of him interrupted them and spoke her final words to him.

"Pray that you find somewhere far away to hide from me," she threatened. "Montague has no excuses left. And you will never get a chance to even think of one."

"Where are you going?" Jenner managed to say, as she turned from the window to disappear into the night.

"I must go," she uttered with contempt. "My Master must know that Jackel is alive."

FIVE

GATHERING THE ARMY

The news that Catherine had brought had not been in his plan. The box was to have been brought to him where he would destroy it, along with the prisoner inside. That was the plan. It was a simple plan. That was why he liked it.

The box had hexes on it, painted and spoken, and only a mortal could lay hands on it and survive. Ingenious it was, hiding the Master away so that no other vampire could go near him and harm him. Flawed it was too, because no other vampire could go near him to help. Alive he was, but forever imprisoned. Or so he had thought.

A mortal had finally found him after centuries of searching, and had brought him almost to within his reach. But the mortal he had paid to lay his hands upon the box and bring it to him had somehow freed him, and now the Master of Kar'mi'shah was free. It was that that would make the killing of him so much more difficult. Difficult, but not impossible. He was weak, after all.

He had been imprisoned for a very long time, and away from the modern world. The vampire Casta Mica'tore, meanwhile, had been spending the time resourcefully, reading and learning, conducting himself so that he would not make the same mistakes again that had cost him so much before.

And what had he lost?

Everything.

All this he turned over as he sat in the darkened knave of the church, his bloody knife still at work on the hardening flesh of the dead victims. He had fed so well on the six of them, passers-by pulled off the streets at random, but it had left their bodies dry and difficult to manage, their joints cracking in his attempts to dismember them, arranging the parts across the cold stone floor. Men and women, it didn't matter what they were, only what they would become. Potential, that's what they were. The word suited them immensely.

The bright narrow flames of the candles guttered around him as the night breeze found its way in through the numerous cracks of the old building, and it was one of these candles that he now picked up to drip its scalding wax over the carved limbs of the dead. The incantations that he had learned rolled fluidly beneath his breath as he worked, pressing his fingertips into the searing wax, leaving his impression behind on its surface. He put the edge of his knife to his arm and drew it slowly back, opening a sharp narrow wound that allowed his blood to drip freely into the marks left in the pliant wax.

It had been a lonely business - the secrecy, the plotting, the deaths of the innocent - and it had all come crumbling down around his ears. No, crumbling was not the word. Fucked up beyond all recognition, that was the truth. All that he had planned, all that he had wanted for himself and his wife, had disappeared in a matter of seconds as his failures turned for the worst. Oh, how those events had haunted him over the years, his deeds, his actions. He knew now what he had done wrong, the incantations he had not made, the safeguards he had not known about. He knew them now, of course, oh how he had studied them. Things would not go wrong again, he had seen to that. Except... things had gone wrong. Jackel was free. He had not foreseen that. How could he have foreseen that? He had thought he was aware of everything. He had eyes everywhere, even where they were least expected. Everything had been taken into account, even things that could not be taken into account, and yet here was something that had not run the way it should. That part was not controllable. It would have to be taken out, and things were already in motion to do just that.

The flesh of the dismembered limbs began to stir and pulse as his spilled blood began to dry and congeal in the wax dripped from the candles. Casta's recitations demanded life return into those parts, return and grow, gestate into slaves worthy of his army. The flesh continued to stretch and deform as he worked, his eyes half-closed now as the words rolled perfectly and controlled from his lips. An arm from a human that had once grasped an umbrella to shield the rain, now became a sprouting torso, limbs growing awkwardly at unnatural angles from joints that defied nature. Teeth bristled from the ankle of a severed leg, long and razor-sharp, a lower jaw cracking open from the lower foot and clamping shut like a vice. Claws germinated from fractured femurs, clenching and stretching like twisting ferns. Eyes formed and popped opened, glistening brightly from the depths of bruised pulp and marrow. And needles of ivory bone raised themselves along ridged spines of ever-ripening sinew, bristling like raised banners of war.

Casta's magic flickered around him like bright orange embers, his army almost complete, and he lifted his head to cast an approving eye over the ragged battalion of wet and foetal soldiers. They looked back at him with fresh and unused eyes, their skins glistening and drying in the breeze of the draughty old church. Their bones still creaked and cracked as joints fought to reach unfinished sockets inside this ancient house of God, and basic maps of veins and arteries continued to pulse and throb as new blood flowed to fill them. Casta stood and gazed up at the motionless undead army, their sight upon him keen and eager for instruction, and breathed a long and heavy sigh of satisfaction. This war would soon start, and his victory, surely, could not be doubted.

SIX

THE HANDS THAT LEAD US

It was a test to his rejuvenating powers just how quickly he had managed to evade the pursuing demon, despite the rain that soaked their clothes and the wind that gusted it into their path. Even with the new-born Emma in tow, it had taken only a few streets to outpace the thing that would destroy them, and he slowed their flight now to a more moderate walk.

It had been two nights previous since he had sired the young Emma, drinking from her until she bordered the threshold between life and death. He had opened a vein in his own arm then, and coaxed her to drink from him in turn, nurturing her to live once again, except now as a vampire, and as a daughter of his. She would gain much in the way of her own power, being a blood-child of his. She would inherit the abilities of the Faraohs, the rise towards Godhood and the blessing of the shape-changer. What shape she would assume would be governed only by her own intuition and desire, and such ability would only develop over time. She had been a vampire less than one night and she was weak. Her transformation had taken just minutes, the time it had taken Jenner Hoard to leave the room and re-enter. She had appeared dead to him then, but the reality could not have been further from the truth. She had been initiated into immortality that night, and would grow into a Goddess of Kar'mi'shah, even if she had never set foot in its rich green pastures, or strolled its bountiful groves of great fertile orchards.

It would be a long road to recovery for her, of course. It had only been shortly before the assault on the flat that she had opened her eyes and recognised him for the first time. It might be days yet before she was even able to form complete coherent sentences. She had murmured a few words already, nothing of significance, but it would come, in time. During the battle where so many teeth had attempted to slice both of them to shreds, he'd had to protect her as well as himself, so helpless was she, and he did not want to lose his companion to that creature so soon after having made her. What hexes he had managed to scrawl on the walls of the bedroom were pitiful safeguards against that thing, he had known, but it had at least afforded him a few moments respite while they had initiated their escape. The creature had been on their heels as soon as they had hit the street, however, but thankfully it was sluggish by comparison, even against their dwindled strength and resources.

And so they found themselves in a dark and oppressive city, wandering the undistinguished grimy streets. Where could they go that would be safe for them? Jackel had set foot on this world only a handful of times, that was a very long time ago, and it was not even in this cold and dank country. Emma stumbled beside him like a mannequin, her eyes looking only forward and uncomprehending, as her body struggled against the living death that he had brought upon her, and the subsequent rebirth he had bestowed. He had needed help, he had realised early on, and she had been the first human that was suitable.

Jenner Hoard was a weak man, that much was plain, and although his blood had been vital, it had not been as nourishing or as clean as Emma's. His hand grasped her damp forearm as she staggered sideways, guiding her along the rain-lashed pavements, and her flesh was so very cold against his touch. She would need to feed again, he realised, and soon, and knew that he would not be able to spare any more of his own blood. They would have to find someone, the next passer-by, and open up their neck to the world.

His memories were all that he'd had during his time imprisoned inside the box. Time had passed the same, it seemed, for those living outside, and it had been a maddening struggle to survive so long intact. With no new stimulus, he was only able to recount over and over those same events that had claimed his sovereignty.

And just what had happened?

He knew so very little.

His address to the clan elders had been imminent, and he had just been about to give them the news that the internal struggles between them all would soon be over. He had finally been granted conditional access to The Blood Of The Ancients, which would mean the foundation of peace between all clans, and the continuing prosperity of the land. But there had been a disturbance. Had there been an explosion too? Certainly there had been shouts and cries. And he had smelt blood, vampire blood, stark and sharp, pricking the air like a cloud of needles. He had seen forms also, or had these been imagined in the years of confinement and solitude that had followed, forms and coloured veils that shrouded those members present inside a violent blanket of death and butchery. Such images, horrific though they had been, had not lasted long.

His sight had misted as though a layer had been brought down between himself and the rest of the world. His hearing became deadened and his sense of smell vanished, until all he could detect was his own aroma. It was so intensely disorientating, that for a few moments he was not sure of what was even happening. Only when it was too late, and he was trapped inside six harsh boundary walls, did he realise that someone had invoked a protective shield about him.

He had waited - what else could he have done? - for whoever had set that shield, to finally release him from it. But that person had never returned, and for a long time he waited, expecting his freedom, and expecting to bestow his blessing on the head of whoever had saved him. But he paid little attention to the amount of time that passed.

He practised that speech of blessing a thousand times, over and over in his head, but the day of its telling would not come, and insanity threatened with each and every thought. Time lengthened, and his hopes of appearing intact began to dwindle, and in his desperation he decided to attempt to calculate the passing of his time imprisoned. Hours were relatively simple to deduce, but when they stretched into days, it became more complicated. After he had counted the first week, his fears began to accumulate, compounding themselves so that he did not know what to do. With no way to even kill himself, death was no longer an option. He was, in the truest ever sense, beyond death.

The second week came and went, and still he had nothing to occupy himself with but his own thoughts. There were no sights, no smells, no sounds. He had nothing to touch nor hands with which to touch. He was simply a mind, a collection of ideas, a store of memories and deductions. Weeks passed into months, and months accumulated, at length, into years. His sanity came into question frequently, and yet he still possessed his own powers, even if they were all trapped inside the same void of his prison. He tried to keep himself empowered as though each day might bring his release, but each day came and went, and his strength could not be maintained. Then the night came when his senses had ignited like a torch, his sight, his smell, his touch, his taste, his hearing, all sparked into life at the same miraculous moment. That had been the night when Jenner Hoard had released him. He had thought his weakened state would have deprived him of all hope when at last he emerged once more into the world. But he had lain in a darkened room for only a few minutes, before he felt the room invigorate and stimulate his senses sufficiently enough to give him flight.

The sight of exposed skin consumed him beyond belief, and he flew at two uniformed blood-parcels, his desire to feed and bathe in raw flesh consuming him entirely. The frenzy lasted only moments until his control returned, but he lay still, with their innards caked to his skin, panting deliriously like a caged beast, looking up at the man who had unbolted the latch.

Yes, that man had been human, and it was only natural that he should have opened up that man's throat too, but he passed over him. This mortal had

233

done what members of his own tribe had failed to do in centuries. He owed him his life, and in return he gave him his. The Master of Kar'mi'shah was free. But he was lost in a strange and mystifying place. His tribe was still a long way away, a world away, and he had no idea how he would ever be able to reach them.

Through the billowing veil of rain ahead he could make out the figure of a mortal coming towards them on the pavement, his head up, his hands thrust deep into the pockets of his dark jacket. Their eyes connected briefly, the human staring back defiantly, oppressively. Emma was swaying with weakness beside him. She would have to feed now, Jackel knew, before she passed out completely from the cold and the hunger.

They were within yards of each other now, and Jackel's sight connected with the youth's once again. A sneer came at the man's mouth, just as his hand swept free from his jacket, a glint of a blade slicing the cold damp air before him in his clenched fist.

"Give me your fucking wallet," the youth spat, slashing the air between them once again, his other hand held out as if to prevent their escape. "Do it now."

Jackel held onto Emma with his right hand while with his left he lashed out to snatch hold of the man's throat. The youth's eyes bulged wide and white as he suddenly choked, startled and afraid, and he lashed back instinctively with his knife. The blade found Emma, its point plunging deep into her chest, but she remained silent as though it had not even touched her. Jackel crushed his grip tighter until the vertebrae in the youth's neck creaked. His arms fell limp at his sides as he loosed a stricken groan, and then Jackel hauled the sodden carcass before Emma, and offered its exposed neck up towards her lips.

"Feed," Jackel instructed, pressing the wet taut skin against her parted lips. "Sink your teeth deep and drink hard upon his blood."

Emma continued to stare blankly down at the pavement, spears of rain splashing circles in the puddles around them, mesmerising her with their random uniformity. She was barely alive, he realised, confounded and possibly even insane from existing so permanently on the edge of death. Jackel let go of her arm and allowed her to slump down into the puddles her vision had been so fixated with. Taking hold of the human, he sunk his own teeth deep into his neck and drew several mouthfuls of the hot rich blood back into his throat. Going down beside Emma as the rain continued to soak them both, he put his own lips to hers and passed the life-giving blood to her. She choked as it filled her mouth, her chest convulsing as her throat tried to reject it, the hot fluid smoking in the cold of the London night air. But Jackel persisted, and drew another mouthful of blood from the youth before attempting to pass it on to Emma a second time. Again she choked, but she did at least take some, and gulped it down eagerly and instinctively. Jackel repeated the procedure a third time, and this time Emma found strength enough to drink without letting the hot scarlet fluid sputter down over herself. It was then that Jackel offered the body up to her lips again, pressing the place where the neck had been opened up against her lips. Emma's teeth grew long as he watched, and he admired her as they found the holes that Jackel had already made there. The arteries reopened eagerly, and the blood flowed freely into her mouth. She gagged at first as more blood filled her mouth than she could cope with, but then she found a rhythm as her strength came, and she clamped her mouth hard to the wound and drank freely.

Jackel stood back and watched as she fed, her eyes clamped shut as she took in the meal that would nourish her so fully. It took only a few moments before the body became too parched for her to drink from any more, refusing to offer more blood, and then she suddenly let the body drop from her grasp and loosed an involuntary gasp of delirium. Her eyes flickered open too, blankly at first as they tried to focus, but then came a sudden and sharp clarity as they searched the dark streets until finally settling on the figure of Jackel El'a'cree standing in front of her.

The rain was beginning to come down harder when they heard the shifting sands of the creature once again. It could only have been a few streets away, perhaps even closer than that, so difficult was it to tell with the wall of rain dampening the sounds of the city. But with Emma stronger than she had been they were able to pick up their pace considerably.

Still blind as to what direction they should be heading in, they covered ground swiftly, away from the terrible sound and the horror that it would bring. The bitter taste of salt came through the wind and the rain, and they soon came upon the expanse of the River Thames, its cruel freezing mass violent and fast flowing. Concrete and steel bridges spanned it at frequent intervals, all of them lit up with bulbs that glittered bright reflections in the falling rain and across the surface of the dark surging waters beneath. They followed its course east beneath a tree-lined route, all the time the sky lightening with the approaching dawn. Daylight would be upon them soon, but if they stopped to rest out of the deadly touch of the sun, they would undoubtedly succumb to the deadly jaws of the creature.

Would the creature itself need to shelter? That was a question that needed to be answered and quickly. If the answer was yes, then that would afford them much valuable time. If no, then they were in greater danger than they had at first envisaged. It was not a good position to be released into, Jackel realised, but better that than another day imprisoned. At least out here, he could play a part. At least out here, he could make a difference, however short-lived that may be.

Out of the dank gloom rose another bridge, and on it Jackel could just make out a dark motionless figure. He seemed to be returning his gaze, this figure, studying him, and as the distance between them diminished, so Jackel observed that this could only be the solitary and breathless figure of another vampire. He realised too that although he was not from his tribe, he was not from any of the other tribes either. This was a vampire sired in this world.

"I've been expecting you," this other vampire said, when at last they met, his glistening leather coat held tightly around his frame as the rain gusted hard across the bridge.

"You know who I am?" Jackel observed, undaunted by the foulness of the night.

"I know of you," the vampire returned, his gaze now settling upon the wretched state of the woman at his side.

"This is Emma," Jackel informed him. "She will be my companion from now on."

"We must be away," the stranger insisted. "There is

little time. Dawn will be here soon."

"But the creature, does it sleep?"

"I fear not, but you will be safe throughout the daylight hours if you come with me now."

"I thank you, friend. In a world where I seem to have no family or subjects, I am glad that the bond of blood-drinkers is still strong."

"Please," the stranger persisted. "We must be quick."

And so they headed north, away from the river and deeper into the heart of the city, beneath black and purple clouds heavy with rain, and rolling thunderheads that promised the worst storms that they had ever seen. Through gusting streets and unlit alleyways, Jackel El'a'cree and the undead Emma followed their new-found guide. The creature was behind them, a long way behind them, but the sound of its shifting forms could still be heard on the foul and grimy wind. Only as the vampire who led them slowed his pace and came to a halt in front of an old abandoned church, did Jackel finally ask him his name.

"Venice," the vampire informed him uneasily, his eyes unable to hold his thankful gaze. "My name is Venice."

SEVEN

SIDES

The vampire Casta Mica'tore stood in the nave of the church, his army of undead soldiers creaking around him, and watched with a satisfied grin as the Master Jackel El'a'cree stepped in through the tall heavy doors. He had waited so many lifetimes for this moment, so many years planning for this final retribution. There could be no salvation for Jackel El'a'cree, he thought with a long hollow grin, not from this. A dozen of his brainless monsters had already taken their station, hiding in the shadows on either side of the doorway, flanking the enemy, with only one instruction to be followed.

Death.

That was all they had to bring.

They could be fought, of course, and maybe even killed, but he had two dozen more waiting behind him, heaving and drooling, and waiting their turn to put that one sole instruction into motion.

It had been such a long time, he realised as he watched the events unfold, waiting and plotting, everything devoted to this one final moment of victory. He'd wanted Jackel's death, and his ascension to kingship, for centuries, almost for as long as he could remember. And now here it was. The moment had come. And it felt strange to him that he didn't feel something more, something greater. The moment seemed almost uneventful.

Casta started forward, his army clanking instantly in ranks in his wake, keeping their formation as best their awkward bodies could manage. Their joints clunked and grated against each other, their teeth rattled inside their malformed and makeshift skulls, but their grisly duty to their master was bound by laws far beyond that of loyalty. Their minds - if what they had could ever be described as such - held no thoughts, or dreams, or fears for anything beyond what Casta's incantation had put there. They could be torn apart and battered mercilessly, and yet they would continue to fight. They would not comprehend their own slaughter, nor their own pain - had not the magic decided against the inclusion of such things as sense or nerve or logic? What were these things in a soldier anyway? Mortals needed training in order to take such things away, and even then there was doubt. Magic simply never made them in the first place. This was purity. It was divine.

Through the flickering half-light of the candle-lit nave, Casta could see his soldiers lurking in the darkest reaches of the church. Jackel El'a'cree had no knowledge of them, of course, cloaked in a magical web as they were. And neither, it seemed, did his mysterious companion. Casta did not know who this woman was, he'd had no reports that Jackel had not come alone, but it just seemed like yet another eventuality of the story that he had not planned for. She was a vampire certainly, he could smell that much at least from such a short distance, but she had no identity as far as he was concerned, and would simply die along with her Master. Casta himself wore a veil of concealment, cast over himself as well as his two dozen troops behind him. The spider did not want

Jackel to find this place occupied. At least not yet.

There were only two routes into this building, the door through which they had entered, and the chambers to the rear. The latter was now structurally unsound, the doorway crumbled into a ragged mound of fallen masonry. Casta had seen to that. He was only yards from his Master now, and he could smell the blood on both his and the woman's lips, fresh blood, less than an hour old. He would be stronger than if he had not fed. But no matter. He would die just the same.

"I'm glad you could make it," Casta spoke for the first time.

Jackel jerked backwards, so too did Emma, and Casta loved the sight of their disorientation.

"I'm so glad you could make it," Casta continued. "I've been waiting such a long time for this, waiting and planning for the moment when I could finally have another go at you."

"Who are you?" Jackel demanded into the empty church.

"All in good time, my Master. All in good time."

Casta made a motion with his hand, and the web untangled at the back of the church. Jackel turned suddenly as his senses finally found the dozen hideous forms lurking in the shadows behind him.

"What is this?" he growled. "Who dares to threaten me?"

Casta made a second gesture, and the dark web covering the rest of his army dissipated into fluttering threads, revealing their twisted limbs and unearthly grimaces. He himself remained hidden, watching the fear wash over his Master's face in wonderful waves, relishing his distress, and studying his sight as it

241

scanned the old building for another route of escape. There were none, of course. He had seen to everything.

"You know that if you had just died like you were supposed to have done, none of this would have happened, don't you? Then perhaps if you had died when my other assassin had tried to take your life, there would have been even less bloodshed. But no, you had to have your protector. You had to have Cal'Beha hiding in the vaults. Well guess what? No sanctuary for you tonight. No Cal'Beha to swoop down and save you. You are mine, this night, and you will die by my hand."

"Just show me your face. Have at least some honour."

Casta made one final gesture with his hand, and the veils that swathed his form lifted like a suppurating cloud. He stood and watched as Jackel took in his face. It was more disfigured than he would have remembered, but remember he did, and the shock was blissful.

"You," he gasped.

Casta grinned at his Master's bewilderment.

"Now you know," Casta said.

"I would never have guessed."

"The guessing is over with now, it will console in your last few moments. Now all I require is for you to die, like you should have done centuries ago."

Casta murmured a few recitations beneath his breath, and watched with gleeful triumph as the dozen soldiers at the back of the church shunted forward along the nave like a single ghostly battalion. He watched too the look of fear wash over the face of Jackel El'a'cree, and could not help himself enjoying this moment, his enemy held so helpless and defenceless, and facing his last few moments of existence.

The flat was empty.

Alexia had gone.

And it looked permanent.

Venice left Knightsbridge swiftly, there was no point hanging around and waiting for her to return, not when the hours left were so few. Regrets took so long, actions even longer, but his decision had at least been made in an instant. No more was he to be a servant or spy. He'd known what he should have been for years, and yet he had not acted upon it. He was acting now, though, and oh how good that felt. His actions tonight might yet cost lives, but it was his speed on the streets that would find the truth in that. Tonight of all nights, he would have to find his courage, would need the strength to fight, to pull in favours, and stop the evil that had been haunting this city. He had been a part of that evil. Unwilling at times, but still contributing to it. But that had to stop, and tonight, before things were too late and before his deeds could not be turned back.

He learned of Alexia's whereabouts from a psychic he knew in Chelsea. She had gone to see the Wraiths who controlled Camden, he'd been told, but what she had hoped to find there was not known, and he only hoped that she would still be alive. There was only one guard at the underground station when finally he reached it, and he intercepted him quickly as he emerged from the building to defend their shelter. This was no time for turf wars. The future of the city and their home was at stake this very night. The guard kept up his offensive, but when Venice mentioned Alexia's involvement, he suddenly allowed him passage, deep into the heart of their underground network.

He found Alexia in a dark cavernous chamber, among thirty or more other vampires, all of them pale, weak and wary. Callie was there too, hidden away in a darkened corner, amid those that would protect her. A commotion rose as he entered, Alexia's eyes finding him too, and now she came to him, concerned why he was here, but grateful too. She was much improved since last he had seen her, but she still showed signs of the conflict that she'd had with The Howler.

"What are you doing here?" she wanted to know, as she reached his side. "It's not safe out on the streets."

"I fear I carry the same news," Venice returned, taking her arm and urging her away from the Wraiths nearby. "I need to talk to you. There are things you must know."

"This is a night for revelation," she told him. "I've learned so much already."

Venice stared at her uneasily.

"I came here to meet with Koulan," she went on, "and he's told me so many things about Kar'mi'shah that I never knew. He is devoted to a suspicion that the creature that destroyed our tribes was conjured not only by one of our own kind, but by one of my own family."

"I fear my news is far graver than that, Alexia."

"What could be graver? Here is news of my own family's deaths."

"That same creature is back."

"That much I know for myself."

"But do you know also that the vampire who invoked it is here as well?"

Alexia stared at him, before offering a shallow shake of her head.

"He is here, and intends to bring about the death of your Master. He lies in wait even now, with an army of mindless slaves, too hideous to describe."

"How do you know all this?" Alexia wanted to know, her eyes searching the darkness of his shadowed features for clues that she knew would not be there. Callie emerged from the shadows then, her expression one of concern as she put a hand to Alexia's arm.

"It is the same man who brought me to London," Venice confessed after a reluctant breath. "He brought me here to watch over you."

"Watch... over me?"

"I've been telling him all that I know of you."

Alexia was staring hard at him now, incredulous, offended.

"Anything else?" she suddenly snapped.

"I have been a spy for your enemy. It is that that I now confess to you."

Her eyes began to burn and well with something close to tears as she took in the sight of this other vampire, but whether they were tears of anger or sadness Venice could not be sure. Callie too seemed to stare at him with eyes of utter disbelief, and all Venice could think of was that this was the truth, he had found it at last. Alexia did not appreciate the difficulty of his honesty - but how could he reasonably expect that? - or how hard it had been for him to tell her all that he just had. He had also placed himself in great danger just by telling her. He knew that Casta had spies everywhere. He was also intelligent enough to realise that he had assassins everywhere too. But Alexia knew the truth now, that was all that mattered. What she did with that truth now was up to her. He just hoped that she would be able to put right all the things that he had made wrong.

"Where is this vampire now?"

"In an old church," Venice replied. "I can take you there."

"No," Alexia exclaimed. "You've done enough. Just tell me where."

Venice relayed the directions to the church where the battle would begin. There was little time left. It might already be over. The downfall of another world could be imminent, if not already over, and the burden for that weighed heavily on his shoulders. He watched her go without another word, slipping back out through the tunnels and heading off to fight an army alone.

The transformation had already begun. No longer did the Master Jackel El'a'cree stand in the guise of a simple man, but now took on the characteristics of those that he'd returned to in the flat of Jenner Hoard, those of the black dog of the desert. Still standing upright, two claws held poised to defend himself with, his head had lengthened into a dark growling snout, fierce fangs dripping saliva beneath a pair of rabid eyes. His back was hunched and bristled with dark fur, and he was ready to make a stand against this terrifying army of the unnatural undead. Stronger than she had ever been, but still too weak to fight, Emma stood her ground beside him. Infused now with the blood of the Faraohs, her ability to mutate had barely taken. Her jaw jutted forward with a more animalistic form, a growl of threat rumbling deep at the back of her throat, and it was certain that she would at least take a few of her enemy with her in order to defend her Master.

The vampire Casta Mica'tore stood before this all, flanked on all sides by his grisly army, enjoying the spectacle of Jackel El'a'cree's final moments. He would soon be dead, and Casta would be here to feed from his veins and take over as Master of them all. Memories came too, of nights spent talking centuries ago, before the massacre, before things went the way they had. They'd spoken often, Jackel and he, of Kar'mi'shah and of the Ancients, of temples and the mortal humans who relinquished their blood. But what had come about had been unfortunate. Still, at least it would soon be over.

"What do you think you are doing?" Jackel snarled. "You are a Faraoh, how can you kill your own kind?"

"It wouldn't be the first time now would it?" Casta countered. "Now just die quickly and let me become Master of all Kar'mi'shah."

"You will never taste my blood."

"I don't think you know your place. Take another look around you. Count the warriors on your side. You think this girl will save you? I will have her neck snapped before she can take her next step forward."

"Why do this, Casta?"

"I should be Master. I would bring strength back to our tribe. You weakened what we had by helping all the tribes to settle together. Peace has forfeited our power. the Blood Of The Ancients is not solely ours."

"So by killing me you will bring terror back to

Kar'mi'shah."

"And bring absolute power under my control. We are Gods, Jackel. Have you forgotten that?"

"Of course I have not forgotten that. I sought The Blood so that it would unite us all, not destroy us."

"That is of little consequence now. I hold the portal to Kar'mi'shah. I will soon be Master. And I will then take control of The Curbane. Everything is within my reach. The centuries of learning and planning will pay off this night, and I will have it all."

This last statement he growled as though barking a promise, and raising his fist as he spoke, he punctuated his intent as he ordered his army forward.

From the back of the church, the dozen monsters shunted forward as one, ragged cries of murder and bloodshed shrieking forth from raw and ill-formed throats. From behind Casta, another dozen leapt forward to kill these two vampires, claws of bone and jagged spines rasping the air in preparation for finding their enemy's flesh.

Jackel hunched back at the sight of this, and then launched an offensive back at them, the new-born vampire Emma at his side and clawing blindly at the beasts that would undo them. Blood sprayed the air as battle commenced, and overlooking it all from a safe distance stood the vampire Casta Mica'tore, grinning and proud, awaiting his victory.

Alexia went not by the directions Venice had given her, but headed south instead towards the Thames. If there was such an army as Venice had described, then by her storming the abandoned church alone, she would only seek her own demise more quickly. She needed an army of her own, and as she knew that Koulan would not risk himself or his tribe in order to save the lives of the vampires he held responsible for the deaths of his own family, she knew that she would need the help of a completely different kind.

There were only a few hours left before dawn, and she knew that her Master would not live long enough to greet it unless she somehow intervened, and quickly. It was perhaps a suicidal risk, and if she was wrong then it might compromise both her own and Jackel's chances of survival. But she knew that she had to at least try. There was simply no other choice available.

Westminster was busy as she reached Parliament Square, and she moved swiftly across the maze of streets and out onto the bridge, negotiating the throng of the early hour traffic. She had taken no more than a few paces before she caught sight of The Howler, standing on the pavement in the middle of the bridge, his hands deep in the pockets of his coat, his face shrouded by the shadows cast by the streetlights overhead. Alexia slowed her pace until she was within yards of him, but he did not advance, or even raise his hands from his coat. There was no threat in his stance, just a statement of frustrated contempt.

"You have returned," was all he said.

She had still not thoroughly worked through all that she was going to say to him when finally they would come face to face, and all that she knew or thought she knew came out in one simple word.

"Cal'Beha," she uttered.

The Howler stared at her in silence for a few moments, long enough for Alexia to doubt that her suspicion was even true, or even to wonder whether she would have time to get off the bridge alive a third time. The Howler, however, still made no move towards her, but kept his distance a few yards away. Had he even heard her, Alexia wondered? He made no response to confirm that he had. But then he took a step towards her, and Alexia wondered if this was where her death would come after all.

"I have not heard that name in a very long time," Cal'Beha murmured. "I had forgotten that it used to be my name. With no one to call me it, it became nothing but a redundant word."

"But it is your name," Alexia said now, "and the one person who used to call you it now needs your help once again."

Cal'Beha stared at her. It was obvious that he did not know the revelations of the night.

"Jackel El'a'cree is no longer a prisoner," Alexia told him. "But he needs your protection now more than he has ever done."

"He is alive?" The Howler whispered, daring to believe the truth.

"But not for much longer. Even now he may be fighting for his life."

Cal'Beha took another stride towards her, and Alexia stumbled back a step as his huge black wings spread out from beneath his long great coat like two colossal sails eager to blot out the sky beyond him. Another stride and he had hold of her, lifting her high up into the night sky as he swooped up and off the bridge.

Alexia clung to him with all her strength as they continued to soar up and over the parliament buildings, before the dark sprawling metropolis of London spread out before them like a carpet of tiny fires caught up in a vast soup of grime and black tar.

"I can't believe what you've done," Callie murmured, as she found Venice standing alone in one of the vaults of the underground station.

"I know," Venice replied quietly. "But what's done is done. I only hope that Alexia can forgive me."

"That's not what I meant," Callie said to him.

Venice had kept his back to her, but he turned now to look down into her young wide eyes. She was studying him intently, those eyes glistening brightly in the half-light.

"What do you mean then?" Venice asked.

"I just can't believe that you betrayed Casta like that."

Venice stared at her.

What was she talking about?

"After all that he gave you, this is how you repay him? And in his moment of triumph?"

Venice suddenly couldn't think. Although she was a vampire and had been one for a few decades, she was trapped inside a young girl's body, and he had always thought of her as one. But these words that were coming from her mouth were strange indeed. They had no place being there.

"How do you know -"

"- that you've been spying for Casta Mica'tore?"

Her right hand had been inside her coat during this brief exchange, but now it was out and in front of her. It was shrouded by shadow, and he could not see what it held, but his hands were suddenly trembling at the intent.

"Because I've been spying on you, Venice," she

251

answered her own question with a grin.

Her hand had already risen, swiftly and towards him, and he watched almost helplessly as she found her target before he'd even had a chance to evade her. She was quick, and keen. He felt the stab of pain explode throughout his body, his thoughts blackening and his senses dissipating rapidly. He had only a moment to register her cruel satisfaction, before he dropped to the ground, and came apart in a ragged shower of dark dry dust.

Jackel's right arm hung at his side, torn and useless, his stomach running with rivers of blood, while Emma lay slumped and shuddering at his feet, her fight gone. Two soldiers pierced his legs with their talons, another had taken hold of his neck, but he had one of their own clamped hard in his jaws and was tearing at their flesh. Screams of rage filled the air on all sides, as did the pop of punctured skin, and a rain of blood filled his sight to soak his body. The image of Casta Mica'tore came only in snatches between their glistening raw bodies, grinning and triumphant, but it was enough to strengthen his fight, even as he felt his knees crack beneath the fresh assault of yet another of his soldiers.

It felt as though a burning lance was searing his innards as something razor sharp penetrated his abdomen. The strength in his legs went momentarily and he dropped down onto one knee, a blood-curdling howl piercing the din raging all around him. But he barely had time to register it, not even as that lance of jagged bone was tugged back out of his body, and he slumped down to the ground. He waited for the final blow to come, but instead of a new agony, he felt the claws withdraw from his legs and neck, and a sudden freedom fall over him. His eyes flickered upward, uncertain and unable to focus through the blinding mask of blood that coated his face, but he could just make out that the undead creatures that had felled both he and Emma had backed away a few yards.

The howl came again, shrill and piercing, but his sight could do nothing but fix itself on the soldiers before him. His strength had all but left him, and he could do nothing but shield himself feebly with his left arm. But as one of the soldiers lunged forward, its claws raised high above its twisted head, it suddenly came apart in a shattering explosion of bone shards and pulp as something came at it from behind. Jackel struggled through his confused senses to make out just what had saved him, but it moved too fast through the shadows for him to unravel its shape. The army continued towards him, ignoring the fall of their unnatural brother, but they too were severed in half by the same lethal force.

Jackel flashed a look past their toppling bodies to see Casta cast another incantation, his spell dispatching his remaining army towards him, urging them quickly to destroy his enemy while he was fallen. He watched in horror as they shunted forward on his word, this group of ragged nightmares, limbs extricated from shins, teeth born from bone, flesh bound, grown and sown.

Yet again his saviour came, swooping down from the dark vaulted ceiling to take hold of one of this last twelve, and ripped its angular head from what shoulders it had been given. Its legs buckled even as its claws sought to tear gashes in the creature that had halted its progress, and Jackel now had a view of who this was that was destroying Casta's army, his eyes able

253

to focus now that he was blessed with so small a respite, and he praised him, just as he had praised him so many years ago. Cal'Beha.

He felt a jagged claw cut deep into his shoulder as one of Casta's squad found him from behind, and Jackel cried out in pain as it began to rip the flesh from his body. The torture did not last long however. He turned briefly to find yet another vampire fending off this attack. Her face he did not recognise, but he knew her instantly as a Faraoh. She took his arm now, and tugged him back away from the frenzy still raging. Even as he looked he could see Cal'Beha snapping the spines of two of the killers as they plunged at him down the blood-washed nave. The remaining eight had already eluded his protector, but it was this woman who leapt past his mutilated body to save him yet again.

She threw herself at them, finding their raw eyes and jagged claws in a fury of aggression, a snarl of her own growling angrily in her throat. She was already wounded from a previous battle, he could see, but still she fought hard with whatever strength remained.

She was struck down quickly, but her attack had been enough to save him. Cal'Beha descended with a fury as he took hold of them all, his flesh bloody and wet from a series of brutal wounds. Still he battled on, even as they overpowered him and sank their claws deep into his flesh, pulling it from his bones as he struggled to destroy them. His howls came again now, but of pain and agony as they broke him. It was eight against one, but still he fought, even as his legs were cracked, and his arms were snapped, and his skull bashed in with rocks and fists.

A ball of light crackled the length of the nave

towards them, stealing the sight of The Howler's demise. But beyond its halo of livid intensity, Jackel El'a'cree could just make out the hunched figure of Casta Mica'tore, his hands outstretched and performing this other terrible magic. Jackel could feel the heat of the furious orb as it sought to destroy him, its heat searing his torn skin, its power boiling his blood. The respite that Cal'Beha and the other vampire had afforded him had at least been enough for him to recoup some of his strength, but even with his physical powers so depleted and torn, he attempted to conjure some of his own magic that he had once possessed.

The light burned him even as he conjured a wave of fire in retaliation. He felt the ground shudder all around him as the two magics met, igniting the wooden seats of the church and rocking the already crumbling masonry of the abandoned building. The beams shook and the ground creaked, the blast of their magic tearing at the very limits of the structure's strength. Through the maelstrom, Jackel could see that his fire had been unexpected, and grinned through his blood-washed mask at the sight of Casta Mica'tore stumbling to keep upright. He saw too, as the other vampire composed himself for retaliation, the second burst of magic as it left his fingertips.

Jackel sprung forward, as much to save those who had fought at his side than to destroy his enemy, and hurled all his energies into a single bolt of fury. The resultant boom as the two magics met this second time, not only shook the borders of the old abandoned church, but also at the very fabric of existence. It shocked the Master Jackel El'a'cree just how much Casta had learned in the years he had been away, and as the floor beneath his feet shuddered and began to pulse like a grisly soup, so he realised that the forces that had been exerted between the two vampires had the potential to destroy them all.

Screams of terror mingled with blood-curdling cries, and creaks and crashes pounded the air as the vaulted ceiling cracked and toppled. Stone shattered and wood splintered, and the world that they had been a part of for so long suddenly came apart beneath the tumult as it refused to sustain such powers that were being forced upon it.

EIGHT

FLIGHT

People would come looking, that was the first thought in Jenner's mind, come to stare at the building with the two gaping holes punched through it. People would gather out in the street, and then would come the police, cars full of them. They would have their questions, innumerable questions, and when they broke the door and found what remained of the two dead officers, those questions would rapidly increase. He had nothing now. No home, no life, no Emma. A decision needed to be made, and it quickly made itself. He had no choice but to leave his home and flee. Going where and to who were just two questions, but they could both only have the same simple answer.

Montague.

The big house was quiet, and there was no reply when he repeatedly buzzed the intercom at the gate. Scaling the tall iron railings, he hurried quickly across the courtyard, only to find the doors all locked, and the windows firmly secured. It seemed that Montague had already taken flight.

Jenner stood in the courtyard staring up at the house beneath a light drizzle that had begun to fall from the night sky. What now, he thought desperately to himself? Of the only person who could possibly help him, there was now no sign. It was certain that he had not simply slipped out for a few hours, because Montague never left the house. There was too much danger for a man of his knowledge to walk the streets. And besides, what was out there for him to go looking for that his sources could not bring to him? No, Montague had already learned of the assault on his flat, the importance of this being far graver than he himself had imagined, and had disappeared out of harm's way. But why would he leave him high and dry? There were so many things that he could still do for Montague, secrets that he was certain Montague would not know of himself. Jenner thought hard, but the same thought kept surfacing.

The coward had fled.

A flickering light from inside caught his attention then, a pale beam passing across the surface of one of the upstairs windows, and for just a fleeting moment, Jenner gave hope that Montague was still inside. As the wind picked up and gusted veils of drizzle across the courtyard, Jenner made his way swiftly round to the back of the house, looking once again for a way inside. The back door, usually barred and bolted, stood slightly ajar, something that just normally wouldn't happen. It only then dawned on him, as he stepped closer to inspect it, that the light coming from inside was not being cast by Montague. With a quickening pulse, Jenner tentatively crossed the threshold, stepped out of the miserable night and entered the warmth of Montague's home.

The building was silent as he entered, and the corridors and rooms were as black the night outside. Treading carefully through parts of the house he had never even seen before, Jenner navigated his way in the direction of the stairs, to at least give him some kind of familiarity, and get his bearings for the ascent that would take him up to the intruder. The nature of this intruder he could only guess at - a customer perhaps, desperate for a fix, or maybe even a common criminal like himself - but he knew that it might be the only lead he might get in discovering the whereabouts of his sometime patron. Montague's house was an exceptional building, built at the turn of the century without the burden of expense. Every part of the building was ornate and built without restriction. The stairs, even with a plush red carpet to soften any footstep, would not creak beneath his step as Jenner began to climb, but nor too would it give up the footfall of the other secret occupant of the house. So it was, then, that Jenner climbed in silence, whilst listening earnestly for sounds that would not come from the upstairs rooms. It was not until he neared the third floor, and caught sight of that same pale shaft of light flickering between the banisters, that he could determine just where the intruder was.

He reached the landing cursing himself for not carrying anything that could be deemed a weapon. He had no idea who this intruder might be, but to be confronted would almost certainly bring an act of panic, perhaps even aggression, and he would only have his own fists to fight with if it came down to conflict. But it was as he eased open the door to Montague's study and caught sight of a figure standing in front of the leaded window, his frame silhouetted against the night sky beyond, that he froze and recognised him.

Jenner only had time to recall the sight of the gun holster and the rifle slung across his back, before he realised his predicament. What he had taken to be a single intruder was now a mistake. This was one of the skulkers from the van, and he realised his terrible situation immediately because he could find no trace of the others. His concerns did not last long, however, for a second later he felt the barrel of a gun at his back and saw the second member pull the door out of his hands and usher him further inside.

"For a thief, you're not particularly stealthy," said the skulker at the window, without looking round.

The partial light dimly illuminated his face but Jenner did not recognise him. This, he presumed, had been the driver of the van, the one that had been named Grunt. He looked round at him now, and his face disappeared instantly into shadow, transforming it into nothing but a talking mask.

"We saw you out in the courtyard," he continued. "It didn't take much to follow your movements."

"I had no idea I had to hide," Jenner replied, defiantly.

"I would've thought you had every reason to hide. And not just from us. Why do you think your boss has run? He knows he's a dead man. I'm just surprised that you haven't figured it out."

"I think I've got a pretty good idea, Grunt. My flat's just been totalled."

"We know," the one who had opened the door informed him. It was Vapour. "We saw."

"You saw?"

"We were outside. Down in the street."

"And you did nothing?"

Vapour glanced across at Grunt, and then back at Jenner.

"That was some pretty hefty creature. We don't know what kind of shit you've got yourself into to be having something like that come knocking, but be sure that we'll find out."

"It'll give us something big to bag," added Grunt, with a smirk.

"Is that why you're here? Trashing Montague's office looking for clues."

"You had your chance, boy," Grunt exclaimed now, from the shadows by the window. "We're doing it our way now."

Jenner stared at him, both angry and afraid. There was so much going on that he could only guess at, and he watched helplessly as the black silhouette of Grunt continued to stare back at him motionless. It was like a still from a movie, the silhouette against the stormy backdrop of night. It was almost surreal how spooky it looked. But little did he know that it was about to get a whole lot spookier.

The scene was motionless. But then something within that scene moved, and it was something that should not have moved. One of the curtains behind him suddenly lifted, almost too slowly to be real, and a third unknown figure glided into view. It was too dark to make out much of what happened, but this other figure descended upon the first in a coming together that reminded Jenner of the embrace Jackel El'a'cree had made with Emma. Here was this figure of Grunt, staring at him without movement, ignorant of the other figure now biting down hard into his neck. One hand seemed to seize his chest, effortlessly restricting any resistance he might have, while a second hand seemed to clutch at his throat as if to break it. Jenner thought he heard a breath slip, a soft breath that could either have carried a note of death or of pleasure. The scene before him lasted only seconds, and then he watched as the body of the skulker

261

slipped from the deathly grasp of the vampire and toppled awkwardly out of sight towards the pitch black floor.

There were already shouts in the air, and it shook him violently from the stupor that the sight had induced in him. He stood helpless and frozen as Vapour pushed past him, Rocket appearing out of the shadows to draw his gun, as they both rushed to save their fallen comrade. Jenner knew that it was already too late, even as he stood and watched the vampire recede back into the shadows, back into the realm that would afford him protection from the eyes of those that would do him harm.

"You will die," threatened the vengeful voice out of the darkness. "You will all die, and soon. I hope you lived your lives well."

The two remaining skulkers fired a series of desperate shots into the shroud of darkness where the vampire had last stood, but there was simply nothing more to be seen, no more to be heard. Rocket and Vapour were shouting now, Vapour attending to his colleague who was already dead, as Rocket rushed forward to search the shadows for the demon who had disappeared inside them as though they were camouflage. The vampire had been there all along, of that there was now no doubt, watching them as they had searched the room, choosing his moment for when he would descend upon them, and take their lives swiftly and effortlessly.

"Shit," Rocket was cursing, stumbling about the room in a futile attempt to find at the killer, his gun sweeping the darkness for the vampire that they knew was already gone. "Shit. Shit. Shit. Fucking vampire. It got Grunt. It got Grunt."

He turned aggressively upon Jenner suddenly, as though it were all somehow his fault.

"Now do you see?" he raged. "Now do you see why we kill these fucking things?"

"I know, I know," Jenner exclaimed, defending himself from Rocket's grasp upon him. "One of them killed my girlfriend, remember? One of them destroyed my flat. There are two dead officers lying in pieces in my bedroom, and when they find them, I'm a dead man."

Rocket gazed hard into his eyes as his words slowly sank in.

"Shit," the skulker relented finally, releasing his grasp upon him. "But know that when we finally meet your friend Montague face to face, we will be having more than a simple chat with him for what he has done here."

"I'd like to argue with you, I really would, but I just don't have an argument. Not any more. I've lost too much."

Jenner backed away and left the two skulkers after that, turning away from them and leaving them to tend to their murdered friend. He had no idea what he would now do, but as he slowly wandered down the stairs, his head whirled with forced memories of conversations had with his benefactor. Had he mentioned the locations of any safehouses? Had he let slip anywhere that might be deemed a shelter or sanctuary? He wracked his brain over and over as he continued down the staircase, but even when he reached the downstairs hallway, he still had no idea.

It startled him as a figure suddenly loomed out of the blackness of the shadows, sweeping out of one of the rooms, and Jenner stumbled sideways before

263

grabbing hold of the banister for support. Montague's name slipped from his mouth as if to address him, but the voice that came back was not from that throat, but from one that he'd not heard in a very long time.

"You guessed it wrong, boy, but it's the same guy that I came here to see, same as you."

Jenner fumbled in his pocket for his cigarette lighter, tugging it from the lining and sparking a flame to confirm that the voice did indeed match the face. The yellow flame sent distorting patches of light across the man's face, and Jenner couldn't help but loose a sigh of relief as he murmured his friend's name.

"Kole," he said.

"The one and only."

"How the fuck are you? I've been looking for you everywhere."

"I been around, boy," the cigarette lighter illuminated a deep grin on Kole's face. "You probably just not been looking in the right places."

"What are you doing here?"

"Same as you, Jen, looking out for Monty."

"Working for him too, huh?"

"Working for someone else, as it happens. I just wanted to show my face."

"Well, good luck. Things have turned to shit and he's run."

"Well that's too bad. I was lookin' forward to showing my gratitude, y'know, for bringing me into the field that we're in. Killing an' that."

Jenner stared at him.

"Killing?"

The cigarette lighter illuminated that grin on Kole's once again.

"Not directly related t'you, o' course, but you've

made your deaths, we both know you done."

"I've never killed anyone, Kole. You've got to believe that."

"I know you don't, Jen, I'm jus' fooling with ya. But your deeds led to the deaths of those two policemen, huh, and let's not forget that lovely Emma now."

Jenner stammered for breath, his system shuddering with the reminder of Emma's death, his stomach turning over with the thought that it was now common knowledge amongst those living in London. Just how did Kole know about that? The question must have been voiced in his eyes or in his silence, because Kole answered it the very next moment.

"The woman at ya window told me. She say you were very upset. Pathetic, I think she say. Bad breaks, boy."

"How -"

"Come on, Jen, you were always quicker than this. Give it a think."

Kole's grin broke again, and was it because Jenner was now searching his friend's face harder than he'd been doing before, or was it simply because Kole was allowing it to be seen, but he could now make out the trace of something glistening across his lips. He saw it plainly now, a smear of scarlet across his lips and chin, traces of it coating his teeth that now seemed to gleam in the brightness flickering from his lighter.

"No -" Jenner stammered.

"Afraid so, boy," Kole confirmed, with a shallow nod.

"When...?"

"Don't worry 'bout it, it were a long time ago. While you were inside, in fact. I took on a couple o' ya duties, delivering some shit to a few willing customers. One o' them fancied the real thing, y'know, and - wham - that was it."

Jenner took a step back as he watched the sight of his old friend. How could this be? First he had lost Emma, and now Kole. It was becoming too much to bear. But then the vampire took hold of his arm, his grip like freezing granite against his skin, and Jenner couldn't help the shiver of fear that came.

"Don't worry, Jen. I'm no here to hurt you. How could I harm my ol' friend, anyway. Not with them marks already upon ya neck. I see someone got there first. Just a little snack, though, huh?"

Jenner felt Kole's fingertips rise up towards his neck, searching out the puncture wounds that Jackel had left there. The thought of it sickened him afresh, but before he could do anything else, Kole spoke his final words to him, words that Jenner could not think of any reply to.

"Was nice to see you again, though, boy. I be looking for you out on the battlefield. Maybe we even share the same side one day, no?"

No, Jenner heard himself say inside his head, but even as the word came, Kole had already slipped away into the darkness and was gone, leaving Jenner to stand alone in Montague's large unlit house.

NINE

LEAVING THE REALM OF THE KNOWN
AND HATED

The heavens opened as Jenner left the house and stepped back out onto the pavement, a torrent of rain falling on the city like an angry sea. Thunder boomed across the heavy skies as it rocked rooftops and shook buildings, lurid flashes of lightning sparking in bright white peals inside the blackest of ebony skies. It was the cruellest night that could ever be imagined, but through it Jenner could just make out the shape of a figure, hunched and watching him from an archway across the street. He might almost have ignored the sight, except that the figure now beckoned to him with furtive curls of his hand. Jenner tugged his collar up against the torrent of rain, his hair already a river cascading harsh rivulets into his eyes, and approached the man cautiously. After all that had happened over the past few days, and all the new players that this city had seemed to have possessed, this stranger preferring to remain hidden seemed like a godsend. Only when he reached the pavement and a flash of lightning lit the scene around him did he realise who this stranger was, and he uttered his name rather more loudly than he'd expected, given those that were seeking out his throat.

"Get off the street," Montague hissed, reaching to haul him into the shadows of the archway.

"Do you have any idea how many people are

looking for you?" Jenner exclaimed, searching the frantic expression of the man and realising the full truth was already painted there in stark colours.

"I thought you would come back," Montague told him, wiping the rain from his face with the whole of his hand. His suit and overcoat were sodden. He had clearly been waiting a long time.

"You came back for me?" Jenner was incredulous.

"Does that seem so hard to believe?"

"Frankly, yes."

"You may not believe this, but out of all those that I have worked with over the years, you were the most loyal, the most trustworthy. And now such commodities are valued above anything else, I came back for you."

"Just what exactly is going on?" Jenner demanded to know, the question that he'd been wanting to ask for days suddenly out.

"We have to get out of this city," Montague confessed. "But not just this city, away from this whole place."

Jenner gazed at him, confused by his words, his lunacy echoing those of the skulker Rocket. Just how exactly were they going to leave the world behind? The world was all they had.

"There are portals," Montague told him, as if to explain his unspoken questions, "gateways between our world and another more dangerous place. You asked me before about the drug that you'd been trafficking, and the deaths that have been occurring, and I think that now might be a good time to tell you the truth."

Jenner's gaze was still all he had, dumbfounded and lost for words, as the rain continued to berate them.

"What you have been supplying to my customers is blood, powerful blood from this other world. The people that buy and sell this blood are mostly from this other world too, and it is the dealing of this blood that has made me my money."

"People are buying blood?" Jenner exclaimed. "What are they doing with it?"

"What do you think they're doing with it? They're drinking it."

"Drinking it? They're drinking blood?"

"These people, they're... not like us."

"No shit they're not like us."

"They're dead, Jenner. They're undead, vampires, or whatever else you want to call them, but they need blood in order to survive."

"So those vials I carried were full of blood? I thought it was called The Blood just as some kind of cool street nickname."

"Its full title is the Blood Of The Ancients, and it is exactly that," Montague attempted to explain, wiping another layer of rain from his face with the whole of his hand. "The earliest vampires in their world are known to them as the Ancients, and it is their blood that is collected and distributed, as far as I can understand. There is a sort of black market, and I simply provide a service. My contacts have grown considerably over time, both my suppliers and my customers -"

"And you've grown rich because of it?"

"Vampires desire that blood more than anything else, Jenner. It is rich, powerful, and they would do anything to drink from the source."

"Is that why they kill each other?"

Montague thought this over for a moment, perhaps

thought it over too much.

"That's just it," he said at length. "I really don't know. Some of the vampire community blame me for the deaths, using the trade of the Blood as an excuse."

"Does that mean they blame me too?"

"I've told them that you're ignorant of what you were trafficking -"

"So they do?" Jenner was becoming anxious as well as angry. "The woman by the window. No wonder she spat those threats at me. Shit. She wants me dead."

"That's why we're leaving."

Jenner looked hard into Montague's eyes now. He did indeed look like a troubled man.

"Look, Jenner, I don't want anything to happen to you any more than I want anything to happen to me, and of course I blame myself for involving you. But these vampires have been misled. I am not trying to have them killed. Why would I? They are my livelihood."

Jenner wiped the rain from his face now and took a haggard breath.

"So where do we go from here?" he asked.

"I have a friend, his name is Coda-Beda, and he will help us. He knew more than I that the situation was escalating, and he's been hanging on for as long as he can while the market lasts. It is he who knows where the portal lies."

"And he'll be coming with us?" Jenner asked, uneasily.

"Not quite," Montague murmured hesitantly. "He said that he'd rather go to California instead."

*   *   *

They went to a small park, just over a mile from Montague's house, and waited for their contact to arrive, during which time neither one of them spoke much at all. What else was there to say that hadn't already been said, or implied, or was even unable to comprehend? The storm had worsened and the rain had started to come down harder, and it took a little over an hour for Coda-Beda to finally appear. He was a small man, plain and unnoteworthy, and he pulled up at the entrance to the park in a small dark saloon. He was nothing like Jenner had drawn in his mind, and hadn't even visualised a vampire owning a car. It seemed all too ludicrous. In his imagination, he had painted the vampire blood-dealer as a huge brutish figure, his face disfigured, perhaps even with only one eye, with a growl in his throat and a sackcloth robe draped across his back. What he got, when he and Montague finally clambered into the car and could see him more clearly beneath the bright interior light, was a well-presented gent in an expensive suit, with neatly trimmed black hair and a single gold earring.

"We've got until sunrise," Coda-Beda explained quickly, as he pulled back out onto the road. "An hour at most until things escalate to crisis point and I'm caught red-handed, so to speak, if things haven't already turned to shit."

"I hear you're going to California," Jenner found himself saying.

He was sitting in the back seat, and the vampire cast him a glance over his shoulder for the first time since he had entered the car.

"Yes," he confirmed his intent in a matter-of-fact kind of way, his cold grey eyes taking in the sight of

271

him quickly, his clothes, his eyes, before returning to navigate the rain-lashed road ahead of them.

"Why California?" Montague asked him this time.

"Can you think of a better place to spend my riches? I risked my life bringing The Blood into this city. Do you think I'm just going to lie low when I retire? Hell, I'm going to live it up. Get fat in the state that never sleeps. Can you think of anywhere more fitting?"

From his place on the back seat, Jenner could see that Coda-Beda was grinning at this point, but when he looked for him in the rear view mirror, he was startled to find that he cast no reflection, and that all that he could see was the leather of the driver's headrest. Even though this so unnerved him, this undead back-street drug dealer driving them to sanctuary, to have him with them at that moment seemed somehow strangely comforting. But Jenner still wanted their time together to be brief. The vampire had promised them swift and safe passage. He just wanted the journey to begin and be out of the city as quickly as possible.

Coda-Beda told them, as they travelled, that the air was agitated - things were coming, things bad, things cataclysmic - but neither Montague nor Jenner could feel anything. Their journey took them deep into the heart of London, through gloomy wet streets and thoroughfares already busy with vehicles and hurrying pedestrians, until they arrived at a hotel in the centre of Kensington. This was surely too busy a place for a dimensional portal, deep amid the bustling streets of one of the most popular areas of London. Even at this hour, cars and vans dashed across lanes, pulled up at kerbs and honked at one another. Jenner kept thinking, even as they clambered quickly out of the car, that there were just too many eyes to see them, too many people that could be more than they seemed, ready and eager to have their necks snapped, out of malice or hatred or both.

But there were no knives or guns thrust at them as they made their way urgently across the pavement, not even as they entered the hotel and took the lift to the fourth floor. The corridor was quiet as they approached room thirty one, and as Coda-Beda pulled a key from the inside pocket of his suit and opened the door, so they all slipped quietly over the threshold, and into a very ordinary room, that apparently would offer them passage into a very extraordinary world.

The portal, when it became known that that was what it was, was not particularly inspiring. Jenner perched on the edge of a bed just yards from it before Coda-Beda explained just what it was and what it could do. It was an old wooden cupboard, standing in the corner of the room, with nothing more than a simple lock fastening the two doors together.

"That's it?" Jenner exclaimed, staring at it.

"What did you expect?" Coda-Beda replied, indignantly.

"I don't know," Jenner stammered, unable to take his eyes off it now, "but at least something with lights, perhaps even glowing or something, and a cool whooshing vortexy kind of noise."

Coda-Beda stared at Montague.

"I think he's taking the piss," Montague explained.

"I know what he's doing," Coda-Beda said, "I just wanted to know why you thought it prudent to save him, that's all."

"Hey," Jenner exclaimed. "It's just not what I expected, okay?"

"Look, I think you'd better say your goodbyes to this place," Coda-Beda told them, raising his voice authoritatively, "because if you're smart, you won't be making the trip back again."

"Are you sure you won't come with us?" Montague asked him, taking his hand.

"No," he replied. "I've been there before, remember? There's nothing waiting for me in Kar'mi'shah now but bloodshed and death. No, California's the place for me. I've seen it in brochures and on TV. Everything a rich man of the flesh could ever want."

It was hard to hear these words and not think of them in the same context as human longing. But this vampire's idea of pleasures of the flesh was surely something completely different, and Jenner couldn't help thinking, even as he watched this vampire at work, that perhaps part of him wanted to go to the west coast of America with him, and lap up the land of endless sunshine and endless beautiful women. There'd be no sunshine for their guide, of course, and no doubt he'd end up leaving a trail of murdered victims in his wake. But it was as he thought this, and as he watched Coda-Beda unlock the cupboard, that the insanity of his situation suddenly loomed once again - they were in the middle of London, talking about horror film rejects that drank blood, and old cupboards that could take you to magical worlds. This was ridiculous. The whole thing. And he was just sitting here in the middle of it all taking everything in.

His eye strayed to the door, and for just a moment

he thought about walking out through it, back out into the world that he had always known. But then his memory conjured up the hideous image of Emma lying dead on his sofa, the sight of the two dead policemen that had rotted on his carpet, and the tiny cell that he had spent those prison years in. Yeah, that was the world he knew, that was his cosy little world that he belonged to. So what if this idiot here thought there was a door to another world in his battered old furniture? So what if he was being dragged through the streets of London because of it? At least it was a distraction from the shit he called his life. Dawn was nearly upon them, the brightening sky outside was proof of that at least. Then the sunlight would illuminate another shitty day for him. Who was to say what was right or wrong? The man in front of him unlocking the cupboard? The man he had known as Montague, now extending his hand again for the other man to shake? It was fucked up, all of it. He felt sick.

"I will miss you, Montague," he heard Coda-Beda say.

"And we are never to meet again?"

"Not unless you find another portal connecting a world of vampires with Los Angeles."

"Who knows then," Montague said with a smile.

Just fucking get it over with, Jenner found himself thinking, as he watched Montague pump the vampire's hand again, before being ushered towards the cupboard door. It was then, as Jenner watched his foot tread upon the wooden base of the cupboard, that the following moment seemed almost to occur in slow motion. He heard the door to the hotel room click open. His head turned, absently, and his eyes fell upon a beautiful pale-skinned lady, her long black hair billowing gracefully behind her. She was dressed all in black, too, a long black cloak that shrouded most of her body, and she seemed almost to glide into the room to join them, her eyes transfixing him utterly. Then his mind connected all the thoughts that were slowly putting these pieces together, and her identity came to him in a shuddering instant.

This was the woman who had clung to his window.

"Catherine."

Her name came not from her own lips, but from Montague's behind him. Jenner turned to look at him, but Montague's attention was already ensnared utterly by the sight of this woman, and his expression was one of absolute terror. He was stumbling back now, his lips repeating over and over the name that seemed to horrify him so. She came after him, however, gliding across the floor, apparently with no weapon in her hand, but with more than enough malice and threat in her intent.

"I have found you," she hissed, "attempting to escape your crimes. Your guilt is proven and I will now have my revenge for all that you have done against us."

"No," Montague managed to stammer. "I have never hurt any of your kind. I swear."

"And you," she turned her icy stare upon the vampire who had led them to the hotel, "you are the one who has traded with this foul creature. You have sold what was not yours and profited by our loss."

"I have brought The Blood to those who could never have tasted it," he tried to reason, but the woman would have none of it.

"You have brought shame upon your tribe," she seethed, "and death upon yourself."

Jenner saw that her eyes, focussed and intent as they had been, suddenly strayed from the two mortals for a moment and settle upon the old wooden cupboard. She began to speak again, threatening them afresh, but then her words simply froze in her mouth. Her lower jaw hung open slightly, as she took in the sight of this furniture again, until she managed to utter a short and simple question.

"Is this it?" she whispered, her breath barely audible, her eyes unable to leave this most precious object before her.

"It is," was Coda-Beda's even shorter reply.

"It leads to Kar'mi'shah? To home?"

"It will take you there, yes."

"Oh," Catherine breathed, drifting slowly towards the wooden doors that still stood ajar. "Could it be true that my home lies just beyond this door?"

"It is true," Coda-Beda told her. "Kar'mi'shah lies within your reach. Just go through. It is so simple to just go through."

Catherine made her delicate breathing sound again, and came to a drifting halt just inches from its threshold, her fingers straying delicately close as though the thing were made of gossamer, and might dissolve at her touch.

"I must... I must kill you," she murmured, without taking her eyes off the dark interior of the cupboard. "I must kill Montague. I have to. For... for Casta."

"Just go through," Coda-Beda repeated. "It is so simple to just go through."

"Yes," Catherine whispered, chanting the other vampires words like a mantra. "It is so simple. So simple."

Jenner watched as the black-haired vampire started forward, entering the cupboard without even stepping up into it. The plain back of the cupboard then seemed to shift and become protean, the wood becoming insolid and allowing this woman the ability to pass through. The journey, it seemed, from one world to another, was just as uninspiring as the portal itself, because the next moment the woman had gone, the back of the cupboard solidified behind her, and there was nothing to even mark her disappearance. She was there, and then she wasn't, her body simply passing through the back of the cupboard that had opened itself up for her. Coda-Beda had been right. It really was so simple.

Montague stood in awe at what he had just witnessed, and it was Jenner who now took the initiative to pass through. He stepped forward, just as Catherine had done, and readied himself to greet this strange new world. Just as he took a breath, however, someone took hold of his arm, and he spun round startled and found the wide terrified eyes of Montague holding him back.

"We should think about this," he began tentatively, his touch trembling against his arm.

"There's no time. You said it yourself, we have to be away and quickly."

"I know what I said. But what if she's waiting there for us on the other side."

"We don't know what's on the other side."

"Exactly. So what if -"

"But we do know what's waiting on this side. We can't expect anything more than to be killed, and we can't expect your friend here to hang around waiting for us any more either, right?"

The vampire shrugged on the affirmative.

"Come on, man," Jenner insisted. "I want to know what's going on in this other world."

Jenner rocked back on forth on his heels now, eager to be gone from this place now that the adrenaline had begun to course throughout his body. Montague still regarded the whole journey with fear and uncertainty, but slowly he began to nod his head, saying that yes, he was right.

Jenner took a deep breath, desperately trying to suppress a lunatic grin that had somehow found its way onto his face, and closed his eyes as he stepped forward into the gloom of the old wooden cupboard. The first step darkened the world behind his eyelids as the cupboard stole the light from the hotel room. The second step made his skin tingle as he imagined the back of the cupboard parting to allow his passage. The third step never even came, and his foot went down into nothingness, and seemed to swim there in a world where nothing existed.

There was no wind against his face, no lights to guide his way - not that he was even certain that there was a way for him to find - and the darkness simply cradled him as the void became complete. He tried to look ahead to find the vampire who had first entered, but of her black hair or black gown there was no sign. He tried to glance behind him to see if Montague had already begun to follow, but even if his eyes did find the space where he had first entered, there was nothing but blackness now in that direction too.

He seemed to hang in an inky black limbo, a void with no content, with no confirmation that he was even moving anywhere, his eyes playing games in the swirling darkness, conjuring shapes and faces in the ebbing soup. Where was he heading, he distantly wanted to know? To a pit of death or a lair of killers, or to a world of wonder and spontaneous redemption?

The darkness seemed to caress him suddenly, and warm currents danced across his skin in dry floating rivulets. Was this the world coming to greet him, he wondered, or the devil's breath inviting him into a never-ending hell of fire?

PART FOUR

DESOLATION

Desolation, *de-so-la'shon*, n. To be deprived of inhabitants; a place made desert; deserted; dead.

ONE

RUINS OF SELF

Casta had stood at the end of the nave, the altar of Christ at his back, and witnessed the scene of his plans crumbling to dust. The man he had called enemy for over sixteen hundred years, who had been just moments away from death, who had been left to writhe in agony just yards from where he'd stood, had remained very much alive. Blood had poured from the wounds that had covered his body, lacerations so deep that white bone had shone through. Injuries had been inflicted so severely that any other creature would have lasted only moments, and would surely have had no hope of survival. His enemy's death could not have been doubted, and yet he had fought, and even managed somehow to find strength enough to retaliate with a furious magic of his own.

Oh yes, his plans had turned to dust.

All of them.

Even though his imprisonment inside a box locked solid with dark incantations had lasted well over a thousand and a half years, Jackel El'a'cree had somehow been reborn stronger and more resourceful than he'd given him credit for, strong enough to put up resistance to his army, strong enough to bring unheard-of comrades into the fray, and strong enough to deliver power that could tear open a breach between them.

Casta had thought that Jackel had somehow conjured a violent threshold to a prison the likes of which he himself had lived out so many centuries inside. He'd thought that Jackel had torn open the world itself, ripping a gash in space that threatened to haul him into an abyss that held no hope of return.

Jackel's magic had stunned him momentarily, and that hesitation had cost him dearly. A burning desert wind had raged from the breach out into the nave, dragging everything that stood before it even as its blinding sands sought to fill the four corners of the church with alarming fury. The army of unnatural zombies that Casta had already seen slain before his eyes, had already become hidden beneath these furious dunes, their severed limbs that had been scattered throughout the old church like scraps from a bloody feast, now gone from sight. He had found himself quickly outnumbered as Jackel's furious sandstorm covered those that had fallen, and had been left to face his enemy's own miscreant army of fools alone.

But Jackel's vengeance lay somewhere beyond the sudden baking dunes that rose higher and higher against the pews and altars, it lay inside the breach that now tugged at his heels. And as much as Casta knew that he had to flee from those who would now seek out his throat, to be denied witnessing Jackel's own death after all that he had planned over centuries of unfathomable hatred, oh, that was simply too much to bear.

His enemies now outnumbered him, and in trying to prevent the escape of his quarry by blocking every other exit in the church, he had unwittingly prevented his own. The chasm torn by Jackel El'a'cree's hateful

284

magic, that even now was dragging broken furniture and unmade bodies deep into its clutching vortex, was to become his escape from death. It would take him away from those that would do him harm, but it would also steal the hope of reconciliation that he had dreamt of for so many hundreds of years.

Amongst the furious battles and the rains of blood, between the walls of fire and the bodies of the dead, his eyes had located the one solitary creature that had become more precious to him than the promise of the rule of all worlds. She had been lying face down in the sordid muck of blood and bone shards when he had finally laid his cold hard eyes upon her, and to see her just yards away, instead of from across a street or park or from the depths of a distant and shadowed alleyway, was simply bliss. But it was to be the most briefest of glimpses, it seemed, because the cruel storm snatched him so swiftly away inside its dry grasp.

But it was in that moment that he had feared for her wellbeing more than his own.

He had seen no movement in her body, no gasp upon her lips. There had been no tang of life upon her cold flesh, and no sign that she even lived. He had wanted to go to her - caring neither for the eyes that gazed upon him with hatred, nor for the hands that would reach out with vengeance for his throat - so that he might speak with her, comfort her, check that she even still lived, and to let her know all that had happened so very long ago in a world that they had once called home. But such pleasures would never come, for the thunderous boom that had rocked the old abandoned church had torn a divide so unstable and so furious, that to do anything but be dragged across its threshold was simply impossible.

Casta had felt himself slip even before he had tried to anchor himself to the dominion in which he'd lived for so long. His magic had been insufficient, and he had gone quickly into its clutching grasp, Jackel's hateful sandstorm eager to carry him away from her and deliver him into a hell destined to burn out all the hatred that he had in his cold dead heart for him.

The journey seemed to sear his skin as the sands carried him. Casta was aware only of an intense dry heat, burning deep into his body, as the raging howl of the wind dragged him through its tunnel. The passage battered his body, so furious was its will to haul him into Jackel's new prison, the portal hurling his frame finally into a hot and arid desert that baked beneath a black midnight sky.

His eyes opened amid a swirling dust storm, and he had to screen his eyes with both hands in order to discern just where Jackel had dumped him. Across a vast expanse of rugged dry scrub, an ominous range of jagged black mountains rose up before him, scything the heavy dark sky, dominating his vision. And as he struggled to his feet, his body bruised and battered, he wondered just what kind of desolate limbo Jackel was capable of conjuring, as he looked back at the chasm that streaked the sky for miles towards the distant horizon.

It was as he searched this desolate horizon and a familiar odour lingered inside his keen sense of smell, that a fear began to creep over him. The air was humid indeed, the wind carrying a heavy cargo of sand and detritus, but through it came the tang of blood, age-old blood, and the dull drone of mystical magic. His fear would not leave him, and as he stepped disbelieving towards those jagged black mountains, the certainty grew in him that such a place was not solely of Jackel El'a'cree's making. What if the portal had been a clash of both their magics, a clash of such immense proportions that -

No.

That was not possible. A clash of magics between himself and Jackel El'a'cree could not possibly rend a gap between two worlds.

Or could it?

The sandstorm continued to berate his body as he gazed across the dusty plains of scrub towards the ebony-black mountains. The smell of ancient blood came more strongly as the wind suddenly gusted, enticing him to believe the truth.

This was his home.

This was Kar'mi'shah.

A shrill cry pierced the wasteland just yards behind him, snatching his uncertain thoughts from a limbo far darker than the night's sky. Casta did not turn, but saw behind him another figure hurtle down out of the portal, dragged surely from the nave of the church, and only registered her tiny frame tumbling awkwardly as it hit the hard baked earth.

Projecting his sight backward, his cold merciless eyes regarded her without compassion and watched her crawl up to her knees, shuddering unsteadily from the ordeal. Even from such a distance, he could discern the taint of vampire blood that marked her hands. He tasted it on the air around her, and recognised it instantly as the lifeblood of Venice. There could be no mistaking it, and in that moment of verification, he had a moment of revelation too, understanding the sudden and unexpected appearance and intervention of Alexia in the church. All this he suddenly knew, even before he saw the face of the assassin, knowing that it was this assassin too, who had brought Alexia into the middle of a battle, inviting her to unnecessary injury.

"You followed me," Casta stated, his voice measured but managing to cut through the howl of the storm.

"Did you not hear my approach?" Callie yelled up to him, pushing her golden curls from her face as the wind snaked it. "I was in the church behind you. I saw your enemies fall."

Casta continued to keep his back towards her as she lay in the dirt. He did not want to look at her. She had brought Alexia into the middle of his battle. She had unwittingly hurt the only person he cared about. She might even have led her to her destruction.

Casta's eyes suddenly glazed as he stared out at the mountains, his sight distant, almost vacant. Callie went to speak again, to plead with him, but Casta merely uttered an answer for her, if only to keep her from speaking again.

"I did not hear you," was all he said.

"Where are we?" she continued, tentatively.

She heard him utter a rasping breath, a growl caught somewhere in his throat. And then he replied, as though the answer was obvious.

"Home."

Callie looked up at him for what could have been an hour, not daring to stand until he invited her, or even gave her reason to, as he gazed ahead into the darkness. She would have attempted to search his features that had been scarred a lifetime ago, but he would not return her scrutiny. She wanted him to say something, to assure her that everything would continue to plan, her deceptions made good, her murders validated, and that the cataclysm that had joined one world with another was just a part of that same plan.

She had heard him speak of another land so many times before, in secret meetings and in unlit hollows, in remembered dreams and insane fancies, but he had always recalled fondly a green world, fresh and verdant, with a vast pale moon that made the trees glimmer with a silver blanket, and the air sing with a bountiful fragrance. They had been Gods of a wonderful world, he'd told her. They'd had temples built in their honour, statues raised in forms of gold and marble, reflections of their image carved and painted and sown. They had been kings of a different order, and ruled a province so vast and divine that its equal had never been known in any other land.

But this was not the precious land that he had described. This was a baking desert of dust and scrub, with little life and no hope. It was dry. It was a hell.

"Are you sure this is Kar'mi'shah?" Callie asked over the storm, her voice hesitant, not wanting to question Casta's uncertainty.

"A cloud has descended," she heard him murmur over the howling din. "It shrouds what light there was. It chokes me, it blinds me, and I want someone to pull the blanket back from my face."

His words made little sense and they troubled her. He had often spoken thus, in riddles and at tangents, but she had never been one to ask for clarity from him. He was more powerful than she ever would be, with

289

magics so cruel and disturbing that he could take off her head if he so desired with a simple movement of his crooked hand.

"This sand has stolen the blossom of life," Casta continued beneath his breath. "Its shroud drowns the promise in its suffocating web of lacklustre lies, confusing the ground, confusing the sky. I can taste the past in the mountains, I can hear its sweet pulse in the rock and in the earth. The Blood is here. *I can still be Master.*"

The storm was beginning to pile shallow drifts of burning sand around her legs as she knelt on the rough desert floor, but her Master stood in silence now, looming over her like the jagged black mountains beyond, his silhouette stark against the midnight sky, dominating her vision. A hollow feeling of emptiness suddenly coursed throughout her body, and a chill crept across her skin despite the burning heat of the night. Callie could sense his anger, his insanity, but even being this close to him, she realised that she was alone. It came as no surprise then, when the vampire ahead of her suddenly started away, heading swiftly into the swirling maelstrom of the storm in the direction of the foothills without her. Swiftly she scrabbled to her feet, following in his footsteps as closely as the desert allowed, as it sought to cloak him in its swirling clouds of dull yellow sand with every yard that he covered.

She had only really asked him one question since she had been hurled into this hateful burning place, and although he had seemed to answer that question, she was not entirely convinced that he had answered it honestly. Could this burning hell really be the sacred land that he had called Kar'mi'shah? Could it actually be the opulent world that he had wanted all this time to fight for and rule? Callie thought that it hardly seemed worth the effort if it was. Surely anyone in such a position of kingship would have simply given this place up, handed it over without any such fight, and deemed themselves blessed that they had finally got rid of such a poisoned land, where nothing flourished but graves and despair. Could this possibly be his fight? A fight to command the dead that could never walk again, and the living who had already abandoned their homes?

TWO

RUINS OF STONE

For a long time Alexia had not been able to take her eyes off the far end of the church where Callie had appeared amidst the battle that had seen Jackel El'a'cree felled. The child vampire had not seen her, that much was plain, but her face had seemed captured by some mysterious frozen moment, transfixed by an event unknown to her. What that event might have been, Alexia could only guess at, but she'd had neither the proximity nor the opportunity to ask her, before she became sucked inside the raging void that had ruptured the building, along with the other vampire who had sought Jackel El'a'cree's life.

Callie's eyes, usually devoid of any human emotion, had seemed to let slip a series of them, tumbling one after the other, as the void took her. Not used to reading them from a vampire's gaze, Alexia had struggled to comprehend their authenticity as she saw them - sadness and fear, victory and regret - so many confusing looks in her wide blue eyes that it became difficult to discern her true nature or even her true feelings. Did she even have feelings, Alexia wondered? Up until this night she would have emphatically said yes. But to have seen her then, come to join this other vampire at the expense of both herself and Cal'Beha, carved a deep chasm of doubt into her mind. But perhaps she was not even reading it right. Perhaps Callie had just appeared and fallen as an innocent victim into the gateway that seemed to tear the very building in half. She would have no way of knowing for sure, not until she finally caught up with her, if ever she would, and be able to ask those questions to her face.

Alexia's own ability to stay grounded in the dominion she had grown used to did not last much longer. It was fierce, the pull of the portal's ethereal talons, and it had dragged her over its burning and deadly threshold before she could grab hold of any anchor, hauling her weak and defenceless body into a void of blinding sand that she had no strength or will to navigate.

It tugged at her body as it drew her deeper into that void, snatching the sounds of those left behind in the church inside the grip of a deafening and howling wind. It negated her senses as it tossed her through, and with neither sounds nor sights nor smells to discern, nothing could distinguish her passage between worlds. Until, of course, she reached the other side of the burning tunnel, where the source of the hot desert wind waited, and a new world rushed up rapidly to meet her.

She had hit the ground hard, the force of the blow knocking her consciousness swiftly from her, but when she had woken, presumably several hours later, her skin had been crawling with the threat of a rapidly approaching dawn. The storm had relented considerably, but still harried gusts of baking dry sand at her with a scathing intensity. Alexia had gazed around her in all directions, her acute sight barely piercing the dust clouds around her, but there had been very little to see anyway, just dry land and a barren vista of coarse bushes. Ahead of her stretched a vast horizon of jagged black mountains, their crests tearing a ragged line between the earth and an unblemished but brightening sky. Behind her were tangled forms, low-lying buildings of a rough construction, shacks or barns, certainly nothing grand. She had checked her senses once again, dazed though they were, and attempted to confirm, as well as she could, just where the portal had delivered her.

It was a rough and dry place, that was all that was certain, and she wondered if this was a hole between dimensions that either Jackel or the other vampire had created, perhaps even both as an explosion of their powerful magics, constructed rapidly to imprison the other. It certainly seemed like some kind of hell-hole where nothing could survive for long. She looked around her as her skin began to itch with the threat of daybreak, and she turned in circles as she searched for the nearest shelter. But in the middle of a desert basin, there was none.

Parched white sand stretched to every horizon, interspersed in places by dry scrub and gnarled trees. Even amongst all this desolation she could still make out a few creatures that braved such harsh conditions. Laying beneath one of the sun-bleached trees stretched a pallid scattering of white-boned lions, malnourished and weak, awaiting a dawn that would bring them better pickings. Peeking cautiously from above stumps of dead bush, rabbits and small fowl gazed in trepidation, hoping to witness that same dawn, if only to mark yet another victorious night of survival. From such a distance across the shimmering plains, and with only starlight to illuminate the expanse, Alexia could see so very little, but knew that at least some things lived, which in turn meant that at least she might find a meal or two.

Her thoughts returned to Callie, and the mysterious vampire to which she had seemed so attached in the crumbling rundown church. She had left no discernible trail behind her, or if she had, the desert wind had simply blown it away beneath its onslaught. Might she have stood on this very spot, watching the desert predators, and wondered about her shelter for the approaching dawn? Might she already have found some place to hide from its lethal rays? The thought of that dawn crept over her mind once again, bringing with it a fetid touch that could no longer be ignored. It would be upon her, and soon, and if she did not want it to desiccate her into the same dust that blew in such great clouds across these burning plains, then she knew that she had only one of two choices - hurry swiftly towards the mountains and hope that she could find some dark cavern to wait out the day, or keep the jagged range at her back and learn the source of the low-lying buildings, and hope that they might at least offer some kind of substantial shelter from the harsh sunlight that would soon be brightening the earth afresh.

She had covered perhaps only a quarter of a mile before she began to fear that she would not reach those buildings before the sun broke the skyline. She was covering vast distances at an immense rate, gliding swiftly across the dry earth at a pace that the desert lion could never have dreamed of. Daybreak was imminent, however, but even the incandescence of the brightening sky was enough to affect her flight. Such was the power of natural sunlight, just the lightening of the sky at her back seemed to cause her hips to grind against themselves, to force her knees to grate, and her shins to creak. The blood that flowed so furiously throughout her veins seemed ready to boil and burst through them, to drain her body of all fluids before drying her rapidly into dust. Her head became thick, forcing her thoughts almost to clot. Her mind defied her, and she stumbled frequently as the sun continued to threaten daybreak above the crest of the mountains behind her. She knew deep inside that as soon as it did, and the first rays of natural light touched her pale white skin, it would begin to burn and ignite her very being.

With the power of the sun forcing her flight into such a ragged pace, she had no idea how she finally reached the first of the rundown buildings and eventually managed to throw herself inside. Her skin was smoking as she entered, her body almost rebelling as the first stray shafts of sunlight broke the skyline. But somehow she made it to cover, her legs finally giving out as she crossed the dusty threshold, her shuddering limbs hauling herself further out of the reach of the sun that would crawl across the sky for the entire duration of the day.

The darkness was alive, that was all she was aware of. It pulsed around her, a soup-like rhythm that went on, and on, never slowing and never threatening to cease. Her eyes were open, of that she was certain, but there was simply nothing for her to see. In the midst of such an ethereal state, for a dream this surely was, she started slowly forward, and seemed almost to pass through shades of darkness, veils of matter that allowed her passage, as though they were doorways, opening and closing as they ushered her from one blissful shade of night to another. And it was blissful too, her being in this place of blackness, the pulse of the void pumping like a heartbeat, caressing like that of a mother's womb, reassuring her that she did indeed belong in this place.

A thought occurred as Alexia wandered between the silken veils, that the feeling of belonging came not from the caress of this dream-womb, or from the nurturing heartbeat, but from another source. The void of darkness offered her more than that. It offered her the comfort of home. And she dared to think that the portal that had dragged her from her beloved London, might actually have carried her across a realm of nothingness and delivered her back into Kar'mi'shah. But the thought was confusing, and even as she gave credence to it, the veils began to shiver with agitation, and the pulse began to shudder. But the seed of doubt had been sown, and Alexia could not recant her train of thought.

Suppose this was Kar'mi'shah, she could not help wondering inside her unconscious state, this blistering land where life had all but died beneath a blazing and merciless sun. But how could such folly be true? Kar'mi'shah had been palatial when she had been torn from its limits. It had been a city of vast and beautiful temples. Great stone monoliths had been raised by its adoring populace. Gleaming pyramids had been erected to honour those Gods that had brought prosperity to the land. Everywhere was good, and everything was splendid.

And then the fear resurfaced.

If this was Kar'mi'shah, just what had happened to bring such calamity?

The void of darkness seemed to thicken, the blackness solidifying to press hard against her skin. The pulse of the heartbeat now boomed throughout her body, threatening to pound the inside of her skull, and turn such rebellious thoughts to pulp. And in the swirling soup of darkness, strange images began to play themselves to her.

A door opened in one of the walls of a great stone temple, and sand began to billow out of the orifice, coating the land in a blanket that devoured everything before it, bringing a plague of death and famine in its wake. As the sand billowed out, so the temple began to crumble, its shards becoming the freight of the storm until nothing was left. The people that had once flourished and prospered inside the city now emerged from the dunes of sand like budding flowers, but as their heads broke the surface and reached upwards for protection, so those heads began to burn and decay, their ash flying skyward on a roaring burning wind.

Further images of death and rot filled the darkness ahead of her as she made her way through the veils that clutched at her skin. She wanted to wake, to take her chances against the sunlight of the day that surely still burned fiercely overhead, but the dream seemed eager to have her within its grasp for a little while longer, and played out yet more scenes of the populace of Kar'mi'shah as they met their ends in the most hideous of ways.

Shrines fell to dust, altars to sand, and all in front of the graves of the dead. Crops withered and choked beneath rising dunes of burning white sand, and the river that had once been the heart of the city ran dry as she watched. Life moved rapidly out of the land, and a sprawling death descended upon everything else that remained. A crushing weight seemed to attach itself around her neck as she struggled to take in all that the dream wanted her to see, and as that weight began to tighten and restrict her throat like a noose, so a cloud of dank matter pressed itself hard against her face like a clammy hand, ready to smother her, and bury her like it had so many others.

Alexia's eyes snapped open to the sight of a large wet snout investigating her face, her senses dispelling the horrible images of the dream as they tried to rapidly discern information about her surroundings. She was alive, that much was at least certain, and after that, there was a cow looming over her. Severely malnourished and swaying on four rickety legs, it teetered over her as she lay beneath its reaching muzzle, staring up at two expanding nostrils as it sniffed the haggard creature before it. As she tried to sit up, the creature became startled, and lurched backwards in fright, darting back towards a pen that stood open as Alexia cried out with a sudden pain.

She put her hands to a number of places on her arms and face, and found patches of skin that had been seared and blistered. She dimly recalled the terror of fleeing for her life across the rough desert plains, images of the brightening earth at her back, the memory of trauma. Turning her head, she gazed back at the doorway to the barn through which she must have come. The calm of night once again dominated the world, and she was glad that the heat had partially receded too. Placing her hands firmly on the ground, she tried to ease herself up into a sitting position, but as she twisted her body, her legs seemed almost to crumble as they threatened to cast her back into the dirt. Her head pulsed with a myriad of thick shapes, mirroring the swirling rhythms of the horrific dream she had just woken from, and she almost slipped back into its eager clutches. The haze began to settle as she lay there for a few moments, and knowing that her body would already be trying to heal itself, Alexia slowly hauled herself to her feet and made her way out of the barn, back into the cloudless night to confirm one way or another, that this barren wasteland of scorched desert was indeed the remains of what had once been her great majestic city.

The silvery wash of the moonlight illuminated her way through the featureless farmland, but as she passed by field after field, she could tell how meagre the bounty was. The land was still tended, that much was obvious, but she had to wonder at the persistence of the farmers. How could anything grow in such desperate conditions, and what possible reward could they reap? Shoots bloomed in paltry clutches in dry tilled rows, but even where they had taken, most had withered from the past days heat.

The farmland gave way to rough tracks as she progressed, the rough tracks to roads only partially covered with the encroaching desert. Here there seemed to be some semblance of her former city's industry, but what there had been once was now mostly weathered or destroyed. The roadway at least afforded some easy travelling for her, her legs complaining less and less as she made her way into an untidy area of huge flattened rocks, heaped up in great piles where they had fallen, like refuse and unwanted rubble. They might almost have been dismissed, except that the moonlight began to cast strange and familiar shadows across their eroded surfaces.

Alexia left the roadway to look closer at these rocks, and as she ran her fingertips across their coarse hard surfaces, found ridges that had been carved into them, pictures and images once set in stone many centuries ago. Sandstorms raging in off the desert had done their best to disguise all traces of the civilisation that had once ruled here, but now that Alexia bent forward to examine such works, memories flooded back into her head, merging with the pictures that her dream had placed there.

Much of the carving belonged to a language she'd long forgotten in the hundreds of years that she'd been away, but as she traced her fingertips across their patterns, certain words and phrases leapt out at her and she not help but raise a smile of wonder at seeing them again.

Across the surface of one of the columns, now toppled and crumbling, she found references to a Moon God, his name partially depleted beneath a gaping hole. Further down, she deciphered a passage outlining his ascension, rising from the depths of this very temple to bless the people of the city. A hollow pang grasped her chest suddenly as she continued to search for words and clues, her intrigue snatching a reaction that she had not felt in a very long time. The dream was true, this was her home, and these images proved that as much as the emotions now tugging at her. After sixteen hundred years of evacuation, she had finally come home.

Alexia only had a vague recollection of the sights and sounds of Kar'mi'shah, that much she now realised, but when the void had dragged her out of a world she had grown so very used to and delivered her into that terrible arid desert, the image that had filled her memory for so long clashed beyond recognition. The rich green land that she had remembered as the province of Kar'mi'shah had been overtaken by dust and sand. The river that had once wound its grand way through the city bore little resemblance to what lay dried and parched just a short distance away. As she stood now and gazed across the panorama of rubble and desolation, a weight seemed to descend upon her shoulders as she realised that the great temples and grand buildings of the metropolis that had once been its icons were now toppled and buried beneath vast dunes of uncaring sand. Kar'mi'shah had simply vanished, replaced by an encroaching wasteland. Even the air was heavy as it blustered across the dunes, with only the promise that it would continue until it had laid all it could find to waste.

This might not even have been her home, except that she knew now deep inside that it was. She might almost have tried to rationalise all that she saw, conjuring stories about wars that might have raged, or battles that may have razed her beloved city to dust. But all that greeted her eyes, all the desolation and the ruins, all of it was just something that no war could ever produce. This was simply death come to wipe the land clean of all that hoped to survive.

What had happened in those centuries she had been away? What could have turned the land so violently? It looked as though a cruel and steady progress of drought and decay had overcome the place, smothering the young and burying the strong. But just how was that possible?

Alexia stood and gazed around at the arid province, her joyous expectation of one day returning home now replaced with a hopeless dread. The land was still home to a few ragged settlements, a series of farms that stood in defiance against the desert, a few streets of mortals that dared to stand against the death that hung over their heads, but it was nothing compared to what had once stood in this very place. It was all a barren dry wasteland.

Even from such a distance, she could see that the portal still stood open across the desert plains behind her, a single dark veil that tore the night sky in half, a bruised threshold between one world and another. A thought entered her head then, tugging at her uncertainty, telling her to return to London, away from this heartbreaking wilderness, and back to sanity. But could she even do that? Would the portal even allow such return passage? And what was there in that dark city that she might ever truly call home? A quiet flat in Knightsbridge, the familiar banks of the Thames, Venice waiting for her on the bridge at Chelsea? Moments of tranquillity all of them, but that was all.

She was finally home now, she tried to keep telling herself, home in Kar'mi'shah. It was no longer the plush and verdant land that she had left some sixteen hundred years ago, but a desert with few motes of life, where death shrouded the scorched land. As she gazed about her, it occurred to her that it had been a barren wasteland for some time. Desolation such as this could not have occurred overnight. Death moved swiftly, but despair took awhile.

It was difficult for her to get her bearings, so destroyed was this place, and if only it had been as she had once known it, she would have been able to travel directly to any one of the many glorious temples within the city that she knew, and taken refuge in its dark subterranean catacombs, the daytime haunt of the imperious Gods, until she regained both strength and composure.

Alexia started away then, away from the crumbling pillars of stone that rose out of the dunes of sand, and on into what she hoped would be the greater parts of the city. Several times she passed what she thought she recognised as architecture of a temple of the Faraohs, but upon closer scrutiny she was disappointed at every turn. The midnight streets were deserted, except for a few scavenging rodents darting across the sands, and Alexia remembered how busy the city used to be, the populace lining the thoroughfares to witness the rise of the Moon Gods. They were hailed as Gods, the mortals fawning on them with every step that they took, offering flowers and incense to honour those that protected them. But to see these streets now, so deserted and lifeless, was almost too much to accept.

The roadway swept round suddenly to her right, on towards the dry banks of the river, and there amongst yet more heaps of rubble, she made out the silhouette of a broken cross. She stopped as she gazed down at it, her eyes making sense of the patterns of rock and debris in the darkness to make out the unmistakable carved figure of Christ adhered to it. A Christian Church, she thought to herself, and one of only a few inside the limits of Kar'mi'shah. She went towards it now, curious to see the shrine so few of the populace prayed to, her sight cutting through the shadows to make out the crown of thorns carved across the face of despair. As she reached the altar and gazed down upon the huge wooden cross, she recalled again the rumours of its effect upon the vampires sired in the other dominion. Perhaps if she had been born a BloodGod on Earth and renounced the church, she might not have been able to stand on this very spot. How many vampires would not have been able to stand where she now stood? And how many would have played on the source of those rumours only to kill the believers prostrate beneath it?

Leaving the ruins of the church, Alexia followed the banks of the river for a while, her mind lost to memories that grew as she walked. So many had she lost when the creature had appeared that night; members of her family, members of her tribe, all gone to dust. She had not dared hope that there might be some left to rule what remained of the city, but the more she traversed the remains of Kar'mi'shah, the more it seemed that they had all gone. Those that had not been killed by the creature in those few moments of chilling frenzy, had been killed by the passage of time. Nothing remained of the province of Kar'mi'shah. No Gods, no temples, no kingship. What few mortals remained, left to scavenge what little they could off the dry burnt land, were only waiting for the inevitable. Nothing was left. Not even hope.

As she made her way slowly along the banks of the river, the moonlight illuminating the dry cracked basin, her attention became suddenly caught by something tall to her left. Alexia idly looked up, her eyes dimly finding the outline of a monolith still standing amongst the dunes. So oppressive were her memories that she hardly took heed of it, or the fact that there was something still upright, defying the onslaught of the desert. But Alexia stopped now to gaze at it, her sight battling the images that whirled inside her head to make sense of the vast stone column. Why had she not seen it before, she suddenly wondered? It was something she recognised, something she knew, but her mind would simply not offer up a name for it, at least not readily. She went to it now, though, crossing the sands swiftly as an urgency came upon her. This was something of hers, something of the Faraoh tribe, and it stood against the desolation and the despair that choked this place.

As Alexia reached it, so her memories relinquished their hold upon her, and let its name finally enter her head. No sooner had it settled there, than Alexia voiced it aloud to the night air.

"Raza."

The monolith was almost entirely intact, and rose up into the heavy black sky like a vast silver needle, holding the honour of the Faraohs aloft for the whole province to see. Across its surface she could now see the once familiar symbols of her tribe, the moon and the stars, the animals of the forests, and the jackal at the highest point looking down upon them all. Her eyes graced every inch of the carved stonework for what seemed like hours, as she took in the magnificence of the sight, the splendour of her family, but when her gaze gradually lowered, she eventually saw the pyramid in which their final meeting had taken place, or at least what remained of it.

The glory of Kar'mi'shah had almost completely been destroyed, the huge stone blocks that had once been laid to stand against any onslaught, broken and scattered into a mound of heartbreaking nonsense. The ornate statues of the Moon Gods that had once dominated the grand plaza were unrecognisable. The elaborate arched entranceways through which the mortal priests had led processions and baptisms of blood had been swallowed, enveloped by the ravenous dunes. Everything was no more. The icon of Kar'mi'shah was gone.

Alexia stood for a few moments gazing across at the heaped mounds of broken rock and shattered stone, a hollow ache in her chest that cried of loss. This was her home, more than the fields, more than the rituals. The Raza Pyramid had been the centre of her world. She went to turn away, to put the terrible ruin at her back and keep it there, but as she went to leave, the desert wind brought something on its back that was not simply death and dry dust. There was a tang, a hint of something having graced this placed, recently, and it tugged at her curiosity. Such a place was crumbled to nothing, razed wholly to the ground. There could not possibly be anyone inside it. Surely.

Her heart, as dead as it was, told her to leave this place, to leave it to the ghosts that haunted its crumbled corridors and the phantoms that prayed to its shattered altars. But the wind brought that something to her senses once again, holding it in the air long enough for her to taste it and verify its nature as vampire.

Her senses froze as the revelation came. A vampire still stood inside the Raza. Could it be one of the Faraohs from the past? Could one of them have perhaps survived the holocaust and be left to rule what had become a hell?

Her sanity contested every hope as they came rocketing into her head, but she disregarded every negating thought, every notion that might disregard all the longing that kept her on that spot, and started away, on towards the broken ruins of the pyramid, with the intention of searching every block of stone and every splintered rock, until she found some way in to the hall of the BloodGods.

WONDERLAND

The ground seemed almost to be alive as they made their way through the forest of bleached white trees. Night had passed uneasily, strange noises coming down off the slopes of the mountains like baying wolves and grunting beasts, but by daybreak, all such sounds relented, and offered the dawn a blissful but heat-filled welcome.

Coda-Beda's old wardrobe in room thirty one of a Kensington hotel had promised them deliverance out of a world that threatened their lives and into a fabled place of ancient blood and immortal beings. The brochure had sounded better than the reality at first, Jenner gasping beneath an oppressive midnight heat and then fearing for his safety in an unknown outdoors, but when the sun had finally crested the jagged black peaks of the mountains, the clear blue skies had invigorated him like he had never recalled feeling before. Gone were the gloomy grey skies of London, the dismal spattering showers of grimy polluted rain, the honking of traffic, the aggression on the streets. The air was hot in this place, there was no doubt of that, but it was clean, and it seemed to burn the very toxins out of his lungs as he breathed it so deeply in.

Montague, however, had not seemed so enthralled, and complained bitterly and endlessly about the home that he had left behind him, his businesses and his monies, and all that he could have bought, his freedom included. Hindsight being what it was, his regrets were useless. It was a one-way trip, of that he was indeed certain, and he had not thought that he would change his mind once they had reached Kar'mi'shah.

Before they had even met with Coda-Beda, Montague had spilled out descriptions of a wonderland filled with triumphant temples and magnificent promenades, a palatial city the likes of which had long since turned to dust back on Earth. But there was no such city waiting for them on the other side of the wardrobe, and as the heat had set in and the baying and growling had drifted down from the slopes of the mountains, Montague had taken to muttering irrationally about life on the busy London streets, where he might have at least found a few new hiding places. Out here in this wilderness, he knew nothing, and knew that he had become nothing.

After a while, Jenner switched off to his benefactor's complaints, and continued to take in more and more of their surroundings. The earth was parched, baked by a sun already hot in the sky, and a layer of that earth skittered across the hard cracked surface beneath the swirl of the wind. The trees of the forest, although affording some partial shelter, were mostly barren and devoid of leaves, their bark stripped to reveal the white streaked trunks beneath. So much of the landscape was white, bleached by a fierce sun that they would no doubt be succumbing to as morning continued to age. The trees would offer some shelter, but Jenner guessed that by midday it would be suicide to stay out in the open, and a better refuge would have to be found. With the mountains being the only option in sight, Jenner suggested they head off into the foothills before the day grew hotter still, hoping that they might spot a settlement from a higher vantage point, or even come upon a community nestled in a hidden valley. They had no idea how long they might be staying in Kar'mi'shah, but they both knew that they had to at least accept the honest truth that it might even be forever.

The climb seemed easy going at first beneath the shallow arc of the rising sun, but as that sun rose higher and higher, so the effort of their journey began to slow their pace to a stumbling crawl. There seemed so many places scattered across the vast range of the mountain slopes that might offer at least some partial shelter, vast boulders and heavy overhangs, and as they reached each one, so they took leave of the day's onslaught beneath them for an hour or so, recouping their strength for the next stretch. Where they were even headed that they should trek across such a rugged landscape, they had no idea, if indeed there might be anywhere to go, but with a barren vista in each direction they might at least visit an outcrop where they might be able to find their bearings and perhaps even locate a populated settlement.

As their exhaustion grew the higher up they climbed, so it seemed that their fatigue began to play tricks on them. Upon reaching their fourth rest stop of the morning, it seemed as if the very rock around them was whispering, communicating with them in a kind of barely audible hush. Montague would have none of it, of course, and perched himself at the back of the shallow cavern as he pulled in air and wiped at his brow. Jenner, however, maintained that the ground was alive, and pressed his face against the walls of the cave in an attempt to decipher the message in the mountain's monologue. It was heat-stroke, Montague repeatedly told him, telling him that it would be more profitable to rest and slow his heartbeat rather than rush from rock to rock and build such hope and excitement. He was not used to such temperatures, Montague continued, living in a damp and cold climate like England. He himself had visited the tropics many times on various business ventures and was more acclimatised than his younger traveller. They would also need to find food at some stage, he pointed out, and just the mere mention of it brought a growl of agreement from his own stomach. Jenner disregarded all his logic and just wanted a straight answer as to whether or not Montague could even hear the whispering. It seemed like a tetchy subject, for Montague would not be drawn on the issue, and refused to answer him one way or the other.

The sun had started its downward arc by the time they reached the crest of the slope and gazed down into a deep valley floor on the other side. The sight was breathtaking after such a hard climb, the sweeping shadows cast by the setting sun almost fluid like a dark ebbing sea of granite. At their backs the hot desert plains stretched out to a shimmering horizon, but in each direction there remained only the same desolate panorama of bleached white sand and scrub. A number of areas showed promise, coarse bushes and trees, a break in the monotony of desert, but from such a distance nothing gave them confidence enough to turn around and head back.

The memory of the baying beasts the previous night returned as the sky continued to darken. The crest of the slope broke away in many places to reveal outcrops and caverns, shelters in which they could hope to wait out the night. Several species of plant life grew on the mountain, sparse and dried, and with some effort, they managed to gather what they could in order to manufacture a fire. Not for heat, of course, but for protection against the animals that might wander the slopes looking for easy prey, lost in an unknown wilderness.

While Jenner had been collecting handfuls of the heather-like plants, he had come across a trail of spattered blood, leading off towards a crease in one of the rocks. Thinking it to perhaps be that of an injured animal, he followed it cautiously to an opening, narrow at the front, and tucked away on the edge of a ravine. But as he tentatively gazed inside, thinking the dying beast to have maybe fallen just out of sight, so he discovered that the crease widened considerably inside, and might offer them both a suitable shelter for the night. With so much space to hide in, he followed the blood trail with trepidation, searching for a creature, either prey or predator, by the partial light still illuminating the uppermost reaches of the mountain, stumbling amongst the rocks in search of something that might at least make a meal.

He stopped in his tracks, however, as his eyes suddenly fell upon a body lying huddled in a corner, a body of a human male, his hands hanging limp just beneath a wound slashed across his neck. He was dead, that much was obvious, and it took Jenner a few moments to take his attention away from his grizzled deathly expression, and down to where his belongings had been scattered across the ground. His guilt surfaced briefly, a guilt that questioned his humanity, passing over the death of a human being in favour of rifling through his belongings in the hope of at least finding something to fill his stomach. With one superstitious eye on the dead man's half-lidded stare, he kept the other on the contents of the bag that lay at his side, and was rewarded as he found not only enough food that would take the bite off both his and Montague's hunger for a few days, but also some kind of protection in the form of a knife, and a hand-crafted book with its pages half written.

The man possessed a diary, it seemed, a journal of his life in Kar'mi'shah, and as he slowly turned the dry pages over in his hands, Jenner learned that the book seemed to cover the past few years, with infrequent entries that told only of hardships and suffering. There was little in the way of maps to civilisation, or indeed routes to major cities, but it did at least show that people still lived in this province, people with a society, a community where they might still find a place that would have them. Slowly Jenner flicked back a few pages, picking one of the entries at random, and began to decipher the rough scrawl of the dead man's penmanship.

Seventh full moon.

The creatures will be coming stronger tonight. Already I can hear them on the mountain. The fierce winds bring their horrible sounds on the back of the sandstorm. Annabella is afraid. She sits with her needlework at the hearth, attempting to ignore them, but I know that she cries when I am not here. Rodane will be here soon, and his wife will take her off to their home for protection. It is a good idea, the wives staying together. The doors are bolted and will keep the creatures out. But we must be strong and kill anything that does not belong here. It is the only way. We have to kill them all.

I asked my question again, but Annabella will still not agree to be my wife. She knows full well the arguments that I have, and knows too the futility in all of them. I promise to work hard to get money, I promise to slave myself to get food. But everyone else in Kar'mi'shah is in the same situation. There is no money and no food, no matter how many hours any of us toil, no matter how much any of us slave, and no matter how much any of us will it. It is a desperate time, and certainly no place for celebration. Extravagance would only invite our downfall more quickly.

I tell her that such things are immaterial, and that the only gift that I need from her is her face to wake to every morning. She tells me that I already have that, and that she wants our love to be known to everyone as well as I, but there is a dreadful curse that plagues our land, and we have barely enough food to live on from day to day, without stockpiling any for a feast for relatives and friends. I know this deep in my heart, but I love Annabella so very much that it blinds my eyes. I have to keep remembering this. Annabella helps me, and for her undiminishing guidance I am truly thankful.

Annabella brought up my want of children again, too, and I could not deny that I so desperately want her to bear me a child, a boy or a girl I hardly care. But she knows that even if she was to conceive, how could we *expect to feed our offspring or help it grow? So disastrous are the harvests, so pitiful the fishing trawls, that we all feel cursed, as though the very Gods themselves have deserted Kar'mi'shah and nothing we can do can help our plight.*

Jenner glanced up as Montague appeared at the narrow entrance to the chamber, his face one of confusion for the others impromptu rest. But then his eyes found the body slumped in the corner, and he dropped his collection of coarse weeds to the floor. There was death here, come to claim this stranger, and neither one of them could think of anything to say. Jenner watched as Montague turned his sight away, unable to see any more death, before resuming his reading of the dead man's journal.

Shallow moon

Kar'mi'shah shakes beneath the second sandstorm of the day. Every day the desert takes a stronger hold of the borders of our province. Crops continue to fail, rains refuse to come, and every sight around us is one of desolation and disease. It is getting harder by the day simply to survive, that is the only true fact. The farmers can barely grow enough food to support themselves, the fishermen return frequently with ever pitiful trawls, and the animals with which we share our world scavenge regularly on what little is left. With so little food grown or caught, the market continues to remain empty. This city was once a thriving metropolis, distant legend tells us so, but now death looms in the harvest and in the seas, and of a hopeful future for us all there is no sign. I pray that something will save us, but I wonder just what could save us from this terrible existence.

Hunger is our greatest adversary. Many have died beneath its withering touch, others have simply packed up their kin and trudged into the heart of the desert in search of a new land, never to be seen again. The market stands barren daily, yet everyday we force ourselves to traverse the same worn route, hoping for a flask of fresh milk, a catch of fresh fish or, should the Gods ever return to save us, a gift of meat from one of the few sheep or cattle left alive in the province. At the moment, Annabella and I have very little sustenance to carry us through the rest of the night. Even the water in the wells grows less and less, as it is consumed so frequently by those with strength enough to draw it. Things can surely get no worse. What hope can there possibly be from such endless hardship? Something must help us soon.

Second shallow moon

Oh, Gods, why have you forsaken us so cruelly. My heart is pitiful and aches with the horrific burden that I have witnessed this night. Death lurks in so many different forms here in Kar'mi'shah, in hunger and disease, in desert lions and the scavenging river crocodiles, but none are so evil or so terrifying as the death that came out of the darkness this night. A monstrous creature came out of the nothingness of the desolate wastelands to take the lives of those we love, killed in the most hideous way imaginable. It is *something that has held us all in the same dreadful grasp, but until last night, I had not known it so close to my own heart before. I need to write it down, to at least pay respect to my departed brother, but perhaps also to bring some kind of sanity back into my head. It was earlier today, when I went to his house, that I found him lying on the hearth floor with his throat torn and bloody. He had been dead for some time, and I found him doubled up and in a position of agony. There had been no swift and painless death for him. He had died slowly and in torment.*

Kneeling sickened and wretched at his side, I wept for him. I had no clue as to how long I even remained there, before I eventually stumbled through into the small bedroom at the back of his house and discovered poor Pip and Isa, brutally murdered in an almost identical way, their veins drained of all blood, their tiny bodies ripped and battered. My memory of such horrid sights are still cruel in my head, and plague the darkness behind my eyes with vivid images, played back from my unfeeling mind.

Daybreak

The desert creeps closer and closer, and grasps our wretched lives both day and night, as too do the burgeoning predators and scavengers that haunt the banks and outer limits of the city, but it is what comes down from the mountains when the sun sinks low that threatens our lives so lethally. We are in danger, each and every one of us, and no one can escape such unnatural death.

They are horrific creatures, prowling through the dry and dusty streets after sundown like evil dogs, lurking in the shadows and hunting mercilessly for those who have not yet returned home; children, adults or the infirm, it makes no difference to such demons. They kill their victims by ripping open their throats, draining them of their blood until they are nothing more than a ragged corpse, leaving a dry grey husk in their wake that begs a humming scab of black flies by morning's early light. There is very little protection against such demons, and even the superstitious who know their talismans or incantations, know that they are no more protected than the rest of us. Any weapons that we can make are of little use, but only as a community have we been able to take a tentative stance against the evil that haunts our homes.

I have been approached by four other men from our district, each of them with stories of death in their own homes. They have started to patrol their dwellings at night, searching their fields and plots of land should one of these unnatural creatures be lurking there, stalking their backyards while they sleep. With anger still gnawing at my belly, I agreed to join them, and since then, the nights have passed without further incident. Perhaps with the five of us scouting through the darkness and the heat, it is our very presence in the darkness that keeps the creatures at bay. We can only hope that our resilience will prevail.

Fifth full moon

Our hopes are dead. We came upon one of the

creatures feeding on a young boy. It was too late to save the child, but the beast is at least destroyed. It had been strong, and it had been swift, and I fear that after a string of nights with no alarm, it had found us horribly distracted and offguard. It had taken all five of us to hold the raging beast down, long enough so that we could beat it with what paltry weapons we had, dismember it roughly with a blunt woodsman's axe, and bash in its disfigured skull. It had struggled to the last, howling a piercing scream that cut through the night like a foul scythe. But when finally it lay dead, its arms and torso crumbled rapidly into the dust that surrounded us, and the sheer sight of this made us feel more afraid. What unnatural creatures are these?

Sixth full moon

Rodane will be here soon to collect me for the patrol. I have insisted that Annabella stay in his house along with the wives of the others in our group, rather than be left alone and defenceless in our own home. I haven't yet listed the names of the remainder of our group, but they are all from our district. The first is a man called Rodane, I have already mentioned him. The second is a farmer called Lemass, a large man with huge hands like shovels. The third is a fisherman from one of the barren docks called Bayle - he lost most of his family in one single night over a month ago. He cries frequently, and we have all looked after him as best we can. The last is the nearest thing we have to a religious leader, a man called Whinter. He prays for us all that we do not come upon any more of these foul creatures. All I have is my axe, and I fear that it is too clumsy a tool to be useful as a weapon. I will, however, use it as fully as I can if I have to. These things of evil must be stopped.

Night

Heaven help us, we are undone. The demon has returned and taken so many of us. There was yet another blinding sandstorm this night, and we stepped out into it unprepared and without a plan. The freight of sand overwhelmed us as we struggled against it in our first search of the area. We were only a few streets away from where my brother had been killed, in a place on the very outskirts where the dunes have piled high against the wooden houses, and continues to grow deeper by the day. A shout rose up suddenly out of the darkness and I realised that I had lagged quite some considerable distance behind the others. Ahead of me through the blinding storm I could just make out the vague silhouettes of Lemass and Bayle as they clambered headlong through a battered wooden fence and into a pen scattered with bleating sheep. I didn't know what was going on, but Rodane took hold of me and yelled instructions over the din of the storm.

There was chaos everywhere, and I don't think anyone knew what was really going on. I tried to make sense of the swirling rage of the wind as it tore up the ground into mini-whirlwinds, but all I could make out was a handful of malnourished sheep, staggering in circles on stick-thin legs, and the vague forms of Lemass and Bayle as they swept the air with their weapons above their heads. It was then that I heard a scream fill the air, sudden and piercing, and raised in absolute terror. But it came not from the confusion of the sand and the animals ahead of me, but from behind, in one of the houses in the street. I searched the lamplight that flickered between the shuttered windows, but Rodane was already dashing out across the dusty street, his great knife wielded high in the air as he yelled his own cry of alarm. I followed as closely as I could, but it was only as I deciphered the layout of the street through the swirling storm, that I realised Rodane's sudden and intense fear. It was his house.

Without Bayle, Whinter or Lemass at my side, I stumbled towards the house in pursuit of Rodane, not daring to believe just what might greet us inside. But by the time we reached the smashed front door, I had my worst fears confirmed as a terrible sight awaited me. The monster that had first attracted us had backtracked and found its way into the small wooden dwelling. I saw it standing hunched over Rodane's wife, its great maw embedded deep into the crook of her throat as it grasped her skull hard against its body as it fed, her neck surely snapped at such a horrid angle. I watched, frozen in the doorway, as Rodane hurled himself at it, his great knife sweeping down out of the air. The beast growled horrifically as it moved unnaturally swiftly to avoid the blow, swatting Rodane away even as the knife caught a glancing blow across its bare arm and sank deep into its foul meat. The creature neither registered the wound, it seemed, nor howled with any kind of pain, but continued after Rodane. Whinter appeared beside me suddenly at the threshold, forcing his way past after taking only a moment to register the assault. He ran then, even as I continued to remain helplessly at the door, into the fray, berating the creature with a barbed weapon so ludicrously ineffective that it was simply too much to bear.

Rodane lay slumped and lifeless in the corner of the room, his back broken, his skull smashed in, and as Whinter beat down upon the beast, so it simply turned upon him and gored him with its sharp and blood-stained fangs. It was only in this brief moment, as the creature ripped at his innards, that I caught sight of the monster's eyes, and I saw them to be exactly that of an animal, neither calculating nor reasoning, but only seeing, raging to sate its endless hunger.

I watched as Whinter was thrown back with considerable force, his stomach opened up in a shower of scarlet, and landed hard on his back next to the twisted body of Rodane's wife. But then I could see, just past this sight of death, the slight figure of my beloved Annabella, crouched between the hearth and the woodpile, cowering for her life. She lay terrified and waiting for this monster to turn upon her, to take out her throat as it had taken out Millie's, but not even this sight of my beloved could provoke me into action.

The sound of splintering wood snatched my faltering gaze from her, and I turned to see Bayle and Lemass hurl themselves through one of the small shuttered windows at the back of the small room, their weapons raised to beat back the creature now bearing down upon what was left of a shuddering Whinter, choking loudly on blood that rose in a river from his own throat. The unnatural creature faltered then, apparently weighing up the vision of yet another meal with the arsenal that confronted it, and afforded me with a clearer look at this thing. It had fed this night, so fully on Rodane's wife if no other, and blood tracked down from a gaping mouth lined with sharp pointed teeth. Its eyes burned with an intensity, black and hollow, but they were devoid of any intelligent thought, and stared out from sockets sunk deep into its head. Of its skin, as dry and white as parchment, little could be seen as it became stretched across its hideous distorted face as the creature growled and snarled with anger. Bayle and Lemass stood their ground, relying on each other for strength as the two of them confronted this monstrosity, a pitiful weapon of wood and iron clutched in each of their hands. They could not have put up much of a fight, I remember thinking to myself as I studied the scene in front of me, but it seemed to at least be enough, for the creature backed away a step in retreat. A growl of threat still rasped from its raw and brutal throat, but then it turned away swiftly, and came charging towards the open door, headlong towards me.

I feel ashamed to even write this now, but I panicked as it came. I knew that I should at least try and swing my axe at it and try and sink its blade into the monster's foul body, but my limbs were leaden and still would not move, not even as this blood-fiend fell upon me, and screamed its banshee cry that tore at my ears. I felt only the demon's ferocious claws and rancid breath against my chest, before I felt the ground hard at my back. Much more than that I do not know, but the creature must have disappeared into night, free to kill again.

Daylight

I still feel the shame of last night. The others have said nothing but it is clear that they hold me responsible for the deaths of their kin, at least because I may have been able to injure it, perhaps even kill it. It is true that I could have done something, but I did nothing, I didn't even try. Harsh words, but it is the truth.

When I had seen that thing come bounding at me, its jaws brimmed with canine teeth and awash with wet muck, my blood had frozen. All I could see was its burning eyes, its fangs that hung down from a ghastly red mouth, and the smear of fresh blood plastered across its lips and throat. What could I have done anyway? It had fed at Millie's neck. It had savaged Rodane as though he had been nothing more than a sick animal. And it had thrown Whinter to the ground like a lifeless doll. Just what could I have done, please Gods tell me? If I had tried, the beast would surely have torn out my throat as well. I am at least alive. Perhaps that is more than I deserve.

My excuses are poor, but they are all I have, and they linger now in my head to haunt me. If that is not poison enough to me, then the look upon the face of my dear Annabella is so very much worse. When I went to her, I tried to take her trembling frame into my arms. She was unresponsive at first, like a hard stone statue, as she stared in absolute horror at the scene of death in front of her. I tried to soothe her, attempting to usher her away from the sickening sight and out into the open air, but she would have none of it, and kept saying the same two words over and over again. "What happened?" she wanted to know. "What happened?"

At first I thought I understood her question, but it wasn't until she asked it with such repetition and with such accusation in her eyes that I suddenly realised the weight of those words. She held me responsible, perhaps not solely, but it was there. I was supposed to protect them, that's what her eyes said to me. I was supposed to protect them, and I failed. Her disappointment weighted more heavily in those few terrible moments, than the deaths of the others, or even, Gods curse me, the death of my own brother. Annabella means more to me than anything, and I failed her so cruelly. I thank the Gods that she was left unharmed, I could never live with myself if she was to come to harm, but to have her hatred kills me inside.

I held her cold hands a while longer after that, but it was apparent that she got no comfort from my touch, and it was then that I realised what it was that I had to do. I left her then, beneath the capable attentions of Bayle and Lemass, and went back out into the street. The sandstorm had let up its assault a little, yet still it howled throughout the dusty streets of the town, blinding me to the sight of the rest of the province. The mountains rose somewhere to the north, but they were just a direction with no sight to give them substance. It would be a day's travelling on foot through harsh desert, I knew, but what other choice did I have? I took up my axe, still lying in the dirt outside Rodane's house where I had dropped it, and set out towards the mountains that I could not even

*see, knowing that I had to find the unnatural beast
that had killed these people's families, and slay it.*

A wave of sickness poured over him as Jenner read
the dead man's journal, his stomach knotting as the
vivid descriptions of death and mutilation at the hands
of the vampire brought sickening memories back into
his head, images of Kole, images of all that Jackel
El'a'cree had done to him, and of course of the death
of his dearest Emma. He glanced up briefly from the
dry yellowed pages to see Montague standing huddled
in the narrow entranceway. Beyond him, he could see
that it was already dark outside the entrance to the
narrow cave, and the knowledge that these things
roamed not only this world but these very mountains,
brought with it a dread that would not leave his skin,
but stayed there with a kind of creeping itch. The
wonderland that he had thought they had been
delivered into, was no more than a world where
creatures killed without mercy or fear of retribution,
or without even the need to hide in shadows. It
dawned on him then, as he watched Montague gaze
out at the darkening sky, that the world they had
found was no safer than the one they had left, and that
the biggest terror was that Montague had been right.
At least back home they knew the hiding places. Here,
they knew none.

There was only one more entry in the journal, and
Jenner was loathe to even begin it, knowing that it
was surely the man's last notes before death had
caught up with him. The text was scrawled more
quickly that the others, hurried, no doubt, with a
petrified urgency.

327

First night of slaying

I saw the shape of the demon high up on a plateau, gazing out across the plains beneath a sharp rocky outcrop. From such a distance, and with only the pale luminescence of the moon overhead, it was difficult to discern whether this was even the same monster or not. It seemed to have long billowing hair, but again, I am not sure of this. It seems to be alone, or lost, and does nothing but look out into the night. It is strange behaviour indeed, but I have been sharpening my axe with each rest stop that I make. The blade marks the stone easily now, and I will kill it when I climb up to its lair. It will soon be dead.

Later

I have reached the plateau, and it is just as I feared. The creature has gone. There are the remains of what seems to be another, a handful of rags and some patches of parched dust and bone shards. Perhaps two of them had fought. Perhaps two of them lived together at this point. Whichever is the truth I do not care. There is nothing here to keep me waiting. I will continue to look for the one that killed Rodane and his wife.

That had been the last entry.

Jenner sat and stared at the page. Perhaps the vampire had been on the plateau after all. But that didn't explain how the man had managed to climb back down to this cave and set up camp for the night.

Perhaps the vampire had followed him down from the plateau to this place and killed him as he slept. Jenner gazed about him uneasily now. That seemed to make more sense, but horribly so. He glanced across the cavern towards Montague, his dark figure silhouetted grimly against the darker sky, and realised how much this must have shaken him, even without reading the words of the dead man. He knew what was going on. He didn't need to have it written down. He'd been dealing with these creatures for a very long time. What surprises could there possibly be for him? He went to push himself to his feet, to go and tell Montague that they should begin to make preparations for their night in the cavern, to light the fire, perhaps even barricade the entranceway. But even as he did so, there came the delicate clatter of skittering rocks from outside the cave. His blood ran cold.

The weight of his heart thudded heavily inside his chest as he gazed stricken at the opening, catching sight of Montague stumbling away from it. Was this the vampire here already, come to kill them both as they slept, come to butcher them as it had butchered the keeper of the diary? Jenner looked round for something to use as a weapon, the knife, the axe that the man had written about, but nothing was within reach, nothing that he could swiftly grasp and swing.

The sounds from outside the cave ceased, and the two of them stood in petrified silence for a long time. But then, at the narrow entrance to the cave, a shallow figure suddenly emerged, gaunt and growling a ragged threat.

The vampire filled the narrow threshold, her eyes gazing out of the night with a piercing and fiery intensity. And then, in the staggering moment that followed, she stared across in bewilderment at Jenner, as his lips suddenly parted, and a single word slipped delicately from between them, without him even knowing that it had come.

"Emma," was all he had said.

FOUR

NOMAD

The rock breathed and the earth yearned, the landscape swelling and shimmering all around them as the two vampires ascended the steep ragged terrain of the moonlit mountains. Even the air at such an altitude seemed to be alive, pulsing with a heartbeat that intensified as the distance between themselves and The Curbane lessened, its intoxicating rhythms enough to make their own flesh pulse, enticing it to change and turn to new forms and possibilities. The vampire Casta Mica'tore could feel that he was at last back home now, could feel the buzz of The Blood in everything around him, and felt blessed as the wash of the vast white moon overhead bathed him in a blanket of holy ethereal light.

This very path may have been a familiar one to his sometime acquaintance, Coda-Beda, traversing between dominions as he collected The Blood Of The Ancients from its source. There had been no reason in coming to this place before the life of Jackel El'a'cree had been finally extinguished, but forces had driven his hand prematurely, Jackel's death could not be assumed, and he knew that he would now have to try and take those energies of The Curbane, forcibly if necessary, if he was finally rise to become Master himself. He had no guide across a landscape he had not set eyes upon in centuries, his rendezvous with

Coda-Beda altered without warning; but his senses were keen, and with the mountains themselves singing like a chorus of energy, he used them as a living map as he made his way to the pivot of the vampire world with the child-vampire Callie stumbling after him in his tracks.

Echoes of the hot desert winds gusted in from the south but The Curbane seemed to brighten even these, bringing a harmony to its heat that seemed to swell the rocks yet further. If Coda-Beda had not trodden this exact path countless times before, he had no doubt taken a similar one, trafficking the Blood from wherever his associates managed to gain access to it, back through a portal to London where it was sold to whoever had the necessary funds. It was not always money either. Properties were handed over for a vial of the potent fluid, tomes of ancient magic, spells, bonds, but most especially Casta's favourite commodities, secrets and allegiances. So valuable were these, that they were beyond price. What good was money when you could not see into your enemy's mind? Such goods had already brought him this far, to the brink of ultimate Godhood, but it had been that tiny unpredictable percentage that had let him down. There was always that percentage. It could not be hidden or gotten away from. It could always be lessened, but it was always still there. That was the true value of things, he knew. The ability to unsettle the balance between luck and control.

"Are we nearly there yet?" Callie whined somewhere behind him.

Casta glanced behind him, suddenly startled by her proximity. He had forgotten that she was even with him, let alone climbing right behind him. He realised that he suddenly despised her presence, and did not answer her at first, loathing the fact that she should see such holy sights when she had achieved so little in her short life with its paltry span of not even a third of a century.

This vampire who had the face of a child but a blood history of some thirty years, had been reporting Alexia's moods and movements to him for over half that time. A great insight, certainly, but not the sort of accomplice to have around for long. Yes, she was a distraction, and she had appeared and offered him just that in the church when he might not have otherwise found one, but she was still fodder, and he would drop her whenever it was most convenient.

"It can't be much further, can it?" she continued.

Casta answered her this time, but curtly.

"No," was all he could stand saying to her.

The interruption had caused a break in the booming of the rocks and canyons around him, but as Casta's senses caught up with their rhythm once again, he became invigorated by them afresh. He was close now, he knew, he could feel it in the ground he walked upon, in the air that sang with a harmonic resonation. He could feel his own flesh begin to creep and contort, the power of the mountain affecting his body as it sought to mould it into new and interesting shapes, to transform him into something other than blood and bone.

But then the ground began to beat a new and more intense rhythm, like a heart forced to pound beneath exerted effort. The intensity escalated rapidly until the very mountains seemed to shudder, and then through the darkness of the night, the pathway ahead of them erupted in a shower of rock as the whole world

333

seemed to come apart.

A form came out of the rock - no, not out of the rock, but of it - a vast giant being of solid granite that thundered into view, standing its ground and permitting no further passage beyond it. A rumble came at the back of its crudely-shaped neck, a growl that boomed along the canyon like a heavy storm, with a din made not with any kind of living throat but with a raking cacophony that rasped like rocks being ground together. This, surely, was a guardian of The Curbane, built to withstand violation.

Casta stumbled back a step as the very ground shook beneath him with a violent fury. His eyes searched for intelligence behind the guardian's hollow gaping sockets, but it was being driven by purpose, not reason, and as it came at him with a bounding howl, so he threw his fist forward and summoned a blow of livid flame that streaked across the midnight air towards it, illuminating the canyon with a blanket of bright fire. The body of the rock guardian, although seeming to be solid, was protean, and divided effortlessly to create a hole inside its chest cavity that allowed the fireball to blaze through untouched, exploding against the rock face beyond it. Casta watched spellbound as the guardian then resealed this cavity, a growl of coarse laughter mocking his pitiful attempt, before it launched its own retaliation.

The ground shuddered afresh beneath Casta now, and great tendrils of rock sprouted skyward like fingers that sought to trap him inside a colossal fist of granite. But the vampire was swift, and dodged them as they came crashing down around him, seeking to bludgeon him, and punish him into the mountain. He heard Callie loose a shriek and caught only a brief glimpse of her disappearing into the darkness. The guardian would have no one escape, it seemed, for a great wall of rock suddenly rose up after her and pounded her hard into the canyon floor like a tidal wave, a brief shower of vented blood filling the air before the rock ceased even that.

Casta didn't even notice. He was already loosing another bout of magic, a whirlwind of lightning that shrouded the fingers of granite and shattered them inside its vortex like brittle leaves. A column of water rose up between shuddering fissures as they opened, fanning the air and spraying out over the rocks beneath the onslaught of the vampire. The swirling vortex of lightning that Casta had created moved on, away from him to shatter the pathway ahead of him, searching out the great guardian that continued to block his path. But even as the guardian stood its ground against the force that would undo it, the shower of water at the vampire's back rose up once again, this time under its own strength, and reared an angular head to look down upon him.

Casta's vortex took hold of the rock guardian in its deathly grip and began to shake him apart, bands of electrical light blistering the air as the entire mountain seemed to share its fate and shudder beneath the furious hold. The guardian battled for a few moments, standing its ground like a unbreachable wall, but then the forces that tore through its very structure broke its back, and unleashed a monstrous howl up into the night sky. Unrepentant and unrelenting, Casta Mica'tore watched without mercy as his magic continued to berate it, knocking lumps of rock off its head and torso as though it was caught in the grip of some terrible fit. The howling din came again, and even as Casta infused more force into his furious vortex, the guardian shuddering harder as its vast limbs sparked and burned in the air like phosphorus, the battle was not yet over.

The water guardian grasped the vampire from behind with a fluid fist, and Casta cried out loud as it then froze and sank ice shards deep into his body. The pain was excruciating, and his control over the vortex of lightning faltered momentarily as he sank to his knees, his head reeling in turmoil. The next few moments he only registered in snatches, the rock guardian ahead of him breaking free of its sparking cradle, the ice surrounding him glistening like a borealis, before he shuddered into blackness from the intensity of the cold now piercing his very being. His unconsciousness lasted only a heartbeat, however, but when his eyes did eventually flicker open, they burned with a fury that almost made the guardians shudder back a step.

He could still feel the knives of ice piercing his body, but now fingers of rock had grown out of the mountain to join them, taking hold of his limbs and crushing them to the point where his bones were actually creaking. His sight located the vengeful gaze of the two guardians, furious and intent on his final destruction, but amongst all this, he felt too the heartbeat of The Curbane, still pounding throughout everything that he could touch and see and hear. He felt it pound inside the rock that held his bones. He felt it pound inside the ice that clasped his innards. And he felt it pound inside his own body, and give it the energy to grasp the possibilities that his own mind could devise.

The great hollow eyes of the rock guardian cracked

open with terror as Casta took hold of its coarse fingers, and forced his already changing blood in between the fissures. The narrow eyes of the water guardian sank into its flowing head in disbelief as he let its course flow directly into his veins, mixing his blood that now began to seethe and boil with the ice of its structure. He could feel the fear grow inside both of The Curbane's guardians as he forced his protean form inside each of them, taking control of them as he fused his being with theirs. He felt their energies enter into him in turn, discovering the weight and the magnificence of the rock, learning its strength and its secrets at the centre of the earth. The beauty of the water too became his to manipulate, its coursing energies, its tranquillity, its states of solid, fluid and vapour. All this he felt as the rhythms of The Curbane coursed throughout his body and gave power to his own intent. The guardians stepped back with breaths of ragged defeat as Casta stood once more under his own strength, and assumed their hold on him to be his own. They were a part of him now, all three of them seemed to suddenly possess that knowledge, sharing too the inescapable fact that Casta Mica'tore now had nothing to stand between him and the source of the Blood Of The Ancients.

"Stop," the rock guardian suddenly bellowed, brute force suddenly giving way to a hopeless discourse. "You must not go further."

"You dare give me orders?" Casta raged.

"I know your power," it uttered. "I can feel the hold you have inside me. I can feel you crushing me. But The Curbane, it is a sacred place."

"You think I do not know its merit."

"You cannot know, unless you have seen it."

Casta stared up at the huge hulking beast,

motionless and carved like a vast living statue. He could feel its fear now too, feel it skittering about inside its huge bulk like a petrified canary in a cavern, darting against the jagged sides. He turned his fist in the air, as though it was inside the guardian and twisting his innards, and watched as his magic burned once more inside its belly, igniting the vortex of lightning once again so that it burned at its core, glimmering intensely between the fissures of its being. The rock guardian shuddered at the invasion of its body, and staggered back a step as it issued a grating sound that bordered on pain.

"Should I call you slave, or prisoner?" Casta asked it, turning his fist further so that the lightning flared like embers in a wind. The creature loosed another grating sound, and then dropped to one knee in agony, the ground quaking beneath the weight.

Casta stood and watched this thing, prostate and trembling beneath the might of his magic. It seemed almost pitiful to see something so mighty, reduced to something so weak.

"Do not kill me," the guardian murmured softly. "I beg you."

Casta turned his head to gaze back at the water guardian, and found this second repentant with its eyes cast earthward. He could see the streaks of his own blood curdling like poison in the fluid motion of its body as it rippled beneath the midnight wind. He returned his gaze back to study the rock guardian, and let up the fury a little, keeping a shallow fire of lightning inside it to glimmer and burn his intent as a reminder.

The cool night air buzzed with the fading crackles of electricity, tinged with the rhythmic boom of the mountain, and once again Casta asked his question of devotion.

"You are kneeling," Casta commented. "Will I call you slave, or prisoner?"

The rock guardian's eyes rose to find those of the vampire, but even with the knowledge of its defeat, the thing remained defiant.

"If you will call me anything, it shall be by my name."

"And what is your name?"

"Call me Nomad," it replied.

Casta looked upon the creature as he turned over the weight of its name in his mind. It seemed to settle somewhere appreciatively, and even as he turned his head to look back at the water guardian, it was already voicing the same response.

"I am Vessel," it said, the streaked channels of Casta's blood burning brightly inside its crystalline body like networks of uniform veins.

He had climbed the mountain with an allegiance of one, but that had now gone. In the wake of Callie's demise he had seen the birth of two new disciples, two vast monoliths of fury that would defeat the crippled form of Jackel El'a'cree with certainty, should the two of them ever meet again, and he see the battered face of his enemy. He looked at the two of them afresh, towering over him but chastened.

"You guard The Curbane?" he said to them.

"That is our function, yes," Nomad replied.

Casta gazed at this thing more closely, this mystical creature that should not even live. It was a great hulking lump of rock, its limbs made of coarse granite, its torso and head of layered stone. Standing against a backdrop of the mountain, it could barely be seen, perhaps because it was of the mountain itself. So too was Casta now. He could feel the weight of the mountain inside him, just as he could feel parts of himself living inside it, his eyes and touch roving through layers that had stood since the dawn of time, before even the Ancients.

"We guard The Curbane against those that would defile its sanctity," Vessel announced behind him, the sound of its motion like waves lapping against a faraway shore. "There have been some who have trespassed this far, some who have persisted against the living heart of this place, but we have met each and every one of them, and we have destroyed them. This canyon is a graveyard to their transgression."

"The spider needs not see the fly in order to kill it," Casta said quietly, "and yet it chooses which to eat and which to treat. Is there reason for taste, I wonder, or do things reach far deeper than its belly?"

There was no response to his fancy, and Casta watched as the guardians exchanged glances, feeling too the ripple of uncertainty as it passed between them. They shared a bond now, the three of them, and all would know what the others felt.

"Tell me, then," Casta continued, "of someone who comes here as frequent as the moonlit nights, a vampire that draws from The Curbane, who takes it out of this world and sells it for whatever is offered. How is it that you do not destroy this particular insect?"

"You speak of a vampire who belonged to my tribe," Nomad began. "We were both once vampires, the same as he, the same as you, but a perpetual existence so close to The Curbane has changed us. You have felt its pull already, its influence, its desire. You have already ceased to be what you once were. You are more like us now. You are part of this place, and will not function away from it."

"That is my dream, the horror of which you speak. Your words you use to try to injure me, but your barbs are like feathers, and I grasp them to my lips like the throat of a child."

"Your dream is mutation?"

"My dream is transition," Casta declared, with a mighty voice. "I am to be Master of Kar'mi'shah. I shall have all this to do with as I please." And then to threaten his point, he ground the rock inside the guardian so that the lightning that guttered there suddenly flared and burned his very being. "Beware my intention now, Nomad, for it will come." It was only a short burst, but Nomad reeled back in agony.

"I'm... sorry," the guardian stammered, sinking its colossal hands into the wall of the canyon to steady itself. "I did not mean to offend."

Casta stifled the electricity, and allowed the force he still held inside it to gutter. He could still see the sparks glittering between the fissures in its body, glimmering behind its eye-sockets like a candle in a jack-o-lantern, but he would leave it there, just as he would leave the tendrils of his lifeblood inside the very fabric of the body of Vessel.

"We were once made of flesh," Nomad continued, its voice haggard, "and walked the lands to feed on blood just as you had done, hunting and killing with my hands and teeth. But my desire for blood changed as I spent time here. The power of the place transformed my needs, and I drank of this power as I would have drank of blood. My flesh became weak and gradually decayed, and the spirit of the rock in which I lived slowly grew to replace it. Rock grows stronger than flesh, and becomes more pliant beneath the will that forms it. What I once was is now gone, and all that I am now is all that you see."

Nomad's words of finality were difficult to accept, and although Casta had already felt the power of this place, the notion that the transformation would not only be permanent, but would also continue to grow from his present state, filled him with a kind of uneasy dread. This was his dream, to venture to the source of the Blood, and what had come of that, to not only have The Curbane accept him but to actually draw him into its being, had seemed too much to hope for. He had only been here a few hours and had felt not only the booming rhythms of The Curbane coursing through his blood, but also the enveloping influence of its power upon his own flesh. All this and he had not yet even reached its source. Nomad and Vessel had lived beside it for centuries, having their form moulded and altered inextricably until no part of their former selves was visible. Could the guardian's words be true? Had his own transformation into another form already started, and if so, what would that final transformation be?

"Are there others like you," Casta asked suddenly, "left to guard the source of the Blood?"

"There are no others," Nomad announced, with a brief shake of his massive head. "No others like us."

"Then with the web left unguarded, shall we not proceed inside, where my dream may reach its end, and my potential be finally rested."

The mountains boomed afresh as they went, with the vampire, now bloated with an influx of rock shards and ice crystals and followed by a subservient pair of monolithic guardians, more confident of his final victory than ever before. The power of the source was infectious, and Casta found his own blood swelling and pulsing to the new rhythm as it grew and grew in both intensity and influence. He felt as though the place had its own notions about transforming him into whatever it desired, with the hint of an agenda that their two desires might not be the same thing. His unease at losing control of his own destiny blossomed in his mind the higher up the mountain he climbed, but the strength that filled his body was more than its equal, and gave him a might that he knew could have no vanquisher, and a renewed desire that was already sowing ambitious dreams for itself.

FIVE

ALL THAT LIES BURIED

The once grand halls of the Raza Pyramid, now fractured and toppled into awkward slabs of ugly grey rock, creaked beneath a wind that howled through its caverns, threatening to collapse in upon her, and crush her bones to nothing. It immediately became apparent, as Alexia crept cautiously through the broken ruin, that the hallowed structure was indeed occupied. The chambers carried a distinctive odour, not one of incense or of fresh blood, but one of decay and rot. She dared hope that one or more of her family might have remained behind in the ruin of the Raza, struggling against the merciless hold of the creeping desert to keep the ideals of the Faraohs alive. But that hope dissolved rapidly as she crept further into its darkness, as she discovered dozens of animal carcasses littering the floor like that of a savage beast's lair.

The smell of death hung heavily in the air, the fetid stench of putrefaction and coagulated blood souring the air further. She noticed too, as she stepped deeper into the main chamber now almost entirely destroyed, that the animals were not only drained of blood, but their flesh had been left relatively intact too.

The blood loss at least suggested the domain of a vampire, but the state of a building once revered as the most holy and sacred temple in the vast kingdom defied such an explanation. This was no place for a vampire of Kar'mi'shah, it was more of a prison or a cage, and it sickened her to see the epicentre of her religion defiled so cruelly.

A low bleating suddenly echoed off the walls of the chamber, resounding towards her in a myriad of sound, confusing her senses as to the true direction of the creature. Cautiously she stepped forward, her keen sight searching the darkness and finding a rough enclosure fashioned crudely from branches and twine. Inside she could see the ragged outline of a sheep, as emaciated and close to death as those she had seen in the fields of the outlying farms. Could this be a vampire's feed, she wondered to herself, as she gazed down at the pathetic bleating creature? A domesticated beast held restrained for later consumption? It dawned on her that her most desperate hope and fear was true. This was the home of a vampire, a vampire that had once held the name of a God. But how then could such baseness have possibly come from what had once been part of a blessed tribe? How could a vampire have grown so low?

As she gazed down into the ragged pen, the life of the animal suddenly overcame her, and brought with it an insatiable hunger along with the recollection that she had not even fed that night. The smell of its flesh came mingled with other smells from its enclosure - fear and excrement, disease and rot - and so foul was the combination that it turned her away from it. But the knowledge of her hunger battled with her nausea, and she found herself stepping once more towards it, her teeth extending in her mouth even as she fought her disgust.

Would the vampire who had claimed the beast for his own even know it was missing? How could he not? There was only this animal present.

Her hands came to rest against the rough wooden handle holding the cage door closed, and even as her mind wrestled with the guilt of taking another vampire's meal, the urge to feed grasped hold of her other senses.

The handle drew back easily beneath her touch, and the animal let out another bleat in the darkness as it sensed the danger of her intent. She could see it better than it could see her, and she went to it now, went to this dumb frightened creature, and took hold of the filthy wool about its neck as she knelt down beside it. Either it was too weak to run, too weak to struggle, or just too sick to realise the danger and make a dash for freedom, because it simply trembled on four rickety legs and allowed Alexia to sink down towards its throat.

The stench of rot and shit grew worse as her lips came within inches of its foul grey meat, but the need to taste blood and drink was greater, and she sank her teeth deep into the flesh of its neck as her teeth ran with water. The taste of its filthy swollen skin sickened her the moment her tongue found it, but she tried not to taste it, and swallow only its blood as it came freely into her mouth. But it was just not possible.

She gagged as she drank, her body convulsing with nausea, and the blood of the creature surged back up into her mouth even as she tried to keep it down. The sheep bucked beneath her assault now, and her strength went in fits as she struggled to keep a tight hold of it. But it continued to pull and buck beneath her faltering grasp, and in a final convulsion, her body rejected all that it had taken and the sheep charged off into the darkness of the chamber.

Alexia fell forward into the muck at the bottom of the cage, her stomach retching the last of the foul blood out of her system. The animal had gone, stumbled its way out towards a comparative freedom. It was close to death when she had found it, and she had drained what little blood it had to spare. It would be lucky if it found its way to an opening and threw itself to the mercy of one of the desert lions. But then the bleating came again, only briefly, and from somewhere near the back of the chamber. And then the darkness lapsed into a heavy silence once again.

Alexia lay there for a moment on all fours, her eyes closed against the sickness as she fought to regain her composure. The stench that still hung in the air around her was not helping, and as she pushed herself up onto her knees and then unsteadily onto her feet, a blow suddenly came at her out of the darkness that sent her hard back into the filth at the bottom of the cage.

Her sight clawed at the darkness as she sought for her assailant, her mind distantly wondering why she had not sensed the presence of another being inside the temple. But even as she thought this, she was grasped by her hair and hauled back up onto her feet, only vaguely able to make out the silhouette of a slight figure. This was the vampire, the owner of the sheep and the dweller of the Raza, and it seemed that he was not pleased at having his last meal taken, despite the foulness of the dish.

Another blow came at her, swinging out of the blackness, but it was clumsy in its aim and Alexia now had the benefit of knowing her enemy and managed to dodge it easily. Retaliating with a furious assault, her fist managed to find her assailant's head, knocking it back on a long thin neck with sufficient force that he relinquished his grasp upon her hair and stumbled back, a rasping growl erupting from his raw throat. Keeping up her momentum, Alexia kicked out hard at him, sending blows into his chest and stomach, and then watched with mixed emotions as his vague form fell sprawling into the soup of rotting carcasses behind him.

"I am no threat to you," Alexia yelled at him, keeping her stance aggressive as she stood over him, her teeth bared brightly as if she would tear out his throat. "I am a vampire, the same as you, and I will kill you if I have to."

The vampire remained on the floor at her feet, a deep growling breath heaving in his raw throat. It seemed he would fight for what little food he had left, even if it meant fighting to the death. But Alexia knew that she could take no chances with him, savage as he was.

"I am a vampire," she said again, lowering her fists. "Don't make me kill you. I only wanted to feed, that's all."

The growling lessened, and Alexia heard him sniff at the air around her like a dog. It seemed as though he was little more than an animal, as base as the creature that he had caught and trapped inside the rough wooden cage. Just what could have happened to descend a vampire from Godhood to savage beast? He suddenly seemed to her so far below her in evolutionary terms, like the desert lion or the filthy livestock, and yet he was still vampire, still a Blood God, and his senses she could not doubt. His breaths suddenly lessened as she gazed down at him, and then

348

he moved forward on his claw-like hands to speak.

"Why are you here?" he growled.

The voice coming out of the darkness startled her, and her eyes pricked the night-black air between them, searching afresh for features that refused to reveal themselves.

"You speak," she murmured, not daring to move any closer to him.

"Yes," he said awkwardly. "But not... often."

"How is it that you come to be here?"

"This is... my home," the vampire stated. "I have lived here for more years that I can count or remember."

"Why bring animals back here to feed like an animal?"

"What else would you have me do? Where else would I feed? Outside in the storm? Up in the mountains with the vermin? I have not lost my way, I travel the path of the Ancient Ones, the way I was commanded to."

"Commanded by who?" Alexia asked him.

The vampire stared at her, his answer unforthcoming, and Alexia wondered just how long he had lived in the shell of the greatest temple ever constructed.

"Who are you?" she asked him, stepping finally out of the muck of the cage and back into the depths of the main hall.

"I cannot remember a name," he told her. "My memory loses words with frustrating ease, like the fishes that once swam the river, slippery, fleeting. I am sure that I knew a great deal once, I know deep inside that I must have done. But such knowledge is no longer mine, my memory cheats me, and each night I meet myself with renewed fear."

"Fear of what?"

She saw through the darkness that he suddenly stared at her, his white eyes piercing.

"Fear that I will become one of them one day."

"One of who?"

"You have not seen them in the mountains?" he hissed.

"No."

"Then I pray you keep away. Nothing lies there but terrible animals, animals that will kill you on sight."

"And you are afraid that by losing your mind, you will become one of these killers?"

"It has already happened to so many. I have seen it."

"How do you know this?"

"Because these halls used to be more populated than this, even after the holocaust, lined with Gods of gold and flowers."

"I remember that too..." Alexia uttered quietly.

She felt the weight of the vampire's stare, incredulous at her words.

"I also lived in this place," she told him, "and wandered these halls that were once so grand. I remember it all, just as I remember the beast that destroyed it all."

"It was not the beast that destroyed this place," the vampire informed her solemnly. "It was the cruel earth."

"What nonsense is this that you speak?" Alexia suddenly demanded. "I saw the creature with my own eyes, and witnessed the destruction that it rained down upon the heads of my family."

"I saw it as you did, sister, but unlike you I did not run from its fire. I stood and fought for my life just as I fought for the lives of those around me, even as it

350

tore at my flesh, and cut down members of my tribe. It fought so many claws and teeth that I thought oblivion had manifested itself from the very rays of the sun. But as it raged through these very halls, blood spraying the air on all sides of me, so the horror suddenly went, and disappeared from all sight."

"It disappeared?" Alexia murmured.

"Out of sight and out of this place, leaving us only to grieve the Gods that had fallen."

Alexia stared hard into the darkness, trying against hope to make sense of the blackness and search the shadows for some sign of the scars on the vampire's face. Surely what he spoke of could not be true, she wondered to herself. Surely his sanity must be in question, living in this most hallowed place alone, time not able to claim his life, only his wits.

"How could this place have been destroyed then, if not by the creature?" she asked him finally.

"I told you, it was the cruel earth, unbidden and seeking to bury us all."

"You mean the dunes?"

"If only it were the dunes," he said. "If only it were that."

"Tell me whatever it is that has happened here."

The vampire seemed to settle himself upon the hard ground, as though the debris of rotting carcasses and fallen stonework was both his blanket and his mattress. A ragged breath came from his throat as he seemed almost to inhale the memories out of the foul air, before he then breathed out the facts of the past that had brought Kar'mi'shah to its knees and almost into oblivion.

"The dust storms come to bury this city is only the final torment the earth has brought upon us," he began. "It started so very slowly and inconspicuously after the creature left us to count the dead that we didn't even notice until it was too late. The ground lost its ability to sustain life, that is the true nature of our end. The fertility of the soil dissipated rapidly, and all with a speed that killed so many of the populace within the first year alone. Crops failed across the entire province, trees withered and refused to bear fruit, cattle died, sheep perished, and soon all that grew out of the soil were the gravestones of the people."

"Surely, you don't suspect the earth held some malice against us?" Alexia asked him.

"What else could we think? Famine gripped our land with a ferocity that could not be tamed or halted. We did what we could to stem the tide of death. We kept back the crocodiles that sought to feed on men and women rather than the shoals of fish that disappeared from our river. We drove back the lions of the north as they encroached on farming land, searching for new sustenance as the wilderness herds disappeared. But the anger of the ground grew, and overcame the diminished numbers of the Gods. What could we do? The earth had defeated us."

Alexia could hardly see his face in the penetrating gloom of the chamber, but she could tell by the calamity in his voice that there could have been no salvation. But his words made no sense. The earth could not possibly have had a conscious agenda, a rational process whereby it had planned a revolt against those that walked upon it and grew foodstuffs in its being. Or could it? She shook the notion away, so ludicrous did it sound.

"I say it was the ground that defeated us," the

vampire continued, "but that is not entirely the truth. The sun joined the vengeance of the earth, and brought its killing heat with it, even to the coolness of what had once been the precious night. It burned the soil and turned it to dust. It boiled the river and dried its banks into hard clay. It seared what few plants survived, and cracked the great buildings of the city, and allowed the sandstorms to blow in at every breach. The world around us seemed to be destroying us, killing everything that was once good, and covering it over with a baking blanket of desert, as if none of this had ever happened. The earth hates us, sister. It will kill us all soon."

Alexia gazed into the darkness at the vague shape that was the vampire. His words told of a madness that had grasped his mind, and yet what other explanation could there be for what had greeted her eyes on her return to Kar'mi'shah? Her home had been a palace when she had left under such harrowing circumstances, but now that palace had become a ruin, a shell almost swallowed by the desert of which this vampire spoke. She wanted to believe that some other force had destroyed her home, some tangible thing that she could put a name to and hate. But she had nothing to aim her anger at. Nothing to blame for all the loss she felt inside. Her home was gone, and for good, and now there was nothing she could do about it but accept the fact and surrender herself to it. She would have no home.

She wanted to leave, to rush out of the temple and go in search of the real Kar'mi'shah, to name this hellish place as a fiction and keep it at her back always. But she knew that flight was not an option, that this place was indeed Kar'mi'shah, and that to run would serve no purpose. She was immortal, and as long as she lived, she would know the terrible fate of her beloved home.

A draft of cool air shifted past her suddenly, like something passing effortlessly through the air, and it carried with it a tang of something familiar. It was slight but her keen senses detected the motion, and it was then that she realised the familiarity. It was the same smell that she had caught on the wind outside the pyramid in the first place. It had been what had attracted her to find a way inside the ruin. Perhaps on some level she had forgotten about it when she had met the vampire, but now she realised that he did not carry this odour - he reeked of decay and the foulness of the death that littered the floor - no, this was a different odour altogether, and she barely had a chance to search the darkness anew before this other vampire made herself known.

"It is a terrible truth that he speaks," the vampire murmured softly, out of the blackness of the chamber. "You know that in your heart because you have seen it for yourself."

"Who are you?" Alexia demanded to know, readying herself for an attack should one be forthcoming. But there was no fight, however, only discourse, and the same resigned melancholy that had gripped the first vampire so assuredly.

"I too once called this place home," the stranger said, "and like you I did not want to believe that the earth could be able to destroy such a vast state. But you only have to walk the sand-filled streets and the dust-littered thoroughfares, and I know that you have done so, to see that he speaks the truth."

Alexia turned over this confirmation as though the

second vampire could not possibly lie to her. So many emotions gripped her inside - anger, fear, loss - and it caused her mind to throw fragmented thoughts about inside her head. She needed something to latch onto, something sane in the middle of all this madness.

"I asked you a question," Alexia managed to say, defying all this honesty that was battering her mind.

"I have no secrets," the vampire told her flatly. "Not now. Not anymore. Everything I ever had has gone."

"So then, give me a name."

"My name, as if that means anything anymore, is Catherine."

SIX

TERMS

The last time Jenner had laid eyes upon Emma, she had been in the arms of the vampire Jackel El'a'cree, her body lifeless, and with her blood upon his teeth. He had woken to find her body gone, stolen from the sofa where she had been laid to rest. But now here she stood, hunched in the narrow threshold of the cave, her eyes fierce and bright, and staring back at him as though she would have his life too.

A growl reverberated at the back of her throat, threatening like that of an animal, and it caused the hairs on the back of his neck to bristle with trepidation. Was this even her, he thought to himself? It wore her face, looked out through her beautiful eyes, and yet she had been dead, he had seen her die. Or had he? A sudden chill passed over his body as a sickening realisation rushed headlong through his mind.

His memory jolted as he tried to drag it back through every horror movie he had even seen, about how vampires were made, and about how they could be stopped. It did not even seem as though she recognised him, so vacant was her gaze. He wanted to move towards her, to comfort her and learn the true nature of the few days they had been apart, but that growl continued to rasp the air between them, and it kept him in the partial darkness of the cave, his hand still grasping the journal writer's knife. Tentatively he said her name.

"Emma?"

The creature, for it seemed the most appropriate word to describe her, continued to stare unblinking at him, but now the growl stopped, and her eyes seemed almost to fill with the reflection of the bright flickering fire.

"Is it you?" Jenner continued, releasing his grip on the knife and moving towards her a yard or two, even as she let out another deep growl of threat. He heard Montague hiss a word of caution but Jenner ignored it. This was his girlfriend. He wanted her back. Even if it was back from death's threshold.

"Do you remember me?" he persisted. "It's me. It's Jenner."

As soon as he spoke his name, the growl dropped altogether from her throat, and something descended over her like a veil, almost like a veil of passivity. In that moment, Jenner felt sure that she knew him, despite all that must have happened to her, and he stepped forward yet again, halving the distance between them this time. He was only within yards of her, and she had yet to utter a single coherent word. But then suddenly she lashed out at him, a claw-like hand that struck his face with such force that it felled him, knocking him sideways into the cavern wall. Jenner fell awkwardly to the hard floor, and put his hand to the wound with shock, stunned to see that it came away bloody. He looked up at her. The ferocity had returned to her gaze, the growl once more at the back of her throat, and he was sure in that moment, that she would fall upon him there and then, and take the blood from his trembling veins.

Her form suddenly loomed over him like a vast silhouette, swift and with a cruel purpose, but as his eyes flickered to register the movement, so he heard a cry from behind him. He only had time to see Montague lunging at Emma with the knife he had dropped, before the whole scene was stolen from his view, and the sight of Emma, Montague, and the resulting skirmish was snatched from his sight.

When his eyes opened again, it was to survey the image of Emma sprawled across the stone floor, Montague standing hunched over her, the knife drooping in his hands. Jenner pushed himself up onto his elbows, a question already on his lips, but Montague was already murmuring his apology.

"I... didn't mean to hurt her," he was stammering. "I didn't mean to kill her."

Jenner hauled himself to his knees now, and gazed across at the woman who had once again been taken so very violently away from him. It did seem as though she was dead, and as he crawled across the cave to sit beside her, he pressed his fingertips to her neck, and grimaced when he could locate no pulse. Emma was dead. He glanced up at Montague, already knowing the truth, and watched as his one-time benefactor dropped the knife to the ground with a dull thud. Jenner turned to gaze back down at the beautiful face of Emma, a splatter of blood marking her temple where the rock had broken her fall. He wasn't sure whether Montague's actions had indeed saved his life, but it seemed certain that she had sought his death. He could only vaguely recall the sight of her coming at him, and yes, her teeth had seemed extended, and perhaps even slick with both saliva and intent. But then, just as he looked down upon her breathless corpse, her eyes suddenly flickered open.

Jenner leapt back with a start, toppling onto his backside with a cry of alarm. Montague too stumbled backward, hitting the wall of the cave behind him hard. The knife was on the ground, just out of easy reach, but Emma seemed more subdued, and put a hand to her back where the knife had opened its wound. From the corner of his eye he saw Montague make a move towards the dropped blade, but he held him back with a swift motion of his hand, and clambered quickly to his feet in order to address Emma once again. She was dead, he was more sure of that than anything now, and that could only mean one thing in this terrible new world. Emma had become a vampire, the same as Jackel El'a'cree.

Her lips parted as though she tried to speak. Jenner could see that she tried, and urged her on by saying her name once more.

"Jen..." was all she could manage, but Jenner continued to press her to say his name.

"Jen-ner." the vampire said, her eyes searching those of the mortal in front of her. "You are Jen-ner. I... know you."

"Yes, you know me," Jenner insisted. "I was your... boyfriend." The word played uneasily on his lips, but he'd used it now, and it seemed almost comforting now that he'd admitted as much to himself.

"No," Emma said.

"Yes," Jenner pressed. "You were my girlfriend."

Her eyes suddenly glimmered with fresh hope, a renewed clarity, and with even a hint of a smile, she added:

"The real Jenner would never admit such a thing."

Jenner turned suddenly to look at Montague, her smile, although fleeting, was infectious and spread rapidly across his face. His expression now conveyed his confidence that the person he had once known was still very much part of this other being in front of him, belaying Montague's fears that she just needed destroying in order to save their own lives.

"What happened to you?" Jenner wanted to know, turning back to look at her.

Emma held her head now, blood from the knife wound now beginning to trickle between her fingers of her other hand, but it seemed that the effort of locating her memories caused her the greater discomfort.

"I see death," she started. "Here on this mountain. I... try to focus, but there is mostly a dull haze."

"You killed this man?" Jenner asked tentatively, indicating the body behind him.

He watched as she followed his finger, her eyes falling upon the slumped figure with no remorse or emotion. He hoped she would look away in self-disgust, perhaps even repent for what she had done, but she simply saw him.

"I have not been here before," was all she said.

"But he has been killed by a vampire," Montague cried. "His blood has been sucked from two puncture wounds in his neck. Do you see?"

"I see. And I smell too his blood."

"You are the only vampire here?"

"No. There was another."

"The journal spoke of another vampire," Jenner said to Montague, "two figures up on a plateau. It must have been him."

"No," Emma told him. "That other is no more. That

360

was my Master Jackel El'a'cree."

Jenner stared at her in bewilderment. The unnatural creature that had killed her, who had torn her neck and fed from her just as he had fed from him, she now called Master. He was a killer, a butcher, and that was all.

"He's dead now?" Jenner asked, wanting her to confirm the deadly truth.

"Yes," she replied, her body motionless, her head not even yielding a shallow nod. It hurt Jenner to look at her in such a condition, and it occurred to him now as he looked at her, how little she did actually move. Her eyes followed him coldly as he moved and shifted his position, but neither her head nor her arms moved for any reason - not even her hand had moved since she had first clamped it to the would in her back - and it suddenly chilled him with its eerieness, seeing her so different from what he had known before. She had been warm before, full of energy and joy, but now she was dead, she had no pulse, and she drank blood from the veins of the living. His stomach turned over, and in a jerk of panic he reached out for her hand. She tried to snatch it away from his touch, but his movement caught her offguard, and he gasped with horror as the skin that he touched was cold.

"What did you expect?" she said to him, realising now the thoughts that distressed him.

"I... I didn't think. I mean, I guessed that you were..."

"A vampire?" she said. Her eyes flickered downward briefly for the first time. "I spent time with Jackel El'a'cree before his final demise, and he spoke to me at length about my condition, about the purpose that he had chosen for me. It is a blessing, Jenner, a calling to a higher purpose."

"Don't speak to me of purpose," Jenner snapped, exposing his neck for her to see where Jackel had fed from him. "I knew my purpose long ago. I was food, fresh blood for him."

"That's all we ever are, Jenner. Blood."

"No," he cried, almost desperately. "We were more than that, Emma. We had a future. We were in love."

It was Emma's turn to stare at him, at his breathlessness, his fervour.

"Is this the same man?" she said, her tone even and measured. "You speak of love, and of a future. You wanted none of that, Jenner. Why say these things to me now? Is this some kind of closure to make you feel better? Does your heart need to rest?"

"How can you say such things to me?"

"It is true, Jenner. You don't mean this. You might miss me, miss what we did together, but you could never bring yourself to say those words before."

"But I'm saying them now, Emma. I've realised what we had, what I had."

"It's too late, Jenner. I'm dead. Things can never be as they once were. You will have to accept that."

Jenner stared at her, not wanting to accept her argument, but knowing that he had no choice. How could he defy her nature now? She was dead, a vampire, and despite how little he knew about such things, he knew enough about himself to realise that he didn't want something like that to affect them. This whole situation was ridiculous, but then he thought that he had lost her altogether. Surely they could work through something like her rebirth as an undead blood-drinker. His head felt numb, swirling.

"What would you have me do?" Jenner said to her

suddenly.

Emma looked at him, her eyes cold and glistening. A frown creased her pale white brow briefly, but it was gone a moment later.

"I do not understand your question," she said.

"For us to be together," Jenner clarified. "What would you have me do?"

"There is nothing, Jenner. You have breath, I have lost that. You can walk beneath the sunlight, I have lost that pleasure. But I now feed on the blood of mortal beings, and you... well, you do not."

"But -"

"This ends, Jenner. I cannot stay here with you any longer. I must leave."

"What do you mean? Where could you possibly go in this place."

"I have something that I must do," Emma reiterated. "I made a promise, and now it is time for me to keep it. Goodbye."

SEVEN

TO BATHE IN FIRE

Hours seemed to pass as Casta Mica'tore continued his ascent, up towards the summit of the mountain and the source of The Blood Of The Ancients, and yet still his body refused to tire. On the contrary, his limbs seemed to become stronger the more he hauled himself towards the summit, the will of the rock stirring his bones with strength, the ebb of the waters coursing vitality throughout his body. He was no longer an individual traversing the mountain, he was a part of it, part of the province as a whole, and he was simply shifting his physical form through different states of being. Even as he climbed, he could feel the exhilaration of The Curbane, coursing throughout his body like sparking events, challenging his flesh to give up its simplistic form and become reborn as rock, sky or ocean.

To anyone else high up on the mountain with a view of the vampire, Casta would have appeared to have made his journey alone, his climb in the darkness of the night solitary up the vertical incline of one of the sheerest heights in the vista of the mountains. But to have witnessed this scene with only one of the senses would have meant not seeing it at all, for the vampire Casta Mica'tore scaled the mountain this night with two unseeable servants, named Nomad and Vessel, their forms so dominated by the will of The Curbane, that they rose towards the source of The Blood inside columns of rock, moving in seams and in channels, their masses contorting the stone around them to give them ease of passage. It was only as Casta reached a plateau and came face to face with a gaping chasm, a dark opening into the very heart of the mountain, that he commanded them to appear before him, and to verify that this was indeed the place that he had waited a lifetime to see.

The ground seemed to swell beneath his feet, even as he started forward, urging him onward towards The Curbane's secrets and energies. His limbs felt the motions of the rock as he made his way, stirring vigorously in his blood and bones as though this most holy of places longed to be inside him fully, to be a part of him, just as he would, in turn, be a part of it.

Oh, but it was such a wonderful feeling, the overwhelming desire for the sharing of space and matter, the unity, the synthesis. He could feel The Curbane more fully now, before he had even laid eyes upon it, as though its heart resounded throughout the very air around him, causing tremors to ripple though the space between himself and the opening.

The darkened threshold in the wall of solid rock ahead of him beckoned, and he felt himself being guided across it, delivered into a black void in the heart of the mountain, and the bliss of such heavenly transport tugged the memory back of the two guardians still waiting at his back. So desirous was he to lay eyes upon the sanctity of The Curbane, that he failed to even address them, failed to concern himself about the safety of the unknown ahead of him, and allowed himself simply to enter the place comparatively defenceless.

Voices seemed to whisper to him out of the darkness as it descended around him like a death shroud, hands seeming to stray from out of the murk, to stroke him, to stray against his face and neck. Was this the bliss of this place, he wondered to himself, his thoughts relinquished to the marvel and spectacle of all that he had hoped and planned for? Was this the final step toward ultimate Godhood, to have The Curbane accept him utterly into its embrace, and to have him be a part of it fully? The promise seemed so close to perfection, and as he offered himself out to the consciousness of the place, so something moved up ahead of him, flitting across his path. As the passage seemed to open up, a gentle scarlet glow began to illuminate the rough rocky walls. His eyes, misted with all that the mountain had offered his senses, suddenly snatched a glimpse of the motion, and focussed rapidly as an ominous dark shadow suddenly streaked along the passageway towards him, a monstrous howl reverberating now throughout the chasm like a banshee's wail.

The touch of the living rock inside his body suddenly stiffened, holding his limbs motionless, fusing his feet to the ground like magnets with a strength that defied his own. The cool whispering fluid of the water that had invigorated his senses and his thoughts, now burned and seethed inside him, as though it had transformed itself utterly to acid, and sought to scorch his mind and burn away all his hopes and intent. Casta swayed disorientated for a moment, caught in a grip that was not his to command. The Curbane had brought him here to this spot, knowing all that had coursed through his head, and now it seemed that it would punish him for that.

The creature lunged at him out of the darkness, its great maw stretching wide, contorting into a hideous gaping chasm that sought to devour him whole. His hands rose to conjure some kind of magic to repel the creature, but the rock in his limbs deadened them, and the fluids coursed quickly to extinguish any fury that his powers might project. The jaws descended upon him, but it was not teeth that came to devour him, but the approach of a deadly heat. His body defied his will as he sought to escape this horror, but The Curbane would have him here and face it, and kept him fast like a cold stricken statue. Black claws sank into his chest, clasping his insides as they clenched to a fist, ripping shreds of matter out of him as the fire from its throat came to burn him. It engulfed him in a sea of yellow flame, illuminating the passageway like a flash of phosphorus, searing his skin so that it ran like the waters that burned in his veins. It was an event that surely only lasted a moment, but he witnessed all that happened as though it was an hour spent watching his own demise. His sight began to darken as he gazed down in panic at the stone floor, his blood spilling out of his body now and running beneath his feet. But as he looked, and as his sight continued to deteriorate, so it seemed that his fingers began to blur and melt. Was he even seeing what his eyes were telling him? His fingers seemed almost to glow, glittering as though a fire burned somewhere inside them. And then a flame came, igniting the back of his hand and licking down towards each fingertip. His arm ignited as he watched, and sheets of bright orange flame spilled across his raw and melting limbs like a slick tide. He felt the weakness of his flesh disappear as such fuel was spent, his bones cracking and disintegrating into ash as the heat intensified, his skin melting and dripping onto the floor like molten wax. Casta loosed a scream suddenly as the sight of all this, but he was sure that the sound

367

did not even make it outside the cloud of fire. He stood frozen to the ground as the fire guardian flayed the flesh from his stricken bones, burning him so utterly that as the cloud of fire dissipated, all that remained of the vampire was a charred and ragged husk that creaked and heaved in the aftermath of the furious furnace.

That same watcher who might have viewed the vampire climbing alone toward the summit of the mountain, might also have wondered why the demon did not crumble to dust, so badly burned was he. That sense would have been insufficient to the observer here too, for the consciousness of Casta Mica'tore was still very much alive. The rock held him inside it, just as the force of the water continued to carry the pulse of The Curbane inside it. His thoughts, once coursing with agonies and pain, now carried nothing but intent, and it was this intent that caused him to urge himself out of the bond that would have killed anything else, and onward inside a state of revenge and defiance.

In front of him, the teeth of the fire guardian still sprang like knives from its murky jaws, snapping at his body like traps, as if eager to continue its assault. He watched it from behind a mask so cruelly destroyed by flames that he could see the smoking hush of the sockets through which he saw. As the motions inside the rock became his to own once more, and he managed to haul a mighty step forward, stunning the creature before him with a defiant step towards it, so the charred husk of what had once been his body tumbled away in great crumbling blocks. It cracked and hissed as it hit the floor and fell apart, and he could not help but feel some remorse for the passing of his state. He no longer felt the intensity of pain that the fire guardian had instilled upon him, only the strength of the rock, the coursing motion of the water, and strangely the fury of the fire that had burned him. But with his mind still conjuring thoughts through the elements of the mountain, he forced his second foot forward, and watched with a furious contentment as the fire guardian shrunk back to allow him passage, the source of its element that now glimmered inside him, echoing the uncertainty and perhaps even the fear that it felt, that it had used the full force of its power, and could still not stop this intruder.

"You are another guardian of The Curbane?" Casta spoke aloud, his voice seething and crackling like burning fat.

The creature of fire and shadow nodded its head vaguely, and Casta could feel the uncertainty that it had, watching this vampire who should be so utterly destroyed, not only continue to stand, but demand answers to questions that he had.

"One of the brothers three," Casta mused, almost light-heartedly. "Give me a name in case I should summon you, the same as I should summon your monstrous kin."

The demon of shadow and fire gazed at him for a moment with both confusion and unease, and then it spoke, its voice guttering like the flames that still glimmered in the shifting veils of its body.

"Rail," it said. "I am called Rail."

"Tell me, Rail," Casta said, turning the smoking husk of his limbs over, studying his flesh as it cracked and fell away from the rock that had become his new arms. "Is this what The Curbane wants me to be? Is this to be my new body?"

The guardian Rail stared at the vampire

369

bewildered, not knowing how to answer such a question from a creature who defied death so hideously. He should be dead, burned into the hard rock of the passageway, no longer able to speak, no longer able to threaten the sanctity of The Blood. And yet there he stood. Defiant and angry.

"I... am not sure," the guardian finally replied.

"You have lived here centuries, entwined with the very soul of The Curbane, and you are not sure? Tell me how such a thing can be?"

The fire guardian suddenly seemed helpless, unable to answer, or even unable to continue facing this thing. But Casta Mica'tore now needed an answer, and commanding the protean rock that now made up his limbs, he cast one of them forward, deeper into the heart of the mountain towards its source.

"Well then," he said finally. "Let us not see for ourselves."

EIGHT

COVENANT

What promise could you possibly have to keep?" Jenner wanted to know, stepping after her into the night.

"Jackel El'a'cree was more than just a vampire. He was once Master of this entire province, but so very long ago. He drank from you so that he might grow strong enough to reclaim what was once his. Circumstances chose me to be his companion across these two worlds. I see that now as an honour. You see it as a punishment."

"He drank my blood from my neck, Emma, how can you possibly see it any other way than that? I will never see it as an honour."

"I know, Jenner, but there is nothing I can do about the way that you feel. You remain mortal, your life fleeting. I share blood with a being who was once the most powerful. I died and became reborn into immortality. I will never age, and through that I have inherited grave responsibility."

"But what of this promise. To who do you keep it? Jackel?"

"Of course."

Jenner wanted to take hold of her hand, to feel her touch and have that comfort him in turn. But he remembered the coldness of that touch, her skin as cold as death, and refused to move nearer to her. To look at her was painful, his heart aching with both sorrow and loss. She was here with him now, together once again, but she was different, so utterly different, that perhaps it would have been better if she had gone to the grave and stayed there.

"What did he ask you to do?" he asked her, at length.

She looked at him as though there was nothing she could say that he would understand. But she spoke anyway, relaying the past day or so, as though the boundary between them, the boundary between life and death, was insignificant or even illusory.

"I remember little after my visit to your flat. You left quickly, shortly after the stranger emerged from the shadows, and I was left alone to succumb to his advances. He was at my side before I was even aware of his movement through those shadows, and I barely heard a word that he said, even as he took hold of me and laid a kiss upon my neck. I could not refuse that kiss, there was something about him that nourished submission, destroyed resistance, and as I felt the sharp stab of pain as his teeth broke the surface of my skin, I was suddenly totally helpless beneath him. He sucked the life out of me, forcefully, and I can still recall the strength of his arms as he almost crushed my body beneath his will to feed from me. My sight blackened and a great void seemed to envelop me. I could not scream or resist his trespass, and my last memory before my heart finally stopped, was the sound of a cry, your cry, erupting distantly from your bedroom suddenly so very far away."

"I'm sorry," Jenner murmured.

"For what?"

"For being so caught up in my own world, for

worrying over what he might have done to my room, to my possessions, that I ignored your plight and the danger that I put you in. I already knew that he had killed two people, and yet I left you alone with him."

"It no longer matters, Jenner. What's done is done."

"But it does matter. I let him kill you."

Emma stared at him for a moment in silence. Jenner wasn't sure whether the words were actually sinking in, or whether she was just regarding him as some kind of lunatic, a superficial mortal lunatic, who was no longer of any significance to her. But then she laid a hand upon his, her skin icy, and he resisted the urge to retract it away from her touch, and found even some little comfort in it.

"It is still me," she said. "We may have lost each other for a few brief moments, but now we are back together once again."

"But it can never be like it used to."

"No, it can't," Emma confirmed flatly. "Although there is another way."

Jenner looked at her, uncertain of what she was going to say.

"Jackel El'a'cree made me like this," she said, "perhaps I can make you the same way."

Jenner's brow furrowed as he sought to make sense of what she was saying.

"We could be together forever," she said.

Slowly he began to shake his head. Images flooded into his mind of Jackel feeding at her neck, of death caused by his hand, of killing in order to simply survive. Could he even be one of them? His stomach suddenly turned with the thought of it.

"No," he said.

"No, what?"

373

"I don't want to be like you. Like him. I couldn't -"

"You couldn't kill?"

Jenner shook his head fiercely.

"I have barely fed since Jackel sired me," Emma said. "I dimly recall a fountain of blood at the back of my throat, the taste of its sweetness, its heat. I think I was repulsed, just as you are now with the thought of it, but I also remember swallowing it and feeling it surge inside my body. It gave me a strength, Jenner, like I have never felt before. My head was like mud then, vague and thick, but as I drank, so I felt clarity and a forceful vibrancy."

"You killed another human being?" Jenner could hardly bring himself to say the words, least of all to Emma whom he had so recently come to think of as perfect, perhaps even someone with whom he could share the rest of his life. A wave of relief passed across him as he watched her shake her head.

"I did not kill that man, but I did feed from him. You must understand, Jenner, I am no longer like you, no longer the person that I once was."

"But you must be, Emma."

"You may still call me by that name, but I am no longer living. I do not breathe, and I no longer have a hunger for anything other than blood. You must accept that."

Jenner searched the bright intensity of her eyes, and knew that all that she said was true. But how could he come to terms with such truth? She was his Emma, his beloved Emma, and when he looked deep into her eyes, as he did now, all he could see was the one woman who had made more sense to him than any other ever had. Perhaps it was his guilt for how he had treated her when she had been alive, he had no idea, but all he wanted was to have her back, knowing deep down in his heart that such an occurrence would never happen again.

"I have to go now," Emma suddenly said, snatching him from his thoughts.

"Where?"

"I must leave the mountain, and cross the plains to where the city of Kar'mi'shah once stood."

"What for?"

"It is what Jackel El'a'cree wanted me to do before he died."

"Fuck Jackel El'a'cree."

"He was my Master, Jenner, and I will pay respect to him."

"But what about us, Emma?"

"What about us?"

"What happens now?"

"Nothing happens. Our destinies no longer follow the same path. I must leave this mountain and find the temple in which Jackel once resided. Upon that altar I will leave his remains so that he will forever be home."

"And then what?"

"Then...?"

Jenner moved closer to her, knowing that he must press some kind of answer out of her before he lost her yet again.

"Then... I do not know," she finally admitted.

Jenner stared at her, not knowing what to say. All things had come to an end, it seemed, and there was nowhere left to go.

"Come with me," Emma said at last. "Travel with me across the desert to find Kar'mi'shah."

"The province is dead. There is nothing to find there."

"There is nothing for you here either. Vampires still

haunt these mountains, Jenner, vampires like the one that killed your journal-writer. Where there is one, there will be another. It is not safe for you here. You have no protection against them. At least with me, you may stand a chance."

"But what of Montague?" he asked, glancing back towards the cave.

"What of him? Do you want to save his soul?"

"We came together," Jenner started. "I can't leave him here alone."

"Then stay and be killed. I must go."

"Wait," he cried, staring into her cold bright eyes as he grasped her icy hand. He knew that she was right. His life had become lower than it had ever been before. Those two years spent in prison had been bliss, an ignorant bliss, compared to any of this. He looked beyond her, across the dark plains that stretched beneath the midnight sky. There were no lights of civilisation anywhere to be seen, no spark of fires, no lamps or hearths. It was a barren wilderness where only scavengers could survive. But surely he would become a scavenger now, searching for scraps of anything that might keep himself alive. Perhaps even he might need to feed on a blood-filled carcass if he was to survive another day. Whatever he would do, there could be no solution in staying on the rocky slopes of the mountain, and to have the protection of a vampire was probably the best protection he could earn in such a terrible and forbidding world. With a dazed mind, he glanced once again at the entrance to the cave, and then turned back, and slowly nodded his head.

NINE

AT THE SOURCE OF THE CURBANE

The Curbane rose high inside the vaulted chamber, a vast seething mass of glimmering rock, buzzing like a vast hive of bees, and Casta Mica'tore stood before it as though he was its king. He could feel the trepidation in the minds of the three guardians, just as he could feel the substance of their being flowing throughout his body; rock, water and fire. It gave his body, (the charred husk that he had known all his life was now gone, replaced by this seething amalgamation), the strength to embrace the source of the Blood Of The Ancients, the most powerful element in Kar'mi'shah, with a certainty that it would not simply destroy him for the blasphemy of trying.

With his arms held out wide to embrace the sheer power that dominated the cavern, the ground shuddering with energies beneath his feet, Casta threw back his head in awe at the mightiness of this one true source of power, dwarfed by its immense magnificence and resounding dominance, and with a motion of his hands, forced them deep into the well of the rock and began to claw himself inside it, as though it was little more than a child's mudpile.

The face of the rock wall resisted his intent at first, flowing and congealing to deny the intrusion, but the will of The Curbane, already eager to transform the vampire's body into new and interesting shapes, had undone itself, allowing him passage where before he would have had none. It had taken his flesh, but it had made the mistake of replacing it with something far greater, a part of itself, and it was that mistake that had led to its present danger.

Behind him stood the three brothers, Nomad, Vessel and Rail, who had become transformed into the guardians of this most holy of places. The Curbane itself had seen fit to resurrect them into vast creatures of rock, water and fire, but it had not always been so. As Casta scaled through the towering hulk of The Curbane, so he felt the wills of the three surge through him, their thoughts, their emotions, their memories, all divining to become a part of him. He saw, in the moments that his new body came apart and reformed, the events that had taken place in the history of their minds, and it was of a history that he himself had only a primary dimensional view.

On the night the tribes had been decimated, there had been confusion beyond measure. They had all witnessed the deaths of members of their families, their brothers and sisters falling beneath a shroud of blood and dust, as a terrible creature devoured them, tearing them unmercifully to shreds. This beast the brothers had not understood, but Casta had learned a new perspective to their memories, knowing that it was his creation that had butchered them, his magic that had gone astray to destroy all that they had known. Casta himself had managed to summon a portal to carry both himself and his wife away from the beast that would endanger even she. It had been conjured to kill only the Master of Kar'mi'shah. But his power had been insufficient, and it had threatened the life of the only person he had truly ever cared about. But even that portal was conjured poorly, and broke into fissures that divided the temple and catapulted several others into its clutches. Where they had been taken was anyone's guess, and his incompetence there, as with the beast, had snatched his beloved away from him, and to a place where he would never lay eyes upon her again for hundreds of years to follow.

Only a few had managed to escape both the beast and the ruptured portal, and Nomad, Vessel and Rail had made it as far as the mountains. There was little to sustain them on the cold bleak heights, but they somehow managed to survive on what pitiful creatures they could find to feed upon. But they stumbled upon a force one night as they travelled higher and higher in their flight away from the terror that had destroyed Kar'mi'shah, a force that called to them, beating with a rhythm too mesmerising to be ignored. That force had been The Curbane, and it had drawn them so very fully into its domain.

But there had been another, a fourth vampire who had fled with them. Casta could see him now in the theatre of his memories as he watched them play out. His face was shrouded by darkness, but then as a wall of flame engulfed the one that would later become known as the guardian Rail, Casta recognised his features, and named him as the trafficker Coda-Beda.

So, that was how Coda had managed to gain access to The Blood. He had been a member of the same tribe, the same family, that had grown to guard The Curbane. The other three brothers had remained to protect it from any others that might have tried to gain access to it; anyone, it seemed, except their brother.

Was this the reason why Coda had been the only one to return to Earth with vials of it? Perhaps others had tried, and perhaps Nomad, Vessel and Rail had ground them into the rock the same way that they had tried with him.

Casta's magic had been lacking then, the events that had dominated the aftermath of the decimation was proof of that. But now, surely, his magic had reached heights sufficient to bring him to ultimate Godhood. His very being here in the halls of The Curbane was undoubtedly confirmation of that. He had triumphed where others had failed. He would have The Blood, and he would rule Kar'mi'shah, drinking in the lushness of its green plains, basking in the glory of its thriving populace, and enveloping himself in all the bounty that the province had to offer. He would be Heaven's king, and soon.

The vampire passed through the layers of rock that pulsed with the heartbeat of the Ancient's Blood, changing his being and making it seethe with renewed energies, the memories of the brothers three surging through his mind - images of burning flesh and swirling vapours - all mingling and congealing to make the final forms that had stood against him. After The Curbane had disfigured them into the wills that it so desired, it had allowed them access to The Blood that flowed there, Blood that had drained from the oldest vampires to have walked the land countless centuries before. It was potent, this Blood, and fabled to be an elixir of heightened experience, and their consummation of it had heightened them even more than they could have imagined. So unstable was the very ground and air around The Curbane, that a portal opened itself up on the heights of the mountains.

Coda-Beda had gone through, and found other vampires who had been catapulted from one world to another, who knew the legends of The Blood Of The Ancients, and who needed, as Coda met their acquaintances one after the other, the source of The Blood from their home world if they were to survive what paltry pickings they could find for themselves in a new and foreign land.

The distribution of The Blood Of The Ancients began then, with Nomad, Vessel and Rail gaining access to The Blood, and Coda-Beda taking it across the threshold to a world called Earth. There was a demand, Coda always told them. Prey was scarce and the land was dangerous. If the vampires were to survive in the new world, then they would need a continued supply. There were portals across the province, he had been told, but what was there to return to? Only death at the behest of the creature that was confirmed as neither alive nor dead. Still to this day, centuries later, the guardians knew nothing of existence, except what Coda would tell them. But what could they ever return to? There would be no normal life for them in the temples any more, nor would they ever be able to walk through the lush plains of Kar'mi'shah, or see its moonlit river or glittering sea. The Curbane was their only home now, and all it ever would be.

Coda was simply another vampire that had worked for him, but without the insight of Nomad's memory, all that he had known of this vampire was now unnervingly superficial. Originated from Kar'mi'shah, he had been one of the few lucky enough to escape, finding himself delivered into the growing hamlets that would later become collectively known as

London. It seemed he had come upon a portal in their home world, he and yet another, and they had kept up its use, periodically travelling back and forth in the hope of renewed safety or unity. It had not come, of course. So it was that they made a home in that strange world, but when feeding upon the local populace had begun to become noticed, and the need for something more secretive in order to survive became a factor, so it was that they became aware of a supply and demand marketplace.

It brought them wealth, and quickly too. Other vampires had found their way to the districts of London and the surrounding towns as well, but it was only Coda-Beda and his associate that knew of the portal, and they soon discovered how much these other vampires were willing to trade in exchange for the most valuable commodity known - The Blood Of The Ancients. How they were managing to even get their hands on it was a mystery, but get their hands on it they did, and power and profit boomed for them.

Only when Casta Mica'tore crossed the Channel out of Europe and found himself delivered by carriage into the docklands along the Thames, did he learn of these two enterprising vampires. He went to work for them initially, delivering The Blood in exchange for safety in the new and dangerous city. He continued to study his arts as he worked, however, and grew in both strength and ability, while he continued to build up a network of Coda's customers. Within a decade, he was strong enough to take a stranglehold of their operation, and killed Coda's associate in a swift murder, but not so swift that nobody knew who had done it. So Casta threatened the remaining vampire, and took a share of the profits as well as keeping a hold over those vampires he had sold to. His name became feared over time as his strength and power grew, until he met a mortal man one night, who had not nearly so many contacts as his own, but enough important ones that it made dealing with him even more advantageous. That man's name was Montague, and if there was one thing that he would curse himself for, it was that he had not kept as tight a rein on him as he would have done decades before.

The ground shook its concerns as the intruder inside its vaults sought to take all the secrets that it had, but as Casta finally broke through into the soup of the Ancient's Blood, learned how it filtered throughout the mountain, recycling and recircling so that the mountain no longer held The Blood, but carried it in its fissures and crevices, like veins in the body of a living thing. He felt it pass into him, surging through his body of rock, igniting in his body of fire, churning in his body of water. It illuminated his innards, glittering in bright iridescent seams that glimmered and burned until his head seemed set to explode. The Curbane sought to reject him, even as he pushed himself in upon it, violating the sacred place with his intrusion, and claiming all that it had to offer. The power was surging through him, he could feel it race through every mote of his being, burning and turning like sparking cartwheels. He could feel the place desperate to keep him back, fighting to reject him at every inch he clawed forward, but as he enveloped himself deeper and deeper into its thick viscous fluid, so he began to understand more of what the legends spoke of.

He suddenly saw a picture of himself, standing in the centre of The Curbane, struggling against the forces that fought to reject him. He realised as he witnessed this, that this was Nomad's view of him, watching him from inside the living rock, spectating as he took hold of the one thing that he had been created into to keep safe from violation like this. Tendrils of rock pierced him in several places, he now saw - he had not even realised that he was being kept in such a way - and so he reached down and simply fused the barriers with his own limbs, increasing the strength of his own mass.

A halo of searing white heat suddenly seemed to pass over him, and he wondered if he even imagined it, his senses coming now in violent and uncertain snatches as The Curbane relented to his presence. Was it even fire at all, or merely just The Curbane accepting him finally and utterly into the mighty and powerful substance of its eternal being?

Casta felt himself become one with its power as he settled into its column of boiling blood, his halo of flame encircling it, drawing from it, learning and deciphering rapidly. He was now a part of The Curbane, and the secrets that it held began to flow into him, filling his mind, flooding his being, until he knew all that made the world work, and all that made the vampires immortal.

TEN

THE BOUNDARY OF DEATH

There seemed no possible way for Emma to navigate their route across the barren desert so accurately, and yet they travelled swiftly and directly. They'd left the mountain together after a long argument with Montague, who'd chosen resolutely to stay behind, claiming that he was going to return to the forest where Coda's portal had delivered them, where he would try and attempt a return journey back to London. Jenner, too, had felt the wisdom of this, wanting as much as his benefactor to return to a world that they knew so well, but he had only just rediscovered Emma and did not want to let her disappear out of his life so quickly again this time.

So it was that they departed, Emma urging Jenner that she had to travel before sunrise and find shelter or else their relationship would be over more quickly than he could imagine. And permanently. Jenner relented, and left Montague before they could properly say any goodbyes. He had a feeling that it would probably be the last time they would ever set eyes upon each other, and although neither of them was sure that either one of them would survive until daybreak, they kept to the decisions that they made.

Jenner pondered the wisdom of their separation as he hurried to keep up with a fleet-footed Emma. He had cursed Montague's name so many times, hourly sometimes, and yet he suddenly felt a pang of loss at the thought of never seeing him again. They had both shared something momentous, a crossing of worlds, something found, something lost, and yet perhaps it was best that they separate, to go further afield and spread the word that there were new dominions to find, new worlds to explore. It startled him when a series of lights flickered on a distant sand-swept horizon and Emma relayed that this was the glimmer of promise that Jackel had discerned high up on the mountainside. Jenner could see little hope of a glorious city, and as they edged closer to its borders, so it was that Emma confirmed the poverty of the province.

There was little to guide her once they passed the first few buildings, partial shelters and farmhouses built and repaired insufficiently against the rigors of the desert storms. Jenner wondered, as he passed the low-level shacks, whether one of these had been the home of the journal-writer, a poor hovel in which the people of Kar'mi'shah had huddled or even perished beneath assaults of the vampires that had come down from the dark mountains to feed. Further ahead through the swirling dust rose a number of stone buildings and monoliths, but these too had been badly eroded and punished by the onslaught of the encroaching wasteland, battered for many many years and offering no hope that at least part of the city still stood its ground defiantly and with grace.

"Jackel's description fits nothing here," Emma announced suddenly as she came to a halt at a junction.

The sky was brightening, and with its early shallow light, Jenner could make out more of the vista of toppled columns and dune-covered temples. If this city had once been great, as he had certainly been led to believe, then it must have been a very long time ago, and without the aid or care of workers to keep back the sand.

"Jackel described many things," Emma went on, scanning each of the routes leading off from the junction, "but I can see nothing of which he spoke. Rivers, oceans, towers, courtyards. There is none of that. All I can see is death and ruin."

"You'll have to find somewhere to hide out of the sunlight," Jenner prompted her.

She turned to look at him.

"Yes," she said. "I must."

Jenner indicated one of the more upright structures, and together they crossed quickly towards it, searching for some way inside, and hoping that there might be sufficient shelter for her.

A passageway still stood upright, the stone archway keeping up the weight of the temple that had toppled awkwardly, threatening to flatten the building completely. Inside was humid and musty, carrying the weight of the heavy desert air like a solid mass. There was little more than a single chamber left standing, two further annexes had crumbled, and a stairwell leading downward into the ground had collapsed partway down. It was almost completely destroyed, but with dawn looming in less than an hour or so they both knew that to look elsewhere might risk Emma's existence altogether.

"You should look for something to eat," Emma said to him, as they made a seat for themselves upon the rubble-strewn floor.

"You too," Jenner replied, failing to locate her face in the heavy gloom.

"I will have strength enough until tomorrow night. You, however, will not. You should leave now and have a look around. The vampires of the mountains should have left every shadow now and headed back towards their sanctuary."

"I don't think I'm going to find any food just lying around."

"There are people here. Find someone charitable."

"I don't think it works like that here. Food is scarce."

"What makes you say that?"

"Can't you see it? Hunger is the biggest killer here. More than -"

"More than vampires?" Emma said.

"Says a lot, doesn't it?

There was silence for a while after that brief exchange, both of them pondering the obvious that without sustenance for either of them, both of their futures were in doubt. Down in the hidden depths of the fallen temple, they were at least together again, and yet the cruel darkness, although protecting Emma from the sunlight that would engulf her in a gown of flame, kept the sight of each other away from them. Jenner longed to touch her, to hold her and both give and gain comfort by such an embrace. And yet the thought of feeling her flesh cold instead of warm as he remembered it chilled him with a hateful unease. Why couldn't he just forget her death and take hold of her? He didn't want any kind of physical love, didn't want to be inside her, (wasn't that called necrophilia, he distantly thought), but just to have her close, and to know that his love was reciprocated. Could they even make love again? He was curious, now that the thought had come into his head, but then his own conscience crept up behind it and demanded the question, had they ever made love?

He wanted to dispel the darkness suddenly, to defy its solid cloak so that he could lay his eyes upon her beautiful face once again, and feel a glow inside him that told him that she was still his. Without the knowledge that she was even returning his gaze, he remained in a kind of isolation, where he could not even hear the sound of her breath, or the movement of her hands or the fabric of her clothes. She was motionless, just as she had been in the cave, and to be denied every sound or sight was simply too much. Through the envelope of blackness that shrouded her from him, he reached out blindly, and grabbed hold of the first part of her that he could. It was soft yet resilient, and not knowing whether it was even her arm or her breast, he followed the direction of his hand and swept forward to kiss her.

Her lips had been warm and sweet when last he had pressed his own against them, but now they were cold and tasteless, and it felt as though he was kissing raw meat. The contact between them was brief, for she snatched herself out of his grasp quickly and swept out into the darkness altogether.

He reached out his arms again to try and find her, but she had moved completely out of his range. The kiss had been rash, but he had wanted it, and to have her repel him was something that he had not anticipated. He stared suddenly into the void inside the temple, the air still hot and stale, and tried to find her form in its shadows. The murk was impenetrable and he could discern nothing. Gently, he spoke her name, but she did not, or would not, reply.

"Emma?" he said again, and wondered if she was even still in the same chamber.

"What did you think you were doing?" she wanted

to know.

She was some distance away, and not even in the direction that he was looking.

"What's wrong?" Jenner wanted to know.

"You," she told him. "Your kiss."

"I'm sorry. I... I just wanted to."

"No. It's me that should be sorry. I always said that I wanted us to be together. It's just that... I didn't think it would be quite like this."

"I heard somewhere that love is never perfect."

Suddenly he felt her words right next to his ear, and jerked back in surprise as he realised that she had moved back beside him.

"Love?" she said. "Where did you hear of such a word?"

It took a moment for him to realise that she was joking. She had not seemed to be in possession of humour. Not since... not since her rebirth.

"It took a while for me to realise," he confessed quietly.

"As well as my death," she said.

"Yes. Losing you was everything. Perhaps kissing you now was wrong."

"No, it wasn't wrong. I wanted to kiss you too. But I am different now. I didn't want you to touch me in such a way. Not with me like this."

"I'd be lying if I told you that it didn't matter."

"I know, Jenner. But remember that I offered you a solution. The only one I can think of."

Jenner took hold of her hand in the darkness, only this time Emma did not shrink away from it.

"But I cannot accept," he told her. "I could never be like you."

"I understand."

"But I do still love you," he told her. "And I always will."

"Always for you is but a handful of years. My love is devotional until the end of time. That is a long time. Perhaps that is why you could never be like me. Commitment is an easy thing in something so fleeting. Being reborn has shown me a road so much longer than the track I saw before. It is a straighter road, but it had less junctions to choose. My path is never-ending. I cannot deviate. That is our difference, Jenner."

Gently he squeezed her hand, but Emma did not, or could not, reciprocate the feeling, and so there was no physical comfort to be had from it. He tried to smile, but wondered if she could even see it in the murk. He could not see her face after all. She asked so very much of him, prompting his death in order to cross boundaries into the world of the monster. He had done some terrible things in his past, but he had only hurt people financially, stealing things here and there from people who could well afford to have some things lifted. But to invite himself into a world that sought the death of innocent people, deaths like those the journal-writer had written of, that was simply too much to ask. He was human, and he wanted to stay that way, even if most of the time he was unhappy or defenceless. He wasn't a religious man, but he thought on occasion that he might have to make his peace with some god some day.

He said no more to Emma on the subject after that, and even drifted into a shallow sleep for a few hours, content that the blood-drinker beside him would respect his neck enough not to feed upon it while he dreamt, the same neck that she had pressed kisses to only days before. They were together again, that was all he thought as he let the darkness take him. It was enough for now too. More than he'd had in what seemed a very long time. More than perhaps he'd ever need.

ELEVEN

REUNION

Casta swept down off the mountain inside a seething cocoon of living rock. He could see all that made up the world, the living and the dead and all that lay in between, and felt the majesty and the magic within it all. The desert had seemed dead when he had first returned to Kar'mi'shah, the sands swirling, raging, seeking to cover everything with its choking blanket. Even the mountains had only seemed alive because of the influence of The Curbane that kept its life-force beating inside it. That life-force he carried inside him now, pounding and churning with a fury that refused to be contained. But his own magic was strong, and the two raged in an unending conflict, sparking throughout his new-found body of living elements like broken power cables.

The night sky above him was still heavy with a humidity that offered no hope of rain, and yet somewhere within the it he could feel the density of its motes, packed and contained and unable to deliver the moisture that might end the relentless drought. No matter, he thought, as he swept onward across the desert, taking in all that the province could offer him, the parched earth, the scavenging beasts, the baked river that had once offered a bounty of life that had outweighed anything that had ever been seen before, in this world or indeed any other.

Casta found his bearings quickly as he approached the toppled buildings of what had once been the city's outskirts. Blocks of stone littered routes drifted high with heavy dunes, columns crumbled into useless shards. His home was now a ruin, but at least he was its Master.

Locating the river, he circled round, searching for the pyramid which had become his last night in Kar'mi'shah. It had been in this temple, in Jackel El'a'cree's temple, that he had called forth his creature, and willed it to destroy the vampire once and for all.

The past brought with it a heavy burden, and even now it weighed upon his back like the broken blocks that littered his fallen city. What could have happened to such a mighty province to have caused such devastation? What could have caused such chaos? And then the ruined form of the Raza loomed into view out of the darkness of the night, less destroyed than most but certainly far from intact, and Casta came to a staggering rest in front of it, his boots of stone absorbing the surface of the ground, and receiving messages of its fate through them and up into his conscious being.

They had shared a proximity, Alexia and Catherine, in a city a long way from home, a city called London, the capital of a cold dank island surrounded by chilly seas. It seemed, as they spoke now, that Catherine had heard of Alexia, but the knowledge was not reciprocated. Catherine had heard her name mentioned frequently, but of details, or who she even was, she had no idea. To meet her now answered a few vague questions of general interest, but even the dismissal of that seemed easy.

Alexia, on the other hand, had never heard of the other vampire, nor indeed had any knowledge of her existence in London. Perhaps she might not have felt quite so isolated from her home world, if she'd had someone to confide in for those very long years. Catherine, however, was quiet, distant even, and viewed any kind of reminiscing with disdain. What was the point, her vague words seemed to say, knowing that their home was destroyed? Nothing could bring back the great city that they had once known. It was all over.

The third vampire, however, the one who had remained at the Raza after the holocaust, said little during their exchange. He had known less and less conversation over centuries that had dwindled into one another, and it seemed awkward for him to participate. Alexia was sure that he could offer some vital insights, but for him to even articulate his memories seemed sometimes beyond him, and so she left him alone, content that one day he might supply answers to all the questions that she had.

Alexia turned to look back once again at Catherine, and saw that she was staring into the murky depths of the temple, the columns and great structures now broken into dust across the vast stone floor. She sat motionless, like a corpse, and Alexia went slowly to her to ask her about the life she'd had previously in Kar'mi'shah.

"I made my home here in this temple," she reluctantly began, "but down in the catacombs, away from both mortals and vampires. I have no need of them now, and nor, I suspect, will I ever want for their company again. I have little desire to tell of my memories, but I also feel that I have much to unload to someone."

"I have nowhere to hide," Alexia said to her. "Not now."

The other vampire stared at her for a moment, and with a movement that could almost have been a shrug of resignation in some other living being, she began slowly to tell her tale.

"My full name is Catherine Calleh, and I was born a mortal human baby in Reesa, a district of the city of Kar'mi'shah. My father was a trader in the local market, selling pottery he made from clay dug near the delta. It was not a lucrative business by any means but we got by. I remember my childhood as a lonely time. There were other children in the tenement where we lived, but their friendship seemed so conditional, and because of that, I rarely played with them. By my sixteenth birthday, I was introduced to a man who was to become my husband, a man called Troy, and after a brief marriage ceremony, I went to live with him in a house a few blocks from my parent's building. It was then that things began to turn bad."

The expression upon her face did not change throughout her dialogue, not even as the destitution of her youth came tumbling out. Alexia felt the sadness in her story, but the vampire relayed it as though it was simply a story, told from old worn pages, not surprised at the ending.

"It was within the first week of our marriage," Catherine said, "that Troy first took his hand to me. I forget now the reason for our argument, but it was something trivial, I am sure. He told me that I had disobeyed him, and that I was not to think that this would be the start of things to come. I still recall the initial shock of the stinging blow as he brought the palm of his hand across my face. It hurt beyond measure, and I was so stunned that he had done it at all, that I did not speak of it to anyone. Months passed without any further incident, and in time I forgot about it altogether. It was only when it happened again, though, and when I slapped him back, that I realised it was to be the biggest mistake I could have made."

She paused after that, and it seemed as though that was the story ended. Alexia wanted to know the extent of that violence, how her own birth into immortality might have compensated for this outrage, but she did not want to push Catherine into anything too regressive. Catherine did continue after a time, however, but it was once again with the same cold recollection, staring into middle distance as though she was relaying someone else's childhood, not her own.

"Troy dragged me screaming through the house by my hair before tying my hands to the great brass handle of the front door. The door was open to the street, but it seemed he was not afraid to be seen by our neighbours and friends, but in fact relished the sight of his disciplining his household. So it was over the threshold to our home that he began to beat me, landing punch after punch to my stomach and face. I wept and pleaded for him to stop but he would not. It seemed that his blows went on for hours, the passers-by in the street glancing my way before continuing past. I remember the pain in my head and ribs as I felt the endless dull blows one after the other until I blacked out."

Alexia stared at her, not believing such a thing could have happened, the events so different to the childhood she had known, of games and laughter, of

397

friends and of pastimes. Behind her, she felt the third vampire listening to Catherine's outpouring, although with so little emotion used in its telling, it was surely far from a personal conversation.

"When I later awoke, I found myself staring up at the ceiling of our bedroom. Troy was sitting on the edge of the bed looking down at me. He was smiling and he held a cup of water in his hand, which he offered to me as I tried to sit up. 'Here, you should drink this,' I remember him saying to me, putting his other hand tenderly to my forehead. The touch brought a stinging pain, and I flinched at the contact. I did not want to take the water from him, but he pressed the cup to my lips anyway and urged me to take a drink from it.

"'It will not happen again,' I heard him softly say, as I struggled to swallow the water. My eyes stung with my hatred for him, but as he continued, I realised that what he had said was not an apology but an instruction to me. 'You will never speak to me again like you did earlier,' he continued, 'and you will certainly never touch me again in anger. I hope you learnt something today. Next time I will not be so lenient.'"

"I did not speak to him for days after that, only simple replies to his comments and enquiries. I went to bed before him, I rose before he woke, and I avoided him around the house as much as possible. A similar incident occurred less than two weeks later, when he returned home one evening and tried to touch me. I moved away but he was adamant that he would enter me that night. When I exclaimed that he would not, he hit me again, and then again and again. I lay still after that, and allowed his entrance inside me until he was done. So it was, then, that this routine continued, week after week, for five agonising years. I could not tell our friends or neighbours because they already knew of my insolence to Troy, and I could not tell my parents because they surely would not have believed such a thing of my husband who was so courteous in their company. The day of my salvation, however, also became the day of my immortality."

"Was it then that one of the BloodGods saved you?"

"In a manner of speaking, yes, but it was as a punishment, not as part of any reward."

"I don't understand you."

"Troy had left the house one night to meet with his friends," Catherine explained, "and I had prepared a knife from the kitchen beneath my pillow in readiness for his return. I lay for hours in the half-light, waiting for him, my eyes growing heavy as my body demanded rest. I fought all urges to sleep, knowing that what I had initiated with the knife must be finished that night. When I heard the door to our house clatter open and Troy climb noisily up the stairs, I took hold of the knife and gripped its wooden handle firmly. He spoke aloud to me as he entered the bedroom, comprehending me to be sleeping, but demanding his intentions anyway. I heard him take off his clothes and drop them to the floor, and then felt the covers being lifted from my body as he tugged them from me. I refrained from rolling over to look at him, but waited until I felt him slide into bed beside me, his hardened member already pressing against the small of my back. It was then, and with a small cry of rage, that I pulled the knife from its hiding place and plunged it backwards and into his body lying beside me."

"You killed your husband?" the third vampire uttered. He was stood beside them now. Alexia had not even heard his approach, so engrossed was she in Catherine's tale.

"I never so much as looked at him as I stabbed him," Catherine confessed. "I had thought before, when I had planned his murder, that I would want to see his face as he felt the pain I wanted to inflict, as he had looked down on me as he had hurt me. But I could not turn to look at him. I felt the resistance of the knife hard against him as it found its way into his chest, and I felt too his hands clasp hold of me in both surprise and alarm. He let out a staggered cry that his lungs would not allow him to finish, and then his body gave up a violent jerk before he fell into a motionless slump. I lay there for some time after that with my hand still holding the knife, his body cooling against my skin. I could feel too his spilled blood spreading out beneath me as it flowed from his body, but still I could not move. I may even have slept a little, I cannot remember, but if I did it would have been my first restful sleep in years."

Catherine turned to look at them both now, and for the first time Alexia could see her mask of coldness lifting, a glimmer of emotion seeping through like a spring of mountain water.

"At sunrise I left the house and went out into the street. I must not have comprehended my actions, for I began to tell people that my husband lay dead in our bed, a knife plunged deep into his heart. At first they passed me by, an insane woman with a bloodstained night-dress, but when one of them stopped to listen, they all stopped, and before I knew what was happening, I had been taken to the temple. I remember my mother saying to me inside the Raza

Pyramid that it was not my fault, but that there was an evil inside me that had to be cast out. To this day I am still not sure if I told her then what had happened within our house during my five year marriage to him, but if I did then her attitude remained unchanged."

"'The Gods will rid you of the evil in your blood,' she said to me, even as she lovingly stroked my hair. 'It is your blood that needs cleansing. You can be saved, my daughter, but your blood must be made pure again.' So it was, then, that the BloodGods took me from the great hall and down into one of the lower sanctums. I remember that it was dark, and that I could see very little, but I was laid out upon a stone plinth and stripped bare. I did not struggle, not even as I felt the cold touch of the Gods upon my skin. All I wanted then was a release from my life, and an end to my tortured past."

"So your birth was a cleansing ritual?" Alexia asked quietly.

"Is there another way?"

Alexia suddenly felt choked, as much for this vampire Catherine, as for herself. She had been sired through love, born into immortality by her husband. She had committed no crime, nor known any reason for having her blood cleansed of all evil. The vampire's tale was indeed sad, and there seemed reason now for her coldness and vacancy of emotion. It was a survival response, a shutting off of all feeling. How could she blame her? Her youth had been a tortured one.

"My entire body clenched as I felt that first bite," Catherine went on, eager now that she had started, to finish her story and perhaps even be cleansed by that, "teeth sinking into my neck and beginning to draw that evil blood out of my veins. I grasped the plinth with all my strength as I let the Gods do their work, drawing my blood out of me until I was dry. My head grew light, my fingers went numb, and my thoughts became elusive and slipped swiftly from my grasp, swirling about me in an easy delirium. But then from somewhere nearby, a voice instructed me to drink, to take back what had been stolen. I became aware of that cold flesh again, but this time against my dulled lips, and as I opened my mouth, I tasted the sweetness of the wound that had been made for me. I'm still not sure whether I was fully aware that it was the blood of the Gods that I was drinking, but perhaps if I had known I would not have done it. But I drank and I drank, until my thoughts began to return, and I began to feel a surge of energy pass through me that could suddenly not be tamed."

"The God's flesh was taken from me and I lay for a few moments just comprehending my ritual. The sanctum was just as dark as it had been before, only now I could see the face of the God standing over me, my sight suddenly keen and able to make sense of the blackness. It was white and without emotion, his eyes simply returning my gaze, his lips and bared teeth stained red with my blood. It was then that I realised that my hearing was keen and alert too, and that I could now hear voices out in the street, talking and chanting, as well as the wind whistling across the great stone blocks of the pyramid itself. The air was sweeter now too, perhaps because it carried on its back the fragrances of both my blood as well as the God's before me. So many new things to see and smell and hear. So much new information to attend to, it stunned me."

"Rats were busy in the great hall, I could hear their tiny claws tapping across the marble flooring. Outside in the eaves of the tenements, I could make out the scratching of wood as owls rocked on clenched talons as the night air ruffled their feathers. Dogs sniffed the air as they picked over debris, cats clawed the bark of trees before testing their balance in the branches, and beneath them all, termites crawled throughout the dirt in search of tiny carrion. My focus gradually returned to me, and I turned my head to look back at the face of the BloodGod. He stepped back away from the plinth and allowed me to find my own feet, and I pushed myself round and slipped down onto the cold ground. Even the stone of the floor had new wonders to bestow upon my bare feet, the pattern of its layers, the texture of its grains, everything was like a textbook to my hungry senses. The BloodGod then took hold of my hand and began to speak."

"'Catherine Calleh,' he said to me. 'You have left your family to join ours. A new and great horizon has opened up for you and it is here that you will learn its secrets.' I think I looked at him without speaking, unable to comprehend anything of what he was saying. He was unblemished in his appearance to me, perfect even, and I was simply in wonder to be able to lay my eyes upon him. 'You now belong to the Faraoh tribe,' he continued, as he led me through the sanctum towards an annex at the back of the chamber, 'and I am your Master.' I sat on the edge of a bed for a while, thinking, before I eventually lay back on the silken sheets. It seemed almost to cradle me, like my mother's arms had done so many years before, and it rocked me gently towards a blissful sleep. My eyes closed, and the world drifted slowly away in the darkness that was left behind. The tapping of the rats ceased, as did the scratching of the owls. The dogs and cats of Kar'mi'shah ceased their nightly travels, and the termites quietened their labours until there was but suffocating silence. My ascension into immortality began that night, but it was only the start of a learning experience that was to go so far beyond religious devotion that I would not have previously thought it possible."

Her eyes had become less vacant, more focussed now upon the two vampires who stood to listen to her story. Her tone was still monotonous, but her sharpness had returned, as though the telling of what had made her, had brought fresh vehemence back into her being.

"I woke the following night to find the BloodGod's hand upon my brow. His face was expressionless as he looked down upon me, as a priest might look down upon his disciple, and I could not help but stare up into his huge eyes in awe. It was not a time for words, those precious few moments that we gazed at each other. It seemed we both understood what had happened the previous night when we had drunk from each other's veins, but I was still very much aware that I knew nothing. That was the feeling that the God had instilled in me - understanding and bewilderment at the same time, knowledge and ignorance, paradoxes melded seamlessly. He made me feel secure, but only in the sense that I needed to learn more from him, and that night was going to be one hell of a first lesson."

"I knew, of course, the religion of my people, (by that I mean the people to whom I had once belonged; the Faraohs were now my family). I watched the people of the city build us our temples, organise our festivals and ceremonies. They kept vigil over us during the day, and sought guidance during our waking hours at night. We were not the blood-drinking killers that some of us were later forced into by any means. We were Gods, and we had responsibilities. No one would worship us if all we did was butcher them, but I am getting ahead of myself. All of this you already know."

"I am a Faraoh the same as you," Alexia said to her. "All that time spent alone in London, we might have spent together."

"I was not to spend time with pleasantries. I had my duties, and I wanted to find those that had done harm to this place, and see them dead. That was my only passion."

"Do you think that I was happy at what happened to my family? Our family? We lost many of the same people."

"I thought that the one responsible, when finally he was caught, would make the hunt necessary, the endless wait worthwhile. But now that I see my home again, see the state that it has fallen into, I find that none of it matters any more. Even with revenge, Kar'mi'shah lies in ruins. Justice will not rebuild it."

"What you say is true, Catherine. But perhaps we can build again."

"How can we do such a thing. It is useless. Kar'mi'shah is gone, and shall never be again."

"There are still people here," Alexia persisted. "Perhaps they will help us rebuild this temple, let them know that at least some of the Gods have returned."

"And what can we do for them? We can offer nothing. So much of the art and culture of the people of Kar'mi'shah was based upon its religion, and the dominant religion of Kar'mi'shah was the worship of the Faraohs. This pyramid itself was once decorated with countless images and pictures of the Gods in many different guises. My Master himself favoured the head of a spider whilst keeping his own body intact, but even those images are gone, crumbled to dust along with the mighty stone walls that once held them high."

"Defeat is not an answer."

"It is the only one we have," Catherine declared, and without any chance for further debate, she turned her back and wandered away into one of the darker recesses of the chamber.

So much of what she said was true. Alexia knew that the province they both once knew was now a flattened ruin, overrun and choked with relentless desert. Nothing grew here, and those that had survived death this long, knew to expect it soon. Hope refused a home here, as did luck and prosperity. There was nothing to be gained by staying in such a place. Nothing, except that it was their home. They were back at last, after so many years away. If they were to leave now, where in this world or any other could they ever possibly go?

Casta did not need an entrance to find his way inside. The broken rock that littered the courtyard swelled and churned as it accepted his passage, embracing his being as the creature that had once been vampire entered the Raza pyramid. It was dark inside, darker than he remembered it ever being, but he had no need for sight, his huge eyes redundant as he felt the stone of the walls all around him, and knew the secrets that it knew. He learned of all the passageways that had crumbled, discovered the parts that had once housed the sacred altars where rituals of blood had been performed centuries ago. But then, as he made his way effortlessly through the heavy stone walls, the ground brought him messages of something that he had not expected to find.

Conversation.

It was faint, even in the silent murk of the broken chambers, and yet the movements in the stale air of the place confirmed it. He altered his course to where three occupants were standing, and as he emerged through one of the walls and into the main chamber, he slowed as he discovered the forms of three vampires; two female, one male.

The male he did not recognise, he was insignificant, but the other two startled him by their very presence in this place, and not only that but conversing in dialogue that should not have even been occurring. He moved, deliberately now, towards them, not caring that his blending of elements should betray himself to them. So this was his final moment, he thought to himself, his final moment of reunion, where everything was to be resolved. It was a moment of epiphany, certainly, and an elation sparked throughout his body like a jolt of electricity.

At last, here was his Alexia.

Her eyes turned towards the darkness where once there had been nothing, and found a face coming towards her out of the murk. Alexia did not know this creature at first, this strange collage of shapes and forms, and a pall of fear passed through her being as she wondered whether this was a sibling of the thing that destroyed them so many years ago. But then she saw a recognition in its eyes, a veil of knowing pass over its expression, and it made her wonder what this thing could possibly be. It came closer, until it was within yards of her, and then it stopped, and softly spoke her name.

"What are you?" she said to this creature of living stone, studying the curves and fluid lines of its angular face, a fire glimmering somewhere inside its living grate.

"You do not know me?" it replied, its voice still coarse and barely audible.

Alexia shook her head, her sight pricking at the sight of its contortions.

The expression flickered briefly on the creature's face as she studied it, but she could still not detect its meaning. The creature came a step closer, almost reaching out a hand to her, but then kept its distance as though to touch her would be to break some unspoken rule.

"No," it whispered. "Perhaps you should not."

Catherine uttered a caution beside her, and Alexia turned to see her stumble back a step, a look of disbelief upon her once emotionless face. To see such a sight startled Alexia in turn, and she turned quickly back to stare at the creature of stone, wondering now if there should be a reason for fear.

"She remembers how I used to be," it said to her. "But all that is gone now. You should know me, though, for I once laid at your side."

Its words stunned her more than anything she could have expected, and as her mind reeled at the sheer lunacy of it, her eyes stared into the sunken hollow sockets of those that returned that stare. Its eyes, if they could even be called that now, twinkled like quartz, rich and full of exotic colours, and somewhere in that glimmer, she could see something of the vampire who had initiated her ascension into bloodhood. But surely it could not be true.

"Casta?" she finally said, her eyes still searching for clues within the transient state of his new body.

The creature slowly nodded.

"Yes, it is me. After so many years apart, we are finally together again."

"But I thought you were dead," Alexia managed to say, unable to take her eyes off his disfigured face. "You've changed."

"This new body? Yes. I have recently come a long way."

"What happened to you?"

"It is a story as long as the path I've travelled."

"We have another lifetime."

The thing that had once been her husband seemed to smile in response, but the angles of the rock just didn't seem to want to allow it, and his face cracked with the effort. The effect was grotesque, but it was certain that this was indeed her Casta.

"You should know that I am Master now," he said to her, at last. "My body holds the secrets of The Curbane. And with Jackel no longer alive -"

"No longer alive?"

"His life was taken. In the church."

Alexia stared at him, not wanting to accept the weight of this, even as it penetrated its way into her mind.

"That was you?" she whispered.

Casta's sight seemed to falter, his eyes dropping away from hers. The sound of rocks grinding together seemed to reverberate around him suddenly, and it seemed to confirm his terrible guilt.

"What have you done?" she whispered. "How could you have done such a thing?"

"I... I did it for you," he suddenly replied quietly, stating his plea as if it wasn't obvious.

"You killed our Master for me?"

"I did it all for you," he said, taking a step towards her.

Alexia backed away from him a step, staring at him in silence as she struggled to comprehend his meaning, his words making no sense.

"Everything I wanted, everything I did, was all for you," Casta went on, his words suddenly tumbling as though caught in the grasp of an avalanche. "You were to be at my side, ruling our world with me forever. We were to be king and queen, we were to govern the Blood, govern The Curbane. I loved you so much. Why can't you see that?"

"What... what are you saying?"

"The slaughter..." Casta murmured, seeming to realise now that she did not know quite what he had done. "In Kar'mi'shah..."

Alexia stared hard at him. Her head was suddenly spinning but she had to try and keep her focus concentrated on this revelation.

"You... didn't know?" Casta said.

"You made that thing?" Alexia hissed, her comprehension barely able to voice the words that laid such unspeakable guilt upon her husband. "That was you?"

"I... I'm sorry. Jackel was doing everything wrong. He wanted what was right by the people. They were just fodder for us, don't you see? There was so much power that he could not use properly. He had magic in

410

his hands that he had never even used. I couldn't stand to watch it any longer. I had to bury Jackel, but I knew my hands were simply not strong enough, and so I studied. I consulted an elder who lived alone in the mountains. He trained me in everything a Master should know - magics and spells, hexes and incantations. The night I thought I was ready was the same night Jackel brought the clans together. My head spilled over with plans and speeches, I barely heard anything of what anyone said that night. I had picked the strongest spell I thought I could deliver, a deadly creature that would prey upon Jackel, conjured not to stop until he had been stripped of all life and all blood. I created it with that one sole purpose, but it was..."

Casta trailed off, his eyes fixed utterly upon her horrified eyes.

"It was what?" Alexia wanted to know.

"It was too much for me," he confessed. "I wasn't ready."

Although he had brought so much death to their home world, he suddenly seemed like an empty shell now before her, an empty shell of shifting rock and broken values.

"What are you saying to me?" she demanded to know. "That the creature that decimated our families was a mistake?"

Casta closed his eyes altogether now, shielding the dazzling display of glittering quartz. It seemed that he could not even bear to think about the bloodshed that he had caused so many centuries ago. He was the butcher of Kar'mi'shah. Perhaps the weight of that was now breaking his shoulders.

"I was not ready," he said again slowly, as if that was his only defence, and it was then that he asked her a question that it seemed he had wanted to ask her for a very long time.

"Can you forgive me?"

The question stunned her into a silence that seemed to last an age. How could he possibly even ask her such a thing? Here was the man responsible for killing her family. Here was the man responsible for destroying her home. She had found herself stranded in a world far from home where she had been forced to find her own way, and it was all because of the one man who had once laid at her side.

"I thought even you were dead," Alexia stammered, "killed by that creature the same as everybody else. The one person who I loved more than anything else, butchered by that incomprehensible thing. I wished death upon myself so many times, Casta. I struggled to survive, more than you can ever know. Now I learn that it was all because of you, and you just casually ask me if I can forgive that?"

"I did it all for you," he yearned again.

"I never asked you for any of that."

"But I protected you. I sacrificed my own body to save yours. I sent you away to protect you from my demon."

"You did that as well?" Alexia gasped in disbelief. It was suddenly all too much. "What other secrets do you have?"

"You hate me," he murmured.

"What did you expect?"

"If I tell you all, you will crush me."

"With all the things that I'm feeling at the moment, I will crush you if you don't."

Casta stared at her for a moment, his eyes of glittering rock studying her intently as though all that he had planned for had both come true and now rocked on the edge of oblivion. This was his wife, his only, and it seemed that she would rather embrace anguish at the truth, than be close to him.

"A few hours earlier and you would have announced a short brief list of friends," Casta began, "but both Venice and Callie betrayed you, your relationship with both a sham that was nothing more than a report brought back in secret to me. They helped me, Alexia, helped me become what I always dreamed would come. That is real now. I possess the world inside me. And yet I remain incomplete without you."

Casta stared at her after that, as if waiting for a response, but there was simply nothing to come. What was there that she could possibly say to such a revelation. It seemed true that he had been plotting his own ascent to Jackel El'a'cree's position of Master of Kar'mi'shah, just as The Howler had told her, but there had been so much bloodshed, so much evil, and it had all been at her husband's behest. Casta was the vampire whose blood Cal'Beha wanted to dance in. He was the one that had brought death to their families, death to the entire province. She'd not known of his greed for such power, not even throughout those many years spent in the heart of London when he had watched her and used such sickening tricks upon her. He had perverted her life, just as he had perverted all their lives, and yet still he continued to bring about the deaths of others in his mindless pursuit of that power, even though now it seemed he had finally accomplished his one and only goal.

She ran at him now, a scream filling her throat as her fists clenched into weapons that would pound his head into the ground. But his face was solid and impervious to her assault, and her knuckles came away raw and bloodied with each and every blow. But still she threw herself at him, desperate to tear this abhorrence from the sanctity of the temple, the cries in her throat now piercing with rage. The fight was pitiful, but Casta did not retaliate, and remained motionless as she bestowed her aggression upon him, his arms of stone dormant at his side, his network of fire that burned inside him tended.

"I cannot fight you," he cried, as she rained down another volley of blows. Her anger was full, but her strength was no match for his. Slowly she ceased her onslaught, and staggered back as if in a daze, her hands broken and bleeding, her mouth bloody where she had tried to rip out his throat.

Despite the pain searing through her crooked hands as she retreated, it was bliss compared to the proximity of her husband. Casta watched helplessly as she crawled back away from him, and it seemed to hurt him more than anything to see the agony she would rather suffer than to be near him. Catherine and the other vampire stood at a distance, their sight fixed upon these two one-time lovers, uncertain whether magic or aggression would rear itself again, or even destroy the temple completely. Casta held the strength of The Curbane inside him, he could feel its strength itching inside his body, eager to fuse, desperate to tear open the ground, but despite the pitiful damage that they could do to him, he would rather have let them simply kill him and be done with it, so great was the pain of Alexia's dismissal of him. That was all Casta could suddenly think. He had claimed the world. But he would readily relinquish it all for this woman.

"Leave me," Alexia suddenly hissed, her voice as cold and bitter as ice.

"I cannot," was all Casta could say. "I will never again be able to leave you."

"Then I will kill myself."

"No," he cried, taking a tentative step after her. "You must never die. Here," he opened his arms to her, as if offering her his embrace. She grimaced at the thought, but then realised that he was not offering her his love this time, but rather all that he had. "Take this. Take it for all that I have done to you. Take it and see that I am truly sorry for all the hurt that I have given you, and all that I have given everyone else. If that will make you happy, take it all."

Alexia stared at him, uncertain of what to do, but in the instant of her indecision, something seemed to make the choice for her, and a column of fire leapt from Casta's body and crossed the void between them, engulfing her in a shroud of living flame that seemed eager to penetrate her. She loosed a scream as she felt its burning touch, lapping across her flesh with a rabid fury, and yet as it caressed her skin, so she realised that she remained unburned and intact.

She looked up at the open form of Casta, still servile in front of her with his arms extended out to her. His body seemed to come apart then, and a flood of furious water burst from every seam and crack, the deluge forcing wider every fissure that came. Casta let out a cry of his own as The Curbane willed itself out of his body and into Alexia's, the torrent too furious to be stemmed, too powerful to be dammed. Alexia staggered beneath the tumult, her mind blackening with reeling thoughts as the power of The Curbane forced itself to be a part of her. Secrets mingled with images of destruction, magics fusing with glimmers of birth and hope. She saw a wide bright moon, a column of stars, shifting sands beneath an ocean of swaying grasses. So many images, one after the other, tumbling through her head like a swirling vortex. It was too much to cope with, so unexpectedly and so forcefully was it dealt, and she tumbled backwards into a heap, her mind blacking out completely as her head hit the ground hard.

Ahead of her in the uncertain darkness, Alexia saw the distorting figure of her husband, his flesh sprouting new limbs of lightning, rock and ice. The consciousness of The Curbane seemed to flow throughout her new body of fire and she instantly knew its will, wanting rid of this intruder of greed and self-worth, battling, she knew, to keep back the power it held, keep it back from the creature that would use it for ill-will. Her fire took her to him, the inferno bearing down upon him from the heights of a vaulted ceiling, and the holocaust of her flame seared throughout his body.

She heard him gasp, almost with something close to resignation, as she engulfed him with her arms of burning white heat, and felt too the bliss of The Curbane as he was forced backward, away from its might. Its will grew in her, unfurling furiously like a thunderhead as it flowed out of his body and into hers. The tendrils of rock that had become his own shattered into fragments of dust, and a blizzard of ice that had raged about him like a shield now swirled hopelessly downward, falling into useless flurries. His eyes opened to gaze up at her as she hovered over him, her vast burning mass crackling like an inferno, her previous form nothing but a distant memory. She resembled nothing more than a burning fire, a cloud of flame, a pyre with no base and no fuel but the will that had created it. She was unidentifiable to anyone that had ever known her, and yet the gaze that Casta held her with seemed to be one of absolute recognition.

"Alexia," he cried. "I give you everything that I once sought. All I ask for now is your forgiveness. Your love would be bliss."

She looked down upon him, uncertain what true form her words might take, or even if she might be able to talk at all in this uncertain dreamstate, for a dream must surely be what this was. Her thoughts turned in what had once been her head, forming somewhere in her dark and clouded consciousness, and she answered him with words that seemed to have been scorched into existence.

"It is no longer a question of forgiving or repentance," came her voice, seething and harsh, startling her as it came, "but one of rebirth and rebuilding. What you did years ago was wrong," Alexia continued, her voice berating the very air between them, singeing him further with the heat of her words. "You killed so many of us. And those that found a way to escape, you continued to pursue with dreams of death."

"I wanted it for us both," he stammered, desperate for her to let him explain, but what explanations could there be?

"You killed everyone we ever knew for me?" she said. "That was your gift?"

"We were to rule Kar'mi'shah forever. I did it all for you."

417

Despite the body lying before her, twisted, deformed and purged of what had once held it solid, Alexia could still feel the strength within him. Any other vampire would have been destroyed long before, but Casta had learnt of ways to keep himself intact far longer than most. She could sense that his magic could do many things, and she wondered why he just lay there, looking up at her with defeat in his eyes.

"Why do you just lie there?" she asked him at length.

"I cannot do anything else but adore you," he said. "You of all people I cannot hurt any more. You were to be my queen. I loved you more than anything. But now you despise me, injure me, and your words destroy me."

His eyes flickered closed then, and in the trembling darkness that came swiftly to sever her vision, she felt her husband slip away from her completely. It wasn't until she realised that his life had gone out of him, that she knew what he had done. He knew that he would never be able to live with the hurt that he had caused her, and without hope, what future could there ever have been for him? She knew that now. Yes, she despised him for what he had done so many centuries ago, but he was still her husband, and she had still loved him. She had thought him dead, and had mourned his passing as she had mourned those of her family, but to find him alive after so long had briefly been rapturous. His words and deeds had clouded that rapture, however, and quickly, and his single-minded purpose had seemed to dissolve as he confessed secrets to her that snatched at her innards. Indeed, it seemed that he had been able to watch her and learn about her movements without ever showing himself to her.

He had done so for thirty or more years, as far as she knew. How much longer then, might he have been watching her? Forty years? One hundred years. A millennium? Perhaps since she had even left Kar'mi'shah? He had even admitted to forcing her away from him, away from her home, away from the creature he himself had created. Yes, he had saved her, but at what cost? He had been her husband, but now he had relinquished his life and his duty to remain at her side, and she would not be able to forgive him that, more than anything.

The Curbane seemed to call to her in the darkness of the dream, a silent instruction that compelled her to leave Casta's broken body and return to her true waking moment. She felt the guardian of rock pass through her, its strength and solidity coursing with wonders. She felt too the tides and rhythms of the water guardian, swell inside her body and show her the motes of life that glimmered in its wake. Her halo of flame encircled them all, brightening her dream world, until her eyes settled not only on the fallen body of Casta, but also illuminated the pallid expressions of Catherine and the nameless vampire standing in the broken chamber of the Raza. It was in this moment that Alexia realised that the dream had merged with the waking, and as she gazed down at herself, realised too that her own body was one that shared the same elements that Casta had worn; rock, fire and water. And throughout all of it, she felt the surging echoes of The Curbane, urging her onward, out of the fallen temple, and into the desert world of what had once been called Kar'mi'shah.

GODHOOD

She was part of The Curbane, of that she was now more aware than anything, and the secrets that it held began to surge through her, filling her mind, flooding her being, until she knew all that made the world work, and all that made the vampires immortal. They were there for more than blood taking, they were there to make the world work, to bring order to chaos, and yes, even to bring life out of death.

The scenes of the past came into her mind, a history showing itself of the province she had called home for hundreds of years, but had not been a part of for far too long, and with the images that she knew came images that she didn't. The decline of the vampire populace in Kar'mi'shah made itself known to her, as though she was watching a rapid history of the years she had missed. She saw the infrequency of the rain clouds, and the drying up of the lands. She saw the baking sunlight of the day grow hotter and hotter, parching the earth as the rivers and seas receded and ran dry. She saw the animals of the land, the predators that would attack the populace, increase in numbers and desperation as their own food chain was depleted. And she saw the desperation claim the people of the city, as their homes became more punishable to live in.

Oh, what had Casta done? His actions had destroyed more than the Gods of Kar'mi'shah. He had taken a beautiful province and turned it to death and dust. He had replaced joy with misery, prosperity with downfall, and left nothing in the wake of his aspirations but desert. This was the role of the immortal vampire, this was the deed that bound the Master of Kar'mi'shah, and now she had inherited it all, the weight of the burden and responsibility sudden heavy upon her shoulders.

Alexia remembered how her feeble body of flesh had been her downfall - she had been battered twice by Cal'Beha, cut down by Casta's unnatural army, she'd even beaten her husband until those feeble hands broke - but now she was renewed, carried inside a body of rock, fire and water, and the strength she now felt was overwhelming.

As she made her way out of the ruins of the Raza Pyramid, Alexia turned her thoughts skyward once again. The night air was still full of the previous day's heat, and it did little to help cool the ground, baked hard by the merciless sun. The dark star-laden heavens carried no promise of cloud, no rainstorms that might bring life to the choked seeds buried so deep beneath the parched soil. But then the fire guardian Rail emerged ahead of her, its dark swirling mass of shadows skulking in the blackness of the hot night, and as she saw him, she knew its meaning and turned her sight skyward, and watched in wonder as the veil of impenetrable heat was pulled back, and wisps of cumulus began to form where she looked, light eerie mists of cloud growing in size and shape. The wisps condensed as they developed, almost as though she willed them into being, and then droplets of water began to form inside them, soon to become too heavy for the clouds of which they were made to hold them.

Alexia watched with wonderment as the rain began to fall, gazing with utter disbelief as they dropped like spears through the dark clear air, cool and perfect, splashing in tiny clouds of dust and steam as they ricocheted off the hard hot earth. More fell as the clouds continued to build, darkening the baked ground as it slowly became soaked with the life-giving rain.

Then Alexia cast her sight downward, deep in the ground, and finding that she could see far beyond the surface, became filled with wonder as she witnessed the seeds begin to sprout, creeping into life, drinking deeply of the moisture in the same way as she had drunk of blood. It invigorated them, she saw, and they flourished both quickly and forcefully. She saw the ground that had only moments before been as hard as rock, begin to erupt and crack open as the seedlings pushed their way to the surface, eager to be free while they had the chance of this most unexpected release. The sun would not touch them for hours yet, but still their stretched skyward, unable to be stopped.

The courtyard outside the temple was suddenly a moving carpet of lush new green, shoots sprouting forth between the broken slabs of marble and polished stone, defying the encroachment of the desert, and bringing life to where before there had been none. Alexia felt the cool moist blades of the grass suddenly beneath her feet as her sense of touch returned in an instant, as the rock that had made up her new body retreated at her will, feeling too the chill of the rain on her arms and face as her flesh returned there also. Oh but it was wonderful, she thought with delirium, to feel once again the crystalline rains of Kar'mi'shah. Returning after so many centuries away from her home and to find it little more than a desert had been devastating, but now to bring forth rain to a rainless sky, was simply beyond words, beyond expression, and she felt truly blessed.

She thought it would take time for the animals of the province to return to their former feeding grounds, but even as she made her way across the courtyard and on towards the ruined streets and thoroughfares at the heart of the city, voles and rabbits emerged from holes that had previously been hidden, taking immediate advantage of the new food source, and darting with abandon from shoot to shoot. She relished the sight of them, drawing as much food as possible into their mouths as though they expected it to be some fanciful dream which would not be there come the morning. Overhead in the rain-lashed heavens, hawks took to the sky, circling the brave new foragers from above, completing the food chain that had been stagnated by the drought and relentless sun. It would be sad to see a few of those brave rodents perish before they saw their first new sunrise, their endless wait for nourishment finally rewarded, but it was the way of things. She knew it, and somewhere deep down inside, they knew it too. Even as she watched them, she began to wonder whether they had even been waiting at all, or whether, like the rain, she had willed them into being too.

The rains grew heavier over the next hour or so, and somewhere further south, the river was already beginning to swell. The dried banks became wet with moisture, and held the passage of the torrent as it came. As she studied the muddied banks, their paths heading out towards the distant seas, with the pitiful harvest of fish that it had born for so long, the water guardian Vessel appeared before her, its form manifesting itself out of the flood-sodden ground. Alexia could feel the echoes of its touch, as though part of its being was already in the seas and rivers, and as she felt that, so everything began to teem with rich shoals of fish, and she could see their silver flanks glittering in a far away moonlight as they flashed and swam with a magical life.

It was unbelievable to see such life exploding where none had been before. The dry and dusty plains where the remainder of the populace had struggled to grow their crops, now brought forth the potential that they had sown there. Not only did they shoot and bloom, but doubled their yield, bountiful crops growing and yearning in a rain that had been held back for years. All this Alexia seemed to have brought forth as she saw fit, her sight the catalyst for all that needed to be done. The rain she yearned for appeared as she studied the cloudless sky. The grass she longed to touch flourished as her own body blossomed to meet it. A myriad ocean of fish came forth into a dead sea as she willed it into being. And the promise of prosperity returned to her beloved city in a single glance.

As the rain soaked the earth and the plants continued to grow, so the desert receded to reveal the ruins of the buried city. Temples had been destroyed and houses had crumbled. Palaces had been reduced to little more than derelict pits, and courtyards and villas no more than rubble. It was a scene of what had once been, and yet it held the promise of what could be again.

And as Alexia gazed down upon them with pity, so she felt the echoes of the broken rock somewhere inside her. Her sight fell upon a broken column, images carved into its flanks of Faraoh BloodGods and sacrificial deities, and as she watched, so she felt her body become part of that column, and she began to give life to it, just as if it was part of her own flesh, until it was once again complete and standing upright with its own majesty once more. It startled her to feel the magic inside her move in this way, and as she gazed all around her, so she could feel the living rock inside every building and every thoroughfare. And as she looked, so she saw the great figure of the rock guardian Nomad standing there, his vast frame of granite towering over her like a monolith.

She was a part of it all, just as this creature given life by The Curbane, was a part of her, and suddenly Alexia realised the fullness of what The Curbane had instilled inside her. She wondered briefly if Casta had known this, that all that he had searched for was to be a central part of all things. She wondered if even Jackel El'a'cree knew the fullness of this secret, or whether Casta had been right all along by saying that Jackel had not been right. Whatever the reason, both of them had perished, and she now held the might of the Blood Of The Ancients inside her body, and it seemed glad to have her there. She could hear the pounding of its rhythms inside her, just as she could feel the pulse of the rock and the fire and the water, even as they reached out to rebuild broken pathways, force back the desert, and replenish the seas.

"My hunger is growing," Jenner heard Emma murmur in the darkness. "My strength is going rapidly."

He reached to take hold of her hand. Her skin was cool and clammy.

"You must feed, Emma," he urged her, and as he pursed his lips, offered himself to her, exposing the two puncture wounds that had barely healed from Jackel's repeated drinking.

It took a moment for her to understand his intent, but when she did, she pushed him away from her, declaring that she would never drink from him.

"You must," he told her. "It's the only way you can survive."

"I will not have your death be my salvation."

"You love me that much?"

The question was immediate, and caught them both offguard, such was the severity that it was asked.

"What I feel for you goes beyond love," Emma said to him, "but I will not drink from you if it means taking your life."

"You do not need to take it all. Just enough to give you strength for another day."

The smell of his flesh was tantalising, especially with it so close to her lips. She could feel her own teeth lengthening inside her mouth, her saliva washing over them in rivers that could suddenly not be stemmed. She so desperately wanted to feed, to have the taste of blood wash over the back of tongue and swell and surge deep inside her being. But this was Jenner, the man whom she had loved for years. She knew that she could drink from him and keep him alive, but a fear nagged at the back of her mind, a fear that cried What if you can't stop? What if you start and the vampire takes over, and you drink and you drink until his life is extinguished?

She gazed down at his neck in the blackness of the crumbled temple, her senses raging, and before she knew it, her teeth were embedded deep into the soft meat of his flesh, and she was drawing hard upon the hot sweet blood that had flowed so uninterrupted in the map of his veins.

Alexia was in the centre of one of the towns now, and she began to look at the people as they came out into the welcome rain, come to save them in the hopelessness of the night. She watched them as they rejoiced, hugging each other and praising anything they could think of for the fortune that had finally befallen them. She passed amongst them now, witnessing every face and every cry of joy, and in each of their hearts she could see how the hope had returned to them, even as they returned her gaze, curious glances falling upon this stranger who seemed not to share their jubilation but simply stand and watch theirs.

As a Faraoh, she was a shape-changer, but unlike Jackel El'a'cree or any of the other shape-changers before her, she would now take on not the guise of an animal, but those characteristics of the elements than ran throughout her being, of rock, fire and water. She walked amongst her people now with a human form, her hair wet and snaking, her flesh exposed to the rain, but this was a turning point for all the vampires of Kar'mi'shah, she knew, and it was wonderful to behold such change and to be at its centre.

Her coming out of the Raza Pyramid as a benevolent force of The Curbane was by no means the salvation of them all, she knew that, but she knew also that it was a start. If her beloved city of Kar'mi'shah was to be great once more, then she would have to devote her time to it. Time was something she had in abundance. And at least now she had the means to do something far more wonderful than she had ever imagined, perhaps more than even Casta had imagined. Reshape a country.

She was home, and she possessed power to bring life back to that home. Even now, her people were out celebrating all that she had done. She would need their help in return, of course, to rebuild fully the culture and civilisation of what had once been before. She could not simply bring a province prosperity just by waving her hand. She would need them to build her a temple to shield her from the sunlight, she would need them to bring her nourishment when she could not get it herself. She would feed on what they gave her, when she did not feed on the predators that stalked them. And in exchange for protecting her people, for they were her people again, they would worship her as their Goddess.

There was no Master of Kar'mi'shah anymore. There was now only a Mistress. She would bring life back to her world, and pride back to her people, and in time maybe recover the scattered members of the tribes who had once lived here. They may have fled to distant lands, and indeed spanned the divides to other worlds, but she would bring safety for them all in Kar'mi'shah. Safety and prosperity. And a new and valued beginning.

Jenner's eyes flickered open as the whole of the temple seemed to shudder around them, threatening complete collapse and to bury them inside its shadows forever. The pain in the curve of his neck was agonising from where Emma had drank from him, and as he thought about her, and about getting them both the hell out of there, he suddenly realised that she was no longer with him.

He sat upright suddenly, the effort bringing pulsing black shapes to his head and a sickness swiftly into his stomach, and yelled her name into the black quaking air. There was no reply at first, but as he hauled himself to his feet, his senses reeling beneath a blanket of light-headedness, he heard her say his name, softly and within a yard of his ear. He reached out to her, and was surprised at how readily she allowed his embrace. He was weak, they both seemed to know that, and even as Jenner confirmed her fears that the building was indeed going to collapse, another shock came as a third voice broke the darkness like something solid, a voice that seemed to hold up the uncertain ceiling, and hold back the debris that should have broken their skulls.

"You no longer have to fear," it said to them, a woman's voice, soothing and confident. "I have you now."

"Who are you?" Emma asked, searching the darkness for the sign of its speaker.

"You are a vampire," the voice returned, "a BloodGod, and this shall be your temple. You shall be worshipped here by the people of Kar'mi'shah. And you will offer them protection and prosperity in return."

Emma gazed around her now, trying to locate the owner of the voice, but neither she nor Jenner could find any living being inside the chamber with them.

The air now sang with a myriad of lilting rhythms, rhythms that seemed to hold back the crumbling chamber and even to rebuild it into something safe, something grand.

"You are a God now," the voice continued, drawing the fallen debris back up into the cracked walls of the chamber, "and I will need you at my side, to help make this city great again. I ask your devotion, and I pray you will give it without condition."

Jenner continued to gaze out into the darkness, his mortal eyes unable to grasp little of what moved there, so total was the chamber sealed from all natural light. He felt Emma's grasp tighten around his, and then clench into a fist, as the ground suddenly shuddered afresh all around them as though the very building was reshaping itself, solidifying what had been insolid, rebuilding what had been destroyed, and re-carving all that had been turned to dust and ruin.

THIRTEEN

THE TEMPLE OF SHADOWS

It was a strange few months of rebuilding what had become visible, uncovering old sites and new wonders, returning prosperity to desolation. Jenner wandered the city daily as the boundaries of the city gradually increased, as those new buildings were offered up by the receding desert, the blanket of smothering sand shrinking back to the wastelands from where it had come. New growth blossomed in every nook and every field, flourishing in any place where it could find a purchase (and it seemed to find one everywhere), until the province that he had first seen, a province that he had first looked down upon as being a dead world, had turned into a plush and verdant land full of pastures and bountiful crops.

It had seemed that only a few defiant members of what had once been a grand population had remained to fight the struggle against the desert, but day after day the numbers seemed to swell as healthily as the produce that began to appear at the marketplaces. Joy filled each face that he came upon, strangely more so with those that carried the heaviest burdens of fish and wheat, testing the strength within their backs.

Jenner had promised his devotion to Emma frequently since the Goddess Alexia had appeared to them in the broken temple, beholding the glorious spectacle of her own temple now, as he stood and gazed up as it crested the banks of the river glittering with the reflection of an adoring sun. Emma could not leave her temple beneath the glare of this sun, of course, and would never see the magnificence of this sight, but when she did appear beneath the wide full moon each night, her beauty seemed as breathtaking as it had always been, and there they would stand for hours simply watching the hours of the night ebb slowly past.

It was during one of those resplendent days, however, that a strange revelation came to him. Several members of the local community had already seen the image of Emma adorning the newly rebuilt temple and entered reverently to offer devotion upon their new Goddess. Many of them were women, and seemed to behold the fact that a Goddess would look after her daughters with compassion and affection, and indeed Emma had nothing but good grace for them. But as Jenner watched them, laying offerings of bread and milk at a shrine that he'd erected for his beloved, he overheard one of the women speaking to another in hushed but insistent tones.

It seemed no different to any of the other reverent prayers spoken that day, except for one of the names that was uttered - Annabella - and it struck Jenner deeply, remembering the hand-written pages that he had read so diligently high up on the mountain. Could this be the same Annabella that the journal-writer had written of? Had this woman's husband inadvertently led him to the rocky outcrop where he had chanced upon his dearest Emma in a strange and mystifying land where he had even thought her dead? He slowly crossed the quiet stone chamber, his soft footfalls barely making a sound off the heavy walls, and asked her in a gentle voice if she knew of a man who had recently entered the mountains. Her reply, when it came, was full of sadness.

"We were to have been married," she replied, "but the night before he left was one of utter dread. A creature of the mountains killed so many of us, and he went after it to destroy it. He has not returned to me, and I can only fear the worst."

"I am sorry that I cannot offer you any news of comfort," Jenner said to her, his voice hushed, "but I believe that I saw him, high up on the mountain."
The woman stared at him, her eyes welling heavily with tears.

"You saw him?"

"I believe so. Tell me, did he carry a journal with him?"

"Yes. Yes, he did."

"I found his book, and read what he had written. He spoke fondly of you. I heard your name spoken just now, and I had to ask."

"You don't need to tell me of his fate. I have already guessed that he is dead."

"That is the sad news that I must unfortunately bear."

Annabella looked at him for a while, and it seemed that even though his message was as brief as it was final, she seemed strangely comforted to have the truth at last. It seemed unlikely that anyone else might happen upon his body, but for her to know that he would not be coming back to her seemed, at least for her, to have some finality to it.

"His journal," Jenner continued, drawing her attention from an unfocussed limbo between the two of them, "did lead me to the one I love, and if it had not been for him, I perhaps never would have met her again."

A tiny smile tried to creep into her mouth, but her sadness would not let it come completely.

"Jacob would have wanted something to come from his death," she said.

"Jacob," Jenner murmured. "I did not know his name."

Annabella went to turn away, but Jenner kept her a moment.

"I still have his journal," Jenner said to her. "You would like it back?"

The woman managed to fully smile at this, but the threat of tears forced it away almost immediately.

"Yes," she said. "I would like to keep it. Thank you."

Jenner touched her arm as he hurried away to collect it, but when he descended the cold stone staircase down into the lower vaults, he came upon Emma, sitting alone in the half light.

"I think there is someone you should speak to," Jenner said to her.

"I heard your conversation."

"Is something wrong?"

Emma turned to look at him now.

"Is this how you saw our future, Jenner?"

"Nothing here is how I imagined things would end up. I thought I had lost you, Emma. I thought you were dead. That realisation brought a lot of things into my head. I missed you, more than I thought could ever be possible. But now I have you back again -"

"Not as I once was -"

"No," Jenner exclaimed. "But still with me. Nothing has changed in the way you feel about me, has it?"

"Everything has changed. I can no longer think of you in the same way, don't you see that? I will continue one night after the next without any discernible change, and I will have to bear the sight of seeing you age, watching the progress of time as you wander the path towards death. I cannot bear the thought of that."

"But what about this moment, now. We are together. Is that not enough?"

"No," Emma said simply. "That is not enough."

Jenner wanted to continue, to express all the feelings that he'd had for her, and perhaps had always had for her. But he knew the truth in what she said. She would live forever. He had maybe forty or fifty years at best. If reversed, the ache at watching her perish slowly in front of his eyes would be insurmountable. Perhaps this rejection was a devotion of love. It would hurt either way. It all came down to those choices once again, choices that just had to be made. It was neither fortunate nor unfortunate that it wasn't he who made the decision.

"What do you suggest then?" Jenner had said, somewhat more bluntly than he'd intended.

"Go back to London," Emma told him. "It's where you belong."

"Is that what you really want?"

"No, but what I want doesn't matter. I've become something different to what I once was. My home is gone. My father is gone. This place now offers me solace, a sanctuary, a tomb where I can sit and think."

"But I would offer you devotion if I stayed."

"We can never be equal partners, Jenner, we both know that."

"But you drank from me, what more intimate relationship could we have?"

"You're clutching, Jenner. Leave me now."

He was getting desperate, and he knew just how pitiful his reasoning had suddenly become. But he also knew that he was about to lose his beloved Emma all over again. He struggled to view her face in the heavy gloom of the lower vault, searching for some telling expression on the deep shadows of her pale skin, but there were simply none to be found. She was something different, something far beyond natural, no matter how hard he tried to see past it. She had become a vampire, a Goddess; her heart had been stopped, and only blood could nourish her and give her strength. He moved across the darkened chamber now and took up the journal that had seemed to lead him to her in the depths of the mountains. And then left her without another word.

He found Annabella still waiting for him close to the altar, arranging her offering of bread, milk and fish, and after a brief exchange of words, he handed the book over to her. He watched with something close to happiness as she clutched it to her breast, before leaving the temple with one of the other women who had accompanied her, despite the pang of loss that nagged at the pit of his stomach.

Taking one last look around the vast vaulted stone chamber, Jenner strode across the marble floor towards the great carved threshold, his footfalls echoing loudly off the walls in his wake. The darkness that clung to the shadows of the place seemed almost to whisper to him, as if Emma herself was urging him to stay, uncertainty even in her own words. Stay. Go. Stay. Go. With a breath, Jenner continued forward, out of the temple and into the orange glow of the day that was steadily drawing itself out towards dusk.

FOURTEEN

MESSENGER

The truth about what had taken hold of the city in such a miraculous way had merged so fully with ancient myths that it was difficult to discern one from the other. Jenner wandered through the newly-laid thoroughfares of bright mosaic tiles in an attempt to sift through just what it was he could do. The portal that had transported him across worlds still hung in the sky above the ever-receding desert like a vast tear, as knotted and as bruised as a ragged wound. His first thought was to try and return to that place, to inspect the uncertain threshold of a limbo he did not understand, and simply hurl himself into its void. That was even if such a thing could be attempted. It had shat him out of its maw like a lump of badly chewed gristle, hurled him down from a great height. Clambering high up into its reaches would not be easy, if it all possible. The choices were few, and he was able to comprehend none of them. Montague had been right in one respect. At least on Earth they knew the terrain. Here, they knew nothing.

Another choice that occurred was little more than a rumour, and yet it had been a rumour that he'd heard on several occasions. It sounded like nothing more than sheer madness, crazed superstition even, and yet it been held aloft as the source of all their salvation, sung in joyful songs and whispered reverently in hallowed prayer. It told of a deity come back from on high to deliver them from a burning hell and into an Eden of tranquillity. The tale rang with heavy echoes of Bible stories, and yet Christianity had barely found a foothold in this province, even with all the heavy labours and rebuilding inside the city's limits.

This deity had apparently appeared in visions before many of the townspeople, and had brought life from where before there had been dust, and substance from drought. Emma herself had already been honoured as a divinity, a temple raised swiftly to her immortality. So how different, then, could such a mystical being be in such a place of wonder and magic such as Kar'mi'shah? The temple that had been built for this deity was not far, and even with uncertainty still prevalent inside his head, Jenner made his way there, not knowing what he might even ask for when at last he would reach it.

"Your request is a strange one," the Goddess said to him, the figure standing before him sleek and tall, her skin blossoming and brightening as though hot embers burned beneath her skin.

"I do not belong here," Jenner explained. "I should return home, and bear the consequences for what I have done."

The Goddess looked at him for a moment and Jenner felt a curiosity in her gaze, although there was no change in her expression, no gesture with her hands, just a brighter glow in the iridescence of her skin.

"I cannot argue with your heart," she said finally,

"for I too know how it feels to be lost. There is, however, one request that I will ask of you in return."

"You have only to ask it."

"I do not ask with words, I have discovered that they are insufficient and hold back the truest nature of things. I will show you what I desire of you. You will learn when your journey has begun."

"So I can go back?"

The goddess nodded only briefly.

Jenner was not sure what is was that she actually wanted him to do, but she seemed almost keen to have him attempt the return journey, and needed no further persuasion to try and open a portal for him.

She took him down a narrow stone stairwell to a darkened chamber where only a handful of candles burned, for his benefit presumably more than hers, and as Jenner watched with both disbelief and wonder, her body began to transform itself as she murmured soft incantations.

A halo of flame seemed to burn around her, illuminating the room with an orange radiance, its fire licking delicately across her protean flesh like ethereal fingers. Her skin, however, then began to take on the form of all manner of elements, first seeming to crystallise into rock, then to glisten like ice, and finally almost to ripple and flow like a babbling stream, all while she stood before him in an uncertain darkness, as she continued to chant her magic.

The threshold, when at last it began to evolve in the centre of the ill-lit chamber, seemed more like a womb than the shuddering gateway that had brought him into this other world, or even like the raging void that it was surely soon to become. Fingers of the ethereal fire that encircled her drifted in waves towards this opening threshold, entwining with the incandescent folds, twisting and opening like blossoming flowers. It grew as it bloomed, this delicate portal, its circles of radiant light threatening to collapse at any moment, and Jenner found himself holding his breath as he watched this magical spectacle unfold before him. Then, when the Goddess's eyes finally flickered open, her pupil's bright with a lurid flicker, her indecipherable murmur ceased, and she stood aside to allow this mortal access to this magical bridge that would span worlds.

The gateway opened up before him like a tunnel of newly-made flesh as he stepped hesitantly towards it, the air jittery, the blackness uncertain. Jenner felt it take him before he could even snatch a breath of the sanctum's dark air, the roiling forms of ether reaching to take hold of him and drag him swiftly into its innermost depths.

The passage itself, however, took him from a shroud of soft light and hurled him into a vista of bright luminosity, and was as swift as it was enlightening, so different from the first voyage of chaos and pain, of brutality and heat, offering a surge of images and emotions as it took him. It seemed almost as though it wanted to explain itself, to offer reason and compassion to the messenger that it carried inside its arms, to convey to those that he would encounter at his journey's end all that it desired to show him now. The passage hurled him through images of civilisations and continents, and he could neither decipher whether it was the past, the present, or some dreamt-of world between. His body became harried by the vortex as it took him, his head throbbing with the intense pulsing rhythm of the limbo, his blood seeming to boil one moment and then freeze the next, his bones seeming to creak and crack beneath pressures as though they were being exposed to heavy altitude.

Bright motes of light began to burn all around him, and inside each one, a portrait of a being sketched out in sepia shades; mortal and vampire, male and female. They seemed almost to stare back at him, some with masks of rapture, others with cowls of death, but all with a look that yearned for him to know the truth and have him act upon it. And he did almost seem to grasp them too, even as he travelled so very swiftly through this flashing cinema, struggling to hold on to the answers and revelations as they came.

Pictures displayed themselves around him as though painted upon living canvasses, changing as instantaneously as they appeared, showing scenes of grandeur, scenes of triumph, scenes of change and poverty. So much seemed to want to show itself to him that it became little more than a blistering palette of perverted banality, too much information shrouded by itself, distorting and contorting into a soup too polluted to be tasted.

The shuddering mess ended the journey, and Jenner staggered out into a swamp of dark grey buildings huddled beneath a spattering grey layer of grim cloud, and realised almost immediately that he had finally returned home to London.

It had not changed as significantly as the province that he had left in the months that he had been away. Its stagnated limits reached beyond his vision in every direction, sprawling and cramped, with a sky that pressed down upon it with an ever-constant threat of rain. It took a few moments to register his being back at all, the wonders of the rebirth of Kar'mi'shah still vivid inside his head, the memory of Emma still fresh, but as the crisp smell of the early England morning bit at his nostrils, and the heavy tang of diesel fumes coated its back, he knew that he was home, perhaps even back where he knew deep inside that he truly belonged. It took only a few minutes of wandering to realise his location, perhaps less than a half hours walk back to Hammersmith, but he took it briskly, and with a confident step that he never would have thought he would have before.

A notion edged in his mind to make a detour and try and find the hotel in Kensington that he and Montague had entered with their vampire guide Coda-Beda. He thought that if he turned the corner of that magical street he might come upon a scene of jubilation, of visitors to that part of the city standing back in awe, beholding a site that offered passage to a wonderful and mysterious land where before there had been no trace. The notion brought a smile to his lips, drawing on his knowledge that he had trodden where so many would clamour to step. But this was not the time to lapse into such false fancy. He knew that he should first return back to his flat, or whatever might be left of it, and make his routes out into the world from there.

The flat, when at last he set eyes upon it, was in a far greater state of collapse than he would have dared thought possible. Cold steel scaffolding and sheets of plastic orange mesh covered most of the frontage, holding up or holding back whatever else was likely to fall from the breach. Of the two storeys below his top floor flat, both seemed to have been evacuated, and even those flats to either side seemed deserted, their tenants presumably having moved out to make way for imminent repairs or demolition. Two huge skips dominated the roadway outside, both filled with rubble and splintered woodwork, and Jenner approached them cautiously, wondering as he reached them, whether there would even be access to his flat, let alone the building itself.

The main door to the block was sealed only by a sheet of the same orange mesh that covered so much of the upper part of the building, and it came away easily from the frame to which it had been nailed. The air was thick with a heavy dust as he entered, but at such an early hour, it was probably just a clinging dust rather than anything stirred up from builders working overhead. The stairs were littered with rubble and crooked nails as he began to climb them, and an unease crept up inside him as he wondered just what desolate sight might reach him when at last he stood before his front door. His flat hadn't been much, but it had been all he'd had.

The cold wind of the morning swirled about the top floor landing as he reached it, and where his front door had stood, now gaped a broken entranceway. Brick shards and splintered timber decorated the ripped carpet underfoot, and Jenner stared at it with something close to disbelief, as though this was not even his flat, but someone else's, and that he'd taken a wrong turn on his route home and found a street that had previously not existed. But this was his flat. And beyond the broken threshold lay the blackened patch of carpet where the two police officers had slumped with opened deadly wounds. Much of that stain had been covered with scaffolding, however, as though no one had even given it a second look. And why should they? That had been their final resting place, a place of sanctity perhaps. But had it been their final place? Jackel El'a'cree had consumed part, if not all, of their bodies. Had he shat them out only to have them drifting in some dank sewer below everyone's feet? The thought still sickened.

The cold early wind whipped up as he entered, gusts coming from breaches torn in all the walls, not just from those that he remembered in the living room and bedroom. Workmen had ripped windows out to allow disposal of rubbish, had torn carpets up to get to floorboards which in turn had been gutted, and to simply take in the state of the place was almost too much to bear. Jenner staggered from room to room, trying not to associate memories with possessions that lay either smashed on the floor or just gone where they had presumably been looted. He went through into the bedroom where thankfully much of the filth that the vampire king had left behind had been taken away; burnt, no doubt, in some medical incinerator where no human should ever see it or smell it again.

He stood in the place where his single bed had been, and gazed out at the dismal rain-threatening sky still hanging over the rooftops of Hammersmith, still grey and noxious, still unappealing and unwelcoming. He felt like smoking suddenly, although he had smoked his last cigarette weeks ago, Kar'mi'shah being short of many things, cigarettes not being a priority. The change had done him good, not at first admittedly, but the clean air of Kar'mi'shah's plains had brought a vigour to him that could not remember ever having. The sight of London sprawling before him seemed almost to drag him back to a state that he did remember, had always remembered, and he suddenly no longer wanted to return to that place again.

He recalled suddenly the memory of the view from this window, the dull blue smoke from a cigarette curling lightly towards the ceiling. It had been a slowly writhing distraction between himself and the city, and perhaps that had been the problem. It had distracted him from what had been real. But he could see that now. Oh yes, he could see what was real, and it was neither good nor bad, but intense and colourful.

There was a fire burning at the centre of all things, and he had been distracted from it, had failed to witness it and become a part of it. And now London and the fumes and the banality of smoking his cigarettes was trying to draw the veil back over his eyes once again.

He turned away from the gaping window and started back towards the door, but halted almost immediately as his eyes found the silhouette of a figure hunched in the doorway. Jenner fought the shadows for a moment, as though the figure had pulled them over himself like a hood, but then he found his features, and uttered his name as a whisper.

"Kole."

The vampire's eyes lifted and found his, and a grimaced smile came to his lips.

"Been a while," was all he could say.

"I've been away."

"You don't keep this place none too tidy, boy. Been a while since I seen it last."

"I should be ashamed."

Kole nodded absently.

"You should."

445

This was small talk.

What did he want?

"I been hearing all kinds of things, Jen. Some good, some bad, some very odd indeed. I think you been keeping some secrets from a lot of people. I think it's about time you tell some of them."

Jenner gazed at him for a while, searching his face for an expression that might have revealed his true motives. He had seen vampires take life, and he had seen vampires bring life. It was certain that Kole was not one of the latter, but as for his motives and indeed true intentions, he had no idea.

"Are you a messenger?" Jenner asked him finally.

"Maybe, boy. Are you?"

It seemed a fairly straight forward question, and he was about to say no, when he suddenly found himself thinking about it. Had that been why the Goddess had seemed eager to have him return? She had shown him images, certainly, or at least that's what he believed now, pictures offered in the journey back to this place, instructions perhaps of worlds in need of reconciliation.

"You're part of a community?" Jenner tentatively asked.

"Of vampires? Be sure o' that."

"But you're not from Kar'mi'shah, though, Kole. Are these others?"

"Is that part o' your message?"

"If it's part of yours."

"Seems like we're singing parts o' the same song, Jen. Yes, they be from this other world. They talk of it often, like a cage within a cage, a paradise within a prison."

"I think I need to talk to them. To help them get home."

Kole looked at him then, with an expression something close to pride. They had known each other for a few years, or at least they had before Jenner had gone inside while Kole had been drafted into the blood-drinking set. He'd heard that the vampire takes over the human host totally, leaving no part of the person behind. But this seemed untrue. In the look Kole now gave him, this most definitely seemed untrue.

"Is there an address?" Kole asked him simply.

"I'm not sure it's as easy as that."

"Seems to me that's all there is," the vampire countered. "Perhaps you should inform me now."

It was Jenner's turn to look at the other, hard now, and with a creeping uncertainty. Kole had once been his friend, but he seemed to have changed now in more ways than one. The vampire took a step towards him. It was a simple movement, and yet it seemed to carry a threat that stole Jenner's courage. The vampire didn't need to ask his question again, his bright orange eyes demanded it all, and yet his lips formed the words again.

"Perhaps you should inform me now."

In the next moment that Jenner gazed at him, the expression on Kole's face suddenly and inexplicably changed rapidly. His eyes, that only just before had burned with a fierce intensity, now glazed, and flickered with a confusion of disbelief and resignation. His lips lost their thin smile, and faltered as though to gasp either an apology or a plea. And then his face rippled with a cracking mask of drought, as within a heartbeat, all life drained utterly from him, and his entire body shuddered into a tumbling cloud of heavy dry dust.

Jenner stared with utter disbelief at the space

where Kole had been standing, as the motes of his parched body circled earthward like dead embers. Beyond the space, in a limbo where his eyes now struggled to make sense of the shadows, stood another figure, a crossbow held tensed in his hands. Jenner's eyes fought to focus upon this new player, but the recognition came swiftly, even as the man entered his ramshackle bedroom, a second bolt already fed into the shaft of his weapon.

"For your own safety," the skulker said by way of reason, "I watched him follow you inside the building. Pretty bad shape, huh?"

Jenner wasn't sure whether Rocket was referring to the flat or to him, but he nodded absently, still trying to take in just what Kole had been prepared to do in return for information about the portal to Kar'mi'shah.

"You're safe now," Rocket reiterated, laying a hand on Jenner's shoulder with a smile. "But I don't think it's a good idea to be hanging around here too long. They might get wind of the kill, you know?"

"I need... to track them down," Jenner explained, looking at him.

"I could do with another helper," Rocket said. "Recruiting has been slow."

"No, not to kill. To help."

The skulker stared at him.

"You got a face that says you're serious -"

"I am, Rocket. Look, I don't expect you to believe me, and to tell you the truth, I'm not sure of what I'm doing either. But come with me, without weapons; I have something to show you."

FIFTEEN

THE RETURN

There were so many questions that Rocket wanted answers to as they both made their way back across London. Jenner attempted to offer those answers, but he just didn't have the information, that was the simple truth of it. All he had been given were snatches that had been left to tempt his imagination as the bridge of the Goddess had carried him home. He wasn't even certain if they had even been left for him; perhaps they had just been fragments of a previous time and place, or even just a fanciful vista of a province dreamed. He only had his instinct now.

The direction in which they were now headed was a dangerous one according to Rocket, and he drove cautiously with a frequent eye on his mirrors. His array of guns and crosses still swung from their hooks in the back of the van, but Jenner had been insistent that he leave them behind when they finally reached their destination. Besides, he had reasoned, a public underground station was hardly a fitting place to be seen carrying an arsenal around. But Rocket had commented, without humour, that it wasn't anything new to him.

It was shortly before ten o'clock when they finally reached Camden. Rush hour was lingering heavily, but it only took the skulker another ten minutes to find somewhere to park up. It was in a back street, behind some dubious-looking garages, and Rocket made only the briefest of comments about having colleagues in the right places. It wasn't until Jenner led him round to the station entrance and down towards one of the platforms, that Rocket realised that they weren't even taking a tube anywhere, but trekking inside one of the tunnels themselves.

"Here?" he exclaimed, glancing furtively around.

Jenner shrugged absently, as he checked for guards on the platform behind him, before slipping down in front of the rails and darting out of the reach of the yellow lights. Rocket added something about having his own people moving about just above their heads, but Jenner lost most of it as he headed swiftly into the rapidly enveloping darkness.

"I can't believe it," the skulker continued, as he finally caught up with his guide. "I know they have their nests all over the city, but I didn't expect to find one here. You're sure you've got your facts right?"

"No," Jenner admitted over his shoulder. "I'm not."

They made their way as quickly as they could through the darkness, their hands tracing their path along the thick grimy walls, passing over layers of filthy cables and wires. It had not occurred that the entrance, if indeed there even was one, would be hidden, or even camouflaged, but after perhaps only a few hundred yards, their progress was halted by a figure blocking the tunnel.

"Where you headed, bloods?" came a low guttural voice.

"We're looking for someone," Jenner managed to reply, his heart suddenly pounding in his chest.

"Down here?" returned the figure. "I think you

made a wrong turn."

"You live here?" Rocket demanded suddenly.

Jenner thought his intent might threaten what he was here to bring, and he put a hand out to him to quieten him.

"We're looking for Koulan," Jenner said defiantly, his words stronger than he actually felt. "I have news.

"You're human," the voice returned. "This ain't no place for you."

"This isn't the place for any of us. Please, if you know where Koulan is, take us to him."

"Are you crazy?" Rocket suddenly hissed in his ear. "You've seen what these things can do. I told you we needed weapons. And reinforcements. We found out where they are, now let's get back."

"We're not going to be killing anyone," Jenner said to him, and turning back to the figure halting their way, said: "There'll be no killing on any side today."

"No?" said the figure.

"No. Now take us to Koulan. I have news of Kar'mi'shah."

The city, now named, brought a change to the guard's demeanour. Jenner could barely make out his features in the murk of the tunnel, but he was certain that they changed now, to one of confusion, and he watched as he slowly stepped aside and allowed these two insane mortals access to the polluted tunnels where the Wraiths had made their home.

It was a grim circle of figures that Jenner found himself standing before, when finally he and Rocket were delivered into the presence of Koulan. Standing huddled, the tribe of vampires looked down upon

451

them as though they were little more than vermin, with both distaste and contempt. One of their number came forward, the crowd allowing him passage, and he carried himself with some considerable authority. To simply be in his presence was threatening, but with his huge great coat billowing around him like deathly black wings and his inset heavy eyes bearing intently down upon them, it was like being in the court of hell itself.

"You risk everything in coming here," the great vampire growled. "Speak what you will, and quickly."

Jenner gazed up at him, his lips parted and dry in the air thick with grime. He felt Rocket stare at his silence, and the nudge in his ribs to hurry him to a speech which might yet save their lives.

"Well?" the vampire asked.

His eyes burned with a terrible impatience, but still Jenner could find no words for him, and realised only now that he'd had no speech prepared, only a desire to come here and meet with this blood-drinker. The vampire gazed down upon him with an unerring temper, and it was only as Jenner saw those two eyes flicker in the direction of the skulker beside him, that he realised that Rocket had drawn a gun. The moment happened swiftly, but not so swiftly that Jenner managed to find the speed in his own hands to knock the weapon that had already been levelled at the vampire before them, away from his heart and sideways into the crowd. He could not stop the bullet as it came, though, and as the shot echoed around the cavern like a furious thunderclap, one of the assembled vampires recoiled in pain from the shot. It did not kill him, but a clamour rose instantly nevertheless, some cowering from further attack, others springing to the wounded demon, others lurching forward to take out the throat of the assassin. Jenner managed to wrest control of the gun out of Rocket's hands, and in that instant, caught sight of Koulan do the same to his clan, holding those that would destroy the two of them back with a single growl.

An uneasy silence fell across the cavern as eyes shifted from one to another, voices hissing, bared teeth white and glistening. Jenner dared a look back at their leader, the one he had been sent to find, and saw that he stood waiting for explanation. He had saved his life perhaps, Jenner guessed, and now it seemed that he wanted to know the reason for that. Rocket stood trembling beside him, and knew that he too would want an explanation of why he had let the vampire live. He was not sure whether he even had answers for them, but then, as he heard the sound of the gun skitter across the hard ground, he glanced absently down, to see that his hand had suddenly twisted at an awkward angle, and that where before there had been flesh and bone, was now rock and a slowly consuming flame.

He felt no pain in the mesmerising fire, only a curious sense of wonder that it should even be there. His eyes rose to find that everyone who surrounded him - the skulker Rocket, the vampire Koulan, and every demon sheltered in the depths beneath Camden Station - was staring aghast at him and at the yellow flame of the fire that was even now beginning to play across his forearm with ambition.

Jenner saw his limb degenerate without anything close to panic or fear. Even as the fire caught his torso and licked feverishly down in search of his belly and manhood, he realised that this was the instruction of the Goddess, the play that she had wanted her brethren to see. There was no message that he had to give. He *was* the message. And as he looked up at the vampire Koulan, saw his confusion dissipate as he too realised that this meeting was something destined by a higher order.

Stepping back with his arms outspread, Jenner let his fireball body continue to open up into the cavern, the brightness of his being reaching out towards every depth, every shrouded corner, until every being inside became touched by his light. It was in that flame that he conveyed their passage home, showed the edge of that portal within his being. And as he stood in a cavern beneath the ordinary grey streets of England's capital, he felt the boundaries between those two worlds merge, the journey of thirty vampires and two humans begin, and his own part in the way of things come together.

Emma would be proud of him, he thought to himself through it all. Prouder still to imagine his route throughout the world, of finding those still lost from the holocaust so many hundreds of years go, of reuniting them with their home.

Oh yes, she would be proud indeed. He would take the skulker too, out into the blossoming city of Kar'mi'shah, and show him a world of wonder where Gods created life, brought prosperity to a nation, and devoted their immortality to more than just the killing of man.

Oh yes, Emma would indeed be proud. He would give her every reason to.

Oh yes, he would see to that.

SIXTEEN

VIEW FROM THE HILL

It is a freezing night, but the cold is refreshing compared to the humidity of the life I have lived. Life, can it even be called such? An existence, that seems closer.

I have existed.

I can see the frost already beginning to glisten across the back of my hand as I sit here and look out over the valley floor. I think I will make my home here in the mountains, away from both mortals and vampires, away from the oppressions and desires of both, a place where I can chart the years I have passed.

Will anyone even miss me?

That is hard to tell. I have no need of them now, and nor, I suspect, will I ever want for their company again. But for them to miss me? Who knows? That is another story, I fear. I may have had impacts on the lives of others, I may have drifted through others without casting a ripple on their imaginations. The notion is irrelevant now. I have left them behind me, and I intend to live here alone.

There is a wind gusting over the ridge now, I can feel the freezing cold of the ice it has blown over to get here, but it does not chill my body. It will perhaps keep others from coming here, and because of that I will tolerate it.

I have little desire to tell of my memories, little

desire to recount my decision to leave what had once been my home, little desire to even tell of how I came to leave that home, and travel a vast divide, to a place so very alien to me. It has been a time lived, a journey travelled, but for my future, I can see nothing. It is uncharted, unlived, and that in itself gives a clearer perspective.

Maybe one day I will tell it all.

Anonymous.

Ascension

Paul Stuart Kemp

Hampton, England 1172: After witnessing the death of her family in a frenzied witch-drowning ritual, Gaia, an eight year old girl, flees for her life. Alone and afraid, she stumbles upon a magical young boy who takes her on a journey to meet Calista, a spirit capable of harnessing both dreams and time, with promises of so much more.

Makara, Kenya 2589: There are desperate times at the end of the human race. Kiala is a man living at one of the last stations on Earth, a planet where all life has been eradicated by snow and ice. With his future hinted at, could he hold the key to preserving what little life remains, and if so, why is Calista intent on stopping him?

London, England 1994: When Carly Maddison's fiance is suddenly abducted under very strange circumstances and her fleeing brother is accused of his demise, she finds herself trapped in the depths of a dark and secret world. Her love for them both draws her deeper into that world, and if she is to discover both its rules and, ultimately, its solution, then she must face the past as well as the future, in order to learn truths that she would previously have thought unimaginable.

Witchcraft, alien abduction, ritual murders; all unfathomable mysteries, all with a human heart. Paul Stuart Kemp's science fiction horror fantasy takes the reader on an extraordinary journey, where such mysteries are found to be sown into the human soul, unable to be removed, and unable to be revoked.

ISBN 0 9538215 0 1

Natura

Paul Stuart Kemp

In the heart of the Jume mountains live Orkhas, creatures who it is believed guard and keep rule over Natura - the city of the dead. A war between two factions has raged for centuries, one side worshipping them as divinities, the other demanding their extinction.

Finding herself caught between both, Jessie McHard - a disillusioned scientist - stumbles upon a bridge spanning worlds to face a battle not only of blood but also of love, on a journey where she will have to make decisions she'd never believed possible. But only at its end can she rest, where mysteries can be unveiled and secrets be made known.

Paul Stuart Kemp's science fiction horror fantasy takes the reader on an extraordinary journey through space and time. Join Jessie as she embarks upon an experience that will lead her, ultimately, into the dangerous and unknown realms of self-knowledge.

ISBN 0 9538215 3 6

The Unholy

Paul Stuart Kemp

In an old forester's cottage in rural southern England, Irene and Michael Rider, a young married couple, decide one night to 'play the ouija'. What they invite into their new home begins to take its toll not only on their lives, but also on the lives of those around them, and the lives of their, as yet, unborn children.

Trapped in a world in which they no longer have choices, they struggle to raise the idyllic family of which they've always dreamed.

The birds in the trees are watching them, waiting for some eternal event, but the ancient evil that sits behind their eyes has time on its hands, time enough to wait forever.

Paul Stuart Kemp is one of England's darkest writers. The Unholy takes the reader into his darkest world yet; a place of demonic possession, of nightmarish visions and creatures, and the destruction of an entire family. But only at the heart of this world can true values be found: the resilience of love, the sanctity of marriage, and what it means to be human.

ISBN 0 9538215 4 4

The Business Of Fear

Paul Stuart Kemp

A young thief steals a mystical deck of cards, only to incur the wrath of their unnatural owner.

A mother is tormented by forms that seem to move within the shadows of her house.

A man stops at midnight to fix a flat tyre and sees eyes watching him from the blackness of the woods.

From malevolent ghosts to carnivorous cats, from street-walking angels to life-loving zombies, The Business Of Fear is a collection of twenty four dark tales that unravels the mind and makes us face our most primal nightmares.

Paul Stuart Kemp is one of England's darkest writers, and with this book, his first collection of short stories, he takes us on an exploration of the human capacity for fear, playing on our emotions, and exploring what it means to be afraid.

ISBN 0 9538215 5 2

Voyeur Café

Jasmine Grace

Book 1: Heartbeats in the Heat

Cover Art by Gary Tussey

First edition 2024

ISBN 979-8-9892533-1-9 (Paperback)
ISBN 979-8-9892533-0-2 (Ebook)

JasmineGraceAuthor.com

For Gary. There wouldn't be a book to dedicate if you hadn't said, "Write, baby. I've never seen you happier than when you write. I'll take care of the rest."

Author's Note

It is my intention for this book to feel like an ooey gooey romantic escape from reality. Real life is hard enough. Let's have a good time while we're reading our romance. That said, I do want to share some content warnings, so you can determine if Voyeur Café will be a safe space for you. Minor spoilers ahead.

Content Warnings

-Profanity
-Explicit sexual content, including voyeurism and exhibitionism
-Brief medical marijuana use
-Drinking to excess
-Mention of injury of a loved one, not depicted on page
-Mention of child neglect and death of a loved one/parental figure. Both happen many years prior to the main story, and neither are depicted on page.

Voyeur Café is a spicy, low-angst romantic comedy with no third act break-up or miscommunication. Intended for 18+

Station Nineteen

Chapter 1
Allie

Today will provide an opportunity to
practice the art of looking on the bright
side, Leo. *-Allie's Horoscope, February 1st*

My mind reels as I jam my fingertip onto my phone screen's
End Call button. Fuck that guy.

Pulse pounding, I close my eyes and take one long, deep
breath in an attempt to calm myself. It does not work. *Suck it up,
Allie. You've got a business to run.* This problem will have to
wait its turn.

Fortunately, there's nothing like helping customers to
take my mind off my problems. Unfortunately, there are no
customers that need my help right now, so I'm left with cleaning
to keep my mind occupied. I reach for one of our branded
Turbine Café cappuccino mugs that's still on the bar from the
morning rush, which promptly slips through my fingers and
shatters on the floor. *How poetic.*

By the time I've retrieved a broom and dustpan from the
back, Hector's already made his way up to the counter. He and

his husband, Brian, spend the mornings of their Palm Springs retirement at *Turbine*. Brian reads the paper in the comfy chairs by the front windows, and Hector usually ends up sitting on the barstool next to the register, keeping me company while I work.

"You alright, Allie?" Hector leans both tawny forearms onto the counter between us. "What happened?"

The *Tur C* and *bine afé* pieces stare up at me mockingly as I sweep up the remains of the wide-mouthed cup. "I accidentally dropped this mug."

Hector leans across the counter, eyeing the ceramic shards at my feet. "Yes, Allie, I can see that. I meant what happened on the phone call."

My head swivels in his direction, sending the tail end of my ponytail tangling into my eyelashes. "You heard that?"

"You had the conversation at sharing volume." Hector waves a hand to gesture at the rest of the shop. "We all heard it."

Carefully unravelling my hair from my lashes, I cringe. "All of you?"

"All of us." Hector nods.

I shouldn't be surprised. No one's ever described me as quiet. Loud, bold, outspoken? Absolutely.

At least, 'All of us' doesn't include many people this morning. A tiny silver lining. Brian's in his favorite orange chair next to the giant potted palm, completely unbothered as usual. Another regular, a pink-haired retiree named Daisy, draws in her sketchbook on the opposite side of the room. She can't hear too well anymore, and even if she could, she's slow to judge.

Actually, the only people in here who don't bring me gifts during the holidays are a couple that's in town from Minnesota on vacation. They wouldn't be out of line in leaving a review to the tune of "The shop owner had a loud argument on the phone for ten minutes. One star." *Yikes*. I'll bring them some free cookies.

Hector waves a hand to get my attention. "You're not getting out of telling this story. What's going on?"

"Fine," I sigh. "You know how Mel always said he'd sell me Station 19 when he was ready to retire? And I've been saving forever, waiting for him to finally give up the building?" Hector nods along impatiently, already knowing all of this. "Evidently, Mel lied." I brace my hands on the counter in front of me and squeeze the edge. "He called to tell me I'll meet my new landlord today."

"New landlord? Today?" Hector's incredulous voice carries through the entire coffee shop. *At least I'm not the only one.*

"Exactly. It's bullshit." I start pacing back and forth behind the register. "Some guy made Mel an offer without Station 19 being listed, and he just sold it to him. Never gave me a chance."

"That's so slimy," Hector gasps. "Why would he do that to you?"

"All he said was he couldn't turn down a good offer." I stop pacing and try leaning back against the counter next to the espresso machine, which lasts about ten seconds before I start pacing again. "I don't get it. I asked him every time we talked when he would be ready to sell, and all he would say was 'someday'."

Hector slides onto a barstool, propping his chin up with a palm while his elbow rests on the bar. "I know you wanted to own it, but would it be so bad to keep renting from the new person?"

"Mel said the new guy wants both sides. He has to honor the rest of my lease, but *Turbine Café* will be gone in six months." Station 19 is split into two units, separated down the middle by a glass wall. My coffee shop is on one side, and Mel runs a touristy gift shop on the other. Or at least he did until this morning.

The glass wall is technically a wall of windows that start a few feet above the ground, just higher than the tops of the row of white, tulip-style, pedestal tables that line it on this side. Brass frames separate the windowpanes from top to bottom every five or six feet, but the overall effect is like having one long window between the two spaces.

Mel's tacky gift shop was such a waste of a unique building design that no one ever bothered looking through to that side more than once. I'm just now noticing the cheap straw hats and palm tree keychains are gone, leaving only empty, dusty glass shelves. He must have done that last night when I wasn't here, so he wouldn't have to face me in person. *Coward.*

My best friend and roommate, Devon, was supposed to move her interior design firm next door when I bought the building. She designed *Turbine* so it blends in seamlessly with the building's mid-century architecture, using pedestal tables, knock-off Herman Miller Eames chairs in sea-foam green, and those funky sputnik chandeliers with bulbs sticking out every which way in a spiky starburst to pull it together. She's had a perfectly coordinated design for her office in her back pocket for years. *That she'll never get to use.*

"Sounds like we have six months to come up with a solution, then." I don't miss that Hector says *we* instead of *you*. He'd do anything to help me, but he shouldn't have to. He's my customer and my friend. It's not his job to figure out my business woes. Still, he's in fix-it mode, and there's no turning that off. "What do we know about the new landlord?"

"All I know is I'm supposed to write my next rent check to Lucas Pine," I say with a sigh and a shrug.

"Lucas Pine?" Hector's lip curls into a sneer. "Sounds like a jackass."

"Lucas Pine *is* a jackass name, isn't it?" My voice is way louder than it should be for talking shit about a stranger, but professionalism is out the window today. "I hate him already."

"As you should." Hector nods emphatically. "I'll hate him in solidarity." That brings a little smile to my face. He takes the last sip of his cold brew, and I get to work making him another. His presence is the only thing besides staying busy that's keeping me from spiraling out of control, although his next question has the opposite effect. "So, do you have any ideas yet on what's next?"

My mind whirls. The shock of losing this place hasn't begun to wear off in the twenty minutes since I found out. "I have no idea." My voice slips out, lacking its usual power. "Station 19 has always been my only plan. I've never had a backup." *Holy fuck. I don't have a backup.*

Hector rushes to reassure me. "Don't worry. You don't have to have a solution yet. You have plenty of time." I wish I could believe him. Six months is hardly enough time to find the kind of solution this massive problem will need.

I know it's not unheard of to relocate a business, especially if you're renting space. But I cannot imagine *Turbine* anywhere other than Station 19. It belongs here. *Fuck whoever Lucas Pine is for taking it away from me.*

Six years ago, when I found this building, it was love at first sight. The mid-century icon oozes character and is generally cool as hell. It was a gas station in the 1950s, and the exterior still has most of its original details, including the old gas pumps on the patio. There's even an oversized triangular awning out front, in true mid-mod fashion.

This place is more of a home to me than anywhere I've ever lived. The community is my family and *Turbine* needs to stay put for them as much as it does for me. I can't relocate it. *I just can't.* I turn to my friend where he sits at the counter. "There has to be a way out of this, right?"

A boyish smile of bright white teeth takes over Hector's face, making him look younger than his sixty-something years. "Of course, there's a way." He's confident I'll figure this out, so that makes one of us.

I pop the lid onto his fresh cold brew and slide it over to him. He tries to pay me, but I insist it's on the house since he's being a sounding board for me while I process my life falling apart. "Seriously, it's on me. Go enjoy your coffee with Brian. I'll let you know if the jackass shows up."

Hector reassures me one more time before going back to sit with Brian in their spot by the front windows.

The oversized mid-mod starburst clock on the wall tells me I have five more hours before I can go home and get drunk about this. Closing my eyes, I take a few more deep breaths and start pulling affirmations out of my ass. *This shit happens all the time. Not to me, but to someone, I'm sure. This is going to be okay. Turbine is going to be okay. I am going to be okay. Every problem has a solution. I can find this solution. I will find this solution.*

One more deep breath, and I open my eyes to find a man waiting at the register. And not just any man, an unreasonably good-looking man who's watching me with focus that borders on scandalous, sending a blush straight to my cheeks. He's all broad shoulders and sharp lines, holding a motorcycle helmet under one bulging muscular arm. Like, *whew.* I have to crane my neck to take him all in.

He wears a faded navy collared shirt, the canvas kind mechanics wear, worn jeans, and work boots. Tousled black hair falls over his forehead in a few places, but it's not quite long enough to obstruct the view of his big brown eyes or the envy-inducing lashes that frame them. *If I had those, I wouldn't be spending forty-five minutes and too many dollars twice a month to get lash extensions.* His face is framed by thick, stern brows and a perfectly square jaw that's covered with a closely trimmed beard, making the smirk pulling at his lips the only soft thing about him.

Oh god. How long was I taking deep breaths with my eyes closed and he was just standing there watching me?

Hector's voice carries over from the front of the restaurant. "So, this jackass named Lucas Pine swoops in and steals Allie's dream!" Love him for having my back, even if it is a little awkward that everyone else heard him too, including this gorgeous man. This gorgeous man who I am fully staring at. *Shit.*

Resisting the urge to ask him to come back to my place and help me get over my rough day, I ask, "Can I help you?"

He stares at me, unmoving, playful smirk gone. *Where did it go? I miss it.*

I try again. "How's your day going?"

Raising his eyebrows, he says, "It's been interesting."

Stifling an embarrassed laugh, I give him a little shrug. "It's been a hell of a morning," I offer. *How long has he been here?* He couldn't have heard my conversation with Hector. I would have seen him. Right? *Shit.* "What would you like?" I ask, unsure how to lift the awkwardness.

He doesn't respond immediately, setting his helmet on the counter before squaring his shoulders and sliding his hands into his front pockets. His forearms flex, and *damn*, what a set of forearms they are. Firm, sinewy muscles define every inch of skin, sun-tanned quite a few shades deeper than the light-olive complexion of his face. He looks so at ease that the awkwardness must be all on my side. *Awesome.* "You were going to buy this building?" he asks. So he *did* hear my conversation with Hector. *Also, awesome.*

Not really his business, but I humor him so I can keep enjoying the view. "That was the plan." I gesture to the skeleton of a gift shop on the other side of the glass wall. "Mel next door always said he'd sell it to me as soon as he was ready to retire. But he must have changed his mind because he sold it to some jackass named Lucas Pine and didn't tell me about it until the deal was already done."

A muscle ticks in his jaw, his expression tight, while he considers my answer. His hands remain in his pockets as he lifts his chin toward the gift shop. "What were you going to do with that side?"

"My friend is an interior designer. Her office should be going over there." The man doesn't respond, only stares through the window briefly before focusing his intense gaze back on me. *So, why'd you ask?* I try again to see what he wants. "Can I get you something to drink?"

He looks up at the menu behind me, considering it before asking, "Doesn't that seem like an odd use of space for an old gas station?"

Okay, rude. Usually, I'm all for chatting with customers, but he keeps prying at the exact thing I don't want to talk about. "Can I get you something?"

He ignores my question again, pulling one broad hand out of his pocket and pointing toward the windowed wall. "And the windows?" I wish Devon were here so she could level him with a proper glare. But she's not, so my wimpy glare will have to do. *Damn my round cheeks and giant Bambi eyes.*

"What *about* the windows?" I ask him, lacing my voice with irritation, before I drop down to the bakery case to consolidate the pastries onto fewer trays.

He eyes me through the curved glass but doesn't speak until I'm standing in front of him again. "Do your customers want to watch interior designers all day?" The smirk from earlier returns, looking cocky this time instead of playful. "People sitting at computers, sifting through floorplans?"

Now he's trying to stick his nose into Devon's business? I won't be having that. "The point of the window isn't for customers to have something to look at." I retort, immediately realizing it isn't the gotcha I'd hoped it would be.

His smirk grows wider. "No?"

I plant my hands on my hips, not caring that it probably makes me look like a petulant five-year-old. I'm done with this guy. "No. It's not."

He takes half a step closer, full of broad-shouldered confidence. "What's the point of the window, then?" He thinks he got me, but he is dead wrong.

I recite the story I've told customers a thousand times before. "In the sixties, a man named Lou bought this old gas station and turned this half into a diner. He rented the other half out to a woman named Nora, who turned her side into a bookstore, and they fell in love. They were so head-over-heels for each other that they had the giant wall of windows put up so they could see each other all day long, never missing a moment of their partner serving lunches or stacking books." I watch for the softening of his posture and the "aww" face that people inevitably get whenever I tell this story, but it doesn't come.

Instead, he scoffs. "You don't believe that, do you?" What is *with* this guy? Of course, I believe it. I just told it, didn't I? Sure, the whole thing is a little far-fetched, but that's what makes it a good story.

"They used to come in all the time. Nora loved to tell the

story about how they got together," I tell him, tightening my hands where they're still planted on my hips. "They're the ones who sold it to Mel. In case you missed it while you were eavesdropping earlier, Mel's the guy who sold this building to some jackass after years of promising he'd sell it to me."

He furrows his brows, bringing a momentary flash of confusion to his sculpted face before it returns to his stern stare. "Sounds like maybe Mel's the jackass."

My cheeks heat with frustration. "Mel is an exemplary jackass, but that's the thing about jackasses. No one has a monopoly on the title. Lots of jackassery going around."

The black-haired man's gaze is heavy on me. He's thinking something really loudly, but I can't decipher what it is. "Do you want a drink?" I ask him a final time. *If he doesn't order now, he can fucking leave.*

His gaze narrows, considering something that probably isn't his order, but actually answers me, "Coffee, black."

Of course, this guy drinks black coffee. There are two types of people who order black coffee. The first type is the easiest, sweetest, lowest maintenance customer you'll ever meet. The second category is the one he clearly falls into—condescending asshole.

"Size, room, name?" I ask. How hard is it to know your entire coffee order, black coffee man?

He doesn't hesitate to respond, "Medium. No. Luke." *So, he knew but didn't say?* He must be the kind of gorgeous person who never had to develop manners. Or a personality. *I bet he doesn't have one of those either.* The muscles in his arm strain against the sleeve of his shirt as he reaches for his wallet and a thick strand of onyx hair falls across his forehead, his deep brown eyes never leaving mine. *Yeah, definitely no personality.*

"Luke," I repeat back to him as my blue marker squeaks his

name onto a compostable paper cup with a turbine printed on the side.

"Yes, Luke." He's smirking again. In the five minutes that I've known this man, I've gone from being dumbstruck over that smirk to being glad it'll be out of my life after I get him this damn black coffee, but then adds, "It's short for Lucas. Lucas Pine."

I almost drop the cup. Of course, this obscenely gorgeous and equally frustrating man is my new landlord. *Of course*. That is precisely the day I'm having. I should have known. He's the one who bought my building out from under me. He's the one taking away Station 19 and everything I've ever worked for.

Stopping the blush from overtaking my cheeks again is a losing game, but that doesn't mean I can't hold my ground. I plant my feet, taking up as much space as my five-three frame can.

Leveling him with my best Devon-glare impression, I say the first thing that comes to mind. "The faucet in the back leaks. The faucet in the bathroom leaks. The door to the parking lot in the back always gets jammed. It's not safe. Speaking of the parking lot and safety, there's only one light out there that isn't burnt out..." I continue to list every little thing that could possibly fall under his responsibilities as a landlord. *Turbine* is still mine for six months, and I'm sure as hell not going to make them easy on him.

Chapter 2
Luke

"Looks good on ya, kid." *-Luke's Grandad,
Ernie Hudson, on Luke's fifth birthday after
gifting him his first bicycle.*

Before Allie and I ever spoke, she decided I was a jackass, and I
decided she was the most stunning woman I'd ever seen.

It only took one look at her through our shared glass wall to
stop me in my tracks. She's flawless. Thick thighs, full hips and
rounded breasts create an exaggerated hourglass shape on her
short frame. Big green eyes pop against her pale skin, and rosy
cheeks and plump lips define her sweet face.

She wears her emotions open, raw, and beautiful for anyone
to see. Hands moving for emphasis, cheeks blushing at the
slightest trigger, chestnut-haired ponytail bouncing along with
every word she says. I was captivated.

When I walked over there to introduce myself, I realized all
the heated emotion I'd seen through the window was directed
at me. She believes I've fucked her over by buying Station 19,
and she tried to punish me with a lengthy "fix-it" list. But I'll fix

anything that needs it. Saves me from doing it later when I've taken over her side of the building.

Allie rushes toward me when I walk behind her counter after retrieving my toolbox from the truck. "What do you think you're doing?"

The counter forms an L-shape, with the register and bakery case on the shorter arm, parallel to the front door. The long arm runs parallel to the glass wall, almost all the way to Turbine's back door, with the entrance to the kitchen behind it. She reaches me in a huff, grazing my arm with her perky breasts as she crosses to block my entrance to the kitchen. *Fuck me, that was nice.*

With only a couple of feet between us, I have a clear view of the freckles that detail her plump cheeks and the nose that curves up a touch at the tip. I know enough about eyebrows from my little sister to understand that Allie's have been perfectly crafted into their shape. She's arching one at me now, which I'm sure she intends to be intimidating. It only makes her look sweeter, or at worst, like she's overly curious about what I'll say next.

I lift my toolbox toward the swinging door to the kitchen. "Figured I'd start with the faucet in the back."

"You can't do that." She puts her hands on her hips in another move that she means to be threatening but isn't.

She's so damn cute. "Can't I?"

"No, you can't." She moves a few paces to place herself more firmly between me and the kitchen door.

"Convincing argument." I take a step closer to her.

"You are infuriating, do you know that?" She takes a step back.

I step closer. "I've been told."

Allie moves again, letting out a frustrated snarl when

she backs into the counter. *Did she just try to growl at me? Adorable.* "You can't do it today." She gestures around the coffee shop as she regains her hands-on-the-hips power stance. "I'm slammed."

There are seven people here, and we're two of them. She's hardly slammed. When I move closer this time, her lips press together and the pupils in her doe eyes flare.

Strange thing to hold her ground about, not having her faucet fixed, since it was three minutes ago that she told me to fix it. I look over her head at the kitchen door and back at her dilated gaze and remember the conversation I overheard. *She's having a shit day.*

Raising one hand in a signal of surrender, I back away from the counter. "I'll be back tomorrow." Walking away toward the jammed back door, I resist the desire to look back for her reaction. She is incredible. Beautiful, feisty as hell, and not someone I need to concern myself with. I have mountains of work ahead of me getting two businesses off the ground. The last thing I need to think about is Allie Walker, no matter how much I want to.

The door to the parking lot is more pressing than a dripping faucet. I need to ensure it's safe. The steel lid to my army green toolbox opens with the same creak I've been hearing since my childhood. The toolbox was my grandfather's, and it went to me when he passed.

Light shines off of the glossy black-and-white photo of him that's taped inside the lid. In it, Grandad's leaning on his motorcycle, the same 1955 BMW R69 that he taught me to ride on decades later, at a gas station surrounded by desert mountains and palm trees. The photo fell off of the lid a few months ago, and I read the back for the first time.

Ernie, Station 19, Palm Springs, 1961

When I read the location, I had to go in person to see the place I'd carried around a photo of for years. Three hours later, my Honda CB had taken me from Ventura to Palm Springs. I was expecting to drive by a gas station that had been renovated to current standards or to find that it had been knocked down completely and replaced with condos. Instead, I found that not only was Station 19 still here, but it had been split into two spaces.

I had to have it. Grandad left me money that I got access to a month ago on my thirtieth. The timing couldn't have been better. The location is perfect. The fact that it comes with a stunning coffee shop owner who doesn't like me yet is just an added bonus.

It only takes ten minutes before I've fixed Allie's door and I'm crossing back into the side of the building that will soon be my shop. My phone rings as I flip the switch for the overhead fluorescent lights. The half that aren't burnt out flicker on. "Hey."

"Hey, Luke!" The energetic voice of my best friend, Cam, comes through. "How's day one of owning the most badass motorcycle shop-slash-bar around?"

"It's something." I put in my wireless headphones and slide my phone into my pocket.

"That good, huh?"

"The fierce little brunette who owns the coffee shop next door has another six months on her lease, so the bar is going to have to wait at least that long." I look around the dusty shell of a gift shop. There's a whole wall of puke-green Formica cabinets in disrepair, worn brown carpet, god-awful wallpaper on every wall covering the original brick, and a dozen empty glass shelves and an oak desk that Mel left behind. "I'm about to start clearing out the shop side. It's not much demo. Should hopefully be done in a few days."

"Fierce little brunette?" he asks, unsurprisingly.

"Turns out she wanted to buy the building, and I 'stole her dream.' She's pissed." Looking through the window, I catch Allie trying to glare at me from behind her counter. *Does she not realize how cute it makes her look?* I lift my chin in her direction in acknowledgment, and she quickly turns away, cheeks flushed and brown ponytail bobbing.

"Sucks for her," Cam says.

"The guy I bought the building from said the community wouldn't miss her place. Looks like he lied. There was a line out the door this morning."

"I can hear in your voice that you already feel bad about this. I won't allow it."

I flip on the mostly burnt-out lights in my office that currently holds three boxes of broken shot glasses, calendars for every year but this one, a stack of empty cardboard boxes, and all the tools I unloaded earlier this morning.

Cam's voice grows even more animated than usual. "You've gotta look out for you for once, Luke. It's not your fault someone you don't know wanted the building, too. It's business."

"I know," I grumble.

"You can be a charming guy if you want to be. You've just got to turn it up a notch for this girl. That'll make life easier, I promise." Cam carries on the conversation without me while I organize my demo tools, giving me unwanted advice about women and catching me up on all the racing stories I've missed this year. He's in the middle of his competitive race season, and it's the first year I haven't been out there on the track as a mechanic.

"Cam," I interject. "I've gotta go." Love the hell out of him, but I need to get back to work.

Cam ignores me. "What are you gonna call the bar?"

"That's what you're keeping me on the phone for?"

"Just answer the question."

I sigh, "Probably Ernie's, or maybe Luke's."

"Very creative," Cam chides. "But you can't call it Luke's."

"Why not?" I slide my work gloves on and pick up my sledgehammer.

"Because you don't run a diner in the fictional town of Stars Hollow."

"Huh?"

"It's from *Gilmore Girls*."

"Yeah, I haven't seen that." I look through the glass at the people sipping their coffee and the brunette behind the counter who's putting on a broad smile for her customers. I wonder how soundproof that glass wall is? Probably not very.

"Since you've chosen not to get your own pop culture education, you'll have to trust me. Luke's is taken."

"Noted."

"Also, if anyone ever asks, you're Team Jess."

"I can't be Team Luke?"

"No, of course not. There is no Team Luke."

"Wh—" I start to ask him why not and remember I don't care. "Okay, Cam. I'm about to swing this hammer."

"Alright, I've got four days free coming up next week, or maybe the week after. Fuck, I don't know. But there's three or four days, and I'll be there to help you." He's a chaotic guy, but he's loyal.

"Alright, boss. Later."

"I'll see you sometime soon. Probably surprise ya," Cam says and hangs up.

～

It's been almost a dozen hours of heavy manual labor by the time I lock up to head home. All I want to do is pick my dog Betty up from daycare, take a long shower, and drink a cold beer on my couch.

But I can't. Because my truck is missing.

What the hell?

I find my answer in the form of a reflective white parking sign that I missed this morning because it's largely covered by an overgrown bougainvillea vine.

TURBINE CAFÉ EMPLOYEE PARKING ONLY
Violators Will Be Towed at Their Own Expense

There's a Post-it stuck to the sign, proudly displaying a single all-caps word in blue marker.

JACKASS

Chapter 3
Allie

Play nice today. Your gut reaction isn't necessarily your best reaction. -*Allie's Horoscope, February 8th*

Turbine's massive starburst clock reads five-fifty-three when Bea rushes through the front door. She's running late for the six AM barre class she teaches at the gym across the street, which isn't unusual. Her dark brown hair, a perfect match for the coffee I'm brewing, is twisted into a fancy Pinterest braid that she definitely did while she was driving here. Her golden-beige skin is make-up and blemish free, and she wears black leggings and a cropped Poison t-shirt that's undoubtedly vintage.

I slide the iced oat milk, half-sweet vanilla latte that I just finished making for her onto the counter. "Morning, gorgeous."

"Bless you, coffee angel," she whispers as she hands me her card. Hugging her latte close to her chest before taking her first sip, she says, "I am Hangover Barbie today. I could never get through my class without this."

"I'll never understand how you do it," I say, copying her

hushed tone and returning her card. In exactly three minutes, she'll be *on* and teaching one of the toughest workout classes in the Coachella Valley. "You're amazing."

"No, *you* are amazing." She takes another deep sip of her drink as she backs toward the door. Before she reaches it, Luke appears and pulls it open for her from the outside. Having his truck towed has not had the desired effect of making him disappear. Instead, he's been back every morning this week for coffee and working next door from sunup to sundown. "Thank you, door angel." Bea says. She silently mouths at me from behind him, *"So hot!"* before checking for cars and sprinting across the street.

A muscular blue pit bull steps in behind Luke, its steel gray fur interrupted in a few places by snowy white, including two front 'socks' and a thick stripe that starts at the width of its nose and narrows between its ears. "She allowed?"

"According to the FDA, it's a hard no, but this early in the morning, I usually let it slide." Rounding the counter, I squat down so the dog can come check me out. "New landlord's a jackass, though, so who knows?" She ambles over and rolls on her back for me to scratch her belly. *I like this dog.*

Luke ignores my jab. "He's good with it. "

Rolling my eyes, I focus back on the sweet face in front of me. "Who is this pretty girl?"

"Betty." She looks up at him and wags her tail when she hears her name. I settle down cross-legged onto the slate gray concrete, the floor cooling my legs from beneath as Betty rolls her warm body into my lap. *What a sweetie.* I keep petting her and soaking up all the doggie love I can until I hear Luke chuckle from right above us.

On the ground like this, with him looming over me, he's even more imposing than usual. I straighten my spine and square my shoulders, pushing my chest forward. I won't be intimidated that easily. "Are we amusing you?"

"Endlessly, but I'm here for a drink. Service is pretty slow." Does he seriously think he's allowed to tease me now that I petted his dog once? *No, thank you.*

"No more pets for you, Betty. Sorry, sweet girl." I point a thumb at Luke. "All this jackass' fault." When I stand up and cross over to the sink to wash my hands and arms, she whines briefly and returns to his side. *How could such a sweet dog belong to Lucas Pine?*

"Jackass? Didn't know you liked me enough to give me a nickname." He smirks. *Cocky* jackass.

"That's not what a nickname is." I roll my eyes while I slide a to-go cup for his drink from the top of the stack.

"I say it counts."

"It doesn't count."

Betty leans her heavy pittie head against Luke's leg and looks up at him adoringly while he scratches behind her ear. *Aren't dogs supposed to be good judges of character?* Maybe Betty's too loving to perceive the truth about her human.

I place his drink on the counter between us. "Medium coffee, no room."

Luke pays in cash and picks up his cup. "Thanks, sweetheart."

"Oh, nope. Nope, nope, nope. I hate that already." A smile takes over his entire bearded face, clearly pleased with himself. *Dammit.*

"Noted," he replies with smooth confidence.

"What are you doing here so early, anyway?" I enjoy the quiet of a solo opening shift, and if he's banging around on his side all morning, he'll ruin it.

"You're here," he says. Like that's a reason.

"I run a coffee shop. Sleeping in isn't a part of my life. But it should be for you."

"Not today. Too much to do."

He's been tearing up Mel's old shop all week, and it's been as loud as his presence in my life is obnoxious. "Whatever you're doing today had better not be so damn loud. I'm losing business over it. How much longer until you—" I twinkle my fingers toward the windowed wall. I have no idea what he's doing over there besides being a nuisance.

Luke finishes the thought. "Until I finish demo and open my motorcycle shop?"

A fucking motorcycle shop? Eew. That's the last thing Station 19 needs. "Really? What for? Is this building even zoned for that?"

Luke takes a slow, deliberate sip of his coffee before he responds. "Sweetheart, you're asking if this old gas station," he lifts his chin and leans toward me, "is zoned for mechanic work?"

I pull my lips in a tight line. "Doesn't make a difference to me anyway, does it? You took the building."

If my words have an effect on him, he doesn't show it. He's completely at ease, strong shoulders relaxed, casually sipping on his coffee and scratching Betty behind the ears.

"What's the plan for my side?" I ask, curiosity winning out over good sense.

His face pulls into something unreadable. "This'll become a bar as soon as you're out."

My heart sinks, and I know it shows on my face. *A bar?* "In the meantime, figure out a way to get your shit done over there without disturbing my customers."

I know I'll have to leave no matter what, but hearing the details of his plan is like flipping through an ex's wedding photos. *If I was still in love with the ex.* It would have been better not to know how Station 19 would move on without me, but I couldn't help myself.

Luke just stares at me for a few seconds and then turns to leave. Betty walks beside him out my front door and back through his, following him happily over to his side. *His side.* That's what it's become. His side and my side. Him against me. We're on opposing sides with a wall of windows running down the middle like a line in the sand.

I pull out my phone and text Devon.

Me: Can you get me curtains for the glass wall?

Me: I don't want to look at his stupid gorgeous face anymore.

Me: I hate him.

Devon: Just got out of my workout.

Me: Oh shit, sorry. Forgot.

Devon: All good.

Me: I'm so bummed it's him over there and not you.

Devon: Me too.

Devon: That's a lot of drapery. Take it you don't want to wait on a custom order?

Me: Ugh I NEVER want to see him again.

Devon: Got you. Be by this afternoon to measure.

Devon and I found Station 19 together. She got a job after college at a design firm in Palm Springs, and I helped her move down here from Beaverton, Oregon, where we grew up. While we were apartment hunting, we drove by this converted gas station that was half diner, half gift shop. The diner side was for rent, and we got the idea that I should open my coffee shop here and move to Palm Springs with her.

Opening my own coffee shop was my go-to daydream, starting freshman year. In high school, people didn't like me much for reasons I never understood. Although even then, no one would cross Devon. She was like a tall, blonde, resting-bitch-faced shield that protected me from teasing glances and whispered insults. The only time I felt accepted when she wasn't around was when I'd sit at *Coffee and Trees*, our neighborhood's coffee shop, to work on my homework. The baristas were always nice to me, complimented my attempts at nail art, and included me in their conversations.

Working there was my first job, and a year after graduation, I became the general manager. Everyone else in my family has a master's or a PhD, but I knew what I wanted to do, and couldn't be convinced to go to college. For four years, while Devon was away at school, I worked at *Coffee and Trees*, saved, and planned.

It took an outrageous amount of convincing, a very thorough business plan, and a lot of Devon's design help, but eventually my parents caved and let me use my college fund to open *Turbine Café*. I still can't believe we pulled that off, especially since whenever I talk to my parents now, they still ask me when I'm going to get a 'real job.'

Turbine has been my life for six years. I love my employees, my regulars, the drinks we serve, the happiness we bring people, and the atmosphere inside my sunny little shop. First, *Coffee and Trees* was my safe space, and then with *Turbine Café*, I've gotten to create my own to share with other people. Every day, I watch my dreams unfold into reality.

But I could never have pulled it off without Devon. When I was starting out, she would cover shifts on nights and weekends all the time. She did the entire interior design for free, which was dozens of hours of work. No matter how hard I've tried, she's never let me pay her. Without Devon, there would be no *Turbine Café*.

Buying Station 19 was supposed to be my turn to give back. I was going to charge her the lowest amount possible to rent the other side so I could help her get ahead like she did for me.

Devon went out on her own last year, splitting from the design firm she moved out here for, and started her own company, *Friday West Interiors*. Working out of our little three-bedroom bungalow is not cutting it anymore.

I was sure this was the year Mel would finally retire, and she could move into Station 19. The perfect solution. Turns out I was only right about half of that. Mel did retire, but Lucas Pine sucked the life out of our plan with his stupid motorcycle shop.

Fortunately, the morning rush keeps me from dwelling on these things for long. The next few hours pass quickly, with a line out the door for much of it. By the time I sit down next to Hector at the barstool closest to the register for a break, I'm dripping sweat from my temples and my face is flushed red, even hotter than I usually am after a go-go-go morning.

"Why's *Lucas Pine* so quiet today?" Hector pronounces Luke's full name in a nasally voice, making it sound like an insult. "What's he up to?"

I look past Hector and see Luke carrying a cardboard box overflowing with other cardboard boxes to the back of his shop. "I told him to keep the noise down this morning, but somehow I doubt that's why he's quiet."

Marisol, a barista who works here a few days a week while her kids are in school, hands me a giant glass of ice water from behind the bar. "You always know exactly what I need, Marisol. Thank you."

"You've been working too hard, and it's hotter in here than usual," she says before hurrying back to work.

"She has a good point, Allie. When was the last time you took a day off?" Hector asks, arching a dark brow at me knowingly.

"I don't have time for days off right now, Hector. You know that." He should know better than anyone. We've been talking all week about options for a new *Turbine* location. Between that and running the shop, I can't afford to take time off.

Hector shakes his head and pulls out a brown paper package with a striped ribbon, handing it to me. "Open this. It's for you."

A gift? Unwrapping it, I find an orange pen and a toffee-colored leather notebook, detailed with floral embossing. "What's this?" I ask, running my fingers over the grooved blossoms.

He taps on the leather cover. "Read the first page."

I open to that page, and on the top, in orange block lettering, it reads:

Allie's I-Can-Do-Anything Notebook

He turns on his barstool, so we're facing each other. "You're starting something big and new. It always helps to have somewhere to gather your thoughts. Oh! And the pen is orange because red is aggressive and black is boring."

I pull him in for a big hug. "Well, dammit, that is really sweet. Thank you so much." I try to imagine my thoughtful friend sitting on a stool here when this building is a bar, not a coffee shop. I can't decide if I'm sad or maybe jealous, but either way, I don't like it.

Hector smiles wide, his perfect white teeth shining against his rich brown skin. "Now, look at this. This is the best part." He reaches across to the journal and flips to the next page. In more orange script, he's written:

134 Cactus Ave - 9am, Feb 13
279 Paseo De Montaña - Noon, Feb 13
2389 Desert Canyon Dr - 10am, Feb 16

He's been sitting at the counter with me this week while I've been scouring online for potential new homes for *Turbine* with attached office space for Devon. These are the addresses of some of the best options. *Did he make appointments for me?* I was going to, but I haven't had a chance yet.

"A little push to get you started."

I don't need a push. I'm already working on this. I force a smile and thank him. His intentions are good, and I know the correct response would be gratefulness. On some level, I *am* grateful, but I don't want anyone else to solve this for me. I reach for my water glass and realize I've already downed the whole thing. "Is it hot in here to you?" I ask.

"Yes," Hector nods emphatically, thick hair that's more salt than pepper these days flopping forward as he fans himself with his hands. "I thought maybe you turned off the A/C."

"It's ninety-five degrees outside. Who would turn off—" My voice trails off as realization dawns on Hector and me at the same time. We turn our heads in unison to see Luke walking from the back of his shop toward the front.

"This should be fun," Hector laughs.

"For who?" I ask, already making a beeline for the thermostat.

"For me!" Hector calls to me as I disappear into my office by the back door. Sure enough, our A/C is turned off, and it's eighty-three degrees in here. There's a lot of charm with a vintage building, but it has its challenges, too. The A/C system isn't up to par with what it should be in the middle of the desert, so whatever the temperature is at Lucas Pine's stupid motorcycle shop is the temperature at Turbine.

Throwing open the back door, I find him in the employee parking lot. He's wearing a gray t-shirt that's practically soaked with sweat, jeans with holes in them that look earned and not store-bought, leather work gloves, and dark boots. I watch the muscles ripple across his back and shoulders as he throws a roll of old carpeting into a giant dumpster that isn't usually here. *It really is inconvenient how attractive he is.*

He heads back into his shop without seeing me, and I follow behind him. "Why the fuck is my A/C off?" He doesn't respond and keeps walking toward the pile of torn-up carpeting, back still to me. I follow after him, getting louder. "Hey, jackass! Why is my A/C off?!"

Still no response. I walk around and place myself between him and the construction trash he's headed for. "Hey!" I wave my hand in his face.

Luke pulls wireless headphones out of his ears and puts them away in his pocket. Maybe he wasn't ignoring me then, just listening to music. *Somehow, that's even more irritating.* "Why are you here, Allie? Am I not being quiet enough for you?"

"You need to turn on my air. It's sweaty as hell over there." I point over his shoulder to *Turbine*.

Luke wipes sweat from his brow with a bandana he pulls from his back pocket, the tendrils of his hair falling back against his forehead in a perfectly imperfect way. "It is?" He raises his eyebrows and tilts his head sarcastically.

"Whatever, I guess it's sweaty everywhere. But that's within your power, Mr. Landlord Man. Fix it." I turn on my heel, but before I can take a step, Luke's gloved hand is grasped around my elbow, stopping my progress. "What?" I shake him off as he walks around to face me again.

"Hold on." Luke's normally harsh brows crease with concern. "It's not safe for you to walk in here."

"I walked all the way from there," I use my finger to draw a path in the air from the garage door to my feet, "over to here, my guy. I assure you, it's fine."

Luke follows my gesture and stares at my feet for a moment before he reaches down and picks up a rusty nail that's an inch away from my tan checkered slip-on Vans. He holds it out in his palm for my inspection as he stands up. "It's a wonder you didn't step on anything. You could have gotten seriously hurt."

I scan his shop. Its footprint is a mirror image of mine, with the front being a bit narrower than the back. This is the first time I've been over here since Luke took over. The carpet has all been ripped up, the brick walls are exposed again, although some are covered with paint, and there are piles of broken-down construction trash against the far wall where Devon's desk was supposed to go.

With the furniture from the gift shop gone, there's nothing obstructing the view of *Turbine*. He's got a direct view from the front door to Brian reading the paper in his rust-colored leather chair, to the plants hanging in front of the far window above the self-service station that needs napkins restocked, to Hector, watching us with rapt attention at the bar, all the way down the entire length of my white quartz counter. *Lovely.*

Putting my hands on my hips, I tip my chin up at him. "Well, I didn't. Now, why the fuck don't you have the A/C turned on?"

He tosses the nail into a trash can a few feet away. "It broke this morning. There's someone coming in a couple hours to fix it."

"A couple hours?" I throw my hands up in frustration. "It'll be a hundred degrees over there by then." Looking through the window shows me Hector watching with rapt attention at the bar. *Great.* "You should have told me."

"I should have. I'm sorry about that." His tone is patient and calm, and he doesn't even argue back. *Doesn't anything upset this man?*

"Fine." I try to take a step toward the back door, and he blocks me with his sweaty muscular frame.

"You can't walk out in those shoes."

That nail did look nasty, but how the hell else am I getting out of here? "I will be very careful and watch every step," I say placatingly as I try to leave again. Instead of moving out of my way, he steps in closer.

"It's not safe for you to walk." His voice is low, intended as a demand. *Too bad.*

"Cool. I'll just learn how to fly real quick." I jump in place and flap my arms in an approximation of flying before I try to step past him again.

Luke smirks. "You're very stubborn." Before I can respond, he's ducked down low, but instead of picking up more sharp things from the ground to clear my path, he wraps his arms behind my knees and throws me over his shoulder.

"What the fuck?" I shriek as he makes his way toward the garage door in the back of his shop. I try to squirm out of his hold, but he has my thighs pressed too firmly against his chest to get anywhere. His shoulders lift up and down against my stomach. "Are you *laughing* at me right now?"

His body moves with the rumble of his laughter, and I feel it in every inch where he's pressing our bodies together. "It's hard not to. You're being ridiculous."

"*I'm* being ridiculous? Put me down!" *I will never forgive him for this.*

"Next time, be more careful." We've reached the parking

lot, and he plops me down on the asphalt, holding his hands out to help me find my balance. I ignore them. *Like hell, I'm letting him touch me again. I'd rather fall over.*

"I am covered in your sweat now." His shirt was soaked from working in the sun without an A/C reprieve, and now I can smell him on me. It's not awful. *What? No.* I refuse to believe that his sweat smells good. I definitely don't like it. *Nope, not at all.* It's not surprisingly pleasant. Or comforting. Or warm and strong. *I hate it.*

He eyes me skeptically. "A little sweat is better than a tetanus shot and bloody feet."

I blow out an exasperated breath, trying to remember if I have a spare shirt in my car. "You're intolerable."

"Thanks for stopping by, sweetheart." He chuckles lightly and turns around, moving back into his shop. I'm staring after him in frustration when I catch the sight of Betty out of the corner of my eye. She's lying on the cool concrete floor in Luke's office next to her bed, directly in front of a fan. She doesn't get up to greet me, only lifts her head and sniffs the air. "Yeah, I'm sure I smell like him. Don't rub it in." She wags her tail. "I do not understand how you live that with that man."

Chapter 4
Luke

"You learn more about people when they think no one's watching than you do in most conversations." *-Grandad Ernie, explaining to nine-year-old Luke the benefit of patrons sometimes treating bartenders like they're invisible.*

Betty and I get to Station 19 well before the sun comes up. It's warmer inside than usual when I unlock the door. *Is the A/C broken again already?* Allie's going to be pissed. But the lights don't flicker on when I flip the switch, either. *Well, shit.* I check a few other switches and confirm the power is out on my side, but the red lights on the espresso machine next door and the safety light in the back hallway by her office shine in the dark, so Allie should be fine.

The breaker box on the wall by the dumpster in the back parking lot reveals a few of mine must have flipped in the night. Maybe there was a power surge. *Easy fix.*

It's too early for overhead fluorescence, so I only turn on the dim light by the back door and move to the leather couch by the windowed wall to get some work done on my laptop. It would be a hell of a lot easier with some coffee in my system, but Allie won't be unlocking her doors for another half hour.

The emails I rarely have to send are the worst part of my job, so I'm lucky. Normally I'm turning wrenches or mixing drinks, two things I love. Now that I have this building, I can do the same work, but for myself.

Lights flicker on next door, and loud music starts blasting. *Maybe I won't have to wait so long for coffee after all.* Looking through the window reveals Allie pulling chairs down off of tables, bobbing her head to the beat of *Killing in the Name* by Rage Against the Machine. Her chestnut hair is down and falls around her shoulders every time she brings her chin forward with the beat.

She plays indie rock and singer-songwriter stuff over the speakers most days, which I don't mind, but this is a welcome change. Her movements build with the music until she's fully dancing. I close my laptop and lean forward, bracing my elbows on my knees. Nothing on my computer is as interesting as Allie.

She bends to pick something up, exaggeratedly arching her back and sticking out her plump ass. Her jean cut-off shorts and simple black tank top hug her curves as she comes back up into a body roll. *Is this song sexy?* I never thought so before, but *goddamn* if she isn't making a case for it.

She sings along to the words, "Fuck you, I won't do what you tell me!" clearly working out some frustration. On the final line of "Motherfucker!" she holds up her middle fingers toward the windowed wall. Toward my shop. Toward *me*. Her eyes don't stay on the glass for more than a beat before she walks to the counter and picks up her phone. She doesn't know I'm over here. The lights must be reflecting off the glass and blocking the view.

She blames me for taking Station 19 away from her. Personally, I blame Mel. I still don't understand what he has against her, but whatever the reason, I have this building now, and Allie's hurt by it. Reaching my goals means she won't be reaching hers.

9 to 5 by Dolly Parton comes on next. What a follow-up to Rage. She's working behind the bar, calmer now, singing along to herself. As the song wraps up, she leans back against the counter and cradles a drink in two hands, pulling it up to her face. She closes her eyes, her chest rising and falling with each deep breath she takes.

When the song ends, she opens her eyes and takes a sip, reaching for her phone and ending her morning meditation of punk rock and good coffee. The volume goes back down to normal, and her regular acoustic style of music comes over the speakers. After tying her short black apron around her waist, she wraps her hair up into a ponytail while she walks to unlock the front door fifteen minutes early.

Goddamn, the way she moves. The way she wears every emotion so transparently on her face. Stunning. I could watch her like this forever.

Scratching Betty behind her ear, I wake her up after she slept through Allie's loud music morning routine. She rolls her heavy head into my hand. "Come on, babe. Let's go." She doesn't move. "I need my coffee." She still doesn't move. "You want to go see Allie?" Betty pulls herself into standing and wags her tail. This dog is already obsessed with the girl next door.

When I open the door to *Turbine*, Betty looks up at me, transferring her weight between her feet and wagging her tail. "Okay." I tell her, and she runs to the front counter. Allie comes around and squats down low to pet her.

"Morning, sweet girl!" Allie says. Her voice is bright, and

her smile is electric. "You're here early."

"Some of my favorite things happen before the sun comes up," I respond, even though she was talking to my dog.

"I agree with you." She cocks her head to the side. "How unusual."

I move over to stand next to Allie and Betty, who are practically cuddling on the floor. *They're adorable together.* "I can't think of one thing we've disagreed on."

She scoffs, looking up at me. "Seriously? Nothing. Nothing at all?"

"Not one, sweetheart."

She huffs and rolls her eyes before she stands up from petting Betty and crosses to the sink to wash her hands. She looks over at the currently brewing coffee and calls over her shoulder to me. "The coffee's not ready yet. I'll make you an Americano."

Spending a few extra minutes here sounds better than going back to emails. I sit on the barstool closest to the register. "I'll wait for the coffee to brew."

She glares at me, or at least she tries. "The Americano's better."

"I know what I like."

She eyes me from the espresso machine, brows raising and chin tipping up as she unhooks a metal piece with a thick black handle. "Have you ever had an Americano?"

"I haven't."

Her eyes widen, and she smiles briefly before she forces her face into something stern. "Well, you're having one today." We sit in silence while she makes me a drink I don't want. She places it in front of me, lid to the side. "It's super-hot, so give it a minute to cool off."

We're back to silence while I wait for the drink to cool and

Allie starts on another, even though I'm the only one in here. The front door opens, and Allie's face lights up at the sight of the dark-haired woman coming inside.

"Allie! My coffee angel!" The other woman yells.

Allie giggles and holds both of her hands over her head in the shape of a halo. "That's me!" The contrast between Allie's reaction to this woman and to me is striking, like she's purposely holding her joy away from me. The other woman pays for the drink Allie just finished making and rushes back out the door.

After her friend leaves, Allie looks at me again and asks, "Have you tried it?"

"I was told it's too hot."

She rolls her eyes and snaps the lid from the counter onto my cup. "I didn't realize I was going to have to babysit your coffee this morning. Hurry up."

She watches me intently as I take the first sip, concerned with whether I'll like the drink or not. It's a nice change from middle fingers and ineffective scowls. I revel in this moment of her undivided attention, her teal-green eyes dancing with anticipation as she bites her lower lip. *Damn.* She was right. This is better than my regular coffee. I bet she's insufferable when she's right. I nod slowly and drag the moment out for a few more seconds before I give her an answer. "My new favorite thing."

She throws her hands up, exasperated. "Told you."

∼

"Let me see your office!" My little sister, Skye's, voice comes through the video call on my phone. She's been bugging me for a tour of Station 19 since day one, and now that the demo's finished, there's something to show her.

"It's more Betty's office than mine," I say, making a slow pan of the small space. My steel desk is pushed against one exposed brick wall, followed by open shelving for parts storage. On the opposite side, a grey drum fan points toward Betty, who's lying flat on her stomach on the cool concrete, next to a cushioned dog bed she never uses, an oversized water bowl, and a rope toy.

Skye leans closer to the camera, grinning ear to ear. "Hi, Betty girl!" Betty wags her tail at the sound of her name. "I love it," Skye continues, "all of it. I'm so proud of you. Now take me over to the other side. I want to see this coffee shop."

"No." The last thing I want to do is walk around *Turbine* while I'm on a video call with my sister, showing off the business I'm displacing.

She waves her hand at the screen. "You're no fun."

"It's okay, Skye, I'll show you later!" The familiar but unexpected voice of my best friend interjects from over my shoulder. He did say it would be a surprise when he showed up.

Skye waves from my phone screen. "Hi, Cam!"

"He will not show you later, but I'll call you soon," I say, and we hang up our call. She's in her last year of college, and we talk whenever she needs a break from studying. I'm sure we'll be on the phone again soon.

Cam tackles me into a hug, nearly knocking my phone from my hand. Releasing me, he pats the top of my head and messes up my hair. "You getting shorter?" I'm over six-foot, but Cam's got to be four or five inches taller than me.

Stepping back, I poke his biceps. "You getting scrawnier?" He may be taller, but I probably outweigh him by twenty pounds.

"I am *lean* for racing," Cam insists. He walks out of my

office into the open space of my shop and gestures over his shoulder to *Turbine*. "If you're so worried about it, come buy me lunch."

I check my watch. "It's not even eleven." *And I was already over there once today.*

"Alright, I'll go over there and meet the coffee-girl all by myself." He walks up to the windowed wall, looking for Allie. "Which one is she? Baggy pants? No. Flannel shirt? Doesn't seem like your type."

I step in front of him to block his view. "Did you come here to hassle me, or are you going to help?"

"Can't it be both?" His eyes light up and he grabs my shoulder with one hand, pointing through the window with the other. "High pony and Bambi eyes! That's your girl for sure. You always were a sucker for the sweet-looking ones."

Pushing his pointing hand down and moving him away from the window, I say, "She is not my girl, and this glass isn't soundproof. Jesus Christ, Cam."

"Sure, sure, but I still want a sandwich," he brushes past me, heading for the front door of my shop. I follow behind him, not about to set him loose on Allie alone. As soon as we're inside *Turbine*, he's analyzing the empty motorcycle shop from this side. "Damn, you really can see everything from over here, can't you?" He waves his hand back and forth. "No secrets between you two, huh?"

"Yeah, boss. That's how windows work. You didn't notice from over there?"

"I did, but it's weird to see it from this side. What're they for, anyway?"

"They're left over from when it was an old gas station. Like the windows they have when you're getting your oil changed or your car washed so you can see what's going on."

"Actually, that's not why the windows are here. Your friend is lying to you." Allie's voice comes from behind us. When I turn, she's standing there with that ineffective glare on her angelic face and her hands on her hips, emphasizing her curvy figure.

Cam leans against the ledge below the windows on the glass wall, trying not to tower over Allie. After I introduce them, she brings up the windows again, teal-green eyes glittering with anticipation. "So, you want to know where the windows really came from?"

At Cam's urging, she repeats what she told me on the first day we met about the couple that used to own Station 19, getting more animated with each new detail. She seems to believe this story, but I can't see how. Windowed walls like this are standard in a lot of auto shops.

While I was cleaning out my office, I found a black and white photo that had fallen behind a file cabinet that proved that at least the couple she's talking about is real. It pictured a voluptuous woman in front of a lit-up Christmas tree with a note on the back.

Lou, now you can see me whenever you want. Quit staring through the window.

"Nora and Lou didn't like each other much at first. He thought she was a spoiled princess, and she thought he was a selfish prick." At that, Allie giggled. "Hearing an octogenarian call her husband a selfish prick will always be awesome," she explains, sharing details I didn't get on the first telling.

"A direct quote, then?" Cam asks, leaning forward and crossing his tattooed arms across his chest.

"Oh, definitely." Allie nods.

"What changed her mind?" I ask. Both Cam and Allie look at me then, like they'd forgotten I was here.

Allie tilts her head to the side, chestnut waves spilling over her shoulder from the end of her ponytail. "Not interested in what changed *his* mind?"

Cam laughs and answers for me. "Nah, falling for the girl next door's a classic."

Allie narrows her eyes, then turns to Cam, answering my question as if he asked it. "Nora never explained it directly," Allie scrunches her nose, considering, "but you can see in the way he looks at her, treats her, he'd do anything for her."

A woman with pink hair and giant, thick, black-rimmed glasses comes up to Allie and wraps her in a hug, ending our conversation. She's probably in her seventies but has the energy of someone much younger.

"Daisy, you look extra fabulous today!" Allie says, genuine delight coming through in her voice. Before walking away with her, Allie addresses Cam. "Nice to meet you, Cameron." Then she turns to me, scowls, and hands me a list from her apron pocket. "There are a few more things in the back that you'll need to get to immediately."

Once she's out of earshot, Cam turns to me. "Wow, she really does not like you."

"I've been telling you…"

Cam waves it off. "She'll come around. I have a sixth sense about these things." Cam's always saying shit like that, and for once I hope he's right.

Chapter 5
Allie

Things are stacking up in your favor.
Patience will see them come to fruition.
-Allie's horoscope, February 16th

The property manager from the third place on my list flashes a
fake smile at me as she gets into her car. We both know it's a
no-go. That makes me zero for three. I pull out my orange pen
to update my notes.

~~134 Cactus Ave – 9am, Feb 13~~
Too small. No windows in Devon's "office"
~~279 Paseo De Montaña – Noon, Feb 13~~
Too much $$$$$
~~2389 Desert Canyon Dr – 10am, Feb 16~~
No personality. Also, too much $$$$$

My phone buzzes with a text from Devon.

Devon: What was this one like?

Me: Stale air and disappointment.
Devon: Stop. It can't be that bad.
Me: It really, really can.
Devon: Don't give up. You've got this.
Me: I won't! Don't worry!
Devon: See you at barre tonight?
Me: ...
Devon: Tacos after?
Me: Okay, yes. I'm in.

Even if finding a new spot for *Turbine* in three tries was wishful thinking, I can't help being a little disappointed. Looks like I'll be spending my afternoon on my laptop searching for new options.

I turn my key in the ignition, and my car shudders but doesn't start. *Oh shit.* I do not have the energy for this today. I try again, holding the key longer this time, hoping it'll magically start. *What was the name of that mechanic again?* This is not how I want to spend my day. I flip the key back and forward again, giving it one more try, and it actually works. *Whew, false alarm.*

When I get to *Turbine*, Marisol greets me from behind the counter. "I know just what you need!" She's uncannily good at knowing what kind of drink someone 'needs' before they order.

In my experience, knowing your drink is like knowing your astrological sign or your Enneagram type. People wear 'Nonfat latte, extra shot' or 'Iced mocha, no whip' with pride, but I can never pick a favorite. It's not fair to the drinks.

A moment after, I sit down on a barstool at the counter and pull out my laptop to start my search again, Marisol puts a small ceramic cup filled with a double shot of espresso on the counter in front of me. Okay, maybe not *uncannily* good. I need something cold and refreshing that'll solve all my problems, not something hot and intense. I take the first sip, making a conscious effort to shake off the morning and bring a smile to my face. My employees know *Turbine* will have to move, but they don't need to share the weight of figuring it out.

A whirring sound comes from next door, and a look through the glass wall shows Luke and Cameron working on something below the eyeline of the bottom of the windows. Cameron is lanky with fair skin that barely shows through the tattoos that start on his hands, cover his arms, and run up his neck. Fire red hair crowns a head that manages to tower over Luke's significant frame. They're quite a pair.

The whirring gets louder. How is the loud part over there not finished yet? This is getting ridiculous. Closing my eyes, I take a long sip of espresso. *This is fine.* The whirring is accompanied by a bang. *Totally fine.*

Marisol reappears, smiling broadly. "Are you ready for the best part of your day?" she asks.

"Absolutely."

She hands me an iced orange drink with carbonation bubbling from the bottom and cream slowly easing down from the top. "Peaches and cream Italian soda. It's tart and playful, and I've never seen you drink one." She points at the espresso I've just finished. "You needed caffeine first, though."

I take the first sip and can't help but giggle. *Uncannily good at knowing what people need.* Never should have doubted her. "Dammit, Marisol. You're right. This is a good time."

"I know." she tsks at me before moving back to the register.

Cameron saves me the trouble of dealing with Luke by being the next customer in line. "What are you doing over there that's so damn loud?" I ask him.

"Not sure if you noticed, but I'm not over there," he says,

laughing at himself. "I'm over here, buying sandwiches."

The whirring gets even louder, and I raise my open palms and jut my chin out to emphasize my point.

"It's not me!" He shrugs his shoulders and points down his long body, to show that it is, in fact, not next door. "Take it up with Luke!"

When I look through the window again, Luke's staring back at me and Cameron, his facial expression indecipherable. Though, I'm guessing it's not an apology. Grabbing my new comfort drink, I hop down from my stool. "I *will* take it up with Luke."

When I enter his shop from the back parking lot, there's a fine layer of dust in the air of his shop, and it smells like a parking garage. The whirring is coming from a machine with a t-shaped handle and a circular base that he's pushing across the floor. Without the barrier of the windows to dull the sound, it's more of an intense scratching sound. *Lovely.*

He continues pushing the irritating machine, not acknowledging me. Between the whirring and the ear protection, he can't hear me, but I know he saw me walking over here. Hell, I'm sure he can see me in his periphery right now.

I am not interested in being ignored, so I move to block his path, checking the floor first because I am also not interested in being thrown over his shoulder like a sack of potatoes again. No rusty nails this time, just a thin layer of water that squelches with each of my steps.

He doesn't slow down, even though I'm in his direct line of sight. So, we're playing some kind of weird game of chicken? *Fine.* I plant my feet and put the hand not holding my drink on my hip, daring him to find out what would happen if he ran into me. Right when he's about to, the noise pitters out, and the base of the machine stops spinning only an inch from my feet. He takes off his ear protection, looking at me with a mix of irritation and a smirk of amusement.

"People are trying to enjoy their coffees over there," I say to him, keeping one hand on my hip and pointing through the window with my drink.

Luke holds my gaze for a moment before looking over his shoulder at my shop. "It looks like they're succeeding, sweetheart." My cheeks flame with indignation. He only calls me that because he knows I hate it. *Fucker.*

"Of course, they're fine now, jackass. You turned it off."

He smirks. "I should be done in an hour."

"You can't do this during business hours. We close at five. You can pick it up then."

"I'll finish sooner if you get out of my way."

He starts to put his ear protection back on, but I'm not done. "No. I have a right to peace and quiet. You can't impede my business."

He points through the windowed wall at the people enjoying their coffees. "I'm not impeding your business."

"You have been since your first day here." I then list all the ways he's already inconvenienced my customers with parking, noise, and lack of air conditioning—even if that one wasn't technically his fault. I'm proud of myself for leaving out the fact that if he hadn't bought Station 19, none of this would be a problem in the first place.

Luke raises his eyebrows skeptically. No one has complained yet today, or any other day actually, but how could he know that? He clenches his jaw, takes a slow breath, and concedes. "Fine. I'll do it later."

Looks like this peaches and cream Italian soda is now my second favorite thing that happened today. I don't try to hide my smile as I turn and walk back to *Turbine*.

~

The last customer of the day leaves, and I have twenty minutes to rush closing before my barre class across the street. I wasn't technically supposed to be working, but I was here all afternoon anyway, so I covered for a part-time barista, when they asked to leave early.

The whirring from earlier starts up again, and this time, I can't help but smile. I peek at Luke through the legs of the chair I'm placing upside down on a table, so I can bask in my mini-victory.

He's pushing what I found out is a concrete polisher slowly across the floor, with his back to me. I allow myself a few seconds to admire the definition in his broad shoulders and sculpted arms as they move under his black t-shirt. bandana hangs out of the back pocket of his worn jeans again, but it's not enough to obstruct the view of his ass. *Of course, that's thick and muscular, too.*

Having a win, even a small one, on Luke should feel amazing, but the sense of victory doesn't come. He shows up by at least six-thirty every morning, so that means he'll have to work an eleven or twelve-hour day while his friend is in town. The sound was, at worst, mildly irritating from my side of the windows. If I'm honest with myself, it didn't have any impact on my business. Still, he should have notified me about all the noise and other disturbances beforehand, so I'm not out of line.

Devon: Here!
Me: Meet you out front!

Fortunately, Devon's text saves me from further self-reflection. She's waiting for me by the front door when I lock up, her tall, slender frame and immaculate posture looking statuesque under the lights of Station 19's triangular front awning. Her platinum hair is styled in chic loose waves that stop at her shoulders, the only person I know who can workout with their hair down and not come out a sweaty mess.

We walk into the barre class three minutes before it starts. It's packed, but Bea is teaching and she saved us two spots right up front. *Guess I won't be phoning it in like I'd planned.*

Devon leans over to whisper to me halfway through the class, "Sadie's coming to visit." Sadie was Devon's roommate in college and quickly became a friend to both of us. She lives in Portland, but one of the joys of living in a vacation destination is that people are always willing to come visit.

"Yay!" I whisper back to Devon, "When?"

Devon whispers, "Next month."

Bea comes around and passes out those blue mini exercise balls that guarantee I'll be sore tomorrow. Squeezing these makes every exercise ten times harder. Looking over at Devon, I fake a whimper. *Somehow, this class is even harder than I remembered.*

"Try to think about margaritas," Devon whispers.

Times like this remind me I don't know what I would do without her. Sure, I never would have moved here without her. But even if I'd never left home, life without Devon wouldn't feel right. Hell, sometimes I wonder how I made it through the years when she was in college, and I was slinging lattes back home. Me staying home, insisting I'd never need a degree, and I already knew exactly what I wanted for my career was not well received by my parents, my siblings, my teachers, or really anyone other than Devon.

She always believed in me, believed I could prove everyone wrong. She'd stay on the phone with me for hours while she did her homework and I daydreamed out loud about what my coffee shop would someday be like. It's her voice in my head that tells me to keep going when I don't think I can anymore, which has been happening more often since Lucas Pine stole Station 19.

Sometimes Devon is there for me by doing something huge, like designing *Turbine* for free. Other times, like tonight, it's the small things. There's no way I would have made it to this workout without her as a motivator to go, but the quaking in my quads is just what I needed to take my mind off my problems.

"This is the last set, I swear." Bea smiles, counting us down from sixteen.

Thirty minutes later, all thoughts of a tough workout are behind me, and there's a margarita the size of my head in front of me.

"Tell me all about your day," Devon says, before scooping her first chip into the guac.

"You sure?" I've been doing a pretty good job of keeping my shit together, smiling, and acting like nothing's wrong every day while I'm at work. But that means every night when I get home, Devon's been a sounding board for all of my stress. "Haven't you heard me complain enough over the last couple of weeks?"

"You could try not complaining," Devon says drily.

I mock a gasp. "Okay, rude." Over her margarita glass, she arches a dark brow at me that's intentionally in stark contrast to her platinum hair. That's all it takes for me to back down. "Okay, fine. Not rude." She has a way of cutting to the point that I can't help but admire.

"Do you need to elongate your pity party?"

"No, you're right." I knock some of the salt from the rim of my glass into my drink with the tip of my knife while I figure out how to positively frame my day. "It's actually a good thing the place I visited on Desert Canyon was so expensive. If it had been cheaper, I'd have been tempted to go with it, and we deserve something with more heart."

"We?" Devon asks, waving a smooth, ivory hand between us.

"Yeah," I mimic her hand motion, "You and me."

"Wait, have you been looking for places we can share?" Devon shocks me with her question.

"What do you mean?" I ask, my voice as frantic as I suddenly feel.

Devon rolls her lips together in thought before responding, "I'm not sure how I missed that, Al, I'm sorry. You don't need to find me an office." I think through our recent conversations. Many of them have been filled exclusively with my complaining. *Ick.* But I never actually *said* I was trying to find her an office. I figured we would still have a place together, since that was the plan for Station 19, and she must have figured the opposite. After giving me a minute to process, she continues, "It would have been incredible if we could have had a building together." She leans forward, her voice a touch softer than usual. "But you're not moving until August, and I need an office before then."

Shit.

A slightly hysterical laugh bubbles out of me. I have been losing sleep over trying to find a perfect building for Devon and me *totally unnecessarily.* "Guess I should've asked you what you wanted, huh?" I ask, between bouts of laughter.

"Might have helped." She nods, cracking a smile, light dancing in her deep blue eyes.

"It's almost like I was making a bigger deal out of this than I needed to."

"Maybe just a little," Devon says, joining in my laughter.

The relief of knowing that Devon wasn't counting on me to find her an office, so I'm not letting her down, is a minor salve to my stress.

"I can help you look if you like, research places, go with you to check them out," she offers, meaning every word of it and knowing I'll turn her down.

"Totally unnecessary." I take a deep draw of my lime-flavored drink. "I've got this."

I catch the slight shift in her eyes the moment she decides to spare me her *you're not any less of a person if you accept help* speech. "Yes, you do," she says, warmth and confidence in me ringing in her voice.

Chapter 6
Luke

"It's not fair that you're the man of the house, but it's true."-*Grandad Ernie, when nine-year-old Luke complained that none of his friends had to do yard work.*

"That's the last of it." Cam collapses backward onto the cushions of the shop's leather couch.

"Move over." I push his shoulder to make room for me and lean back and relax, the work of setting up the shop finally done.

"This was not a very restful vacation," he groans. Betty leans up against his leg and rubs his hand with her head until he gives in and pets her.

I fold an arm behind my head, looking over at him. "Was it supposed to be a vacation?"

"Yes! I'm in Palm Springs. I should be lying by a pool, or golfing, or enjoying the company of," he covers Betty's ears with his hands and lowers his voice, "a woman with only two legs and no tail."

"Should've thought of that before you came out here in the

middle of my remodel."

"I'll make sure you have a lazy week planned before I come next time," Cam says, and we both laugh because I've never had a lazy week.

"It means a lot that you made the time to come here and help. Thank you."

Cam eyes me warily. "Fine, if we're being emotional, I'm proud of you for making this happen for yourself. You deserve it after everything you've done for your mom and Skye."

Not wanting to talk about my family, I look through the window for Allie. She's leaning across the counter between two barstools, with one toe pointed on the ground and the other kicked behind her into the air, giving me a direct view of the soft, rounded ass she's squeezed into tight jeans that gap at the waist.

"Are you listening to me?" Cam asks.

"No."

He readjusts his position on the couch, so he's blocking my view of Allie. "Skye and your mom are both doing great."

"I wouldn't say Mom is doing great." I shake my head. "She keeps asking when I'm moving back to Ventura. I've only been gone a month."

"You know I love your mom, but you don't have to do everything for her."

"I know that. I don't help Mom because I have to." Cam spent more time at my house than his own when we were kids. He knows better than anyone how hard it was for my mom. My dad dipped before my first birthday, and Skye's dad was only around for a year or two after she was born. Mom had a lot to carry between me and my sister, and money was always tight.

She never asked for my help, but I hated that she was struggling, so I started working as soon as I could to take some pressure off of her. Mom struggles to keep jobs for long. She either gets overwhelmed, bored, frustrated with management, or any number of other things. We got her house paid off years ago, which is the only reason I felt comfortable leaving. Still, I kept everything in the house fixed and her car running. No one's there to do that anymore. "It's not her fault I taught her to rely on me."

Cam sighs and reaches a long arm up to rub at the back of his inked neck, pulling his lips into a tight line.

"If you've got something to say, say it."

"I've said it all before." Cam sighs again. "It's not your job to take care of your mom. It was her job to take care of you."

I sit up straighter on the couch, bringing my eyes level with his. "And she did her best."

Cam sits up straighter, too, matching my posture. "I know she did. I know. I'm saying you don't have to feel guilty for having your own life. She should be happy for you." That last sentence sticks. Her response to my moving away and buying Station 19 doesn't surprise me, but it stings that she's not supportive.

"She'll come around."

Sensing I'm done with the topic, Cam suggests, "Next time I visit my folks, I'll go by and check in on her." The tension falls out of the room as quickly as it came.

"I'm sure she'd love to see you." I lean forward enough to see Allie, who's still pointing her ass in my direction, and scan the coffee shop to make sure I'm the only one enjoying the view.

Cam chuckles at me, leaning into my line of sight again. "Of course, she would. She always liked me better than you. Plus, who wouldn't want to see this?" He holds his hands up, creating a frame around his face.

I narrow my eyes at him. "I know I've seen about enough of it for this week."

"Bullshit. You love seeing this face."

Standing up, I wave at him to do the same. "Come on, let me

buy you one more sandwich before you hit the road."

~

> *Allie: I need another set of keys.*
> *Me: Can it wait until tomorrow?*
> *Allie: If it has to.*
> *Me: Great. I'll get them to you tomorrow.*
> *Me: Have you had any issues with your power going out?*
> *Allie: No.*
> *Allie: Why?*
> *Me: Having some troubles on my side.*
> *Allie: k*

That was the second time she's asked me for a new set of keys in the last month. I get texts like that every couple of days, with more questionably legitimate things to add to my to-do list. If she's trying to get under my skin, it's not working. I like seeing her name light up my phone.

Cam left six or seven hours ago now, and I've just wrapped up my punch list and put the finishing touches on the shop. It still smells like a warehouse, but soon it'll smell like a proper shop. Steel, oil, exhaust, and sweat. Tomorrow, I can get back to the closest thing I have to meditation—getting my hands dirty in a motorcycle engine.

Sitting down in the center of my newly polished concrete floor, I pop the cap off of a bottle of beer. Betty lies down next to me, leaning her boxy head against my hip. "Look what we did, babe," I say as I hold my beer out and motion around the room.

The wallpaper is gone, leaving most walls in their original exposed brick, and the rest is painted a simple white. Dark brown leather couches, a low coffee table, and a vintage, traditional-style red and blue rug take up the spot closest to the glass wall by the front windows. On the opposite wall, the refinished oak desk I repurposed from Mel serves as the front desk.

About halfway back—parallel to Allie's counter closest to the glass wall—is the wide wooden work bench where I'll disassemble, clean, and rebuild engines and parts. We added new black cabinets with butcher block countertops and a utility sink, with easy access from the workbench. On the opposite side are two motorcycle lifts, toolboxes, and loads of open shelving storage. Above that, a massive green neon sign shines *Voyeur Motors*.

The wider back section is still split into three areas like it always was. There's a small bathroom that shares a wall with *Turbine's* bathroom, a large open area with a garage door that opens to the back parking lot, and Betty's office on the opposite side. "First half of our plan is in motion."

I raise my beer to the sky, in a sort of cheers to Grandad. Building the shop is for me, but running the bar will be for him. I'm one step closer to honoring his memory the best way I know how.

Grandad ran a biker bar by the beach in Ventura until the day he died. I spent more time behind that bar than a kid has any business to because he couldn't drop work to raise me. He died when I was fifteen, but before that he helped my mom with everything.

She sold the bar almost immediately after he was gone. I had to know what the new owner did with it, so I rode over on my dirt bike—a Yamaha 125 two-stroke with a duct-taped seat and bald tires, that I'd bought from a friend's dad with money I'd saved up doing odd jobs and mowing lawns.

When I got there, the building was boarded up and marked for demolition. Whoever bought it felt the community would be better served by a strip mall than a classic biker bar. They knocked down his legacy, and I decided then that I'd open a new one to honor him one day.

I knew cheap beer, leather cuts, and lines of Harleys wasn't what I wanted, which is why I knew I had to have Station 19. I'll have a bike shop and a bar that work together, but each will have their own identity. *Voyeur Motors* can be entertainment for people at the bar, but they won't have to be bikers to enjoy a drink there. The windowed wall between is the key that makes it work, and the reason I moved to Palm Springs.

Betty and I sit in relative silence for quite a while, her sleeping with her head against my hip, and me resting my forearms on my bent knees, holding the beer suspended loosely between my fingertips while I reflect on Grandad. The only sounds are the subtle buzz of neon and Allie's Taylor Swift playlist coming through the windows.

Her place is closed, but she hasn't left yet. She was already here when I showed up at six-thirty this morning, making this the third time this week we worked simultaneous twelve-hour days. She's dancing to the music, ponytail bobbing to the beat, lighting up the whole place. She's got to be exhausted, but her mouth is stretched into an electric smile, anyway.

I wait to leave until she heads out, so she's not in the parking lot alone at night. I wave to her, and she lifts her hand in the least enthusiastic version of a wave a person could muster. Chuckling under my breath, I open the passenger door for Betty. I've earned myself a place as the only exception to Allie's kindness.

I shouldn't let myself dwell on it. She won't be the girl next door for long, but I spend the whole drive home trying to figure

out how to get in her good graces without giving her the one
thing I have that she wants—Station 19.

Chapter 7
Allie

Take time today to reflect on this saying,
'Can't see the forest for the trees' -*Allie's
Horoscope, March 12*[th]

"You need a break," Devon says to me over her laptop screen.

I take a quick scan around *Turbine*. "Seems like it's about that time, doesn't it?" Grabbing my latte from behind the counter, I sit down on the barstool next to Devon's.

She holds her hands palm-side up and swivels on her stool. "No, you need a break from *Turbine* in general."

"Yeah, that won't be happening," I laugh.

Devon rolls her lips together, thinking before she responds, "It needs to."

"Why, though?" I copy her earlier motion with my hands palm-side up, gesturing around me at *Turbine*. "I want to be here."

She narrows her eyes at me. "When was the last time you went twenty-four hours without coming through these doors?"

"When was the last time *you* took twenty-four hours off of work, Ms. Friday West Interiors?" Devon is the last person who should be lecturing me on work/life balance. "When was the last time you ignored an email or a text from a client?"

"I can't ignore my clients." Devon's tone is unamused.

"You could let them wait for more than twenty minutes."

"You know I'm trying to hire an assistant designer. After that, I can consider a day off." Devon has been conducting interviews at *Turbine* all week since she hasn't found an office yet, either. "Quit changing the subject."

I try to glare, but it comes out more like a pout. "I like it here."

"You haven't answered my question. When was the last time you spent twenty-four hours away from this place?"

I consider it for a moment and can't remember. *Dammit.* "I don't know, Dev." I wave my hand dismissively.

"You're more than *Turbine*."

"Of course, I am." I snap back, my tone more defensive than she deserves.

She isn't fazed. "Name one thing you're passionate about that isn't this coffee shop."

This shouldn't be hard. I'm a passionate person. I'm passionate about lots of things. *Except none of them are coming to mind at the moment for some reason.* If I wasn't on the spot, I'd have a long list of passions. Devon's face gets a teensy bit smugger with every second that passes. I look down at the drink in my hand, and it comes to me.

"Coffee! Making people drinks. Making people feel safe and at home." Three solid things. *Take that, smug-face Devon.*

"You just explained why you're passionate about *Turbine*." She shakes her head. "Doesn't count."

"Why are you pushing me so hard on this?"

"Because I care about you. You're wearing yourself out trying to solve the problem of what happens when this lease is up. You need a break."

"Let me get this straight. Last month, you told me I needed to quit moping and move on. Now, I'm spending too much time trying to move on?"

Devon takes a measured breath. "There's got to be a middle ground. You did a 180. You're pushing too hard in the other direction."

"No one else is going to solve this for me. I can't ignore the problem and hope it goes away." I push my chin forward and look through the window to Luke's side, and Devon's gaze follows mine. That big, muscular pain in my ass has been over there all morning, working quietly, so I can't even complain that he's fucking my shit up.

"Spending every waking minute here won't make him go away, either."

"I'm not taking a break, Devon." Heat rushes to my cheeks as I get more frustrated with this conversation. "*Turbine* is mine. I *need* it, and I don't know if I'll get to keep it after my lease is up. I've been searching for a new building, and there's nothing. I'm not wasting a moment of the time I have left with this place."

My voice threatens to crack if I keep talking, so I pull out *Allie's I-Can-Do-Anything Notebook* and show her the latest updates. It turns out that finding a building without Devon is not any easier.

367 Red Vista Ln- 9:15am, March 6th
Reasonable price. Vibes are off.
124 Quail Nest Drive- 3pm, March 10th
Not worth the drive.
89 Sunny Day St- 8:45am, March 11th
Too much $$$$$
323 Vista View Way- 10am, March 11th

Guy never showed. Ugh.

Devon looks it over. "This is only proving my point that you need a break."

"Fine, but you have to do it, too."

Her posture is always perfect, but somehow, she straightens further. "I'm serious. I cannot take a break right now." Her voice is firm, not allowing room for argument. "Sadie will be in town next week. It's perfect timing for *you*. You'll get three days off, not just one."

"How did we get to three? And don't think I'm letting you off the hook about this."

"Nope. This is about you, but I can try to be on my phone less," she nods her head to the side, like she's making some great concession.

"If *I* can, then *you* ca—"

Screeech!

A loud metal scraping sound comes from the covered patio out front. Devon and I exchange a *what the fuck* look and then hustle outside together.

Screeeeeeech!

Screeeeeee—

The sound stops as we come out the door. Luke is standing under the large triangular awning, broad tanned hands braced against one of my metal patio tables, obscene forearms flexed. *He's moving my outdoor seating.* Heat spreads from my neck up to my ears. I squeeze my hands onto my hips and knock my head to the left, leveling him with my best *don't fuck with me* glare.

It doesn't land. Luke stands up to his impressive full height. "Hey, sweetheart." He is totally fucking with me. *I've got to work on this glare.*

"Sweetheart?" Devon asks me, raising a brow.

"Devon, I swear to god—"

Luke interrupts me and reaches out to Devon for a handshake. "Devon, lovely to finally meet you." *Lovely? Finally? Who the fuck is this guy?*

"And you are?" Devon shakes his hand, but keeps a scowl on her face, not giving him an inch.

"I'm Luke."

"Mm." She loads the single hummed syllable with unmasked judgment.

"So, what the fuck?" I ask, pointing at my displaced furniture.

Luke has the audacity to act confused. He looks back and forth between Devon, me, and the tables and chairs. He furrows his brow. "You know you have furniture in front of my shop, right?"

"I have furniture on *my* patio."

Luke braces one hand on the table behind him, leaning back against it. "And *also* in front of my shop."

"The whole damn patio is *Turbine's*." I barely resist the urge to stomp my foot.

His brown eyes spark, and his brows raise in a look that oozes arrogance. "Not anymore."

This fucker. "You can't just decide it's not mine anymore." My hands clench into fists at my hips. My ears, cheeks, and neck are all hot with an angry blush, but I'm holding my ground.

"I didn't just *decide*." He crosses his arms low over his hips and drapes one foot casually across the other. "I own this building. It's all my patio."

I'm about to lose my shit on this guy. I know he owns this building. It's all I can think about. That doesn't mean he can take it away from me early, though. "And you have to honor my lease." My voice is barely concealing my anger, volume just this side of yelling. "I am here for four and half more months, so for four and a half more months my tables will stay right where they were."

"Allie, I am honoring your lease. It doesn't include the patio."
The look on his face borders dangerously on pity.

"Of course, it does." I enunciate each syllable.

Luke closes his eyes and presses the heel of his hand into his
forehead. "It's not my fault you never read your lease."

"Don't tell me what I have and haven't read, you jackass."
It's been years since I read it, but I shouldn't have to memorize
it. *Fuck's sake.*

He points at a seam in the sidewalk that follows the same line
as the windowed wall, effectively separating the patio into two.
"You can keep using the patio from this line over." Before I can
respond, he stands up and starts walking away.

"You can't touch my stuff!" I yell after him.

Devon breathes a silent laugh, and only loud enough for me to
hear, she says, "Are you five? 'Don't touch my stuff?'"

"That's not helping," I admonish her, but I'm giggling too.
"I hate that motherfucker." I whisper-yell at her and point in his
direction.

Devon looks across the patio to Luke, and she gives him her
version of a *don't fuck with me stare.* It's way more intimidating
than mine. I wish she was here all the time to do that. "We'll
move the rest," she says, making one swift sweeping movement
with her hand, shooing him inside the building. He nods and
disappears inside the door.

"It's like he's taking everything he can away from me," I
say to Devon, my mind beginning to spiral, heart beating faster.
*This is actually happening. I am losing my building. I've lost my
building. I don't have a new plan. I only have four—*

Devon interrupts my impending breakdown, stepping between
me and the door Luke just disappeared into. "Allie. This is okay.
You are okay."

I nod, taking a deep breath. *Fuck. Maybe I do need a few days off.*

"I'll make this work. It'll be a cozier patio situation now."

"It's fine, Dev. I'll find places for everything."

"Can't let you do that," she scoffs. "*Turbine Café* is featured prominently on my website. I can't have people driving by and thinking I just threw the tables out here haphazardly into corners."

"I wouldn't throw them haphazardly." I say with some level of defeat. We both know I have no design sense.

Devon surveys the area, finding solutions I don't have the skill or current mental capacity for. "I'm helping. Deal with it." She walks around the patio, humming to herself meaningfully while she considers the new layout.

She points to the large window next to Turbine's front door. "We can put three tables together right there, so it's like one long community table." Then she points to an empty space in the corner. "I've always felt that needed a potted plant. Now's the time." We spend thirty minutes rearranging furniture and trying out different ideas before she folds her arms across her slender waist and smiles in approval. "There, it's perfect."

It may even look better than before, but I'm not about to admit it. We have one table pushed right up against the line that Luke pointed out on the sidewalk. I move it three inches across the line, just to fuck with him. "There, now it's really perfect."

Chapter 8
Luke

"It's still not fair that you're the man of the house, but it's still true." -*Grandad Ernie, to ten-year-old Luke, after Skye's dad left.*

The breaker box creaks as I pull the door open. It's common enough for sections of my power to go out during the night that I check the box before I even go inside the shop now. Six on my side are flipped today, and like usual, none on Allie's. *Doesn't she realize how obvious that is?*

Me: Still no issues with your power?
Allie: I'd tell you.
Allie: Keep the noise down today.
Me: Noise?
Allie: Engines and stuff.
Me: I have to test motors.
Allie: Customers are complaining.
Me: No they're not.
Allie: How would you know.

Me: Allie. I know everything.

~

"Looks great over there. Really came together." The man waiting next to me for his coffee says, pointing through the window to my shop. He looks to be in his late sixties, about my height with fair skin and iron gray hair accented with streaks of silver. His thick, black-rimmed glasses and light blue oxford shirt give him a distinguished quality. We haven't met before, but I see him every day reading his paper in a leather chair by the front window.

"Thank you," I nod. "Feels good to have that part finished and finally be working on bikes again. I missed it."

"I'm Brian," he says, offering his hand. "I don't think we've met officially."

"Luke," I say, smiling as I return his firm handshake. He's the first regular to introduce themself to me. Everyone is fiercely loyal to Allie, which I can't blame them for.

"Join us for a bit?" Brian offers warmly once we both have our drinks. He points toward a man with copper-brown skin and full, graying black hair, who I imagine is his husband, sitting by the front window. He wears a navy button-down polo with white stitching and tailored khakis. I recognize him, too. Allie was talking to him the first time I heard her call me a jackass. He shot me some dirty looks in those first couple of weeks, but right now, his expression is neutral.

"Hi, Luke. I'm Hector." He introduces himself as I take the seat across from him and Brian takes the one next to him. He acknowledges the surprised look on my face before I realize I'm making it. "Of course, I know your name. Don't be ridiculous."

"So, Luke, tell us about yourself," Brian says, interlocking his fingers and leaning forward in his seat. The conversation immediately takes on a *meeting the parents* tone I wasn't expecting, and I instinctively run my fingers through my hair like a nervous teenager. This seating area even lends itself to a living room feel. A large, decidedly mid-century modern, green and blue, geometric rug anchors four rust-colored leather chairs arranged around a coffee table that holds Brian's discarded newspaper and a few art and design books.

"Where are you from? What's with the motorcycles? Why Palm Springs?" Hector elaborates. "Allie mentioned you want to turn *Turbine* into a bar." His voice is kind, but his shoulders stiffen.

"That's part of the *why here* answer." I give them a brief explanation of growing up in Ventura and my reasoning for moving to Palm Springs. Neither is surprised I'd move out here for Station 19.

Brian tries to hide a smile by taking a sip of his drink.

"Dammit," Hector says, throwing his arms up in the air. "That's sweet. It's inconvenient for us that you're not actually a jackass."

I can't help but laugh, feeling like I passed a test. "How so?"

Hector leans back in his chair, crossing one ankle over the opposite knee before he responds. "Aside from the fact that we can walk over here from our house to spend all morning drinking coffee," he pauses and takes a deep breath, "We love Allie." Brian nods in agreement as Hector continues. "She's a special girl. She's got such a big heart. It's crushing to see her lose this place." He's pulling no punches, and I appreciate him for it.

The 'living room' grows quiet with the facts laid out. This is Allie's place, as much as I don't want to think of it that way. It's important to more than just her. *Turbine* is the home of a community, and Allie is its cornerstone. No matter how you look at it, my being here is the catalyst for an unwelcome change.

"Listen, we're not trying to make you feel bad," Brian says.

"Well, maybe a little," Hector adds. Brian sends him a scolding glare, but I smile at him. I get it.

"We're worried about our girl," Brian says. "She's been—"

"So, what's the deal with all the motorcycles?" Hector cuts Brian off at a volume much higher than we were using before, clearly changing the subject. I don't have to turn to know Allie is walking up behind me.

"I fix bikes that don't run, so that's most of what'll go on inside the shop," I say, pointing toward it with my shoulder. "I also build bikes on spec and sell them, mostly café racers. Those are the ones out front."

"The ones that made it so necessary for you to take over the patio?" Allie asks from behind me, voice thick with irritation. I have to suppress a grin before I turn around to face her, resting my arm across the back of my chair.

"Hey, sweetheart."

"You're the worst. You know that?" she asks, hands propped on her hips.

"I know you think that, yes."

"If it weren't for Betty, I'd never let you over here." Allie rolls her eyes, then looks around and realizes Betty isn't with me today. "Where is she?"

I point through the windowed wall. "I put a bench on my side under the window for her, so she can watch." Two high schoolers sit at a round white table on the *Turbine* side, right underneath the window, waving at Betty through the glass.

"That is one patient dog," Brian's voice surprises me. I almost forgot he and Hector were sitting with us.

"She really is," Allie says, speaking over my shoulder to Brian. She's standing close enough that the warmth radiating from her heats my neck. "I adore her. I have no idea how this jackass has raised such a lovely creature."

Brian gives her an indulgent smile. "Oh, he's not so bad."

She opens her mouth in protest, but Hector stands up and wraps her in a big hug before she can respond. He whispers something in her ear, and she tries and fails to stifle a laugh.

"Allie," Brian says, "sit with us for a little bit." She eyes the empty seat next to me and hesitates a moment before crossing in front of me to sit down, giving me a tempting view of her lush ass on the way.

"Luke was about the tell us what the fuck a café racer is. Weren't you?" Hector asks, returning to his seat.

"Never tried to define it before." I've got three lined up on the patio by the front door of my shop, but I know if I asked them to come and see for themselves, Allie would stay behind, and I'm enjoying her closeness too much to lose it.

"It's a type of motorcycle, right?" Brian asks.

"Yeah." I nod. "Most café racers start as vintage bikes, and then they're modded to make them simpler, faster, lighter." Hector and Brian both listen intently. Allie is the quietest she's ever been, but I doubt it's due to interest. "Once I'm done with them, they're naked bikes, stripped of their bullshit. Mostly vintage leather and chrome. Nothing that comes out of my shop will have a windscreen, a radio, or a fucking heated cupholder."

"So, you're an artist who likes to get his hands dirty," Brian says, thoughtfully tapping his coffee mug.

"Didn't take you long to figure me out."

"Brian is annoyingly good at reading people," Hector says, smiling over his shoulder at his husband. "It's impossible to hide anything from him."

"That's true," Allie chimes in for the first time, agreeing with Hector.

"I pay attention. That's all," Brian says.

"You are hard to miss," Hector adds, sharing a look with Allie that's too brief for me to decipher.

Sometimes I forget that my view of Allie is a package deal with everyone at *Turbine* having a view of me. Turning my head, I point my chin toward Betty, who's now snoozing on her bench next to the teenagers on the other side of the glass wall. "I guess I set us up as the unofficial entertainment for the day."

Allie's mouth widens into a knowing smile. "Not for long, Pine." She pats my knee, then stands up and walks back to the counter, leaving Brian, Hector, and I to exchange confused looks. *She doesn't want me here, but she can't think that it's enough to make me leave.*

Chapter 9
Allie

You'll burn brighter if you allow others to add sparks to your flame. *-Allie's Horoscope, March 23rd*

Luke's truck isn't here yet. *Good.* I get to play my favorite little game. The man is stoic, steady, and unbothered *all the fucking time.* No matter what I do, there's never a twitch of irritation. But he's asked me a couple of times if I'm having issues with my power, so I think this is getting to him. If I keep at it, he might even call an electrician.

Locking my car, I rush across the parking lot, so I can do this before he shows up. The metal door of the breaker box creaks open, and my smile drops. There's a post-it note stuck carefully above the top line of his breakers, written in a simple, clear hand.

Morning, sweetheart.

~

This is a little precarious, I'll admit. My arms are full of the curtains that finally came in after Devon ordered them for me weeks ago, and I'm standing on one of our white, plastic tulip tables trying to hang them on my new curtain rod. The table is circular with a singular pedestal base, so when I lean my weight too far in any direction, it wobbles.

Not being tall enough to reach, I've resorted to hopping on top of the table and swinging the curtain rings toward the rod. So far, three of them are hooked. The three-day *Turbine* hiatus Devon is forcing on me starts tomorrow, and I need to be at the airport to pick up Sadie in an hour so I'm in a hurry to finish. With a little more oomph than last time, I jump to hook my fourth ring.

"What the fuck are you doing?" Luke's voice sounds from the front door, startling me mid-hop. I miss the rod with the curtain ring and lose my footing, throwing the table completely off balance. Time slows as the polished white surface rocks out from under me, my head careening backward toward the concrete floor and my feet flying up toward the ceiling. *This is not going to be good.*

I squeeze my eyes tightly shut. *If I can't see the crash, it can't hurt me.* The curtains drop from my hands, and I flail for purchase, but find only air. *This is going to hurt.* The crash of the table hitting the concrete floor echoes around me, and I brace for impact.

My body doesn't hit the ground. Instead, it slams into a solid, muscled body. Luke's arms grapple around me, pulling me clear of the fallen table. He keeps me pressed tightly against his chest as he pulls himself upright, adjusting me in his hold until his thick arms cradle me under my knees and shoulders.

Luke's chiseled face is inches from mine, tendrils of wavy

black hair falling loosely across his stern brow. His gaze locks firmly with mine, a wildness in his deep brown eyes. Pressed up against my ribs, his heart beats hard and fast, almost as intensely as my own.

He must have run from the door to catch me in time. I try to crane my neck to gauge the distance, but he pulls me tighter into his warm embrace, surrounding me with the smell of soap and steel. A muscle ticks under the thick stubble of his square jaw.

He releases my gaze, slowly scouring my face and body. "Are you alright?" he asks, voice low and husky.

I blink a few times, but words don't come to me. I nod in agreement. *Get it together, Allie.*

"Did you hit your head?" Luke leans his forehead toward mine in question.

Words still don't come, so I shake my head *no.*

He looks down at where my hip is pressed firmly against his stomach. "Am I hurting you?"

Your abs aren't that hard, Jesus. But apparently, being pressed against his chiseled torso does make it difficult to speak. I shake my head *no,* again.

His heart continues to thunder against my ribs, holding me against him protectively, like there'd be a danger in putting me down. He speaks slowly, deliberately. "You have to be more careful with yourself."

He's scolding me? All at once, I'm thinking straight. My entire body is wrapped up in his arms, and not for the first time. *This is ridiculous.* "Put me down." He narrows his gaze at me, like he's considering if he'll comply. "Put me down. Now." I wiggle against his hold, but just like the last time he held me against my will, I'm unsuccessful in freeing myself. *Why on earth has this happened more than once?*

He smirks—*that fucking smirk*—and walks me a few feet

away from the fallen table, setting me down on a chair and lowering himself in front of me, so his eyes are level with mine. He carefully rests his broad hands just above my knees. *Dammit, why is that so comforting? I do not need to be comforted.* "You're not dizzy, are you?"

"I told you, I didn't hit my head. Why would I be dizzy?"

He glares at me, grumbling, "Reckless," under his breath before standing up. "What the fuck were you doing up there, anyway?"

I stand up too, following him across the room. "What was *I* doing?" *Is this guy serious?* "What were *you* doing? You basically knocked me off the table!"

"If it wasn't for me, you would have fallen off on your own. I caught you. Or have you already forgotten?" he asks as he rights the table he made me knock over.

"I wouldn't have fallen at all if you hadn't snuck up on me."

"Snuck up on you?" Luke holds his arms out at his sides. "The door was open."

"And now, thanks to you, I have to start over," I say, pointing an accusing finger toward the pile of curtains now crumpled on the ground.

"You're trying to hang curtains by jumping up and down on an unsteady table? That's your plan?"

"What else am I supposed to do? It has to get done. I have to do it." Stress and adrenaline have my pulse pounding loudly in my ears. The curtains are the only line of defense I have against Lucas Pine until I find a new building. *But what if I can't find a new building? I'll lose my business—my safe space, my purpose— to this jackass.*

Luke presses a flat hand to his t-shirt clad chest and points through the windows to his shop with the other. When he speaks his voice comes out with an irritating level of calm. "I'm right next door. I can help you."

Squaring my shoulders, I move close enough he has to tilt his head down to look me in the eyes. He may be taller than me, but that doesn't mean I can't take up space. "I don't need your help. I don't *want* your help." The words pour out of me, fast and loud, like the dam holding my self-control has burst. "I don't want you here at all. I don't want you next door. I wish you'd never moved here and taken everything away from me."

His face goes stony, the muscles in his jaw flexing underneath his short-trimmed beard and the wildness in his eyes flattening out into cool indifference. He presses in even further, our foreheads almost touching. "Is that what you think happened, Allie? That I took everything away from you?"

"It *is* what happened. This building was my dream." Heat has flooded from my neck to my ears, and I know I'm flushed red with frustration, unable to hide my feelings from anyone. I fucking *loathe* that my voice cracks on the next word. "Everything was hanging on it." It's not his fault that pursuing his dreams happened to randomly fuck me over. *But if I don't blame him, who do I have to blame?*

Luke stares at me for a long moment before he steps back, leaving me blinking against the bright lights I hadn't realized he was blocking with his height. He heads toward the door without a word. I should feel vindicated, but something in my chest tightens instead. The brief moment of catharsis that came with speaking my mind fades into guilt. *Fuck.*

I'm still staring out the door that Luke disappeared through when a welcome and joyful figure appears. "Allie!" Sadie squeals and rushes toward me from the doorway, rolling a sensible black carry-on suitcase behind her and balancing a canvas bag of groceries stuffed to the brim on her hip. Her long golden hair is styled to perfection in loose curls that are supposed to look effortless, but I'm sure took at least thirty minutes to create.

"Sadie!" Her presence is like a burst of sunshine that breaks the heavy cloud hovering over me after my interaction with Luke. She sets her grocery bag down on a table and pulls me into a tight hug. "You're early, right? I was planning to pick you up in an hour. Did I mess the time up?" My mind races. Did I have it on my calendar wrong? Was she waiting at the airport for me, and I blew her off? *Fuck, how long was I working on these curtains?*

"No, no, no, you're wonderful!" My joyful friend rushes to reassure me, "I got an earlier flight and wanted to surprise you." She holds her hands out by her sides and spins in a circle, sending her sunset-colored floral skirt into a twirl. "Surprise!"

I pull her in for another hug and let her familiar scent of vanilla and orange blossom flood my senses. "I love this surprise. What do you need? Are you hungry? Do you need a drink? We get to start *Turbine* girls' night early now!"

Turbine girls' nights have been a tradition since the night before our grand opening. Devon, Sadie, and I popped a bottle of champagne, or three, in celebration and stayed up laughing and talking in the empty café until the late hours of the night. We all worked my opening day together, hungover, on three hours of sleep. Over the years, we've repeated the event every time Sadie's in town, with a couple of tweaks. Now we include food and make sure no one has to be up early the next day.

"I'm good. Just happy to be here. I'm *so* overdue for a vacation." Sadie walks over to the table and opens the canvas bag of groceries. "I brought the yummiest charcuterie spread." She pulls ingredients out one at a time to show me. "You will not believe this aged cheese I just discovered, and I got this honey the last time I was visiting my family in Idaho. I've been saving it for you to try."

"You're so good to me." At some point, I decided a charcuterie board was my favorite meal, and no one has been more supportive of that than Sadie. "Tonight's cocktail special has Sadie written all over it. I'm making lavender gin sours." Coffee is my job, but there's a special place in my heart for a craft cocktail, too. "Even made lavender syrup from scratch."

"That sounds incredible. I truly…" Sadie's voice trails off as Luke's impressive frame casts a shadow through the glass front door. He props it open and a moment later walks in with a full-sized ladder under his arm. He doesn't say anything or make eye contact with either of us. Sadie gives me a confused look, and I wave a hand to say, "I'll tell you later."

Unfolding the ladder, he sets it right where the problematic table was, perfectly lined up for me to hang the curtains. Sadie and I both blink at him, silently, as he walks past us again and back out the front door without saying a word.

Chapter 10
Luke

"If you quit running around, I'll show you how this works." -*Grandad Ernie, to five-year-old Luke, while he was tightening the chain on his BMW R69*

"Wow, looks incredible in here," Brian says as he walks in the front door of *Voyeur Motors*. He tucks his hands into the front pockets of his neatly pressed chinos and tilts his chin up, taking in the space's exposed brick walls, functional wooden furniture, buzzing neon sign, and the latest addition—a fern in a matte black pot on the front desk that my friends, Kiara and Rick, sent as a congratulations gift.

I thank him, rounding the Triumph I've been working on all morning. "It's good to have you in here."

"Can barely remember what the gift shop looked like." He walks up to the Triumph and leans down to inspect it. "Looks like you're already busy with work, too."

I wipe the grease from my hands with a shop rag. "People were more ready for a motorcycle shop than I anticipated. I've got a queue of work lined up that'll last me all month."

"Glad to hear it. We want you to do well."

He must mean him and Hector, because Allie sure does not wish me well. She was livid with me the other night when she fell off that damn hazard of a table, and I haven't seen her since. The next morning, the curtains were hung, and one of her baristas dropped the ladder back off to me. The curtains have been drawn ever since, leaving me isolated inside *Voyeur Motors*. Brian's visit is a welcome surprise.

He takes a step back, continuing to check out the shop. "We mentioned my dad's motorcycle to you the other day," he pauses briefly, glancing over his shoulder toward *Turbine*, probably deliberating Allie's parting statement from that conversation. It's pretty clear now that she was referring to these fucking curtains. "I was hoping you'd have time to talk about it now."

"I'd love to hear about it." I keep my mouth shut about the salty brunette next door.

"My dad had a motorcycle when I was a kid," Brian starts, adjusting his black-framed glasses where they sit on his nose. "He bought it brand new in 1959." My eyes grow wider at that. "I remember my brother and I would always sit in the front room before dinner so we could hear it coming down the street. It only had one seat, no room for someone to sit behind."

"A lot of the old bikes are like that," I chuckle.

"He used to put me in his lap and take me for rides through the neighborhood." The look in his eyes is wistful as he recalls the long-buried memories, and the story brings up similar memories I have with Grandad. "He probably never went faster than thirty-five or forty, but to a five-year-old boy it felt like flying."

Brian smiles, and his clear blue eyes meet mine, coming back to the present. "After he passed, the bike ended up in my garage. It's been out there for decades. Last time I checked, it didn't run."

He laughs at himself then. "It probably didn't fix itself since then, so I'd imagine it's still not running. Would that be something you could fix?"

"I bet I could. Do you know what kind of bike it is?"

Brian laughs again. "A black BMW. That's all I know."

We make arrangements for me to bring it into the shop on Tuesday, so I can get a better idea what needs to be done.

Brian nods thoughtfully on his way out the door. "Good to see you today, Luke. Don't be a stranger."

As soon as I've been back to work long enough to dirty my hands again, my phone buzzes. Then it buzzes again. And again. I wipe my hands off and pull out my phone to see my mom's number flashing across the screen.

"Luke? Are you there?" Her voice comes through as soon as I answer.

"Hi, Mom." I put my wireless headphones in, so I can work.

"What took you so long to answer?"

"I'm working."

She huffs, unhappy with that answer. "Cameron came by yesterday. He is such a vibrant young man. Handsome too. His hair is green now. Did you know that?"

"No, must be new. Did he help out with your list?"

"Yes, he's so sweet. Not quite as good at fixing things as you are, but he makes a much better margarita." *Sure he does.* I'm the one who spent over a decade bartending, but Cam makes a better margarita. "He mixed us a whole pitcher and told the funniest race stories. You know, I got my hair cut two weeks ago, and he's the first person who noticed."

"He's a charming guy."

"He gets that from me."

"From you?" I ask, torquing down a head bolt.

"Yes. I spent more time raising that boy than his own mother did. Lucas, don't act like you never heard me say nurture is more powerful than nature. You know that."

I hear her screen door slam in the background. It shouldn't be doing that. The slow-close mechanism must need to be replaced. I take a break from the engine rebuild while Mom moves on from Cam stories to filling me in on the life of every girl I went to high school with, including extra details for the ones that still live in Ventura.

"How do you know that Marissa's single?"

"Social media. I'm friends with all of your old girlfriends." *Should've known.* The screen door slams again.

"I just ordered you a new hydraulic door closer for that screen. It should be there by Wednesday," I tell her.

"Thank you, honey, but it won't do me any good. I can't fix the door myself, and you're not here anymore to help me." I check my watch. We made it a whole forty-five minutes before the guilt trip kicked in. Impressive.

"Cam should still be in town. I'll ask him to come by again. Maybe he'll make you more of his *amazing* margaritas."

"That sounds nice, but it's not the same as having you home." Her voice is sweeter than normal, laying it on thick.

"I know, Mom. I'm sorry I can't be there."

"It's okay. I understand you have your *priorities*," she says, the last word dripping with condescension. The temptation to argue with her is heavy, but I know it won't get me anywhere. And part of the guilt she's throwing my way is sticking. She has to be lonely with Skye and me both gone.

"I'll visit you as soon as I can, definitely for your birthday."

"That'll be nice," she sighs. "I just never thought we'd be one of those families that only see each other on birthdays and holidays."

My phone buzzes again, and I'm grateful for the excuse to get out of this conversation.

"Alright, Mom. I have to go."

"Okay, little goat."

"I love you." I convey as much warmth and sincerity as my voice will hold.

"I know. I know. I love you too."

I feel like shit about how sad she sounded, but my life was stalled out in Ventura. I couldn't live fifteen minutes away from her forever. She'll have to come around, eventually.

When I pull out my phone, Allie's name lights up the screen. She hasn't been here for three days. What could she have to complain about?

Allie: Luke.

She starts and stops typing a few times, and then the next texts come through in rapid-fire succession.

Allie: Lucas
Allie: Im sorry im mean..
Allie: I lov you
Allie: you dog
Allie: i love you're dogg

Holy shit. She's drunk texting me. At three o'clock on a Monday.

Chapter 11
Allie

Share your energetic spirit with those
around you, Leo. -*Allie's horoscope, March 25ᵗʰ*

Devon, Sadie, and I show up at our favorite boutique hotel pool
shortly after it opens for a Monday of poolside day-drinking.
We snag a spot with the perfect mix of sun, shade underneath
lemon-colored umbrellas, views of desert mountains, and
proximity to the bar.

"This drink is pure sunshine and happiness," I say, admiring
the yellow tiki concoction in my hand. Devon was right. I
needed a break. This is the third full day I've been off from
Turbine, and my stress level has lowered with each one.

"You told me an hour ago that *I* was like sunshine and
happiness," Sadie says.

"You are! You and this drink are kindred. That's why I love
you both so much."

Sadie settles back into her lounger. "It's only eleven-fifteen;
Isn't it a little early to start drinking?" she asks, eyeing her own
tiki treat warily.

"Absolutely not," I say. "First of all, late morning is a perfectly acceptable drinking time in any social circle that I care to be a part of. Secondly, you're on vacation. And thirdly, you look adorable with that drink in your hand."

Sadie giggles and beams under the brim of a chic Panama style straw hat, striking a pose and taking an indulgent sip of her drink. She *is* the embodiment of happiness and sunshine, wearing the hell out of a yellow high waisted bikini that shows off her slightly curvy frame. I snap a few pictures and show her on my phone. "See? You belong here."

"I do look really good," Sadie says bashfully.

"You want to send one to your man?" I ask.

Sadie nibbles her glossed-pink lower lip. "No, he won't—he doesn't need—no..." She starts her sentence three different times but never lands on an answer.

"Sade, you've been here four days," Devon says, leaning forward in a taupe one piece only she could pull off, "and you haven't said Jared's name once. Are you going to tell us what's happening, or are we all going to pretend he doesn't exist together?" Sadie has been dating Jared since they were in high school, so they were already together by the time we met her when she was in college. There's nothing necessarily wrong with the guy, but Devon and I have always shared the opinion that he's not good enough for Sadie. And Devon is always quick to say as much.

Sadie sighs and takes a deep draw from her drink.

"To be clear, I'm all for pretending he doesn't exist," Devon adds, sending Sadie and I into a fit of giggles.

"No, no. I should talk about it. He just," another sigh and another long sip, "We're not...things aren't," she pauses to consider before landing on, "We're good." We stay quiet, waiting for her to continue. "He takes care of me. I live in his house. He takes me on vacations, and we have all the same friends back home. It's uncomplicated."

"Is that all you want, uncomplicated?" Devon asks.

"Not really." Sadie drags out the word, holding her hands in the air like opposing scales. "I'd like it if he were more interested in the things I am. And he's honestly not a great listener. And the sex is blah. But otherwise, I have it pretty good."

Devon's wearing dark-lensed tortoise-shell designer sunglasses, but I know her eyes narrow into a judgmental glare by the disdain that radiates from her slender frame. It can probably be felt by Jared all the way up in Portland. "Not a great listener? Blah sex? That's not pretty good. That's an idiot who doesn't understand the gift he's been given by being with you," she says, slicing harshly through Sadie's statement.

"Jesus, Dev," I hiss at her.

"No, it's fine. She has a point," Sadie says, resigned. "We've been together for so long, and he loves me. He *does*. He's a part of me, and I can't picture my life without him."

Her heart-breaking confession hangs heavily in the air around us. Sadie fidgets with the edge of her black and white striped towel, clearly uncomfortable.

"Okay, I'm going to say one thing, and then we can move the fuck on," I say.

"Yes, let's please move on," Sadie breathes out, relieved.

"Sade, you are a magical, thoughtful, kind, beautiful person. You deserve everything in the world, and you don't have to stay with anyone who doesn't believe the same." I watch her for a reaction, and she only tugs her lips into a weak smile. "Okay," I clap my hands, closing the subject for now. "If there was ever a time for tequila shots, it's now." I jump up, adjust my cheeky pink gingham bikini around my tits and ass, making sure I've at least got the goods covered, and rush over to the bar.

When I return, Devon is filling Sadie in on the latest updates for *Friday West Interiors*. "I signed a lease for an office. We start moving things over the middle of next month."

We went to check out the building last week. It's in a sweet little office park with a courtyard in the middle, close to a few design showrooms. It's perfect, and it pains me to admit, but it's better than Station 19 would have been for her. No matter how much my world was rocked by losing the building, at least it was the catalyst for Devon finding her right thing.

"I haven't told you this part yet, Al. Bea's going to be my assistant," Devon says with a rare, excited smile broadening her lips. "We finalized everything after her class yesterday."

"What? I am obsessed with that!" My voice comes out loud and boisterous, even more so than usual, the alcohol starting to take effect. "I had no idea she did interior design."

"She'd never mentioned it to me before either, but her portfolio is impressive. She's precisely what I've been looking for."

"Dev, she is so fucking cool." A selfish thought finds its way to my lips. "Wait, is she going to quit teaching barre now?"

Devon tilts her head, giving me a censuring look from behind her sunglasses. "No, she loves that. No need to give it up."

"Ooh, you know what I want to hear about?" Sadie interjects, a little buzzed herself. "I need more details about sexy ladder guy."

"Is she talking about Luke?" Devon asks.

I glare at them both and make a show of tightening my lips to indicate that I'm keeping all words on this subject to myself.

Sadie's straw sputters loudly as she sucks up the last of her tiki drink.

"You know what? I'm getting more drinks," I say, pushing up from my lounger, and settling my pink bottoms back into place on my hips once more.

"I'll catch Sadie up," Devon says as I walk away.

And she does. When I return, she's deep in the details of me having his truck towed on that first day. Then she continues to spell out every interaction with Luke I've told her about. *It takes quite a while.* Evidently, this man has been taking up more space in my life than I realized. Hearing Devon's perspective on the whole situation adds to the twisting feeling that I've been unnecessarily mean to Luke. *Dammit.*

"There. Dev's got you all caught up." I wave a hand when she finishes explaining why we had to move my patio furniture.

Sadie shifts on her lounger to pull one leg up against her chest, turning toward me with an expectant look in her caramel-colored eyes. "No, I want to hear what *you* have to say. Let me live vicariously through your work crush," she pleads.

My jaw drops open. "He is not my work crush. How did you get work crush from," I tick off each offense on my fingertips, "he stole my entire building, stole my patio, stole my damn *dreams*, and is the loudest work neighbor ever?"

Sadie smirks at me under the brim of her hat. "Sounds like you'd better set me straight."

I narrow my eyes at her. "Fine. But I will require at least one more tequila shot and another one of these sunshine magic tiki drinks immediately."

"On it!" she squeals and runs over to the bar.

I turn and glare at Devon. *Why did she have to say all that?*

"You've got to narrow your eyes more if you want to look mad. And you're smiling. Did you know that? Flatten your lips." I try both. "This isn't working. Maybe suck in your cheeks?" I try that too and end up in a comical fish face. We both double over laughing. She coaches me on how to look intimidating while we wait for Sadie to return with the next round of drinks.

"You need to reapply," Devon passes me a tall white spray

can of sunscreen after another failed attempt at glaring.

The spray comes out like a fine foam and disappears into my sun-warmed skin without leaving a greasy sheen. "Are you sure this is sunscreen?" I ask.

"Yes, I got it from my dermatologist." Devon *would* have fancy dermatologist sunscreen.

Sadie returns with the drinks, and I hold the can out to her. "Sadie, you've got the check out this sunscreen sorcery. It doesn't even smell bad!"

Once our SPF is reapplied to Devon's satisfaction, we throw back the round of tequila shots.

"Now, details about sexy motorcycle guy, please," Sadie chimes.

"He *is* sexy, isn't he?" I agree and then gasp, throwing a hand over my mouth when I realize what I've admitted. The second tequila shot has eased my apprehension, and the third tiki drink doesn't hurt either. *Hmm. That's kind of a lot of drinks. How long have we been here? A few hours?* Words flow easily, and pretty soon I'm spilling every detail that's happened between Luke and I. Sadie eats it right up, and Devon smiles knowingly as my stories go on.

They indulge me with my usual complaints. The smug smirk he always wears and the fact that he's impossible to upset. He's a cocky know-it-all. He's always around. Like *always*. He acts like he owns the place. Devon interjects to point out that he does own the place. *Not helpful.* He doesn't know anything about Palm Springs. Sadie points out that I didn't either when I moved here. *Again, not helpful.*

"In the moment, when he threw me over his shoulder because the floor was *unsafe*," I interrupt myself, "which, by the way, I call bullshit. The floor was fine. I fucking had on shoes." *Does that make sense?* "Had fucking shoes on." *That's better. Right?* "My feet were fine! He just wanted an excuse to manhandle me. Anyway, I was livid. But I haven't stopped thinking about that strong, sculpty" *Is that a word?* "Scultpled. *Sculp-ted* body ever since. And then when he was holding me again the other night—"

Devon cuts me off. "Again?"

"What other night?" Sadie asks.

Trying to avoid this exact interaction, I've kept my mouth shut about the whole falling-off-the-table incident. Now, though, I can't remember *why* I didn't want them to know. They're my best friends. *They should know.* I giggle to myself, and then I give them every detail, even how it gave me butterflies when he walked back in with that ladder.

Something clicks, and for the first time in months, I run out of insults and bad shit to say about Lucas Pine. The alcohol releases the tight hold I've been keeping on every kind or soft thought that dared to bubble up about him, *and there have been plenty*, and now I'm thinking them out loud at my friends. *Why was I keeping this in?*

I confess how attracted I was to him the first moment I saw him, that by the time I found out who he was, I'd already pictured him fucking me in three different positions. Sadie chokes on her drink at that little detail. I point out that he changed his order from coffee to Americano after I made him an Americano *once*. He's a good tipper. He holds the door open for everyone. He has a skill for showing up in the parking lot exactly when I'm carrying something heavy and always carries it for me.

The floodgates are open now, and I gush about him and Betty, showing Devon and Sadie all the many, many photos I've snuck of Betty on my phone when Luke wasn't looking. "He's good to his dog, like *sooo* good to her. She adores him."

"Dogs are supposed to be good judges of character," Sadie says, nodding along with me.

"Ezzackly! It's so weird. How can she be the sweetest, best cared-for dog I've *ever* met, and he's a jackass? It doesn't make sense!" The people in the spot next to us look over at me. *Maybe I yelled that last part.*

"Maybe he isn't a jackass," Sadie shrugs.

"Shit," I grumble, "If he's not, that means I am."

"You're not a jackass," Devon says, adjusting the umbrella above us for maximum shade, "but it's time to move on. Hating Luke isn't a great look on you."

"You have a really irritating habit of being right all the time. You know that?" I ask, moving from laying on my back to sitting up on my lounger, pulling my legs into a crisscross. I'm dizzy for a moment as my vision takes a second too long to catch up.

"I do," she says, with a self-satisfied smirk.

She was right about me taking a few days off, too. I needed this. Time outside with my friends, relaxing, laughing, and spilling secrets. Having a good drink. *Or five or six good drinks. Whoops.*

Devon passes me a glass of water. "Drink this, babe." *Where did that come from?* I don't remember her getting up. I down it in a few gulps, and she immediately passes me another.

"Should I apologize for being so harsh?" I ask, and I can hear my words slur. *Shit.*

"Of course," Sadie says.

At the same time, Devon replies, "Absolutely not."

~

I wake up on the couch in our living room, my vision fuzzy and a sharp headache pressing into my skull. My eyes focus on the clock on the wall, and it reads seven-eleven. *Ooh, now I want a Slurpee.* I lost count of how many drinks I had by the pool, but apparently it was enough to warrant a hangover that timed up with the sunset. There's a full glass of water and two Advil on the coffee table that I'm sure Sadie set there for me. She's on the other side of the powder-blue tufted sectional, wearing an oversized cotton t-shirt, and tucked under a cream-colored knit blanket, scrolling on her phone.

Sitting up, I down half the glass of water in one go, followed by both Advil. I tap the rim of the glass. "Thank you for this."

"Of course." She smiles broadly.

Part of our conversation from this morning comes back to me, and I realize this is likely my last chance to chat with her before she leaves. "Sade?" I ask. "Are you really okay about Jared?"

She plops her phone down in her lap and rubs her hands together nervously. "Yeah, he's a good guy. Sometimes I just need a break. Being here with you and Devon has been so nice. It's like an escape."

An escape from your boyfriend? I resist the urge to push her further about that. "We'll have an office for Devon soon enough, so our third bedroom will be empty if you ever want it," I offer.

"Yeah, right," Sadie laughs without mirth, "I could never."

"Could never what?" Devon asks, coming down the hallway. She's fresh from a shower, smelling like clean laundry and peppermint soap. Her face glows from doing the kind of nighttime skincare routine that I've never mastered. *Is she not hungover? How the fuck?*

"I was telling Sadie she should move in with us."

"Yes, you should. Dump that loser boyfriend, and get yourself out to the desert," Devon agrees, cutting through the bullshit, yet again.

My phone buzzes, and I'm confused by the name on the screen.

Luke: Feeling okay?

I'm Day Drunk Hangover Barbie, to use one of Bea's phrases, but I'm not about to tell him that. *Why is he texting me?*

My eyes focus on the rest of our text conversation, which should be details about dripping faucets and burnt-out lightbulbs. But it's not.

Me: Luke.
Me: Lucas
Me: Im sorry im mean...
Me: I lov you
Me: you dog
Me: i love you're dogg

And then an hour later

Me: dont hate me plss

My heart plummets to my stomach. The sounds of Devon and Sadie's voices fade to nothing. *Holy fuck.* I look on in horror. I drunk-texted him from the pool today. *And now he's checking on me.* I am beyond mortified.

"Oh, my fuck." My words come out in a breath.

Devon's face snaps to mine. "What happened?"

"I drunk texted Luke."

"Noooo." Sadie drags the single-syllable word out into a long gasp.

"Oh, yes." I hand my phone over to Sadie so she and Devon

can read through the texts.

"Allie." Sadie's voice is a shocked whisper. "You told him you love him."

I bury my hands in my face. The leftover smell of the rum on my breath fills my nose as I mumble through my fingers, "I know."

"And you used the wrong form of your." Devon adds, and I roll my eyes. She's *such* a Virgo.

"It's a good thing I have to move *Turbine* because I can never face that man again," I groan.

"What are you going to say to him now?" Sadie asks, handing my phone back.

Devon answers for me, "Absolutely nothing. She is going to walk into work tomorrow, tits up, chin held high, and act like nothing ever happened." She turns to face me, holding both of my hands in hers. "You are a queen who doesn't drunk-text your irritating work neighbor, no matter how hot he is. It never happened."

I like that plan. I look back at my phone and review the short conversation again, wincing at every word. *Yeah, Devon's plan is my only option.* There's absolutely nothing I can say to make this better.

Chapter 12
Luke

"If you keep pointing the flashlight at everything but the lug nuts, we'll never get this spare on."-*Grandad Ernie, teaching seven-year-old Luke how to change a tire on the shoulder of the PCH.*

By the time I finish working on my last bike of the day, the building is quiet. The curtains are still drawn at *Turbine*, so I'm not sure when the last people left, but the light stopped coming in at the edges hours ago. I spend a few minutes scrubbing my hands with pumice soap to get the day's grease off before I grab my helmet and lock up for the night.

The parking lot out back is empty except for my Honda CB and Allie's silver Toyota Corolla. *What's her car doing here so late?* She wasn't at work today and hasn't been since she essentially told me to fuck off after I caught her when she fell off that table last week. Those adorable drunk texts yesterday are all I've heard from her since.

Her headlights come on, illuminating the cinderblock wall on

Allie's side of the parking lot, but instead of driving away, she gets out and walks toward the hood. The lights and shadows of the parking lot display her silhouette, soft shoulders narrow to her waist, then flare into thick hips and thicker thighs. *Goddamn.*

She reaches to lift the hood of her car, and my feet move immediately. I'm not leaving her alone in a parking lot with a car that's not working.

"Oh!" She makes a startled little scream and presses her hand to her chest. "You scared me."

"Didn't mean to." Closer now, I can take in the full sight of her. Hair damp around her forehead. Little beads of sweat sitting on her collarbones above the neckline of her shirt. A cropped white shirt stops a few inches above the waistband of her tight black leggings. She's coming from a workout. *Shit, that's sexy.* Seeing her slightly disheveled and sweaty sends a shock of awareness through me.

She looks up at me, wide eyed, with a look on her face I can't decipher. After a few moments of silence she speaks, her voice coming out weak. "My car is being mean."

"Mean?" I step closer, holding up a flashlight over her shoulder at the engine bay, and catch the faint scent of her sweat. It makes me want to smell every inch of her.

"Oh!" she yelps in surprise again, her back brushing against my chest when she turns to look up at me. "Where did that flashlight come from?"

I hold open my hand to show her the light is on my key ring.

"Oh," she replies, voice quieter than usual. "That's handy."

I nod in agreement. "What's the problem?"

"Won't start." She shifts her weight from one foot to the other, running her fingers through the tips of her hair. *Is she nervous about her car?*

"Is it turning over?" I ask.

She looks at the engine bay, confused, then back to me, "I don't think so?"

"Let me have your keys," I say, holding my hand out.

A flash of defiant irritation crosses the round features of her face, but then she motions towards the cab. "Still in it."

I hand my motorcycle helmet to her and push back the driver's seat to make room for my legs.

"What are you doing?" she asks, looking between me and the helmet in her arms, lips pursing in confusion.

"Figuring out what's wrong." I press my foot to the brake and turn the key over in the ignition. "It's most likely your starter."

"How do you know?" she asks, and I'm glad to hear some of her usual fire return to her voice.

"You realize I'm a mechanic, right, sweetheart?"

She moves to put her hands on her hips but ends up propping my helmet on her curvy waist instead. "Don't you work on motorcycles?"

"An engine's an engine. I'll show you." I wave at her to come closer, which she ignores, and turn the key in the ignition again. "You hear that clicking?" I ask, and she nods. "That means it's not turning over. I have to get something out of my shop, so I can confirm. Come with me?"

She tilts her head to the side, making her precious attempt at a glare. "Why?"

"So you're not alone in a dark parking lot."

Surprisingly, she follows without argument. We get a screwdriver and a second helmet from my shop, which she eyes warily but doesn't say anything about when we set them on the asphalt by my bike.

I hand the flashlight to Allie when we reach her car's open hood. "Will you point it right here?" I ask, tapping the starter with the screwdriver. She holds it up and presses in closer to me in order to see what I'm doing. *Closer than necessary.* The thought settles nicely into my mind. "If you're ever doing this by yourself, make sure you use something with a plastic or rubber handle like this one. Otherwise, it's a good way to get electrocuted."

She looks up at me with intent teal-green eyes, bringing our faces only inches apart and swinging the flashlight off its target. I hold her gaze, reaching across her to wrap my palm around her delicate hand, and direct the flashlight back to the starter. "Keep that there." Her cheeks flush pinker. Memories of Grandad scolding me for not holding the flashlight correctly remind me to soften my tone, adding, "Please."

She blinks a few times before she turns away and holds the flashlight steady. I use the rod of the screwdriver to connect the positive and negative posts on the starter. The same clicks sound, as I thought they would.

"Is that good or bad?" she asks.

"Pretty good. Means it's not your ignition, which would be a pain in the ass to fix. Starters are a lot easier." I make sure her hands are clear and shut the hood. "The part's not hard to get. I can take care of it in the morning."

"What?" She sounds bewildered and steps back, looking up at me. "No, you don't have to fix this. I'll get it figured out."

"I don't have to, but I'm going to."

"It's fine. I can handle it." She looks around, like a different solution is going to materialize in one of the empty parking spaces.

"Hiring a mechanic is handling it, Allie." I don't have any intention of accepting her money, but she doesn't need to know that right now.

She purses her lips and props her hands on her hips in a familiar stance, the look on her face flashing from irritation, to concentration, to deep thought, and back to irritation before taking a deep, exaggerated breath. "Okay, thank you."

"Come on. I'll give you a ride home." I take a step toward my bike, but she doesn't follow.

"Where's your truck?"

"At home. I dropped Betty off a few hours ago and came back on my motorcycle."

She plants her feet firmly on the ground, hands going to her hips. The strong stance makes me grin. "There's no way I'm getting on that thing."

"Why not?"

Her mouth drops open, like the answer should be obvious. "Because motorcycles are dangerous."

"You have nothing to worry about. I'll keep you safe."

"Safe? *Safe*?" She juts her chin forward, voice incredulous. "Have you ever had, like, even one conversation with an ER nurse? That is a sexy death machine."

"Sexy death machine? I like that."

"You are impossible." She throws her hands up, but the act is more teasing than frustrated. "It wasn't meant as a compliment."

"You don't have to ride the bike if you don't want to. I'll go home and get my truck, but you have to promise to wait for me inside."

She steps closer to me. "You can't go home for your truck. That's ridiculous."

"Allie, you're afraid to ride the motorcycle. I'm not going to force you onto it. I'll be back in fifteen minutes."

That does it. "I am not afraid," she says, indignantly enunciating each syllable.

"You're not?"

She crosses her arms over her stomach, pushing her rounded breasts up. *Fuck.* "No, I am absolutely not afraid."

"In that case, let's go." I hold a helmet out to her.

She shifts back and forth on her feet, staring at the helmet ike it may bite her. Her emotions have ranged from nervous, to rritated, to curious, to irritated, and back to nervous in the last ten ninutes. Her raw expression is one of my favorite things about ier.

"Have you ever been on a motorcycle?" I ask, arm still extended with the helmet.

"No," she says quietly.

"You'll probably love it. There's a reason people ride them."

She waits a few seconds, and then slowly unfolds her arms, curiosity winning out, and takes the helmet from me.

Chapter 13
Allie

It's in your nature to make the most out
of new situations. Get outside and try
something different today. *-Allie's horoscope,
March 26th*

Dammit. Of course, he's here when my car breaks down and I
need help. I should have gotten it fixed last month when I first
noticed it having trouble.

Devon's advice of *tits up, pretend nothing happened*
regarding drunk-texting your work rival is harder than it sounds.
I may have even taken an extra day off of work in order to
postpone facing him. *Why isn't he saying anything?* It has to be
fresh in his mind. It was yesterday.

And he's being nice. And helpful. And protective, *which I
don't hate for some reason.* And standing close to me, smelling
like steel and something soapy and citrusy. Between all of
that and trying to shut off the *lov you, you dog, i love you're
dogg* cringe-loop in my brain, I'm too distracted to come up
with a solid reason why I shouldn't be getting on the back of a

motorcycle.

"I'll take it easy," Luke says. "You can trust me." I *have* to trust him, whether I like it or not. I committed to this, so there's no way I'm backing out.

"This is yours," he says, tapping the padded seat in the back of the bike. Then he reaches over and pulls down two pegs towards the back of it. "These are for your feet."

The pegs are a couple of feet off the ground, which makes me uneasy. "They're way up there."

He looks at them, like he's never considered their height before, then looks back at me. "Won't matter. You'll be holding on to me, anyway." *Oh fuck.* He's right. I'm going to need to press my entire body against his for this to work, which both horrifies and excites me. I'm suddenly very aware of how sweaty I am from my workout. *Why didn't I think of this earlier?*

"Ready?" he asks, exuding warmth and kindness. Cocky smirk nowhere in sight.

"Sure," I say, infusing my voice with all the confidence I don't feel.

He nods toward the helmet in my hands. "Safety first."

I pull my hair down out of its ponytail and fluff the roots. Not that it matters, because the helmet's soft fabric padding smooshes snugly against my head. Luke lifts the visor of my helmet up, then reaches under my chin and tightens the strap. It's a warm night, but his hands are warmer when they graze against my neck. "Is that snug enough? It should be good and tight," he asks, his voice slightly muffled by the helmet.

"Yes, I'm tight," I say, grateful for the helmet hiding my blush when I realize what I've said. "I mean, it's good and tight." *Shit. That's not much better.* "I'm ready for you." *Jesus Christ.* Adding this exchange to the cringe-loop immediately. I look up at Luke right as a cocky smirk takes over his mouth.

He grasps the bottom of my helmet and tries to wiggle it, making sure it won't budge. "You're all set," he says and then drops a playful tap onto the top of my helmet. *Did this man just bonk me?* He slides his leather jacket off, revealing a black t-shirt and those fucking ridiculously muscular forearms, then holds it out for me.

"No, no. I am very wet." His usually stern brows raise into a surprised arch. *Oh. My. Fuck.* Can I say anything that isn't an innuendo right now? Everything was so much easier when I was focused on hating him. "Sweaty. I am very sweaty."

He shakes the jacket, indicating I should slide my arm in. "Don't care."

"I'm not getting my sweat all over the inside of your jacket."

"You were worried about safety, right?" he asks, being so fucking patient with me. I nod. "You're safer with the jacket than you are with bare arms." He steps close to me and brushes his unoccupied hand against my ribs where my cropped tank meets the skin on my back, sending a chill up my spine and a drop in my stomach. I remember my sports bra is soaked underneath, and I cringe. The look on his face suggests he's not grossed out by it at all, though. He tugs on the hem of my shirt. "Plus, as soon as we get going, this little tank top will fly right up your back."

Then he walks around behind me and eases me into his jacket before I manage to respond. It's warm from his body heat, the structured sleeves hang all the way past my fingertips and then some. Even from inside my helmet, it smells like leather and *him.*

"Now you look like you're ready for me to take you for a ride." *Did he have to phrase it like that?* He must be fucking with me. Luke puts his helmet on and tightens the chin strap before he settles smoothly onto the motorcycle. He looks over at me. "Well?"

With my bravest face on, I set my left foot on the peg. *Now what?* I look at Luke and try to figure out a way to do this without grabbing him all over.

"You have to touch me if this is going to work." Luke reaches over and puts my left hand on his stomach, flexing his abs underneath my touch. *Show off.* I take one deep breath and then place my right hand on his shoulder and hold on to him as I swing myself onto the bike. My body naturally slides flush against his, and my hands settle on his hips.

"A couple more things before we go." He turns in his seat, speaking to me over his shoulder. "Where do you live?" I laugh as I realize a phone GPS is not going to suffice in this situation. After I give him brief verbal directions, he says, "I've got it, but you can point in front of me to show me where to go if you need to. Tap my right shoulder to turn right, my left to turn left."

"Okay."

"When I told you to hold on, I wasn't kidding." Luke takes my hands off of his hips and pulls them together against his stomach, causing my chest to press tighter against his back. "It's safer for both of us if you stay connected to me. Follow my lead, like a dance. If I lean into a turn, you need to lean into it, too. Do you understand?" he asks.

"Yes. You lean. I lean. Got it."

"For some people, the first time the bike dips into a turn, it scares them, and they jerk up. You can't do that. It's dangerous. Trust me. Trust the bike. I won't drop you on a turn, okay?" His voice is serious, and I've rarely experienced this stern version of him before, but it's working. I do feel safe.

"Okay." I nod, and my helmet knocks into his.

Luke smiles, and his abs flex under my fingertips again as he laughs. "You're going to love this, sweetheart." His usual teasing tone returns. He flashes me his cocky half smile one more time before he slides my visor down. Luke fires up the engine, and the entire bike vibrates underneath me.

All the nervousness fluttering around inside me shifts into excitement the moment Luke pulls forward. He doesn't leave the parking lot immediately. Instead, he snakes around the spaces, turning left, then right, then left again, teaching me how to lean with him. *He was right.* It feels like the bike is going way lower than it should, but I follow his instructions even when my instinct is to pull up.

When he accelerates onto the street, the evening desert air blows against us, his body blocking the brunt of it. *Are his arms cold?* He shouldn't have given me his jacket.

Luke reaches back and squeezes my knee as we pull up to a stoplight. "You're doing so good, sweetheart," he says, a thrill ringing through my body at his touch.

The light turns green, and the bike gets up to speed immediately. The wind blows against us harder, feeling like we're going eighty-five miles per hour. I look over his shoulder at the speedometer, and it reads only forty. I tap his right shoulder to remind him to turn. The speed limit on this road is higher, and again, we get up to speed in an instant. I can't help but giggle as we ride down the road. *Shit. He was right. I fucking love this.*

The motorcycle continues to rumble underneath us, and holy hell, between that and the brawny man wrapped in my arms, I am turned the fuck on. *How does no one ever talk about how very stimulating riding a motorcycle is?*

Luke reaches back and squeezes my leg just above my knee again, offering reassurance I no longer need, but the touch still sends butterflies into my stomach. I've finally given myself permission to stop hating him, and without that lens, I'm afraid I'm falling quickly in the opposite direction.

Standing in that parking lot was the most I'd ever heard him speak. He's usually clipped sentences, smirks, and what I assumed was quiet judgment. *But is he just observant?* He oozes confidence and self-assuredness. I try to ignore the very real possibility that he barely talks to me most of the time because it's been my habit to shut him down.

Luke turns into my neighborhood, and when he pulls up in front of my house, I'm disappointed the ride is over so quickly. He turns toward me and slides up his visor before doing the same to mine. His cocky smirk is gone, replaced with a broad, full-mouthed smile that makes him look like a kid on Christmas morning. "I was right," he says.

"About what?"

"You loved it."

My smile is giving me away, but I still try to pull it down. "Maybe."

"Bullshit. I could feel you giggling."

"I didn't hate it." That's the only admission I'll give.

"You loved it. It's a good thing, too." He tugs at my chinstrap. "It'd be a damn shame for you to look so cute in that helmet if you weren't going to wear it again."

"What makes you think I'll be wearing it again?"

"We parked a while ago, and you're still on the bike. Either you like riding it, or you like holding onto me."

Releasing my hold on him, I scramble off as quickly as possible, pressing myself fully against him once more.

He laughs, getting off the motorcycle effortlessly and taking off his helmet to set it on the seat. With one shake of his head side to side, his hair falls back into its perfectly imperfect style, dark tendrils draping across his forehead.

I pull up on my helmet, forgetting it's still strapped on, and end up yanking hard on my chin. Luke laughs, saying something under his breath that sounds suspiciously like, "Adorable," and reaches under to loosen the buckle before sliding it off my head.

My hair must look completely ridiculous between the sweat, the helmet, and the wind. I rush to smooth and tousle it into shape. *How does his hair look so good immediately?*

I thank him for the ride, and he follows when I move toward my front door. "You're really on that gentleman shit tonight, aren't you?"

He shrugs as he tucks his hands into his front pockets and chuckles. "What time should I be here in the morning?"

"For what?"

"To give you a ride to work."

My eyes flash to the motorcycle behind him, bringing a blush to my cheeks that I try to hide by messing with my hair. "No, you don't need to do that," my words rush out. "You've done enough. Thank you. But Devon has a barre class across the street in the morning, so I'll catch a ride with her."

"Alright, sweetheart. You know how to reach me if you change your mind." He dips his chin at me in a movement that echoes a cowboy in an old western, tipping his hat to a lady, then walks down the driveway. I close the front door and collapse back against it, listening to the sound of his motorcycle disappearing. *What just happened?*

～

"I would've come to pick you up," Devon says, as she pulls out of our driveway onto the street the next morning. "I wasn't even asleep yet."

"I know, but he was just *there* being so helpful and—insistent. And *muscular* and—I don't know. I couldn't think straight."

"Mmhmm." She smiles, infusing the two hummed syllables with pages of unspoken observations.

Pulling my purse into my lap, I dig around for my red lip liner, lipstick, and cherry gloss. "You can say it. Go ahead."

"Do I need to?" she asks, flipping on her turn signal.

"No. You don't. I'm fucked. I know I'm fucked. And he's going to fix my car, even though I really don't want him to. So I'm going to *owe* him." I find the gloss in the little zipper pocket and tuck it into my palm.

"You won't owe him anything but money, which you have," she says, firmly.

"I know, but it's a huge favor anyway, which sucks." I hold the lipstick next to the gloss as I continue searching.

"It's okay to ask for help," Devon says, insistently, for the probably the millionth time in our friendship.

"I know," I drag out the word in a way that I'm sure makes me sound like a petulant child. "Ah!" I exclaim when I locate the lip liner. I flip down the passenger-side visor and apply a bright red lip. "I'm going to make him teach me," I say, admiring my cherry-scented crimson smile. "That way, I'll never have to ask anyone to help me with a starter on my car ever again."

"And the lipstick is for…?" Devon asks, glancing over at me when she stops for a stop sign.

"It's part of my *I'm a pin-up girl fixing a car* look, duh," I say waving my hands over my denim romper, fitted navy t-shirt, and white low-top Converse. I don't dare pull out the red bandana for her to judge me.

"Oh yeah, very necessary for fixing a car," Devon smirks.

Chapter 14
Luke

"As soon as you get it running, I'll teach you how to drive it." -*Grandad Ernie, to twelve-year-old Luke, after handing him the keys to a rusted-out Oldsmobile*

"Morning, Luke! Morning, Betty!" Allie calls from behind the counter when Betty and I walk into *Turbine*. Usually it's only Betty she greets. *Interesting.* She slides an Americano across the counter to me. This is the first time she's had my drink ready before I ordered. *Very interesting.*

She stops me when I reach for my wallet to pay. "Nope, free coffee. You're fixing my car."

I drop cash in the tip jar instead. "Can I get your keys?"

"You're fixing it right now?"

"Yeah, I picked up the parts on the way here. Want to get it done before it's too hot out."

"Oh, sure," Allie says, cheerily, before leading me back to her office, giving me a view of short denim overalls that barely cover her ass cheeks. I've been watching them since Allie pulled the curtains back open this morning, mercifully restoring my view into her life.

Sitting down at her desk, she pulls her purse into her lap and digs around for her keys. Her hands pause, and she speaks into her bag, instead of looking up at me. "Would it be alright if I helped you today? I'll probably slow you down. And I know it's actually extra work to have someone help who doesn't know what they're doing, but I'd—"

I cut her off, "Of course, I'll teach you."

She smiles, cheeks blushing, as she thanks me.

Grandad taught me about fixing motorcycles and cars as soon as I could grasp a wrench. I complained once when my little sister said she wanted to help too, thinking it would take too long, and he told me he was teaching Skye no matter what, because *'only assholes hoard knowledge.'*

After locating her keys and holding them out to me, Allie pulls out a red bandana, rolls it into a two-inch strip, and ties it up into her chestnut brown hair, using a mirror on her desk to get it adjusted correctly.

"I figured I should try to *Rosie the Riveter* it up today. I wish I had those blue coverall things, too. This was the best I could do on short notice." She waves her hands in front of her overalls, and the tight, low-cut shirt she has on underneath. She even has on bright red lipstick, which is something I've never seen on her before. *Fuck, she looks good.*

Allie has a simple wardrobe like jeans, t-shirts, and cotton dresses, but the way she wears them makes her stand out. She uses clothes to show off her body instead of using her body to show off clothes. "It's working."

Allie's different today. She's as strong and gorgeous as always, but instead of being bristly and argumentative, she's being sweet and considerate. I'm finally getting the version of her she gives everyone else.

"Lie down on the creeper and roll under there."

"I'm sorry?" Allie puts her hands on her hips, scoffing a laugh. "Lie down on the what?"

"It's called a creeper." I point at the flat, four-wheeled dolly by her feet.

"The fuck it is."

"Why would I make that up? Lie down and roll under there."

Eyeing me skeptically, she lies down carefully and glides underneath the car. My biceps rubs against her, from hip to shoulder, as I roll into the tight space next to her. We got started early, but the desert sun is closing in on us fast.

Allie rolls her head to face me, bringing her nose within inches of mine and the scent of coconut, lemon, and cherry with her, cutting the drab smell of asphalt and road dirt.

She listens intently as I talk her through the steps of removing the old starter. Nodding emphatically to show her understanding when I finish, she knocks her forehead solidly into the underside of her car and immediately bursts into laughter. "Ow! Fuck!" She presses her hand to her forehead. "I bet you've never done that."

"It's more common than you think." I ease her hand off her forehead. "Let me see. Close your eyes so I can check with the flashlight." I roll my chest against her side, careful to keep my weight off of her. With her eyes closed, the light lets me view every detail of her face close up. Her defined brows, a few shades darker than her hair, are arched and serene at the same time. Dark, thick eyelashes cast long shadows over her round, freckled cheeks.

Plush, pouty, reddened lips part, asking me, "Can I open them now?"

Shit. I'm supposed to be checking her head. "Almost." Carefully smoothing my thumb across her hairline, I find she has a bump forming on her forehead already. *I'm an asshole.* I should have warned her how tight it is under here. I should never have let her get hurt. I should have had ice on this already instead of getting lost in her eyelashes. I swing the flashlight off her face. "Alright, sweetheart. It's not bleeding, but you've got a decent-sized bump already."

She opens her eyes and lifts her hand back up to touch her forehead, wincing.

"Are you dizzy?"

"Nope," she shakes her head side to side to emphasize her point.

"Vision blurred?"

"Also nope."

"That's good. Now we need to get you some ice."

"No, no. Don't worry about me. I can ice it after we're done. I want to learn how to do this."

No sense of self-preservation in this one. "You can learn how to do this after we get ice on that." I roll out from under the car, but she doesn't follow. "Come on, Allie." I say, tapping her foot where it sticks out under the hood.

"I'm fine!"

Stepping around, so I'm standing between her legs where they're extended out from under the car, I wrap my hands around her ankles. "You can do it after your head is taken care of." Sliding my hands over her calves, I pull her forward until she's no longer underneath the car, and my hands are hooked behind her knees, holding her legs on either side of mine.

She squeals, and her words come out in between delicious

bursts of laughter. "Lucas Pine! Put me down!"

Fuck, she looks good like this. It takes control I didn't realize I had to give up the view and lower her feet to the ground. "Can you sit up?"

She accepts my offered hand but scoffs, swinging herself upright. "Yes, I can sit up."

"Wait here for me." I head into *Turbine*, and by the time I return with a bag of ice, she's back under the damn car. Rolling in next to her again, I say, "You were supposed to wait," as I plunk the bag of ice on her forehead.

"Shit, that is cold!" she protests, but leaves the ice in place while she continues to work on removing the starter.

She sings along to music that plays from her phone, tucked into the front pocket of her overalls. I don't recognize the artist, but it's something poppy with female vocals, and she knows every word.

Enjoying the show, I don't intervene unless she asks for help. She remembers my explanations from earlier and tries things out a couple of different ways, getting the old starter off without any physical help from me.

Beaming, she holds the starter out to me. "We did it!"

Turning it over in my hand, I say, "You did it."

Her smile grows wider. "Little fingers. Makes it easier," she says, wiggling them for emphasis.

"You were serious about wanting to be able to do this on your own, weren't you?"

"Oh very." She nods again, the ice pack sliding from her forehead into her eyes, stopping her movement just in time to avoid hitting her head again. "This is very inconvenient," she says between giggles.

Removing the plastic bag of ice from her nose, I find that it's melted, anyway. "We'll get you a new one when we're done."

"I think it's almost ready," she says as she immediately goes back to work.

Reaching one arm across her body to brace on the dolly she's lying on, I lean in to confirm her progress, reveling in the feel of her body pressed against mine. "You almost have it, should only be a few more minutes. You're picking this up really quickly."

"Mm, thanks," she mumbles, focusing back on her task. Once it's finished, she helps me remove the jack stands and pack up my tools. The morning heat has grown intense, and we're both relieved to move into the cool air of my shop.

"How much do I owe you?" she asks over her shoulder, as she washes the grime from her hands in the shop sink. Smudges of grease and engine dust remain on her cheek, collarbone, the front of her overalls, and her white tennis shoes, making her the picture of adorable disarray.

"Nothing. You did all the work."

"Stop it. You bought the parts, and you spent your morning teaching me." Wild pieces of her hair curl out behind her bandana as she shakes her head.

"And you gave me a free drink. We're square."

"We are absolutely not square." Allie's posture straightens, and if she weren't vigorously scrubbing her hands, I'm sure she'd have them planted on her hips. "I'm going to pay you."

Taking money from her isn't right. Taking *anything* from her isn't right. But if I don't let her pay me, it'll insult her independence. "You can pay me for the part."

She turns to face me, drying her hands on a blue garage towel. "I'm paying for everything, including your time." Her voice is stern.

"No." I have to draw the line on that point. "I didn't do any work."

"You are impossible, Lucas Pine." Allie huffs. "How much for the starter, and how much for your time?" I give her a dollar amount that's a quarter of what I paid for the starter and half my hourly rate. I hate charging her, but I'll find a way to discount her rent or something to make up for it. Luckily, she doesn't know the price of car parts, and pays me without protest and goes back to work on her side.

For the rest of the day, her smile is even more electric than usual, red lips adding to the effect. And a couple of times, she's already looking back at me when I find her through the window. I try not to count the days that I have left of this and enjoy her presence while I can. I'll have to let her go in a few months, because the only way to keep her would be scrapping the idea of Grandad's bar, which I can't do.

Chapter 15
Allie

No one is better suited to handle
today's challenges than you are. Your
natural creativity and resilience will have
opportunities to shine. *-Allie's horoscope,
April 4th*

"This neighborhood has a wave of darling little restaurants popping up," Hector says as I pull into the parking lot of the building we're touring. It was a smoothie place for a few years but has been vacant for five or six months now. It's in a funky foodie location about twenty minutes from Station 19.

The two major downsides are that it's only available for rent, and a lot of locals who walk to *Turbine*, including Hector and Brian, wouldn't be able to come as often. So far, I haven't considered something so far away, but it's time to broaden my search.

I nod excitedly. "Devon and I tried that Indian place on the corner last week, and I haven't stopped daydreaming about the samosas since."

Taking a few solid days off of work has renewed my perspective on my situation with *Turbine* and my search for a new location. I was gone long enough to miss the café, but I didn't miss the building. I missed gossiping with Hector, hearing stories about Marisol's kids, and seeing Daisy's latest drawings. None of these people will go away completely when we move, so the heart of what matters will still be there.

Ideally, I want to find a place that has character, a unique aesthetic—maybe some vintage appeal—but that's also in the same part of the city we're in now, doesn't cost too much, and is available for sale. *So—Station 19.* I've rejected every place that hasn't met those criteria, but I'm slowly accepting that I don't have to find the *ideal* solution. If I find *a* solution that works well enough, the people will make up the difference.

The property manager has to step outside to take a call shortly after he lets us in the building, so Hector and I are left to wander around on our own. The floors are a drab linoleum, and every wall that isn't covered in lime-green tile is in need of a good coat of paint. But it *is* a corner unit with lots of windows and natural light.

"Honestly, this is the best place I've toured."

"It *is*? You cannot be serious." Hector makes no attempt to mask his shock.

"Yes," I laugh, "It really is." Leaning against the wall, I dig in my purse to find my phone so I can take a few pictures. "Everything's in good shape. It's not too expensive. The floors and walls can be changed. It's not *our* neighborhood, but it's a good one."

Hector moves around the space, one hand propped under his chin, considering. "Maybe I was being a touch too judgmental." He paces quietly for a couple of minutes, trying to see its potential. "Our chairs would look okay right here in the corner, and you could put tables along that wall, but it would be a tight squeeze."

Moving behind the counter, I join him in imagining the space. "The espresso machine could go here. This place is bigger behind the counter than what I currently have, which would be really nice." We spend the next twenty minutes taking pictures and visualizing how to make it work.

"You don't love it, do you?" Hector asks, concern rimming his chocolate brown eyes.

"No, not yet." I scan the empty dining room again, trying to imagine the smell of freshly brewed coffee and the sound of friendly conversations. "But I could if I had to—"

"If you *had* to? Yuck."

I wish he loved it. Maybe then, I could love it. I'm running out of time. "So, you don't think this place could work?" I wave at the windows, which are its best feature.

"I want to hate it because it's far away, but you could make something special out of this space if you *had* to," Hector begrudgingly admits, as he inspects one corner of tacky tiled wall.

"I may *have* to make the most of something. If not this place, then something like it. Nothing will beat Station 19, but," I spin around in a circle, taking in all 360 degrees of the old smoothie shop, "honestly, I'm starting to see it. This could be really good." The weight on my chest lifts a little. For the first time, I found something that *could* work. "It's big enough, not too expensive, has lots of outdoor space, and the rest I can work around."

The property manager comes back in right as I'm ready to tell him I'm interested in the building. "Oh, good! You're back," I say, smiling widely at him.

"Hey, guys," he says in a slow, cautious voice. He closes his eyes, wincing, and I know what's coming before he says it. "So, my business partner just leased this unit this morning. I'm so sorry to waste your time. I didn't realize."

Of course. I'm flooded with warring feelings of disappointment and relief. I wanted this to be it so I could be done trying to solve my problem. But at the same time, I'm holding out hope that something better will come.

"Perfect!" Hector claps his hands together. "Now you can't settle. Let's celebrate with samosas."

For him, the matter is closed, but my mind can't shift to lunch. "Hector, what if I can't do this?" I ask him, as we step outside the latest building that will not be housing *Turbine.*

Hearing the tone in my voice, he swivels and pulls me into a warm hug. The smell of his cologne, woodsy and bright, brings me comfort.

"Alice Walker," he uses my full name, one of the few people who knows what Allie is short for, "you have already done this. *Turbine* exists. Right now. Because you made it."

"But what if I fail this time around?" Emotion rises in my throat, the loss of this building that I only wanted for forty-five seconds, and not even that badly, the final straw that makes me break.

"Nothing about this could make you a failure. You could close *Turbine*'s doors forever, which I *know* you will not have to do, and you would not be a failure. Who are you really worried about failing?"

My family, *who I barely speak to*, my friends, *who couldn't consider me a failure even if I never earned another dollar in my life*. Me. *No caveat there.* I'm worried about failing me. I can't say it. "Maybe I am ready for samosas."

Hector's lips widen into the whitest toothed smile of anyone I know. "Alright, let's get lunch, and in a few days we can go check out that place on Avenida de los Arboles and Third." He pronounces the first street name in his Mexican accent the same way he always does when he pronounces the Spanish street names around here, and it makes me smile.

"Hector, that place is twice my budget," I laugh.

"You know Brian and I would help if—"

"Absolutely not," I cut him off.

"Fine," he sighs. "Had to at least try."

~~433 Sierra Vista~~
Too late :(

~

A group of women who are in town for a bachelorette weekend have populated the row of white pedestal tables that line the glass wall, shamelessly watching the dark-haired, broad-shouldered, muscle-armed, motorcycle mechanic show next door.

"Good lord. I didn't know we were getting coffee and a view," a woman with red hair and a pink *I'm with the bride* tank top says.

"It didn't say anything about a viewing window into blue-collar sexiness when I looked this place up online," the maid of honor, marked by her matching white-lettered, pink tank top and air of *I'm-the-planner* authority, replies.

"*Voyeur Motors*, indeed," a third woman drinking out of a flask I pretend I can't see adds.

I'm tempted to draw the curtains and cut off their view, but when we had them closed before, customers complained. They missed seeing Betty. *And probably also Luke.* Plus, ever since he fixed my car, it doesn't feel right to shut him out.

"Who has forearms like that? I can see the definition from here," a bridesmaid adds, leaning forward on the table to get a better look.

Luke has parts and pieces of something metal and mechanical laid out on a towel on his workbench, forearms flexing as he picks up each piece to polish them, or maybe file them? All I know is nothing on that table is a starter for a Corolla.

"Excuse me?" The maid of honor waves me over from where I stand behind the counter. "Would you take a photo of us?"

"I'd love to." Sending tourists home with a memory that isn't off center and blurry is such a special little joy. She hands me her phone and then arranges her group into a pose, making sure the bride is prominently featured in the middle.

"I can pull that curtain if you want," I say. "It'll make for a nicer photo background."

"Oh no, we want him in the background," the redhead says, pointing at Luke, and the rest of the group giggles in agreement. *Has he noticed them fawning over him yet?*

My height won't allow for a good photo angle, so I climb up on a sea-foam green Eames chair to get a better shot. After I take a dozen photos with slight variations—making sure Luke is in the background—one woman smacks the window to get his attention, like she's a child, and he's a gorilla at the zoo.

The sound gets his attention, and he looks up from his work, brows narrowed, and lips flattened in irritation. I wonder if he'd be offended by a *Please don't tap the glass. It disturbs the mechanic* sign? I'm smiling to myself about the idea when his eyes catch mine. His face is stony, and he points to my feet, where I'm standing on the chair.

Some of the women try to get his attention, but his eyes stay on me. I hold up four fingers, trying to express that the chair has four legs, not just one like the table I fell off of, so I'm safe. He cocks his head slightly, probably confused, and continues to glare.

I hold my hands flat in front of my chest, palms parallel to the ground, and swing them out straight to the sides, making the *safe* motion from baseball. It's not supposed to be funny, but immediately, his brows soften, and his lips curve into a smirking grin.

The same woman from before bangs on the glass again, gaining Luke's attention for the briefest moment before he looks back to me. I shrug apologetically and pantomime that they want him in a photo, pointing at the phone, then at the bachelorette party, and then at him. He smiles at me, then disappears below the workbench and reappears, holding all sixty pounds of Betty as if she weighs no more than a grocery bag.

The bachelorette party makes a collective, "Aww," and if I'm honest, I join in. Betty is too adorable for words. Luke settles her on to an empty space on the workbench, and she sits proudly at attention next to him. His gaze fixes back on me, even though there are ten other women staring at him through the window.

We take another round of pictures, this time with Luke and Betty proudly in the background. Again, a little like a zoo. His eyes stay locked on me the entire time, and I can't fight the blush that spreads to my cheeks at his attention. I twinkle my fingers at him to let him know we're done, but he keeps watching me until I've climbed safely off of the chair.

The redhead who first pointed Luke out leans on the glass wall next to me, tilting her head in Luke's direction. "So, what's his story? Is he single?"

The question catches me off guard. The only person I've seen next door who isn't a customer is Cameron, and they're definitely not dating. That doesn't mean he isn't dating *someone* long-distance from wherever he moved from, though. The thought twists my stomach in a knot. *Why do I care?* He's only the distressingly good-looking man who works next door, and I've just barely forgiven him for taking Station 19. After my lease is up at the end of July, he'll be out of my life.

"I honestly don't know," I tell her as she watches me with hungry eyes.

"Oh, I thought maybe you two were…" she says waving her hand between me and Luke, raising her eyebrows suggestively.

Where did she get that idea? I look through the window at Luke. As if he can feel my eyes on him, he immediately looks up from his workbench and smirks at me. My ears burn with embarrassment, and I turn back to redhead and glass-tapper.

"Nope. We just work next door to each other. I barely know him."

"Oh, good! Can I get his number?" she asks.

"Um—I, um," I stumble over my words. *What the fuck? Why are they asking me?*

"Oh my god, Aspen. You're so rude," another bridesmaid chides. "She can't give us his number." She grabs the redhead by the hand and pulls her out the front door of *Turbine*. A second later, they're inside *Voyeur Motors*.

Good, now they can talk to him, and I won't have to be involved. They can get his number and meet up with him later tonight or something. That wouldn't be an issue for me. *Not at all.* I move back behind the register and wipe down the already clean counter. It doesn't matter what they're talking about. It's not my business. *I don't care. I don't care. I don't care.*

I look through the window, but only to check if they're being nice to Betty. I can't see her, of course. There is a three-foot wall at the base of the windows, and she's not that tall. But it looks like Luke is scratching her ears, based on the movement of his arms. He's leaning back against his leather couch, and the two women are both giving him their best flirtatious looks. What are they saying? *Why can't I read lips?*

Their conversation only lasts a couple of minutes, and as the women turn to leave, he faces me and waves. *Dammit. How did he know I was watching?*

~

Luke's locking the back door to his shop when I step out into the parking lot to leave for the day.

"You're heading out early," he says.

"Happy hour." I nod in confirmation as I walk over to pet Betty. "You're leaving early, too. Crashing a bachelorette party?"

He doesn't respond, so I look up from petting Betty to find him staring down at me. He holds eye contact for a few seconds before asking, "Would it bother you if I was?"

"No, of course not," I respond too quickly. "Why would it bother me? You can spend time with anyone you want. It's not my business." *Why am I still talking?*

"I'm not meeting up with them."

"They were attractive."

"Were they?" he asks, dryly.

"What do you mean?" I stand up from petting Betty, and she leans against my leg. "Of course, they were attractive. You saw them."

"Didn't notice."

"Sure you didn't." I roll my eyes.

"I noticed the attractive brunette who was taking my picture."

Did he just call me attractive? Blush floods from my cheeks down my neck. Hopefully the sun's too bright in his eyes for him to notice.

I talk to Betty, since apparently, she's the only sane one in this parking lot. "Good night, sweet girl. Love you," I say, waving at her as I practically sprint to my car.

"She knows, sweetheart. I did read her your text," Luke calls out right as I shut my door.

Chapter 16
Luke

"Are you listening? We've got a legacy here, kid. Someday this bar will be yours. Pay attention." *-Grandad Ernie, teaching eight-year-old Luke how to run an industrial dishwasher.*

Allie has on a dress today. Most days, she wears shorts and tank tops, clothes that are only made special by the privilege of displaying her curvy body. This dress is different. I've watched its butter-yellow fabric shift against her thighs all morning as she floats around *Turbine*, chatting up customers and wiping down tables.

Standing on her toes, she does a little hop to get onto a barstool, causing the dress to ride up much higher on her legs.

A throat clears behind me, and I turn around to find Brian standing by my front counter. "Hey, kid," he says, smiling knowingly.

"Perfect timing," I say, redirecting his focus from my obvious attention on the girl next door to his bike. "I've spent the whole morning with this beauty and got it running." I pat the single headlight of his 1959 BMW R60. Turns out his dad had incredible taste. "You ready to take this bad boy out for a quick ride?"

Brian laughs quietly. "I've never actually ridden one myself." He puts his coffee and a white paper bag on my front counter before crossing over to check out his motorcycle. "I kept it after my dad passed because it felt like keeping a piece of him, but I didn't know what to do with it after. Guess that's how it ended up sitting in the garage for decades."

"I've got my grandad's old BMW, too. I don't ride it much anymore but seeing it in my garage always makes me feel closer to him." I grab his key from the lockbox. "Even if you never ride yours, you've at least got to hear this motor. It's fucking beautiful."

"I'd love to."

Getting on the bike, I twist the gas, flip the kick starter out, and give it a few solid kicks. The R60 rumbles to life underneath me. *Braaap.* The sound reverberates off the walls and rumbles around the shop, waking Betty. She lifts her head from where she's lying on the cool concrete floor, yawns, and settles back into her nap.

I give it a few more good revs, *braaap braaap braaap,* watching Brian's smile widen with each one.

He shakes his head slowly from side to side as I cut the engine and move off the bike. "That's something I haven't heard in years," he says as he stares wistfully at the bike. "Many, many years. Sounds just the same as it did when I was a kid. This is incredible, Luke. You have no idea what you've given me just by making it run again," he finishes, reaching out to shake my hand.

We discuss the details of the remaining work on the R60, and he takes all of my suggestions on the aesthetics, teeing me up for a dream project.

"What about you? How have you been?" Brian shifts the

conversation to me, adjusting the sleeves of his white oxford shirt.

"Been real busy with the shop, haven't had time for much else," I respond, leaning back against my workbench. "No complaints, though."

"Any updates on the bar?"

"Currently, it's boring paperwork and prep."

"Do you mind if I ask," Brian looks through the glass wall, then back to me, "Why a bar? The motorcycle thing I get." He holds an open hand out, gesturing between me and my shop. "It suits you, but what's the motivation behind the bar?"

Brian's presence makes my venture in Palm Springs less isolating. I met most of the people I know here through *Turbine*, and they're understandably apprehensive about trusting the guy who's unseating a local favorite. A lot of the regulars have warmed up to me, but my bar is still a taboo subject. Brian's the first one to show any interest.

"My grandad—the one who left me the BMW—ran a biker bar, and I spent a lot of time there with him as a kid." I leave out the details of why I was always at a bar as a small child. Grandad was the closest thing to a dad I've ever known, and Mom left him to do most of my parenting. I can't blame her. No one should have to raise kids alone, but it doesn't always reflect well on her when I share those details. "He always told me that everything worth knowing can be learned behind a bar."

"Never would have thought of that, but he had a point," Brian laughs.

"I'd perfected pouring beer with the right amount of head before I could reach the taps on my own." My hands mimic the proper form, holding an imaginary glass at a forty-five-degree angle, showing the pouring motion I've repeated thousands of times.

"Did he hold you up to show you how to pour?"

"When I was real little, he did." I point to a battered wooden stool against the far wall. "Eventually, we made that stool over there for me to stand on."

Brian walks over and inspects the decades old piece of homemade furniture. "Solid construction." He taps a wooden leg, smoothed with age and use. "He taught you well. Impressive that you still have it."

"I kept the pieces of him I could. That's the answer to your question about the bar, too, by the way." I run all ten fingers through my hair before sliding them into my front pockets, shifting my weight against the workbench. "He died when I was fifteen. It made sense to me at the time that opening a bar was the best way to keep him close and learn the lessons he never got to teach me. I did a lot of dumb shit as a teenager, but that kid had at least one good idea."

"Sounds like it," Brian agrees, nodding as he moves to leave. "I'm looking forward to seeing how it comes out." He pauses by the front door. "I'll let you get back to work."

"Don't forget," I tell him, pointing toward the coffee and white paper bag he left on the counter.

"Those are for you." He smiles.

"Thanks, Brian. You didn't have to do that."

"I didn't," he says, pointing over my shoulder.

"Allie?" I ask.

He smiles and nods with knowing amusement before turning around and walking out the front door of my shop.

Watching Allie, who's having an animated conversation with Hector, I take a sip of the coffee. It's an Americano, of course. The paper bag holds a turkey sandwich on rye and a bag of BBQ chips, my usual order. Her memory is perfect, like the rest of her.

It never made sense to me why the guy I bought Station 19

from wouldn't sell to her. I finally had the opportunity to ask him last week when he came by to see how things were going. Evidently, he didn't believe she was serious when she brought it up because the dollar amounts she talked about were too low.

He got cagey and changed the subject when I asked why he told me no one would care to see *Turbine* go, making it obvious he was afraid I'd rescind my offer if I found out how upset the community would be at losing Allie and *Turbine*. It doesn't sit right with me. This town deserves better. *Allie* deserved better.

My eyes lock on the movement of her yellow dress as she walks behind the counter. I scan the curve of her body from the short hem of the dress, over her ample hips and soft belly, up to her electric smile, and land on giant teal eyes that stare right back at me.

Holding up my drink, I mouth *thank you*.

She waves her hand in the air dismissively, cheeks flushing, before turning back to Hector, chestnut ponytail bouncing along with her animated hand motions.

The temptation to extend her lease and surrender the idea of opening a bar in Grandad's memory comes to the forefront of my thoughts. *It's been coming up with a disturbing regularity lately.* But asking Allie to stay would mean giving up on Grandad, and I can't do that. He raised me, and there are too many things I never got to learn from him. Working behind a bar is the most connected I feel to him, and it's the reason I bought Station 19 in the first place.

My phone buzzes, lighting up with Allie's name.

Allie: Eat! It's 1:30 already!
Me: You didn't have to do this.
Allie: You can't go all day without eating. I won't allow it.
Allie: 1:36 now. Eat!!

Me: I'm not a man who takes well to being bossed around.

Grabbing the lunch she sent me, I move over to the couch to take a break. Betty comes to lie on my feet, hoping I drop something.

A teenager sitting by herself at one of the white round tables by the glass wall asks Allie a question, and my daily visual companion moves over to take the seat across from her. From my angle, I can see her profile, filling with a warm smile as she talks with the younger girl. After a brief conversation, Allie brings her something from the bakery case, and by the girl's response, I can tell it's a gift.

Allie's a natural host, making each person at *Turbine* right at home. I've seen her take countless photos, spend twenty minutes building a full itinerary for lost tourists, and remember the names of people who only come to Palm Springs twice a year.

Allie returns to the counter, and my phone buzzes again.

Allie: I can see you eating the sandwich. You're taking it just fine.

Me: This sandwich is the tits. I made an exception.

It takes her a few minutes before she's able to look at her phone again, but when she does, her shoulders shake with laughter.

Chapter 17
Allie & Luke

April 7th

Luke: What did you do different with my coffee today?

Allie: It's the literal same thing I always make you. Is something wrong with it?

Luke: Nothing wrong. It's better today.

Allie: No it is not.

Luke: Agree to disagree?

Allie: Never.

April 10th

Luke: Honestly surprised you're a Sex Pistols fan

Allie: WHAT

Allie: LUKE

Allie: You can hear my music???

Luke: Clearly

Allie: WAIT. Always??

Luke: Always.

Allie: Why didn't you ever say anything? Fuck I can turn it down.

    Luke: Don't. I like it.

April 11th
Luke: How's the car running sweetheart?
Allie: Starts every time. No new sounds. So good?
Luke: Good. You'll tell me next time something comes up?
Luke: Right?
Allie: Ugh.

    Luke: Why do all of your customers today look like they're ready for a photoshoot?
    Allie: Coachella this weekend. They are.

April 13th
Luke: Are you in the back?
Allie: Yeah why?
Luke: There's a dog out here you'll want to see.
Allie: WHAT
Luke: It has floppy ears.
Allie: I'm coming right now!! Don't let them leave!

April 15th
    Allie: That's the prettiest motorcycle you've had. I like the sparkles.
    Luke: Sparkles won't last. I'm sanding and repainting it.
    Allie: Boo. Sounds lame.
    Luke: It'll be prettier when I'm done. Promise.
    Allie: Doubtful.

April 17th
    Luke: Your friend scares me.

Allie: Devon?

Luke: Is she the blonde glaring at me from the bar?

Allie: Oh yeah. She's terrifying.

Luke: Did you leave already?

Allie: Yeah?

Luke: You shouldn't be alone in the parking lot at night. Tell me next time?

Allie: Not necessary.

Luke: Allie. It's not safe.

Allie: I walked to the parking lot by myself for years before you showed up.

Luke: Good thing I got here when I did. You never have to again.

April 18th

Allie: Is that a new shirt? I like it.

Luke: I have 9 of this exact shirt. They come in packs of 3. I wore one yesterday.

Allie: Whatever.

Allie: The correct response is Thank You.

Luke: Looking for a comment on your new shirt?

Allie: Of course not.

Luke: Looks perfect on you.

Luke: 10/10

Allie: I hate you.

Luke: The correct response is Thank You.

April 21st

Luke: Is that a new dress? That color looks incredible on you.

Allie: You don't have to comment on everything I wear.

Allie: But thank you :)

April 22nd

Allie: Are you actually taking a day off for once?

Luke: Why? miss me?

Allie: People are asking about Betty.

Luke: Sure they are.

Luke: Be there this afternoon. Went to Ventura last night for my mom's bday. Heading back soon.

April 24th

Luke: What do you think of this bike?

Allie: Ooh, shiny. Very sleek.

Luke: Maybe even pretty?

Allie: More than pretty. Beautiful.

Luke: So I was right. It does look better without the sparkles. Noted.

Allie: Dammit.

April 25th

Allie: Are you even working today?

Luke: You're looking right at me.

Allie: You've been sitting on that couch for hours.

Luke: You've been watching me for hours?

Allie: That's not what I said.

Luke: Sure it is.

Allie: Whatever.

Luke: Doing emails and bullshit today. Don't worry. The motorcycle show will be back tomorrow.

April 26th

Allie: That lady by the window practically fell out of her chair when you rev'd that motorcycle.

Luke: Shit. Sorry.

Allie: It was fucking hilarious.

Allie: It was like Grrr rrrr RRRR and she yelped.

Luke: Is grrr supposed to be the motor?

Allie: Yeah cause it's growling.

Luke: You're adorable.

Luke: But just so you know. if you're ever texting anyone else about motorcycles we use braaap instead of grr.

Luke: I changed my mind. Never text anyone else about motorcycles.

April 27th

Luke: Coffee is extra good again today. What are you doing to it?

Allie: Nothing. You're ridiculous.

Luke: You're ridiculous if you think I believe that.

Allie: I haven't changed anything.

April 28th

Allie: You left your step stool over here.

Luke: No I didn't.

Allie: It's right here.

Luke: It's yours. Try it out. You'll love it. Furniture designed for standing on.

Allie: Let me pay you for it.

Luke: No. It's not even new. I've had it forever.

Allie: Free coffee all week then.

Luke: I'll accept it if you tell me what you're doing to make it better.

Allie: It's not different!

April 29th

Luke: Looks like you were slammed this morning.

Allie: Holy fuck, yes. That was brutal.

Luke: Want to come test drive this Ducati with me when you're ready for a break? Got to make sure it'll handle with two.

Allie: Be there in 30 seconds.

Luke: Leaving soon?

Allie: Yeah, in like 10.

Luke: On my way to walk you out.

April 30th

Allie: Hector and Brian are over here talking about you.

Luke: What are they saying?

Allie: I'm no snitch.

Luke: You just snitched.

Allie: I told you they're talking about you. Not what they're saying.

Allie: It's barely a half snitch.

Luke: Remind me never to tell you any of my secrets.

Allie: You have secrets??

Luke: Of course.

May 1st

Luke: It's an extra shot, isn't it?

Luke: That's why my drink is better?

Luke: Allie.

Luke: I'm right, aren't I?

Allie: I don't know what you're talking about.

Luke: You're so cute.

Luke: Okay, this song I don't like.

Luke: Did you just turn it up?

Allie: That motorcycle is the actual prettiest one.

Luke: You should tell Brian that. It's his. '59 BMW R60.
Might be the prettiest bike I've ever worked on.

Allie: Since when does BMW make motorcycles?

Luke: Since before they made cars.

Allie: Sharing a glass wall with you is very educational.

May 2nd

Luke: It's nice on the patio.

Allie: It's 90 degrees out.

Luke: 80 in the shade.

Allie: Practically winter.

Luke: Come sit with me. You need a break.

Allie: Fine, but you have to split the BBQ chips with me. You
got the last bag.

Luke: They're all yours.

May 3rd

Allie: You should start charging for these bachelorette party
photos.

Luke: I don't mind. I like the photographer.

Luke: I didn't give these ones my number either, in case
you're wondering.

Allie: Wasn't. You can give your number to every single girl
in Palm Springs if you want.

Luke: I'll pass.

Allie: Leaving in 5!

Luke: Be right there.

May 4th

Allie: When's your birthday?

Luke: January 11th, 1994. 6:10am

Allie: I didn't need all that.

Luke: Sure you didn't.

Luke: When's yours?

Allie: August 11th

Luke: Leo. Should have guessed.

Allie: Who taught you this??

Luke: My mom, don't worry sweetheart.

Allie: I wasn't worried.

Luke: Sure.

Allie: A triple Capricorn?? What??

Luke: Mom calls me her little goat.

Allie: She sounds awesome.

May 5th

Luke: What's my horoscope say today?

Allie: How would I know?

Luke: Come on.

Allie: "Luck is on your side today. Big risks will have big rewards."

Luke: I like that one.

Allie: Let me know what you decide to risk.

Luke: I'll try my turkey sandwich on sourdough.

Allie: So risky.

Allie: Does that blue bike need to be tested for two top?

Luke: Two-up.

Allie: What?

Luke: It's called two-up when there's two people on one bike.

Allie: I like two top better.

Luke: Works for me.

Luke: The blue one isn't ready, but the green one is. You want a ride?

Allie: I don't want a ride. I just want to help if you need to test it for two top.

Luke: I need to.

Allie: Good thing I asked.

May 6th

Allie: Do you ever take a day off?

Luke: And miss the view through this window? Not a chance.

May 7th

Luke: What's my horoscope today?

Allie: You could look it up yourself.

Luke: I could.

Allie: "You are on the right path. Keep pushing forward, but don't ignore the thorns that snag you on your way."

Luke: Mm. Lots to consider.

Allie: Did you get Betty BOOTIES??

Luke: It's getting too hot for her feet. I'd rather not carry her everywhere until fall.

Allie: They're so fucking cute.

Luke: You should've seen the first time I put them on her.

Allie: Tell me there's a video.

Luke: There is.

Allie: Send it!!

Luke: Come over here. I want to see your reaction.

Allie: Coming right now.

Luke: You ready to walk out?

Allie: Yup!

Luke: Be right over.

May 8th

Allie: You got a haircut, didn't you?

Luke: I did.

Allie: You look good.

Luke: Thanks for noticing. Got a horoscope for me?

Allie: Ooh, be careful today. "Small changes can cause big feelings. Think before you act."

Luke: Are you having big feelings about my haircut?

Allie: I think it means your feelings.

Luke: Doesn't answer my question.

May 9th

Luke: Are you alright?

Luke: Allie?

Luke: It's 7:30 and Turbine is still locked.

Luke: Is someone supposed to be here? Don't you usually get here first on Thursdays?

Luke: I'm worried about you.

Luke: Are you okay?

Chapter 18
Allie

Some surprises are better than others.
Be prepared for all kinds today. -*Allie's
Horoscope, May 9th*

Knock! Knock!

What the fuck? My body hurts. All I want to do is sleep.

Knock! Knock! Knock!

Who knocks on a door anymore? *Rude.*

Knock! Knock!

"Allie, are you okay?" A booming voice calls, barely muffled by the distance between my bed and the front door. It sounds familiar. A little too familiar. *Why is he here?*

The awful noise continues as I force myself out of bed and painfully move toward the front door. My cramps are so intense, I'm practically limping.

Looking through the peephole confirms what I suspected. Luke is the motherfucker who forced me out of bed. Betty whines and wags her tail, probably smelling that I'm close.

"Allie?" he yells again, not catching Betty's cues.

Reaching for the brass doorknob, I catch my reflection in the entryway's full-length mirror. My hair is loose around my shoulders, kinked from yesterday's ponytail. The gigantic t-shirt I'm wearing that reads *Death Before Decaf* is barely long enough to cover the biggest, comfiest granny panties I own. *No notes.*

Luke's broad chest rises and falls with a full body sigh of relief when his wild eyes land on me. Then his jaw clenches under a freshly trimmed beard and he tenses up again. "You don't keep your door locked?"

"Can you fucking not?" I roll my eyes at him, exasperated already. "What are you doing here? The last thing I need right now is to be dragged out of bed. For fuck's sake, you have my number. Text me if you need something. This is the most—"

He cuts me off, running a hand through mussed black hair. "You're not answering your phone, sweetheart. I texted, and I called."

"So what? Calm your tits. Jesus. I don't have to answer my phone. You don't have to come banging on my door at," I reach for my phone to check the time, but realize I left it in bed, "whatever the fuck time it is."

"Allie, I was worried," Luke says, the tension around his eyes corroborating his assertion.

"Just come in. It's hot out there."

As I'm shutting the door behind him and Betty, another wave of angry cramps tightens around my uterus. I can't suppress the pained whimper that passes through my lips as I collapse at the waist, pressing a hand against my stomach.

"What the fuck, Allie?" Luke crosses to me in an instant, wrapping an arm around my waist and supporting my weight as I lean bodily against him. "What is going on?" he asks, angling his face, so his concerned espresso-colored eyes meet mine.

"It's literally just cramps."

"Just cramps? This isn't *just* anything. You need to lie down. Let me help you."

"I was lying down before *someone* came banging on my door for no reason."

Letting me lean on him, Luke guides me over to the blue sectional and holds my hand, steadying me while I lie down. He grabs two patterned throw pillows from the other end of the couch and tucks one under my knees and the other behind my head. Betty sits on the ground next to me, settling her sweet face onto the cushion next to my head.

"Shit, Allie." Sitting on the walnut coffee table next to me, Luke leans forward, bracing his forearms on his knees. "I'm sorry. There's no one at *Turbine*. It was an hour and a half after you were supposed to open." Squeezing his eyes together, he runs his fingers through his messier than usual hair. He continues, voice quieter than before, "You weren't there. *Turbine*'s never closed in the morning. I was afraid something had happened to you."

"My uterus happened to me."

The tension falls out of his jaw, and his eyebrows furrow. "I can see that now."

If I wasn't preoccupied with hating one of my reproductive organs, I might be touched by his concern. "Marisol couldn't make it in to cover for me until nine. Sorry, I should have told you."

"Don't apologize to me." He shakes his head. "That's not the point. I just, I'm glad you're okay."

"Okay." I blink at him, unsure what's supposed to happen next.

"What can I get for you? What do you need?" He leans back and looks around the room. "Where's your heating pad?"

Normally, I loathe needing help, but right now, I don't give a shit. I'm just grateful he's here to take care of me. "My room is the one down the hall with the door open. Will you get my yellow blanket, please? And the bottle of painkillers next to the bed? The heating pad is in there too."

"I made you get out of bed." He runs his fingers through the dark tendrils of his hair yet again, forearms flexing. "Shit. I really am sorry, Allie. Do you want to move back there?"

"No, no I'm good." He'd probably carry me to my bed if I asked him to, which would sound appealing under *any* other circumstances, but now that I'm settled into the couch, I'm not moving for anything.

Luke skeptically narrows his eyes   but turns and disappears down the hallway. Betty stands up, wagging her tail, and whines at me. She nuzzles her head into my palm, so I pat the couch by my legs to encourage her to jump up.

"She's not supposed to be on the furniture," Luke says, emerging from the hall.

"She seems different today. She's nuzzling me more and whining. Is she okay?"

Luke drapes my cozy yellow blanket across my legs. "She's worried about you. She can tell you don't feel well." He reaches down and scratches her behind the ears. "Isn't that right, babe? You're worried about Allie, too?"

"Dogs can tell that?"

"I don't know about all dogs, but Betty knows."

"Are you sure she isn't allowed up here?" I push my lower lip out in an exaggerated pout and make a show of batting my eyelashes. My face may not be good for intimidation, but it's perfect for getting exactly what I want.

"How could I say no to that?" he asks, his familiar smirk tugging the edge of his mouth. Luke tells Betty, "Okay," and gestures to a spot on the couch that she immediately jumps onto. When I reach to pet her, she scoots closer and cuddles up close to me, resting her blocky gray head with the thick white stripe down the middle on my hip, and curling into the space behind my hooked legs.

"She's an excellent snuggler," Luke says. The mental image of Betty curled up in his arms feels ridiculous and endearing at the same time. "Figured you'd want this, too," he says, handing me my phone. He sets me up with the heating pad, painkillers, a glass of water, and even pulls the tray of remotes across the coffee table, so they're within my reach. Taking his spot across from me again on the edge of the coffee table, he asks, "Is there anything else you need? You want? Snacks?"

"No snacks," I groan.

"Have you eaten anything?"

"No, but food sounds awful right now."

"Okay." Luke's voice is damn near sweet. He's fully in caretaker mode, and it makes me wonder how many other women have seen this side of him.

The idea of Luke draping a blanket across another woman's legs and letting her cuddle Betty makes me irrationally jealous. I look down at Betty, who's snoring not so quietly against me. She probably knows all his secrets. *Fuck*, I bet Luke's the kind of guy who brings soup when you have a cold—or he comes over and *makes* soup.

"I've never had a dog before," I say, trying to distract myself from the direction my thoughts are headed.

"No? You're so good with Betty."

"I don't know about that. I think she's just good with me."

Luke's smirk turns to a full smile as I watch his eyes pass from me to Betty and back again. "What else do you need?"

"Will you grab me an edible? They're in the cabinet above the fridge." Lying down has taken some of the pressure off, but I'm still in a lot of pain. All I want to do is sleep until the worst of the cramps have passed.

When Luke returns with the pink package of gummies, he's also carrying a bowl of cashews, some crackers, and an apple. Setting them on the coffee table, next to where he sits, he says, "Hopefully you're hungry soon."

"Why are you so good at this?"

"At what?" he asks.

"Knowing how to take care of me."

"My little sister gets bad cramps, too." His tone is matter of fact, like any big brother would take care of their little sister in the same situation.

"I didn't know you had a sister." *How have I missed something this basic?*

He laughs, "Skye is finishing her last year at UC Davis. She's coming to visit next week." His voice carries clear affection for his sister. "You'll meet her then. I bet she'll like you more than she likes me."

"I doubt that, but I'd love to meet her." After how awful I was to him for so long, I'd be shocked if she liked me at all.

"You'll see soon enough." He reaches across me and pats Betty's head before standing up. "Alright, sweetheart. I'm heading out, so you can rest." I try not to let my disappointment show. It felt good to have him here, and I'm convinced Betty's cuddles have some kind of magical healing properties. "Is there anything else you need before I go? I'll be back to check on you this afternoon."

"You don't have to do that."

"I have to come back for Betty, don't I?"

"Would you really leave her with me?" I ask.

"Of course. Doubt she'd be willing to come with me right now, anyway."

"Thank you for coming to check on me," I say. "It was totally unnecessary, but sweet."

Luke scoffs, walking toward the door. "It was necessary." He opens the front door and looks back at me over his shoulder. "Text me if you need anything, okay?"

"Okay." The response is a reflex. I have no intention of asking for more help. He's done far too much for me already this morning.

I'm not sure how long it takes after Luke leaves before I fall asleep, but when I wake up, it feels like it's been hours. The pain medication has started to wear off, but the edible has definitely kicked in. Betty's still cuddled tightly against me, but I wake her up, let her outside, and fill up a bowl of water by the back door.

Fifteen minutes later, we're cuddled up together on the couch again, and I'm halfway through the snacks Luke left out for me. I take a picture of Betty curled up against me and send it off to Luke, who replies immediately.

Luke: She taking good care of you?
Me: The best.
Luke: You hungry yet?
Me: Nope.

I'm really hungry. But he's already done enough.

Luke: That's not true. I'm bringing you food. Any requests?
Me: I have food here.
Luke: See you soon.

I must have fallen asleep again, because the sound of Luke rapping lightly on the door startles me awake.

"Coming!" I call. Betty groans when I push against her to get up. Catching my reflection in the mirror again, I realize I'm still not wearing pants. Probably should have done something about that before he came back. *Oh well.* Pulling on the door to open it, I realize he locked it on his way out.

"You don't check to see who it is?" Luke asks.

I roll my eyes. "Come in."

"Was she good for you?" Luke asks. Betty wags her tail and goes over to greet him, while I settle back into my cozy spot on the couch under the yellow blanket.

"She was a dream."

Luke unloads a paper bag onto the coffee table, pulling out a bag of chocolate-covered pretzels and then handing me a tub of mac 'n' cheese from the deli down the street. *He made two stops.*

"Fuck me. This looks incredible," I say, popping off the top of the macaroni. "Thank you so much for doing this. I'm sorry you had to go out of your way."

He chuckles at my response. "I like helping you."

My cheeks heat at his statement. "Seems like I've been needing a lot more of it since I met you."

He smirks, taking a seat next to me on the couch and pulling out his own tub of mac 'n' cheese. "No, you're just more likely to accept it from me." *Dammit. He's right.* I keep finding myself in situations where Luke is helping me, and rather than fighting it, I'm leaning into it.

Luke sitting on my couch, eating takeout in the middle of the day, shines a light on how segmented my knowledge of him is. How does he know about the deli down the street? Is it close to his house, too? Where does he even live? We don't sell mac 'n' cheese at *Turbine*, so I didn't know he eats it with a fork instead of a spoon.

I know how he treats strangers. But what about his family? He's so good with Betty, but how did he get her in the first place? I know the hours he keeps at work, but what time does he go to bed? I know what he looks like, polishing stuff and twisting tools around. *I should really learn more about his actual work.* But what does he look like laid back after a long day, drinking a beer? *He has to be a beer guy, right?* Does he like to grill?

Looking up at him, I see that he's watching me, with a grin on his face, not a smirk, nothing cocky about it, just genuine pleasure. "Something on your mind?" he asks.

Well, shit. I'm just staring at him. How creepy of me. I land on the least invasive of my questions. "How did you end up with Betty?"

"She found me. Four years ago, she was sleeping in the shade under my truck when I was leaving my friend Rick's house. She was underfed and a little skittish," He reaches down and wraps a thick arm around her neck, kissing her on top of the head, "but already such a sweet girl. Instead of running away, she wagged her tail and whined. I stood and waited, and after a few minutes she came and leaned up against my legs. I checked for a tag or a microchip and asked around to the neighbors, but I already knew she was mine."

He pulls out his phone, and I lean in close as he shows me pictures from their first few days together. She's thinner, scarily so, but the same dog with the little 'socks' of white fur on her front feet and already looking at him with adoration in her eyes.

"Maybe someday a dog will find me, too," I say.

"Would you like that?" he asks, setting his phone on the coffee table, but not leaning away from me.

"Hopefully, someday. I'm so busy with *Turbine*, it wouldn't be fair to one now. They'd be home alone all day."

"You'd be great with a dog. Too bad you can't tell the FDA to eat shit and get one, anyway."

Or, it could hang out at Luke's with Betty all day. The idea crumbles as soon as it materializes. In three months, Luke and

Betty will both be out of my life.

Chapter 19
Luke

"Pay attention to this idiot in the hat, and you'll learn what not to do to keep a lady interested." *-Grandad Ernie, pointing out a guy crashing and burning on a first date at the bar.*

"Dude. I can't believe you made me get out of bed this early," Skye complains. "And without coffee. You're a monster."

"It's ten o'clock," I say, holding open the passenger side door of my truck for her, "and we're going for coffee right now."

"It better be as good as you said."

"It will be."

As I'm pulling onto the road, she asks, "Are we gonna talk about mom?"

"If you want."

"She's doing better than you think."

"I know how she's doing. Just saw her a few weeks ago." I reach across the truck cab to point the vents so the A/C hits her, but she bats my hands away.

"I can adjust my own vents. Did she tell you she made

friends with the new neighbors? And she adores the handyman you hired to work on her bathroom? I know she's always trying to guilt you into coming home. She even asked me to help convince you. I told her to get the fuck over it, by the way. She's not being fair to you."

"I've always been the one who takes care of her."

"Do you hear how fucked that sounds? She's your mother. She should have been the one to take care of you."

"And she was, in every way she could manage."

"I call bullshit. She saw how much easier it was to let you manage the house, raise me, finish raising yourself and just coasted."

"Be careful how you speak about Mom." Each time we have this conversation, Skye pushes harder toward my mom being in the wrong, but she was so young when it all started. She wasn't old enough to comprehend how much it fucked with mom when Skye's dad left or when Grandad died. I was. She was a wreck. Maybe it wasn't right for me to be the one to help her, but there was no one else to do it.

"You know what's not fair? Staying up late to help your little sister with her homework and then getting up at five the next morning to work a job before school while your mom gets to go to bed early and sleep in."

Pulling up to a stoplight, I briefly look her in the eyes. "It wasn't fair that both of our dads skipped. It wasn't fair that Grandad died so young. But that doesn't mean it wasn't reality."

"You're enabling her."

"Did you take a psych class this year or something?"

"Two, actually," she says, flipping her dark, curly behind her shoulder with the back of her hand. "You know, you're allowed to put yourself first. You're not doing anything wrong, living out here, doing things you love."

"Never said I was."

"Grandad would have been proud of you."

"He's the one who told me to take care of her." Grandad taught me almost everything I know about fixing and building while he was fixing and building things for Mom. He always said he wouldn't be around forever, and I'd have to pick up where he left off, eventually. After he died, I did exactly that.

"I'm sure he didn't mean for you to do it at the expense of living your own life."

"Is there a point to this?"

Skye pokes me in the arm. "The point is you shouldn't feel guilty."

"I don't."

"You're impossible," she huffs, crossing her arms over her chest.

"Common opinion these days."

"Who else says that?"

My silence answers her question.

"It's Allie, isn't it? I cannot wait to meet her. Do you think she'll be there today? Do you think I'll like her? Do you think she'll like me?"

"She will. And you will. And she will."

My prediction about the two of them is proven correct within seconds of entering *Turbine*.

"Is this your sister?" Allie squeals, coming around the counter. "It has to be. You have the same eyes."

"Yes! And you're Allie, right?" Skye reaches out, pulling Allie into a hug. Her eyes flash with surprise, probably at my sister knowing who she is already, but she returns the hug with enthusiasm. They look like old friends, not two people meeting for the first time. Allie fawns over Skye's curly hair, and Skye asks where Allie got her silver necklace with a lock and key pendant, because she has to have one too.

"I am dying for coffee. He's deprived me all morning," Skye says, glaring at me over her shoulder.

"He didn't let you have coffee at home?" Allie asks, voice incredulous.

"She wasn't awake to drink it."

"You should have woken her up with it," Allie scolds, leading us over to the register. "Coffee is the only acceptable reason to wake someone up."

"Noted."

The two of them have a lengthy conversation about flavored syrups and seasonal specials, with Allie helping Skye pick the 'perfect Palm Springs vacation' coffee before Allie trades off her duty at the register with Marisol and joins us with a drink of her own at a round table by the glass wall.

"So, how has my brother been as a work neighbor?" Skye asks, dimples showing in her mischievous smile.

I expect Allie to explain how she finds me infuriating, but she doesn't. "I wish I could tell you he's an impossible jackass, but he's not."

"It's irritating how calm he is, isn't it?" my sister asks, glaring at me accusingly.

"It's like he's totally unrufflable," Allie agrees.

Leaning back in my chair, I sip my coffee and watch them volley excited conversation back and forth.

"What's with the windows?" Skye asks. "He said it's cause it's an old gas station?"

"He would say that." Allie rolls her eyes at me. "The real story is sweet and adorable and includes people falling in love."

That's my cue to leave. I push back my chair. "I've got some work to do, so I'm going to head next door before she starts on this fairytale."

"It's a real story," Allie insists, sitting up straighter in her chair, a slight rosy blush coming to her round, freckled cheeks.

I don't bother arguing. The story makes her happy, and the last thing I want to do is take away any more of her happiness.

~

Allie: Today's horoscope says little goats make very good big brothers.

Me: Is that so?

Allie: "Those around you look up to you, even if they don't realize it. Or you don't deserve it." So pretty much?

Me: I'll take it.

My eyes meet hers through our glass wall. Her cheeks flush, as they often do when I pay attention to her, but she holds my gaze and shines her electric smile at me instead of looking away like she used to.

She and Skye talked for an hour before Skye borrowed my truck to go shopping at the places Allie recommended. It only took my feisty brunette neighbor two minutes to text me after my sister left.

Me: Thank you for keeping Skye company.

Allie: I'm obsessed with her. She's like a funnier, cooler version of you.

Me: So you're obsessed with me?

Allie: That's not at all what I said.

Me: It's basically what you said.

Allie: You're impossible. Can you see me glaring at you?

Looking through the window, I see her round cheeks, bright

eyes, and plush lips trying to suppress a smile. She may be trying to intimidate me, but I'm only reveling in her focus.

Me: I see you.

Opening my laptop on the workbench, I settle in for a few hours of working on plans for the bar. I've been connecting with beer vendors, working on the cocktail menu, looking for staff, and I applied for the liquor license weeks ago. But when it comes to the actual physical design for the space, I get stuck.

Looking up from my laptop, I see Allie's chestnut ponytail bob in time with her laughter, reminding me why. She belongs over there. Every time I try to imagine changing out countertops, adding in beer taps, or revamping the kitchen, all I can picture is her standing there, disappointed.

She's wearing a dress again today, mint green with thick straps and a short skirt. I don't know if it's the extra heat of late spring in the desert, but she's been wearing them more often than not. Probably inconvenient for her work, but I'm not complaining.

Me: That dress looks perfect on you by the way.

When she sees my text, she spins in a circle, showing off the dress, its hem ruffling just barely below her ass.

Allie: It's nothing special.
Me: You make it special.
Allie: Jesus, sometimes I think you're trying to make me blush.
Me: I am.

Chapter 20
Allie

You can't make old friends, but don't let
that stop you from making new ones. *-Allie's
horoscope, May 17th*

"It looks good right there to me," I say to Devon, who's been
moving the same chenille pouf around her new office for ten
minutes, uncharacteristically indecisive.

"Love you, but you're wrong," she replies, picking it up and
walking back to the window she first set it under. She and Bea
have been working out of this space for the past month, but all the
furniture and decor have to be placed to perfection for their grand
opening party tomorrow night.

My design skills are sorely lacking, so I've been helping by
providing coffee and an extra set of hands. "What's next, boss?"

"The guys from the showroom should have been here an hour
ago with the sofa and the rest of the furniture. There isn't much
else today." Devon twist her almost-white blonde hair together
into a clip, before she holds up her wrist, checking her black
athletic watch. Most days, she wears a cream-colored leather one,

but today she changed it to match her outfit, essentially dressed for a workout in white Adidas, black wide-leg sweatpants, and a fitted brown crop-top that shows off her flat stomach. "Yeah, they said between one and two. It's quarter after three, I'm calling again."

While Devon is on the phone, Bea pushes open the front door, balancing a cardboard box on her hip. She's wearing loose-fitting olive-green pants, tan Nikes, and what I'm assuming is a t-shirt of a band I've never heard of. Seeing her outside of barre class and workout gear still surprises me sometimes. Her vibe is much less Workout Barbie, as she calls it, and much more Cool Girl Barbie.

"Hello, angel!" she greets me in her low, sing-song voice.

"Hi, gorgeous! Let me help you." I take the box from her.

Bea slides off her rectangular orange sunglasses. "You're perfect. Thank you," she says, moving to style a bookshelf that holds exactly six books and a bunch of other *stuff*.

"I still can't believe I took your classes for years and never knew you were a designer."

"I'm a woman of many mysteries," she says, moving a bronze vase down two shelves. "But my degree isn't one of them. I just like to keep this part of my life separate from the gym."

Devon walks back into the room. "I am very stressed," she says instead of greeting Bea.

"You don't look stressed," Bea responds. "You're playing it off beautifully." And she's right. Devon's moods are often hard to read. She has an enviable poker face.

"Thank you for that," Devon says. "I just got off the phone with the showroom who sold me the sofa and the rest of the rugs and furniture we need. They over-committed their delivery schedule, and they can't deliver until Monday."

"Do you need all that for your grand opening?" I ask.

"Not technically," Devon says, and I can tell she's frustrated by the tiniest change in the shape of her mouth.

"We need them," Bea disagrees. "It's the grand opening of *Friday West Interior*'s first office. It matters. We'll figure it out," she finishes, with the comforting authority of someone who knows how to pull a solution out of thin air.

"The showroom closes at five, and they're not open tomorrow. I've got an hour and a half to figure out a way to get it picked up," Devon says.

"*We've* got an hour and a half," Bea corrects, pulling out her phone.

"How do I not know anyone with a truck?" Devon asks.

"Oddly enough, neither do I," Bea says, "but rentals exist. I'll start calling around."

"I kind of know someone with a truck," I volunteer.

"Who?" Devon asks. It's a fair question. We have all the same friends.

"Luke."

Neither of them looks surprised. Maybe I'm not playing things as close to the chest with him as I thought, but I haven't said a word to either of them about him since the day he helped fix my car. I don't fully understand what's happening between us. He's sweet to me, keeps *fucking* taking care of me, and I don't even blame him for taking the building anymore. So, I guess that makes us friends? But he flirts with me. A lot. And I might flirt back. But nothing could ever happen between us. *Right? Right.* I'm moving *Turbine* in a few months. Although I'm still not sure where, which is another—

"Al," Devon interrupts my thought spiral, "are you going to ask him?"

"Of course." It makes me extremely uncomfortable to ask anyone for a favor, especially him, but I would do anything for Devon.

Me: How would you feel about me owing you a big favor?

Luke responds immediately.

Luke: You could never owe me anything. What do you need, sweetheart?
Me: I feel so bad asking this.
Luke: Ask.
Me: You're my only friend with a truck.
Luke: What do you need me to move?

"Are you texting him?" Devon asks. "Can you not just call him?"

"We aren't on phone call terms yet."

"Well, I'm about to be," Devon says, voice steady and firm, not losing her cool.

"Give me three minutes." I walk to the other side of the room as Luke and I finish the conversation over text with him agreeing to pick everything up immediately.

"He's on his way to the showroom." I tell Devon.

"Really?"

"Yes, really."

Devon's façade cracks for the first time, her shoulders slumping in relief. She walks across the room and wraps me in a tight hug. "Thank you, Al. I don't know what I'd do without you."

"Literally, all I did was text a man."

"A man who you're frenemies with," Devon says.

"At this point, he's pretty much all friend, and no enemy," I say.

"Interesting," is all Devon says, but I know her analytical mind is already thinking about what that means.

We work together to unpack every item Bea brought from the house. The space is practically unrecognizable from the bland white walls they started with a month ago. They've added paint, wallpaper, and new curtains. There's even a little kitchenette that now has tile and freshly painted cabinets with new door hardware and, of course, a killer coffee set up. The place feels like Devon. She got to implement design ideas I've heard her daydream about for years.

An hour and a half later, Luke's truck rumbles up. I check my reflection in Devon's leather-framed "statement" mirror. White Converse, black bike shorts, black cropped t-shirt, and my usual ponytail. Nothing he hasn't seen me in before. *Not that I care.* I finger comb my wispy hairs into place as I follow Devon and Bea outside to meet him.

He opens the passenger side door, and Betty bounds out, then runs up to me in her little blue pavement shoes, wagging her tail, and wearing that broad open doggy-smile of hers.

"It's pretty definitive that she likes me better than you now," I tell Luke as I squat down low to the ground to hug Betty. He only laughs in response.

"Thank you for doing this," Devon says. "How can I repay you? Actually, can I pay you?"

"Absolutely not." His answer is immediate and firm.

"Ooh, bossy," Bea says, walking past him on her way to check out the furniture in the truck bed.

"It is hot as fuck out here," I announce, standing up from my place on the ground with Betty. "Let's get this unloaded."

Luke's truck is loaded down with enough furniture and boxes to fill a small apartment. "Holy shit, Luke. I had no idea how much I was asking you to move," I say to him and then shoot Devon a glare. She rolls her eyes, raising her hands in a *sorry, not sorry* shrug.

Luke takes a step closer to me and slides a hand around my bare waist as he leans down to speak into my ear. "It's alright, sweetheart. I like doing things for you."

I turn my face to hide my blush and catch eyes with Devon, who's analyzing us. "Well, thanks," I stutter out awkwardly to Luke before reaching for a box in the truck bed.

The heat makes the task of unloading the truck twice as daunting, but between the four of us, it goes decently fast. Luke takes the lead, and much to my surprise, Devon lets him. After his truck is unloaded, he hangs around to help get everything placed, genuinely happy to help.

"Luke, you saved me today," Devon says to him as we're heading to our cars. "Truly, thank you."

"No point in having a truck if I'm not willing to use it," he says.

"Are you free tomorrow night?" Bea asks, shooting me a conspiratorial grin. "We're having a grand opening party. You should come."

My eyes grow wide, but I try to hide the surprise on my face. It's the right thing to do, inviting him. *Didn't we just decide he's my friend? Why am I so nervous? I see him every damn day.*

Luke slides his hands into his front pockets, and his familiar cocky half smile appears across his face. "I'd love to come."

Chapter 21
Luke

"Same as most things, kid. Don't rush. This works better if you take it slow." -*Grandad Ernie to twelve-year-old Luke after he cut himself while learning to shave.*

Hector and Brian find me the moment I walk in the door of Devon's party, Hector wrapping me in an unexpected, but appreciated, hug before I have a chance to look for Allie.

"Well, doesn't Mr. Motorcycle clean up nice?" Hector says half to me half to Brian, who nods in agreement behind him.

"Is that my nickname?"

"No, I just tried it out for the first time and I don't like it. It's officially retired. You deserve better," Hector says, making all three of us laugh. "I'll come up with something in time. Or not. Luke suits you. Anyway, I'm thrilled the girls invited you."

"It's good to see you outside of Station 19," Brian adds.

"Love the name of your shop, by the way. Don't think I ever told you," Hector adds. "*Voyeur Motors*. Very sexy."

Brian moves past Hector's comment. "I'm sorry I haven't

picked up my dad's motorcycle yet. I'm afraid it'll just go back into the garage for another thirty years."

"It's a gorgeous machine. I don't mind keeping it around," I say, scanning the room behind him for a chestnut ponytail. "I could help you sell it if that's what you decide you want to do. It's worth quite a bit."

"Oof," Brian says, putting a hand to his chest, "It's probably the best idea, but it hurts to consider."

"You don't have to part with it. There're motorcycle shows you could submit it to."

Hector interjects, waving a hand between our faces. "This is a party. Let me show you the bar." He squeezes my shoulder once before leading the way across the room.

Following Hector through the packed crowd, we pass a couple of people I recognize from *Turbine*, but still no Allie. *She must be here somewhere.*

"The line for the bartender is right here," Hector says. "We'll see you in a bit." Brian taps my shoulder and points to the far corner of the room before he and Hector walk away in the opposite direction. Following the line of where he pointed, I finally lock eyes on Allie.

Her body is turned, showcasing her profile. Chestnut hair styled in loose curls falls around her face. No ponytail tonight. She throws her head back in a laugh that I can hear all the way across the room, hair sliding away to reveal bare shoulders. The crowd between us blocks my view of what must be a strapless dress.

"Sir?" The bartender's voice grabs my attention. "What would you like?" His tone implies this isn't the first time he's asked me this. After apologizing, I order both of the event's specialty cocktails. Drinks in hand, I find an empty space against the wall with a view of Allie talking with some people I don't know, her laughter repeatedly echoing throughout the room.

She looks over her shoulder toward the door, trying to be discreet, but obviously waiting for someone to arrive, which I take as my cue.

Once I've cut through the crowd, the full sight of her from head to toe nearly steals my breath. Her strapless pink dress has a straight neckline that sits low on her chest. The bottom of the dress lands just above her knees, which would make it seem modest if it weren't for the slit that runs up the front of one leg. It's much tighter than her usual clothes and shows off every one of the lush curves that I'm dying to run my hands over.

Steep, tan high heeled shoes lengthen her exposed legs, and a gold necklace lands in the divot between her collarbones. Most days, Allie strikes an adorable balance between casual and put together. Tonight, she's all sex and power.

She looks over her shoulder, checking the door again, and I step closer, so I'm standing beside her when she turns back.

"Waiting on someone?" I ask.

"Luke," she gasps, face lighting up with a smile when she sees me, eyes growing wide. The warm blush I crave fills her cheeks.

"Hey, gorgeous."

Her cheeks blush brighter. "I'm so happy you're here. Is one of those for me?" she asks, indicating the drinks with a pale, freshly manicured hand.

"Or both. Whatever makes you happy."

She giggles, reaching for the rosemary whiskey sour, leaving me with the greyhound. "I like this one better." And then she wraps her free arm around my waist, pulling me tightly against her for a hug, barely avoiding spilling both of our drinks. Her high heels bring her head up just above my shoulder and the familiar scent of coconut and lemon with it.

When she pulls back, I let my hand linger on her waist for a few extra breaths. "You look incredible."

She giggles again. "Thank you. You look," she pauses for a moment, looking me up and down, taking in my combed-back hair, freshly trimmed beard and fitted dark-gray suit. "You look incredible, too." She cocks her head to the side, unabashedly staring at me.

"Hello, darlings." Bea's voice comes from my left, and I reluctantly give up eye contact with Allie to greet her. They squeal over each other's outfits while I sip my drink.

When another friend of theirs joins, they include me in the conversation by sharing how I moved furniture yesterday. The story paints me in a better light than I deserve. Allie asked me for help, and I know how hard that is for her. There's no way I'd pass up the opportunity to come through for her, to be someone she can count on.

The rest of the evening plays out similarly, Allie shining brightly while she and her friends exchange stories and make each other laugh. She's more relaxed than she is at Station 19. Without the weight of being in charge, she's letting loose.

"Don't think just because you helped out last night, I'll go easy on you with my girl." Devon speaks quietly enough from her position next to me that only I can hear.

Suppressing a smile of admiration for Devon's fierce protection of her friend, I invite her critique. "Tell me what you're worried about."

Devon narrows her eyes at me skeptically. "I don't know you. She doesn't either, really. But she likes you, and she trusts you." Her words come out like an accusation. "To be clear—I do not like you, and I do not trust you." She pauses, staring at me with searching blue eyes that are level with mine with her heels on, while she considers her next words. "You will be careful with her."

Her words are firm and deliberate, but not practiced. Still, I wonder if Devon has ever had this talk with another man. Or men. The thought stirs a level of jealousy in me deeper than I knew I was capable of.

"I am careful with her, and I will continue to be," I respond, keeping my voice respectful and not defensive.

Devon persists, either not satisfied with my answer or her own warnings. "She gives a lot more than she takes. Do not take advantage of her."

"I would never take anything from her."

"You've already taken the one thing her entire future was hanging on."

"That's fair." We both know what she's talking about, and I don't bother defending myself. The idea of Allie moving *Turbine* is more distasteful to me every day. Watching her struggle to find a new space keeps me up at night.

I glance down at Allie, where she stands to my other side, and she flashes a brilliant smile up at me before returning to her conversation. I'm amazed that she's allowing me into her life despite the trouble I've caused her.

When I look back at Devon, she glares at me and sighs in frustration. I half expect her to ask me my intentions next, but she says, "She likes peonies. The season is short, so don't miss it."

My eyebrows rise in surprise. "Thank you for that."

Devon's eyes narrow at me again, judging. "Don't fuck this up."

I nod in affirmation before returning my attention to Allie. Leaning down, I whisper, "You want to grab another drink and get some air with me?"

She squeezes my wrist and whispers back, "Yes, please."

We get two fresh cocktails and find a quiet spot with a bench in the courtyard outside. It's May in the desert, so the days have been blazing, but the nights are warm with a slight breeze occasionally blowing through.

Settling my arm across the bench behind Allie, I consider her little pink dress and all the skin it exposes. "Are you cold?"

"No, it's perfect outside." Still, she inches a little closer to me. "Warm desert nights like this are my favorite," she says, smiling up at the sky.

"This will be my first desert summer," I look down at green eyes framed by thick black lashes that beam back at me, "but I can already tell I'm going to love it."

"I bet you will," she responds, watching the stars above as we lapse into an easy silence.

Devon's words repeat in my head. *You've already taken the one thing her entire future was hanging on.* If I hate the idea of taking anything away from Allie, how do I justify letting her lease run out? What am I offering her if I'm the source of her biggest problem? I see her strength, keeping a brave face for everyone around her, but she's being brave about losing something that I've taken away from her.

Allie points the toes on her right foot, admiring her strappy tan shoe. "You have a nice talk with Devon?" she asks, the laughter in her voice showing she knows it was anything but.

"Nice isn't the word I'd use," I answer.

Allie laughs, setting her cocktail down on the bench beside her. "She really loves me."

"She really does," I agree. "You want to know what we said?"

"Nope. Doesn't matter. I trust you. She likes you." Allie squeezes her hands on the edge of the bench on either side of her partially exposed legs. Now that she's sitting, the top of the slit reaches nearly to the fold of her hip.

"That's not the message I got."

"You must be confused, silly."

Moving my arm off the bench to rest across her shoulders, I ask, "Agree to disagree?"

"Have I ever?" Allie crosses her legs toward me, leaning into my hold. She's so close now and she smells *so damn good*. Warm and sweet. "Agreeing to disagree would be admitting I'm wrong. Which I never am."

"I'll keep that in mind."

"Good, don't forget it." Tapping her fingers lightly against my chest, she adds, "For the record, I'm happy Bea invited you tonight."

"So am I, sweetheart. You shine so brightly when you're with your friends. I've never seen you laugh so much."

She tries to bury her face in my shoulder to hide her blush, but I catch her chin between my fingers, drawing her eye to eye with me. "Why do you do that?" I ask, smoothing my thumb across the silken skin of her jaw before releasing her face.

"Do what?" she asks as she blinks up at me.

"Hide from me when you blush."

"Didn't know it was obvious."

"Hard not to notice."

"Blushing is so embarrassing. When I was in high school, kids used to make fun of me for it, and then my cheeks would turn even redder, so I started hiding my face. I guess I never stopped."

"I hate that they did that to you." The thought of anyone making her feel bad for one of her most adorable, and vulnerable, traits makes my own cheeks red, but for a different reason. "You're not looking for revenge, are you? I could help."

"No, but you're very cute," she laughs, the sound sugary and full.

I brush a loose curl behind her ear. "Try not to hide from me when I say this next part, okay?"

Turning on the bench so she's facing me directly, she brings her legs all the way across my lap, resting her feet on the other side of my thighs. "Okay," she nods emphatically, sending her hair out of place again. "I'm ready for whatever you've got."

I resist the urge to explore further as I run my fingertips up the length of her thigh, so I can make my point. "Your blush is beautiful. It's beautiful that you wear every emotion raw on your face. When you're happy, your smile is electric. You radiate joy. When you're laughing, your ponytail bobs, and your whole body dances. And when you're mad at me, and you try to glare—"

"Ugh, damn Bambi eyes and round cheeks," she interjects.

"Allie Walker, I never want to hear you curse your perfect features again." Clearly, I haven't gotten through to her yet. "It's fucking adorable when you do your little glare thing. I know you're mad. You get your point across, but you're too good inside for it to overtake your face. Bambi eyes and round cheeks are exactly what you should have. They suit you. Your remarkably kind heart. You are so thoroughly good from the inside out."

Allie blinks up at me, cheeks brighter than I've ever seen them, but she makes no move to hide. I can tell her mind is whirling behind her teal eyes, so I continue tracing a path up and down her leg and wait for her to speak. "That was—I'm not—I don't even—," taking a deep breath, she clasps her hands together across the top of her knees and tries again. "You make me feel seen. And not just right now. Always. Every day at our building."

The sound of 'our building' on her lips cuts me to my core. She's forgiven me for taking Station 19, but I haven't forgiven myself. Devon was right. She gives magnitudes more than she takes, and I refuse to be someone who takes from her. I want to be the man who gives her everything, no matter what I have to give up.

"You're impossible to miss, Allie." I tap her chest above her heart to emphasize my point before tracing her bare collarbone with my fingertip. "Did I tell you how much I love this tiny pink dress?"

"You didn't."

"Shame on me. You look delicious."

She blushes, giggling, as she reaches across me. She picks up the cocktail I took two sips of before abandoning in favor of having my hands all over the chestnut-haired goddess in my lap. "Can I have this?"

"It's all yours. You're not driving, are you?"

"Oh, fuck no. Devon's taking me home. She never drinks at work stuff." Through the windows of Devon's office, the party is winding down, meaning my time with Allie is almost up.

"How would you feel about playing hooky with me tomorrow?" I ask, continuing to run my fingers up and down her lush thigh.

"Hooky?" She leans her head onto my shoulder, giggling more.

"Yeah, blow off work. Spend the day with me."

"Would I get to sleep in?" she asks, but her playful tone suggests I've already got her.

"I want the whole day. I'd pick you up at seven."

Allie reaches across my body and wraps her right hand around my left wrist, pulling it up so she can read my watch. "That's almost nine whole hours away. Plenty of time for a good night's rest."

"So, that's a yes?" I ask.

"It is." She smiles. "Are you going to tell me what we're doing?"

"You'll find out soon enough."

Chapter 22
Allie

"You can be the life of every party, but it's okay to take a step back and give someone else a chance to shine occasionally." *-Allie's horoscope, May 19th*

Luke: You make me coffee every day, but I don't know how you take yours. That's not right.

Me: I'm indecisive. Different every day.

Luke: What would you like today?

Me: Lucas Pine, are you bringing me coffee?

Luke: That's the idea.

Me: Cold brew with a splash of sweet cream please.

Luke: Perfect. See you in 30.

Me: How am I supposed to know what to wear if you won't tell me where we're going?

Luke: We'll be outside. Maybe wear a hat. And lots of SPF.

Me: A hat?? And sunscreen. Not exactly a complete outfit.

Luke: It's casual. Anything you wear will be perfect.

Me: You continue to be infuriating.

Luke holds my hand as I jump down from his truck onto the gravel parking lot. He's enjoying keeping today's itinerary a surprise, so I didn't push the subject during our hour and a half drive. The smells of hot asphalt, burnt rubber, and engines revving are my first clues. "Is this some kind of car show?"

Reaching into his truck bed, he opens a cooler and tosses me an ice-cold bottle of water. "Stay hydrated, today. Okay?"

"Wait, did I guess right?"

"Let me have my fun, sweetheart. You'll find out soon enough," he says, leading me toward the sounds of revving engines. Luke walks with even more confidence than usual. Muscular chest proud, steps sure, and a permanent grin on his bearded face.

My stomach has been filled with butterflies ever since Luke asked me to spend the day with him, my mind wandering with the possibilities of what it could mean.

Luke's been teasing and flirtatious with me since we first met, but I wrote it off as something he must do with everyone. The way he's treating me lately feels different, more intentional. Affectionate even.

"Did I tell you how fucking cute you look in this?" Luke asks, tugging playfully on the bill of my hat. After his entirely unhelpful wardrobe suggestions this morning, I landed on cutoff denim shorts, cropped white tank top, white low top Converse that are still scuffed from the day we worked on my car, and a black baseball cap, silver anklet, and a little black backpack filled with Devon's good sunscreen and oversized sunnies for accessories. *Trying to look like I'm not trying. Not sure if I succeeded.* For his part, he's dressed the same as always, navy t-shirt and worn jeans.

"Yes, Lucas, it was the first thing you said when I opened the door this morning," I say, his attention making me giggle.

"Good, I don't want you to forget it." He slows his steps,

leaning closer to me. "Stick with me today, alright?"

"Who else would I be with?" I ask him, confused.

"I'm serious."

"Me too."

Luke shakes his head and laughs, picking his pace up again. "They're going to love you. Maybe too much."

Before long, a rainbow of canopy style tents, like the ones at a BBQ or the beach, comes into view. There are trucks and trailers everywhere, a lot like a tailgate party, except this one has motorcycles peppered throughout. Underneath the tents, people are sitting on lawn chairs and drinking beers out of koozies.

"Fucking Luke!" a boisterous voice coming from somewhere in between the tents yells. "Bringing a girl to race day?" The owner of the voice appears, and I recognize him immediately as Luke's friend Cameron. He's hard to miss. Excessively tall with wild red hair that fades into a washed out green, and colorful tattoos covering almost every inch of exposed skin other than his face.

Cameron rushes us, like he's about to scoop Luke up in a hug. I step back to give them room, but at the last second he turns toward me instead, wraps his arms around my waist, and picks me up all the way off the ground to spin me around in circles.

"Okay, that's enough," Luke says to Cameron after the second spin. "She probably doesn't remember you, Jesus."

"I remember Cameron," I say, laughing as he sets me back down on the ground. Luke moves next to me, wrapping his heavy, muscular arm around my shoulder in an undeniably possessive move.

"See? She loves me," Cameron says.

"Actually, I said I remember you," I correct, causing Luke to smile.

"One and the same, love. One and the same," Cameron says,

every word out of his mouth bordering on laughter. "But will you call me Cam, please? Or Hack?"

"Hack?" I ask him.

"Cameron Hacker," Cam says and then lowers into an exaggerated bow in front of me. "My mother calls me Cameron. My friends call me Cam, and my race friends call me Hack."

"I'll go with Cam."

"After today, we'll be race friends. Is this your first time racing a motorcycle?" Cam asks me.

"Wait, hold the fuck on." I hold my palms up flat in front of me and try to step backwards away from them, but I only land more solidly in Luke's hold. "Nope, nope, nope."

"Quit being an ass," Luke scolds Cam before squeezing my shoulder reassuringly and looking down at me. "He's fucking with you. We're only here to *watch* races."

"He's right. I'm sorry," Cam says, with a gigantic smile and not a stitch of remorse in his voice. "Although this shit is addictive. I'll bet you ten bucks and a warm beer that you'll want to try it yourself by the end of the day."

"Those are low stakes," I say.

"Exactly. That's how I get people to play along with me. Did it work?" Cam asks.

"Sure didn't," I deadpan, causing Cam and Luke to both laugh louder than the joke deserved as we head toward the tents.

"Are you racing today, too?" I ask Luke.

"Our boy gave up racing years ago," Cam answers for him. "He had to, otherwise no one else would ever win."

"Lies." Luke shakes his head. "I was not that good."

"He was that good."

"I haven't raced since juniors. Switched from racing to fixing bikes pretty quick," Luke explains.

The scene around us becomes more chaotic as we reach

Cam's tent. People are rushing between the enclosures, yelling things about missing parts and how little time they have left. The revving engines become more frequent, which Luke informs me is people testing their bikes before the races.

Everything in Cam's area is black and yellow, like an oversized bumblebee. His canopy tent is bright yellow with black metal legs. He's backed his truck, which is also bright yellow with black stripes along the sides, up under the edge of it next to a big black box trailer with yellow decals on the side, including one that says, *"Race Naked."* Luke slides two camping style folding chairs out of the bed of the truck and sets them up for us next to Cam's chair.

"What'll it be?" Cam asks, holding up two different beers, one in each hand.

"It's not even nine o' clock," I answer.

"Are you going to sit there and tell us you're against day drinking?" Luke asks, mistaking my pleasant surprise for judgment. He settles back into his bumblebee-colored folding chair like it's a throne, with his chest broad and chin held high, smiling wide. The cocky half-smile I've grown used to hasn't made a single appearance yet this morning.

"This is hardly day drinking," I say. "It's *morning* drinking. It's different. Arguably better." I'm all-in on whatever Luke has planned for the day, so I pick a beer, and Cam gives the other option to Luke.

"It's all coffee and water for me until I'm done racing, but you should enjoy," Cam says, handing us each a warm breakfast burrito wrapped in foil before disappearing from the tent.

Luke raises his can in cheers. "Thanks for being up for this."

"Of course!" I tap my can against his. "I can already tell I'm going to love it."

"And we haven't gotten to the good part yet."

"No?"

"The races are the real fun." He smiles broadly again, carrying himself with the kind of happiness I've never seen on him before.

"Even though you don't race anymore?" I ask him.

"Absolutely. I prefer it that way."

"You really like to watch, don't you?"

"You have no idea," Luke responds. I turn away and take a sip of my beer to hide the blush I can't quite explain.

"LP!" a young voice yells from behind us. A girl and two boys, probably pre-teens, walk into Cam's tent. They all have on leather coveralls that are unzipped and hanging from the waist over the top of their regular clothes. It's got to be eighty-five degrees out already. They must be sweltering.

Luke hugs each of the kids and introduces them to me. The girl with two long dark-brown braids and rich bronze skin is named Addison. The boys, Joshua and Dylan, look so similar with their shaggy long hair and sandy sun-tanned skin that I'm sure they're brothers.

"Where have you been this year? I almost won last weekend, and you missed it!" The taller of the two boys, Dylan, asks Luke.

"Fourth place isn't almost winning," Addison teases him.

"I got passed twice in the last turn. Wasn't fair," he argues. "Still better than you placed."

"One time. You've placed higher than me once this whole year," Addison scoffs at the boy and moves a few steps away from him. *Are these children racing motorcycles? Is that safe?*

"You're gonna watch today, right?" the shorter boy asks Luke.

"Of course. We both are," Luke says, sitting back down in his chair next to me and waving a hand between us. "Why else would we be here?"

"Are you his girlfriend?" The shorter boy asks me.

My cheeks flame red, and I choke on my beer. *Very smooth.*

Luke responds before I have to, "Allie is my friend." I have no right to feel the twinge of hurt in my chest that rises at his quick denial, but I feel it just the same.

"That's dumb. LP never has a girl," Dylan, the taller and likely older boy, replies. *Never has a girl? How is that possible?*

"Do *you* have a girlfriend?" Luke asks him, playful accusation in his voice.

The boy shakes his head no. "Yeah, that's what I thought," Luke says. "Worry about yourself." The other two kids laugh, and I do my best to stifle my own.

"Does my dad know you're here today?" Addison asks.

"I gave him a heads up," Luke replies, turning back to me. "Addy's dad is Rick Weaver. He's one of the best guys out here, on and off the track." Addison's posture grows proud at Luke's description of her dad. "I was his lead race mechanic for years." I nod along like I know what a lead race mechanic is.

"Yeah, and then he ditched us to move to the middle of the nowhere and open a bar," Dylan adds.

"Oh, I was there for that part," I say, taking another sip of my beer.

"Now, get out of here." Luke waves them away. "You're going to be late for your qualifier."

"Oh, shit!" The taller boy exclaims. He yells over his shoulder at us as the kids hurry away from the tent, "I'm number 383! Look for me, I'll be the one out front!"

"It seems like they really like you," I say to Luke after they've cleared the tent.

"Fuck if I know why." Luke shakes his head.

"They're racing motorcycles?" I ask, nodding in the direction the kids went. "They're so young."

"They're probably twelve or thirteen," Luke explains, like that's a perfectly normal age to be racing anything. "Cam and I were that age when we started."

"We were what age when we started what?" Cam asks, reappearing and sitting on his truck's tailgate.

"We were the same age as Bill's boys and Addy are now when we started racing," Luke says.

"Oh, shit yeah. Probably younger. Fifteen, twenty years ago now," Cam agrees. Picturing Luke and Cam at that age, hanging out around racetracks and visiting the adults they liked, just like those kids were, brings a smile to my face. I bet they were adorable. "Of course, our parents didn't have money like their parents do. Luke and I were always coming up with new money-making schemes to support our motorcycle habit." Cam laughs. "Some things never change."

Luke reaches over and places a light squeeze on my thigh just above my knee, the same way he does when we're riding two top. "Did I tell you Allie's a great mechanic?" he asks Cam, pride clear in his voice.

"I am not!" Leaning forward in my chair, I clarify for Cam. "Luke replaced my starter, and I helped a little."

"She did the whole damn thing herself. I barely touched the car," Luke says.

"Bull. Shit," I say with exaggerated emphasis on both syllables.

"I dunno, Allie. Luke's the best mechanic I know. If he says you're good, I'm with him," Cam says, jumping down off his tailgate. Well, stepping down is more like it. *He's so fucking tall.* "I'm going for a walk to clear my head before qualifiers. See you two cuties later." He pulls cordless headphones out of his pocket and pops one in each ear before disappearing from the tent again.

"He never sits still, does he?" I ask Luke.

"No, never." He chuckles and smiles warmly in the direction of his best friend. "Never has. Cam's all energy. Gotta get it out somehow. Today's a big race for him. He's lined up to get a couple of big new sponsors, and he'll be able to move up to a higher racing league for next season depending on how this one plays out. His last two races didn't go as well as he wanted, so he's got to pull it out today."

Luke speaks about Cam with genuine care and affection. The way he knows so much about him, his struggles, the specific details of his life, reminds me of how close I am with Devon. For the first time, I'm realizing how much he's had to do by himself in Palm Springs. I've always thought he was kind of a solitary guy, but maybe that's not it at all. Maybe his community is somewhere else.

My phone buzzes in my pocket, and I pull it out to see a new group text.

Devon: Your location is showing as the middle of nowhere. Do I need to come out there?

Sadie: I wanna see where you are! Share with me too!

Bea: You'd better write back soon. Dev's losing her shit over here.

Me: Sorry!! forgot to check in. I'm safe. We're watching motorcycle races.

Sadie: Thank you for sharing!

Sadie: Wow, that really is nowhere.

Me: I'm being rude. Got to go.

Sadie: Have so much fun, Al! Call me tomorrow, so I can hear all about it!! Eeeee, I'm so excited for your motorcycle date!

Me: I don't think it's a date.

Bea: It's a date.

Devon and Sadie both like Bea's last text, and I shove my

phone away.

Luke gets stopped multiple times while we're on the way over to the track. Evidently, every single person here is thrilled he's back and they all say racing isn't the same without him. Dylan wasn't joking when he said, 'LP never has a girl,' either, because each person expresses shock to see me with him or does a terrible job of trying to hide their surprise. Luke makes a point to include me in conversations and occasionally drapes a mildly possessive arm over my shoulders.

His warning to stay close to him makes a lot more sense now. There are not many women here, and a lot of single guys. More than a few of them start to check me out and then turn away when they notice Luke. The introduction of me as his 'friend,' stinging a little more each time.

The juniors' qualifier is first, and Addison places higher than both of the boys, filling me with a little girlie pride. After juniors, we get to the "good" races, and Cam places third in his qualifier.

I'm stunned at how much fun the races are to watch, far more exciting than I'd expected. Kind of like riding on one with Luke was so much better than I'd imagined it could be. His passion for motorcycles is making more and more sense to me.

On our walk back to Cam's tent, we run into Rick, the man who Luke used to be a mechanic for. He wraps Luke in a huge hug, just like everyone else has. I never would have guessed a race day would include so much hugging. *But maybe that's Luke's way?*

When we reach Rick's trailer, Luke introduces me to Rick's wife, Kiara, who's almost a twin image of her daughter, with the same rich-bronze toned skin, long dark brown hair, and welcoming smile. When Luke leads me to 'go see what kind of mess the new guy had made of Rick's bikes,' she stops him.

"I'm sure she's seen enough motorcycles today to last her

a lifetime." Stepping in between us, as if the matter is already settled, she says, "Come on. Let's sit and talk instead."

Luke checks with me briefly, making sure I'm okay staying with Kiara before walking away with Rick. It's the first time he's left my side all day, and even though he's leaving me with a married woman who seems perfectly nice, he's still protective.

Kiara gets us both giant cups of iced tea, and we settle into chairs in the shade of a canopy. "This is the first season I can remember that Luke hasn't been at the track every weekend. He always talked about opening his own shop or opening a bar like his grandpa's. When we heard he found a way to do both, we were so proud. As much as we wanted to, we couldn't hold it against him that he was leaving our team."

Skye mentioned their grandpa being Luke's motivation for opening a bar the day she visited, and now Kiara's bringing it up, too. This woman knowing him so much better than I do leaves me jealous. *What was his relationship with his grandpa like? What was so significant about this bar?* I was awful to him for so long about Station 19, it's no wonder that he's never mentioned it.

"Luke worked on Rick's bikes for years. He used to take care of Addy when she was really little so I could watch the races, he'd even babysit occasionally so we could do date nights," she says, giving me a knowing smile when I'm way too obvious about adjusting in my seat to get a view of the subject of our conversation.

"I got to meet your daughter earlier. She was with a couple of boys who race juniors, too."

Kiara sips her iced tea, smiling. "They all admire him, grew up with him. He has such a big heart, that man, but I'm sure that's old news to you."

My cheeks heat. It would have been old news to me if I'd been seeing him clearly from the beginning, but I was blinded by my anger about Station 19.

When it's clear I'm not going to pipe in with recent anecdotes about Luke's big heart, Kiara continues, "We miss him terribly. We all knew it was coming, but it's hard to imagine him being happier doing something other than working on bikes at the track."

Kiara tells me stories about Luke fixing bikes in record time and getting into trouble with Cam when they were younger. He was even at her and Rick's house the night he found Betty. I learn more about his history in this one conversation than I've learned from him in the last few months. Her family has a significant role in his life, and I'd never heard of them until a couple of hours ago. The realization stings that Luke had this whole life before Palm Springs that I know nothing about. *Because of course he did.*

"We're all planning on coming out for his grand opening at the bar. Does he have a date set for that yet?"

Holy fuck. The question is like a punch to the gut, but not because he's opening a bar where *Turbine* currently is, but because he hasn't even mentioned it to me. Of course, he's planning on doing a big grand opening, and of course his friends know about it. *Of course, of course, of course.* I've been disappointed every time he introduced me as his friend today, but am I even that? "Um, well," I stumble over my words, trying to mask my flush of embarrassment with literally any information. "My lease is up July thirty-first, so a month or two after that?"

"Oh." A flicker of understanding passes over her face, and her tone softens. "You own the coffee shop. That's how you two know each other."

I nod in affirmation.

"You weren't planning on leaving until he came along, were you?" I shake my head no. Kiara nods and then says the last thing I'd expected. "I bet that's just killing him."

Killing him? No. That can't be true. "I don't think so. He's never said anything like that, anyway."

She scoffs then leans in close to me, her kind face bordering on stern. "I'm going to fill you in on some things, Allie." *Doesn't she realize how much she already has?* "Luke is one of the best men I know. I guarantee he's one of the best men you know. He brought you out here today for a reason." I wonder again what that reason might be. "You're the first woman he's ever introduced to us, and we've known him a long, long time." She looks over her shoulder at him and Rick walking toward us and then back to me. "He will do anything for the people he cares about, especially the women. You are on that list now." With another quick glance to make sure he's not close enough to hear, she finishes. "Do not waste it."

He has done a lot for me, but that doesn't mean he cares. It's in his nature to be nice. He brought me the ladder when I was trying to hang curtains, curtains that he knew I was only hanging to block him from my sight. *Curtains that only got used for one weekend, but that's beside the point.* He took care of me when I had cramps. He walks me out at night. He moved all that fucking furniture for Devon. That's normal stuff to do for someone you don't care about. *Right?*

Chapter 23
Luke

"Some things you don't want your Grandad's advice about." - *Grandad Ernie, after twelve-year-old Luke discovered a stack of Playboys.*

"Join me for dinner, sweetheart?"

"Of course," Allie replies with a scoffing laugh, as if having dinner together is something we do every night. "Where should we go?"

"I have that handled."

"Handled? Like you made reservations?"

"Handled." We aren't going to a restaurant. I've spent the whole day introducing her to people, catching up with friends, and trying to keep every guy at the track from ogling her. Tonight, it's only the two of us. I'm not sharing her with anyone, and she is getting my full attention.

"When you picked me up, I figured we'd be going to brunch or something. This was so unexpected."

"In a good way?"

She beams up at me from her spot on the other side of the bench seat in my truck. "In the absolute best way. I think I might be totally obsessed with motorcycle racing now. Actually, I know am. I'm totally obsessed with it. The energy at the track is electric." I chuckle at her use of electric, the word that always comes to mind when she smiles. Every time I looked at her today, it lit up her entire face. "When can we go again?"

"Whenever you'd like." My plan in inviting Allie today was to let her experience my world. I hoped she would like it, feel the excitement of it, and her response was better than I imagined. "They have races every weekend during the season, always at different tracks. I can check the schedule, but I think the next time they're out here is in July."

"Count me in," she says, pulling her left leg up onto the bench seat between us and turning to face me. It's a struggle to keep my eyes on the road when I can feel the full weight of her attention on me.

Reaching across, I squeeze her knee. She doesn't shy away from my touch, and I realize she never has. Well, not since that first time I threw her over my shoulder and carried her out of my shop. I can't blame her for that one. She could have walked out without getting hurt; I was just being a dick. And I wanted to hold her. "I liked having you by my side today."

Watching Allie at the track revealed a new side of her, the side that fits into my world. Seeing her on the backdrop of asphalt and motorcycles that I've defined my life by, felt like snapping the final piece of a puzzle into place.

A sense of pride filled me more and more with each new person who was captivated by her presence. Cam's been sold on the idea of her for months already, telling me he's never met someone more perfect for me and asking when I'm going to get my shit together and make it happen.

Even Kiara, who can be tough to impress, liked Allie. Kiara's protective, like a big sister, after watching me grow up at the track. I wouldn't be surprised if their conversation was a mirror of the talk Devon gave me last night. Although, it couldn't have gone too badly. Before we left, she told me, "She's got it bad." It's tempting to believe her.

"I liked being there with you," Allie says, tempting me further. She's still turned sideways on the seat, watching me, but when I turn on a dirt road, she pulls back and swivels around. "Where the fuck are we?" She laughs. "What happened to dinner?"

"We're on our way to dinner."

"You know I'm not going to be fishing for my dinner or some shit, right?"

"You won't have to kill your dinner. We're almost there."

"I didn't expect you to be so big on the surprises, Pine, but I'm into it." She moves on from the subject of dinner immediately, settling back into her seat and recounting the details of Cam's race for me, the way someone would recount the highlights of a movie when they're walking out of a theater. "I thought there was no way he'd make it, but then he finally passed that guy on the blue bike." She covers her pouty pink mouth with her hand, interrupting herself. "Don't tell him I said that. I always believed he'd win. But anyway, it didn't look like there was space for him to fit his bike past the other guy, but he fucking did it!"

The amazement in her voice when she talks about my best friend shows yet another reason she fit in so perfectly today. She knew nothing about racing, but jumped right in. "He's notorious for going for the tightest gap, pulling off passes no one else would dare to try."

"That doesn't surprise me one bit. He's really..." Her voice trails off as I park the truck. Dozens of massive wind turbines come into view, each tower topped with three long propeller-like blades. The setting sun casts a yellow light against the white behemoths, creating an impressive view. She points up through the windshield toward one that's casting a shadow across the truck cab where we sit, only its tower visible. "You know these are the reason I named my coffee shop *Turbine*? I'm obsessed with them. I even have a tattoo of one."

I had a good idea that's how she picked her coffee shop's name, but the tattoo is a surprise. "Oh? I've never seen it."

She raises her eyebrows suggestively and bites her lower lip in a way that tempts me to peel off every piece of clothing she's wearing until I discover where she's got that tattoo hidden.

"I fell in love with them the first time Devon and I drove down here from Oregon. I'd seen some before, but out here there are so many, and they're lined up so perfectly, like gigantic protectors of the desert." Allie's speaking picks up speed in the adorable way it always does when she's excited about something. She unbuckles her seatbelt and slides closer to me on the bench seat, waving her hands to emphasize every other word. "Did you know they're like twenty-something stories tall? I looked it up once. And the tips of the blades are moving way the fuck faster than the center part that's connected to the tower. Like, 200 miles per hour, I think. I bet you can't even get that fast on a motorcycle."

She can't really think that. "Of course, I can."

"Bullshit!" she exclaims, mouth dropping open incredulously.

"What's your guess at my top speed, then? Since 200 is out of the question."

In a move that's rare for Allie, she takes a breath and considers my question for quite a while before answering.

Finally, she says, "135."

I don't bother stifling my laugh. "I've done that in a car. Motorcycles are light. They have a higher horsepower to weight ratio than anything else you can drive. There's nothing to stop you from getting over 200."

"Except maybe sanity. Or a will to live." Allie lengthens the last word in each sentence. "Self-preservation..."

"You worried about me, sweetheart?"

"No." She answers too quickly for me to believe her, "But I am worried about your concept of a restaurant. Aren't we supposed to be having dinner? As amazing as these bad boys are," she gestures up toward the turbine's blades again, "they can't feed us."

"I told you there'd be dinner. Never said anything about a restaurant." I get out of the truck and walk around the hood to open her door, but she's already getting out by the time I make it around.

"You could let me open your door."

"Oh, didn't realize that's what you were doing," she says, accepting my hand as I help her down. Immediately, she has her phone out, and she's snapping pictures of the turbines and the increasingly vibrant sunset.

Leaving her to enjoy, I lay out pillows and blankets in the truck bed, pull a full spread of meats, cheeses, fruits, and crackers from my cooler, and put on a band I know she likes on a Bluetooth speaker. Then I sit on the tailgate and lean forward to enjoy my favorite view— Allie Walker. She snakes through the field of precisely lined wind machines, their shadows growing longer with each minute as the sun settles closer to the horizon.

When I moved to Palm Springs, romance was the last thing on my mind. I've been saving and prepping for fifteen years, getting ready for my shop and my bar, so as soon as that inheritance kicked in I'd be ready.

Station 19 is an ideal situation, one I never expected to find. I chose it because I wouldn't have to sacrifice my passion for bikes in order to fulfill my dream of opening a bar and becoming the kind of man Grandad wanted me to be.

But Allie is a wrench in that plan in the worst and best way. Her joy is more important to me with every moment she's in my life. How can I take anything away from this woman? What kind of man would I be if I took away the thing she wants most? Grandad wouldn't have been proud of that, and neither would I.

We're the only ones around for miles, and Allie's wandered far enough into the desert that I could cover her from view with the tip of my thumb. Turning around, she calls something out to me and jogs in my direction. Her loud, bubbly laugh carries all the way to me.

Allie reaches the truck, still laughing, and braces her hands on her knees to catch her breath. "Sorry about that. Didn't realize I'd gotten so far away."

"Don't be sorry. You're adorable," I say, getting down off the truck bed to greet her and tugging on the bill of her baseball cap. *She looks so fucking cute today.*

She blushes at my words, and instead of turning away, beams a smile at me. "Is there food?"

"Sure is." Wrapping my hands around her soft waist, I lift her onto the tailgate before getting back up to join her.

She squeals in surprise at my touch before scanning the meal I've laid out. "Did you make me a truck-bed-charcuterie dinner?"

My intention was to cook Allie a proper meal for dinner tonight, but my little sister talked me out of it. Skye's *I miss my stupid big brother* call came through while I was in the produce section at *Ralph's* on my way home from Devon's party. She told me taking Allie back to my place was very presumptuous, even if my intention was only to cook for her, and insisted I do something 'casual and cute' instead. She then spent ten minutes on a video call directing me to which cheeses, jams, and tiny pickles I needed.

"Skye said it counts as a proper meal."

Allie's ear-to-ear smile tells me it's a good thing I listened to my sister. She kicks off her shoes and says, "She was totally right." Getting on all fours, she makes her way deeper into the bed of the truck toward the blankets and food, and I swear she points her ass directly at my face to fuck with me.

We each get comfortable in makeshift cushioned seats, using the truck bed's walls and the back of the cab for support. I resist the urge to draw her into my lap and feed her every bite myself, so we end up sitting across from each other, snack-meal spread out between us.

Allie comments on how *yummy* or *tasty* each bite is, never eating the same combination twice. Every few minutes, she declares a new favorite and makes one for me to try. The appeal of this slow, interactive way to share a meal becomes clearer each time she holds out a new tiny sandwich offering.

"Why did you invite me today?" Allie asks as she hands me a gorgonzola, salami, and spicy mustard on a poppy-seed cracker combo.

For months, Allie and I've been living parallel lives through our shared glass wall. Even when we don't talk, she's a constant presence in my day, making drinks for regulars before they even walk in her door, while I'm on my side of our building turning wrenches and polishing chrome.

I've memorized her wardrobe to the point that I know every time she wears something new, which is often. She notices when I get a haircut. I know when she has a new favorite album, because she plays it on repeat over the speakers at *Turbine* for days on end.

We've spent so much of our time together while we're both working that I meant what I said last night when I asked her to play hooky. I needed to get her out of Station 19. All day there's been an undercurrent of energy like we're getting away with something. Like we've put away all our responsibilities, so we can play.

"I wanted more of you." It sounds greedy, but that's where I'm at with Allie, greedy for more.

"You always say things that make me blush."

"It's intentional."

Allie's blush turns even pinker now and she turns away to examine herself in the reflection of the cab's window. She takes off her hat, makes a sound of disapproval, and fingers through her hair before securing it up in a big claw clip. Her blush returns when she looks back at me and realizes I'm watching her.

"I know you thought the hat was adorable, but I was over it. Sun's down now, anyway."

"I like this too. I can see you better."

"You see me every day."

"Trust me, I know it's a privilege that I can look through that window and see you whenever I want." I scan her face for any sign of apprehension at my words, but she only smiles and leans toward me. "But today was even better. You're usually so busy taking care of everyone else that you don't get a chance to slow down and enjoy things for yourself. I've never seen you so at ease with yourself."

Allie doesn't respond immediately, instead reaching for a sleeve of crackers and returning it to its box. Following her lead,

I open the cooler and start putting away the meats and cheeses. *Is she ready to leave, already?* I watch her twist the lid back onto a jar of jam. Her motions are easy, body language loose. She doesn't look upset, but it's unusual for her to stay quiet for this long.

"What do you mean when you say, 'at ease with myself?' Do I not normally seem like that?" Her voice is curious, timid, like the concept of ease isn't something she's considered before this conversation and she's worried about what I meant by it.

I take in the now empty space between us after packing up our dinner, four feet of blanketed truck bed. *Too far.* Moving closer, so we're side to side instead of facing each other, I lean against the cab of the truck. She adjusts in her spot, making room for me and resting her knees against mine, the casual closeness like a gift.

When I press a comforting squeeze onto the bare warm skin of her thigh, just above her knee, she visibly softens. "You're in your element at *Turbine*, but you're always *on*. I only get to experience one side of you." Her brows draw together in concern, or maybe confusion. I give her leg another squeeze, leaving my hand to rest on her knee.

"It's a good side. You make people feel seen, and that's really something. You're always thinking about what you can do for someone else. You're in control when you're at work, so everyone else can relax and have a good time."

Allie nods her head slowly, agreeing with each point I make.

"Today, I got to see what you're like when you're along for the ride and relaxed. You let me run the show." She let me take care of her today and didn't fight me for a second.

A timid smile, one that's new to me, spreads across Allie's lips. "You were different today, too."

"Oh?" I raise my eyebrows in question.

She giggles. *And fuck, it's adorable.* "You were more relaxed than usual. Those people are really *your* people, aren't they?"

"They are."

"You were bolder with me than usual today, too," Allie says, quickly enough to show her nervousness at the words.

"Yeah?"

She cocks her head exaggeratedly to the side, nervousness gone as soon as it appeared. "Yeah," She leans in toward me, "and a little possessive." Leaning in to match her brings me close enough that her scent fills my nose.

Most days she carries with her the stoic scent of ground espresso beans, filled out by lemon and coconut. Today, the espresso is missing. The light smell of her sweat from being in the sun all day comes through, combined with the lemon and coconut, making her smell like summertime and spontaneity. It's impossibly sexy.

I lean in another inch, soaking up as much of her as I can. Her eyes register my closeness, and she sucks in a quick breath.

"Do you like that?" I lean closer still and ease one hand underneath her bent knees, the other behind her back. She makes a surprised squealing sound and smiles up at me. I'm close enough to catch her pupils dilating when I pull her legs across my lap. "When I'm possessive?"

She laughs quietly, her breath skating across my jaw as she leans her head back further to look me in the eye. "I usually hate that shit, but I like it with you."

Pulling Allie closer until she's sitting sideways across my lap, the warmth of her skin tempts me. I indulge myself in it, running my nose all the way down the column of her neck, starting behind her ear and ending at her collarbone. She hums in pleasure as I do.

The press of my hand against the small of her back causes

her to arch deliciously into my hold. Inhaling a deep breath against her chest, I cannot resist tasting her for another moment. Opening my mouth against her smooth skin, I trace the lines of her collarbone with my lips. She hums a satisfied sound and presses more firmly against me. *Fuck.* I make another pass, this time letting my tongue taste the salty sweetness of her skin.

Her whimpers get louder as I taste up her neck with light kisses. She swirls her hips, the heat of her center pressing against my leg.

"Luke." Her voice is a needy whisper that runs straight to my cock.

I ghost my lips back and forth along the column of her neck. "Yes, Allie? Is there something you'd like?" She whimpers again and presses herself harder against me. When I draw her earlobe between my teeth, she twists her fingers into the hair at the base of my skull and says my name again, this time an all-out whine.

Pulling my face up so it's level with hers reveals wild eyes and cheeks that I'm sure are flushed with a delicious blush that's only hidden by the evening's fading light. I run the back of one knuckle down her cheek and across her jaw. "Fuck, you're incredible like this."

Allie leans into my hold, her desire palpable. "Like what?"

"Undone." I lean in as if to kiss her, and she closes her eyes in anticipation. I place a soft kiss just to the side of her mouth instead.

Long lashes part, and her eyes fly open, giving me the closest thing to a glare she's ever managed. "Tease."

"Needy," I say, before I place a kiss on the other side of her mouth.

"Luke." She whimpers my name, dragging it into three syllables.

Resting my forehead against hers, I speak against her lips. "Absolutely incredible." My cock is straining hard against my jeans, and Allie's whimpering and writhing in my arms. *I've teased us both enough.*

She whimpers one more time, loudly, and I capture her mouth with mine, swallowing the sound with the kiss we've both been aching for.

Chapter 24
Allie

"Don't ignore the person who's right in front of you. Great love is within your grasp." -*Luke's horoscope, May 19th, that Allie conveniently forgot to share with him.*

Finally. Luke presses his lips against mine with such tantalizing intent. He kisses me slowly, deliberately, reveling in each second just as much as I am.

There's always a special thrill the first time my lips meet someone new. But this is different. This isn't the rush of gaining the attention of the hottest guy at a party, or a chaste kiss on my doorstep after a first date.

This is powerful. There is deeper meaning behind this kiss than any kiss I've had before. *And the feel of it.* His lips are firm and soft, teasing and insistent. He's rocked me to my core, and I haven't even gotten any tongue yet.

While Luke is slow and tender with his lips, he's buzzing with desire for more at every other point in which our bodies meet. For more of me. The muscled arms I've admired time and time again through our glass wall are wrapped firmly around me, crushing me against his body as his thundering heart beats against my ribcage.

He places one soft, teasing kiss against my lips after another. Each time I think he'll deepen it, he pulls away briefly, then picks it up again with another sweet, closed-mouth caress. *It's infuriating, and I love it.* Luke's lips moving against mine feel like a new beginning and a perfect ending at the same time.

From the first moment I saw him, I've been drawn to him, captivated by him, impossibly turned on by his stern face and all the muscle that's currently wrapped around me. When I found out who he was—what he'd done to me—my desire was overshadowed with a mix of hatred and jealousy, though I never stopped imagining all the things our bodies could do together. With each second his lips are pressed against mine, I melt a bit more. *How did I ever hate this man?*

I'm growing needier and more impatient. He holds me up, one hand behind my head, the other at the small of my back, but from my position sitting sideways across his lap, I can't get the contact I want.

He stops our kiss and draws back from me, his cocky grin sexier than ever only inches from my face. He raises a thick brow at me. "Is there something you want, sweetheart?" He leans down to kiss me, but instead of my lips, he goes back to the tender spot behind my ear. I moan, loudly. "Mm," he hums, grazing his lips along the curve of my jaw. "I want to learn everything you like. Give you everything you want."

I open my eyes wide. "Is it not clear? I want you to kiss me."

He drops a light kiss into the dip between my lips and chin. *So close.* "Am I not kissing you?"

"I was just thinking about how you've made it impossible

for me to hate you anymore. But you're no less infuriating than you were three months ago, Lucas Pine."

He rubs a slow, grazing circle on my back with his fingertips. "I love it when you say my name like that."

"Are you even listening to me?"

He grazes his lips across my jaw on the opposite side. "I am." A light kiss behind my other ear. "I promise."

"Then why aren't you—"

He kisses my lips again, cutting me off. His tongue teasing against mine for just a second before he pulls away again. "I know what you want. You want me to kiss you." He presses his lips against mine in another agonizingly short kiss. "Properly."

"Then why did you—"

He cuts me off with a kiss again and then speaks against my mouth. Our lips touching with every syllable. "You like it when I'm in control?"

He places another quick kiss to my lips before I can speak, so I only hum an agreeing, "Mmm," in answer.

"Then let me be in control, Allie." Another kiss. "You can't make me rush this. I've been dying to have you pliant in my arms since the moment I first saw you. I *will* savor you." He kisses me again, properly this time, open-mouthed, allowing our tongues to ease against each other. *Fucking finally.*

The feel of his tongue inside my mouth, of him inside of me, ratchets up my desire even further. The tentative, teasing kiss of moments ago is gone, and it's replaced with a kiss of visceral desire. I am melting beneath his arms further and further with each second he holds me pressed against his lips.

"Is that better?" he asks.

"Mmhmm." I nod. He holds me there for long moments, stern brows suddenly not so stern, jaw still chiseled, but without its usual tension. The sound of music cuts through the tension of our locked gazes. *How long has that been on?* "I love this song."

"That's why it's playing."

"I never told you that."

He places a tender kiss to my forehead. "You've played it every morning for three weeks."

"Before you get there, though."

Luke chuckles, his breath ghosting against my lips. "Allie, I'm always there in the morning. I work by your lights and don't turn mine on."

"Stop it. You're lying."

He smirks. "You knew."

I suspected. When I do more dancing in the mornings, I get a lot more texts during the day. *Okay, I knew.*

"Will you dance with me, Allie?" His question surprises me.

"Right now?"

"Right now, sweetheart."

"Okay." I never liked it when he called me sweetheart until this moment. Now, I feel the sweetness in it. The tenderness. Like I'm dear to him.

He removes me from his lap with control and gentleness before helping me to my feet and pulling me close to his chest. Wrapping one arm tightly around my waist, he holds my hand up in the air near our shoulders with the other and rocks me gently with the beat of my current favorite song. We're dancing in the bed of his truck, right underneath one of my favorite local landmarks, which I never told him about, but he guessed; listening to my favorite song, which I also didn't tell him about; and we had my favorite dinner, which I never told him about either. *He's far more observant than I gave him credit for.*

"What's on your mind, sweetheart?" he asks, placing a kiss on my temple.

"How come you introduced me to everyone as your friend all

day?"

"It felt presumptuous to introduce you as anything else."

What a perfectly reasonable answer. Ugh. Luke releases my waist and spins me around before pulling me flush to his chest again and bending forward so our foreheads press together.

His voice is low and measured when he speaks again. "Would you have preferred I told everyone that you're the woman who's occupied every moment of my thoughts since I first saw her? That I work early and stay late every day, so I don't miss a glimpse of your electric smile or your ponytail bobbing when you laugh? That I want you as close to me as possible? That your presence in my life has turned every plan I've ever made upside down? That watching you exist is the greatest joy I've known?"

He patiently awaits my response, guiding me in a slow, easy dance as I roll his words over in my mind, trying to commit each of his confessions to memory. *The greatest joy he's known* beats the hell out of *my friend Allie.* "That would have been preferable, yes."

He chuckles, not expecting that response. "I'll keep that in mind for next time, but for right now," his smile skips right on over cocky, flirtatious, and teasing and lands firmly on predatory, "I want to find that tattoo."

In an instant, he's picked me up and wrapped my legs around his waist. He's kissing me again, tongue insistent between my lips as he walks me backward and sets my ass down on top of the truck's cab, still warm after baking in the sun all day.

My legs fall to the sides of his hips as his hands waste no time peeling my shirt up from the hem. When he releases our kiss so he can pull the shirt over my head, I laugh, telling him, "It's not under there."

He places a finger to my lips. "Let me have my fun."

"In that case, you should probably check under here, too," I say, hooking my thumbs under the straps of my butter-yellow lace bra and dropping them down my shoulders.

The light of the nearly full moon reflects in his chocolate brown eyes as he takes me in, running his warm, calloused hands over every inch of my exposed skin in a slow perusal from my waist and tummy, over my back and shoulders, then smoothing over the pillowed tops of my breasts, before finally coming to rest around my ribs, thumbs teasing against my lace covered nipples. "You are exquisite."

He leans in close, pretending to search for a tattoo he knows isn't there, dropping kisses on each place he's inspected. "I want to kiss every inch of this lush body," he says before removing my bra and drawing one of the soft mounds into his mouth while massaging the other.

A wave of tingling warmth spreads through my body. I want to tell him—*Fuck, I can't remember what I wanted to tell him.* Every word I try to say dissolves on my tongue and all I manage to get out is a moan as he trails kisses across my sternum and sucks my other breast into his mouth.

"No tattoos there," he says with a satisfied smirk as he comes up for air.

"You're never going to find it if you keep checking with your mouth," I laugh.

"Are you complaining about my methods?" He cups his hand against the front of my shorts, rubbing against my clit with the heel of his hand. "I was planning to try the same thing here, but if you'd rather I didn't, I can stop."

"Please don't stop," I plead, thrusting against his palm for more friction.

"I was hoping you'd say that," he whispers against my

lips as he pulls off my shorts, revealing the thong-half of my matching set. *Did I put these on today, just in case I wasn't alone when I got undressed later? Of course not.*

After inspecting my right leg from ankle to hip and finding no tattoo, he kneels down and kisses all the way up, "Just to be sure."

"You know tattoos don't taste like anything, right?"

He looks up at me from between my thighs, "If I didn't know better," he kisses higher up, at the soft junction where my leg meets my core, "I'd think you don't want my lips all over your delectable body," he says, before his warm mouth meets the center of my soaked panties, and my hips instinctively rock against his face.

"Goddamn, you're delicious." He licks my glistening arousal from his lips while splaying the fingers of his broad hand across my stomach, pushing me flat on my back against the roof of his truck.

Standing over me, he hooks his fingers into the sides of my panties and draws them slowly down and away from my body. I wish I could bottle up the look in his eyes as he takes in my fully naked body for the first time. With his pupils blown, he stares at me in awe. "Allie," he utters my name in a long, slow whisper. Running a reverent hand from my jaw all the way down my body, he dips his fingers between my thighs and weaves teasing lines through the wetness there, causing my eyes to flutter in pleasure.

I'm laid out bare before him, while he stays above me, his cock cutting an impressive outline against his jeans. I'm aching to feel it moving against me, moving in me, but when I reach for it, he stills my hands.

"Not yet, sweetheart. Let me take care of you."

He draws a finger up to my clit, now slick with my wetness,

making slow, rhythmic movements that drive me wild.

"Okay," I gasp, tugging at the hem of his shirt, "but this has to go at least."

Without a word, breaking eye contact or slowing the hand at my clit, he uses his other hand to rip his shirt over his head, tousling his already mussed hair further. *Good fucking fuck. Is he serious with this body? Like, I knew something incredible was under there, but sweet fucking hell.* He's a tree trunk of a man. Imposing, thick, and muscular. I'm going to lick every inch of him as soon as he lets me.

His cock strains hard against his waistband as he continues his movements on my sensitive bud, not entirely unphased by me practically drooling over his chiseled torso. *Good.* He keeps up the motion at my clit, unrelenting, while I move my hips to match his rhythm.

Usually, shortly after someone has me naked, they're covering my body with theirs, pressed against me, and getting inside as fast as possible. But Luke is leaving me exposed in the warm desert air, eyes bouncing over my moonlit body with heated adoration, unable to choose one place to focus.

"Fuck." Luke runs his unoccupied hand through his hair. "I could watch you like this forever." His gaze focuses on the hard peaks of my breasts. "Touch your nipples for me, baby."

Baby? That's new. His command sends a jolt to my already throbbing sex. I obey immediately and enthusiastically, rolling each of my nipples between my thumb and forefingers as tantalizingly as I can.

"You're such a good girl."

Good girl? Fuck, I am so into that. A gush of wetness swells in my sex at his words. His movements at my clit pick up speed, building heat. *He better not move his fingers away from this exact spot.* "Yes, just like that, please," I beg him, continuing to roll my nipples between my fingertips.

Luke listens, keeping the same movement, pressure, and speed. *What a concept.* Using a finger from his other hand to dip inside me, he moves both hands in tandem, working me close to my peak faster than I thought possible. His eyes are trained on mine now, watching for my reaction to every one of his movements.

He curls the finger that's deep inside me, drawing a cry from my lips. My own hands still, no longer able to focus enough to toy with my nipples.

"You make the most delicious sounds for me." He adds another finger inside my wet heat, massaging the extra sensitive tissue there. "I knew you would."

He lowers to his knees, unrelenting in his attentions, and presses harder with his fingers, working me even closer to orgasm. His name escapes my lips in a cry this time. Luke kisses along my hip bone all the way down to where his fingers move against me. "You smell delicious." He inhales against my sex, and then his tongue replaces his finger on my clit, expertly maintaining the same rhythm and pressure without missing a beat.

The added moisture and texture of his tongue is exactly what I need. He keeps the fingers inside me curved, hitting my g-spot over and over in time with his tongue on my clit. "Oh, yes! Right there. That's it." Words of praise spill from my mouth. "Oh, fuck, Luke. Don't stop. Please. Yes!"

I twist my fingers into his hair, pressing into his lips as my orgasm burns through me like a wildfire, starting at my center and running in a frenzy all the way to my toes. He keeps working me through every wave, and doesn't stop until he feels me relax again.

Gathering me in his arms, he pulls me off the roof and sits

down in the bed of the truck, nestling me across his lap, his hard cock pressing against my ass. He makes a show of licking the wetness of my orgasm from his lips as he presses me tight against his chest.

"Never did find that tattoo," he says, running his hand up my left leg.

Turning in his lap, I point my bare hip and its turbine tattoo up at him.

"Well, that's the cutest fucking thing I've ever seen," he says, caressing it softly.

Eagerly, I graze my fingers across his hard length. "Your turn?"

Luke's hand stops my movements again. "Believe me, I cannot wait to have you wrapped around my cock in every way imaginable, but tonight is about you." He kisses me, and the taste of my orgasm on his lips makes me even more wild for him. "Plus, if I leave you wanting more, I know you won't turn me down for a second date."

Chapter 25
Luke

"Hate to break it to you, kid, but sometimes your mother does know what she's talking about." -*Grandad Ernie, to thirteen-year-old Luke, after his mom's advice about a girl in his class turned out to be right.*

Me: Morning gorgeous.
Allie: Morning handsome! Interested in today's horoscope?
Me: Interested in anything you have to say.
Allie: "Trust your intuition Little Goat."
Me: It did not say little goat. Where are you getting these?
Allie: Don't question my methods.
Me: When do I get to see you today?
Allie: I'll be in at 10.
Me: I'll be waiting.

Fixing bikes is not only my work, but also my meditation. Working with my hands calms my mind and helps me focus.

Well, it does on every day but today. I've been looking at

the same four cylinders all morning, barely making any progress because all I can focus on is the time crawling by until I get to see Allie again.

Betty whines by my feet, looking through the window for the woman who occupies my mind. I scratch her behind the ears. "I know, babe. Our girl will be here soon."

It hasn't even been twelve hours yet. Apparently, now that we've crossed the line from friends who pretend they don't flirt with each other over to people who are honest about wanting each other, I've lost my ability to wait patiently.

I thought I was fucked before, mind constantly occupied with Allie, but now that I know how she looks laid out before me, playing with her perfect nipples and responding so thoroughly to every touch of my hands? I'll never be able to think of anything else again. Nothing could be better than Allie, vulnerable in my arms and trusting me to take care of her.

The moment I first saw her through our shared glass wall, I knew she was gorgeous. Then I spoke to her, and she spit fire at me, and I knew she was special. The idea of fate always seemed like a copout for people who don't want to take responsibility for their own choices. That was until I heard Allie call me a jackass, and instead of pissing me off, it made me want to hear every word she'd deign to share with me. The feeling in my gut that she's meant to be in my life started building right then.

My mom would say it's intuition. She's always insisted that she has feelings about people, and I've always dismissed it. She believes when she meets someone, she can sense what their purpose in her life will be, what their 'story together' will be.

She claims the intuition extends to me and Skye, too. The first day she met Cam, she told me he was going to be the brother I never had. Even at thirteen, I told her that was a load of woo-woo bullshit. She couldn't possibly know that about this kid after spending three minutes with him. But, as often happens with my mother, she was right.

I wrote it off as one of many lucky guesses. For every time my mom's intuition is right about something, it's wrong about another. After Skye's recent foray into psych classes, she told my mom she didn't have intuition—she had confirmation bias. It did not go over well.

Still, I've avoided mentioning Allie to her, half because she might confirm that Allie is destined to be in my life, half because she might contradict it.

Unmistakable movement from the other side of the glass wall catches my eye. *Allie.* The swing of her hips is just exaggerated enough that I know it's intentional, making her walk look like a dance.

The sight of her brings me immediate relief. She laughs at something a customer says, throwing her head back and revealing the delectable neck I now know the taste of. I take a step closer to the window, watching her as she tucks some wild hairs behind her ear and twists her fingers around an earring that hoops around her soft earlobe. I know the taste of that earlobe now, too. Every inch of her is salty and sweet.

She's wearing a cut-off band t-shirt and a yellow skirt. It has to be her favorite color. She wears it so often and so well. After seeing her wrapped in that soft yellow lace last night, it's mine, too.

She laughs, her chestnut ponytail moving expectedly along with her shaking shoulders, and then her eyes catch mine. She blushes but doesn't look away. I could watch Allie all day, *and most days I do*, but this time I need to be closer.

A minute later, Betty and I are standing at the register, up close with the girl of my dreams. When she comes around, squatting down low to greet Betty, she looks up at me, beaming her electric smile.

"Morning, Lucas Pine."

"Morning, Allie Walker. You look perfect today."

She looks down at herself, as if she forgot what clothes she had on and laughs. "I slept in this shirt last night."

"Pity I missed that."

"Lucas Pine!" she says my full name again, this time with a little censure and a big smile.

"Alright, Betty," I call my dog back to me. "It's my turn."

Allie laughs, standing up, "Your turn for what? You want me to pet you?"

Closing the two-foot distance between us, I draw both of her hands around my neck. "Yes, please." Then I pull her close with one arm around her waist and the other cradling her head. She melts into my touch, rising up on her toes to meet me for a kiss.

I didn't think it was possible, but her lips are even more plush today than they were last night. I release the kiss reluctantly.

"That was yummy," she giggles, squeezing my hand before turning and moving to the espresso grinder. "Someone left peonies on my desk," she tells me over her shoulder.

"Did they?"

"How'd you know they're my favorite?"

Sitting on the closest barstool, I reach down and scratch Betty behind the ear as Allie gets back to work. "Devon, wants you to be happy more than she doesn't like me."

"I told you she likes you," Allie tsks.

"She doesn't."

Allie throws a loose coffee cup sleeve at me with accuracy that would have hit me in the forehead if I wasn't quick enough to catch it. "She does."

"Agree to disagree?" I hedge.

"Have I ever?"

"Not yet, but I'm not giving up." She's too much fun to tease.

She tries to glare at me, sparking laughter in both of us.

"How was your morning, sweetheart?"

Allie grumbles under her breath before pasting a smile on and saying, "It was great."

"Bullshit."

"What? It was. I got to sleep in."

I soften my voice. "Tell me what happened."

She sighs, setting the black handle into the espresso machine much harder than usual. "Can we not?"

"Sure." I lean forward on the counter. "If that's what you need. But it seems like it's not what you need."

"You're so annoying," she huffs and doesn't say anything more until she sets an Americano on the counter for me. I spin the cardboard cup between my fingers, seeing the turbine in the *Turbine Café* logo in a new light. *It's the same one she has tattooed on her hip.* She speaks up again before I can comment on it. "I toured a building this morning, and it was fine." Her voice is all wrong. Tight and quiet. "Just like every other building I've toured. Nothing is special like," she lifts a hand up, waving it around to indicate that nothing is like Station 19.

Makes sense she was trying not to say anything to me about it. She loves this building. She belongs here, but I'm the one who gets to keep it. *It's not right.* "Sounds shitty. I'm sorry."

"Don't feel bad. I'm figuring it out."

"Do you have any other places lined up?"

She hesitates, unsure. Yet again, I want to scrap my bar and make this all go away for her. "I'm going to check out a place in Joshua Tree next month that seems promising," she finally says, quietly enough for only me to hear.

"Isn't that an hour away?"

"Forty-five," she hedges, "—ish. But the building looks incredible, and I could buy it, not just rent."

Moving *Turbine* an hour away? To another city? Is she going to live there too? *No. That can't happen.* "I'll go with you to see it."

"Would you really come?"

"Of course." I may loathe the idea of her moving that far away, but I'm not making her continue this search without help.

She rounds the counter, squeezing her arms around me in a tight hug, and speaks into my chest, "This helps a lot. Thank you."

~

Me: I love watching you through the glass.

Allie checks to make sure no one else has eyes on her and then shimmies her perky tits at me.

Allie: Really? I hadn't noticed.
Me: You mean it had nothing to do with your skirts getting shorter over the last few months?
Allie: Don't flatter yourself. It's the heat.

But she tugs up the waist of her yellow skirt, making it that much shorter. I haven't accomplished anything today; all I can think about is her taste on my lips. How wet and hot she was, pulsing around my fingers as she came. I've been half-hard all day.

Me: Want to get out of here?

Allie: I wish. But I already told my new barista he could leave early. Gotta close.

Me: Can I have you after?

Allie's talking to a vacationing family, probably making up a detailed itinerary of the right things to do, like stop by the visitor's center to see the architecture, and the ones to avoid like afternoon hikes, because it's way too hot for that, before checking her phone. The wait is worth it. Her eyes go wide, cheeks flushing, as she looks for me.

Allie: Goddamn I hope you mean what I think you mean.
Me: I do.
Allie: Should have never let the new guy leave.
Me: We'll make do.

Allie starts rushing through the familiar motions of her closing routine a half hour early. I try to focus on stripping the engine I'm rebuilding this week, but her flirtatious green, doe eyes and teasing little skirt won't let me.

Me: Can I make a song request?
Allie: That sounds fun.
Me: Killing in the name
Allie: You think playing Rage will clear customers out? You're underestimating how much people love punk.
Me: It was the first song I saw you dance to.

Allie stares at her phone in confusion, blinking slowly, before realization dawns.

Allie: YOU WERE HERE THAT DAY?? YOU SAW ME???

Me: I was. I did.

Me: You were perfect.

Allie: I cannot believe you. That is so embarrassing. I'm not putting it on.

Me: Missed an opportunity to say fuck you I won't do what you tell me

Allie: Motherfucker

She holds up her middle finger, blows me a kiss with it and turns away fast enough that her skirt flutters up, revealing more than a hint of ass cheek. *Fuck. How much longer until those cheeks are in my hands?* She only has one customer left, sitting in Brian's chair by the front window. He stays there, scrolling on his phone for the next half hour, and still hasn't moved five minutes after the official closing time.

Me: Want me to make that fucker leave?

Allie: Lucas Pine. He is a nice guy. He's probably just not paying attention.

Me: A nice guy would pay attention to the closing time.

Allie walks around, pulling the dark shades for every outside window. When she has to reach across the guy to get the last shade, he finally gets the picture and leaves. She locks the door behind him.

My girl is within my reach now, the glass wall between us a feature, not a flaw. Leaning back on my workbench, I watch. I've been watching Allie since February, but this is the first time I've had her to myself like this in our building.

Allie: You just gonna watch me work?

Me: Hoping to watch you do more than that.

Allie looks at me, opening her mouth wide to feign a scandalized response, before running a teasing finger back and forth across her waistband.

Allie: You're on.

She turns up the music enough for me to hear it very clearly, right as it switches to a Miguel song. Her hips move in tune with the beat, teasing me with the occasional body roll, as she finishes up her final closing tasks.

Her laugh comes through the window, carrying over the loud R&B music. *Goddamn, she's perfect.* Allie's all confidence, joy, and soft curves. She's thriving, putting on a show for me. No woman could ever be more perfect.

Me: You are incredible. so sexy.
Allie: I know, right?

Allie flips a switch, so only dim overhead lighting remains.

Allie: I'm all done, I'll come to your side.
Me: Stay. I need to watch you before I get to touch you again.

She walks over to me, stopping just on the other side of the row of tables that line the glass wall, close enough to show me the pink blush of her cheeks, lust-filled doe eyes, her full chest rising and falling with anticipation. Untying the apron at her waist, she drops it to the floor as she takes a step closer.

Allie: Tell me what you want to see.

Me: Take your hair down for me.

She releases her hair, letting it fall around her shoulders in sensual chestnut waves. I imagine the smell of fresh coconut shampoo as she shakes it out, using her fingers to comb it into place. Closing her eyes, she drags her fingertips down, starting at her temples, combing through her hair to graze the column of her neck, cupping around her breasts, sliding past her hips, and coming to rest on the sides of her thighs.

A pleased smirk crosses her lips when she clocks me running my hands through my own hair, keeping them occupied until I can touch her.

Allie: How was that?
Me: It was perfect. you're perfect.
Allie: What's next?
Me: Take your shirt off for me.

Allie plants her hands on the table in front of her, one of the damn pedestal tables, like the one she fell off months ago.

"Stop! You'll get hurt!" I yell through the window.

She laughs as she pulls herself up onto the circular tabletop that wobbles briefly before settling, placing herself directly in the center, so it'll hold steady beneath her.

Me: Fuck. that was dangerous.
Allie: Calm down. You wanted my shirt off. yes?
Me: God Yes. but do you have to do it up there?
Allie: It's the best view. Promise.

She brings herself up to kneeling on the table, making us eye level. Running her hands up from her thighs, she squeezes and touches all the way until her fingers catch the bottom of her cropped shirt on both sides. She's slow about it, pulling first one side, then the other, lifting it just high enough to show me the light blue lace bra she has on before dropping it and running her hands down and up her body again.

She continues teasing me, taking half a song to tantalizingly peel her shirt off over her head, before throwing it across the room. The dim light shines like a halo over her increasingly exposed body.

Arching a brow in question, I point to her hand and draw an invisible line up her body to the pink nipples that are visible through the sheer material of her bra.

Allie bites her bottom lip, worrying it between her teeth as her painted fingertips pull her bra straps down around her shoulders. She traces all along the detailing on the top of the cups before circling each hard nipple with her index fingers over the taunting blue fabric.

Sinking down on to her heels, Allie spreads her knees wide, barely avoiding exposing her sex to me. She writhes on the table as she draws the lace down, exposing her perky breasts.

"You're incredible," I say aloud, even though I doubt she can read my lips.

But she mouths back, "I know," as she begins to play with the rosy tips of her nipples. *She knows exactly what she's doing to me.*

Me: Are you wet for me sweetheart?

She notices the vibration from the phone on the table next to her, but holds up a finger, as if to say, "Give me a minute."

I watch with rapt attention as she plays with her body, her hips continuing to grind in the air above the table as she twists,

olls, and pinches her nipples. She removes the bra and tosses
t to the floor next to her apron and shirt before picking up her
phone again.

Allie: Of course.
Me: Show me.

Allie's face has been flushed pink since she dimmed the
lights, but that text is the thing that makes her ears flame
ed. Still, she doesn't shy away. She clearly loves sex, loves
ouching, loves her body, and she's discovering in real time how
much she loves an audience of one.

She runs her right hand down her body, in the now familiar
easing trace along her curves, before using it to pull her skirt
up, achingly slowly. When she reveals herself to me, I stand,
aking a step closer to the glass.

Her skirt is folded up over her waist, knees still spread wide
on the table, exposing light blue underwear that matches the
bra she just tossed across the room. *Does she wear exclusively*
coordinating underwear? Fuck. Allie draws her bottom lip
between her teeth, swiveling her hips impatiently.

Holding up two fingers, I point to the junction of her thighs,
hen turn my hand, making a curling motion in a mimic of the
movement I want to watch her recreate.

She does as I asked with no teasing preamble, as turned on
as I am. She slides two fingers underneath her panties, moaning
t the contact. Drawing them out, she holds up her fingers for
ne, glistening with her wet arousal in the low overhead light.

I run my hands through my hair as I take a step closer. I'm
lying to touch her, but I've imagined this scenario with Allie
dozens of times, and I'm not done with her yet. I lift my two
ingers to my mouth, and Allie's lips curve into a wicked smile

before I've even finished the motion. She sinks both of her fingers between the pouty lips of her mouth, turning so I have a full view of how deep she's pushing them down her throat.

I clench my fists at my sides. *Not yet.*

Allie: Hurry the fuck up and get over here. I want you inside of me.

Fucking hell. I can't wait to get that filthy mouth wrapped around my cock.

Me: One more thing I want before filling you with my cock.
Allie: Goddammit you're hot.
Me: Show me how you make yourself come with those sweet little fingers, baby.

Allie wastes no time, pulling her panties to the side, revealing herself to me fully. I step all the way to the windowed wall now, my hands grasping against the glass. She starts playing with her clit, first with slow circles, gradually building up speed.

Allie moans, loud enough that I hear it through the window, then dips the two fingers she's been teasing herself with into her glistening lower lips. She pumps them in and out, in time with the fingers that work her clit.

She's mesmerizing. An angel. A vixen. A goddess. I don't deserve her. Don't deserve to watch her. Care for her. Salivate over her exposed body.

But somehow she believes I do because she is showing me everything. No shyness. No inhibition. She's in ecstasy, holding eye contact with me while she pleasures herself so deliciously, moaning as her hips move, riding her fingers.

I press against the glass as both of her hands move faster and she comes apart, never taking her eyes off of me. The second she pulls her hands away, I'm moving for the back door.

Chapter 26
Allie

"You can accomplish anything you put your mind to, but you may find it more satisfying if you allow someone else to help you along the way." *-Allie's horoscope, May 20th*

I'm on my knees, bra pulled down, panties to the side, skirt folded up at my waist, coming down from the best orgasm I've ever given myself when Luke comes in the back door of *Turbine.*

He watched me with hungry eyes while I touched myself, devoured every movement of my impromptu striptease. *Well, impromptu for me at least.* He was ready for it.

It has not escaped my notice that Luke likes to watch. At first, I thought maybe he hated me just like I hated him, so he watched to catch me fucking something up. Every time I felt myself starting to crack under the pressure of losing Station 19, I knew I couldn't let it show, because he would see.

But as time went on, I recognized the way his features would soften when he watched me. Jaw less tense. Brows less stern.

He wasn't watching because he hated me. It was the opposite. Eventually, when the stress got to me, I'd find him through the glass wall, and our eyes meeting would bring me comfort. I started wearing dresses because I knew he would be watching. I even bought a couple of new ones. *Okay, more than a couple.* And he commented on every single one.

And of course, he's been flirting with me since day one. So, *show me how you make yourself come* shouldn't have been a surprise. I'd never masturbated in front of anyone before, but I loved touching myself for him.

Now, I'm left craving his touch so badly, I can barely stand it. I watch as he takes determined steps toward me, seconds feeling like minutes. The hard cock that's been taunting me all night strains against his pants. *Fuck, he looks powerful.*

He's always in control, almost stoic.

Doesn't raise his voice. Doesn't lose his cool.

I've tried to get a rise out of him in every way imaginable, starting with towing his truck on that first day. Turns out, all it took was giving in to this attraction for him to come unraveled.

When I start to turn away from the window toward him, my table wobbles a little, but he's there in an instant, balancing it and stopping me from moving. In one motion, he picks me up and presses his lips to mine.

It's only been a matter of hours since he kissed me last, but I've craved his lips on mine every second since. He kisses me deeply, and I sink into it, only letting go when he sets me down on a nearby chair.

"You have to get rid of these tables." Luke shakes his head.

"Why? I love them."

"They're dangerous, Allie," he says, dropping to his knees in front of me.

"I've never gotten hurt."

"Only because I keep saving you." He pulls me so far forward on the chair that I have to balance on him to keep from falling off as he draws one of my nipples between his lips, sucking, kissing, massaging with his tongue. When I run my fingers through his hair, he moans, sending vibrations into the sensitive tissue of my breast. Once he's satisfied with the treatment on that side, he looks up to me. "Although, I would like to keep that one." He points over his shoulder at the table I was kneeling on moments ago, the same one that has a chip out of the finish on the edge because I fell off it and knocked it over. "For memories."

"I think I'll keep them all," I say, trying to be light-hearted and flirtatious, but his attentions have my voice coming out breathy instead.

Still on his knees before me, Luke nips at the tight bud between his lips before pulling back, rubbing his thumbs back and forth across my thoroughly ravaged nipples. "I'll take you shopping. I'll buy you new ones. I'll *make* you new tables if you'd like, but I won't allow you to get hurt."

"You're impossible," I murmur.

"So are you," he laughs, rising up to kiss me. Holding me steady, he feels around my skirt until he finds the zipper and pulls it down before immediately peeling off it and my ice blue thong. "You wear the sexiest things under your clothes, sweetheart. Do you always match like this?" he asks, stretching them across the fingers of one hand, fascinated, before tucking them into his back pocket.

"Hey! Those are part of a set. Give them back." *Part of a set that I bought weeks ago in case he took my clothes off one day. But still.*

"Your matching lacy sets are sexy and adorable, just like you." Where has this man, with the praise pouring from his

nouth, been all this time? *I'm obsessed.* "And I'll get you as
nany as you want. A replacement for this pair, even. But I will
be keeping these."

"Lucas Pi—" My protest is cut off by his face, diving
between my legs. The coarse hairs of his beard tickle roughly as
he kisses up the tender skin inside my thighs, over my mound,
and sucks my clit between his lips.

He squeezes my thighs in approval as I cry out. The man
obviously loves the sounds I make when he touches me, and
my body has never responded to anyone else the way it does to
Lucas Pine. He looks up briefly, saying, "You are delectable,"
before bringing his mouth back to my clit. My fingers twine into
his hair, and he moans again. *He really likes that. Good to know.*

He draws one broad hand away from its spot at my hip and
slides two fingers into my wet heat. My second orgasm builds
quickly, still sensitive from the first.

His tongue makes rhythmic swipes across my clit, in time
with the fingers he's curling into my g-spot. *Goddamn, he's
good at that.* He's on his knees before me, broad shoulders
flexing as he draws me closer to another orgasm.

"A little harder," I whimper, and he immediately increases
the force of his movements inside me. When I feel myself pulse
around his fingers, I moan, pulling hard on his hair, and he
responds with a growl of his own. I break apart, legs shaking, as
my climax vibrates through every inch of my body.

Luke pulls back, kissing along the insides of my thighs
before rocking back on his heels and standing to his full height.
Most of the time when he stands over me like this, I feel
intimidated. *But not now. Right now, I feel safe.*

"Am I finally going to get to touch you?" I ask, breathless.

He pulls his shirt over his head with one hand, dropping it
to the ground behind him and revealing abs I want to run my

tongue over. *Holy shit. I bet I could.* Reaching out, I pull him closer to me by his belt loops and lean forward. I run my tongue against his torso, starting with one defined ab muscle, before moving on to the next, making a point to rub my bare breasts against the hard rod of his cock through his jeans.

"Fuck, Allie," he breathes out, twining his fingers in my hair in the same way I had mine in his a moment ago.

I continue licking across his muscled body while my hands join in my exploration, running across his low back and around his hips, before coming around to his belt. I look up at him, wanting to lick something else. "You going to let me touch you tonight?"

"Fuck yes, I am. Any way you want to, sweetheart."

"Then lose the pants, Pine."

He kicks off his work boots, then pants, leaving him standing before me in nothing but boxers.

"Those too." I pull at his waistband, and he drags them off, revealing a cock that is frankly, beautiful. *Like, this cock is art.* I want to learn how to paint so I can make a portrait of it and put it on my nightstand to admire before bed. He's long, thick, and hard with a bead of pre-cum on his rounded tip that I cannot resist licking off.

I get on my knees before him, drawing his length between my lips and swirling my tongue around the head. The hard concrete floor bites at my knees, but I'll take the bruises if it means I get to indulge myself with Luke's glorious body.

"Fuck, Allie. That is so good. Have I mentioned how perfect you are?" he asks, breathless.

"You have, but I can't hear it enough."

He tucks a stray lock of hair behind my ear. "You are flawless."

Bringing both of my hands to his base, I take him deeper

into my mouth, working his entire cock. Luke has been my fantasy for longer than I'm willing to admit. But finally being with him, touching him, getting to do everything I've imagined doing, has me turned on beyond reason. My sex is throbbing after two orgasms, and I still want more.

Luke groans, moving his hips in time with my mouth, holding my hair a little tighter. I suction my lips and hollow out my cheeks as I move faster on his cock.

"Sweetheart," his voice is strained. "You're going to make me come if you keep doing that, and I need your sweet cunt wrapped around my cock before that can happen."

The moment I release him, he picks me up and wraps my legs around his waist. He squeezes one of my ass cheeks. "You've been flashing this juicy ass at me all day. I've been dying to get my hands on it." Sliding the hand lower, he continues. "And these thighs. Damn, every inch of you is a temptation."

Adjusting me in his grip, he slides his cock against me. "Still so wet for me. You have a third one in you, gorgeous?"

"Mmhmm," I nod and moan, making no effort to mask my enthusiasm. *I want him inside me. Now.*

"I've been tested recently. I'm good. You want me to wear a condom?" He nods over his shoulder to where his jeans are discarded on the floor.

Writhing myself against him, I answer in rushed, breathless words, "No STDs. On birth control. Fuck me, please."

He chuckles low but wastes no time walking me back and pressing me against the windowed wall. The cold glass is a pleasant shock compared to the heat radiating between our naked bodies. Lifting me, he lines himself up with my entrance and brings his lips to mine, searing me with a kiss as he pushes his ludicrously immaculate cock into me.

I moan against his mouth, feeling myself stretch around him. He pulls back, then pushes in a little further, repeating the motion over and over, going a touch deeper each time. When I bite his lower lip, his hips jolt, and his thrust finally brings him fully seated inside of me.

"You are perfection," he whispers against my lips as he continues to pump in and out in slow, deliberate strokes. "You're taking my cock so well. I've been thinking about this tight little cunt," he punctuates the word cunt with a punishing thrust, "since you were squeezing around my fingers last night." He continues, shifting his hips, and hitting me deep and hard with every stroke. "You're so good at being mine."

At being his? I like the sound of that. Before I have a chance to analyze it further, he captures my lips in a fierce kiss, and I'm lost in the feel of him, pulsing, throbbing, aching, the tension in my body building up with every hard thrust.

With one hand planted on the glass above my head, and one wrapped firmly around my waist, he looks down at where we're joined. My eyes follow his, and we watch his cock slide in and out of me. "Look at you, Allie. So gorgeous when you take me."

"I want to come on your cock," I whimper against his lips.

"You'd better," he says, bringing me down onto his length in a brutal thrust.

Pleasure buzzes in my body from my center out to my limbs every time he hits my g-spot. I lose track of the sounds escaping my lips. Whimpering, moaning, crying out. He's relentless.

"That's it, sweetheart. Such a good girl for me."

The praise is what pushes me over the edge, and I'm an explosion of electricity, pulsing around the cock he continues to slam into me as I cry out his name with my climax. He pulls me closer, holding me against his chest as he groans, finding his own release.

His arms loosen their grip, letting me lean back against the glass, but he stays inside me, looking down again at where we're joined.

"Holy fuck. You are good at that," I tell him on a breathless laugh.

He tucks another rogue strand of hair behind my ear. "You are unbelievable. You're everything."

Chapter 27
Luke

"Told ya, should've had Luke do it. He's a damn good mechanic, better than the hacks over at Joe's shop." - *Grandad Ernie, about fourteen-year-old Luke, to a bar patron whose motorcycle broke down two hours after getting it fixed.*

Me: Morning gorgeous. When do I get to see you today?
Allie: Morning handsome! Got here early to clean up or else I would have gotten the worst kind of "Who closed last night" text from Marisol.
Me: Be there in ten.

There she is. The sight of Allie brings me immediate relief. She stands in the middle of her shop with her head thrown back in laughter that I can't hear through the window but that's also now familiar enough to echo through my mind.

My eyes shift to the table she kneeled on when she touched herself for me, the chair she sat in while I tasted her, and the part of the window she was pressed against when I got to have my cock inside her for the first time. Not a single smudge or fingerprint.

Me: Did you climb on that goddamn table to clean the window?
Allie: Someone gave me a wooden stool to use instead.
Me: Did you use it?

Voyeur Motors' back door opens, and Allie walks in. "I brought you breakfast," she calls, her bright voice bouncing around my shop as she walks over and places two coffees and a white paper pastry bag next to the disassembled Honda engine I'm working on.

Bouncing up on her toes, she twines her fingers into my hair as she comes up for a kiss. *Fuck, that is good.* Framing her waist with my hands, I lift her and set her on the tall wooden workbench next to the Honda's cylinders. "Allie Walker. No more crawling on wobbly tables."

"You're no fun." She pushes out her lip in an exaggerated pout, but she's only able to hold the look for a couple of seconds before she breaks into laughter. "Okay, fine! If you insist. I'll use the stool you gave me."

"Look at that. You will do what I tell you," I say, kissing her forehead.

Her protest gets caught in her throat, laughing. "For fuck's sake."

"You're a very good girl." My voice is teasing, but her eyes still light up at my praise as if I've unlocked the code that makes this feisty doe-eyed brunette melt for me.

Crossing her legs underneath her, she pulls a bacon and egg breakfast burrito from the bag and holds it out for me to take a bite. The smell must reach Betty because she emerges from my office a moment later. "Ooh, there she is," Allie squeals when Betty comes over, wagging her tail.

"No human food for Betty." I make my voice and my glare as stern as possible, but I know she'll toss the dog a piece as soon as I turn my back.

Watching Allie yesterday had me too distracted to accomplish much on this engine. Her comforting presence allows my mind to focus on the task at hand. She giggles and talks to Betty, giving her half of my gifted breakfast while I work on reassembling the engine.

"I have a question for you, Mr. Pine."

"I'm interested."

"I guess it's not a question," she hesitates, "Kiara mentioned that you're having a grand opening party for the bar."

My hands still. The grand opening is the last thing on my mind. I've avoided focusing on the bar lately, outside of the bare minimum I need to do to make it happen. The liquor license will be ready in time, and I've met with a few of the reps and vendors I'll need, but that's all. I know opening this bar means Allie losing *Turbine*, and me losing the literal window into her life that let me fall for her.

"Skye suggested it, and I told her to run with it."

Allie nods silently, encouraging me to continue.

Moving closer, I rest my hand on her knee. "This is the first I've thought of it since then, but if Kiara knows, Skye must be making progress."

"I'll just text Skye and ask her how I can help," Allie smiles. The heart on this woman. I'm taking away her building, tearing apart her business, and she's going to help me celebrate it.

"You don't have to. I know this has to be hard for you." I run my fingers back through my hair. "If it helps any, I feel like shit about it."

She rubs her hands up and down my arms. "It does not help. I don't want you to feel bad." She pauses when I avert my gaze. "Hey, look at me. Of course, you love this building. It's incredible. Any idiot would want it. How could you have known?" she asks as she grabs my face to bring me back to her. "No more of this, okay?"

"I don't like you comforting me because I did something that hurt you. I'm the last person who should be hurting you."

"Get over yourself, Pine." Holding up one arm horizontally in front of her chest, she says, "This is the bridge," then pushes her other hand underneath the *bridge,* saying, "Water under it. Let's move on, okay?"

Fuck, she's adorable. I won't really move on until I've found a solution for her, but I drop it for the moment. "Wait, you have Skye's number?"

"Obviously."

"Do you talk much?"

"Wouldn't you like to know?" She pushes on my shoulder. "Now, get back to work. I know you didn't get anything done yesterday." Smiling, she takes a long sip of her iced drink and stays sitting on my workbench, keeping me company long after it's gone.

～

The front door to *Voyeur Motors* dings as I finish scrubbing my hands before lunch.

"Hey there," Brian calls.

"Come to visit your bike?" I ask, pointing toward the rear corner where his restored BMW shines under the overhead lights.

"Something like that. Figure it's about time I make a decision about it."

"Oh, yeah?"

"I can't bring myself to sell it." He adjusts his black glasses on his nose. "Doesn't feel right, but I can't leave it to rot in my garage again, either."

"Any other ideas?" I take a seat on the leather couch and wave for him to sit in the chair across from me.

"You've done a beautiful job with it." He smiles broadly, crinkling the skin around his eyes. "Even better than it looked brand new."

"That's high praise."

"I mean it. People stare through the glass at it every day."

"They do," I agree. "Could be my favorite project ever, Brian."

He leans forward, looking back and forth from the bike to me a few times. "What if I leave it here for good? You could use it as a showpiece, couldn't you?"

I'd thought this exact thing myself, but it was too selfish to ask. "You don't have to do that."

"I know," he says, firming his posture. "I'm offering because I appreciate you, and I want the bike to have another life. It's right for you to watch over it."

"That's amazing." I take a breath, gathering my thoughts as I run my fingers back through my hair. "It's already helped me sell a few projects and would help show off what I can do."

"Exactly, and I can still see it whenever I want."

"Come with me." I stand up. "Let's figure out how we should display it. I could build a stage or a table, even put it on the wall."

Glancing through the window, I see Allie leaning across *Turbine*'s counter, talking with Hector and smiling over at me.

Chapter 28
Allie

"Don't be surprised when things start going your way. Eventually, your hard work will pay off." -*Allie's horoscope, June 12th*

Luke: You need to wear pants.
Me: PANTS?! It's already 90 out.
Luke: You know I love you in a skirt but if you want a ride to joshua tree on my bike you'll wear pants.
Me: You're infuriating. I hate you.
Luke: I'm not. No you don't.
Luke: Bring a backpack with a change of clothes.
Me: You could have said that in the first place.

The ride out to Joshua Tree is the longest I've been on a motorcycle, even with all the time I've spent two-topping them with Luke. My ass is a little numb, and it's a long time to go without getting to talk to each other, but it's mesmerizing too. It's amazing how much of the desert I miss when I make this drive in my car—with a roof.

Luke reaches back and squeezes my knee, melting me with his touch. I squeeze tighter around his torso in response, like I always do. We've fallen comfortably into step with each other. Being together is the most natural thing in the world. Decisions like how much time to spend together, what to eat, where to go, all come to us easily.

Four months ago, sharing a glass wall with the unfairly hot man who stole my dreams felt like a curse. Now it's a blessing. He's still unfairly hot, but he shares his body with me, so no more complaints on that front. And I know he didn't steal my building. He pursued his own dreams, and I can't fault him for that.

We're in a happiness bubble of watching each other all day while we work, sending naughty texts through the window, and sitting together at lunch, but it has an expiration date. Two more months of this bliss, and then I'll be somewhere else, maybe as far as Joshua Tree, and he'll be running a bar in my old place.

I'm trying to find the balance between reveling in the present and figuring out the future. *So far, I'm terrible at it.* But it helps a lot that's he's coming with me today.

Luke leans heavily into the turn as we pull off the highway onto a side street. *I swear, he's exaggerating the turns just so I have to hold on tighter. I don't hate it.*

We pull up to the building I've been stalking on Google Maps street view for weeks, the corner unit of a strip mall featuring sand colored stucco walls and a red tile roof with a covered patio that wraps around the front and side.

I've been harping on about character during this search and rejecting places in Palm Springs for their lack of it. While strip mall doesn't exude unique character—Joshua Tree does. There's something magical and undeniably vibey about this corner of the Coachella Valley. Being a part of this community could be a great consolation prize.

"Do you want to change?" Luke asks me.

"Feels a little odd to ask if I can use their bathroom and come out in a totally different outfit, doesn't it?"

Luke shrugs.

"I'll survive in pants, but thanks." Truth is, I don't have a change of clothes in the backpack. Figured I could surprise him with a backpack-desert-floor-picnic-lunch since he surprised me with truck-bed-charcuterie-dinner.

He handles the backpack and the helmets, so my hands are free to take notes and pictures and explore the building. The real estate agent gives a small pitch and hangs back to let me explore on my own. Luke doesn't say a word, letting me come to my own conclusions while he inspects structural things I'm not particularly interested in.

This unit was once a coffee shop, then a taco shop, and has been empty for a few months now. The interior is plain. Cream walls, concrete floors, and big windows on the corner walls that line the patio. My spot in Station 19 is an odd triangular-ish shape that Devon described as a design nightmare. This one's a normal rectangle. A blank slate.

Tables here, here, and there. I walk around, imagining the setup. *Couch here, more tables by the back wall, big plants on the east-facing window, and Hector and Brian's comfy chairs could go by the front like they are now.* A twinge of sadness tightens in my gut. Hector and Brian would come out here once to congratulate me, but who's going to drive forty-five minutes to hang out at a coffee shop all day? Not even those two. Not that I'd blame them.

Moving *Turbine* out here would be starting over in just about every way. Devon said it could be good for me. Maybe even force me to have a better work-life balance. Work a real schedule.

I could tweak the menu and finally drop the damn Cookie Explosion blended drink that I added on a whim years back without realizing what a pain in the ass it would be to make. Cookies, peanut butter cups, chocolate-covered espresso beans, dates, caramel drizzle, and sprinkles on top of the whipped cream. It's a monstrosity, and people love it. I took it off the menu once, and people continued to order it, due in large part to the "Quirky Things to Try in Palm Springs" article that's been making the rounds for ages. I even kicked up the price of every size. It's the most expensive thing on the menu, but people still order it.

The idea of burying the Cookie Explosion once and for all is appealing, but it's still nothing compared to losing Hector and Brian. *Not to mention Daisy. Or Marisol. Or any of my other staff. And there's no barre studio across the street for—*

"It's a little bigger than what you've got now, right?" Luke asks into my ear, his arms wrapping around me from behind, calming my racing heart. *How did he know I was about to spiral? Am I that obvious?*

"It is," I say, with forced cheer in my voice, leaning into his hold. His biceps press in around my arms, the hard planes of his chest firm against my shoulders. Arching my back, I rub my ass against him. "Maybe we should get out of here and trash this whole idea."

"Sweetheart, I cannot wait to have you again," he whispers into my ear, dark and low. "But we're here for a reason. Tell me more about what you see."

He's right. *I hate how often that happens.* "I love the windows and the patio outside."

"Where do you think you'd put the register?" He kisses my temple, letting go of my waist, so I can walk over and show him.

Once my feet are planted, hands up in the air to show I'm in the spot, he says, "Oh, I see it. You look good there."

"You think I look good everywhere."

"You do, but that spot is particularly good. You could make this work, sweetheart. Here, watch," he says, going out the front door and out of sight before walking back in fifteen seconds later. There's a little bell tied to the door that rings when he walks in. Seeing him there in his worn jeans and gray t-shirt from my spot behind the *register* I'm suddenly able to picture what it would be like to move *Turbine* here. From this spot, I could keep an eye on the whole place, but it's far enough from the door that I wouldn't get a wash of heat every time someone came in. I have a view of the mountains in the distance and cars going by on the highway.

There would be new faces. New regulars, lots of out-of-towners—which I love. Luke stands a few feet inside the door, hands in his pockets, sly smirk on his face, and it clicks that one of my regulars *would* still come here. *Luke.* No one else is coming forty-five minutes for coffee, but I bet he would. Could get here in thirty on one of his motorcycles, I bet.

We spend another half hour investigating the place, pondering the possibilities and taking pictures. Luke only speaks up to ask a few questions about safety and security, and when we leave I am truly, honestly encouraged and excited about moving *Turbine Café* for the first time ever.

～

Tapping on Luke's shoulder to signal he needs to turn right at the next street, I rush to get my hands back around his waist. He cocks his head to the side, in a silent, "Really?" but makes the turn, anyway.

I told him I knew where we should go for lunch, but it was easier if I gave him directions on the way. I'm sure he was confused when we drove away from town, but that's the beauty of being on a motorcycle. He can't ask questions. Much easier to keep my little surprise a secret this way. I guide him further into the desert for twenty more minutes, onto side roads and up to a hiking trail.

"We hiking in jeans today, sweetheart?" he asks once our helmets are off.

"Fuck no. There's a shady spot behind those rocks over there." The hiking trails within the actual national park are incredible. Stunning. And often crowded. Where we are now is just as beautiful, *according to me*, and much more private. Luke follows me for the three-minute walk to the shade. It's 105 out, not a cloud in sight, so that's all it takes to have both of us breathing heavily with the heat.

Pulling out the cooler bag that's in my backpack, I toss him a cold water to drink while I lay out the blanket, but he helps me set up our picnic instead. We have turkeys on rye, BBQ chips, and potato salad from the deli with the good mac 'n' cheese.

"This is adorable," he says, settling down onto the blanket and finally taking a big swig of the water.

"You seem to have a thing for surprise picnics. Felt like it was my turn."

His laugh is rich and full. "I have a thing for *you*."

Chapter 29
Luke

"If you don't ask for what you want, someone else will get it." *-Grandad Ernie, encouraging seven-year-old Luke to speak up at a family dinner when the mashed potatoes were almost gone.*

"It's too hot. I can't take it anymore," Allie says, fanning herself with the leather notebook she uses for notes about new buildings.

"Alright, sweetheart. I'll get you home."

"Don't be ridiculous. We've barely been here three minutes. I'm just taking off my pants."

Raising my eyebrows, I scan the area for other people. No other cars in the parking lot. No one on the trail.

"Don't worry about it. I picked a secluded place on purpose." Waving a hand towards my lap, she says, "You've got to be burning up. Takes yours off, too, and we can talk about the building."

"You want me to take my pants off so we can talk?"

"I want you to take your pants off, so you don't overheat," she laughs.

But I'm not thinking about taking off my own clothes. My eyes are locked on her, leaning back on the blanket, unbuttoning her jeans, working them off her hips and shimmying them down her legs, revealing smooth thighs and curved calves.

"Ahh," Allie sighs, "that is so much better." She sets the jeans aside, leaving herself sitting on the blanket, wearing pink and orange striped panties that probably have a matching bra under her pink cropped t-shirt. She pulls her hair back into a messy bun, pats around it with her hands, decides she doesn't like it, takes it down and ties it up again.

She goes about unpacking her backpack, like this is a normal occurrence. This fiery woman—who can't be bothered to wear pants—has me mesmerized with every swivel of her hips and shake of her hands.

"Lucas," she waves her hand in front of my eyes, "did you hear me?"

"You look like that, and you expect me to hear you?"

"Yes, I do. Get it together," she waves her hand towards my lap again, "and take off your pants."

"So we can talk. Right. Got it." Removing my pants reveals the evidence of her effect on me, hard and trying to escape my boxers. I'm pleased to see her staring, too.

"We're never going to have this conversation, are we?" she asks, inching closer to me on the blanket.

"It'll go better if we're not distracted. Maybe you'll be able to focus after an orgasm or two," I say, pulling her close to me and slotting my lips against hers.

She straddles me, swinging her legs around my hips and setting her striped panty clad ass in my lap, without breaking our kiss. She's warm, soft skin and tempting curves in my arms that still can't believe are familiar to me.

"I've been aching to feel you all day," she says, breaking the kiss only long enough to speak. She tugs at my boxers, releasing my cock then moves her hips, sliding her hot sex against my hard length repeatedly. *Fuck, she's magnificent.*

Pulling her panties to the side, my fingers find her soaked. Lubricated with her arousal, I move my thumb over her clit as she continues rocking against me. "You're so wet for me already, sweetheart," I say against her ear, biting the lobe, and showering kisses down her neck, kneading one of her perfect breasts through the fabric of her shirt while I keep up my movements against her clit with my other hand.

"Faster," she whimpers.

"You sound so pretty, telling me what you need." I increase the speed against her sensitive bud, watching her face, feeling her legs tighten around my hips, focusing on the rocking of hers that slicks her lower lips against my cock.

When I increase the pressure with my thumb, her entire body twitches, and she moans, gasping, "Yes, please," and writhing on my cock.

"Are you going to come for me, sweetheart?"

"I want to come around your cock," she practically screams, and it echoes in the surrounding valley.

"You can have whatever you want."

"Lay back and watch," she says, pushing on my chest.

Leaning back, I slide the fingers soaked with her delicious arousal into my mouth and watch as she lines herself up to take me in. The wetness of her entrance welcomes me as she lowers herself down. Her perfect, tight cunt squeezes around my cock, and I watch her lift herself up and lower back down again, riding along my length, using me for her pleasure.

Once she finds her rhythm, my thumb returns to her clit, and she shudders around me, stuttering in her pace for a moment before moving again.

"Show me your nipples, gorgeous?"

Hands flying to her shirt, she throws it down to the blanket, revealing a pink and orange bra that matches the panties she's pulled to the side, half framing the view of my cock sliding in and out of her. She pushes the cups of the bra low, showing me her hard rose-colored nipples.

Bracing herself on my chest with one hand, she uses the other to play with her nipples as her rounded breasts bounce in time with her movements.

She's a vision. Stray strands of hair escape her messy bun every time she brings herself down on me. Her cheeks flush with a mix of heat and arousal, freckles standing out against the pink of her cheeks. Teal-green doe eyes focus as she watches me watching her.

"You love being watched as much as I love watching you." It's a statement as much as a question. I want to hear her say it.

"I fucking love when you watch me," she says around gasping breaths.

"I could never look away."

Her eyes roll back when I find the rhythm and pressure with my thumb that I know will bring her over the edge. A touch faster than before, not too hard, tight circles. She continues to ride me until she breaks, crying out and pulsing around my cock. Holding her steady, I take over, thrusting up into her until I've found my own climax, and she collapses against my chest.

I run my fingertips up and down the length of her spine, never wanting Allie any farther away from me than she is with me still inside her. *This is where she belongs. Where I belong. We fit together perfectly, and she is mine.* "You were incredible. You look so beautiful when you make yourself come on my cock."

She giggles into my chest. "Not sure beautiful is the right word."

"It is."

She lasts for about thirty seconds after we're cleaned up and at least partially re-clothed before she starts the conversation back up. "What did you think of the building?" So business-minded when she wants to be.

"Your thoughts first. You've got to process it without my interference."

She details everything she likes about the place: size, windows, patio, view, charm of Joshua Tree, relative affordability compared to real estate in Palm Springs. I try to understand her points, to be the support she needs, to consider this as a serious option, like I have all morning.

But my mind keeps returning to Allie, *my Allie*, out here. So far away from me. How am I supposed to keep her from climbing on wobbly tables if she's an hour away? *What if someone tried to rob her? Or what if she gets cramps halfway to work and has to drive in pain like that? What if she's lonely?* She doesn't belong out here. She belongs at Station 19.

It's up to me if she gets to stay or not. I can make all of this go away for her, and I'm the jackass she used to say I was if I don't. Yes, Grandad told me I could learn anything behind a bar, but he also taught me being good to the people I care about is what matters most. He never told me I had to spend my inheritance creating a bar in his honor. Fifteen-year-old Luke decided that and never looked back. *Until Allie.*

I bartended for a decade and learned countless lessons. It wouldn't be rejecting his plan for me if I chose not to open the bar. And even if it were, it's time to let *my* plan matter. Wasn't that the whole point of moving to Palm Springs, to stop doing what everyone else wants and start doing what I want? I want Allie in my life. I want to be the man she deserves. And she should be with someone who wouldn't put her second to anything.

"I don't want you in Joshua Tree."

"Oh, I don't want me in Joshua Tree either," she laughs. "And it's not like I'd move, just have a drag of a commute. Believe me when I tell you I have scoured Palm Springs for a better solution." The tightness of her smile causes an echoing tightening in my chest. "This is the best option I have, and I will love it."

Drawing both of her hands into mine, I hold her gaze. "You do have a better option. Stay. Keep *Turbine* where it is. You belong there. Station 19 would be nothing without you. It's not right for me to take it away. I need you more than I'll ever need to open that bar."

Saying this to her lifts the weight from my chest I've been carrying around for months. It's the right thing to do. Allie gets to keep her spot, and the idea of her being close to me, indefinitely on the other side of our glass wall, washes over me in a wave of relief.

"Oh, you're so sweet. But I'm not staying," she laughs.

"What?" *Did I hear that right?* "Why not?"

She kisses me on the forehead like she's placating a two-year-old and explains, "Because I'm figuring this out on my own. I'm not taking anything away from you. Are you kidding? You've told me about your Grandad and the bar. It's a beautiful idea, and it's important to you. There's no reason for you to give it up."

"You're the reason to give it up, Allie. No bar could be more important than you are."

"Of course not. I never thought it was."

I'm at a loss for words, stunned. *Shit.*

"You don't get to be the hero this time, Pine. I found a solution. I found Joshua Tree. Everything's going to be okay. I get to keep *Turbine*, and you get to have the bar." Crawling into my lap, she kisses me soundly. "Don't worry. This is a good thing."

"When did you decide you were doing Joshua Tree? I thought it was only an option?"

"It makes the most sense—" she starts to explain but hears my phone ring and waves at me to answer. It's a number I don't recognize.

"This is Luke."

"Lucas Pine?"

"Yes."

"Darlene Pine's son?"

"Yes."

"She has you listed as her emergency contact."

Chapter 30
Allie

"There's a reason people stay loyal to
you, Leo. Allow yourself time today to do
something extra for someone you love."
-*Allie's horoscope, June 15th*

"You're just alone in his house? He left you?" Sadie asks
through the phone.

"I'm alone at his *mom's* house. He's at the hospital with her.
It's not like he's blowing me off."

"Hmm," she considers, "I guess that's fair. At least you have
lots of time to snoop. Are you snooping?"

"No. I'm sitting on the deck." Pulling my knees into my chest,
I rock slowly on the porch swing on the overhanging roof. Betty
is curled up in a tight, snoring, ball a few feet away, and the sun is
about to set. The scene is almost idyllic, just missing Luke. "You
can smell the ocean air from here. It's delightful."

"I can't believe you're not snooping. Don't you want to know
more about him?"

"Of course, but I don't need to snoop. He showed me around

he house, his old room, childhood photos."

"I snoop through Jared's stuff all the time, and we live ogether." Sadie says this casually, like everyone should be doing t.

"Sadie, what the fuck. Can't you just ask him things?"

"He hates emotional conversations, you know?" Defensiveness edges her usually bubbly voice. "If I don't snoop, have no clue what's going on with him."

Fucking Jared. Maybe if he wasn't an asshole, she wouldn't ave to snoop. Fuck that guy.

Betty's head lifts when seagulls honk as they fly overhead, ringing her close enough that I can reach down and scratch behind her ears. "Listen, I want to be in your corner so badly. You ave a right to be with who you want to, but for fuck's sake, Sade. What are you even getting out of this relationship at this point?"

Sadie laughs uncomfortably, and I feel bad. *But also, no I don't.* Someone has to have this conversation with her. "Allie, I don't know how to be without him. We've been together for nine ears. *Nine.* We were in high school when we met. I've never been an adult without him helping me."

"In what way is refusing to talk to you, refusing to share his ife with you, helping you?"

Luke's truck turns onto the street, and I watch it rumble toward ne and pull into the driveway as I wait for Sadie's response.

When it comes, it's quiet. "I don't want to talk about this nymore."

"Neither do I. I never want to have this conversation again. want you to be free. You're capable of so much, Sade. Give ourself a chance. Devon and I are not joking about you living with us."

"Allie, please. Let it go."

"Fine, I'll drop it. But please know, I hate him."

Luke hears my last statement as he walks up the weathered wooden front steps. Pointing at his chest and raising his eyebrows playfully, he mouths, "Me?"

Rolling my eyes and shaking my head, I scoot over to make room on the swing. He sits, squeezing me tightly to him and kissing me on the temple.

"I kind of hate him, too," Sadie admits, before making up an excuse about being busy, even though she called me to talk just twenty minutes ago, and we end the call.

"Who do we hate?" Luke asks.

"Fucking Jared, my friend Sadie's boyfriend. He's the fucking worst, and she is a beautiful ray of sunshine who won't leave him. It's heart-breaking."

"She's lucky to have you."

"A lot of good it does if she won't listen," I pout, and Luke pulls me closer, squeezing my knee reassuringly, a move he does on and off the bike now. *He's comforting me after spending all day at the hospital with his mom. Shit.* "Enough about me. Tell me about your day."

"Let me grab a couple of beers from the fridge. We can take a walk on the beach while I fill you in."

The evening is cool enough that I get to wear a hoodie for the first time in months. It's Luke's, so it hangs past my wrists and hits my upper thighs, cozy as fuck. *He's never getting it back.*

"How was she today?" I ask as we reach the beach. Betty wags her tail, shifting her feet back and forth impatiently as we slide off our shoes, leaving them in the sand to be picked up on the way back.

"My mom's a little tough," Luke says, reaching for my hand as we start towards the water's edge.

"Isn't that a good thing in this situation? Fighting to heal?"

"Not quite what I meant, but she is healing quickly. Pretty

banged up from the car accident and exhausted from everything, but she should be out of there in a few days." I squeeze his hand, encouraging him to continue. When he does, his voice is tight. "She's a tough person to get along with. For me."

He's only brought up his mom casually before, mentioned she's into astrology, that Skye looks exactly like her—*which must mean she's a curly-haired knockout,* she lives in Ventura, and he occasionally drives out here to visit and fix things. The only other hint I've gotten about their relationship is that she hasn't come to visit.

I stay quiet, letting him process as we continue walking in the wet sand, the edge of the water rippling over the tops of our feet when the waves roll in, occasionally splashing onto the bottoms of our rolled-up jeans. Betty walks alongside us, happy as can be.

"I never want to say anything negative about my mom." Luke breaks the silence. "She's tough in the good ways, like you said, and she got dealt a shit hand with my dad and Skye's dad. They both left when we were still babies. My Grandad, the one who used to own a bar, was her dad. He did everything for her, fixing her car, keeping the house from falling apart, babysitting me at the bar almost constantly."

"Sounds like he was pretty incredible."

Luke's smile is warm and proud. "He was incredible," his smile fades, "and it was awful losing him. After he died when I was fifteen, mom didn't have any help. So I stepped up. It needed to be done."

The picture of fifteen-year-old Luke fixing cars and mending broken furniture slots perfectly into my understanding of him. Babysitting his little sister, who was probably four or five at the time, suits him perfectly too. It all informs his intense need to fix, care for, and meet my needs before I know they're my needs.

"I never stopped taking care of Mom, and she's angry that I

moved away. She's acted like," he takes a deep breath, choosing his words carefully, "like I did it to hurt her. I should have done a better job of prepping her before I left. It probably felt sudden to her. She's been lonely."

"She doesn't have friends?"

"She does. Lots of them. But none who know how to repair a broken floorboard or replace her brake pads. For fifteen years, she's called and I've answered. Her problems were fixed. Now I'm two to five hours away, depending on traffic, and she feels abandoned."

Does this woman not know how to google a handyman? Never heard of paying a mechanic? My cheeks heat, reflecting my rising frustration on his behalf.

"Mom went through a lot to make sure Skye and I were happy and healthy. She worked really hard to make sure we didn't grow up and turn into jackasses." He pinches my ass cheek then, teasing and lightening the mood a bit. "And now she's hurt, physically, and it took me three hours to get here."

Considering we were freshly post-coital on a hiking trail in Joshua Tree when he got the call, I thought three hours was impressive.

"At the hospital, she was trying to guilt me into moving back."

He doesn't want to say anything negative about his mom, but I sure do.

"That's part of why I haven't brought you there. And I just told her about you today," he rushes to explain, "because I wasn't ready to share. Wasn't ready for her opinions."

Balancing on my toes, I give him a sweet, soft kiss. "I'm not offended, promise."

Dropping Betty's leash and tucking his beer bottle into the sand, he cups both broad calloused hands around my face, holding my eyes locked with his. "You sure?"

"I'm sure." I nod.

He kisses me again, and *goddamn* I love this man's lips, the scruff of his close-trimmed beard, his hands on me. I can't believe I spent all that time hating him when I could have had this instead. A cool breeze blowing off the ocean makes me shiver, and Luke blocks my body with his until it passes, even though I already stole his hoodie and he's only wearing a long-sleeved baseball tee.

We turn around and head back down the beach, quietly watching the sun dip below the horizon line of the water as we hold hands and sip on our beers. He doesn't speak up again until we reach our shoes. "It's a financial thing too, with my mom." He steadies me while I knock the sand off of my feet. "She needs help sometimes. Another thing I took over from Grandad. I know she won't be able to handle the medical bills, a new car, any of it without help."

"Hmm." There are so many things I want to say right now, but I doubt, *'Doesn't she have a fucking job?'* would be helpful. "Sounds like a lot for you. How do you feel about it?"

"It's fine. How it's always been. I got my inheritance from Grandad on my thirtieth earlier this year, been saving for the bar for ages. It'll be fine."

"None of that was how you feel," I say as we step back onto the street toward his mom's house.

"You perceptive little thing," he teases, tugging lightly on my ponytail. "I'm not sure how I feel about it yet."

"That's fair." Squeezing his hand, I add, "I'm in your corner, whatever you need."

~

"I'm ready for a shower. Got to get all the hospital and

beach off of me," Luke says after we've fed Betty and scarfed down a dinner of cheap pizza and cheaper beer. He's exhausted, his beard looking scruffier than usual, his posture a bit lax, chocolate-colored eyes starting to show dark circles beneath. *The man needs a break.*

"Alright, I'll shower after you. I'm all beachy, too."

"Sweetheart," Luke picks me up off the couch, and I squeal as he throws me over his shoulder with energy I didn't realize he had, "that was an invitation."

"Not sure how I missed that," I say into his shoulder, giggling as he carries me up the stairs, down the hall, and all the way to the bathroom. Our clothes come off in a flurry of laughter and teasing. The shadows under his eyes persist, but his broad, effortless smile is present in full force. He needs a distraction, and I'm happy to oblige.

We laugh and play, probably making a mess of the whole bathroom while we wash each other, each of us stopping the other if we get too handsy because, "We have to get clean."

"Let me wash your hair," I say, scanning the bath products.

"That sounds incredible," he says, lifting me by the waist and setting me on top of a teak stool in the shower. "Be careful up here."

"I promise. Now turn around." I spin my finger in a spiral over his head, he follows, then leans his head back and closes his eyes. The beach sunset was beautiful, but it had nothing on the bird's eye view of water sluicing down Lucas Pine's brawny naked body.

"Mmm," I hum in admiration.

"Like what you see?" he asks, smirking.

"Obviously. You're a babe." I select a blue bottle from the shower's shelf. "Now keep your eyes closed, unless you want shampoo in them."

He groans the second my fingertips begin to lather the shampoo into his hair, scratching my nails back and forth over his scalp.

"You really love this, don't you?"

"Mmhmm," he moans in response, a soothed smile ticking up the edges of his mouth for the entirety of me washing and conditioning his hair.

When I reach across him to adjust the water temperature, he turns into my chest, kissing across my collarbones and down the soft mounds of my breasts. *Fuck, that's nice.* The hard rod of his erection rubs against my leg, taunting me. "You're not taking care of me tonight, Pine."

"What do you mean?" He looks up at me, pushing his lower lip out in a pout that's comically at odds with his stern brows, angled jaw, and coarse beard.

"I mean, tonight I'm taking care of you. That's it."

"That's not fair."

"Isn't it? You've had a tough week. You need to relax."

He growls, narrowing his eyes. "I don't like to be selfish."

"You're not being selfish, *Jesus*." Luke stops me when I try to get down from the bench and lifts me off while being pointedly careful not to touch me anywhere fun.

He's in the middle of scolding me for being *reckless* with my safety when I drop to my knees in front of him. "Allie, you don't have to."

Water runs over his head, past his shoulders, across every ridge of his pecks and abs, in an obscene river. A few lucky streams pass across his glorious cock before I draw the tip between my lips. His hands go immediately to my hair, tangling his fingers between the wet strands. "I'm never going to forgive myself if you don't come."

"I never said I wasn't going to come," I scoff and swallow

him down whole, or as whole as I can as the tip of his cock brushing deep in the back of my throat for just an instant before releasing him and finishing my thought, "just that you weren't allowed to help."

"Goddamn, Allie." He shakes his head, voice tight. "And I get to watch?"

I nod, arching my low back as I take him back into my mouth, giving him a view of water sliding over my rounded ass cheeks as well as me bobbing my mouth over his cock. His eyes lock on me, watching me with intense desire as I swallow him down. I alternate between closing my eyes and looking up to gaze at him when the position allows it.

My own arousal builds, adding slickness to my lower lips. Touching Luke, pleasing him, taking care of him, and watching him lose control turns me on enough to make my clit throb without a single touch.

Over and over, I slide my lips down and back up, massaging with my tongue as I go, the taste of pre-cum disappearing into the wetness of my mouth. With one hand, I toy gently with his balls while the other works the base of his shaft where my lips don't reach. His broad shoulders block most of the water until it pools around his feet and runs past my kneeling legs. Each time I come forward on his cock, my breasts brush against his thighs, the rough hair teasing my hardening nipples.

Luke groans, removing one hand from my hair to brace it on the tile wall behind me, and I know he's getting close. Dropping my hand from his balls, I make a show of running my fingers down my throat, across my chest, plucking at my nipples before settling between my legs onto my clit.

Luke tracks every inch of the movement, offering encouragements and naughty praises as I go, adjusting his stance to get a full view of my hand on my sex. "You look perfect when you touch yourself for me, sweetheart. Do you know how many times I imagined what you would look like, pleasuring yourself? I got off to picturing you teasing that delicious cunt while thinking of my cock countless times before you ever stopped calling me jackass."

The fingers at my clit pick up speed, moving in time with the slide of my mouth over his cock. His words add to the tension in my throbbing sex, bringing me closer to the edge.

"When was the first time you thought about me, gorgeous?"

I look up at him, unable to respond with a mouth full of his divine cock, deciding I need to shut him up, too. My mouth, the hand on his shaft, and the hand on my clit all ratchet up in speed. I take him deeper, hitting the back of my throat on each forward thrust. The look in his eyes grows wild, muscles tensing across his thick neck, broad shoulders, sculpted arms, and unfair abs.

I lose myself in the motions, focused on getting both of us there. My core clenches around nothing, and I ache to be filled. I'm sure he'd take over in a second if I asked, but this time I'm determined to take care of him. My fingers slide down my seam and inside myself, even hotter and wetter than the steaming shower around us.

My hips rock, riding my fingers as I work his shaft with my throat, lips, and hand. "Fuck, baby," he breathes, hips stuttering as his cum spurts down my throat. Tasting him, feeling him come apart at my mercy, sends me over the edge, and an orgasm quickly ripples through me before I release him from my mouth.

Luke drops to his knees in front of me, water spraying over both of our heads, curls of steam twining past our shoulders. He pulls my lips to his, kissing me fervently, holding my mouth to his with sensuous pressure. "You are perfect, in every single way." Then he takes the fingers I was just riding and sucks them into his mouth, licking and tasting every drop the shower hasn't already washed away. "Every. single. one," he says, placing a kiss to a different fingertip after each word.

"The first day I met you," I say.

"Hmm?" he asks, leaning his forehead against mine.

"The first day I met you was the first time I came with your name on my lips."

Chapter 31
Luke

"Your mother has a soft heart. After I'm
gone, sometimes the hard things will fall to
you." *-Grandad Ernie to fifteen-year-old Luke
during one of their last conversations.*

Careful not to make extra noise, I close the blue painted cabinet
door. Allie is upstairs sleeping, and I'd like her to stay that way
until I have her coffee ready.

She insisted on taking care of me last night, including
playing with my hair as I fell asleep with my head on her chest.
I'm about as good at accepting help as she is, but she knows
exactly how to make me take what I need.

Grandad charged me with taking care of mom half my life
ago. Which, admittedly, was a sort of fucked up thing to do
to a fifteen-year-old. But I can't blame him. *How else was he
supposed to make sure his daughter was okay with him gone?*

Being here this week and spending countless hours at
the hospital with mom, then coming home to Allie has my
perspective shifting. I can honor Grandad and make sure Mom's

okay without having to do it the same way he did. Mom's young, barely in her fifties. She doesn't *need* me here all the time. She's rarely kept a job for more than six months, but that doesn't mean she can't try again.

I can still have Station 19, *Voyeur Motors*, all of it. The bar is happening in a couple of months, though I like the idea less and less as the days with Allie next door at *Turbine* race by. I don't have to sacrifice myself to make sure Mom's okay. The trick will be getting her to see it that way, too.

"Are you making me coffee, Lucas Pine?" Allie asks, emerging from the hallway at the top of the stairs. Morning light beams in, shining golden on her sweet face and mussed chestnut hair. One of my faded black racing tees hangs off one smooth shoulder and rides up just enough to show some cheek as she comes down to the kitchen.

"I am. Was planning to bring it to you in bed. Heard that's the only acceptable reason to wake you up." I retrieve the creamer from the fridge to add to her coffee. "But it's tough to wake up earlier than you."

She climbs onto a stool at the kitchen island and says, "I do love coffee in bed." Her voice still sleepy.

"Then I'll keep trying." I place the warm cup of coffee in Allie's waiting hands and a kiss to her temple. "I'd like you to come see Mom today. How would you feel about that?"

"Sure," her response is immediate and enthusiastic, the first sip of coffee already lending her energy. "I've been wanting to meet her. Will she be okay with me being there?"

"Oh, yeah. After I told her about you yesterday, she scolded me for not bringing you by sooner."

She squeezes my hand across the island. "Then we'll definitely go together." Bringing Allie to the hospital with me today will make the entire ordeal with mom feel less daunting.

Her presence this week has already brought me peace where I normally wouldn't have had any.

While she's upstairs getting ready, I search the house for things Mom might need help with. Cam did a good job of putting in the hydraulic slow-close mechanism for the screen door to the front porch. The stair railing the handyman repaired feels sturdy. None of the plumbing is leaking. The gardener's doing a good job, better than I ever did. Things are not in the kind of shape that I expected, which is a relief. And also a bit irritating, since Mom is always saying how much she needs me to do.

I grab the last few days' worth of mail on my way back into the house. While I'm sorting the junk out, I come across an official-looking pink envelope. *Shit.*

~

"So, my little goat tells me you're a Leo," Mom says, ten seconds after being introduced to Allie. "But he didn't know your rising or moon. Men can be so useless."

Allie doesn't join in with Mom's laughter. "Some men can be, but Luke isn't."

"Oh, I didn't mean anything by that," Mom says, waving it away like it's nothing. And her comment *was* nothing to me. I would have forgotten it immediately, but Allie's refusal to agree with insulting me? *That was something.*

Leaning against a bland, gray cabinet along the far wall, I let them fall into easy conversation. Allie's warm and inviting as she listens to Mom with genuine interest. I've seen her win over hundreds of customers in an instant, but this is different, more raw. She's letting Mom in deeper than that.

For her part, Mom warms up to Allie immediately, smiling

at me knowingly after *every* sentence out of my girl's mouth.

I try to listen, wanting to know what they're connecting about, but my mind keeps going back to that pink envelope. After looking through Mom's desk, I found that it was one of many. *She knows.* She knows exactly what she stands to lose. Was she not going to ask me for money? Or is that why she keeps asking me to come home, so she could ask me in person?

We've spent hours upon hours together in this hospital room this week, and she never said a word about financial problems. Mom has never hesitated to ask me for help before. *What's different this time?*

"How long will you be in town for Luke's bar's opening?" Allie's question draws me back to their conversation. "I want to show you around. I can plan the perfect trip for you. There's an aura photographer who comes through sometimes."

Mom's face lights up as Allie describes all the different things they should do together. I hadn't realized Mom was committed to coming out to visit, but I've also buried my head in the sand about the bar. Skye's been working hard to make sure things come together, and she's forced me to make decisions. The menu is set. We picked the name *Ernie's*, after Grandad. But it doesn't feel right. None of it is worth what it's costing Allie.

She told me *no* when I asked her to stay, but it's hard to believe that's what she wants. *How could her opinion have changed so drastically since that first day she found out I'd bought her building?*

After a long conversation with Mom, Allie squeezes my hand and balances on her toes to kiss me on the cheek on the way out of the room to find us some food.

"She's a very special woman," Mom says, not waiting for her to be out of earshot.

"She is," I say, moving forward to take the seat Allie just vacated.

"You know she's all in, right? She's yours?"

"I know that." I nod.

"Forever. Have you figured that part out yet? You get to keep her. She's your person. I could feel it the second she walked in this room." I knew all of this, but it's fun to watch Mom figure it out, too. "You know I have intuition about people."

"I know, Mom. I love her. I'm keeping her."

"I always knew you'd end up with someone magical and free." She squeezes my hand tightly.

Mom gushes about Allie, repeating the conversation they just had while adding in her observations about Allie's fiery spirit, powerful energy, and even calls her smile electric.

Running my fingers back through my hair, I interrupt her. "I wish we could talk about Allie all day, but I've got something else I have to ask you about."

"What is it, little goat?" Mom tilts her head to the side, her dark brown ringlets even wilder than usual from days in a hospital bed. Her comforting smile, marred by a cut on her chin, her perceptive eyes, same as Skye's and mine, edged with yellowing bruises. The car accident really fucked her up, but nothing could stop her spirit from shining through.

"The property tax on the house, Mom. How long do you have?"

Some people might be angry about me going through their mail, sticking my nose in their business, but not Mom. We've been a team for a long, long time. Her business is my business. "Until the end of the month."

"That's all they give you? That's bullshit."

"No, I've known for a long, long time, honey."

Anger clenches my jaw, my hands flexing in and out of fists.

I take a few deep breaths before asking, "Why didn't you tell me?"

She looks at me, for a long moment before she says, "You may not believe this, but I never liked taking money from you." She takes three deep breaths, which she does when she needs to steady herself, before continuing. "I hated that my son was the only man who stayed. Hated myself for not being able to handle everything on my own, not being able to get out of bed some days. While at the same time, being grateful you were such a capable and hard-working young man." Her voice cracks with the weight of long-held emotion. "I don't know how we would've gotten through those years without you carrying us."

We've never put a name to mom's *issues*. Neighbors called her flighty and irresponsible. Grandad called her troubled. Skye has a whole list of diagnoses she thinks it could be, and has been pushing for her to get help, but to me, she's Mom. That's enough information. She's strong in every way she can be, and I'm strong in all the others. It's how it's always worked. Or at least, I thought it was working until I moved away, and she's had so much trouble with the change. *And then I found those pink envelopes.*

"You work so hard," she continues, squeezing my hand again. "I kept trying to figure it out myself, the money for the taxes, but I just couldn't come up with it. I've been working for Gabriel, doing service writing at his shop for a few weeks now. You remember him, right?"

I nod. Gabriel's a good guy, a local who's been around for decades. He was a regular at Grandad's bar. If mom can hang on to that gig, she'll be in good hands.

"But that's the best thing I've had in years. There just isn't enough money." She pauses, tilting her head to the side. "I know this building, your motorcycle shop, the bar, they mean a lot to you," her voice trails off, almost dismissively.

"Yeah, they do, Mom. But if you would have told me this in the first place, I would never have bought that building. I would never have left." Saying it out loud turns my stomach sour. *If I'd never gone to Palm Springs, I wouldn't have Allie.*

"People are complicated, Lucas, your mother included. I kept thinking I'd figure it out on my own. I really thought I could, but I knew if I didn't, you'd handle it. And by the time I figured out I needed you to step in, you were already making plans to leave. If I talked you into staying here, it wouldn't be such a big deal for you to give up the money," she says, matter-of-factly. "Maybe if I could make you think you never wanted to leave," she trails off. "I don't know. I've always counted on you. With you gone, I didn't know what to do. I'm caught between being a good mom and losing my house. What am I supposed to do?" The question is rhetorical, and also an admission that she doesn't have a plan other than *wait for Luke to fix it.*

I run my fingers through my hair, one hand after the other. "I'll figure it out, Mom. You're not losing the damn house."

"I knew you'd come through for me," she says, warm affection in her tone. "But even if you decided not to, I wouldn't hold it against you."

I narrow my eyes at her in response.

She tilts her head. "I hate that you left me, but I don't begrudge you spending Dad's money on things you want. Even if those things are in the middle of nowhere, far enough away from your mom that she can't pop over for dinner anymore."

"That's not why I picked Palm Springs."

She laughs, shaking her head. "Of course not. You picked it because you were meant to. Your soulmate is there." Mom's right. She is a complicated person. She resents that I left her. She expects me to come back and fix her problems. But she also believes I was meant to leave… Meant to find Allie. To her, none of these things are contradictory.

I arch a brow at her. "I don't believe in soulmates."

"Doesn't mean you don't have one."

"I didn't know she was there when I moved there."

"Doesn't matter. She's the reason you were drawn there. Things happen for a reason. Your Grandad probably didn't realize when he stopped for gas in Palm Springs seventy years ago that it would lead to his grandson's destiny, but it still happened."

Chapter 32
Allie

"Don't let your ego block your happiness.
In some situations, they are mutually
exclusive." -*Allie's Horoscope June 18th*

"Joshua Tree?" Hector asks incredulously. "You can't be serious. Brian!" he yells over his shoulder from his spot at the counter to his husband who's sitting by the front window.

"I heard," Brian says at a normal volume, not looking up from his paper. "Not worried about it."

"Not worried? Are we supposed to carpool with Daisy now?"

Daisy looks up, smiles, and goes back to her drawing.

"Why am I the only person who's concerned about this?" Hector throws his hands up. "What did Devon say?"

"Devon doesn't *love* it," I admit. "Although, she thinks it may force me to have healthier boundaries with work. But you know better than anyone how hard it was to find a place in Palm Springs."

"I didn't realize we'd given up," Hector says, arching a judgmental black brow at me.

"We didn't give up." I set a consolation iced coffee on the counter for him. "This is a really good option for me."

"I hate it. *Loathe* it. Detest it." He takes a long sip of his coffee. "I am vehemently opposed to the idea of *Turbine Café* moving to Joshua Tree."

I lean forward on the counter. "The building isn't going anywhere. We can meet here for happy hour at *Ernie's* instead."

"The fuck is *Ernie's*?" Hector asks, lip snarling in offense.

"Ernie was Luke's Grandad's name," I explain. "It's what he's calling the bar."

"What's the point of sleeping with your landlord if he's going to kick you out, anyway?" Hector asks, still incredulous.

I point through the window at my landlord-boyfriend. He's lifting something metal, maybe a motorcycle engine. The details of his broad muscular shoulders show through his grease-smudged t-shirt and tendrils of black hair fall across his forehead. "I promise, it's worth it, even without the building."

"Okay, fine," Hector admits, begrudgingly. "I can see the appeal."

Truth is, I'm still heartbroken about leaving Station 19. But knowing that leaving helps Luke, makes it okay. I only have a month and a half left here, and I'm spending every second reveling in it while I still can.

Luke: Any chance you'll bring me a turkey on rye?
Me: Sure thing, Pine. Be right over.

I say goodbye to a cranky Hector and head over to have lunch with my sexy motorcycle mechanic boyfriend. Betty greets me when I come in the back door, wagging her tail excitedly as I sneak her extra pieces of turkey while we wait for Luke to finish scrubbing the grease from his hands.

When we sit down on his leather couch together, his body language is stiffer than usual. *Not angry, but maybe nervous?* He's been a bit on edge since we left the hospital a couple of days ago. He's never short with me, but it's evident he has a lot on his mind.

"I want to talk to you about something," he says.

"Anything."

Luke runs his fingers through thoroughly mussed black hair, one hand after the other. "Before we talk about this, I need you to know two things." I nod, encouraging him to continue. "One: I heard you when you said you don't want to extend your lease. I know you're excited about Joshua Tree and owning a building, and I'm not trying to guilt you into changing your mind."

That is not the caveat I was expecting.

"Two: More than anything, I want you to stay. I would give anything I have to make you happy." *Fuck. Why did I tell him No* again? He got the call about his mom while we were in the middle of that conversation, and we never got to finish it. I open my mouth to make an excuse, but he silences me with a calloused finger to my lips. "You don't have to say anything yet." He takes a deep breath. "Mom's about to lose her house."

"Oh, fuck," I whisper.

"Yeah, fuck. House is paid off, but she hasn't paid her property taxes in years. I found out while we were out there."

I know he takes care of a lot for his mom, but this is a weight he shouldn't have to carry. I bite my tongue, wanting to let him talk this out without my opinions influencing him.

"It's a lot of money, and I have it, but…" his voice trails off, looking through the window at *Turbine.*

"It's the money for *Ernie's?*"

"Yeah." He nods.

I wait for him to continue, but when it's still silent after a few moments, I ask, "You know, you don't have to take care of this for her, right?"

"I know that."

"But you *are* going to take care of it, aren't you?"

Luke cocks his head, a knowing smile spreading his lips. "Ernie was her dad, and it's his money. It's the only way for him to take care of her anymore."

"It's your money now, so if you do this, it's you taking care of her."

He furrows his brows. "I guess."

"You've spent a lot of money on her over the years, yes?"

He nods.

"So, maybe if you hadn't, you wouldn't have needed your Grandad's money to do all this?" I wave both hands in the air, indicating *Voyeur Motors* and Station 19.

He nods again.

"You're a very good man, Luke. It's admirable how much you love your mom." He grunts, uncomfortable with the praise. "What does all this have to do with me?"

He reaches down to where Betty lies on the ground by his feet, scratching absently behind her ears. "*Ernie's* isn't happening."

Fuck, I hate that. It's not fair. It's not right. "So you need someone to rent that side?" I ask, my heart fluttering with a mix of excitement about maybe staying and a twinge of anxiety that he's losing his dream.

"I had another idea, actually." He stands up. "Wait here. I have something for you."

He walks back to his office and returns with a thick stack of paperwork. He hands it over, and I flip through, seeing my name, his name, Station 19, and lots of legal jargon. "What am I looking at?"

He returns to his spot next to me. "I've been working with the bank to split the deed for Station 19. I want to sell you your half. Then you can own your space, like you always should have."

Why would he give that up? I never imagined. Overwhelmed, tears well in my eyes. I push the paperwork back towards him. "Luke, I—" I stop and start, struggling to find words. "It's just so—I...Luke, I can't do this to you."

"You're not doing anything to me. You'd be helping me. I need the money to help Mom." He sets the paperwork down on the nearby coffee table and squeezes both of my hands in his. "But that's nothing compared to how much I need you." He pulls me closer to him until my folded legs are leaning against his, his hands cradling my face. "Allie, I love you. I need you close to me always. I don't want to look through that glass wall and see anything but Allie Walker or *Turbine Café*. Do you understand?"

He loves me? He loves me. Holy shit, he loves me.

"Luke, I—" Struggling with words again, I opt for kissing him. My hands go to frame his face, and he pulls me across his lap until I'm straddling him. Our lips crash together in a searing kiss that rocks me to my core. The kiss of a man who *loves me.* Who wants me more than anything. *Who I love.* And who I want more than anything. Breaking the kiss, I stay curled in his arms on his lap, but pull back far enough that we can see each other clearly. "Luke, this could actually work."

He runs his hands up and down the sides of my waist, chuckling. "I know, sweetheart."

An idea materializes immediately, one I can't believe I never thought of before. "But I need you to know two things before I accept."

He nods, a smirk curving his lips.

"One: I love you too."

His smirk turns into a full, broad smile.

"Two: I will not let you give up the bar."

His smile falters. "Allie. No. You're not giving up *Turbine*."

"Have you ever noticed that *Turbine*'s only open during the day?"

"Of course," he laughs, "I hate working late because I don't get to see you."

"What if it was *Turbine* during the day, and *Ernie's* at night?" I smile, giddy with excitement at the prospect.

He squeezes my knee, a broad smile taking over his mouth. "I like that idea, but it has a couple of flaws."

I tilt my head to the side, pretending to rethink my proposition. "Pretty sure it's flawless, actually."

"Calling it *Ernie's* isn't right anymore. The bar will be ours, not his."

"Ours?"

"Oh, yeah. We're about to be business partners, sweetheart. I'm not running a bar in your space without your help. We'd be opening a bar together."

Oh, fuck. He's right. That is *better.* I squeal in excitement, tapping a hand on his sculpted shoulder. "Okay, so not *Ernie's*. I'm good with that. What's the other imaginary flaw?"

"Those fucking pedestal tables." He points through the window, and I collapse against his chest, laughing. "I refuse to run a business with those hazards. They're out. All of them."

"All of them?"

"Well, the *one* will be at my place. The others can go to a landfill for all I care."

"Hmm," I take my time, pretending to consider even though we both know my mind is solidly made up. "Alright. You have a deal, Lucas Pine."

Chapter 33
Luke

"Proud of you, kid." -*A note from Grandad Ernie that thirty-year-old Luke found tucked into a copy of Zen and the Art of Motorcycle Maintenance at his mom's house that was intended for him as a sixteenth birthday present.*

"Today is your day, Capricorn. You will find success in love, business, and family. Step outside, and don't waste the opportunity to revel in your luck." -*Luke's horoscope, that he now reads in bed next to Allie every morning, August 1st.*

Opening the door to my bedroom, two coffees in hand, I find Allie still sleeping. *Finally.* I've been trying for months to wake up early enough to do this. Stepping quietly into the room, I set the coffees on the nightstand and slide back under the covers next to her.

She's perfect, as always. Morning light shining across the

smooth skin of her naked body. Chest rising and falling with the steady breaths of sleep. It's tempting to keep watching her, but the draw of kissing her sweet face is stronger. I kiss along her jaw down the column of her neck, tracing my hand up and down the side of her soft waist, easing her awake.

"Mmm." Her sleepy voice comes as I'm kissing back up the other side of her neck. "Morning."

"Morning, sweetheart," my hand at her waist traces lower over the slope of her hip, smoothing down the curve of her round ass cheek. "I know you've said the only thing worth being woken up for is coffee—"

"That's because it is," she giggles quietly, eyes still closed.

"I'd like to test that theory." I kiss down her sternum, stopping to suck and nibble on each round breast on my way lower. "I have something you may want to add to that list." My fingertips travel across the top of her thigh, dipping between her legs.

She gasps my name at the contact, rolling her hips eagerly to meet my touch. "You may be on to something." Her voice comes out breathily. I rub a finger in circles around her slicking entrance, loving the way my touch affects her. "But I won't know for sure until you show me."

"Of course, sweetheart. You should have all the information." I dip the finger inside her, only a knuckle deep, sliding back and forth, as I kiss lower on her body, tasting the curves of her soft stomach.

"Fuck, Luke, you're going to make me lose control like that."

"That's the idea." I dip the finger further on my next pass, still not giving her quite what she needs. "By the way, there is coffee on your nightstand. If you'd like to enjoy that, too."

She looks over, smiling, "I thought I smelled coffee. Better not, though. Wouldn't want to spill."

I slide my finger free. "I could wait."

"You better fucking not," she scolds, grabbing my wrist and pulling it close to her again.

This time I fill her with my finger like I have something to prove. My lips leave their final kiss on her belly and drop down to her clit. She cries out the moment my mouth is on her.

"So responsive," I mumble against her sex before my lips are on her again, sucking lightly as my tongue starts to swirl her sensitive bud.

Her hips rock on my finger, slick with her arousal now, so I add a second.

"Yes, please," she cries.

The feel of her, hot and wet, soaking my fingers and lips is intoxicating, her pleasure the most delicious thing.

Looking up, I watch her, head thrown back as she moans in ecstasy. Curling my fingers, I pump harder, and her moans reach a peak at the top of each thrust.

I increase the sensation at her clit, more insistent with my tongue, lips sucking harder.

"Yes, that. That. *Yes*." She hits her fist against the bed, punctuating each word. "Fuck, don't you dare stop."

She starts to pulse around my fingers, squeezing me tightly, and I keep up the motions exactly as she asked. She keens, making the most delicious sounds as she encourages me to continue. I could live and die between her legs, but it only takes another minute before she's coming apart.

Once I'm sure she's fully satisfied, I pull back, sitting up to take in her blissful face, flushed from the exertion of her orgasm.

"Well?" I ask.

"Hmm?" she asks, dazed.

"Is that an acceptable reason to wake you up?"

"Oh, fuck yes."

~

Our place is buzzing with people by the time Allie and I arrive. As of today—the soft opening of the bar—Allie is closing *Turbine* at two rather than five, so we have a couple of hours of downtime to switch gears until the bar opens at four.

"This showed up this morning," Devon says, handing me a wide, flat cardboard box. "It needs to be hooked up and hung in the front window, please."

"Please? That's new. Are you finally willing to admit you like me, Devon?" I give her my best smirk, even knowing it won't have any effect.

She scoffs, "I like exactly four people. Allie, Sadie, Bea, and my massage therapist, Sam, who allows me an hour of blissful silence each week."

"She likes me too, but won't admit it," Rhett, a carpenter we hired for the remodel, interjects, brushing against her as he passes by with a case of pint glasses. He's friends with our lead bartender and is helping out as extra staff tonight.

Devon glares at him in a way that would have most people cowering, but he only laughs and continues on his way.

"What is this, anyway?" I ask, taking the unmarked cardboard box from her.

"Your neon sign," she says, annoyed. "What else goes in the front window?"

"I didn't know there was a neon sign."

Devon breathes out, annoyed, her perfect posture slipping for just a second. "He should have told you already. It's a gift from Cam. Try to act surprised."

"Alright," I say, carrying the box with me to the back, where I hear Cam's voice. He's been in town for a few days, helping get things ready. Mainly running errands for Allie before she has a chance to freak out about things not being ready in time.

"Ooh, what you got there, boss?" he asks.

"I'm told it's a gift from you."

"Oh, fuck yes!" Cam grabs the box and leads me toward the front of the restaurant. Betty, who's been following him around since he got here—which Cam assures me has nothing to do with him sneaking her human food—follows along too. "Took you guys so long to pick a name. It barely got here in time."

We rolled around name ideas for the bar for weeks, and ultimately, the one we chose was Hector's idea. A combination of Turbine Café and Voyeur Motors. Maybe not the most conventional name, but it does have a full kitchen. And most importantly, my Allie loved the idea.

Cam unpacks the sign carefully before plugging it in to show me the details. The neon buzzes to life. It's custom with two different names. We can switch it on in the morning to read *Turbine Café*, and at night, when the bar opens, it'll read *Voyeur Café*.

"This is awesome." I pat him on the shoulder. "Really great of you to do this for us."

"Tried to order it for you months ago, but you wouldn't give me a damn name. Guess it was never meant to be only yours, huh?" Cam asks, pushing fire engine red hair out of his eyes.

I shake my head. "No, never was."

Betty gets up from her place on the ground and meets Allie as she comes over, *oohing* and *aahing* over the sign before wrapping Cam in a big hug that he has to practically bend in half to participate in. "It's really happening!" she squeals, bouncing on her toes as he lets her go.

"It really is, sweetheart."

"Okay," she claps her hands loudly in front of her chest,

holding them together as she doles out orders. "We have exactly one hour and forty-five minutes before we open, and there is still a big heap of goodies in the truck out back that needs to be unloaded, please."

"We're on it," I say, gathering up the cardboard trash.

"You got it, boss!" Cam agrees, wide mouth drawing into an exaggerated smile.

"Thank you!" She rises to her toes to kiss me and bounds away to take care of the next thing on her list. Watching Allie lock into her planning brain these past weeks has been amazing. She's loud, giggly, and happy, but she's not scattered. Everything has a place and a time. I had a plan for *Ernie's*, but it would have been nothing compared to what Allie and I have been able to pull off together.

"You did good, Cam. Thank you." I pat him on the back as we walk out to the truck.

"*You* did good, boss," Cam scoffs.

"Me? We're not even open yet."

He dismissively waves his hand. "Oh, that'll be great. I'm not worried about that. I mean, Allie. It was touch and go there for a while, wasn't sure if you were going to pull it off."

"You told me you had a sixth sense that she was into me the first time you met her." I follow him through the back door.

Cam's laugh echoes around the back parking lot. "Oh, I made that shit up to encourage you. I could see it in your eyes that you were fucked up about her. Had to make sure you took a run at it."

"She was already into me then, for the record."

"Sure, she was," Cam laughs, passing me a box down from the truck.

"Luke!" Allie calls out the back door of *Turbine*. Well—of *Voyeur Café*, now.

"Yes?" I ask, around the box I'm holding.

"Get in here. I want you to meet someone." The door closes behind her before I have a chance to respond.

"I'll finish this up," Cam says, taking the box back from me. "You heard the lady. Get in there."

I find her in Brian's chair by the front window, Betty laying by her feet, and an older couple sitting in the two seats across from her. Lots of retirees in Palm Springs, but I don't know these two.

"There you are," Allie chimes. "This is Nora and Lou!"

Nora and Lou. The names sound familiar, and I realize there's an old photograph of this woman in my desk drawer that I can finally return to its owners. I'd recognize that mischievous glint in her eyes anywhere. "Hi, son," Lou says, extending a hand to me. "We're the ones who used to own the place. I ran the diner here, and Nora had the bookstore on that side."

"You knew that." Allie bats at me playfully in the chest before indicating we should share the leather armchair. She gets up just long enough for me to sit before leaning back into my lap.

"We heard there were big changes, and I told Lou we had to come see for ourselves," Nora says, waving a hand toward the counter.

There have been big changes. Devon and Bea worked non-stop getting the place ready for our opening. The wall behind the bar, that used to be painted a crisp white, now boasts sunflower-yellow two-by-six tiles stacked in crisp lines up to the ceiling, brass sconces, and a set of taps. The counter itself is still white quartz, which was a battle I lost against Devon. I would have preferred concrete to match the floors, but she said that was, "Industrial, unnecessary, and incongruent with the mid-century modern flair of this space."

There's a second register at the bar, framed black and white photos of vintage bikes, including a blown-up version of the picture of Grandad that lives in my toolbox, and the fucking white pedestal tables are finally gone, replaced by sensible black ones with four legs. More hanging plants have been added around the glass wall and the windows to the outside. The sputnik lights and the massive starburst clock remain, but the black barstools have been replaced with walnut ones with back support.

The kitchen in the back also received a hefty facelift, now boasting a full chef's set up.

"I tell people your story all the time," Allie beams.

"That she does," I nod. I found the original blueprints for the building while I was working on splitting the deed. They confirmed there was always a window, so people could see the work being done on their cars. But I tucked them away. The story brings Allie so much joy. No harm in her believing it. Still, I wonder why this couple lied.

"He's so silly. He doesn't believe it." Allie squeezes my hand.

"Allie, can I borrow you for a minute," Devon calls from behind the bar, voice firm in a statement, not a question.

"I'm sorry," Allie apologizes to Nora and Lou. "I have to see what she needs, but I'll be back." Betty lifts her head and watches as Allie hurries away.

"Don't worry, sweetie," Nora says. "It's a big day. Take care of what you need to." Looking at Lou, she says, "I'm going to visit the little girl's room," and follows Allie toward the back of the restaurant.

As soon as they're both out of earshot, I lean forward, bracing my forearms on my knees. "Lou, I have to ask," he smiles knowingly, before I have the question fully out. "Why the story about the window?"

"Nora and I didn't always get along. She hated me for a long time." He shakes his head, laughing to himself. "I came in one day, and she'd boarded up the windows from her side, still won't tell me how she pulled it off by herself. She's tall, but not that tall. Couldn't have done it without a ladder, and I know she didn't have one of those. The boards she used were nasty and splintered. Took me hours to get them all down."

"How'd you get her to let you take them down?"

"Oh, she didn't let me." He smiles warmly, reminiscing.

"I broke in after she left that night. And the night after that, while I was gone, she put them up again. The next night, I threw the boards away a few streets over. She found new ones. Went back and forth like that for an entire week."

I glance over to the curtains that Allie put up months ago, still hanging next to the glass wall, that she only used for a weekend. Mild in comparison.

"The final night I went in to take them down was New Year's Eve, and I had a party to get to. Nora was waiting for me, and we had it out. She yelled and told me how I was a selfish prick, and I told her why she was a spoiled princess." A sly grin tugs at the edge of his mouth briefly. "Well, we worked it out. I didn't make it to the party. She didn't make it to whatever plans she had. The boards never went back up, and she's been mine ever since. I told her she could build an entire wall to block the windows, and I'd just put in new ones."

"Well, that explains it," I chuckle, and I can't help but smile.

Lou nods. "That's where it comes from. The windows were already there, but if they weren't, I would have had them put in the moment I laid eyes on that woman. I was never going to miss a second of Nora."

Chapter 34
Allie

"Celebrate today. Big things, little things. You know how to throw a party better than anyone. Take advantage of that fiery center-of-attention energy." *-Allie's horoscope, August 1ˢᵗ*

"Heels may have been a poor choice," I say, brushing my hands over the ruffled hem of my short dress and assessing my look in my office mirror. I look hot as fuck in tan, chunky heels and a fitted yellow cocktail dress with a sweetheart neckline, but I'm about to be on my feet behind a bar for eight to ten hours.

Luke stands behind me, hands coming around my waist. "I do like how easy it is to kiss you when you're up here," he says, dropping a soft kiss on my lips. "But I put a pair of your Vans in the truck, in case you change your mind."

"I knew I liked you," I smile up at him. He's dressed up too, in his own way. His hair is combed back, beard freshly trimmed, and he has on dark wash jeans, and a dark gray button up shirt. He still smells like steel and soap, though—just the way I like him.

Devon opens the office door, statuesque in a navy column dress, nude matte lip, and platinum hair smoothed back into a low bun. Her brows are defined in their usual dark espresso color, as if to say, *Yeah, I bleach my hair. Mind your business.* "You two planning to make an appearance?"

"We still have three minutes," Luke says. "You can trust me to get her out there on time."

"Huh." Devon's blue eyes turn thoughtful for a flash of a second as she tilts her head to the side. "I do trust you. Didn't see that coming." And then her face is back to its usual mix of RBF and otherworldly beauty, and she's on her way back out my office door.

"You know, Lucas Pine, I'm really happy you came to Palm Springs and stole my dream, because now I'm living a new one with you, and it's better than I could have imagined."

"I love you," he whispers in my ear.

"I love you too," I whisper back.

Then he pinches my ass cheek. "But I can't let you be late. Let's get out there."

He follows me, and we take up a place behind the bar, the place already filling with friends and family.

Marisol is here with all three of her kids. I promoted her to *Turbine*'s GM. First, because she deserved it, and second, because Luke insisted I loosen the reins a bit saying, "No one needs Allie Walker working twenty hours a day, every day." *Whatever.* We even hired two more baristas, so I don't have to open anymore. Although, I'll miss my not-so-solo morning dance parties.

Daisy is in her usual spot, wearing a dress the exact shade of her pink hair, and she has a handsome older gentleman on her arm she's never brought in before. We share a conspiratorial smile.

Bea's sitting at the bar, wearing an orange striped dress that has to be vintage, more jewelry than I could pull off, and sipping on a honey whiskey cocktail from Luke's custom menu. Turns out, he knows what the fuck he's doing behind a bar, and those flexing forearms look just as good with a drink shaker as they do with a wrench.

Bea, Devon, and Skye have been here every day this week after hustling to pull the design together to turn *Turbine*'s space into *Voyeur Café* in record time. Devon even let me pay her for once, saying that Luke doesn't get the best friend discount. *Yet.*

Hector and Brian sit on the barstools closest to Luke and me, both looking extra dapper for the occasion.

"Can I get a Cookie Explosion?" Hector asks, teasingly ordering the coffee drink I hate and will never escape.

"Absolutely not." My hands go to my hips, emphasizing my authority. "The blenders are busy making margaritas. Would you like one of those?"

Brian holds up the cocktail menu, adjusting his black-framed glasses as he studies each drink intensely.

"He's picking out the only thing he'll ever order here, so don't rush him." Hector pats Brian on the shoulder.

"I appreciate a man who knows what he likes," Luke says.

I roll my eyes. "One of these days, I'll get you away from black coffee."

"I drink Americanos now. It's an entirely different experience," He scoffs.

Cam drapes himself casually into the seat next to Hector, spinning the stool around backwards so he can rest his arm and chest on the backrest. "I want one of those Cookie Explosion things, too. That sounded good."

Luke puts a draught beer down in front of him. "You'll drink

"Sure, but I'm having a Cookie Explosion for breakfast."

"Fine by me. I won't be here," I laugh, shifting my weight between my feet.

"You want me to get your Vans?" Luke whispers in my ear.

"Not yet." I smile up at him.

Cam pauses the swiveling of his barstool, staring slack-jawed at the front door. "Which one of your friends has pink hair?"

"Huh?" Looking up to see who he's talking about, I find Sadie standing in the doorway. Her hair is indeed pink, at least at the ends and it's a good eight inches shorter than it was last time I saw her.

"Holy shit!" I yell when I see the giant roller bags in her hands. I push out from behind the bar and run to her at the door, unconcerned with the bar full of people whose attention I'm gathering. Pulling her in for a tight hug, I ask, "Is that a fucking break-up haircut, Sadie Winslow? Did you finally leave that motherfucker?"

She laughs against my hair because I still haven't released her from the hug. "Yeah. I left that motherfucker."

I squeal, picking her up and spinning her around. "Are you moving in with us, too?"

"I am. Worked it out with Devon, but we thought it'd be fun to surprise you." She's smiling brighter than I've seen in years. "Plus, I heard you may be moving in with the bartender over here who won't stop looking at your ass."

Turning around confirms that Luke is standing behind the bar, staring at my ass. I blush and blow him a kiss. Sadie and I start making our way back to my office with her suitcases, but Cam intercepts us. "I got these. You two grab a drink. I heard the Cookie Explosion is top-notch."

"Cam, don't you fucking dare," I try to scold him, but he's gone with the suitcases before I finish my sentence.

I get Sadie settled in on a barstool right next to Bea.

When I cross back behind the bar to get back to work, I hear Bea saying to Sadie, "Look at these angels. Aren't you glad you they worked it out?"

"I like to think I helped. If I hadn't encouraged her to text him while we were at the pool that day—"

"Sadie!" I gasp. "You remember that part? I thought we were both blacked out."

"Oh no, just you," she laughs, brightly. "I thought you should apologize, and Devon didn't, so I waited until she went to bathroom and brought it up again."

Luke places a tiki drink, that's definitely not on the menu, in front of Sadie. "She told me these were what caused it. Now I know I have you to thank."

Putting my hands on my hips, my mouth drops open in offense, "You pretended you hadn't seen the texts when I showed you!"

"Oh, I didn't realize what you'd actually written," Sadie laughs.

"What did she write?" Bea asks, hazel eyes sparking with excitement.

Luke scrolls immediately to a screenshot of the text conversation that only recently stopped making my stomach clench with embarrassment and passes his phone to Bea.

I can't help the exasperated expression I give Luke. "You just have a screenshot ready to go?"

"It was the first time you told me you loved me. Of course, I saved it."

"I said I loved Betty."

"Sure, sure." He pats me patronizingly on top of the head.

"Well, those were magnificent," Bea says, passing Luke's phone back to him. "I sent myself the photo, so we can blow it up. There's a spot on the wall right over—"

"You wouldn't dare," I laugh, unable to tell if she's serious, since it would actually be hilarious.

Before I'm able to find out, another familiar voice calls my name. Skye and her mom are standing by the front door, spitting images of brown-eyed, dark-ringleted beauty.

Darlene's eyes are wide, scanning every inch of the bar with an awed smile on her face. She's completely recovered from the accident, not a bruise or scar in sight. I wave at Luke to grab his attention and we weave our way over to his family.

"Lucas," his mom's voice comes out in an impressed breath. "Honey, this is amazing."

"Thanks, Mom. It's really Allie's doing."

"No, it's not." I draw his mom into a tight hug. "He's done so much."

"It's the two of you together," she says, moving to wrap her son in a maternal hug.

"Yeah, Luke wouldn't have pulled this off alone," Skye laughs.

"Dad is so proud of you," Darlene says.

"Communing with the dead now, Mom?" Luke laughs.

"Oh, hush." She waves a hand in Luke's face. "He wanted you to run a bar, take care of me, take care of Skye, but more than that, he wanted you to have love." She steps back, looking between Luke and me. "And just look at you two."

Walking around our new bar, she gushes over him, over me, and over the building. This is the first time she's been here, and I can practically feel the pride rolling off his chest at his mother's approval. He takes her for a long tour, showing her every inch of the building, including the *Voyeur Motors* side.

After their tour, Luke finds me, and we move back behind the bar and work side by side as the minutes disappear into hours. Our favorite people filter in and out, sampling every item on the menu we've lovingly pulled together. The music gradually gets louder along with the laughter and conversations, and before long my cheeks are sore from smiling.

Luke reaches around me far more often than necessary, and I rub my ass against his dick every chance I get. "If you keep doing that, you're going to miss the rest of your party, Ms. Walker," he whispers, squeezing my ass cheek.

"I've worked with couples before," Rhett says, reaching for the top-shelf whiskey, "but you two are next level."

"That's because she's not just my girlfriend," Luke says, pulling my back flush against his chest and wrapping his arm tight around my waist. "This is the woman who's occupied every moment of my thoughts since I first saw her."

My cheeks heat as I recognize the words, realizing he's going to repeat the entire speech he gave me in the bed of his truck after the races.

"I work early every morning and stay late every night, just so I don't miss a glimpse of her electric smile or her ponytail bobbing when she laughs. I want her as close to me as possible. Her presence in my life has turned every plan I've ever made upside down. Watching her exist is the greatest joy I've known."

Rhett passes us each a shot of whiskey and raises one of his own high in a toast. "May we all be so lucky."

~

"I heard an interesting rumor tonight," I say to Luke, as he holds open the back door of *Voyeur Café* for me. It's two-thirty in the morning, and our bartenders just kicked us out, saying it's easier to close down if your boss isn't up your ass.

"You did?" Luke asks.

"Yeah, apparently, we're moving in together. Have you heard that one?"

"I may have been the one who started it," he says, the overhead lights of the parking lot highlighting his growing smirk.

"Were you planning to ask me about it?"

"Eventually." He squeezes my hand.

We reach his truck, and a rustling noise sounds from the nearby bushes.

"Do you hear that?" I whisper.

"Hear what?" he whispers back.

I wave him over, inching closer, waiting for the sounds to happen again. When it does, it's accompanied by a few quiet yips. I look over at Luke, raising my brows in question. He nods to confirm he heard it, too.

The rustling gets louder, and the yipping picks up, and a little pink nose emerges from the bushes, followed by a tangle of brown fur. *It's a puppy.* I suppress a squeal and sit down on the warm asphalt, forgetting the dress I bought especially for today's occasion.

"Sweetheart," Luke whispers at me, "Be careful."

Be careful? Of what? The puppy? Silly man. I sit very still but try speaking sweetly to the tiny dog. "Hi, little one. Are you scared? You're safe now. You found us."

The puppy inches closer to me, then freezes in place again. I look up at Luke making a silent, *'Look how fucking cute this sweet baby angel is'* face.

Luke kneels next to me, dropping a handful of treats in my lap. *Where did those come from? Whatever, I don't care.* I hold one out, flat-handed to the puppy. "You're okay. You can eat this. I'll take care of you."

The brown fur-baby inches closer, finally getting the courage to eat the treat out of my hand, its little tongue lapping up all the crumbs. "Poor baby. Are you hungry?" It comes closer, then scrambles into my lap and starts nosing at the pile of treats there. "Oh, you are." I wrap a protective arm around the little baby, scratching behind its ears, just like Betty likes.

"Hey, Luke?" I ask him quietly.

"Yeah, sweetheart?" His warm hand rubs soothingly across my back.

"Did you hear the rumor that me and my new dog are both moving in with you?"

~

The End

Epilogue

One Year Later

Gravel crunches under my truck tires as I turn on to what Allie now calls 'our road.' Both dogs pop up to standing in the back seat, shifting their weight around in anticipation of being released to run free.

My girl snuggles into my side from her spot in the middle of the bench seat. "Tonight's sunset is going to be so good," she giggles. "Thank you for agreeing to an impromptu picnic."

Pulling her tighter against me with the arm I have draped across her shoulders, I kiss her temple. "Of course. We were overdue for a night off." The thing about falling in love and then starting a business with another person who never takes time off of work is that if I don't take time off, neither will she. Mixing drinks back-to-back with my girlfriend—my partner—is a unique joy I would have never predicted, but it can't replace actual rest.

An excited whine comes from the back seat.

"She knows it's her 'gotcha' day," Allie says swiveling her head to look back, "Don't you, sweet girl? My pasta girl."

Pasta girl. The scraggly puppy that Allie found in our back parking lot is now taller than Betty, but not nearly as thick. She's covered in curly tan-brown fur that Allie described as, "Day-old pasta," the first night we brought her home. I made the mistake of saying, "No, you can't," to Allie Walker about giving the dogs rhyming names, so we now have Betty and Spaghetti.

"Your 'pasta girl' is going to scratch up the upholstery," I say before telling the dogs to settle down. Surprisingly, they both listen. Spaghetti is a wiry ball of energy, not easy to train, but we're making progress. Our dogs spend their days at my shop, and the hardest thing has been teaching Spaghetti not to whine at the glass while Allie works on the Turbine side. I can hardly blame her for wanting to be closer to Allie.

"Isn't this truck like a hundred years old?" Allie laughs.

"No," I scoff. "It's barely older than I am."

"Most people drive vehicles made in this millennium."

"Most people can't fix their own engines."

She leans forward, checking the odometer. "235,197. Come on, nothing's supposed to last that long."

"We'll have to agree to disagree on that."

"Okay," she chirps, smiling up at me.

It takes a few moments to register what she says. "Did you just agree to disagree with me?" I ask.

"Sure did," she says, thoroughly pleased with herself.

"How the—"

She cuts me off, "You had a good point. I don't care enough about truck mileage to hold my ground."

"So you fully agree with me, then? Not just agree to disagree?" I slide the shifter on the column into park.

She narrows her teal-green eyes, glaring ineffectively in the adorable way that I love. If she wasn't seated, I'm sure her hands would be planted on her hips. "Don't go that far. I'm agreeing to disagree only."

"Well, it's the first time that's happened, so I'm calling it a win."

She pats my chest and kisses me sweetly. "You should," she says before undoing her seatbelt and setting the dogs free to play in the desert. While she runs and plays with them, I gather up the picnic bedding from its permanent place under the back seat and lay it out in the truck bed.

Half an hour later, I've lifted Allie and two very tired dogs into the truck bed. Betty and Spaghetti curl up together, sending us matching puppy dog eyes when they smell the food we brought for dinner.

"Don't worry, babies," Allie tells them, pulling a foil wrapped rectangle from the cooler, "I have something special for you."

"I was wondering what that was," I say, leaning in for a closer look.

"I made a birthday cake for Spaghetti Girl!" Allie beams, electric smile taking over her pink lips. "It even has peanut butter frosting." She cuts the cake into two meticulously even pieces and puts them in dishes for the dogs, who gobble them down in seconds.

"I knew you'd be great with a dog of your own."

Allie moves over, sitting as close to me as possible without crawling fully into my lap. Her phone rings, and she answers it on speaker.

"This is not the best," Devon's voice comes through without a greeting.

"What's not?" Allie asks.

"The plumb and level of everything in your kitchen is off," she says, irritation thick in her voice. She's been working on the kitchen remodel for the house Allie and I bought earlier this year. The kitchen was dated, but functional. It could have stayed untouched without a problem, but Allie and Devon wouldn't hear of it.

"Everything?" I ask.

"She doesn't mean everything," Allie says at the same time Devon says, "Enough things are off that everything looks bad."

"I wish Rhett wasn't so busy at the ranch. This wouldn't have been a problem if we'd had him do the work," Devon continues.

"It's okay. They'll come back to fix it," Allie reassures her.

"And, if not Luke can fix it."

Allie and I exchange a glance as we wait for Devon's response. Her idea of 'everything's off' and our ideas of 'everything's off' are undoubtedly different. "Luke could. He's capable," she says, voice flat, "but he won't have to." And then she hangs up.

"I told you Devon likes you," Allie says.

Tilting my head to the side in confusion, I ask, "What gave you that idea?"

Allie turns to face me directly. "She just said you're capable."

"Yeah, but she sounded pissed about it. She doesn't like me."

"Yes, she does," Allie insists.

"Agree to disagree?" I ask.

"Of course not."

What's Next?

You've just finished *Voyeur Café*, book one in *Heartbeats in the Heat,* a series of interconnected standalone spicy romantic comedies. Book two will revolve around Devon and Rhett, and it will be releasing in late Spring 2024.

The best way to make sure you have all the details for the next release is to sign up for my newsletter at JasmineGraceAuthor.com. I'll send out the title, cover, blurb, release date, and all of the other details as they become available.

Thank you for reading book one! I hope to see you again for book two!

Acknowledgments

Thank *you* for reading my debut novel. You've changed my life by giving me a chance, and I am so grateful you did.

Thank you to every single person I sent the first two chapters of Voyeur Café to in the summer of '23. Your thoughts, critiques, and encouragements helped shape this story into what you now hold in your hands.

Gary, I'm already crying and all I've written is your name. I know you keep saying I could have done this without you, and you're right. I can do anything, but any love story I would have written without you by my side would have been a shadow of what we've accomplished together. Thank you for cooking me hundreds of dinners, bringing me mini charcuterie snacks when I was up late writing, drawing my beautiful cover, creating our Station 19 floorplan, reading every word of Voyeur Café multiple times over, being my motorcycle mechanic expert, learning InDesign with me and helping me figure out how to send a newsletter. I never once doubted I'd get to the finish line, because I knew you were supporting me.

The rest of these are listed in alphabetical order, because ranking them any other way feels icky.

Ashli, you've been *Team Jazzy* through every moment of my life since 2015. Knowing that you're cheering me on through every moment that I've spent figuring out what being *Spicy Writer Jazzy* means has been an incredible encouragement and safety net. Thank you.

Diana, thank you for saying "You should be a writer," during each of my many career crises. It took me almost twenty years to listen, but those suggestions are a major reason I felt confident enough to write this book.

Erica, thank you for your enthusiasm and curiosity, your willingness to give me critical feedback, and for always giving me space to talk about my book.

Erin, you've been a champion for me since the day we met. Thank you for being a champion about this book, all of your ideas and encouragement around the story, and believing in me as an author.

Jenica, I love every moment when our lives cross. Thank you for sharing your thoughtful feedback about my story with me. Without all the romance novels and other spicy books we got into during sleepovers as kids, I probably wouldn't be here.

Lauren, your enthusiasm and support have helped me tremendously. Thank you for always holding space for me to think out loud.

Pat, thank you for always believing in me. You'll be the first to know if I ever write a murder mystery.

Samantha, thank you for working with me as a debut author on the edits of my book. You were so kind and understanding. Voyeur Café wouldn't be what it is without you. Readers, I assure you, any grammatical, formatting, etc. issues in this book are all author error. Samantha Swart is a gem.

Soph, thank you for your willingness to listen, your direct feedback, and for giving me hugs when I needed them. So grateful you're in my life.

Steph, thank you for always reminding me of my value and my capabilities and encouraging me to reach higher. Your thoughtful conversations about the story and my author journey have been a tremendous help. I know you've been telling everyone who would listen about Voyeur Café for months and months! You mean the world to me.

Terrio, your emphatic enthusiasm when I said I wanted to try writing a spicy rom-com was exactly what I needed. Thank you for always being willing to exchange spicy book and cheesy movie recs with me. Your thorough feedback, thoughts, and suggestions for Voyeur Café made an incredible difference. You gave me help I needed. This story wouldn't be what it is without you.

Banjo & Shadow, my doggies. I know you can't read, but your constant presence in the office with me while I write helps more than you could understand. I don't deserve you.

About the Author

Jasmine Grace writes sweet and spicy escapist love stories filled with all her favorite things and none of her pet-peeves. You will find *Forced Proximity* and *He Falls First* tropes in most of her stories, and you will not find a third act break-up or a miscommunication trope in any of them.

She lives in Denver, Colorado with her husband, Gary, stepdaughter Sophia, and their two dogs, Banjo and Shadow.

I'd love to hear from you!
TikTok - @JasmineGraceAuthor
Instagram - @JasmineGraceAuthor
Email - Jasmine@JasmineGraceAuthor.com

Printed in Great Britain
by Amazon

37870378R00179